ADAM WILLIAMS

The Emperor's Bones

HODDER

Copyright © 2005 by Adam Williams

First published in Great Britain in 2005 by Hodder & Stoughton
A division of Hodder Headline
This Hodder Paperbacks edition 2006

The right of Adam Williams to be identified as the Author
of the Work has been asserted by him in accordance with the
Copyright, Designs and Patents Act 1988.

A Hodder paperback

1

A CIP catalogue record for this title is available from the British Library

ISBN: 0 340 82815 3

Typeset in Monotype Sabon by Palimpsest Book Production Limited,
Polmont, Stirlingshire

Printed and bound by
Mackays of Chatham Ltd, Chatham, Kent

Hodder Headline's policy is to use papers that are natural, renewable and
recyclable products and made from wood grown in sustainable forests.
The logging and manufacturing processes are expected to conform to the
environmental regulations of the country of origin.

Hodder & Stoughton Ltd
A division of Hodder Headline
338 Euston Road
London NW1 3BH

In memory

of the Muirs and Newmarches, missionaries and railwaymen, who lived through the turbulent early years of the last century in North China;

of my grandmother, Catherine, who once, like her red-headed namesake, browbeat a warlord who had the temerity to camp troops on her lawn;

of my mother, Anne, and my godmother, Jilly, who brightened my childhood with stories of their own adventures as they grew up in Tientsin and Chinwangtao before the Second World War;

of my father, Peter Gordon Williams, a taipan of a Hong Kong trading house who wanted to be a writer;

And to my wife, Fumei, and children, Alexander and Clio, the fifth generation of my family to be living in China.

Contents

CHINA 1922
Distribution of Warlord power on the eve of the First Fengtien-Chihli War

SOVIET RUSSIA

MONGOLIA

HEILUNGKIANG

KIRIN

CHAHAR

① FENGTIEN

JEHOL
● Mukden
● Shishan

SUIYUAN

KANSU

PEKING ●
CHIHLI
Tientsin

SHANSI
Yen
Hsi-shan

SHANTUNG

KOREA

KWANTUNG
COLONY
(Japan)

SHENSI

HONAN
② KIANGSU

JAPAN

SZECHWAN
(fragmented)

HUPEI
ANHWEI
Shanghai

HUNAN

CHEKIANG

KIANGSI

Liu
Hsien-shih
KWEICHOW

FUKIEN

YUNNAN
T'ang Chi-yao

KWANGSI
(fragmented)

KWANGTUNG
Chen Chiung-ming

FORMOSA
(JAPAN)

FRENCH
INDO-CHINA

Canton
(Dr Sun Yat-sen)

SIAM

① Fengtien Clique (Chang Tso-lin)

② Chihli Clique (Wu P'ei-fu)

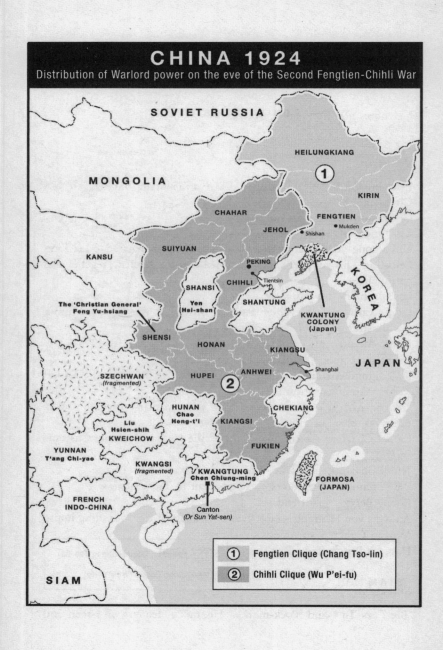

CHINA 1924

Distribution of Warlord power on the eve of the Second Fengtien-Chihli War

SOVIET RUSSIA

MONGOLIA

HEILUNGKIANG

①

KIRIN

CHAHAR

FENGTIEN

JEHOL

• Shishan

• Mukden

KANSU

SUIYUAN

PEKING •

CHIHLI

Tientsin •

The 'Christian General'
Feng Yu-hsiang

SHANSI

Yen
Hsi-shan

SHANTUNG

KWANTUNG
COLONY
(Japan)

KOREA

SHENSI

HONAN

KIANGSU

JAPAN

SZECHWAN
(fragmented)

HUPEI

ANHWEI

②

Shanghai →

HUNAN
Chao
Heng-t'i

CHEKIANG

Liu
Hsien-shih
KWEICHOW

KIANGSI

YUNNAN
T'ang Chi-yao

FUKIEN

KWANGSI
(fragmented)

KWANGTUNG
Chen Chiung-ming

FORMOSA
(JAPAN)

FRENCH
INDO-CHINA

Canton
(Dr Sun Yat-sen)

SIAM

| ① | Fengtien Clique (Chang Tso-lin) |
| ② | Chihli Clique (Wu P'ei-fu) |

The Characters

* Denotes non-fictional characters

Tientsin

Lei Chuang-hsi ('Old Man Lei') – a Tientsin banker, an old Confucianist

Grandmother Lei – his mother

Lei Tang – his elder son

Yu Fu-hong – daughter of Old Man Yu of Shishan, married to Lei Tang

Lei Ming – his younger son, a returned overseas student, teacher and nationalist

Lei Lan-hua – his daughter

Dr Edward Airton – chief medical officer at the Kailan Mining Administration, a former missionary

Nellie Airton – his wife

Catherine Cabot – her goddaughter

Dr Edmund Airton – Airton's son, a doctor working for the Kailan Mining Administration

George Airton – Airton's younger son, working for the China Railways, champion jockey

Lionel Charters – a commissioner of the China Maritime Customs Service

Jenny Charters – his wife, daughter of Dr and Mrs Airton

Willie Lampsett – Reuters correspondent in Tientsin

Robby Berry – his friend

Andreas von Henning – employee of Wilson & Co., a trading house

Martha Cohen – an American teacher

Douglas Pritchett – a British intelligence agent

Shanghai

'Big Ears Tu'* and 'Pock-marked Huang'* – leaders of Green and

Red Gangs respectively
Tommy Hsu – a rich young cotton-mill tycoon and owner of a cinema chain; head of a playboys' militia
Wang Yi – a student activist, Yu Fu-kuei's first husband

'North of the Wall'

MUKDEN AND DAIREN

Dr and Mrs Gillespie – missionaries in Mukden
Henry Manners – former British intelligence agent, now working for the Japanese
'One-armed Sutton'* – English mercenary in charge of Chang Tso-lin's arsenal

SHISHAN

Yu Hsin-fu ('Old Man Yu') – a soy-bean tycoon
Dr Richard Brown – missionary
Professor Ralph Niedemeyer – an American paleontologist

Tsinan

Bishop Huber – Catholic missionary
Hsiung – his Taoist friend

The Russians

REDS

Mikhail Borodin* – Comintern agent, Lenin's and Stalin's emissary and adviser to Sun Yat-sen
Fanya Borodin* – his wife
General Galen* – military adviser to Kuomintang
'Mr Behrens' – a Russian spymaster
Mr Barkowitz – a go-between for the Comintern in Shanghai

WHITES

Baron Ungern von Sternberg* – leader of a Cossack army in Mongolia
Colonel Sergei Ilyanovich Kovalevsky (Serge) – Russian soldier down on his luck in Mukden

Oleg Priapin, Samsonov, Ordochev – officers on the armoured train 'Shantung'

The Japanese in Manchuria

General Taro Hideyoshi – head of the Kempeitai, the secret police in the Kwantung army
Colonel Doihara* – intelligence officer in the Kwantung army
Colonel Machino Takema* – Chang Tso-lin's military adviser
Tadeki Honjo – manager of the Southern Manchurian Railway (SMR) in Shishan
Captain Fuzumi – commander of the SMR garrison in Shishan

The Nationalists (Kuomintang) in Canton

Dr Sun Yat-sen* – leader of the Nationalists, founder of the Kuomintang Party
Madame Sun Ching-ling* – his wife
Sun Fo* – his son, communications minister in KMT government
Liao Chung-kai* – Dr Sun's vice-president, assassinated 1925
Wang Ching-wei* – sometime prime minister
Eugene Chen* – foreign minister
General Chiang Kai-shek* – director of KMT's Whampoa arsenal, later generalissimo and leader of the Northern Expedition
General Tang Sheng-chi* – commanding KMT 8th Corps attack on Wuhan
General Chien Chung* – commanding 6th Corps attack on Nanking
General Pai Chung-hsi* – commander of army investing Shanghai
General T. K. Wang* – commander of Nationalist troops attacking Hsuchow
Colonel Loong – head of 6th Corps logistics department
John Soo – Oxford graduate and engineer attached to Whampoa arsenal

The Chinese Communist Party (CCP)

Li Ta-chao* – founder of CCP
Chen Tu-hsiu* – formal leader of CCP

Chou En-lai* – deputy commander of Whampoa arsenal under United Front with KMT
Li Li-san,* Mao Tse-tung* – young CCP leaders
Comrade Lee – Labour leader and CCP activist in Shanghai
Chin Hong-chi – young CCP activist in Shanghai

The Warlords

FENGTIAN CLIQUE (MANCHURIA)
Marshal Chang Tso-lin* – warlord of Manchuria, 'The Tiger of the North'
General Chang Hsueh-liang* – 'The Young Marshal', his son and heir
General Chang Tsung-chang* – 'The Dog General', Chang's subordinate, later notorious warlord of Shantung
Wang Yung-chiang* – Chang Tso-lin's prime minister
General Kuo Sung-lien* – one of Chang's senior generals, who betrayed him in 1925
General Lin Fu-po – a minor Manchurian warlord, ruling in Shishan
Yu Fu-cheng – Lin Fu-po's chief minister in Shishan, son of Yu Hsin-fu, brother of Yu Fu-kuei
Colonel Yen – commander of General Lin's regiment

CHIHLI CLIQUE (CENTRAL AND NORTHERN CHINA)
Marshal Wu Pei-fu* – warlord, head of Chihli clique
Lieutenant Ti Jen-hsing – an officer in Wu's army, who later changes sides and joins Shishan forces

ANLI CLIQUE (EASTERN CHINA PROVINCES)
General Sun Chuang-fang* – warlord of Kiangsu, Chekiang, Kiangsi and Shanghai
Major Yang Yi-liang – officer in Sun's counter-intelligence arm in Shanghai
Yu Fu-kuei – his mistress, daughter of Yu Hsin-fu of Shishan

NORTHWESTERN WARLORDS
General Feng Yu-hsiang* – 'The Christian general', warlord of Shensi
General Yan Hsi-shan* – warlord of Shansi

SOUTHERN WARLORDS
General Chen Chiung-ming* – southern warlord threatening Canton

The Emperor's Bones

PROLOGUE

Green Thoughts in Green Shade

Catherine, 1917

An English nurse was napping in the sunshine, her head resting on the root of a silver birch tree. Her wide skirt and apron, emblazoned with the red cross, billowed over the bed of bluebells and foxgloves like Ophelia's kirtle in the Millais painting. The tresses of auburn hair slipping from her scarf added a touch of untidy colour, which would have been attractive to a knight of the Pre-Raphaelite school, had one happened to stumble on the scene. As it was she was unobserved. She had come here to escape the bickering of nurses and orderlies with little work to do. The glade hummed with the natural sounds of a continental European summer.

On her lap were letters from her mother – old letters, since the postal service, like the railways, had been in paralysis since the February Revolution that had toppled the Tsar and brought the fighting on the Galician front to a standstill. In the distance a solitary gun was firing (even now some soldiers heeded Kerensky's call to arms) and once or twice in the last hour the whine and crump of enemy projectiles had exploded in the trench lines, but these tired sounds of half-hearted human hostility seemed inconsequential in the timeless music of the forest. It was as if Nature was mocking man and his wars, mimicking the staccato of machine-gun fire with the elegant tap-tap-tapping of a tiny woodpecker, parodying the wail of shells with the fluting of birds, and substituting for the silent death of the gas clouds the buzzing insect life hazing the surface of the pond.

Catherine let herself relax in the embracing heat and the warm breeze that brushed her cheeks. Above her head the dark leaves rustled against a clear blue sky. Her limbs were heavy with languor. For a while the words she had been reading hovered in her mind:

Darling, *please* forgive me. I really can't BEAR to stay in this city any longer. Life under the so-called 'Provisional Government' is just TOO boring. With my Pyotr away, and the rationing, and the meanness – the VULGARITY of it all – St Petersburg is really no place to be. I will be quite safe with the Dashkovs, who have organised a special train to take us over the border to Sweden. I am *not* abandoning you, my darling, headstrong girl. I really am not. I know that you will look after yourself, my brave Florence Nightingale, and join me in Paris when you can. How long, after all, can this war last? General Romalov says that the front is collapsing, and despite the boastings of that *awful* Kerensky and his VAIN military posturings, I am sure that must be the case. So you WILL certainly be coming home soon, and *as an Englishwoman* I am sure that you will have no problem with travel passes or whatever bit of paper it is that these revolutionists demand nowadays. I know I will see you soon, my darling, and in the meanwhile, can you forgive your foolish mother for her weakness and selfishness? Can you?

'*Sestritsa*! *Sestritsa*! Sister! Sister! Please don't leave us!'

She heard the agonised voices as if from far away, and even in her sleep she shivered as the familiar nightmare welled from the depths of her unconsciousness. She could not block out the images of white faces and flailing, stretching arms. She felt again the weak fingers pulling at her skirt, and Pavel Alexandrovich behind her, with his spade beard and world-weary frown, standing impatiently by the door of the convent cell that had become a makeshift surgery, beckoning her outside to where ambulance carts loaded with patients were waiting in the snow-speckled courtyard.

She knew she was dreaming. She could feel the sun on her limbs and face, the rough wood of the birch tree under her head. If she could only open her eyes . . .

'Water,' whispered Feodor, the golden-haired boy, the young officer from the 62nd Division, whose stomach had been torn open by shrapnel, and whose intestines two nights before she had held in her hands while Pavel Alexandrovich, exhausted after three days without sleep, had performed another of his surgical miracles. Must she just abandon him? When and where would this retreat end?

'Nurse Cabot, it is time to go,' the doctor was saying.

'Water,' moaned Feodor.

'*Sestritsa, sestritsa*,' pleaded the other patients.

'I'm coming,' she had told Pavel, and a German shell had burst close to the convent walls. The paraffin lamp swung on its hook casting shadows while plaster fell from the ceiling.

'You must come now, Katusha,' said the doctor. 'There is no time to make farewells.' He left the room. She felt the blazing eyes of the patients as she lifted her leather satchel on to her shoulders.

'Water,' pleaded Feodor. His voice was hardly a whisper.

'I can't give you water,' she said. 'You have a stomach wound. Water will kill you.'

'Water. Please.' His blue eyes widened. She saw the dimming pupils, the sign that death was near. 'I'm so – thirsty.'

She heard the ambulance wheels on the cobbles, the screams of whipped horses, the patients' howls of anguish. She felt the scrabbling hands. She made her decision and filled a cup from the pail. 'I shouldn't be doing this,' she said.

'Thank you,' sighed Feodor, as she put the water to his parched lips. She had only intended to wet his mouth but, with surprising strength, he clenched her hands and the contents poured down his throat. There was a beatific smile on his face. 'Oh, Lisabetta,' he whispered. It had not been the first time she had been called by the name of a dying man's sweetheart, and in these last moments she gazed into his blue eyes willing him to live, although she knew it was impossible. For a moment Catherine was indeed Lisabetta, and Feodor became her own lost Nicky. Then, suddenly, his body began to shake, and green bile gushed from his mouth and nose, as she had known it would. She closed the staring eyes. It was as if she had surfaced out of a deep pool. She heard again the moans and cries of the others. '*Sestritsa*, don't leave us.'

'Nurse Cabot, you must come. Now.' Pavel Alexandrovich was back and shouting at her. She knew he had seen what she had done. At this moment she did not care. With an effort she shook away the hands clutching her skirt and ran out of the door into the courtyard.

Into pandemonium. Walking wounded who had not found places in the carts were struggling with the orderlies. Her colleague, Marya, hunched among bags and blankets, was screaming at her to hurry. Leonid, the Tatar driver, hauled her up onto the seat, then cracked his whip at the horses and the desperate humanity crowding round them. Somehow they made it out of the yard and through the muddy streets to the road where a mixed procession of soldiers, vehicles and refugees was slowly winding its way from the fighting. Catherine leaned over the side of the shaking cart to look behind her. A soldier with a crutch was trying to keep up with their ambulance. His bandage, unrolling behind him, made a white trail on the churned yellow snow. Other men, crawling, were left behind. She heard the fading, pleading cries: '*Sestritsa . . . sestritsa . . .*'

Smoke was rising into the pale blue sky from the burning cottages. Catherine could see Cossacks throwing torches at the thatched roofs. Peasant women ran out of the blazing buildings clutching bundles, babies, chickens.

It was in this confusion that Pavel Alexandrovich had ridden up beside them. 'Nurse Cabot!' His face was angrier than she had ever seen it. 'It won't do. We are healers not murderers.'

She stared in astonishment at his wild, accusing eyes. Marya, frightened, clutched her arm, and Leonid turned his dark face to look at her. What was he talking about? Murderers? Murder was in the air, in the ground, all around them. It was a world of death and destruction. Pavel Alexandrovich was having difficulty controlling his horse, but even as it reared he was shouting: 'You know the regulations. You received training at Princess Golitsin's hospital. How could you give water to a stomach patient? You killed that boy.'

'He was dying, Doctor.'

'Without your assistance he might have lived. This will go in my report.'

'He was already dying!' she screamed. Marya clutched her hand.

'You're no nurse. You're a murderer,' spat Pavel, and Catherine knew that something in him had snapped. She and the other nurses had relied on the austere calm of this magisterial surgeon, the father figure in their little world. No matter the chaos, the horror and confusion, Pavel Alexandrovich had provided a point of order. Now the world was cracking around her.

A shell burst in the field beside them, and for a moment all was fire, flying mud and snow. The cart rocked in the blast, and Leonid had to use all his skill to hold the horses. Around them soldiers were running and leaping for cover. Marya was screaming – but Catherine had eyes only for Pavel Alexandrovich. His mount had sunk to the ground, yet somehow his body remained in the saddle, but where there had been a contorted, accusing face, now gouts of blood fountained from the stump of his neck. And ringing in her ears was the sound of the last word he had spoken: 'Murderer.'

She woke with a start, and heard the chatter of the forest. She shivered, and wondered why this dream always returned to haunt her. She had seen much, much worse in the months that had followed. That retreat of 1915 had lasted for more than forty days, all the way to Minsk. A whole countryside had been uprooted and many of the fleeing peasants had died of hunger and cold. Why did she not dream of the burn victims, whose skin had hung from their raw bodies like discarded clothes? Or the cholera epidemic, when they had piled bodies like logs because the ground was too frozen to dig a pit? Or the woodshed in Chertoviche where they had stacked the amputated limbs? Or the surreal drive through the cleared-out trenches during the advance of 1916, when she had stumbled on soldiers in all the contortions of death, the corpse of an officer kneeling against the barbed wire in an attitude of prayer, Russians and Austrians killed in the hand-to-hand fighting, embracing in the mud of the trenches where they had fallen? Why did she not dream of all the other boys who had held her hand and called her by the name of their mother or lover or sister before they died?

Because she had not been accused of murdering them. Oh, it was unfair. If only Pavel Alexandrovich had not been killed she might have been able to explain to him. His death had exonerated her in the eyes of officialdom: Marya and Leonid had not reported what they heard; but Pavel *had* died, and sometimes she thought she would never be free of his accusing stare. His ghost returned to haunt her nightmares.

7

Especially now. She had had no difficulty sleeping when the war had been fought in earnest. When every hour brought new patients from the front line, there had been no time to think of horror or hardship or anything but the task at hand. When the guns had thundered their loudest, shaking whatever accommodation they had been allotted, be it the straw-covered floor of a rat-infested stable, or a four-poster bed in a commandeered mansion (she had experienced both in her time and everything in between), then she had slipped into dreamless oblivion, waking refreshed to take on another day.

The revolution had changed all that. Now that the front was quiet, it was impossible to sleep at all – even in a beautiful glade like this, which recalled the world before the war, the dream *dacha* she and Marya had fantasized about so many times, while shells whined and men slaughtered each other less than a quarter of a verst away. This unnatural peace had released every nightmare she had bottled up for two years.

It was not only that. The war had given meaning to her life. For the first time in her peripatetic existence she had found a home, a sense of belonging – but now she did not know this army any more. Only yesterday she and Marya had passed a group of soldiers on the road. They had been drunk, and when they saw the two nurses they had stopped, and one had made an obscene gesture. The others had laughed, and Marya whipped the horses on. Mercifully the men had not followed, although a tall, bearded brute, had staggered after them for a few paces, yelling, 'Aren't we good enough for you aristocrat bitches? You can't put on airs with us any more, you know. We're free men now.'

The abdication of the Tsar had shocked them all, but she attributed the beginning of the rot to the ridiculous instruction, which had come down from St Petersburg, that officers should no longer use the familiar 'thou' when ordering their men. Then rabble-rousers had arrived from the cities – the Bolsheviki – who made speeches telling the men not to fight any more, not an aristocrat's war, they declared, and the officers had done nothing.

Two years before, when Catherine had arrived at the front, there had been camaraderie and a cause. She had believed there was nobody nobler or more magnificent than the peasant soldiers with their simple faith in the Tsar and Mother Russia, no hardship they would not undertake. They could be defeated, as in 1915, but not broken. She had tended several of these heroes, and been amazed by their uncomplaining fortitude. One bayoneted man had walked two versts holding his guts in his hands, then waited his turn in the queue until an orderly had noticed the seriousness of his hurt.

In the old days it had been an honour to serve them. A privilege. She was an Englishwoman, a foreigner, but they had treated her as one of their own, calling her *Rizhi Angelochek*, the Little Red Angel, because of the colour of her hair and – they added – the warmth of her heart. She in turn would have done anything for them. They had been her people.

She had loved one of them – briefly – during the Christmas celebrations in St Petersburg in the first year of the war, an officer, but a Russian soldier, and through him she had come to love them all. That was why she was here.

She recalled the night of the Dubaishev party, St Nicholas' Eve. She had not wanted to go, and neither had Nicholai. He had been on leave. By then she and her mother were enrolled as nurses at the fashionable Princess Golitsin hospital. For her mother it was an opportunity to wear uniform, when everybody in her set wore uniform, striking a noble pose at soirées and balls. She had helped Catherine to enrol too, confirming the lie that she was seventeen, and, through her contacts, providing the papers to prove it. ('Well, you look seventeen, my darling. Or even eighteen. And the officers you'll meet as a nurse will be much more dashing than the pimply schoolboys of your own age. And what else am I to do with you if I'm away tending sick heroes?')

Nicky had not been dashing. He had been shy, serious, and deeply affected by what he had already seen at the front. They had met because they were the only ones not dancing. He had a curl of black hair over one eye and translucent white skin, and he had shivered despite his military greatcoat in the cold of the balcony when they watched the candle-lit procession below. She had kissed him, crimsoning afterwards. Pretending experience she did not have, imitating her mother, she had led him by the hand to where the *izhvochiks* waited by the sleighs. He *was* seventeen, and unsure of himself. She did not tell him that she was not yet fifteen. Under the rugs they had clumsily made love. She remembered how afterwards she had looked into his grey eyes and seen the expression of wonder there. The broad back of the driver was still hunched over the reins; the gas lamps shone palely through the night mist; the sleigh bells tinkled. Nothing and everything had changed. She traced a finger over the film of his boy's moustache. 'Katusha,' he whispered, pressing her knuckles to his cold cheek. 'We have such a short time. My leave . . .'

'We have forever,' she had told him. 'Forever.'

He had dropped her at the palace of her mother's friend, and promised to pick her up early the next day – but all she had received was a letter, delivered just before noon by a sleepy corporal from his depot. The message was brief, almost formal, written in a precise schoolboy's hand. He had received urgent and immediate summons to go back to the front, he wrote. Could she come to see him off at one o'clock? She rushed to the station and saw the steam of his train as it pulled away. Three weeks later he was dead, killed somewhere in the Carpathians.

Her mother had mentioned it casually. They were in their *droshky*, returning from the ballet. 'Oh, I quite forgot to tell you,' she said. 'I was having ices this morning at the Angleterre with Mrs Dubaishev. She told me her nephew had been killed. I think he was that wan-looking boy you were talking to at the party, Nicky Something-or-other. I suppose I had better write a condolence letter to his parents. You can't remember what his surname was, can you? I still get so confused with these Russian patronymics. My dear, whatever's the matter? Were you sweet on him? Oh, dearest, what a shame.' And later: 'Catherine, please, do control yourself. Of course it's very sad, but you can't be sentimental about every death in this awful war. You hardly knew the boy. I've such a headache.'

The next day Catherine submitted a formal application to serve in a front-line unit. Her mother had been horrified – but Catherine was accepted. She arrived in Gorlitse only ten days before the great retreat.

And now she was a veteran. Few nurses had had such relentless front-line experience as she. She had never taken any of the leave due to her, except once when she joined Marya, who was recuperating from influenza, at a spa in the Crimea. She had not returned to St Petersburg to see her mother, whose life disgusted her now. Parties, dances, spiritualist séances, betrayal by Prince This and a new infatuation with Prince That; she had no idea who Pyotr was. It was all one and the same.

Her mother had always been feckless. Catherine's whole life had been spent in hotels, with occasional sojourns in palazzos and spas. She was fluent in four languages before she was ten, and after her mother had followed her new banker friend to St Petersburg in 1913, she had added a fifth, Russian. At least her mother had got her lovers to pay for tutors, and there must be few girls of her age, she thought, who had such first-hand experience of geography, and none with so many stepfathers at various times of different nationality. She had had no difficulty in passing herself off as seventeen. Sometimes she thought that she had never had a childhood. She smiled: she had been a woman with a past before most girls had even begun to consider their future.

Even her birth had been exotic. She had been born in Mongolia when her mother was fleeing from the Boxer Rebellion. What she had been doing in China Catherine did not know; nor had she much idea of whom her father had been, except that he was called Cabot and that he had died before she was born. Her mother had told her he was 'a hero. A martyr, darling. Far too good for me. We met on a boat. He liked cricket.' That was all she knew, all that her mother would tell her – except that he had come from a wealthy family who apparently provided her with the cheques that fuelled her lavish lifestyle. She had a vague memory of spending one Christmas with grandparents in Lincolnshire as a small girl – at least, with an old couple whom her mother had said were her grandparents. They had been kind, as had another old couple they had visited in Scotland, her godparents – but that had been long ago, and her mother would never speak of those days.

Her earliest real memories were of Japan, where her mother had lived with a tall man, who had twinkling blue eyes and a black moustache, in a wooden house with a grey-tiled roof that looked over hundreds of islands. He had been the only one of her mother's lovers who had treated her like a daughter, telling her stories about tigers and maharajahs' palaces and genies who knew the secrets of great treasure troves, as he paced back and forth beside her cot. He walked with a limp, she recalled, which seemed odd in such a powerful man. She could not recall a time in her life when she had been happier – until the quarrels began with Mama. With a wet finger she had made a hole in a paper door so she could see into the room where they were arguing. She had been sad, because she loved this man, and she hated it that her mother would scream at him so. He had not come to see them off when they had left on a liner for England, and that had hurt her more than she could say. Now she could not even recall his name. If her mother had one rule, it was that she would never speak of her past lovers.

Catherine glanced at the watch hanging from her apron. It was after four. She supposed she had better return to the tents. Mamasha would probably scold her anyway. She hoped that by now the argument between Marya and Olga might have subsided. Olga's case, containing her winter boots and leather jacket, had been stolen and she blamed Marya for leaving it outside their tent. These days, if it was not one thing it was another. They were not the happy little group they had once been.

She picked up her letters, which had fallen on to the grass. Would she follow her mother to Paris? On the face of it there seemed little future for her in Russia. Not with these Bolsheviki who, day by day, were becoming more powerful. Their leader, Lenin, had already attempted a *coup d'état*, and although Kerensky and the army had driven him for the moment from St Petersburg, she knew that the influence of professional revolutionaries like him was as strong as ever. Perhaps it would be sensible to leave now before the situation in the country deteriorated further. Yet how could she abandon her duties? How could she abandon Marya and her other friends? This little nursing unit was the only real family she had ever known. She felt sudden terror; she could not imagine a life beyond this war. What meaning could she possibly find in her existence? Her work unit was her world. It was the only time she had ever belonged. Even the bickering was that of a close family. If she became cast off from them what would there be? She had a sudden vision of driftwood, tossed on a raging sea.

She shivered, though the late afternoon was still warm, and the colours of summer blazed within the glade. A squirrel scurried up a tree. It paused, half-way up the trunk, as if listening for something. Then she heard it too – the scream.

'We will hunt them down, *Sestritsa*,' said the officer. 'They are animals, and will be hanged when we catch them. That I promise you.'

One of his Cossacks, a bushy-bearded man with red cheeks and a tear in the corner of his eye, offered her a mug of tea. She took it but did not raise it to her lips. Hunched on the camp stool she was only aware of the grey blankets that covered the bodies of her friends. The one over Olga did not quite extend to her feet. Catherine could see the pointed red boots, which her friend had loved, protruding from the cloth. A part of her mind told her that this was untidy. Marya and Natalya, smaller girls, were completely covered. Poor Olga. So tall and ungainly, always criticised by Mamasha for her clumsiness. Catherine glanced at a blanket slightly further away. The grass was bloody around it. Mamasha would not be criticising any of the nurses in her charge again.

'They were deserters.' She heard the officer's voice from far, far away. 'Infantry,' he spat, as if this were important.

Catherine looked at him dreamily. 'Russian soldiers,' she murmured. 'They were Russian soldiers.'

The officer stared at her, then he hung his head. 'Yes,' he said, after a moment. 'They were Russians.'

Catherine sipped the tea. It burned her lips. A group of men were crouching close to where the horses were haltered, at the side of the clearing. 'Who are they?' she asked.

The officer followed her glance. 'They are part of a work battalion,' he said quietly. 'Kirghiz volunteers. We're escorting them to the lines. A queer lot, aren't they?'

She peered at them, squinting against the rays of the setting sun. She had never seen anybody quite like them. They wore colourfully striped robes. They had knives in their orange silk sashes, and their shaggy fur hats were cocked at a rakish angle on their heads. Some were lightly bearded with fierce, hawk-like features, browned and cracked from exposure to the elements. They were observing her solemnly, impassively, from warm, hazel eyes. These were not the Tatars she was used to. They were alien, other-worldly.

'We're dredging the empire for men,' said the officer. 'They are nomads from Turkestan. The great Mongolian steppes.'

'I come from there,' murmured Catherine.

The officer was confused. 'But, *Sestritsa*, you are English . . .'

'I was born there,' she said. Her voice broke. 'In the wilderness . . .'

Suddenly she was weeping, bent double, and the mug of tea slipped from her hands. Her shoulders shook. The control she had exerted over her emotions for two years of war tumbled like logs smashed from a coffer dam. She saw Marya again as she had found her only an hour ago, violated, stabbed, mutilated, the familiar half-smile and black, shadowed eyes gazing up slyly in death, as if the obscene position in which her lower body was twisted over the bayonet had been one of the naughty pranks she had sometimes played on Mamasha. She saw Mamasha herself, and Olga, and Natalya – her beloved sisters – as they were now: anonymous grey bundles on the grass. There had been so much death bobbing in the turbulent stream of her short life; everybody she loved seemed condemned to die horribly, or go away, like the man with the black moustache in her childhood had gone away. And now the family she had made for herself in this war was also lost to her. Oh, it was pointless, pointless. 'You can't be sentimental, my dear. There are plenty of fishes in the sea.' She heard the terrible drawl of her mother over the wash of angry waves sweeping the debris of her mind. And she groaned. Because in a deep part of herself she knew her mother was probably right. Nothing did matter. There was no meaning, no purpose. Only the wild winds blowing over a sea of grass in the wilderness in which she had been born.

'*Sestritsa*,' she heard the officer say, 'is there anything – anything we can do?'

'I'll be fine,' she said, 'in a moment.'

She took the handkerchief he proffered, and dabbed her eyes. The Kirghiz tribesmen were watching her. One was smiling at her, a jagged, kind smile of immeasurable understanding.

Yu Fu-kuei, 1921

Yu Fu-kuei had two more weeks to go before she had to submit the first draft of her thesis. For two months now she had been writing it, and she had hardly left her rooms in St Hugh's. However, this afternoon promised sunshine, after weeks of summer rain, and she had asked John Soo, an earnest, bespectacled young compatriot from the engineering faculty, to meet her at Magdalen Bridge and take her punting. She was aware of how much he admired her, and perhaps if her life had been set on a different course, she might have responded to his shy advances. She liked his reserve (uncommon in a southerner, especially in a Cantonese). He would be content to pole the boat along quietly while she reclined against the cushions and read her books of poetry. She had brought with her today a well-thumbed copy of the English *Helicon*, annotated in the margins with her neat calligraphy, and also volumes of Marvell and Herrick. Strictly speaking, the metaphysical poets did not belong to her period, which was the high age of Elizabethan pastoral, but in their treatment of nature they exhibited a subtlety and whimsicality that had parallels with some of the verses of Wang Wei and Li Po.

Idly, she trailed her hand through the chill green water. She loved the Cherwell: this gentle stream winding like the nave of a cathedral under a vaulted ceiling of leaves; sunshine dappling through the canopy like flashing jewels of light through a stained-glass window. She revelled in the silence of this enclosed little world made up of tranquillity, flowers and shade, where there were no extraneous sounds but the plop of the pole pulling through the water, and the occasional scurry of a small animal or bird in the bushes or reeds. For Fu-kuei, the Chinese student of English pastoral, this little tributary of the Thames represented Arcadia. It inspired the sort of philosophical musings on Nature, which, in a poet of the stature of Marvell or Donne, became a symbol of order in the universe

and society. Quickly she thumbed through the book until she found
the lines she remembered:

> *. . . The Mind, that Ocean where each kind*
> *Does straight its own resemblance find . . .*

Yes, this was the passage she had marked.

> *. . . Annihilating all that's made*
> *To a green Thought in a green Shade.*

Fu-kuei sighed and closed the book. 'A green thought in a green
shade'. So evocative.

Was an appreciation of beauty reactionary, she wondered.
Bourgeois? Wang would have thought so. He would never have
approved of what she was doing now. Poor Wang. So pure. So
certain. So simplistic. So . . . dead. It was rare now that she thought
of him, which was strange, because he had been her husband and
had once meant everything in life to her. Wang, her revolutionary
lover.

With a push of its powerful webbed feet, a swan propelled itself
into the water, rocking the punt with its bow wave. Its cold eye
glared at Fu-kuei as it sailed by.

She remembered the last time she had seen Wang alive: his defiance when they had been captured, how he had spat at the officer
arresting them, his spittle flying accurately the length of the room.
How proud he had been of his peasant habits. They had beaten
him, but had not been able to erase the scornful smile from his
bleeding face. His lips were still curled in an arrogant sneer when
they had beheaded him three days later. She knew that because they
had thrown his head into her cell. They had waited to see her reaction and she had not disappointed them. She had heard their
mocking laughter through her screams. That had been the last time
she had satisfied them. By the time they had begun to rape her,
they were playing with an empty shell, for some time during that
first long night she had drifted away from the pain; what remained
had been the register of each indignity and torment from far away.
Whatever feelings or emotions had motivated the old Fu-kuei had
never truly returned. Only her mind still functioned, and the

memory of each injury, which she had filed in her subconscious like an examining magistrate patiently preparing a prosecution for revenge. It was a cold simulacrum of her former self that was punting on an English river today.

With a shrug of disgust she dropped her book on to the duck-board at her feet.

'Are you all right?' asked John Soo, looking at her with concern from the prow.

'Oh, I'm fine,' she said.

He nodded, and poled on.

Marvell had been a revolutionary, she recalled. He had supported Parliament against the King, in that mild upheaval the British called their civil war. She smiled, thinking of the civil wars her own country had experienced – the Taiping rebellion, in which twenty million people had died; the Boxer uprising, which had taken place when she was a child – she still remembered the vengeful Russians riding past her house and the fear in her parents' eyes; the 1911 revolution against the Manchus and the bloody countermeasures taken by the warlords in her native Fengtian Province; the beheadings that followed and the purges in her own town of Shishan. What did the English know of civil war?

She had found them a shy, courteous people, their manner as temperate as their climate. She wondered what force turned these gentle farmers, shopkeepers and scholars into the brazen, over-bearing imperialists they became abroad. She was well aware of how the British Empire exploited the poor cotton farmers of India to provide cheap materials for its capitalist mills. She knew, first hand, how it had exploited her own country, siphoning away its wealth through the Maritime Customs Service. Many nations had conspired to plunder her country, but the British had been the worst. There had been a time when her friends had believed that things would change after the dreadful world war that had strained Britain's resources to breaking point and squandered the blood of its young on the battlefields of France. There had been optimism in her university campus in Peking that the Versailles Peace Conference would create a new order in the world, restoring China's lost territories – but the victors had merely apportioned the spoils.

President Wilson and the others had spoken of the abolition of the extra-territoriality laws and the dismantling of colonial concessions; yet they acceded to Japan's Twenty-one Demands, and approved this new colonial power's seizure of vast tracts of territory in Manchuria and Shantung.

Fu-kuei had abandoned her studies and marched in protest with the other students to the Tiananmen Gate on May 4th 1919. It was there that she had met the young peasant trade unionist, Wang Yi, falling under the spell of his fiery oratory as he harangued the crowds. It had seemed that his denunciation of feudalism and complacency had been directed at her. Afterwards she had gone to him and asked how she could help, and he had looked her up and down insolently, laughing at her for her modest manners and her fine clothes. He had accused her of being a member of the privileged bourgeoisie, and asked what she knew or cared about the suffering proletariat. She had blushed with anger and shame but she had told him she would do anything. 'Anything?' he had questioned her, smiling. 'It's a hard road for dainty feet.' And in her anger she had kicked him, to prove that her feet were anything but dainty. 'Oh, you'll do,' he had said, and that had been the beginning of her education.

She remembered their wedding night, the wretched tea-house in a back alley in Hatamen, above which Wang had his lodgings, and how he had carried her up the rickety stairs while his friends shouted and banged their bowls of *gaoliang* on the tables, and how Wang, swaying at the top, had led them in a drunken rendering of the 'Internationale'. Her arms round his broad shoulders, she had gazed into his shining face and thought he was god-like, unconquerable, and wondered what miracle had made him hers. Later, behind the thin hanging that separated their corner of the attic, she had lain on a straw mattress with this hero in her arms, and discovered that he was only a boy, as inexperienced as she, and from then on she had loved him the more.

Yes, she thought now, they had been children. They really had believed that they were immortal, and that anything was achievable simply through the power of their love. They had imagined they could refashion the world to their dreams. They saw themselves as the vanguard of a revolution that would bury capitalism and injustice in the dawn of a new age. They would dare each other to ever bolder deeds, drinking in the admiration of their fellow students and agitators, as if this was the aphrodisiac they needed when they returned to the little world of their attic. Their very lovemaking had been revolutionary. Angry and chipped like a granite statue when he was addressing a crowd, Wang's rough manners would soften as he undressed her and she would see wonder in his eyes when he held her, tenderly, as if she were priceless porcelain, while she, fired by his touch, would lose all remaining vestiges of gentility, and violently pull him by his hair to her breast, moaning and biting his smooth skin. 'Every time we fuck, you and I,' he once joked with her, 'we betray our class origins.'

She had rolled her head back and laughed. 'Oh, how I love you,' she had cried. 'You're so beautiful, so strong.' And he had smiled and told her, hush, she would disturb their room-mates beyond the curtain. 'I don't care,' she had shouted, for sheer joy. 'I'm happy. We're changing China. Changing the world!'

She wondered sometimes what had become of that innocence. In the distance, she saw the spire of Magdalen chapel fading behind the trees. No, she no longer believed in dreams. It would take more than love and idealism to change China.

Her colleagues at the university still spoke admiringly of Confucius's 'Golden Mean' and the fair and impartial bureaucracy of scholar officials, of meritocracy chosen by Imperial Examination, of moderation and order that had lasted millennia. She had never contradicted them but she knew the reality: the Confucian system was at best an aesthetic misrepresentation of an order that did not exist, at worst a brocade gown veiling the bloated body of a corrupt, oppressive feudalism, stinking in its misuse of absolute power. It had been that corrupt system which Dr Sun Yat-sen had attempted to overthrow in 1911. All he had done, though, was to strip the covering from the patient, revealing the sores. Worse, every garrison commander had become a power in his own right. Warlords extorted taxes mercilessly at the point of a gun. There were the trappings of a government in Peking with a president and a prime minister, but it was immaterial which clique of gangsters happened to be in official power: they were all the same, worms crawling over each other in a tangle of greed. That was China now, and the only beneficiaries were the foreigners, whose gunboats prowled the inland waterways, giving them a free hand to conduct their all-important trade, using cheap Chinese labour in their sweatshops and factories.

She and Wang had believed they could do something about it. They had left Peking, and organised little sabotages of factory machinery in the Shanghai cotton mills, and strikes among the workers. They had returned, giggling and embracing, to their tenement hideaway, with triumph in their eyes, imagining they had brought the revolution a little nearer. All that they had accomplished was Wang's death, her torture.

Once a week she was invited to drink sherry with Miss Murtry, her tutor, and some of her fellow students. Nice, blue-stocking girls, mostly from wealthy homes, with bobbed hair, spectacles and gleaming, curious eyes, who asked her questions about China. She answered as was expected of her, with descriptions of temples or on-the-spot translations of Tang poems. 'Oh, I hope I have the chance to go there,' they would squeal, pressing their hands together and lifting their shoulders in the girlish manner she had noticed that well-brought-up English girls affected. 'Would you really like to see my country as it is?' she sometimes thought of replying. 'Then let me show you what it is like to be stripped naked in a basement cell, with your hands tied behind you to your ankles for three days, while a brute in uniform beats the soles of your feet with a bamboo rod. Or what about being raped in rotation by the prison guards? Would you like that? Ten of them, one after the other, round the clock. How would you like it if one of them afterwards forced open your mouth when you pleaded for water, and urinated down your throat?' But instead she sipped her sherry and smiled her demure smile, murmuring that she would be pleased to escort any of them round the sights of Peking if ever the opportunity arose.

She was jolted out of her reverie when John Soo, who had misjudged one of the bends in the river, bumped the punt into the bank. He pushed it off with the pole, his boater over his eyes.

Fu-kuei laughed. He looked comical, like Buster Keaton in one of the movies.

'You looked far away just now,' he said, when he had recovered his balance.

'I was thinking of China,' she answered.

'Ah, China.' He gave the boat a hard shove up the stream. 'You'll be going back, then?'

'After I hand in my paper. I was only going to be here for a year to do my thesis.'

'I was hoping you would stay on for a doctorate. Didn't your professor offer you a place?'

'A conditional one. But I have to go back to Shanghai. It's my duty,' she added.

'Duty,' said John. 'Then you have no choice, have you?'

Poor Soo. He was so conservative. He probably thought she was returning for an arranged marriage. Well, she would marry Captain Yang if he insisted. She would do whatever was necessary. Her instructions were clear.

Was she fond of Captain Yang? She was grateful to him. He had saved her life. He had been the new commandant of the prison, taking up his post some five weeks after she had been arrested. He had come to the cells on a tour of inspection. She remembered the door crashing open, and his smart uniform, his shiny boots, his spurs. She had hunched with her arms clutching her knees, wondering what new torment was in store for her, and at first she thought he was shouting at her. It was some moments before she grasped that his anger was not directed at her but at the guards who stood cowed by the door. She could hardly believe her ears. 'Are we animals?' he was shrieking. 'Do we keep women chained naked like beasts?' He rounded on the corporal-in-charge, slapping his face. 'Look at those bruises. This is the new China,' he roared. 'We do not treat our prisoners like animals. I want clothes for her, and I want a doctor to examine her. Now!' Something about this had struck her as funny and, painfully, she had begun to laugh. The officer had stared at her in amazement. She moved a hand to her face expecting him to strike her, but instead he knelt down beside her, resting his gloves on her shoulders. She spat in his face. Even then he had not hit her. He shook his head and closed his eyes. 'I want a doctor. Now,' he had ordered. 'If this woman is touched again, whoever is responsible will be on a charge.' Then he had stamped out of the cell.

There had been no more beatings after that, no more rapes. In fact, the guards who had abused her now treated her with cautious respect; even, in some cases, with kindness. Slowly the bruises healed; she was given better food. One day she had been taken out of her cell to the captain's office, which terrified her more than the beatings had done, and she sat nervously, waiting for a sentence of death – but the young officer had said, 'Let us introduce ourselves properly. My name is Yang Yi-liang. We're roughly the same age. You started studying at Pei Ta at about the same time as I was graduating from the Chiangnan Military Academy. You interest me. Listen, I serve my general because that is my duty, but that doesn't mean that I don't applaud the May 4th Movement or want to create a better country. I suspect that we come from similar backgrounds. Your father's a rich merchant, isn't he? So's mine. What makes an educated, intelligent woman like you want to associate with firebrands like Wang Yi and destroy factories?'

Of course she had told him she had nothing to say. 'I'm not interrogating you,' he said. 'This isn't an attempt to disorient you in order to get information out of you. Soft treatment after hard. And I'm not seeking information to construct a case against you. We're satisfied that you and Mr Wang were operating on your own, so we are not looking for the names of accomplices. I just want to understand why you did what you did.'

She had refused to answer him. 'All right,' he said, smiling kindly. 'It's probably too much to expect you to trust me immediately. But don't go down to that cold cell yet. Sit for a while in the sunshine. Don't mind me. I've plenty of work to do,' and he had set to the papers on his desk, whistling to himself, ignoring her, which had disoriented her still further.

It had not been a normal friendship. Slowly, however, over the following weeks, she had relaxed enough to answer his questions, and engage in the debate he seemed to want. She found that he was well-read. He had even studied Marx, but he rejected the argument that capitalism had caused the world's problems. 'Yes, we must do more for the ordinary people,' he told her, 'but not by destroying everything first. I agree with you that China's wealth should be controlled by the Chinese people, and when our own house is in order, we must do away with these extra-territoriality laws and the pseudo-colonialism of the concessions . . .' There were times, she realized, when she enjoyed herself.

One afternoon he had told her she would not be returning to her cell. He had spoken to his leaders, he said, and persuaded them that she was not a dangerous criminal, only misguided. He had been given permission for her to move into his quarters. 'You'll have your own room, the *amah*'s room, but it will be more comfortable than the cell. Officially you are on housekeeper duty. You won't try to escape, will you? You're still a prisoner.' She was staring at him in amazement. 'Look,' he said, 'I have no intention of molesting you. I just thought that you'd like the chance to sit in more airy quarters and read books that are denied you at the moment.'

Ten days later they became lovers. She had slipped into his room one night when he was asleep. He had not resisted. Instead he had cried and told her he loved her.

Three months after that she was free. He had made her sign a self-criticism, stating that she regretted her actions and now abjured Communism and all other forms of revolutionary thought. 'I have to give this to my general, who's prepared to consider a pardon,' he had told her. 'He trusts me and has agreed to this favour. He believes you have seen the error of your ways but he needs something in writing from you. It's the truth, isn't it? After all our talks . . . By all means say that you believe in Nationalism. That's fine. So do I . . . But revolution? That's all in the past, isn't it?'

'No, it's the truth,' she had told him, looking him levelly in the eyes. 'Thank you for saving me. I love you,' she added, and had signed.

It had been his idea that she study abroad. He wanted her to finish her education, he told her; he wanted her to fulfil the potential of her life that had been cut off through her reckless flirtation with politics. He would be happy to pay. No Chinese university would take her now, he said, but she could find a college in America or Europe. She had chosen Oxford, applied and been accepted. The assessors had thought that her proposed comparison between sixteenth century English verse and the poems of the Tang would be interesting. Yang Yi-liang had seen her off at the International Pier, and there were tears in her eyes as well as his when the ship moved away from the dock, and the streamers parted.

That night, in the first-class dining room, she had met the German businessman, Mr Behrens, who, she later discovered, had asked to be seated at her table. It had been many deckside conversations later, when the ship had turned into the Red Sea on the way to Suez, that she discovered he was an agent of the Third International, the Comintern as he called it, Lenin's organisation to spread revolution overseas, and that he had orders for her from Moscow. 'We are pleased by your association. We have been watching your Captain Yang,' he had told her. 'He is a rising man. We want you to keep this relationship. One day it may be useful to us. For now you are to have a holiday. Pastoral poetry? It will be most pleasant for you, I think.'

She focused on what John Soo was saying. 'We're not going to have the river to ourselves, it seems,' he was murmuring. 'Navigation may become a bit tricky in a minute.'

Three punts were floating abreast down the river towards them, covering the width of the stream. The students at the poles were laughing and shouting, and their companions were having a party; she could see the champagne glasses in their hands. One young man, dressed like the others in white ducks and blazer, was strumming a banjo. Children, thought Fu-kuei. Spoiled, privileged children.

Her attention was caught by the one female in the group who was reclining in the seat of the middle punt. She was wearing a wide-skirted white dress with long cotton sleeves. Ripples of red hair framed her face, and on her head she wore a garland of dandelions and poppies. One of the young men was lying with his head in her lap. The others appeared to be paying court to her. She was the centre of this moving, laughing world. Fu-kuei was suddenly reminded of one of the illustrations in her copy of Tennyson's *Morte d'Arthur*. If the woman had not been holding a glass in one hand and a cigarette in the other she might have been Guinevere surrounded by her knights a-Maying.

As the punts drew nearer Fu-kuei could see her face more clearly, pale but with touches of crimson in her cheeks. She had a delicate nose and her lips curved in an ironic smile. She was young, but there was a watchfulness in her green eyes, as if she were somehow detached from her companions. The faint lines on her forehead and mouth suggested that she had suffered, or at least been marked to some degree by hard experience. One of the young men said something to her and the woman laughed – rather harshly – but her eyes softened in humour as she delivered what was obviously a tart rejoinder, causing a burst of merriment from her admirers, and a dig in the ribs to the boy who had spoken.

There was something familiar about her. Fu-kuei was sure that she had seen her somewhere before.

The boats were upon them. John Soo had observed a narrow gap between the left-hand and middle punts, and made for it. Wood grated as he scraped past, and for a long moment all four punts were locked together. Fu-kuei ducked as the steersman on the woman's boat staggered and his pole swung wide. Droplets of water showered her head.

There were good-humoured cries of 'Whoa there!' and 'Boarders!' and 'Steady on!'

The boy with his head in the girl's lap opened his eyes and raised himself on one elbow. 'I say,' he drawled, 'am I dreaming? It's a couple of Celestials. Where did they come from?' He raised his boater in mock-politeness, narrowing his eyes in the manner of a music-hall Chinaman, and launched into a meaningless chatter consisting of 'Haw! Ching chang chong.' The banjo-player broke into a vaudeville song:

> *'Chin Chin Chinaman muchee muchee sad,*
> *Me aflaid all' a tlade velly velly bad.*
> *No joke stony bloke, have to shuttee shop,*
> *Chin Chin Chinaman chop chop chop!'*

Fu-kuei glanced away from them, concerned about the effect this might be having on John Soo. His features were set in an impassive mask, so she could only guess at the depth of his anger. She turned back to look into the level green eyes of the girl, who was now beside her. She had not taken part in the antics and was frowning, apparently with displeasure. As Fu-kuei watched, the girl viciously slapped the young man who had started this jape on the side of his head. 'Ow, that hurt,' he yelped.

'I meant it to,' she said, in a strong voice that carried above the laughter.

With a heave John Soo broke his boat clear of the others, which drifted downstream. As the gap widened, the girl turned to keep her eyes on Fu-kuei. Before they had disappeared round a bend of the river, Fu-kuei had remembered where she had seen her before.

It had been at a lecture organised by the Fabian Society in a tea-room in New Inn Hall Street. An economist from London University was speaking on Russia's New Economic Programme. John Soo had persuaded Fu-kuei to attend. 'This is relevant to our country's struggle,' he had told her. She had been subjected to a lacklustre eulogy on the achievements of the Bolsheviks, a wordy paean on how they had created a new industrial society out of the feudalism of the past. She had been trying to conceal a yawn when the lecture had been disrupted by a group of rowdy hecklers jeering the speaker in that braying manner of upper-class English students, chanting 'Go back to Moscow' and 'We don't want Bolos here.'

The speaker, an earnest little man with an untidy moustache and spectacles, had attempted to handle the interruption humorously at first. 'Oh, yes?' he had shouted in his reedy voice. 'And how many of you fine young ladies and gentlemen have actually been to the Soviet Republic, as I have? Or is your own eloquence on the subject derived entirely from the propaganda in Lord Beaverbrook's Liberal Party rags?' He had smiled smugly at his witticism, buoyed by the nods of approval from the faithful in the front row. The hecklers roared abuse, but rising out of the tumult came a clear female voice, 'Well, I was there, Mr Know-it-all Speaker, right through the revolution. Does that count?'

Fu-kuei had turned her head and seen a girl with striking red hair. She was wearing a short, fashionable frock. She had an egret plume on her head and a fox fur draped over one shoulder. Her face was heavily made up. She was leaning on the arm of a smiling young man wearing white tie and tails. They looked as if they were dressed for a ball.

In the expectant silence that followed her outburst, the speaker smiled. 'If you'll forgive me, my dear, you look a little young to have been in Petrograd in 'seventeen.'

'Old enough to have served for three years as a nurse on the eastern front. Did you serve in the war?'

He puffed himself up to his full five foot three inches. 'I served honourably enough in one of His Majesty's prisons, where they incarcerated those conscientious objectors brave enough to stand up and make known their horror of the slaughter of the working man for capitalist interests.'

'Lucky you were in a capitalist gaol,' said the girl. 'I don't think you'd have survived long in a Bolshevik one.'

'Madam is speaking from experience, perhaps?'

'As it happens I am. In Moscow just before Brest Litovsk. I was questioned when my train arrived from the front. I was still wearing my nurse's uniform, you see, and that branded me with the officers. They were shooting officers in those days, your Bolsheviks.' The room had stilled. 'I wasn't imprisoned then. Not immediately. They let me go on that occasion, allowing me to stay with a friend. I had a chance to see what life was like in the Workers' Paradise. No food. No fuel. Hunger. Cold. More frozen bodies – just as dead as the ones I saw at the front but this time in the heart of the city – and nowhere to bury them because the graveyards were full and the crematoria didn't work. You could say there was equality of treatment. Everybody starved. Well, that's not quite right, is it? Because everybody didn't starve, did they? The Cheka were well fed. The members of the Party had fires . . .'

'Propaganda!' cried the speaker.

The woman ignored him. She had the floor. 'Of course they came for me. I was a foreigner and therefore a spy. The house in which we were keeping a beggar's existence in the two servants' rooms they allowed us to use was a mansion that had belonged to my friends, and therefore we were class enemies. We all had an idea what would be in store for us by the time we arrived at the Lubyanka.

You surely know what the Lubyanka is, Mr Know-it-all-Speaker? Or perhaps it wasn't on your tour. No, it wouldn't have been, would it? A pity. You'd have been impressed. Their prisons are full of scientific techniques – torture as an industrial process. Very efficient. Quite in keeping with your New Economic Programme.'

There were a few nervous titters. 'Luckily I managed to avoid the full treatment,' she continued. 'I was recognised by one of the Cheka commissars interrogating me. He'd served at the front and been wounded. Apparently I'd saved his leg. He remembered. I didn't. I'd treated thousands of wounded legs, you see. Amputated most of them.' She giggled. 'Couldn't remember his. Couldn't remember much at all by that stage – hadn't slept for days. Difficult to sleep in a six-man cell crammed with forty people. Ironic, isn't it? The whole point of torture is to get information out of you. Hard to confess when you've forgotten who you are.' She ran a hand over her forehead. 'Anyway, Mr Cheka helped me, and later he even found me the papers to get me on a train across Siberia to Vladivostok. Wasn't that a nice Bolsheviki kind of thing to do?'

'An honest official,' declared the speaker. 'An example of the good Soviet citizen.'

'No, a corrupt gangster,' the girl had said, in a different, harsher tone. 'Like all his kind. You don't think he did this favour for me for free, do you? Do you?' Her voice had suddenly become shrill. 'And do you suppose that I had any choice but to give him what he wanted?'

In the horrified hush that followed, Fu-kuei had seen the anger in the girl's green eyes, her shaking shoulders, the glint of a tear, and knew that she had been through experiences similar to her own. She was clearly implacably opposed to everything in which Fu-kuei believed, but she suddenly felt a bond with her beyond any ideology. They had graduated from the same school.

'Come on, Catherine, that's enough.' The young man in the white tie took her by the arm. The fire had gone out of her, and she allowed herself to be led out of the room. A hush accompanied their departure. Then there had been a pandemonium of shouts over the speaker's squeaking denunciations of 'Lies. Propaganda of the rightist press. Don't believe her, ladies and gentlemen.'

But Fu-kuei did. 'Please take me home,' she had asked John Soo. 'I hate politics.'

'That woman,' she said now. 'With the red hair. She was . . .'

'The one at the meeting. I know,' said John Soo, shortly. He was poling the punt quietly. There was no trace of anger in his expression but she could see that he was tense from his rigid shoulders.

'I didn't recognise her. The makeup she wore that night . . .'

'I recognised her immediately,' said John. 'Look, I don't feel like punting any more. Shall we go back?'

The punt had half turned in mid-stream when, on the bank, Fu-kuei saw the woman they had been speaking about. She was standing with her back to the sunshine, her arms hanging loosely by her sides. Fu-kuei could see her limbs and the contours of her body through the white light of her dress. Her dark red hair, with its crown of flowers, blazed in an aureola of colour. She was panting: she must have run back along the towpath after being let off her own punt. To Fu-kuei she looked like a spirit of the river, or a shepherdess who had strayed out of her sixteenth-century poems.

'Here. You there,' she heard the woman cry. 'Do you speak English?'

'Very well,' said John Soo, acerbically.

'I'm so glad. Listen, I want to apologise,' called the woman. 'We were unforgivably rude to you back there.'

'You were not rude,' Fu-kuei heard herself say.

'Well, the others were.'

'Children's games,' said Fu-kuei. 'We understand.' She could feel John Soo glaring at her.

'Yes, they are children,' the woman said. 'A lost generation, really. Some of them were in the war, the last year of it, at least.'

'As were you, I believe,' said Fu-kuei. 'For longer.'

'So that *was* you. I thought I saw you in the audience. You heard my outburst, then. How embarrassing.'

'I thought you were very brave to speak in that way. I was moved,' said Fu-kuei.

'Were you? *Were* you? Listen, I do want to make it up to you. Please let me make amends.'

'There really is no need,' said Fu-kuei.

'Yes, there is,' she said. 'My name's Catherine – Catherine Cabot. I'm at Somerville. It's my last year. You *will* come and see me, won't you? For tea or something?' She laughed – the harsh laugh that was at odds with her smile. 'Come on, you're Chinese, aren't you? You must drink tea. Oh, gosh, what a thing to say. Now you'll think I'm laughing at you. I'm not, though. Please say yes.'

'It really isn't necessary.'

'But it'll be fun, won't it? I'd love to know you better. Do say yes. Tomorrow or the day after. I won't take no for an answer, you know. If your grumpy friend steers your punt away I'll leap in and swim after you.'

Fu-kuei could not help but laugh. 'All right, Miss Cabot. After I finish my thesis perhaps.'

'That's marvellous,' she cried. Her brow furrowed as if she had something else to say and her eyes fixed on Fu-kuei, who thought she caught a look of fascination, uncertainty, a hint of vulnerability. The girl smiled. 'I'd better run back and catch the others. Remember, it's Catherine Cabot at Somerville.' And she started off in the direction from which she had come, running lightly, a maenad among the flowers.

'I don't think I'll ever understand the English,' said John Soo, as he lifted the pole.

Fu-kuei did not hear him. She was considering the ironies and contradictions of her own life, the one she had chosen – or the one that had chosen her. A sudden breeze shivered the surface of the water and for the first time the thought of returning to China filled her with fear. She saw doors closing, options denied her. Wearily she reached for her poetry books, seeking – if only for a last fleeting moment – the illusory certainty of a green thought in a green shade.

PART ONE
The Parasol Wars
1921–1926

I

Journey Through a War

From the journal of William Lampsett, Reuters correspondent, Shanhaikuan Front, 28 July 1922

1.00 p.m.

I find myself in a narrow strip of land between the mountains and the sea while two armies prepare for battle. A breeze ruffles the millet fields, and the grey tiles of a deserted village glint in the sunshine. It's a pretty scene: the wild grass on the hillsides enclosing the small valley buzzes with the sound of crickets. To the west rise the escarpments of the Yanshan Mountains, jagged parapets that merge with the even higher battlements of cloud pavilions, which billow upwards until they in turn are lost in wisps and pennants against a clear blue sky. A careless white line of waterfall is scratched on a black cliff face in the far distance, and if one peers closely one can see that some of the rocky crags are sentinel towers of the Great Wall, which tumbles not far from here into the ocean. It's certainly not the first time in China's history that armies have faced each other in these passes, and neither is it likely to be the last.

Today it's not the forces of civilisation facing barbarians. These are two Chinese armies, evenly matched. The warlord of the northeast, Marshal Chang Tso-lin, is challenging the warlord of the south, Marshal Wu Pei-fu.

I am with a group of officers, who are examining their enemies' positions through field-glasses. They look as if they have been fitted out by a theatrical costumier. Spurs are de rigueur. One or two sport sabres with hanging gold tassels. The display of medals and stars is considered quite seemly on a battlefield. Feathers and plumes on caps and kepis wave in the breeze. They all wear tinted spectacles against the glare of the sun. The grey, bushy-moustached general is swathed in a cape. I could be among the chorus in an Offenbach farce.

2.20 *p.m.*

Ah, action at last. The general has shuffled his cloak. A gloved hand has emerged from its folds and flopped forward, the fingers pointing vaguely towards the enemy. The staff officer beside him snaps to attention and the order goes down the line to the most junior in rank, who summons a dispatch rider. A motorcycle bounces and growls across the hillside to where the officer in charge of the gun emplacements awaits his orders. There is a shouted command, a cheer that floats and fades like the croak of a faraway crow, and activity bustles round one of the cannons. A sharp retort follows, and moments later a flower of pink and black smoke mushrooms on the opposite hill. There is a long silence. The staff officers peer through their binoculars. After an interminable wait, there is another crack and smoke puff, a wail in the air, and the crash of an explosion on an unoccupied outcrop. With these formal exchanges, the battle for the railway has begun.

4.10 *p.m.*

I was premature. I should have realised that the manuals these officers have studied at their academies are specific that no battle should take place without an artillery bombardment first. So for the last two hours the air above the valley has whined with projectiles, which invariably explode harmlessly away from the actual ground on which the enemy forces are crouching.

But just now the general has checked his timepiece and cast an eye at the sun. It's time to get on to the next stage if anything is to be decided today.

Company sergeants shout and the ranks deliver a dose of concentrated volley fire. If the intention of this display is to encourage the opposing force to capitulate it is clearly ineffective. The general consults with his staff officers. Apparently they have decided that an assault will have to be made.

There is a rattle down the lines as bayonets are fixed to rifles. A trumpet blares. A feeble cheer rises from the opposing hillsides, and the soldiers begin their descent. The steel of the bayonets flashes in the sunshine. Field officers shout encouragement. Some of the more enthusiastic raise their voices in the old Chinese battle cry: 'Sha-a! Kii-iil!'

Suddenly both armies are halted in their tracks. A strange new sound is echoing in the valley. It comes from the east, a long-drawn-out bray, followed by the clatter of an approaching train. Its hooter sounds again, closer.

The officers press their binoculars to their eyes. Moustaches bristle. They swing their binoculars back to the battlefield, where the first echelons of the attack are approaching the railway line. After a long pause, the general's glove rises into the air. The command to 'Halt the advance' is sounded.

Round the V of the hills marking the entrance to the valley a steam train pounds into view, dragging behind it a long procession of carriages. On the cylinder of the shiny black engine can be made out a label, in bright red lettering and characters, English and Chinese: 'Mukden – Peking'. Two white flags flutter on either side. One of the officers looks at his watch. 'It's the twelve forty-five from Newchwang, Excellency,' he tells his general.

The general's face puffs a dark purple. 'Foreigners!' he snarls, in his vexation. Within moments the soldiers have sunk into the grass.

As the carriages rattle by, the men, knowing the way that armies work and that it will be some time before any further attack can be organised, fill their kettles from their billycans, and gather branches to make small fires. They settle into comfortable positions in the grass and pull their parasols out of their backpacks.

The bewildered foreign faces staring from the first-class carriages light up with wonder as the hillsides on either side of the track suddenly mushroom into a flower garden of pink, white and yellow paper umbrellas . . .

* * *

'Did you see that, Catherine?' The American girl turned from the dusty window. 'There's a battle going on out there.'

'Looks more like a picnic to me,' said Catherine.

'Well, I haven't had your experience, have I?' said Martha, cheerfully, settling back into her seat. 'Of wars, I mean.'

Catherine put down her magazine and observed her companion. There could not have been a greater contrast between the two women. One was tall and pale, the other dumpy and dark. While Catherine's long red hair flowed naturally over her shoulders, Martha had tied hers into a frizzy bun. Catherine wore an elegant white dress, which highlighted the curves of her figure, and Martha's black smock was draped sack-like over her heavy breasts and protuberant belly. They had met when Catherine had arrived at the door of the small cabin she had been allotted on the tramp steamer from Yokohama to Newchwang. She had been carrying her hatbox, the steward behind her straining with her trunk, and Martha had risen from her bunk. 'Oh, my God, what do you know? A fashion queen! Are you really the Miss Cabot I'm going to be sharing with? There go my chances with the crew. They'll be calling us Beauty and the Beast! Hi, I'm the Beast. Martha Cohen. Pleased to meet you.' She had stretched out a slim hand that appeared incongruously delicate when compared to the rest of her robust figure. Close-set brown eyes above a fleshy nose and plump cheeks crinkled with merriment as her thick lips curved in a wide, toothy smile.

But the glimpse of soldiers through the window had stirred uncomfortable recollections in Catherine, and suddenly, with the dark-complexioned girl smiling opposite her, she recalled another dark, laughing face, one she had tried to burn from her memory, along with the blood-soaked blankets in the forest glade. Suddenly, she was annoyed with her new friend for displaying the same innocent curiosity, enthusiasm and foolish zest for experience that she associated with her long-dead Marya. 'I think you should count yourself lucky you haven't experienced a war,' she said coldly.

'Aw, Catherine, don't you think it's exciting? Scary? Funny, even! Those parasols.' Martha giggled. 'What do you think it's all about? Who's fighting whom?'

Catherine grunted and pretended to read her magazine.

'You know, you can be very boring at times, Miss Oh-so-superior Cabot. For a humble Jewish teacher from the Bronx this is as exciting as it gets.' Martha slumped in her seat, folding her arms. 'You know what you are? You're impossible.' After a moment she added, 'And you know what else you are? You're a snob.'

Catherine hid a smile behind the glossy photographs. Martha always became grumpy when she did not react to her enthusiasm. Not that she felt over-sympathetic to her at this moment. It had been Martha's idea that they travel in a second-class carriage from Newchwang ('so we can be with the real people') and an uncomfortable ride in these closely packed wooden seats it had been. Catherine's back and neck were aching, and she was disturbingly aware of the proximity of the young Chinese gentleman squeezed next to her. She had deliberately avoided looking at him, although she was conscious of his interest in her. He must be a fashionable young man, she thought idly, glancing at his spats, shining brogues and the crisp trousers of his Western seersucker suit.

Most of the other Chinese passengers in the crowded coach were dressed in traditional clothes – the men in ankle-length cheongsams with embroidered silk waistcoats and pillbox black caps with a button on the top; many were smoking a foul tobacco in long, thin pipes. The air was heavy with stench and heat – her nostrils were still not used to the sweet pork scent of perspiring Chinese bodies, which underlay the spicier smells of garlic and vegetables emanating from the lunchboxes that every passenger had brought with them. Wherever she looked, somebody was biting into a mutton dumpling, pulling apart a chicken's foot, or slicing a watermelon. The floor was sticky with rinds, bones and melon seeds. On the small table by the window cracked porcelain mugs were filled with sticks of tea, one for each passenger. Occasionally the monotony of the journey was broken when the steward came by with the kettle. Standing in the rocking aisle like a surefooted sailor on a pounding deck, the man would expertly pour a jet of boiling water through the long brass spout. Catherine was in terror of being scalded each time but he had perfected his technique to a fine art. Martha was thrilled by this performance and would bravely hold out her cup. Eventually Catherine had done the same – but she hated it. In fact, she hated everything about this journey.

Of course, this was sublime comfort if she compared the conditions to those of the train journeys she had made in Russia after the collapse of the front. Then she had been squeezed for days among lice-ridden soldiers, forcing herself to stay awake because she was afraid of their intentions towards her. And she preferred not to think of the journey across Siberia in the closed cattle truck . . . When she had arrived in Vladivostok and experienced the relief of seeing a British warship anchored in the harbour she vowed that she would never again travel in discomfort. It would be first class or not at all. And she had kept to that pledge, even during her student days. Until now.

There hardly seemed any point in meeting 'the people', she thought, since they could not communicate with them. Worse than the stench or the heat was the racket. It was like being locked into a cage full of crickets. A drinking game was going on behind her: intoxicated young men were extending their fingers in some complicated version of stones-scissors-paper, yelling at the top of their voices. Nobody else in the car seemed to mind. At least the Buddhist monks had stopped their interminable chanting. There was a knot of them by the door, in their yellow and red robes, clustered obsequiously round a bald young man, who seemed to be wishing he was somewhere else: there was a miserable droop to his mouth and his nervous eyes kept flitting towards the two exotic foreign ladies in the carriage, who clearly fascinated him far more than his acolytes' prayers. At another time she might have been curious about why such reverence was being paid to a boy in his teens: he must be one of those reincarnated spirits whom Yu Fu-kuei had once told her about; *rinpoches* who had been born with the soul of a deceased sage and were brought up in monasteries to be divinities themselves. At this moment, sitting on an uncomfortable seat in a stuffy carriage, steaming through a dusty north China with a battle going on outside, she did not care.

She thought longingly of the first-class seats only a carriage away. She had passed through them to the lavatory, imperiously ignoring the guard who tried to block her way, and found a world of quiet and calm. Englishmen in tweeds reading the newspaper or smoking their pipes. Women in stoles settled comfortably on the plush seats watching their neatly attired children playing halma. A young woman, a redhead like herself, smoked a cigarette ostentatiously in a tortoiseshell holder, and laughed with a knickerbockered young man. They were her sort of people. That was where she belonged – if she belonged anywhere.

She thought back over the events of the last few months. The telegram from Nice containing the news of her mother's death in a car accident. Her arrival among strangers in the South of France. Her interview with the young Venezuelan in hospital – her mother's latest lover, who had survived the crash. He had been more than usually loathsome, with his effeminate good looks and his petulant whinings in deplorable English. She had paid him off with a cheque. She recalled the shabby funeral, and the uncomfortable meeting in the notary's office. More debts. More cheques. She had gathered her mother's personal effects from the tiny villa. A trunk of clothes: fluffy feather boas, shoes, and dresses of a style that would not have been appropriate on a woman of half her mother's age. Poor Helen Frances. Catherine had kissed the cold forehead in the open coffin in the undertaker's chapel of rest. The still beautiful features had been moulded into an unfamiliar expression of serene composure. It was if she had been making her farewell to a stranger. And when it came to it, her mother *had* been a stranger to her. Catherine realised that she had known little about her, or what had motivated her frenetic flight from one tawdry love affair to the next. Her end had been so sordid.

At the bottom of the trunk she had found a small valise containing letters, documents and photographs. At first she had been reluctant to look at them, but she had steeled herself on the train ride back to England. As the French countryside flitted past the window, she had opened the case and laid the papers on the table in the dining car. What she discovered was not the collection of love letters and *billets doux* she expected but a record of her own life. There was her birth certificate, stamped by the British consul in Peking. A photograph of herself in a perambulator. Drawings in a childish hand. Herself in fancy dress sitting at the head of a table at the smart tea-party her mother had held for her sixth birthday in Vienna, proud matrons standing behind their solemn children, a gorgeous Helen Frances gesturing to her to blow out the candles; later, older photos of herself making sandcastles on the beach at Leghorn; letters she had written to her mother on the many occasions when she had been left alone with a nanny while Helen Frances had travelled with her lovers round Europe ('I miss you, Mama. When are you coming home?'). Her mother had kept every one. She had leafed through them, trying to hold back her tears.

She saw herself growing out of childhood to adulthood: the studio portrait of herself in her new nurse's uniform before she left for the front; the cold letters she had written to her mother from the front (their long estrangement had started then); a photograph by the tent lines at Gorlitse, taken a few days before the Great Retreat – she recognised Pavel Alexandrovich, Mamasha, Marya, Natalya and herself. Then she had wept silently to herself, and for herself, only half conscious of the curious stares of the waiters and the other diners.

The last photo in this little pile was of her matriculation group at Oxford, which Helen Frances had clipped to the letter Catherine had received from her college accepting her into the university. She had kept even that, as well as Catherine's cutting response to her mother's rapturous letter of congratulation when the newspapers had published her first year's results. Three neat lines, which must have broken Helen Frances's heart. 'Thank you for your interest.' Could she have been so callous? There were no more letters. She had not written to her mother again, though she saw now that Helen Frances had never lost interest in her, and had kept the three cuttings from *The Times*, where Catherine's name had been mentioned in the diary page among the list of bright young socialites who had attended the varsity balls.

For a long time Catherine had gazed out of the window at her reflection in the glass, unaware that evening had fallen or that she had smoked almost a whole packet of cigarettes. Listlessly she had gathered together the papers, and noticed a manila envelope she had not yet opened. She had poured the contents on to the table, and seen the photograph that had brought her to China. It was of a small wooden house with an Oriental tiled roof. In the distance, islands floated in an inland sea. In the foreground stood a slim young woman dressed in a striped blouse with puffed sleeves and a long black skirt, a ribboned boater balanced at a jaunty angle on top of her piled hair. She held a parasol in one hand and, in the other, the arm of a grumpy little girl aged three or four. A tall man wearing a white suit stood beside them. He had a black moustache, and was leaning on a walking-stick, though he held his shoulders erect as if he was standing to attention at a military parade. He was smiling, and there was a merry twinkle in his dark, pouched eyes. Her mother's attention was fixed on him: there was a radiance in her expression and a softness in her eyes that Catherine could not remember having seen before. This was the face of a woman in love.

Sitting in the shaking dining car as the train trundled through France, Catherine looked at the fading, sepia-coloured photograph and felt all her childhood yearnings return to her. She knew who this man was. She recognised him immediately as the kindly uncle who had told her stories, the father she had yearned for, who had been taken from her. And her mother had kept his photograph all this time. There were none of any other lover. She could not take her eyes off his handsome face; suddenly, she remembered what he was called. Henry. Uncle Henry. In that moment she was a child again, looking up into his blue eyes as he bent over her cot.

There was another photograph of him, in a slim brown leather case that opened to reveal two framed portraits. It was a studio study in the style favoured in the 1890s. In it he was younger than he had been in the other photograph. He was wearing uniform and looking out at the photographer with a proud, almost supercilious stare. Catherine noticed a cruel downturn to his lips, but it did not repel her; rather, it fascinated her, as did his compelling, watchful eyes. There was a name printed under the portrait: 'Lt the Hon. H. R. Manners, Coldstream Guards'. Henry Manners.

At first she thought the other portrait in the frame was of herself, but then she recognised that it was her mother, as a young woman of no more than eighteen or nineteen. Catherine was struck by the mischievousness of her expression, the eager, amused curiosity in her eyes. This, like the other picture, was of a Helen Frances she had never known.

There had been a bundle of letters tied with pink ribbon. The first was from a woman called Nellie, who appeared to be attached to a mission in the north of China. The embossed letter-heading read 'Dr Edward Airton, Scottish Medical Mission, Shishan'. It was dated 11 January 1902, a gossipy letter about converts and gardens. Catherine's eyes passed over it quickly, but her attention was caught by the postscript:

'I should tell you that a mutual friend passed through our mission not so long ago. He was as well as could be expected, saturnine as ever – but I sensed a sadness in him, Helen Frances, a lack of his old confidence, and he changed the subject whenever I spoke of you and your child as if this were a matter too painful for him to contemplate. It is none of my business, of course, but as you know I am a tidy person by nature and I do not believe that loose ends should be left hanging. I realise that you are contemplating an engagement. Not knowing this Mr Belvedere, I can hardly comment on the suitability of the match; I am sure he is a fine, upstanding fellow, but since you ask me for my advice, I can only observe that you have hardly known him for very long. Of course, happiness can be found in Perivale as in any other place. On the other hand, I feel impelled to inform you that your other friend of longer standing will shortly be leaving for a new – and I fear a lonely – life in Japan. I attach the forwarding address he has given me. You must do whatever is in your best interests, and that of Catherine, whom I need not remind you is also his child, at least in the sight of God – but dare I say, nothing ventured, nothing gained? There. Edward will no doubt inform me that I am a busybody. In this case, my dear girl, I am not ashamed to be thought a busybody, or anything else for that matter. My only concern is for your happiness, and for that of a brave, lost man, who still loves you despite himself.

'Child . . . in the sight of God?' Quickly Catherine had read through the other letters, all of which had been from Henry Manners himself, most of them dated 1902. They were hardly love letters. The man's style was brief to the point of asperity. The first, addressed to her mother in Sussex, had been almost hostile: 'I thought that we had buried the past, and I was content with that . . . No, honestly, I don't want you to come to Japan. You made clear to me what your feelings were before you left Peking . . . I probably sound selfish, but another rejection would be more than I could bear . . .'

The second expressed cautious assent: 'Come then – although I fear we may both live to regret it, even on the terms you propose. And of course you must bring Catherine. I long to see her . . . Never mind what I hope or feel. You must ascertain for yourself whether this is wise. You must be sure, absolutely sure, for your own part. Have no fears on mine.'

The third letter contained comments on the P&O timetable, suggesting that a train across Russia and a boat from Vladivostok to Yokohama might save Helen Frances weeks of travel. It was signed 'Written in haste, H.' but there had been a postscript: 'Thanks portrait C. An angel. Glad she inherited mother's looks, not mine.' That 'not mine' had sent a shiver down Catherine's spine. Yet she still sought firm confirmation.

She read on. The next few letters had been addressed to various *postes restantes* in Aden, Colombo and Hong Kong. It was obvious that her mother had taken the P&O after all, and most of these missives contained contact addresses in the various ports, and recommendations for sightseeing. There had been one sardonic postscript, however: 'I hope you don't think I'm being impertinent offering these tourist guides. I nearly forgot, you came this way once before with Tom, didn't you?' Of course. Tom Cabot. Her father, whom her mother had told her that she had 'met on a boat'. But had he been her father? The letters suggested something else. She had realised with a shock that she was already beginning to think of her true father as Henry Manners.

The letter to Hong Kong had been the first to reveal any real passion:

My darling Helen Frances, I can hardly believe that when you read this you will only be a strait's distance away. You will see me on the pier in Yokohama. You will recognise me by my game leg. I will know you when

I see a goddess descend the gangplank. *Et vera incessu patuit dea.* Do you remember, my Venus? That is how I still think of you. That is how I have always thought of you, and I always will. Yet I am afraid, for a goddess when she manifests can reveal a terrible beauty, which burns and blinds her supplicant. How I long for your presence despite my fears. By the way, when you are in Hong Kong, do stop in at Salvadors in Ice House Street. They serve an excellent roast pigeon there.

That had been the end of the 1902 correspondence. The next letter, one of only two more, was dated February 1904:

I am writing to your aunt's address in the hope that this will reach you. I have had no news of you for months. I had not at first intended to write to you. You made yourself very clear before you left what you think of me, and what you expected of me, and how I had failed you. You are nothing if not forthright, my dear, dear girl. Yes, I still think of you with undiminished love, affection and pride. I blame you for nothing, though I still cannot understand why you should take me to task for an act of God, or of the Devil. In fact it was neither. A human tragedy, an ordinary human tragedy, although it broke our lives. I realise now that in my own grief and sorrow I withdrew from you at a time when you needed me. I did what weak men do when their grief is unbearable. I should have been at your bedside. Instead I abandoned you because I could not face accepting what we had lost. I left you and Catherine in your darkest hour, and when I had returned, when my drinking madness was over – although you said nothing then – it was already too late. I had lost you. I had thrown you away. Well, both of us are proud, my darling, and I am not crawling to you for forgiveness. Anyway, we've been through all of that. I cannot bear to think of that devastating month of quarrels and recriminations. And you are right. My loneliness, this empty house with its memories, like accusations, is what I deserve. I've reaped what I've sown. That sounds self-pitying, doesn't it? But I state it as a fact and I accept it. We both of us know how to look reality in the eyes. It's probably why we were attracted to each other in the first place. Well, don't worry. I am looking reality in the eyes. By God I am. To my sorrow.

Do you know? I pass the churchyard every day and every day I stand by the little plot where our happiness is buried, sometimes for ten minutes, sometimes for an hour. I talk to him. I tell him about you, the wonderful mother he might have had. And about his sister. Sweet Catherine. Of course I never hear a reply, only the sound of the wind blowing through the cypress trees. But it comforts me to be by his grave. Knowing that a part of you is buried there with him, along with a part of me. The greater part of me.

I ask only one thing of you, Helen Frances. For we have another child in whom our blood and our love is mingled. You took her away from me once before. Even now she bears another man's name. Yet for fifteen precious months I knew her as my daughter. I do not ask you to tell her about me. It is probably better that she grows up as a Cabot – spare her our squalid past – but please, Helen Frances, write to me, if only now and again, to let me know how she is getting on. She carries within her my heart. For all that we once meant to each other, promise me this. I find that I am pleading with you after all. My goddess.

From your eternal supplicant, Henry. [And in an untidy scrawl, a repetition of that Latin phrase:] *Et vera incessu patuit dea.*

The last letter, dated December 1904, read simply:

My goddess, it seems, has turned her dark face upon me. You have not answered any of my letters. So that is the way it is to be. I will not plead with you again. I am leaving for Manchuria. There is a war there, and my old masters think I might be useful. Kiss my daughter for me one last time. May you both be happy, wherever you are, whatever you do, Henry.

Catherine had launched herself on her quest. She had returned to Oxford and finished her exams, somehow scraping a second, which had disappointed her tutors, but she had not revised. Neither had she partied, although she found that she was spending increasing amounts of time with her strange new Chinese friend, Yu Fu-kuei. In her mind, Fu-kuei had become associated with her quest. Whatever was the secret of her birth it would be found in China, where Henry Manners and Helen Frances had met. It was a providential coincidence that Fu-kuei herself came from Shishan, a town that featured in her parents' story. The Chinese woman was surprised, no doubt, by her curiosity but she patiently answered her questions in her quiet way.

Over the summer and autumn, Catherine had used the few clues in the correspondence to make her own search. She had looked up the addresses of every Scottish missionary society she could find, and one had replied that a Dr Edward Airton had indeed conducted a mission for them for many years in Shishan but that he had now retired from his proselytising activities. They were reliably informed, however, that he was still in China in private medical practice, in an association with the Kailan Mining Administration, which had its headquarters in Tientsin. The letter suggested that she write to him in China, through the company or the Tientsin Club. She had followed their advice, and a few weeks later had received a telegram from Dr Airton.

MY DEAR CATHERINE STOP DEVASTATED BY NEWS OF YOUR MOTHER'S DEATH STOP WE LOVED HER DEARLY STOP WILL ENQUIRE MANNERS'S WHEREABOUTS OUT OF TOUCH BUT BELIEVE HE STILL RESIDES MANCHURIA STOP MUCH TO TELL YOU AND DELIGHTED YOU INTEND TO VISIT CHINA AFTER JAPAN STOP OUR HOME IS YOURS STOP YOU ASK WHO IS NELLIE SHE IS MY WIFE AND YOUR GODMOTHER SENDS BUCKETS LOVE STOP OVERJOYED TO HEAR FROM YOU AFTER SILENCE OF MANY YEARS STOP E.A.

On a cold November morning she had taken a train to Oxford to say farewell to Fu-kuei. She had found her in her rooms at St Hugh's. They walked for a while in the grounds, their footsteps crunching on the frost-covered lawn. A distant church bell rang, and above them they heard the flutter of crows leaving their nest in one of the bare oaks.

'I'll be glad to get away from England,' Catherine had said suddenly. 'I hate the winter.'

'Do you?' murmured Fu-kuei. 'I will miss it. There is an honesty about winter.'

'What on earth do you mean?' Catherine had asked.

'Look at those trees, beautiful in their nakedness. You see them for what they are – their age, their strength, the ravages of wind and weather on the bark. Don't you think there is a deception when they hide themselves in summer clothes?'

'You are a strange one,' smiled Catherine. She rubbed her hands. 'Give me summer any day.'

Fu-kuei appraised her, then urgently took her hands. 'Yes, you are a creature of summer and light, Catherine. Do not change. Don't let the cold winds of the world harm you.'

Catherine had been a little embarrassed. 'They will, if we don't get back to your warm study.'

Fu-kuei had watched as Catherine toasted crumpets on the grid of the small electric heater. 'I'm determined to make an Englishwoman of you before I go,' Catherine had said, over her shoulder.

'You have already been successful,' said Fu-kuei. 'I don't know what they will think of me when I return to Shanghai and pour milk into my tea.'

Catherine had turned her head. 'You're not going back for a while, are you? Your thesis is not to be handed in till January. I'm sure they'll give you a *viva* and a distinction. You're made for academic life.'

'I've already finished my thesis,' said Fu-kuei, quietly. 'Catherine, there was something I wanted to tell you. When you telegraphed me last week telling me your departure date, I – I booked a berth on the same passage. Catherine, I'll be travelling with you to China.'

Catherine had dropped the crumpet and stared at her, open-mouthed.

'Have I offended you?' asked Fu-kuei.

Catherine had bounded across the room and hugged her. 'Oh, darling!' she had cried. 'I can't think of anything I would like more in all the world.'

Two weeks later they had been at sea. During the long journey their friendship had matured, and Catherine had learned much about China, but strangely, despite the warmth of their friendship, little more about Fu-kuei. She had never known anybody who could be so intimate and so distant at the same time. She could sense the affection Fu-kuei felt for her in the warmth of her attention, and the concentration in those soft, Asiatic eyes, whose understanding seemed to penetrate her soul, and she was reminded of the Kirghiz tribesmen she had encountered in Russia on that terrible day. There was a sadness in Fu-kuei's still face, however, which to Catherine indicated knowledge of terrible suffering – yet there had been nothing in Fu-kuei's brief life story that could account for it. Catherine had pressed her, more than once, to tell her about the life she had lived in China, and Fu-kuei had told her about her family, her university days, her betrothal to a young officer in Shanghai whom she was returning to marry.

'Do you love him?' Catherine had blurted out.

'Yes, very much,' Fu-kuei had murmured, bowing her head modestly, but in those sphinx-like eyes, Catherine had seen pain, regret, sadness.

Usually Catherine ended up talking about herself, and this was unusual, because Catherine very rarely revealed herself to anyone. Those eyes, she decided, seemed to draw out her deepest secrets – and it was calming, cathartic, as if in telling Fu-kuei her troubles she was laying them to rest.

One night, sitting in Catherine's cabin, they had consumed a bottle of wine. They had already had a few glasses over dinner, and were flushed and talkative. It seemed that neither wanted the evening to end. For the first time Fu-kuei had asked about her experiences in Russia, and Catherine spoke of the war. She even told her about Nicky, and later, about Marya. The alcohol numbed the pain. Fu-kuei listened attentively, her eyes never leaving Catherine's face. 'What really happened in the Lubyanka, Catherine? And afterwards?' she asked gently, as she poured Catherine another glass. 'I know about the man. How he used you. But what else did they demand from you?' She paused. 'Before they let you go.' Fu-kuei had waited patiently, then she asked, 'Did they make you sign a confession?'

Catherine looked into Fu-kuei's eyes, so sympathetic, and nodded. 'How – how did you know?' she asked.

'You told them what they wanted to hear about your friends,' said Fu-kuei. It was a statement, a logical conclusion to her own question. 'You're not to blame. Really, you're not to blame . . . But was that all, Catherine? Did they – did they ask you to do anything for them afterwards . . . after you returned to England perhaps?'

Catherine shook her head, confused. 'No,' she whispered. 'Nothing like that. What do you mean?'

'Did you meet anybody from the Comintern?' prodded Fu-kuei. 'The Third International?'

'No,' said Catherine. 'I told you what happened. It was only that man. From the Cheka. He took me to his apartment, and he – and he – he made me—' She was shaking. 'He was an animal,' she hissed. 'And I was grateful to him. Oh, God, help me,' she wailed. 'I was grateful to him. For five whole weeks, I was grateful to him . . .' Tears were running freely down her cheeks.

'I'm sorry,' said Fu-kuei. 'I had to ask. Quiet now. It's all over. It's all right.' Catherine felt the delicate hands fold round her own, and when she looked up she had been surprised to see tears in her friend's eyes. She felt the touch of a kiss on her forehead, and a slim arm round her shoulders. 'It is good to unburden yourself of memories such as these if you have a friend who understands,' Fu-kuei had said, when Catherine was calmer.

'You understand what I just described? How could you?'

Fu-kuei had smiled, and gently smoothed Catherine's hair. 'Don't think that my life is any less complicated than yours,' she said. 'Perhaps I, too, have a quest ahead of me.'

Catherine had looked at her quizzically. She was very drunk. 'I thought you were returning to Shanghai to get married. What sort of a quest is marriage?'

Fu-kuei gave a tinkling laugh. 'Marriage is a sort of quest,' she said. 'Only in fairy stories or in one of your Western medieval romances is it a happy ending. In life it is all too often the beginning of a long journey.'

'That's very romantic.' Catherine smiled sleepily.

Fu-kuei's eyes hardened. 'No,' she said. 'It is not romantic in any way.'

She had looked at her watch and made an excuse that it was late; Catherine, left alone in her cabin, wondered about her friend's strange questions. Had she finally revealed something of the mystery behind the mask? Even if she had, Catherine did not understand remotely what it signified. What on earth could Fu-kuei possibly know about the Third International? As she stumbled about the room, looking for her nightgown, she saw Fu-kuei's full glass of wine, and tried to remember when, during the evening, she had seen her put it to her lips.

Next morning, while they shared a late breakfast, Fu-kuei had been her demure, polite, self, only she was paler than usual and claimed to have a headache.

'You too?' Catherine had been sick in the night. 'I thought I was the one who overdid it.'

'I think we matched each other glass for glass,' said Fu-kuei. 'I don't remember how many bottles we finished, or even what we talked about.'

'I think I was telling you about Russia,' said Catherine, carefully, a warning bell thudding in her mind.

'Were you?' said Fu-kuei, and sipped her tea. 'I can't remember what you said. Can you?'

Catherine had remembered every word, but something urged her to be cautious. 'No,' she replied. 'Not a thing. What a pair we are.'

And they had laughed. But for the first time in their relationship, Catherine had detected a note of falsehood in her friend. And in herself.

The incident had cast a shadow over their last few days on the ship, yet they had continued their promenades on deck, dined together, and made excruciatingly polite conversation. For all that, Catherine had felt a pang of regret when she parted from Fu-kuei in Hong Kong (Catherine was changing ships for Yokohama, while Fu-kuei was continuing to Shanghai). They had exchanged addresses – Catherine gave as her contact the Airtons' – and she had promised to visit Fu-kuei in Shanghai at the first opportunity. Nevertheless, much remained unsaid.

In Japan she had completed the first part of her quest. It had taken some sleuthing but eventually she had found a man in the British consulate in Yokohama who had recognised the seashore in the old photograph. It had been an easy journey to Kyoto and from there by stages to the Inland Sea. She had stood for a long time on the shore, thinking of her mother, her childhood, the strange course of her life. She could not identify the house in which they had lived – there were many wooden bungalows, each one prettier than the next. She had found the graveyard, though, where she had been received by a bowed Japanese attendant who spoke a little English. 'This is probably a waste of your time,' she had said. 'I don't know even if he's here. His surname would probably be Manners if he is.'

The old man had smiled at her. 'Oh,' he said, 'you talk of the little English boy nobody visits. Oh, yes. Oh, yes. I look after that one for nearly twenty years. He lonely little soul. Must be very happy you come today. Oh yes. Come, come with me.' He had hobbled away down the neat footpaths between the graves, beckoning her to follow. He led her up the hill to a small grave, strewn with freshly cut chrysanthemums.

There was a simple wooden cross, which bore the name TOMAS MA RES and some characters in Japanese script. Catherine's eyes misted with tears. 'Who – who put these flowers here?' she managed.

'Oh, very sorry,' said the old man. 'Hope you not angry. But I think this is sad little boy. So I put flowers, and make cross. Sorry, cannot afford stone one.'

Catherine had fallen to her knees and wept – for her parents, her brother, herself, and for the unexpected kindness of this ancient attendant, who wrung his hands in confusion at her distress while a fragrant breeze rustled through the cypress trees.

That had been ten days ago. She had not lingered in Japan, although it was a pretty country full of courteous people. She had negotiated a ticket on the first packet boat to China and on board she had met Martha. She had enjoyed having a travelling companion again – although Martha was very different from Fu-kuei, with her mysterious secrets. She had never met anybody as frank or forthright. Catherine had been delighted to discover that she was also going to Tientsin, where she had secured a teaching post attached to one of the city's synagogues. 'You don't look very Orthodox to me,' Catherine had said, and smiled.

'Yeah, well, my uncle's a cantor and he fixed it.' Martha had sighed. 'A job's a job. At least it gets me out of the Bronx. And who knows? Maybe I'll meet some rich China trader who'll buy me diamonds and all, and I'll become a lady like you.'

'I'm no lady,' laughed Catherine.

'Sure you are,' said Martha. 'You have a hatbox, for God's sakes. Who do I know who travels with a hatbox?'

Sitting now in the Chinese railway carriage, Catherine recalled this and many other jokes they had shared. Suddenly she felt a surge of happiness. Shortly she would arrive in Tientsin, where she felt certain she would find the answers she was looking for. For once in her life, things were working out as she had planned. She giggled. Martha, still pouting, shot her a glance. 'What are you laughing at all of a sudden?' she asked.

Catherine poked her with her toe. 'You,' she said.

'There's a nerve. I thought you'd gone into a coma. Well, now you've decided to become a human being again, come on, Catherine, tell me – you know about these things. What's this war that's going on? And why'd they stop fighting when we appeared?'

'Be-be-be-because nobody dares to upset you f-foreigners. Be-be-because in China you f-f-foreigners have the economic power.'

Both women turned in astonishment. The young man in the seer-sucker suit had spoken. He was blinking rapidly behind his round spectacles.

'Hey, whoever you are,' Martha reacted first, 'what do you mean by us foreigners having economic power? Not this foreigner, pal. Want to see my purse? I got zilch.'

The broadside put the young man into an agony of confusion. His face reddened.

'Calm down.' Martha was smiling broadly. 'I was only joking. Hey, you speak English. That's terrific. Listen, I'm Martha Cohen, from New York City. And this is my friend, Catherine, from Oxford, England. She's not as arrogant as she looks, believe me. And we want to talk to you, because you're the first person we've met in this country who speaks a known language. So, why don't you take it slowly, and tell us your name?'

It took him several attempts, but under Martha's coaching, they established that he was Lei Ming and that he was returning to his family in Tientsin after studying abroad, in Hawaii.

'Well, Mr Lei, that's great,' said Martha, clapping. 'So you've lived in the US of A? And you obviously know more than we do about what's going on in China, so why don't you just tell us slowly now about these wars and economic powers and all, whatever it was you were saying before I interrupted you? First of all, who were those soldiers we saw out there? Which were the good guys and which were the bad?'

The young man was relaxing now and his speech became more

fluent. 'G-good guys and bad guys? Like in the cowboy westerns, yes? T-Tom Mix!'

'Sure. Tom Mix,' said Martha, smiling with him.

'No, Miss Cohen, we have no g-good guys here. They are all b-bad guys. W-warlords. It is terrible the way our country has descended into civil war. But in the battle we have just witnessed I support the n-northern troops belonging to Marshal Chang Tso-lin.'

'Yeah? Thought you said they were all warlords?'

'He is one of the w-w-worst of them. Originally a b-bandit, and very ambitious. I think he wants to make himself emperor, and return our country to f-f-feudalism.'

'Is that right?' Martha rested her plump chin in her hands. 'What makes you support him, then?'

'B-because the w-warlord he is fighting, Marshal Wu Pei-fu, is even worse. He s-supports the c-corrupt government in Peking. He is a − a − C-Confucianist.'

'That's bad?'

'Very bad,' smiled Lei. 'Though my father is a C-Confucianist too. We must get away from all of that b-backwardness of thinking if our country is to p-progress.'

'I get it. So this other warlord, Marshal Chang, he's not a Confucianist − but he wants feudalism. Isn't that worse?'

'It is the same thing. Chang Tso-lin is also C-Confucianist, although he is no s-scholar like Wu Pei-fu. He is uneducated. A bandit, as I told you.'

'I'm lost.'

'Marshal Chang who was a b-bandit, and still is in his heart, wants power only, and that is g-good because with his l-limitless ambition he will unite the country. He is so unscrupulous that he is prepared to acc-acc-accommodate the forces of p-progress if he thinks it will get him what he w-wants, and in this war he is in alliance with Dr Sun Yat-sen in the south.'

'Who's he?'

'You do not know Dr Sun Yat-sen?' Lei's mouth fell open in wonder, and in his excitement his stammer all but disappeared. 'It was Dr Sun who led the revolution against the Manchus. He is the father of our republic – but he was b-betrayed by the m-militarists who took power. Now he has established a power base in Canton, where he is building a coalition that will one day create a Nationalist government to unite the country. Dr Sun is a great man.'

'He's not a Confucianist, then?' asked Martha.

'No.' Lei's eyes gleamed. 'Like any statesman, he will make compromises – with the militarists, capitalists, foreigners, the bourgeoisie – but I b-believe that in his heart, he is like me – a s-socialist!'

'Wow,' exclaimed Martha. She appeared impressed. 'Is that some kind of revolutionary or something?'

'Not n-necessarily, Miss Cohen,' beamed Lei Ming, proudly, 'but we do believe in the equality of m-mankind, and the creation of a b-better, fairer society free of abuses. It is what China needs. And I believe that Dr Sun and the Nationalists will bring us that.'

'Equality of mankind, and a fair society,' Martha repeated thoughtfully. 'I go along with that. Sounds like good old American values.'

'Oh, God, spare me.' It was Catherine's first contribution to the conversation, to which she had listened with mounting impatience.

'Catherine!' growled Martha. 'Be nice.'

'I'm sorry, Martha, and – what's your name? – Mr Lei, but I'm just not interested. I'm afraid I've had my fill of politics and wars, and I probably know more about socialism than you do, Mr Lei. I've seen the sort of paradise on earth it creates. Go on, both of you, plan your Utopias, but I'm going back to my fashion magazine.'

'B-but M-Miss C-C-Catherine,' he was stammering badly again. 'D-don't you believe in s-struggling for a b-better life for ordinary p-people? I kn-know that G-Great Britain is a c-colonial power, but Eng-Eng-England was a c-cradle of s-socialism. John S-Stuart Mill. B-Bernard Shaw. R-Ramsay MacDonald . . .'

'Don't bother, Mr Lei. She's lived through the Great War, and the Russian revolution,' said Martha, acidly. 'She thinks she knows all about it.'

'The R-Russian revolution?' exclaimed Lei, his eyes widening. 'You were – you were th-there? You saw it? Oh – but that is wonderful. Please tell me . . .'

'Some other time, perhaps,' muttered Catherine, and reached for her magazine, but as she opened the pages she was propelled forward, as was everybody else in the carriage, by a sudden halt. Immediately they had recovered from this, they were jolted backwards as the train began to reverse. After a moment she realised they were being shunted off the main line into a siding. The brick buildings indicated that they were on the outskirts of a town. Over a wall they could see grey roofs and in the distance some cranes against a blue line of sea, as well as some ships at anchor including a small grey-clad destroyer or frigate.

'Where are we? What's happening?' Martha asked Lei.

'This is the port of Chinwangtao,' he said. 'I don't know why we have s-stopped here. There is the attendant. I'll ask him.'

The steward was in a hurry to get through the carriage. It was not only Lei who wanted to know what was going on and he was pulled and shouted at from dozens of directions. Eventually he raised his arms above his head and yelled something at the top of his voice. There was a great collective sigh from the passengers, then they rushed towards the windows on the other side of the carriage, clambering over each other in their excitement.

Lei came back breathlessly to the women, his face pink with exhilaration. 'C-come,' he said. 'Come quick to see. In a minute M-Marshal W-Wu Pei-fu himself will be going by in his special train.'

Martha leaped to her feet, and made to follow him, then noticed that Catherine had not moved. 'Come on, Catherine. Don't you want to see a warlord?'

Catherine was staring intently at something she had noticed outside her window. A grubby tent had been set up beside the railway line, with a large red swastika painted on the canvas. Through the flaps she could see men in white doctors' coats with little white caps on their heads smoking and playing mah-jongg on a wooden table. They were ignoring the activities around them – but it was these activities that had so fixed Catherine's attention. She had witnessed similar scenes during the war, but never had she seen such inhuman callousness.

A cattle wagon was parked on the next siding and soldiers were unloading wounded men. Two men stood by the open doors lifting them off bloodstained straw and passing them down to more soldiers waiting in a chain. Some were stretched out on the muddy ground in a row beside the tent, where they twitched and groaned in pain. Catherine saw head, leg and stomach wounds, some extremely serious. They had obviously received treatment at a front-line first-aid station, for she noticed rudimentary bandages and primitive tourniquets – but whoever had given it had been disgrace-fully lax. She watched in mounting horror as more men were unloaded. The soldiers were handling them with the sensitivity of longshoremen swinging sacks of grain on to a wharf. She knew that if she had been able to hear anything through the thick glass window and above the noise in the carriage it would have been screams of pain. Meanwhile, unbelievably, the doctors played on, oblivious to the misery outside.

'Oh, my God,' she heard Martha's whisper behind her. 'Looks like a butcher's yard.'

'They're not being very professional, are they?' said Catherine, in clipped, angry tones. 'Aren't you going off to have a look at your warlord?'

Martha silently shook her head. The two women stared through the window.

As they watched, one of the men on the wagon lost his footing as he lifted a body. For a second he wobbled in the doorway, trying to right his balance. The soldier who had the head and shoulders of the wounded man tottered – then all three fell to the ground. The two soldiers were unhurt. They stumbled to their feet, then simultaneously exploded into laughter. The others in the chain had put down their own loads and, leaving the wounded men where they were lying, sidled up to see what was going on. Catherine tried to make out what had become of the one they had been lifting. Clearly, they had forgotten him. Finally she saw him protruding from under the wagon where he had rolled. The tourniquet had slipped from his wounded leg, and she knew that his life-blood was pumping out over the rocks on the track.

'Hey, where are you going?' Martha cried, but Catherine was opening the door of the carriage, and jumping on to the sleepers.

Ignoring a twisted ankle, she raced to the wagon on the other siding. She heard someone running behind her, thought a guard must be trying to stop her, and was startled to hear an English voice, panting with exertion: 'Steady on there. Where are you going in such a hurry?'

'I'm a nurse. Who are you?' she shouted back.

The running man beside her was wearing a brown fedora and a trench coat. His heavy brown shoes crunched on the stones. He had an untrimmed moustache and unshaven cheeks, and warm eyes that smiled at her from a tanned face. 'A nurse?' he puffed. 'You're rather elegant for the average nurse. Where did you appear from?'

'Second class,' she retorted. 'Where do you think?'

'Then at least the proprieties are being observed. I'm a doctor, from first class.'

The soldiers stood aside, bewildered by the appearance of two foreigners. They knelt by the wounded man. 'We can't lift him on our own,' muttered the doctor, then, in fluent Chinese, ordered the soldiers to help him. The tone of authority seemed to restore a sense of responsibility in them. Carefully they lifted the wounded man on to the embankment. He was unconscious, but alive. The doctor reached into his black bag, which he had brought with him, and passed Catherine some scissors and a clean roll of bandage. 'Cut off those rags,' he said curtly, 'while I prepare a new tourniquet. That's right. Press the artery to stop the bleeding.' Her hands were already red with blood: she was acting automatically, as she had a thousand times before in a previous life.

At one point the man looked up at her. 'You've treated wounds like this before. Where were you?'

'Galicia. Eastern front,' she muttered, dabbing iodine on the wound. 'Look, they haven't even bothered to remove the bullet from the leg. You can feel it. Here.'

'Pass me the forceps, then, and the scalpel from the bag. There we go. Easy now. Salve. Gently does it. Were you with a British unit?'

'Russian,' she said.

'I was in Flanders,' he said. 'There. He'll do for now, though I don't see much hope in the long run of saving his leg. Should have been treated within half an hour of tying on that hopeless tourniquet. Can you finish off here while I look at some of the others?'

As he spoke the train's whistle blew. Beyond the knot of soldiers surrounding them they could see a station guard gesticulating at them to get back on. They looked at each other.

'I'm staying,' said the man. 'What about you?'

Catherine nodded and continued bandaging.

'Good girl,' he said, getting to his feet. 'I spotted a rather nasty stomach wound back there. Bring the bag, will you, when you're done?' The soldiers stepped aside to let him pass. Catherine knotted the bandage, rinsed the instruments in the doctor's antiseptic, then rolled them hurriedly into their cloth case. The soldiers stared at her with amusement and wonder. For a long moment she looked into their fresh faces. Boys, she thought. It's always boys. 'Will you please let me pass?' she said quietly. Nobody moved. Finally she had to shoulder her way through them, stepping briskly towards the tent.

She found the English doctor standing by the body of the stomach patient, but he was not treating him. He was confronting the Chinese doctors, who were shouting at him angrily. He was replying, quietly but firmly, in his fluent Chinese.

'What's the matter?' she asked, when she reached him.

'Apparently they don't need us,' he answered. 'The devil with them. At least two have been smoking opium. Look at their dilated pupils.'

'They should be glad of our help.'

'You'd have thought so, wouldn't you? Look, here comes trouble. Don't say anything. Let me do the talking.'

'I'm only a nurse from second class, Doctor,' said Catherine, sweetly. 'Trained to be quiet until spoken to.'

A squat, moustached officer had pushed his way to the front of the group of doctors, a squad of soldiers behind him with fixed bayonets. He screamed at the Englishman in a high-pitched voice, and at one point prodded his chest with his gloved finger. The Englishman responded calmly, occasionally pointing at the Chinese doctors and the row of wounded, and once at his medical bag in Catherine's hands. Catherine thought he had carried the argument. The officer stepped back, glaring at him, then barked an order at his men. The soldiers with the bayonets stepped forward. Catherine found herself looking at a line of steel, levelled at her chest.

'Well, that's emphatic enough,' said the man. 'We'd better get back to the train.'

'But the wounded, Doctor? Many will die without treatment.' Catherine was outraged.

'Most of them will die. But in China life's cheap. Come on. Let's retreat with what dignity remains.'

'Dignity!' snorted Catherine, as she followed him across the tracks. 'They don't know the meaning of the word.'

'I share your feelings.' He turned towards her. Catherine estimated that he was in his early thirties: the rough moustache and the slight furrow on his brow had made him look older. 'I don't know what to call you,' he said.

'Nurse,' said Catherine, smiling, despite her anger.

He lifted his hat to wipe away a bead of sweat and she observed a shock of untidy brown hair. He was obviously careless about his appearance. Nevertheless he had a trim body, and when he had been running earlier, it had been with an athlete's ease. He had the self-contained look of a man who knew how to handle himself in rough situations and whose natural element was the outdoors. He had beautiful hands, but the fingers were hard and calloused. She remembered the brisk efficiency with which he had used his scalpel. The kindly, intelligent eyes that frankly held her gaze were relaxed now, but when he had been facing the officer, they had burned. There was a quiet formidability about him that was in itself attractive.

'Ah? From second class?' He was also smiling. 'Well – Nurse – I'm grateful to you. If I may say so, at the risk of sounding patronising, you handled yourself magnificently. You know, we first-class doctors can always do with some expert help, wherever it comes from. And you were very professional.'

'Thank you,' said Catherine. 'You didn't do badly yourself. Excuse me, I'm going this way.'

'And I that. Goodbye. I hope we meet again. Perhaps next time it will be in more equitable circumstances. Enjoy slumming it for the rest of the journey.'

Catherine was still laughing as she climbed into her carriage, but the stench of bodies and food in the crowded compartment, and the curious eyes upon her as she walked slowly down the aisle, made her feel faint. She edged to her seat and slumped down on the wooden board. She was conscious of Lei Ming grinning at her, as Martha's hands clasped hers. 'You were great, Catherine. You were just great.'

'Yes, Miss C-Catherine, what you did was noble and brave.'

She passed a hand over her forehead. She was tired, and still bitter about her experience. 'Oh, Lord,' she said. 'I'm still covered with blood. No matter. I suppose the tea man will come by soon with some hot water. Luckily I've got a coat to cover this dress. Did you see your marshal go by? Was it a grand spectacle?'

'Hey, sister, you were the spectacle,' said Martha. 'I don't think anybody was even aware of the marshal after you started your performance.'

'Miss C-Catherine,' Lei was stuttering. 'The c-care you showed for the ordinary p-people, I – I think that you, too, are a s-socialist, w-whatever you s-say.'

'Who was the guy you were with?' Martha was asking. 'He looked kind of cute – well, in a hunky sort of way.'

There were no more interruptions to their journey, and within two hours they had reached the ugly brick suburbs of Tientsin. Catherine had been locked in her thoughts, attempting to control the turbulent and conflicting emotions that the incident in the railway yard had stirred in her. For Martha and Lei Ming, however, the excitement had deepened their intimacy, and they had chattered without stop.

Catherine, half listening to their conversation, had discovered that Lei came from a wealthy banker's family in Tientsin. He had told Martha he wanted to be a teacher because he believed that education was the answer to China's problems. He urged her to meet his younger sister, Lan-hua, who was a student and a radical like himself, and invited them both to visit his family mansion. By the end of the journey he had Martha's promise that she and Catherine would come regularly to take lessons in Chinese, to which Catherine had assented because she was too tired to resist. As the train clanked over the points on the way in to the station, Lei was writing his address on pages torn from his pocketbook.

Their arrival was chaotic. Everybody in the carriage rose as one to get their bags, then shuffled and pushed towards the exit. Catherine found herself squeezed up to the delighted young priest, who was pulled away angrily by his acolytes. Eventually they reached the platform, loudspeakers blaring the times of departures. It was a busy, crowded terminus, reminding Catherine of a miniature Victoria station, where she had begun her journey with Fu-kuei.

She saw Lei bowing to an elderly couple in traditional dress. Behind them was a girl, with bobbed hair and a long red scarf round her neck, who flung her arms round his neck. This must be the sister he had mentioned, Lan-hua. She was a pretty, doll-like creature, thought Catherine. She did not look like a radical. Beaming, Lei waved and departed with his family.

Two elderly bearded men, in black hats and frock coats, with ringlets in front of their ears, were waiting patiently for Martha. She hugged Catherine goodbye, then picked up her bag, and Catherine found herself alone on the platform, in a circle of her luggage. For a moment she felt relief that she was on her own, but an elderly European couple were approaching her: a bent man with a thick white moustache and spectacles, and a tall, dignified lady with a severe expression and keen, rather intimidating eyes.

Suddenly the woman ran forward, and the next thing Catherine knew she was clutched in a fierce embrace. She was startled to feel dry lips pressing kisses on her cheek. Then the woman held her at arm's length, observing her features penetratingly. The eyes widened and, in an attractive Scottish brogue, she made a remark to her husband: 'Look at her, Edward. She's the image of Helen Frances as we first knew her. Catherine, my sweet darling godchild. I'd have recognised you anywhere. Yet it's been so many – so many years.'

Vaguely she became aware of Dr Airton fussing over her baggage and calling to someone for help. She turned and saw that a man in a trench coat was holding her hatbox, and grinning at her. 'You won't be offended, will you, Nurse, if a first class doctor takes the liberty of carrying your luggage for you? Perhaps now's an appropriate time for us to be properly introduced. I'm Edmund Airton, and that's my mother, who can't seem to take her hands off you. Welcome to Tientsin.'

2

Tientsin Follies

From the journal of William Lampsett, Reuters correspondent, Tientsin, 15 August 1922

My Chinese colleagues took me to the opera this evening, and for four hours I watched the incomprehensible antics of bearded generals with pennants on their backs shadow-boxing to the jangling of cymbals. I could see little difference between this pantomime and the war from which I've just returned. After a month's posturing in the mountains, General Chang Tso-lin retired behind the Wall with his tail between his legs. China goes about its business as before, except that now the remains of several thousand peasant soldiers are fertilising the hillsides, and a new chapter has been written in China's sad, unchanging history, which one day, no doubt, will become the theme of a heroic opera like the one I yawned through tonight.

Meanwhile, I am feeling the usual despair when I meet the 'Old China Hands'. They read my articles at their breakfast tables or in the club, then grunt over their cigars, 'If it's not a war it'll be kidnapping, piracy or flood, but China will always be China,' and turn to the back pages to check the share prices of their rice, tea, soy beans, cotton, silk, pig bristles, duck feathers, coal, bauxite and what-have-you being carried by sweating coolies over the mountains and waterways to make them their comfortable fortunes. What I write for them isn't news. News is George Airton's victories at the racecourse on his mare China Coast, or the great debate over whether imported bloodstock should be allowed to compete with the traditional Mongolian pony. The day my piece on the expulsion of Sun Yat-sen by the local Canton warlord, Chen Chiung-ming, was spiked, they have christened 'Black Saturday' because three stewards resigned over the racing issue. What a lotus land we live in, but who cares? There are balls and bridge evenings, golfing and paper chases, and in the summer everybody flocks to the beaches at Peitaiho, where the sailors of the Royal Navy adorn their ships with lights and bunting for the most fabulous of carnivals and parties. I sometimes wonder why I bother.

Tientsiners liked to attribute the founding of their city to the great General Charles Gordon, later of Khartoum fame, who, shortly after he defeated the Taiping rebels with his 'Ever Victorious Army', mapped out the boundaries of a model Western settlement on the marshy banks of the Peiho river.

By the time Catherine arrived, sixty years later, the city had grown into a large, smoky metropolis. Prints and lithographs of the airy colonial buildings that had first lined the Bund adorned the wood-panelled walls of the club, but the original buildings had long ago been replaced by the granite-colonnaded edifices of the proud merchant houses, the great hongs: Wilson and Co., Jardine Matheson, the Kailan Mining Administration, the Hong Kong and Shanghai Bank, Union Insurance, Butterfield and Swire that loured arrogantly over the teeming Victoria Road. Behind these monumental symbols of mercantile power stretched godowns, warehouses and rows of grey tenements, with little steps and black iron railings. These – and the lumbering iron bridge that linked the concessions on either side of the river, lifting now and again to allow the passage of tugs and barges that puffed up from the port at Taku – would not have been out of place in an industrial town in the English Midlands. Tientsiners, if they ever thought about it, would have been proud of that: their city had grown during a pre-war era of imperial confidence, when order and civilisation had been synonymous with steamships, the telegraph and the gold standard, and they considered the transposition of the Liverpool docks, or the city centre of a Manchester or a Glasgow, to heathen lands to be a triumph of God-given progress.

In walking distance from the *taipans'* offices was the grand municipal square, over which brooded a garish red and white brick Gothic folly, the Gordon Hall, with its stained-glass windows and crenellated turrets. It was here that the heads of the leading trading houses gathered on Wednesday afternoons to take their seats in the Legislative Council, which regulated the affairs of the city on behalf of the rate-payers, for Tientsin, like most Treaty Ports, was self-governed under the Laws of Extra Territoriality; later, these latter-day merchant princes would take their sundowners in the equally imposing British Club, or, if they were meeting their wives, in the airy tea-room of the Astor House Hotel. Later still, their Rolls-Royces and Humbers would convey them westwards to their gabled villas off Racecourse Road, where they would change into evening dress and sit down for a sumptuous dinner of roast beef and Yorkshire pudding, served by their solemn Chinese butlers in white livery.

Meanwhile the army of Chinese compradors, clerks, typists, accountants and interpreters, coolies and godown men, who did the work that made these trading houses their fortunes, vanished back to the Chinese town, originally a walled city, and even now safely separated from the concessions by the mile-long Taku Road. Here was another world, full of colour and smells, which the more daring Europeans sometimes visited on their days off to sample the famous pigeon in one of the few salubrious restaurants, or the dumplings on the market stalls, or to explore the curio shops and temples – but this parallel Chinese universe did not impinge too much on their comfortable lives: for most of the time, they were content to leave the Chinese city to the missionaries and the police.

Perhaps the only sub-stratum that found acceptance among all levels of society was the corps of foreign correspondents. Of these, Willie Lampsett was the journalist that the Tientsin *taipans* most liked to invite to their homes. It was not because of his under-standing of the Byzantine politics of warlord China, but, rather, that he was a nephew of Lord Stokes, the Liberal peer. For the parvenus who found themselves at the head of the various trading houses, Willie's presence on the right-hand side of the hostess was a flattering acknowledgement of the social heights to which they had climbed, and the fact that, as a humble correspondent of

Reuters, he earned less than their own griffins gave them an opportunity to patronise as well as preen. When, at the end of the evening, he would shyly make his departure, they would thrust an extra couple of cigars into his top pocket, or promise to send round to his bungalow a case of the wine that he might courteously have praised during the meal.

For his part, Willie was careful never to show contempt for the vulgarity of the merchant princes. He was a professional journalist and they provided him with inside information useful for his financial reporting, the bread and butter of his bureau. After only a few months into his second China tour (the first had been interrupted by Kitchener's call to arms and a spell in the trenches) he had observed that civil war and political chicanery, though it fascinated him, merited just inches in published copy, while a surge in the price of duck feathers or cotton futures ran to columns. He accepted this philosophically when it came to what was printed overseas. Chinese politics were Ruritanian, after all, the names of the warlords unpronounceable, and he understood that they were of small interest in London or Birmingham – but he was surprised that the local expatriates could dismiss them.

There were times when he was appalled by the blindness and frivolity of his fellow Europeans. Sometimes he felt like Gulliver in the land of the Lilliputians. Did they really not understand the forces of change that had been unleashed in this vast country? Could they be unaware that their bastion of privilege was being undermined?

Willie appreciated, even if they chose to ignore it, that a secret Tientsin was hidden among the European buildings. Many of the mansions with their gables and red tiles, which peeped over high walls in the Italian concession and along the boulevards of the French concession, were not the stockbrokers' houses they appeared to be. They had been bought quietly by Chinese merchants and warlords to hide their White Russian mistresses and provide boltholes in case the political tide turned and they had to retreat to the safety of international territory. Because of this, Tientsin was a hotbed of intrigue. Willie knew that there was a story to tell, if only he could lift the veil, of drug-smuggling, arms-dealing, spying and power-broking. The glimpses he had of darkened limousines slipping through the dusk tantalised him. He liked to join George Airton and his reprobate friends on their rampages to the sleazier clubs of the city because there he would sometimes spot politicians or generals he recognised from their photographs in the Chinese papers. He felt closer then to the real China that he had come to report. Chinese politics were puzzles within puzzles, an ever-changing balance of patronage, self-interest and power, and glimpses of the players excited him. He despised them for their corruption or brutality, but they were the future kingmakers, the men on whose whim the fate of millions rested.

It was perhaps for this reason – the suspicion that he was in tune with the darker undercurrents of the city – that Willie appealed to the smart set, of which George Airton, Tientsin's champion amateur jockey, was the acknowledged prince. They were a hard lot, scarred by the war, and all they wanted now was to forget, and enjoy life to the full. They all held down good jobs: Andreas von Henning worked for Wilson and Co., Tientsin's prestigious trading company; George Airton was employed by the China Railways, and Robby Berry . . . well, he had no job, but he compensated in other ways. Sometimes Willie felt that their lives only began after six o'clock, when the black flag flew up the mast in Ewo Road, outside the bungalow he and Robby shared. This was the signal that work was over for the day and drinks were served. Here they would gather, to lounge on Willie's rattan furniture, and sip the lethal martinis and Manhattans that Robby poured. If there was a ball or a party to attend, they would slip home to dress and reunite later. Usually they drifted into their evening adventures, hailing rickshaws or squeezing into Willie's battered old convertible. Sometimes they got no further than the Astor House Hotel, where they drank cham-pagne in the bar, and dined, then returned to the bar for whisky and brandy. If they had women with them they would dance to the lulling music of the Negro band. On other nights they went into the Chinese city for billiards or fantan in one of the clubs, where warlords and gangsters played mah-jongg or cards under clouds of cigarette smoke at a round table, and taxi-dancer girls, with shad-owed eyes and bright lipstick, waited listlessly on the benches by the dance floor for a customer to buy a wad of tickets from the prowling *mama-san*, and a Chinese band jangled out the latest love songs from Shanghai.

It was usually George Airton who led the charge. Willie had known him for several months now but still could not make out his contradictory character. The younger son of a staid missionary couple, George lived well beyond the means provided by his job. He was always cadging from his friends, but Willie did not begrudge this because he valued his company. He was certainly a phenomenon on the track. Willie had heard that he had been taught to ride as a boy by a Mongolian herdsman. Roy Davis, the doyen of the racecourse who, in partnership with the strange Swedish missionary Duke Larsen, had bought most of the Mongolian ponies that raced in the club, had once said that George was like no other rider he had known. He never used a whip. He talked to his horses like a lover. He had spent the war in India, with a cavalry regiment on the North-west Frontier, and was reputed to be the finest horseman in the army. 'But even then they said his style was more that of a Cossack than a lancer. You'd think the blood of the nomads runs through his veins,' Davis had said admiringly. 'Don't be fooled by his clubland manner off the track. There are depths to that boy. Real depths.'

If there were, Willie had never plumbed them. To him George was a cross between court jester and holy fool, blessed with an almost total incapacity for sincerity or seriousness, unless it had to do with his horses or his wardrobe. Even his waspish wit was not malicious, because nothing was important enough to him to merit anything as burdensome as ill-will. Nor could others offend him: his skin was so thick that he never dreamed anybody might dislike him. Life was a theatre designed for his amusement. Utterly selfish and self-centred, his generosity was unlimited because everybody he came across had a role to play in the entertainment he perceived around him. It was difficult not to be drawn into his circle because, as far as he was concerned, you were there already. He and Robby had hit it off from the moment they met, and after a while Willie, too, had become a close friend. He was one of the few people who could take on George in argument and win, and George, who had been a little supercilious towards him at first, had warmed to him with mounting respect. For his part, Willie appreciated the access to Tientsin's society that George provided. His reputation on the course meant that he fitted as easily into the *taipans*' set as he did into the younger crowd's, and Willie had made use of his contacts.

Willie suspected there was a cruel side to George, which came out in his treatment of women. He was rarely without female company, but they were usually vapid society girls, the Roses, Myrtles and Elspeths whom the society hostesses tried unsuccessfully to press on him. Unlike Willie, George took up the challenge. It was his habit, Willie noticed, to charm them with his egregious flattery, wine and dine them in style, then take them on inappropriate excursions to the seedier bars and drop them when they expressed shock and alarm. According to Robby, George's collection of broken hearts matched in number the trophies he had won on the racetrack, and Willie, who was almost pathologically shy when it came to women, had at first disapproved – but George had the remarkable ability to keep the goodwill of the people he seemed to hurt most. Willie couldn't decide whether his friend was a cad or a clown.

There was no such ambiguity when it came to Andreas – 'the Beast', Robby called him. There was no doubt where his interest in women lay: the rougher the better. There was rarely an evening when he did not return to his flat in the ICI block over the river, squat cigar pressed between his fat lips, with two, sometimes three White Russians or Chinese whores in tow.

Tonight, however, as Willie was standing on the small stretch of lawn to run up the black flag, it was neither George nor Andreas who concerned him. It was – as usual – Robby. He did not know what to do with him.

His friend was an alcoholic, which was bad enough. He was also – although, thankfully, he did not advertise it – an invert. Probably Willie had known it subconsciously when they had boarded in the same house at Winchester. He had been left in no doubt of it during the brief period that Robby had been a subaltern in his company near Arras. There had been the time Robby had clung to him, sobbing, after the suicidal night patrol in which he had lost nine of his twelve men. Willie, the captain in charge, had tried to stop the show: he had pointed out to the colonel that there was a full moon and the men would be silhouetted as they crossed their own barbed wire, but Headquarters had been adamant. Willie had watched impotently through the periscope, as they had died one by one in the slime of no man's land. Robby had made his way somehow to the lip of the enemy's trench, bombarded a section and captured three prisoners; it had been a remarkable act of soldiery. Willie had been only too anxious to embrace him on his return, as a comrade who had survived the impossible, and at first he had thought little of it when Robby clung to him longer than was decent. No wonder the man was emotional after what he had been through, he had told himself. It was in keeping with Robby's sensitive character – he had always been liable to affectionate displays, posing as an aesthete in the house prefects' common room, not that he had ever been unmanly. But that night – perhaps it was the spaniel-like look in his eyes, the way he nestled his muddy head against Willie's chest – Willie had felt revulsion: he had pushed him away and shaken his hand perfunctorily. He had talked to the MO, persuaded him (and himself) that Robby was suffering from nerves, secured his discharge and a spell in a convalescent centre somewhere in the Lake District, then used his influence with his uncle to get Robby a Headquarters job for the rest of the war. Robby had been pathetically grateful – he had written to him, and Willie had replied rather formally. He had not seen Robby on his leaves home and had thought the friendship was at an end – until one day, five years later, Robby had appeared with his trunks, suitcases and golf bags and installed himself in Willie's bungalow in Tientsin.

At first he had said he would stay for a month. He was on a world tour, he explained. America would be next, once he had explored all the vices of the sinful Orient, but he had not left, and Willie had been forced to accept him as a permanent lodger. Now, eighteen months later, he was lending him money. Nothing was ever said and Robby behaved himself, but Willie sometimes caught those spaniel eyes in the red drinker's face following his movements with yearning absorption . . .

Willie supposed he felt sorry for him. More to the point he felt guilty. Robby, unlike most of Willie's other close friends, had survived the war, but he had been destroyed by it all the same. It had made him into a drunk. And, deep down, Willie blamed himself. Perhaps the cushy job he had finessed for him had been worse than the danger of the trenches: it could have done nothing for his self-esteem. Robby had never mentioned it, but in his eyes there was a constant '*j'accuse*'. Yet Willie couldn't turn him out: Robby had nowhere else to go.

And he was useful. He charmed everybody. The women adored him, and there was no secret in the community that he didn't know and pass on indiscreetly to Willie, the newsman. More than one of Willie's scoops had originated in tittle-tattle Robby had picked up at dinner parties. And, dammit, it wasn't as if he didn't like him. He was always amusing and, he had to admit it, it had been Robby who had given him his *entré* into society. He would never have got to know George Airton and his crowd had it not been for Robby and his cocktails.

'What do you do all day?' Willie had once heard one of George's flappers ask him.

'Do, my dear? I do what every artist does. I sleep and dream of my next creation,' Robby had replied.

'What? Your cocktails?'

'Indeed,' he said. 'Do you not believe there is an artistry in making cocktails? That a Michelangelo, if his materials had been limited to rums and grenadines, might not have attempted his Sistine Chapel in a shaker? It is my life's work.'

Willie chuckled. His life's work! Robby was irrepressible.

With a crack, the black flag unfurled at the top of the mast, attracting a swirl of bats flitting in the gloom as dusk fell. It was a smoky evening, which hazed the faint pink glow to the west. The dull slate roofs on either side seemed even more like gravestones than usual.

'What are you making today?' he asked, as he stepped back through the french windows into the sitting room.

'Something extra special,' murmured Robby, and gave him a dazzling smile. 'For somebody very special that Georgy-boy's bringing along with him this evening.'

'Who's that?' asked Willie.

'George has a new filly, of the two-legged variety.'

'Well, go on, then. Tell me.' He flopped down on a sofa under the fan, and idly picked up a magazine. 'Who's George planning to torment this time?'

'Made you curious, have I?' said Robby, archly. 'Well, I'll tell you, she's a redhead, she's delicious and her name is Catherine Cabot. And what is most delicious of all is that she is the ward of the saintly Dr and Mrs Airton and young Georgy-boy is debauching her under his parents' roof.'

'Oh, really?' murmured Willie.

'I would hope he is,' said Robby. 'I'm sure I would if I were that way inclined and had the opportunity. I'm sure you would, too, if you could get over your gentlemanly diffidence. She is the most debauchable young thing I've seen in years, male or female.'

'You've met her, then?'

'Oh, yes, I was invited round for tea when you were away covering those warlord battles of yours. Georgy couldn't keep his eyes off her, and neither could that prudish elder brother of his, the doctor. Oh!' he exclaimed. 'How exciting! There might be a love triangle in the making.'

'What nonsense,' chuckled Willie. 'You're making it up. The only missionaries' wards I've ever seen were horn-rimmed blue-stockings with prayer books in their woolly jumpers.'

'Well, that's where you're wrong. This is a goddess. Educated, too. An Oxford girl – but no blue-stocking. She's been around. She's very experienced in every way, I would have said. This is no Presbyterian do-gooder, I assure you. There was nothing good about her at all. That was why I liked her.'

'I'm put off already.'

'My dear boy, that's because you're a sad, repressed Englishman,' said Robby, 'which George, of course, is not, but I suspect that he may be facing a bit of a challenge this time. I rather doubt that this young lady will be easily shocked. I detect an element of spice behind that peaches-and-cream complexion. A dangerous, albeit delicious, bite behind those soft lips. Here, taste this and tell me what you think.'

With a flourish he shook the cocktail shaker and poured a tawny liquid into a glass.

'Not bad,' said Willie, sipping. 'What's under the gin? It has a sort of acrid quality.'

'It's going to be my welcoming cup for Catherine, a little character portrait. An auburn tint for her hair, maraschino for her cherry lips, and a touch of gall – Gunpowder tea from Fukien to be exact – to illustrate the fiery qualities underneath.'

'What's she doing in Tientsin?'

'She's come to find her father, or so George told me. Seems there was hanky-panky before her birth – one of those ghastly, tight-lipped Victorian scandals – and the fellow whose name she carries wasn't the one who planted the seed in Mater's womb.'

'Does she know who did?'

'She thinks she does. Fellow by the name of Henry Manners.'

'Did you say *Henry* Manners?'

'Yes – do you know him?'

'I know of *a* Henry Manners,' said Willie. 'He's an Englishman gone to the bad, journalist of sorts, who lives in Manchuria and is entirely in the pocket of the Japanese. Writes propaganda for their English publications, odious, ranting articles about Bolshevism and the spinelessness of the Western powers. He whitewashes Japanese land-grabbing as some holy racial crusade to protect the nations of the East now the white man has laid down his burden. In our disreputable profession Henry Manners is about as disreputable as you can get.'

Robby gave a hearty laugh. 'How absolutely splendid. Poor Catherine. I'd love to be there for the happy reunion. It won't be for some time, I gather, because George says that Dr Airton made enquiries and the fellow is away in Tokyo until the end of October. There's your Japanese connection. It must be the same chap. George has apparently taken it upon himself – for the three months or so that she has to kick her heels here – to rescue her from the dreary clutches of his saintly parents and virtuous elder bro, and tonight's entertainment is to be a gentle introduction into the joys of good living.'

'Oh, God, we're going on to the Starlight, then.' Willie groaned.

'After my cocktails and a good dinner – but I thought you liked the Starlight?'

'I don't mind it – but I've had a long day. I'm tired. Look, I might beg off tonight. I have a complicated piece to do tomorrow on the breakaway Manchurian Provinces.'

'Who cares?' smiled Robby. 'You know nobody ever reads a thing you write. Anyway, you'll forget your tiredness once you meet Catherine. That I can promise.'

'Oh, really?' muttered Willie, sipping his auburn cocktail.

'Aha, voices,' said Robby, rubbing his plump hands and heading for the door.

In they came: George, boyish features and brilliantined centrally parted hair, wearing a natty pink-striped blazer, his brown eyes twinkling; glowering, heavy-limbed, brush-blond Andreas, eyes still shadowed from the night before; and behind them, a vision of long bare arms, fish-scale silver lamé, ocean green eyes and fiery red hair cascading from a silver cap, the most beautiful woman Willie had ever seen.

The Starlight club was well hidden in one of the back-streets of the Chinese town. A grinning Indian let them in. They went down some rickety steps and came into a room bathed in red light flickering off a revolving ball of mirrors. Catherine could make out tables, chairs and a small dance-floor. Behind it there was a stage on which a troupe of scantily clad Russian girls were performing the can-can for the Chinese clientele.

Catherine knew about the plight of the Russians who had fled the revolution to poverty in China. She had seen some at the station when she arrived in Tientsin as Edmund and his parents had led her out of the crowded concourse: knots of Europeans, dressed in peasant costume, bearded men hugging their boots, shoeless blond children reclining against their mothers' long skirts, watching over their few possessions with the same listless look in their eyes as could be seen in the faces of their Chinese companions.

'White Russians, my dear, hoping to get a ticket to Shanghai,' said Edward Airton. 'Refugees from their civil wars. There are thousands, I'm afraid. It's very distressing and nobody knows what to do with them.'

'Very distressing indeed,' said Edmund. 'Begging on the streets. Prostituting their women to the natives. Let the side down. We can't pretend to be superior any more, can we?'

'Edmund!' Nellie had warned. 'That's not called-for.' Edmund had laughed good-humouredly as he threw their bags into the back of his car.

Catherine had been wondering how she would react tonight. She had heard that the nightclubs were full of Russian girls, many of them middle-class or even aristocratic. In the shadowy alcoves, she could see some now, sitting at tables with their Chinese clients.

George was planning something with the *mama-san*, a gold-toothed woman in her forties with cruel, squinting eyes. Catherine nodded politely to her as the woman appraised her, and Andreas laughed. The nice young journalist, Willie Something, Robby's friend, took her arm and led her to an empty table. 'George is buying taxi-dance tickets and the hostesses will join us soon,' he said. 'Look,' he added. 'Damn George. He's always trying to make an impression. If you don't like it here, I'll take you home.'

'No,' she said, flashing him a smile. How oddly conservative he was among George's hard-living friends. 'I'm enjoying myself. I'm game. Really I am.' She was also very tipsy. It had been quite a night, with an uproarious dinner in the sedate Astor House Hotel. George had been as ridiculously amusing as usual. Thank God for George, she thought suddenly, remembering how his elegant appearance in his parents' sombre sitting room had lifted the claustrophobia that had been growing in her since the old couple had met her at the station.

Edmund had driven them to a detached house in Meadows Road, near the junction with Racecourse Road. It was a dark brick dwelling of three storeys with a gabled roof. A small patch of garden led to a pillared portico and an oak door with a stained-glass window panel. To Catherine it looked like the sort of grand mansion a banker might have built for himself in Esher or Epsom. The door opened as they approached and a wrinkled, black-gowned Chinese servant ushered them into a dark-panelled hall, which smelt of floor polish, old leather and dusty carpets. Catherine had felt the shadows close round her. It reminded her of a Victorian manse in a Gothic novel. Only a scroll of calligraphy on the wall and one or two porcelain pots on a shelf indicated they might be in China – and the grinning, white-haired servant, of course, extending a horny hand towards her portmanteau. 'Catherine, this is *Lao* Tang, our head boy,' said Nellie. 'He'll show you to your room. Edmund, help him with the bags. I fear he'll injure his back if he attempts to take that heavy trunk up those steps on his own.'

'No, Missy,' smiled the old man. '*Lao* Tang still velly strong. Can do by sel'. You go sittin' room, and *Hsiao* Meng bring tea by'm'by.'

'All right, *Lao* Tang, as long as you're sure,' said Nellie, and whispered to Catherine, 'He can't be less than sixty if he's a day, but he's strong as an ox, and he considers it a severe loss of face if we lift a finger in the household. He was a muleteer – probably a bandit – whom Edward converted in Shishan and has been with us ever since. You'll find out soon enough who's in charge of our little family. And since he's given us firm instructions to take tea, I suppose that's what we'd better do.'

She led Catherine into a Spartan sitting room, with french windows facing on to a neatly kept lawn ringed by flowerbeds and tall Siberian pines that let in little light. Edward Airton followed them. Despite *Lao* Tang's protests, Edmund had taken the other side of the trunk and they could hear the two of them arguing good-humouredly as they thumped up the stairs. 'Now, sit with me on the sofa,' said Nellie. 'I cannot wait to hear your news. It must be fifteen – no, sixteen years since I was last in touch with your mother. And the last time I saw you, my dear, you were an adorable little creature in pinafores, only so high. I want to know everything about you. Everything.'

'By golly, so do I,' said a pleasant voice behind her, and Catherine turned to see a dapper man, whom she judged to be in his late twenties, leaning against the door. He was wearing a dressing-gown over his trousers, and a cravat held in shape by a pearl tie-pin. He was smoking a cigarette in an ivory holder, and she could see the end of a silk handkerchief tucked into his sleeve. His dark hair, parted in the centre, was sleek and shining, and a wide smile lit his face. His brown eyes shone with mischief. 'Mama, is this ravishing vision really the same little Catherine Cabot I once dropped into that bathing tub the sailors set up for us on the deck? I'll be blowed. Don't worry,' he added, stepping into the room. 'You were never in any danger. I wanted to be a hero, you see, the boy who saved the drowning baby. Problem was, the baby had to be in the water first for me to do so. It all worked a treat. In you went, bubble, bubble, swaddling clothes disappearing into the murky depths. In I jumped, having shouted the alarm. You're out in a jiffy, hardly swallowed a drop of the brine, and I'm all ready to take the bows from the cheering crowd, when Mother here pulls me by the ear to the cabin where she spanks me rotten and locks me in. The upshot is I miss the camel riding at Suez, which is the next port of call. Of course it was dear Jen, my sister, who blabbed on me, but I blamed you at the time. Now that I see how stunning you are, though, I'm inclined to forgive you. I'm George, by the way, the family incorrigible. How do you do?'

As she reached for the outstretched hand, and felt his firm grip, she had looked levelly into the laughing eyes and decided that Tientsin might not be so dreary after all.

Later that evening the Airtons had led her into the doctor's study, and there had been an emotional interview in which Nellie had confessed what she called her terrible secret.

She had started by describing Helen Frances's arrival in Shishan with her fiancé, Tom Cabot. Their appearance had coincided with that of another man, Henry Manners, an adventurer, 'a dark horse', as Nellie described him. Unknown to the other residents of Shishan, said Nellie, Helen Frances and Henry Manners had already become attracted to each other when they first met in Peking. In Shishan this flirtation had developed into a full-blown romance. They met secretly, over several months, taking advantage of Tom's long absences in northern Manchuria. It was during this period that Catherine had been conceived. The Boxer Rebellion had erupted in Shishan about the time that the foreign community had discovered Helen Frances was pregnant. There had been a siege of the mission station. Henry Manners had saved the Airton family and Helen

Frances, although many of their friends, including Tom Cabot, had been massacred. However, things did not go to plan. Their small party became dispersed. Nellie had believed that Mr Manners was killed during their escape, and many months later, as fugitives in Mongolia, she had told the Russian officers who ultimately rescued them that the child born to Helen Frances was the daughter of Tom Cabot. She had invented a marriage in an attempt to shield mother and daughter from the stain of illegitimacy. Helen Frances had acquiesced in the deception because she also believed that she had lost her lover, and nothing seemed to matter to her any more. Nellie had realised her mistake when they returned to Peking and discovered that Henry Manners was very much alive, but by then it had been too late. For reasons of their own, Catherine's parents had decided not to stay together. As far as the world was concerned, fiction had become fact, and Catherine had grown up with the name Cabot.

Catherine had been embarrassed when the old woman burst into tears. 'You cannot imagine, my dear, the remorse Edward and I have felt over the years for the harm our thoughtless action has caused your family. That one lie . . . I cannot help but feel that ultimately I was responsible . . .'

Catherine had been surprised by her own calm and detachment. She felt neither relief nor excitement, only a quiet satisfaction that her conjectures about her parentage had been confirmed. It was as if she had presented a set of accounts to be reconciled and the numbers had balanced as she expected them to. Now, though, seeing the grief and guilt in the old woman's face, she felt a rush of emotion and sympathy. 'Aunt Nellie, you have nothing to be ashamed of. I know how much you loved my mother, and I'm sure that what you did was in the sincere belief that it was in her best interests – and mine. In any case, you tried to effect a reconciliation – I have your letter. It was you who suggested my mother go to my father in Japan.'

'Oh, Catherine, that grieves me more than anything else. I suspect that my intervention brought only greater hurt. Your mother afterwards – oh, poor, dear Helen Frances. The self-destruction, the despair . . .'

Catherine had a vision of her mother in her coffin, and her sympathy turned to anger. 'The life she lived was the one she chose,' she said coldly. 'I'm sorry, Aunt Nellie, I don't wish to sound callous, or to hurt your feelings, but you have no business, no right, to blame yourself for anything that happened to her.'

Things had deteriorated from there. When she eventually pressed them, Edward admitted that he knew where her true father was now – he had made enquiries through his missionary friends, the Gillespies, in Manchuria – but then had started on a long homily about how the man he once knew had changed for the worse: he was no longer the noble character they had respected. She might be disappointed by what she found.

'Uncle Edward, what are you trying to say?' Catherine had asked, her patience fraying. 'That my father has become evil?'

'Evil is no longer a term I like to use,' said the doctor. 'I fear he has fallen into a moral darkness occasioned by despair. He may no longer be the man who would recognise you as his daughter or whom you may wish to recognise as your father. I fear that in achieving your quest you will be disappointed.'

Catherine's anger evaporated in a burst of laughter. 'Uncle Edward, you're basing your judgement of a man you haven't seen for twenty years on a few scurrilous articles you've read in a magazine. I am sure you mean well, but this isn't going to stop me looking for him. I don't care if my father is a rabid monster. He's the only father I have.'

'I'm sorry, my dear, then I may have misunderstood your quest. I thought you were seeking a father's love.'

Catherine was uncertain how to take this. 'I'm not sure what I'm seeking but, with respect, I don't believe that that is any business of yours,' she said finally. 'I am grateful for your help – and for your kindness – but I'm not . . . I'm not your child. If you give me my father's address I'm sure that I can make all the necessary arrangements to get there.'

'Oh, Catherine.' Nellie had moved over to the sofa to sit beside her. 'You must pay no attention to old dunderheads like us. Of course you must seek your father, and do it in your own way. Edward, you really have gone too far. The poor girl.'

Finally they had worked out what Nellie had called a plan.

'A plan?'

'Yes, my dear. I'm afraid that there is no point in gallivanting off to Manchuria until October at the earliest, because another thing my husband neglected to tell you is that Henry Manners isn't there now. The Gillespies found out he's gone to Japan, and won't be back for a couple of months or more. That will give you plenty of time to prepare. You can write to him warning him that you will be coming, and in the meantime you will stay with us and enjoy Tientsin. When it is time, we'll go with you. You know, my dear, Edward is retiring next year, so it will be good to have the opportunity to visit our old haunts one last time.'

'You're very kind,' Catherine said, but the thought revolving in her mind was that she would have to stay in this dreary house for another three months.

She had been thinking of packing her bags and taking a boat back to Japan to find her father there, but as she had left the study, she had bumped into George in the hall. 'I say, old girl. You look down in the dumps. What's wrong? I can guess. The mad old boy's been lecturing you on comparative religions, hasn't he? Always does when he gets anybody into that study of his. Come on, I know what'll cure you. Get your coat. I'm going to take you for a sampan race across the river.' His enthusiasm had been infectious, and he brooked no refusal, and somehow, by the time she had returned with the dawn light to Meadows Road, she had found herself reconciled to staying three months in Tientsin.

And life in the three weeks since then had been a party. She did not know what Edward or Nellie thought of their returns home in the early hours of the morning, her non-appearances until the afternoon (although George somehow managed to get to work in the morning) and her hangovers. She did not really care. She liked George's friends, loved Robby, and George himself was unlike anybody she had met before. She was still not sure what was his game, although she sometimes caught him looking at her with an imponderable expression in his eye. She was used to men falling head over heels in love with her, but there was a diffidence behind George's blatant flirtatiousness, and on the occasions when he had strayed towards the physical – on the dance-floor or in the back of the car on their way home – it had been in a manner of self-parody, as if he knew that she knew this was nothing more than a joke. She had treated his advances with cool humour, and much disdain.

Edmund, she realised, was a different proposition. She had not seen much of him since her arrival in Tientsin. He was often out on house calls in the evenings, and spent days at a time at the Kailan Mining Administration hospital near the mines in Tangshan, as well as in the company clinic he and his father ran in town. When she did see him, it was usually in the presence of his parents, at meals, or in the sitting room after dinner. Once he had asked her if she would like to visit the Kailan hospital, but she had told him tartly that her nursing days were over. He had no interest in joining them in their nightly escapades, but he never expressed disapproval, as Nellie sometimes did; he would merely raise his eyebrows or wink at her. He was a man disinclined to judge others, she decided. A man who was comfortable with his own thoughts and content with his own company. He had a deep knowledge of China, and sometimes Catherine found herself listening, fascinated, to the serious conversations he held with his father. With her he was rarely serious, but his remarks usually contained a kernel of irony, and sometimes outright sarcasm, especially when he was talking about Tientsin society, which he appeared to despise.

There was still an unspoken understanding between them, a mutual respect that she thought was founded in their common experiences of the war, but she sensed that, like her, he wished to put those memories behind him. Neither did they refer again to the incident at the railway depot, although he would invariably call her 'Nurse' and if anybody should happen to mention that the wine, for example, was 'second class', they both burst out laughing, to the bewilderment of his parents and George. It was extraordinary how comfortable she felt in his company, as if they had known each other all their lives. There were times, if their eyes met, that they smiled at each other for no reason Catherine could identify except that they were happy to be together.

She would wonder occasionally whether his affection towards her was similar to that of a man of the world for a favourite younger cousin, a rather frivolous cousin who liked to tear up the town with his reprobate younger brother, and whose follies amused him; or whether the obvious regard in which he held her had a deeper root. Once or twice recently she had caught him looking at her with what seemed to be tender inquisitiveness, the half-smile of a man in a gallery lost in the beauty of a painting. At first she mistook it. She knew well enough the expression of a devotee, and it amused her that she might have got under his skin – but on reflection she decided it was not as simple as that. She sensed something else in his intensity. She could not place it. It was as if he was appraising her, challenging her, demanding in some obscure way that she match his honesty. It disturbed her, although she could not define why. It was easier being with George, who questioned nothing, so absorbed was he in himself.

She had sometimes wondered what it would be like to have an affair with either brother, and laughed when she thought of the logistical difficulties. Bedroom capers between the creaking landings of the Airtons' upper floors would be a nightmarish proposition, and the thought of bumping into Edmund in the corridor on her way to an assignation with George presented all the elements of a vaudeville farce. Not, however, as farcical as if the situations were reversed and George in his silk pyjamas surprised her on her way to Edmund. George, being George, would probably take it in his stride, but his laughter would wake the household, and the elder brother would be mortified.

The idea of going to bed with either of them had at first been an amusing diversion, a whimsical reaction to the strait-laced Airton household, but it had a certain appeal. She found both brothers attractive, Edmund more so than George. One weekend early in her stay, when George was away on business, the senior Airtons had organised an outing to the beach at Peitaiho; Edmund had joined them from Tangshan on the Sunday afternoon. From her deckchair, she had watched him as he ran in and out of the surf, playing ball with the children of Dr Airton's missionary friends. She had admired his trim, fit body, the flat muscle under his bathing dress, the tuft of chest hair peeking above it, the virility and grace of his movements. There was a stillness about him when he waited for the ball, a spare self-control, that reminded her of a falcon or a well-trained hunting dog conserving its energy. This was in contrast to the more pronounced physicality of George, whose self-indulgent sensuality was that of a predator, replete after feasting. There was also a depth to Edmund that did not exist in his brother, and his very probity was provoking – but she knew he would not take seduction lightly. She had met men like him before, men for whom even a kiss was a form of holy communion. He would never get into her bed unless he had persuaded himself first that he was in love with her and, second, that his love was returned, but Catherine had no love to give. It would be nice to know Edmund better, but if she were to have an inconsequential affair – and she was not sure she wanted one – it would have to be with George.

On the few occasions at university when she had given herself to a man it had always been on her own terms. She chose her partners carefully. Sometimes she regretted her incapacity to love – it was the least of the emotions that had shrivelled inside her soul in Russia – but she recognised it existed in others, and had learned to steer away from the heart-smitten and the impressionable, choosing, almost unconsciously, more selfish men as her lovers. George's thick skin and limitless conceit, she imagined, would make him impervious to any psychological or emotional damage that she was capable of inflicting. And, there was no reason to deny it, he was devastatingly handsome. A strong, firm body moved under the elegantly tailored suit. He smelt delicious. She liked him. Even when he was at his most maddening, he made her laugh. Furthermore, she shared something with him. It was not as deep or intense as the experience of war that brought her close to Edmund, but George, as she had learned from Nellie, had been present with his parents at her birth in the wilds of Mongolia.

But to take him as a lover? Well, she would see. He was certainly raising the stakes. Tonight he had promised her a surprise at the Starlight club. There he was now, still plotting with the sinister *mama-san*. She could see from Robby's sly grin and Andreas's sardonic sneer that they, too, were in on it. Nice, gentlemanly Willie, whom she had met for the first time today, would tell her, but she was too proud to ask.

George was returning in the company of three Russian girls, whom he introduced as Olga, Svetlana and Vera. 'First things first,' he said, lighting a cigar. 'Champagne for these dear ladies, then we'll see what happens.'

Catherine addressed the girl with the darkest hair in Russian. 'How do you do? My name is Catherine – Katusha,' she said. 'It is charming to meet you. I must apologise for the barbarity of my friends.' She nodded towards Andreas, who was already groping Vera.

Vera shoved him away, her attention now fixed on Catherine. Her eyes were sparkling with delight, as were her friends'. 'You speak Russian!' they cried.

'Of course.' Catherine glanced sidelong at George, evidently miffed that he had been tipped so easily from centre stage. For the next fifteen minutes the four women chattered like birds. They might have been at a St Petersburg salon in the old days. Within moments Catherine had their life stories, and was pleasantly surprised by the equanimity with which they treated their new circumstances. They were all refugees, all from good families, but, they shrugged, now they were whores. That was life. It was all very Russian, Catherine thought.

'All right, all right.' George clapped. 'Introductions over. *Mama-san*,' he called. The girls giggled. Catherine realised that they were in on the game too. The sour-faced Chinese woman was by his elbow. 'You have a new recruit,' he said. 'It's time she went to work.'

So that was it. She stared at George coldly.

'Catherine, you don't have to do this,' she heard Willie mutter.

'It's all right,' she answered. 'I told you. I'm game.'

Andreas and Robby stood up to let her pass. 'Now, don't let the side down. Bat straight and all that,' called George.

Catherine followed the *mama-san* across the dance-floor. Svetlana and Vera hurried up behind her. 'We're to show you what to do,' said Svetlana. Actually, Catherine was thinking, I'm going to show bloody George. I'm going to enjoy this.

Svetlana led her to the sofas where the girls waited for custom. Catherine rolled up her skirt, revealing her long legs, smoked a cigarette from a holder, and imitated the disdainful expression of the others. Within moments she had been invited by a short, white-suited Chinese man on to the floor. They performed a decorous waltz, followed by a foxtrot. The man danced well, although his head only came up to her chin, and his movements were mechanical. He avoided eye-contact, or any other physical intimacy. She did not know if she was relieved or disappointed: she had expected to be pawed. He bowed and walked back to his table. It was only after she had sat down that she noticed the wad of dollar bills he had placed in the cleft between her breasts.

Svetlana grabbed and counted them. 'Oh, darling, he likes you,' she laughed, 'or maybe it is not he but someone else,' and pointed at the table. The man in the white suit was whispering to an older man, in a traditional gown, who was examining her through half-closed, sullen eyes.

This is getting interesting, thought Catherine.

He had a handsome, hawk-like face, but when he turned she saw that one side was disfigured by a livid red scar that ran from his eye to his drooping mouth. 'That's General Lin,' said Svetlana. 'If you were really one of us you'd consider yourself lucky. He pays well, though I've never been with him myself. He only ever chooses natural redheads like you. Nora dyed hers to attract him but it didn't work ... Look, here comes his pimp again. What are you going to do?' she whispered. 'Are you going to sit with him?'

'Why not?' said Catherine.

She winked at George as she followed the man across the floor. 'Warlord!' she mouthed silently. Only Willie looked concerned. The others were still enjoying the joke.

An empty seat was offered her next to the warlord, who nodded curtly as she sat down. She settled her features into what she thought was a seductive expression, but he turned away and ignored her, conversing quietly with his friends. She sipped the tea, which was all she had been given. One dance followed another. The men continued to ignore her.

Eventually boredom gave way to anger. She slapped the wad of money she had received from the white-suited man on to the mat in front of the general, stood up and bowed in parody of the curt nod he had given her. Then, head held high, she marched to her friends' table, feeling the general's eyes on the back of her neck.

'Bravo,' George cried, kissing her. 'That showed him what's what. You were magnificent. I never thought you'd go through with it.'

'Well,' she said, 'if I'm to whore I want to be noticed doing it. Give me a glass of champagne, will you? That poisonous tea . . .'

'I wouldn't laugh too loudly,' murmured Willie, lighting his pipe. 'That chap's one of Chang Tso-lin's clique. Commanded one of the brigades in that last little war of theirs and did a bit of fighting. Took Jehol before the whole Fengtian lot had to retreat. He's a dangerous man to cross. Well done, Catherine. You've made an enemy of a warlord. Got him to lose face.'

'If I had a face like that I'd want to lose it,' giggled Robby, who was as usual very drunk. 'Did you see it? One half Jekyll, the other Mr Hyde! Oh, God, what have I said?'

He looked up into the face he had been describing. The general, flanked by the man in white and a large, bearded man in uniform, had left his table and paused by theirs on his way to the door. His expression was impassive, but he was holding the wad of money. As her eyes met his, he bowed and, in an elegant but deliberate action, placed the notes in front of her. He bowed again, spat one word, then left, followed by his men.

'What did he say?' asked Catherine.

'He said "down payment",' Willie told her.

'I say, we'd better not come here again,' said Robby, blinking nervously.

His panic made them laugh, which eased the tension, and they called for more champagne. Willie had quietly apportioned the general's tip to the delighted Russians, who drank with them until the club closed.

'I've seen that fellow before,' said George, as Willie drove them home in the twilight before dawn.

'What fellow?' asked Catherine, who was sitting on his knee.

'Your general,' said George, puffing at his cigar, 'Dr Jekyll. Can't think where, but I feel I know him.'

'No, you don't,' said Catherine. 'He's my warlord. I found him.'

'Whatever you say, my darling,' he chuckled, 'but don't worry,

I'll protect you. You know that St George will always be there to charge to your rescue.'

'I think at the moment the only attentions I need to be rescued from are those of St George himself.' She removed George's hand from her thigh. 'What would your mother say? Or Edmund?'

'Bugger Edmund,' said George, and threw his cigar into the road across a snoring Robby. He covered her neck with wet kisses, but within moments he had fallen asleep on her shoulder.

If she was going to start an affair, Catherine thought, it would not be tonight.

Willie could not sleep. He sat in front of his journal, a thought going round in his mind. A gentleman never takes a friend's girl.

In his rear-view mirror, driving home, he had seen George kiss Catherine, and she had apparently responded. Well, that was that, he thought.

When she had returned from the general's table he had known he was in love. He had never met a woman of such courage, such panache, such beauty – but she belonged to his best friend. Had he imagined Robby's look of derision when they parted in the corridor and went to their separate rooms?

Towards dawn he walked out on to the lawn, and pulled down the black flag. He watched the grey slate roofs and black brick buildings catch the first light of a pale sun, and heard the toot of a tug from the river three blocks away. How he hated this city, and his thankless job. How he loved to be in this great country, which was struggling to enter a new century with all its contradictions and new ideas. As an observer, he thought wryly. That was all a journalist could ever be. He must stand in the wings and watch while others made history.

Or took the girl.

Wearily, he stepped back into his sitting room, where Robby's cocktail glasses lay scattered on the table among the current-affairs magazines.

A thousand miles to the south, in a grander metropolis also originally built on a marsh, a young Chinese woman, tiny in her mink coat, with a veil hanging from her pillbox hat to half cover her face, was sitting in the back of a Rolls-Royce Silver Ghost. Her eyes were fixed on the peaked cap of her chauffeur. She looked to neither left nor right as they clattered across the iron bridge over the Soochow Creek on to the Bund. She ignored the British Consulate General, and seemed hardly aware of the offices of all the great hongs, the same that Edward Airton had pointed out to Catherine on her arrival in Tientsin. In Shanghai, though, they had even more commanding premises. Jardine Matheson, AEA, Chartered Bank, Union Insurance. The existing buildings were impressive, but what could be seen in the large construction sites at the entrance to Nanking Road, and further on, just after the tall Customs Building, defied the imagination. At the one, the Baghdadi billionaire, Victor Sassoon, was laying the foundations for what he intended to be the most magnificent hotel in Asia. At the other, cranes were towering over the granite heights of a Hong Kong and Shanghai Banking Corporation headquarters that would dominate the whole water-front. These emblems of merchant wealth and power were designed to fix Shanghai as the New York of the Far East. The cafés and department stores behind these great façades – not to mention the bars and brothels in streets further back – had already styled the city as the Paris of the Orient. Yu Fu-kuei, in the back seat of Major Yang's Rolls-Royce, could not have cared less. She had a job to do.

Anyway, she had seen this skyline when her ship had docked at the International Pier. Standing on the deck, she had tried to view these buildings as symbols of imperialism and oppression, which she had come here to undermine, but she had felt empty of emotion. She caught herself in the inconsequential, and bourgeoise reflection that such a pretty scene would make a good picture postcard to send to her tutor and former classmates at Oxford. Then she realised that she *should* be cultivating such thoughts, if she were to play her role. Safety lay in her ability to be bourgeoise. She smiled wryly. In a short while, she would be with Yang Yi-liang, and then she would be expected to speak the sentimental language of love. Perhaps her studies of English pastoral poetry over the last two years might prove helpful.

He had been standing on the pier, in roughly the same position from which, two years earlier, he had waved goodbye to her. When he saw her, his face lit up with boyish excitement. He had been trained, of course, in Confucian etiquette, so it would not have been proper to reveal his emotion in public with an embrace or a hug, but in the back of the car, he had quietly clasped her hand. 'You have returned,' he said simply.

'Yes, I have returned,' she answered, and responded to the joy on his face with a smile she did not think had been entirely false. She had been surprised that part of her was pleased to see him, and by how comfortable and familiar it felt to have him at her side. She noticed small care lines on his forehead, and additional creases near his eyes. He had sobered a little while she had been away. He looked harder. More mature. 'You seem to have prospered,' she murmured, indicating the chauffeur and the Rolls-Royce.

'I've been promoted,' he said. 'General Sun Chuan-fang has been kind to me. I'm a major now in his intelligence division. In charge of counter-espionage and anti-subversion.' He spoke casually, but she had detected a question in his eyes. She had leaned over and kissed his cheek. 'I'm very pleased for you,' she said. 'You will have my hundred per cent support.'

'Some of your former friends . . .'

'I have no former friends,' she said firmly. 'My life began when I met you.' She squeezed his hand. 'Don't you remember? The document you made me sign? "I abjure Communism . . ."'

'Yes,' he said, relaxing. 'You did, didn't you? Oh!' he exclaimed. 'Oh, I have missed you, Fu-kuei. And you're so beautiful. More beautiful than . . .'

'Shush,' she whispered, and kissed his lips. In the driving mirror she saw the chauffeur smile as Yi-liang took her in his arms and returned her kiss with passion.

'You've picked up some European manners,' he said, when they had disengaged.

'Isn't that why you sent me to England?' She smiled. 'I think you'll find me very European.'

He had laughed in sheer delight.

He took her to a large, Western-style house he had bought in the Chapei District. With childish pride, he showed her round the rooms, which, he said, he had had decorated by a Japanese designer 'in the European manner'. The drawing room was a mish-mash of marble and chintz. Two bronze hunting dogs of the Napoleon III school flanked a stuccoed fireplace, in front of which lay a carpet featuring the Statue of Liberty. Bottles of expensive brandy and a row of gaudily kimonoed Japanese dolls were arranged on the shelves of a glass cabinet.

'It's beautiful,' she murmured.

'Do you think so?' He preened. 'Perhaps it is not entirely to your taste. After your time in Oxford you may wish to make one or two alterations.'

'One or two, perhaps,' she said, looking at the orange curtains hanging on purple walls.

He had called the servants in to be introduced, then shown her his study. 'Now come upstairs,' he said, 'and see your wardrobe. I think I have remembered your size correctly.' He had opened cupboards and cupboards of dresses, ballgowns, cheongsams and fur coats, then slid out drawers that seemed to be full of jewels.

'You have spent a fortune.' She was amazed.

'In my new job I receive more than is usual for a major. General Sun is generous. But do you like them?' he asked. 'Are you happy to be home?'

She had kissed him again. It was the easiest thing to do. 'Make love to me,' she whispered urgently.

Afterwards, lying in the big brass bed looking up at the fan revolving on the ceiling, the sounds of the city coming through the open window, he had talked of marriage.

'You don't have to marry me,' she had said to him.

'But I wish to,' he said, after a long silence. 'I thought that you . . .'

'You have to think of your career,' she said. 'Marriage in politics is an alliance of power. I bring you nothing.'

'That's not true. You—'

'Listen to me,' she said. 'I will always be here to love and support you. You are my life. It is an honour for me to be your mistress. That is all I want. You . . . you saved me. I belong to you. No, don't speak. Listen to me. Yours is a rising star. You already stand high in the warlord's favour. One day there will be a National Government, and you will have an important role to play. Then you may want to choose a wife who will help your ambitions, as I cannot. I can only love you,' she said. 'For always.'

'I did not send you to Oxford to come back and be my whore,' he said.

'I am not your whore. I am your mistress and concubine. And proud to be so.'

'I could not face life without you,' he said softly.

'You won't have to,' she said. 'How could I leave you? That would be the end of my existence.' She noticed that his cheek was wet with tears. 'Make love to me again,' she said, moving her hand under the sheets.

And so her life in Shanghai had begun. If it was an act, she did not find it difficult or unpleasant. Yang Yi-liang could not disguise his pride in her. He took her to banquets with his fellow officers, once with the general himself. The old man had enjoyed her intelligence and flattery, and congratulated his subordinate on his choice of concubine. She had bowed her head, blushing and smiling demurely. One evening she organised a dinner party to which Yi-liang had invited some foreigners: the deputy chief of police of the International Concession; a missionary and his wife; a professor of English from Shanghai University; the principal of St John's College and his sister, who was a sinologist from Princeton and an expert on Song paintings. Yi-liang had sat at the head of the table, contributing little, gazing half in admiration, half proprietorially at his Fu-kuei, who was dazzling his guests with her wit and her knowledge of Chinese and European culture. By then she had redecorated the rooms in a more restrained style and the evening had been an unqualified success.

After a month or so she found she was becoming used to the comfort and luxury of her surroundings. She began to develop the habits of a lady of leisure, sleeping late in the mornings, shopping in the afternoon. Her other life she had internalised – that was the modern word. Only once had she ever revealed herself: to her English friend, Catherine Cabot, on the boat trip to Shanghai. She regretted that, but had briefly suspected that Catherine had been a plant of the Third International sent to spy on her. Now she knew it was not so. Catherine, whom she liked for her free spirit, and with whom she felt an affinity, was no more or less than she claimed to be. She did not think she had given away too much. Catherine had been very drunk and Fu-kuei doubted she would remember – and now worried about it only occasionally. What concerned her more was that since her arrival in Shanghai she had not been contacted. She waited patiently, keeping her ears open, filing away Yi-liang's occasional indiscretions in a deep recess of her mind.

One afternoon, as she was coming out of the Wing On department store with her chauffeur carrying her parcels, a beggar had bumped into her. The chauffeur shouted him away, but she already had the strip of paper in her hand. She had read it quickly in the back of the car and memorised the instructions. At first she experienced a flutter of fear – everything had been theoretical up to now, but from here on there would be no going back . . . Then, slowly, she had felt her blood warm, and her cheeks burned. She experienced an arousal similar to sexual ecstasy: not the simulated passion of her couplings with Yi-liang but the release she vaguely remembered having experienced in the arms of her husband. It was as if her awareness had heightened, she saw each brick and granite block of the office buildings she passed shining with unusual clarity in the sunlight. It was as if she had woken from a deep coma. For an instant she was the avenger that, in their innocence, she and Wang had only dreamed of being. She was empowered. That scrap of an address was a weapon in her hands.

The elation had lasted only a moment. She had caught her reflection in the chauffeur's rear-view mirror, and was satisfied that her mask had not slipped. She saw only what anybody else would see: an elegant society lady with time on her hands after her shopping. There was nothing in the serene forehead to suggest the turmoil of thought and calculation that the message had unleashed; no hint of her set purpose in that gentle, sphinx-like smile. When they pulled up in the courtyard of Yi-liang's house, the Fu-kuei who allowed her chauffeur to take her mink-coated arm as she alighted, and inclined her head graciously to the servant who opened the door was the elegant persona that she and Mr Behrens had designed between them with the care of playwrights – but this was no longer a dress rehearsal: the play had begun, and she had already worked out a plan.

She had thought it wise to tell Yi-liang about the new dress shop in Avenue Joffre. She had perched on his knee as he sat at his desk and asked him what colour ballgown he preferred. Surreptitiously, he moved his inkstand to cover a document on the table, but she had already glanced at the heading and the list of names, and memorised them. 'Go away.' Yi-liang had laughed. 'If you don't let me work I won't be able to afford any ballgowns for you. Get a blue one *and* a red one.' A few kisses later she had gone out.

It was a small shop on the Avenue Joffre in the tree-lined French Concession. As she went in, the doorbell tinkled. A short, bearded man in a skullcap, a tape measure round his neck, was arranging a dress on a mannequin. 'Yes, Madame?' He bowed to her, and smiled, showing jagged yellow teeth. He had soft, watchful eyes in a sallow face. 'How can I be of service?'

'I am looking for a Mr Hoffman,' she said, as instructed. 'I am told that he has a range of the latest fashions from Warsaw.'

'Ah, you are talking about my partner, Mr Hoffnung,' said the man. 'From Cracow. Sadly he is not with us today. He had to return to Poland.'

'I hope that was not due to any bereavement in his family,' said Fu-kuei.

'On the contrary, Madame,' said the man, 'it was for the wedding of his daughter.'

Fu-kuei nodded, waiting.

'Perhaps I can be of assistance to Madame?' said the man, who also appeared satisfied – Fu-kuei saw his shoulders relax. 'My name is Barkowitz, and I, too, am from Cracow. Was there any particular fashion in which Madame is interested?'

'I wish you to make me a ballgown,' said Fu-kuei.

'Excellent,' said the man. 'You would perhaps wish to study some of our patterns. May I suggest that you enter our dressing room, where we have some pictures on the walls?'

He led her past bolts of silk and muslin to a small curtained alcove at the back of the shop. A female assistant glanced at her incuriously. 'There is a seat inside where Madame may be comfortable,' said Barkowitz. 'Madame will pleased to take as long as she likes.' He left her, pulling the curtain closed behind him.

There were indeed patterns on the wall, beautiful drawings of elegant women in silk creations, each lovelier than the last, but Fu-kuei was more interested in the blue carpeting on the floor, looking for a tear in the fabric. She saw some frayed strands, and cautiously lifted a small flap to reveal a white envelope. Quickly she scanned the letter inside it, then withdrew from her purse a folded piece of paper, on which she had written the names of the political prisoners she had seen on Yi-liang's desk that morning, and the prison in which they were held. She took out her pen, and added a few sentences describing a conversation she had heard at the general's house the week before. She put her note, with the letter, back into the envelope, replaced it under the carpet, and pulled aside the curtain. 'I have found a pattern that may be suitable, Mr Barkowitz,' she said.

'An excellent choice, if I may say so, Madame,' said the tailor. 'Perhaps if you will allow me to take your coat, I will ask my assistant to write down some measurements. I will probably be able to arrange a fitting for you in a week's time.'

'A fortnight would be adequate,' said Fu-kuei. 'There is no hurry.'

'Indeed, Madame. Let us say two weeks.'

Twenty minutes later Fu-kuei was back in her car. It glided away in the direction from which she had come. She sat wrapped in her fur, her veil over her eyes. She looked to neither right nor left as they drove past the Western offices on the Bund.

3

Splendour of an Autumn Moon

From the journal of William Lampsett, Reuters correspondent, Tientsin, 19 September 1922

I went racing yesterday in the Charters's box. Lionel was as pompous and his wife, Jenny, as vacuous as ever. How she and her brother, George, could be siblings I can't imagine. George was, of course, the hero of the hour, magnificent in his maroon and green silks, his body curved in an elegant bow above his saddle as China Coast came in six lengths ahead of the field. Quite the showman afterwards – hugging the neck of his pony in the pouring rain, tipping his dripping cap to the crowd when he was led in by Catherine and Jenny to receive the cup.

With the Charters's blessing, Catherine had brought an American friend, a rough-edged Jewish girl called Martha, who had once been her travelling companion, and with whom she now shares Chinese lessons. I found her intelligent and amusing, if not blessed by good looks or social graces. The problem was that Martha had brought along, uninvited, their teacher – a stammering young man of the type you see quite often nowadays, a half-Westernised, half-radical idealist, trying to find an identity somewhere between the Confucian heritage of his family and the new ideas he picked up at his foreign university. I rather approved of him, but the Charters didn't, and it was amusing to watch Jenny's contortions as she avoided her unwanted guests, who were not only 'from the wrong side of the track' but had also, in her prejudiced view, crossed the racial divide.

Catherine was kindness itself: she never left them alone except

94

when she was called down to the paddock for George's triumph, but I could see that she was furious with Lionel and Jenny. Martha seemed unaware of the tension, determined to enjoy herself, and added insult to injury by treating everybody with what might be termed 'Yankee egalitarianism'. She also became tipsy early on, because as usual the wine was flowing. When she won some money, she hugged young Mr Lei, planting kisses on both his cheeks. It all seemed innocent enough to me but this was noticed, as was the way, afterwards, she sat huddled next to him, her arm through his, as they studied the racing form.

They left early, despite Catherine's protestations that they should stay for the last race. I think the sensitive Mr Lei had felt humiliated. Catherine accompanied them to the exit, then came back, her face a picture. I watched her stride deliberately to the bar, where she ordered a stiff drink. She turned and surveyed the race box, where knots of racers were laughing and joking, it was quite obvious what about. In one of those unfortunate silences that sometimes falls over a crowded room, Jenny's lisping voice could be heard: 'And did you see them? Kissing! I nearly died. What is the word, Lionel?'

'Miscegenation, my dear,' was her husband's reply.

Catherine walked up to him and threw the contents of her glass in his face. Lionel was dumbstruck. I doubt whether a commissioner of the Maritime Customs has been treated with such indignity in all its history.

I don't know what would have happened had not George, who had showered and changed after his ride, entered the box at that moment. 'Good shot, Catherine,' he cried. 'I've been wanting to do that to Lionel for years.' Somehow, that broke the tension and everybody laughed, although it took an hour to calm Catherine.

Later, we all went out on the town. I danced with her, but as usual I was the stand-in when George was off the floor. She has eyes only for him, worse luck.

To occasional visitors, who had never been allowed to penetrate into the Great Within beyond the first grand courtyard, the Lei family mansion had all the mystery and inaccessibility of an ancient civilisation – one subject to wear and tear: the paint on the red pillars was cracked and peeling, and there were signs of moss among the grey tiles. However, the grime on the bricks suggested centuries of continuous habitation, and the busy comings and goings of servants, messengers and cooks embodied an elaborate hierarchy and the unchanging order of a great feudal household. The gold leaf on the patterned ceilings (only a little flaked) and the fine filigree on the carved window-frames and doorways (only slightly chipped) revealed an opulence that had been allowed to spill into the remotest parts of the establishment. Even the small rooms of this outer courtyard were decorated with great beds, imposing blackwood wardrobes, lacquer cabinets and clothes boxes, flamboyantly carved tables and chairs inlaid with marble and mother-of-pearl. The stone-cut tablets in the outside walls and lintels depicted flowers and fruits of the seasons, *ch'ilins* and lion dogs and other mythical beasts, gods and fairies. They spoke to Catherine of traditions and beliefs emanating from the deepest wellsprings of Chinese culture.

As she sat in the side-room off the courtyard, sipping fragrant green tea, her attention sometimes wandered from Lei Ming's attempts to get Martha's tongue round the vocabulary exercises Catherine had already mastered, and tried to imagine what greater luxury was concealed in the courtyards beyond the first reception hall. Here Ming's father, Lei Chuan-hsi, and his elder son, Lei Tang, had their banking offices.

From Ming and Lan-hua's enthusiastic descriptions, Catherine understood that the mansion consisted of three main courtyards, each more impressive than the last. The family lived in the cluster of rooms off the final courtyard. They had told her that the most spacious quarters were reserved for the dowager of the household, Ming's grandmother, who, it seemed, was the real ruler of the establishment. Officially she shared her quarters with her son, Ming's father. Actually, everybody knew that Lei Chuan-hsi – Lei *Lao* or Old Man Lei, as he was often called – had outlived both his wives; he spent his nights in one of the various subsidiary side-courtyards, where he had installed three, four or five concubines. (Neither Ming nor Lan-hua knew the exact number: they were not allowed to visit that part of the mansion.) Ming's elder half-brother, Tang, as befitting the heir to the dynasty and son of Old Man Lei's first wife, had a whole wing of the courtyard for his own wife and two children. Ming and Lan-hua, who were offspring of Old Man Lei's second wife, had rooms on the other side. The courtyard garden that separated their apartments provided just enough space to allow them each to lead their own private lives. 'Sounds like an Oxford quad,' said Catherine, when Ming had explained all this.

'Really?' replied Ming. 'Is Oxford so c-claustrophobic? It's our tradition, I suppose. I intend to move out at the first opp-opp-opportunity.'

The shrine to the Lei family ancestors was in the great hall off the second courtyard. The mansion dated back to the early eighteenth century, but Ming's grandfather, who had established the family banking business, had taken it over from a bankrupt client. 'So, you see,' laughed Ming, 'we're only p-parvenus. We've been in this house less than fifty years. Not that F-Father or Grandmother sees it in that way. For them it's already an ancestral home – but for Lan-hua and me, well, we're the w-wasteful third generation. What do they say? "Slippers back to slippers in three." As younger son I think it my d-duty to s-squander the family wealth.'

'You'll have little chance of doing that while Elder Brother runs the counting house.' Lan-hua shook her fringe out of her eyes. 'He has no intention of us going back to slippers for several genera-tions to come. Look how hard he works.'

'P-perhaps he w-won't have a choice,' said Ming. 'If a – a certain sort of g-government comes into p-power, which s-seeks to distribute wealth more equitably.'

'Long live the revolution!' cried Martha. Ming and Lan-hua laughed. 'Oh, come on, Catherine, it's only a joke,' she had added, but her companion had ostentatiously picked up her textbook.

Ming had introduced the two foreign women to his father and Lei Tang on one of their first visits. He had led them up to the hall dominating the first courtyard and ushered them over the step into the small passageway that divided the building in half. Through the doorway beyond, Catherine had caught a tantalising glimpse of a garden, dominated by two gnarled ginkgo trees, their fan-shaped leaves shading a walkway lined with strangely shaped stones and flowers. Within the hall, moon-shaped openings in latticed wooden partitions revealed the rooms on either side, the shelving hidden among the lattice-work laden with porcelain vases, statuettes, and amber or jade stones chosen for their resemblance to mountains and natural scenery. Through the opening on the left, Catherine could see a long table where elderly clerks made calculations with their abacuses. Ming led them round a lacquer screen into the room on the right, and there, beyond a blue Tientsin carpet, and walls whose every square inch was covered with scrolls of calligraphy, she saw two imposing teak desks. Behind the larger sat a sparrow-like man with cropped silver hair, and deep pouches under his sad eyes. He was wearing a simple black gown, and was fanning himself against the heat. Catherine, recalling the glimpse she had had of him at the station, recognised him as Ming's father. A younger version of him leaned over his shoulder to study a letter. 'P-please l-let me introduce my honourable father, and my b-brother, Lei T-Tang,' said Ming formally. His usual exuberance had deserted him. 'T-together they run our family b-business.'

Two pairs of sad eyes gazed up at them from blank faces. Catherine, in her fashionable, lilac frock, suddenly felt alien in this traditional Chinese sanctum. Ming, in his knickerbockers and bright red tie, appeared even more outlandish than the foreign women.

The two men rose solemnly to their feet, and bowed.

A flicker of panic crossed their composed faces when Martha stepped forward stretching out her hand. 'Hi, pleased to meet you,' she said, smiling broadly. One after the other, the two men took the proffered hand. Catherine noticed that the younger man's initial look of confusion had been replaced by distaste.

There was a brief exchange in Chinese between the old man and Ming. 'My f-father says you are b-both very w-welcome,' said Ming. 'Sh-shall we go n-now that we've had our meeting?'

'You call that a meeting?' asked Martha, incredulously, a few moments later.

'I t-told you my father was a Confucianist and conservative. They are not used to foreigners. Don't w-worry. They will become so in time.'

They had not met the father again, but sometimes, on their way to or from a Chinese lesson, they passed Lei Tang in conversation with a client or messenger in the courtyard. He would make a condescending bow, but otherwise ignored them. 'I'm sorry,' Lan-hua once told them, 'Elder Brother's like Father. He doesn't approve of our Western habits. He's always criticising Second Brother and me for being bananas.'

'*Bananas?*' asked Catherine, wondering if she had heard correctly.

'Yes.' Lan-hua giggled. 'Yellow on the outside, white inside. He thinks we're turning into foreigners.'

'Well, he can hardly approve of Catherine and me, then,' said Martha, glancing at Ming. 'Certainly not me. I really am a hairy barbarian.'

'He'll c-come round in time,' said Ming, quickly. 'And – and you're – you're n-not a – what you said you were. You're – you're very b-beautiful.'

'Why, thank you, Ming.' Martha pecked him on his blushing cheek. 'That's just what a girl wants to hear.'

In view of the antipathy of the elder Leis, it had been a surprise, therefore, when one day Lei Tang had knocked at the door while they were in the middle of a Chinese lesson, and solemnly handed to each of the two young women red scrolls. He held another with which he fidgeted as he muttered a few gruff words to his brother. By now Catherine was fluent enough to recognise the meaning in the sounds. He had said something about an invitation. Surprisingly, she heard 'Shishan', and then '*daifu*', meaning doctor. That was odd, she thought. Could he have been referring to Edward Airton?

Ming said something in reply, and his elder brother nodded. He thrust the scroll at Catherine. 'T-take it,' said Ming. 'He wants you to deliver it.' Lei Tang waited for her to take the scroll, then made an abrupt bow, and withdrew, relief evident on his face.

'What was that all about?' asked Martha, looking at her scroll. 'What are these?'

Ming laughed. 'They're invitations,' he said, 'for you b-both to join our family for the celebration of the Mid-autumn Festival next Sunday. Dr and Mrs Airton are also invited.'

'Tang's inviting us to a party? Why? He hates us,' said Martha.

'I d-doubt it's Tang,' smiled Ming. 'I sus-sus-suspect it's my g-grandmother. She's h-heard of the two f-foreigners who come to our house, and she wants to see you for herself. My father and Elder Brother c-can't go against G-Grandmother's wishes.'

'But why the Airtons?' asked Catherine. 'I didn't realise your family knew them.'

'They d-don't, but we have a s-special guest. My b-brother-in-law, Yu Fu-cheng. His sister is Tang's wife, Yu Fu-hong. Fu-cheng is now a very important man in Shishan, which is his family home. It seems that his father, Yu Hsin-fu, who is a rich merchant there and a p-partner of my f-father, knew Dr and Mrs Airton well when they were missionaries there. You see? So my f-father is inviting Dr Airton to come in order to f-flatter Yu Fu-cheng.'

'I do see,' said Catherine, doubtfully. 'How complicated.'

'It is very C-Confucian,' laughed Ming.

'Wow,' sighed Martha, who had opened her scroll. 'A Mid-autumn Festival. I can't wait.' Her brows furrowed. 'Ming?' she asked. 'What *is* a Mid-autumn Festival?'

The little man who stepped out of the rickshaw was not conventionally imposing. Tiny feet in immaculate black brogues clicked on the pavement. A comfortable belly wobbled under a black silk gown and two pudgy hands flapped in greeting. A round, pink-cheeked face under an enormous Homburg radiated well-scrubbed cheerfulness, energy and considerable self-satisfaction. He looked more like a successful dumpling-seller than a mandarin.

As one the three Leis, father and sons, with their two rows of servants, bowed deeply. The little man quickly raised the elder Lei by his elbow. 'Uncle, Uncle,' he laughed, '*bie kechi*. No formalities, please. How delightful it is to see you all so well.' The clever eyes, magnified behind horn-rimmed spectacles, twinkled benignly.

'My dear Fu-cheng, it is you who are looking well,' said Old Man Lei. 'You honour our unworthy household by sparing your valuable time to visit us. Your esteemed father has written to me of your great achievements in Shishan. My pride also overflows.'

'Uncle, you embarrass me. Whatever I have achieved would have been impossible without my connection to your family. Lei Tang,' he said, turning to the elder son, 'you are growing more like your honourable father every day. Is that Lei Ming behind you? Just look at you in your white suit! A man of the world! I have received your letter, by the way. Thank you. Full of most interesting ideas.' He grinned as Old Man Lei and his elder son exchanged startled glances. 'No, you should be proud of him, Uncle.' He beamed. 'Where would we be without youth and idealism? Ah,' he said, noticing that the servants were unloading his bags and boxes, 'you must tell them to be careful. Father has included several small gifts from our farm. Apples. Pears. And, of course, one or two pitchers of last year's *gaoliang* wine. Refined from the best Shishan crop. Distilled with water from the Black Hills.'

Old Man Lei smiled. 'My old friend is ever solicitous, as is his son. But come, I fear you are tired after your long journey. Your rooms are prepared. It is only a humble little courtyard . . .'

Yu Fu-cheng took his arm. 'Uncle, everybody knows that to experience the hospitality of Lei Chuan-hsi is to enjoy a taste of heaven. Oh!' he exclaimed, as they entered the second courtyard. 'Your ginkgos! I had forgotten how magnificently they towered . . .'

It was two hours before Old Man Lei had his guest to himself. Yu Fu-cheng had paid his respects to the grandmother, and had spent a short time with his sister, Lei Tang's bovine wife, Yu Fu-hong. The old banker could see that it had been a painful interview. Fu-hong had waddled, heavily pregnant, towards her brother on her lotus feet, and had wept on his shoulder, her homesickness evident. Old Man Lei had been struck by the contrast between the two siblings. He had never been particularly impressed by his daughter-in-law. His own mother was always complaining about her, telling him she was no better than a peasant. Not that his placid elder son seemed to mind: she had given him three fine sons already. Whether the parents were happy or not was neither here nor there. What mattered was that, as a seal on his alliance with the Yu family, the marriage had paid dividends. He congratulated himself on his acumen in identifying the woman's father as the man who would help his business in the north-east.

He had known Yu Hsin-fu for more than twenty-five years. As a young banker, Lei Chuan-hsi had interviewed several Shishan merchants involved in the then growing soy-bean business. Yu had been the roughest of the many rogues whom he had encountered in that wild province – he suspected that he was in league with bandits – but he had been struck by the man's intelligence as they drank raw spirit together in a shabby inn in the suburbs of the town. Yu had remained sober, understanding the potential of the scheme. Within a year, using a mixture of the bank's loans and strong arm methods, into which Lei did not feel it was appropriate to enquire, Yu had acquired from the local farmers the land rights to the main bean-growing areas in the county, from the Black Hills to the banks of the Liao river. By the time of the revolution in 1911, Lei's *protégé* had become the undisputed soy-bean king of western Fengtian. Lei, as his banker, had profited from every transaction. They had become firm friends. When Yu had suggested a marriage between his daughter and Lei's eldest son, Lei had agreed, despite his mother's objections.

What had worked out even better had been Lei's investment in the education of Yu's son. The first time he had seen the lad in Yu's home, the tiny ten-year-old peasant boy, with bare feet, brown cheeks and snot on his upper lip, had looked him full in the eyes without fear. His mind was quick and agile. Over the old mule-teer's scepticism, Lei had paid for his schooling, taken him into the bank as an apprentice, then persuaded his father to allow the boy to study for three years at a university in Japan. Lei had not been disappointed. Yu Fu-cheng had chosen to work in a Japanese mining company and had risen quickly to a position of influence.

In 1915 the young man, now a prosperous merchant in his own right, had come to him in Tientsin with a proposition. A new warlord was establishing himself in Shishan and trusted Yu Fu-cheng, who told him he could arrange a loan that would make the warlord's position pre-eminent and give him the wherewithal to buy arms. Old Man Lei had considered the proposition carefully. As a banker, he had always been careful to avoid involvement in politics, but in this case he determined to make an exception. He had assisted him to set up a syndicate that would finance General Lin Fu-po's ambitions. Yu Fu-cheng's position as the warlord's financial genius had been secured, and now he was the chief minister in Shishan. The little man, grinning and calling him 'uncle,' was one of the powers of the land.

'And how is your honourable father? And Shishan?' he asked him, sucking deeply on his pipe.

Yu Fu-cheng was smoking a cigarette from a tortoiseshell holder. In his new plum-coloured robe, perched on his chair, he resembled an exotic bird. 'You must visit us more often, Uncle. You will see many changes. The counties around Shishan are wealthy, and there are revenues to spare for several social schemes in which General Lin is interested. A new drainage plan for the old city. Schools. Hospitals.'

The old banker gave him a shrewd glance. 'The Japanese are happy about these developments? It must be difficult for you that there is an independent Japanese garrison town located in your territory.'

'It is something we are used to in the north-east. The Japanese railway cantonment does not bother us. Our interests coincide, Uncle. The Japanese are interested in developing the resources of the region too . . .'

'For their own ends.'

'And ours, Uncle. We also benefit from the increased prosperity.'

Old Man Lei spat into the spittoon by the side of his chair. 'The Japanese provide subsidies to keep the warlords in power – as their puppets.'

Yu Fu-cheng smiled. 'One might ask who is using whom. For the moment, the Japanese presence in the three north-eastern provinces makes us unassailable from the south. As you saw, in the recent war Wu Pei-fu did not dare follow up his victory beyond the Wall. Now that his government in Peking has stripped Chang Tso-lin and all the other generals of their official titles, Marshal Chang has been forced to declare Manchuria independent of China. We may keep all the taxes we collect for our own use. Our eventual aim is still to unify China, but in the meanwhile we can undertake much-needed reform, building up our strength and our wealth. Believe me, Uncle, future historians will write that the regeneration of China came from the north-east.'

'And the Japanese?'

'How can they object if the Chinese territories undergo modernisation and reform? We will establish our own hospitals and schools. A new generation will grow up reliant on themselves, proud to be Chinese. How then can even railway colonialism survive?'

'My dear Fu-cheng, I had never realised you were such an idealist, or a patriot.'

Yu Fu-cheng laughed delightedly. 'Uncle, I have you to thank for my education. You sent me to university in Tokyo, and it was there that I began to learn, from the Japanese themselves, how a free and independent nation functions. Now I can put those ideas into practice and truly serve my country.'

'Fu-cheng, I am proud of you.'

'You honour me, Uncle, but, you should also be proud of your own son.'

'Lei Tang? Of course I am proud of him.'

'Lei Tang, surely. That goes without saying. But I was thinking of Lei Ming. I mentioned that he had written to me. Do you know what his letter was about?'

'I am embarrassed to think of it. He boasts that he is a socialist.'

'He is young, and these are the fashionable ideas of the times. He impressed me. I think he will make a fine teacher. Uncle, I told you that I intended to establish a school in Shishan. With your permission, I would like to invite Lei Ming to be its principal.'

Old Man Lei's features did not reveal his surprise, or the rapid calculations that clicked through his mind. On the face of it, such a generous offer was an appropriate expression of the gratitude the official owed to the Lei family. On the other hand, Old Man Lei had always made it a principle that, in his relations with the Yu family, credit should always be weighted down on his side. In the past, his bank had profited from its alliance with the Yus and the balance had always favoured him, but now Yu Fu-cheng's influence in the north-east was tilting the scales. Would this patronage of his younger son mean that the Leis were under obligation to the Yus? And what favour would Yu Fu-cheng ask in return?

He could not deny that he was worried about Ming. His son had come back from Hawaii with a headful of dangerous political ideas, mannerisms and attitudes, shameful in a Confucian household.

He and Tang had concluded there would be no role for him in the family business, and he had been cudgelling his brain to think of an educational establishment that might take a radical on its staff, since it was clear that his son had set his heart on teaching. The universities in Peking were obviously to be avoided: his daughter had been infected there with modern ideas, but a girl was easy enough to dispose of in a suitable marriage. He had found a match for her: young Ti Jen-hsing, the son of a business acquaintance, was a presentable young man with a promising career in the army. Yes, daughters were easy to handle – but sons?

A terrible thought crossed his mind. Not all daughters were easy to handle. He had suddenly remembered that Yu Fu-cheng had once had a younger sister, from his father's second marriage to a school-teacher. Old Man Lei had tried to dissuade his friend from marrying such a troublesome woman, but Old Yu had been besotted by her refinement. The daughter, as he feared, had been brought up with unbound feet and the most modern ideas. At university she had been involved in the May 4th Movement and had run away with a peasant agitator. Subsequently, she been disowned by her family. He did not know what had become of her. The sooner his own little Lan-hua was married to this Lieutenant Ti the better.

He had another disconcerting thought. His younger son had not only come back with a ludicrous fondness for Western clothes and ideas but a penchant for Western women. He shuddered as he remembered the two specimens who had been introduced to him in his office: the one black-haired and fat like a pig, the other pale and red-headed like a fox-fairy. He must remove his son from their influence.

It was then that he realised Yu Fu-cheng was offering him a perfect answer. No matter if the debt balance shifted, he had more than enough credit remaining from the past. And what if Yu Fu-cheng were to ask a large favour in return? It would deepen even further the Lei family's relationship with a prominent official. They could not lose.

All these reflections occupied the old banker no longer than it took him to relight his pipe. When he turned to face his smiling interlocutor, his decision was made – although he made sure that his features revealed nothing of their satisfaction. 'I appreciate your generosity and consideration for our family, but I could not allow it.'

'Why ever not, Uncle?' The official's eyes were twinkling behind his glasses.

'How could I burden you with the responsibility for such a weak-willed, stammering youth? It would be a poor reflection on your kindness. He has picked up anti-social ideas in his studies overseas.'

Fu-cheng laughed. 'I, too, am considered a radical by some, Uncle.' He patted the old man's knee. 'Come, it is his heart's desire. He wrote to me asking for such a post.'

'The impertinent rascal!' exclaimed the old man. 'It is shameful that he should impose on you in this way.'

'On the contrary,' said Yu Fu-cheng, 'we need resourceful men of education and talent in the north-east. Come, Uncle. Agree.'

'You are so kind to an old man.' As he took the younger man's hands in his, the old banker adopted a tremulous tone. Both smiled, each calculating the advantages they would gain through this intensification of their relationship.

Catherine stepped through the inner doors of the counting house into a garden of hanging lights. The path was lined with fairy lamps, each candle twinkling in a tinted jade bowl; it was as if a necklace of jewels had been laid on the ground, shimmering in flickering variations of green, blue and amber. Orange flames licked and smouldered from two shadowy bronze braziers. Above her head, red and yellow paper lanterns shone like constellations among the leaves of the ginkgo trees, drawing her eyes to the velvet sky in which she could make out the needle pricks of the Milky Way. Over the roof tiles of the hall behind her rose the brightest lantern of them all, the shining yellow orb of the harvest moon, whose mysterious shadows, Catherine now knew, concealed the palace of Ch'ang-E, the virgin princess of Chinese legend, who lived here with her friends: the bent old man, Wu K'ang, condemned for eternity to lop off the branches of an ever regrowing cassia tree; and the Jade Rabbit, who had been rewarded with immortality for having offered itself as a meal to three hungry sages. It was

Ch'ang-E, however, to whom they would pay their respects tonight: she had saved the world from everlasting tyranny by stealing from the power-corrupted archer, Hou-I, his pills of eternal life, eating them and floating upwards to the heavens; now she looked down on the earth she protected, a symbol of chastity, virtue and hope for all generations of mankind.

'What lovely stories,' Catherine had murmured to Edmund earlier, as he drove her to the Lei family mansion. Edward Airton had come down with a head cold, and Nellie had elected to remain behind to look after him, so Edmund would represent the Airton family at the banquet. He had been answering her questions about the Moon Festival. 'Yes, it's marvellous how folklore accumulates round these great family gatherings. Rather like our Christmas,' he said, 'this one probably started as a common or garden harvest festival.'

'I quite envy Ch'ang-E,' said Catherine dreamily.

'Really?' said Edmund. 'To be stuck on the moon for eternity?'

'Yes, I imagine it would be peaceful,' said Catherine. 'Beyond care . . .' She laughed, shortly and sharply. 'Not that I would qualify as a symbol of chastity or virtue. Or hope,' she added.

'Rather morbid this evening, aren't we, Nurse?' said Edmund, quietly.

'Is it morbid to think of eternity?'

'Depends what sort of eternity you're contemplating,' said Edmund. 'Do you have this sort of conversation with George?'

'George is not the sort of person with whom you have conversations,' said Catherine.

'Have you and he had a falling-out?'

'No,' said Catherine. 'George is not the sort of person with whom you have fallings-out.'

The car turned into Taku Road. Edmund had to concentrate as he steered through the busier traffic of handcarts, rickshaws and pedestrians in the narrower streets of the Chinese town.

'Go on, tell me more about the Moon Festival,' said Catherine, after a while. 'What are these confections you've brought?' She tapped the tin that lay between them on the seat.

'Ah,' said Edmund. 'Moon cakes. Traditional gift that you

exchange at this time of year. You'll like them. Lotus-seed paste and salted eggs in pastry. At some stage of the evening we'll all sit down together and eat them as we look at the moon and recite poetry.'

'I hope you're joking,' said Catherine.

'That's what you do. Actually there's a story about the moon cakes as well, historical this time – revolutionary, even. Shall I tell you?'

'Aren't you going to anyway?'

'All right, then. In 1368, at the end of the Yuan dynasty, the Chinese planned a rebellion against the Mongols. The leader of the conspiracy, Chu Yuan-chang, decided that the best way to pass secret messages about their attack would be inside these traditional cakes. The rebellion was successful. On the Mid-autumn Festival all the Chinese rose up as planned and the Mongols were overthrown. End of the Yuan dynasty, beginning of the Ming. They've celebrated it ever since.'

'Fascinating,' said Catherine.

'You are in a mood tonight, aren't you?' chuckled Edmund. He leaned over quickly and kissed her cheek.

'Why did you do that?' she asked, surprised.

'Wanted to cheer you up.' Edmund grinned. There was a twinkle in his eye. 'Did it work?'

'Yes.' She was laughing. 'I think it did.'

And, oddly, her annoyance with George had disappeared. What had she to blame him for, anyway? Especially since it had been she who had behaved stupidly. After the races and the celebratory dinner at the Astor House Hotel, they had danced as usual to the lulling music of the band, and George had seemed to hold her more intimately, more tenderly – more seriously, even – than he had in the past, and the kissing had been natural, or she thought it had been, as they swayed, arms hanging over each other's shoulders, breast to chest, pelvis to pelvis, the warmth of his breath on her neck. She had believed that they had passed the indefinable shadow-line in a relationship that separated friend from imminent lover, and had felt within her the delicious beginning of desire. It had lasted until the moment George had clapped his hands for the waiter to bring a cigar, then nudged Willie in the ribs. 'Next dance is on you, old boy. Don't know what's got into Catherine tonight. She's hot as a tigress. You'll have your hands full. I'm pooped.'

Somehow she had recovered from the cold douche of shock and shame, had pushed George playfully and made a joke about heroes unappreciative of the tributes of victory. And Robby had laughed and told her that maidenly charms were wasted on Georgy-boy, and George had grinned benevolently as he hugged her shoulders and puffed at his corona. 'It *was* a good race, wasn't it?' She had listened to him boast until finally she escaped with Willie to the dance-floor, where she had charlestoned until dawn.

Her anger with George had smouldered for a week, although she doubted that anybody had noticed – least of all George. Her remarks to him became perhaps a little more barbed than usual, but that was all.

Eventually, though, she had decided to punish him. She would seduce Andreas. She didn't like him – he was a self-centred brute, charmless, with an ugly impatience that made waiters nervous when he ordered his complicated cocktails. One evening she declined George's invitation to go to the *fantan* tables, and took a taxi to the ICI flats by the river where he lived. She knew he would be at home: two nights before, he had injured himself in a madcap rickshaw race. They had found him by the water's edge in a tangle of broken shafts, and washed the mud off his wound with champagne they had brought from the Astor House Hotel – after the Austrian's equally drunken challenger, George Airton, had pulled the other commandeered rickshaw, with a grumpy Catherine inside, to the hotel door and victory. Andreas's friends had thought it a wonderful joke when Catherine had set his leg by the riverside, waiting for the ambulance.

George and his bloody japes, she had thought, as she rang his doorbell on the second floor. It took Andreas an interminable time to answer. He was on crutches, wearing only a dressing-gown, his plastered leg protruding beneath it. What had mortified her was that he had shown no surprise to see her. He had been drunk, of course, and stank of sweat and cologne. He had led her to a sofa. On the table beside it was a bottle of brandy, a third full, a tumbler, a tray of melted ice and an ashtray overflowing with cigarette stubs. He thumped down beside her, the crutches falling to the floor. He poured brandy into the dirty glass, and offered it to her. When she refused, he drained it. 'Well?' he said. It was the first word he had spoken to her.

'Well?' she answered. She was preparing to recite the excuse she had prepared for the visit, something about feeling sorry for you, dear old thing, and how is your poor leg, when he had embraced her. She gasped and felt his lips on hers, his tongue pushing into her mouth. One hand was on her thighs, pushing up her skirt, as the other rubbed her right breast. For a moment she had felt trapped, suffocating. Then she had kicked wildly at his cast. He had slapped her face, swearing in German. Somehow, she had got off the sofa, and swung her handbag at his face, knocking him backwards. The bag opened as it hit him, so her cosmetics, hairbrush and wallet fell on to the floor, but she ignored them and ran to the door. As she lifted the latch and slipped out, she had heard his mocking laughter.

Of course she had had no money to pay for a rickshaw so she walked the two miles back to the Airton home, feeling like a prostitute who had been robbed by a client. Her shame was compounded when she had to invent a story of a fall to account for the bruise on her face. George, and later Robby, had teased her mercilessly about her 'accident', but thankfully she had not seen Andreas since. She knew, though, there would come the day when she would find herself standing next to him, glass in hand, and could envisage the knowing smile he would give her, as he bowed politely in his aristocratic European way.

Well, it served her right for fantasising in the first place. In another month they would set off for Manchuria and then there would be an end of it. She had still not received any reply to the letter she had sent the publishing-house, which was the only address she had for Henry Manners, but the doctor's sources were confident that he was still in Japan, so that was not surprising. She could not imagine what her father's response would be, how she would react when she met him, so in her practical way she had not thought about it, just enjoyed the wild life of Tientsin. Now that had palled, and she had begun to feel the weight of obligation to the Airtons. Also, it occurred to her that her father, this stranger Henry Manners, might have no interest in meeting her. In the week since her rejection, as she saw it, by George, and her subsequent folly, she had become depressed. Edmund's unexpected kiss, the kindness and humour in his face, had reminded her that at least she had one friend who made no demands on her emotions. And in a *volte-face* that surprised her she felt merriment warming her cheeks, and determined to enjoy this Chinese evening, which until that moment she had dreaded.

Edmund and Catherine followed the bobbing lantern held by the servant through the rock garden to the Ancestral Hall. The oilskin-paper windows gave off a burnished glow, which revealed that the hall must be brightly lit within. As she stepped over the spirit board in the doorway, her first impression was of a blaze of gold. Yellow and amber-tasselled lanterns hung from a ceiling decorated in squares of gold and blue. Bronze standing lamps in the shape of dragons, with bulbs hanging from their jaws, shone pools of light on blue and orange carpets. The crude electric lighting highlighted the shining characters on the huge ancestral tablet and glinted on the bronze incense bowls and statues on the shrine, which was covered with yellow cloth. The hanging arches and friezes behind the shrine – even the tall-backed chairs on which the family and guests were seated formally – were painted creamy gold. For a moment she was stunned, blinking in the light, then became aware that Ming, dressed in a Chinese gown, was leading her and Edmund to their hosts.

Edmund knew the etiquette. He bowed briefly to Old Man Lei, and more deeply to his dowager mother, who sat smoking a narrow-stemmed pipe on the seat beside him. What he said clearly delighted the old man, whose wrinkled face was wreathed in smiles. Catherine even saw a twitch on the dowager's severe face. The old man waved his arm in the direction of the chair to his right, on which sat a small, sleek, smiling man whose feet, in laced-up brogues, barely touched the floor. Catherine imagined that this must be the important official from Shishan of whom Ming had told her. Edmund reached into his pocket for a letter, which he ceremoniously passed to the little man. She recognised some of the words he was saying: 'regards from my father and mother to your honourable father', 'intentions to visit Shishan soon', and, following a fruity laugh, the official's reply, 'Old friends. Old friends. Welcome.'

Catherine was still a little disoriented by the formality of the setting. The solemn figures seated on their chairs were like temple idols. She was suddenly conscious of her dark blue, high-collared dress in the cheongsam style, and the caked powder on her cheek with which she had tried to hide the bruise. But Edmund steered her gently by the elbow, and she bowed. Vaguely she was aware of Ming's voice behind her: 'My father and brother you know. And this is my g-grandmother. And M-Minister Yu Fu-cheng.' Then she faced a girlish youth in a pale grey uniform with shining brown boots, twiddling an officer's cap on his knee and grinning shyly at her. 'Let me introduce our other honoured guest, Lieutenant Ti Jen-hsing,' Ming said. She was relieved when he led her to a seat next to Martha, who winked at her as she sat down, 'Thought you weren't coming. We've been sitting here like statues for the last half-hour.'

Catherine accepted a cup of tea from a servant. Edmund had been seated in a place of honour next to the Shishan official. Now he and Ming's father were exchanging polite formalities. Catherine watched him admiringly, envying his ease with the language.

'So where've you been? Where's George?' Martha was whispering.

'He didn't want to come.'

'Surprise, surprise. Hey, what do you think of soldier-boy over there?'

'The lieutenant?' asked Catherine. 'Who is he?'

'Didn't you know?' Martha made a *moue* of conspiratorial astonishment. 'That's Lan-hua's fiancé. Guess she only found out tonight – and she isn't happy about it. Can't you feel the atmosphere?'

Catherine looked at the row of chairs on the other side of the hall. Lan-hua was sitting next to a pregnant woman and three little children, whom she had guessed were Lei Tang's family. Lan-hua was indeed unhappy: she was leaning forward rigidly in her seat, her knuckles white on the armrests, her fringe hanging low over her eyes.

'Ming told me when I came in. There was a real Chinese ding-dong going on before I arrived,' continued Martha, 'but ever since I've been here, we've all been smiling at each other and gazing at our navels. Keeping face in front of the foreigners, I suppose.'

'Surely, nowadays . . .' Catherine was shocked.

'That's what I said, didn't I, Ming?' He had taken a position behind them. As she spoke, Martha reached up and took his hand, which was resting on the back of her chair. 'A girl nowadays doesn't have to submit to an arranged marriage. Ming, you'll stop it happening, won't—' She broke off, aware that the conversation between Edmund and Old Man Lei had ceased, and that all eyes in the room were staring at her and Ming's clasped hands. She let go. 'Oops,' she said, as Ming's own hand snaked to his side. His face blushed red. '*Nan nu shou shou bu qing*,' she muttered. It was a Confucian phrase Ming had taught them. 'There should be no physical contact between youth and maiden in public.'

'Quiet,' said Catherine. If Martha had intended this remark as a joke to lighten the atmosphere, it failed to achieve that effect. Nobody laughed. If anything it had made matters worse. Even Catherine had been startled by the hand-holding in public: it implied a depth of intimacy that even she had not suspected. She was grateful when Edmund dexterously started a conversation with the important official, in which Old Man Lei joined, but she saw that the grandmother and Lei Tang were still staring coldly at Martha.

Martha was not abashed. Eyebrows raised, she looked up at Ming, who indicated she should be silent. Catherine sensed that unspoken messages were passing between them, and with sudden intuition realised that they had as much to do with their own relationship as with Lan-hua's predicament. She had had no idea that things had developed so far.

Old Man Lei stood up. It was time for the banquet. He left Lei Tang to help his lotus-footed grandmother to her feet. The young soldier, Ti Jen-hsing, hurried to support her other arm, and she gave him a gracious gold-toothed smile. Clearly she favoured the match with Lan-hua. Old Man Lei linked his arms with Yu Fu-cheng and Edmund, then led the way to another room, where servants were lifting aside a heavy brocade curtain.

Catherine took the opportunity to catch Martha's arm. 'Martha, tell me, what's going on?'

'I told you, Lan-hua is being married off to a stranger.'

'No,' said Catherine, conscious that Lan-hua herself was behind her. 'Between you and Ming. I know there's something you're not telling me.'

Martha's slim hand touched Catherine's cheek. 'Don't worry, sister. You'll be the first to know.' She turned to face Lan-hua, who seemed near tears. 'You poor darling. Ming told me,' she said, put her arms round the Chinese girl and hugged her, to the consternation of Yu Fu-hong and the wide-eyed children behind. 'I know. I know. *Shou shou bu qing* and all that.' She smiled kindly at Lan-hua. 'But I'm American, and I'm allowed to express what I feel, and I'm telling you, honey, that nobody's gonna make you do anything you don't want to do while Ming and I are around to prevent it.'

Lan-hua pushed her away angrily. Catherine could see that the brown eyes under the fringe had brimmed with tears. 'There is nothing you can do,' she said bitterly. 'Please, leave me alone. You foreigners cannot understand.' She picked up the smallest of Fuhong's sons, pressed his bewildered face to her wet cheek, took her sister-in-law's hand and hurried into the banqueting room, leaving the two foreign women facing the smiling servants, who were urgently beckoning them to enter.

'Martha, she's right. We can't interfere,' said Catherine. 'It's not our country or our culture. They're not our family.'

Martha froze, then turned to her. At first Catherine had the impression of an angry badger ready to attack, but her friend controlled herself and surveyed her with coal-hard eyes. 'Sister, they may not be *your* family.'

Ming came up behind them. He had been delayed by one of the servants. Catherine noticed that his face was unusually grim, and that he did not stammer when he said, 'Quickly, they will be waiting for us.' Martha seemed to lean against him – that intimacy again – although Ming stood stiffly in front of the servants. Martha's eyes searched his face. 'Ming?' she said, in a soft, almost beseeching tone.

'I know,' he answered. 'Don't worry.'

'When?' she asked.

'Leave it to me,' he said. 'Come, let us go in now.'

As she followed them through the curtains, Catherine was confused, and disturbed – shocked, even – by Lan-hua's misery, but also a little amused by the muddle and complexity of relationships in this Chinese puzzle of a family. It was the sort of imbroglio that the doctor and Nellie chuckled over at dinner, and which aroused George's scorn. As she entered the dining room for the Mid-autumn Feast, she suddenly thought of Chang-E in the moon. If this evening was to be a success, it needed her every blessing. Which made Catherine think of the other reason Edmund had given for the festival: the revolution against the Mongols. She wondered what rebellion Ming and Martha were concocting in this household tonight.

Lieutenant Ti Jen-hsing did not feel comfortable. The dining room unnerved him with its grandeur. The enormous round table and the high-backed chairs were made of the finest rosewood; the carpet under his feet was rich and soft; and the side tables were loaded with moon cakes, wine, fruit and flowers. The centrepiece on the dining-table was a gigantic plate of cut meat and vegetables, arranged by the cook in a pattern that consisted of ham and cucumber dragons, chicken and cherry phoenixes and pink prawn clouds surrounding a round carrot moon. He had never seen anything like it in his life.

It was not only the luxury that disconcerted him but also the barbarians: the authoritative man who spoke formal Chinese with the skill of a scholar official, and the two women, one exotic and red-headed, the other striking, brazen, loud. This was uncharted ground for a simple soldier from the provinces.

But what perturbed him most was his own predicament. It was a simple enough problem, but it seemed impossible to resolve. A marriage arrangement had been formally agreed, but now he had discovered that the prospective bride was set against it.

She was certainly as pretty as his father had described. Her hair was bobbed and fringed in the modern Shanghai style. She had soft sloe eyes, and phoenix eyebrows, a pert, well-shaped nose and pearly teeth. The figure under the pink cheongsam was delicate and rounded, and the proximity of her slim, bare arm excited him.

Yet her expression was cold. At first he had not been unduly surprised: a little reserve was only to be expected – she must be as nervous of him as he was of her – but the glare in her eye, the sullenness of her responses, the frigidity of her expression went beyond any appropriate degree of maidenly modesty. When their eyes met, it was he who turned away. In that moment he had seen hatred and, more alarming still, intelligence. There was none of the passive resignation that he saw in the face of the wife of the elder son, seated opposite him with her children, familiar to him because it was the habitual expression of the women in his own family. This was a young woman who knew her own mind. It confused him – and made him resentful.

He knew the value of this match to his family, who were textile manufacturers from Kaifeng. His father had ambitious plans for which he needed the Lei Bank's financial support. An educated bride would also be of immeasurable use to him in his own chosen career. Several of his fellow officers from the military academy owed their promotion to the influence that clever wives had brought to bear over a game of mah-jongg with the wife of the general. This was important to him: up to now, promotion had eluded him.

He had had high expectations of the Fengtian-Chihli war earlier this year, but he had been sent to command a supply depot in Anhwei, nowhere near the fighting. His faction's victory had brought no benefits his way. He had been a little worried that the Lei family's connections were with the Fengtian faction in Manchuria, his theoretical enemies, and the finance minister of the famous General Lin Fu-po was here this evening. In the event Minister Yu Fu-cheng had laughed good-naturedly at his embarrassed admission that he served the Chihli clique, and had as good as told him that he would speak in his favour with General Lin, should he decide to change sides. The minister's visiting card was in the upper pocket of his tunic. This was undreamed-of luck. He had not even married the Lei daughter and fortune was already favouring him. It had already made the proposed match worthwhile. If it took place.

Well, it would, he told himself. Should her father insist, she had no choice. He had heard that after the 1911 revolution new laws had been promulgated, protecting women's rights, but nobody he knew had ever considered that they applied to arranged marriages. But how would he control such a woman when he did marry her? He felt daunted.

Her disdain made him feel like a country bumpkin, which galled him. He considered himself a modern young man. He had read the current anti-Confucian literature. The collection of stories by the writer Lu Hsun, *Call to Arms*, was in his pocket. He had brought it with the idea of discussing it with her, intellectual to intellectual, but now he did not dare, knowing she would snub him.

Finally he gave up all attempts at polite conversation: Lan-hua had turned her back on him and entered into an intense conversation with the red-haired foreign girl on her right; they were murmuring in English, which he did not understand.

The servants had taken away the half-devoured painting. The moon was in quarter eclipse, the dragon had lost its tail and claws, and the phoenix resembled a plucked quail. The dishes that followed were delicious. They were also expensive: abalone, shark's fin, sea cucumber, crab, mud-baked chicken, camel hump, bear's paw. Ti was grateful to the old dowager, who made sure that his plate was piled high with each delicacy, and he ate heartily. There seemed nothing else he could do.

He amused himself by making faces at one of the little children opposite him, who shyly nuzzled into his mother's side. At least the children were enjoying themselves, he thought, and so they should. This festival was designed for them. They must be looking forward to the fireworks in the garden.

When the last dish had been cleared, and the servants were preparing plates of fruit, sweets and slices of moon cake, Old Man Lei stood up and made a short speech, honouring Minister Yu, and raised a glass of *gaoliang* wine to his health. They all drained their glasses. Then he toasted his honoured Western guest, Ai Er-mun Daifu, and his parents, the famous Ai Er-tun Daifu and his wife, who could not be there tonight. They drained their glasses all over again – but Old Man Lei had not finished.

He smiled as he waited for the servant to refill his glass. 'Today we are gathered for the Mid-autumn Festival,' he said. 'It is a traditional time in China for families to be close together. It is also a time to celebrate old friendships.' He nodded at the grinning Yu Fu-cheng. 'It is also an auspicious time for marriages and engagements, which are blessed by the harvest moon. Today I am delighted to welcome a new addition to our family, Lieutenant Ti Jen-hsing, the son of one of my oldest friends. He has graciously agreed to be bound in marriage with my daughter, my dearest Lan-hua. Lieutenant Ti is a young man with a bright career ahead of him in the army. The Lei family is honoured by such an alliance, and I ask you all to stand and to drink with me to the health and future good fortune of this lucky couple.'

Ti felt his cheeks burn as he pushed back his chair to stand with his glass. He was conscious of the smiles on the faces of Old Man Lei, the minister and the foreign doctor, but was startled to see that Lei Ming and his black-haired foreign friend were glowering with anger. Then he noticed that Lan-hua had remained in her seat, her hair hanging over her face like a shroud.

There was a long pause, as everybody stood uncomfortably with their glasses raised.

'Lan-hua,' said her father gently, 'you must stand too. We are drinking to your engagement.'

She did not move.

'Lan-hua!' snapped the old man. 'Stand up!'

Slowly she raised her head. Ti could see that her face was streaked with tears, and that there was a frightening vacancy in her eyes.

There was a horrified silence.

'Stand up,' said Old Man Lei. It was almost a squeak.

'I will die,' she said slowly, 'before I marry this man or any other man you order me to.'

Ti felt a shiver down his spine. It was not the insult to him and his family, but that such a breach of decorum was out of his experience. He was shocked, and at the same time fascinated, transfixed. He saw the old grandmother pulling feebly at Lan-hua's sleeve in a pathetic effort to force her to stand. He saw the old man place his brimming glass on the table. He saw his own stupefaction reflected on all the other faces in the room.

Suddenly the old banker roared, 'You have shamed us!' He propelled himself clumsily round the table to his daughter's chair and pulled violently at her rigid shoulders. The chair crashed to the floor and the two stumbled against each other. Panting, the old man slapped Lan-hua hard across the face.

She staggered back, then shoved her father so that he fell against her grandmother. 'I will die!' she screamed, and ran out of the room, pushing aside the bewildered servants holding their plates of fruit.

In a tangle with his mother on the floor, the old man shouted at his elder son, 'Tang! Follow her, and lock her in her room. Get the servants to help you. We are disgraced. I'll kill her!' Lei Tang, his napkin still hanging from his neck, ran out to do his father's bidding.

It was then that the younger son, Lei Ming, spoke up: 'Father, I w-warn you, if you harm my sister, I'll leave this family. And I won't come back. N-never. You'll lose a son, as well as a daughter – and a daughter-in-law.' He put an arm round Martha's shoulders.

Old Man Lei, who had been struggling to his feet, helped by Yu Fu-cheng – the foreign doctor was supporting the grandmother – froze. 'Daughter-in-law?' muttered the old man, a trickle of saliva running down his chin. 'That?'

'Yes, Father, "th-that", as you call her, is my wife. We married secretly because I knew you would never agree. We love each other.'

Ti heard a long-drawn-out sigh, and turned to see the foreign doctor fanning the face of the old lady, who had fainted. Old Man Lei staggered to his seat and slowly sat down. 'Get out,' he whispered. 'I never want to see you again. We are shamed. The Lei family is shamed.'

'Come, Martha, l-let's go,' said Lei Ming. He turned his back on his family and left the room. His wife, the foreign woman, paused only to put her napkin on the table and pick up her bag. The old man's head fell forward on his folded arms.

Ti left shortly after that. The Mid-autumn Festival was clearly over. He paid his respects to Old Man Lei, but the broken old man had nothing to say, beyond 'Apologies. Apologies to your father.'

The minister walked him to the door. For once, a frown replaced his habitual smile. 'Remember to write to me when you have considered my offer,' he said. 'I do not take it back.'

Ti did not know how he would explain all this to his father. For the moment he did not care: he remembered Minister Yu's words and felt elated. His figure cast a tall shadow along the moon-lit street. His spurred boots clicked on the stones as his steps moved unconsciously into the rhythm of a march, and he began to whistle.

For the first few minutes of their drive home, Edmund and Catherine were silent. Edmund spoke first. 'Well, a scene like that's not something you'll come across every day in a Confucian household. I suppose we're privileged to have witnessed it. Talk about the new China!'

'Don't Chinese families have arguments and rows?'

'All the time,' said Edmund, 'but usually behind closed doors, not in front of foreigners, and certainly not in front of a government minister. Poor old Lei. It'll be difficult for him to recover from such loss of face.'

'I'm rather more concerned about his daughter – not to mention Ming and Martha,' said Catherine. 'Didn't I hear the old man threaten to kill her?'

'He won't do that,' said Edmund, 'but he'll keep her under lock and key. Clip her wings, poor thing. And there's not much we or anybody else can do about it. Feudal practices didn't go away with the revolution, I'm afraid.'

'You seem remarkably cool about it, all the same.'

'Didn't you know, Nurse? We doctors are cold-blooded brutes. Sorry, I don't mean to sound facetious. I'm probably inured to the injustice of it all. Born here, you see.' He pressed the horn viciously, and a startled rickshaw-puller scuttled out of the way. 'Did you know that Martha had married Lei Ming?' he asked.

'No!' said Catherine. 'No, I didn't. Sorry. Martha and I aren't as close as we once were.'

'Poor you,' murmured Edmund. He squeezed her hand. 'What do you think they'll do?' he asked.

'I don't know. He'll find a teaching post somewhere, I suppose.'

'They've taken a brave step. The Chinese are less sympathetic to interracial marriage than we are.'

'Beyond the pale,' murmured Catherine.

'Something like that,' said Edmund. 'We'd better make sure we keep in touch with them. They'll need all the help they can get.'

This time Catherine squeezed Edmund's hand.

'What a world, eh, Nurse?'

After a moment's silence, Catherine said, 'I had a long talk with Lan-hua over dinner. She told me she would never accept an arranged marriage. She plans to leave Tientsin, go to Canton, and work for the Nationalist Government under Sun Yat-sen. She believes that his party, the Kuomintang, is the hope for a regenerated China and wants to play her part.'

'Doing what exactly?' Edmund kept his eyes on the road ahead.

'She thought that there might be a job for her in their propaganda department, perhaps. With her education . . .'

'We've certainly heard enough propaganda to last us a lifetime,' muttered Edmund. 'I suppose she's influenced by her brother's socialist ideas.'

'I – I don't think so.' Catherine frowned. 'She's more intelligent than Ming. She was at university in Peking in the tail end of the May 4th Movement. She told me about a friend of hers, an older girl, whom she admired, one of the student leaders. A Marxist. Lan-hua used to go to rallies where this woman would speak. She came from a similar background to Lan-hua, but she married a trade-union agitator – and was cut off by her family.'

Edmund turned his head. 'This is ringing a far-off bell.'

'She was the sister of that official we met tonight. That's how Lan-hua knew her. She originally came from Shishan.'

'Of course.' Edmund whistled. 'My parents told me about that scandal. Old Man Yu disinherited her but I never heard what eventually happened to her.'

'Lan-hua told me she died in prison,' said Catherine. 'She and her peasant husband had fled Peking and ended up in Shanghai, where they organised strikes in the foreign factories. The secret police caught them. The man was publicly beheaded, and the woman was tortured. She was never heard of again. Anyway, she's now the inspiration for Lan-hua, a revolutionary martyr. She feels she owes it to her memory to carry on the struggle.'

'So Lan-hua's a secret Marxist? Well, well. What did you say to her? I know your views.'

'I told her I could never agree with her politics, but I didn't press the point. It didn't seem to be the occasion.'

'Probably not,' agreed Edmund, 'but somebody needs to give her a talking-to. Rejecting an arranged marriage is one thing but skipping off to Canton to wave the red flag . . . That's madness. Besides anything else, she appears thoroughly confused. Sun Yat-sen may want to be all things to all men – but I doubt that he would accept Communists in his ranks.'

'Edmund,' said Catherine, in a tiny voice.

'Yes?'

'I knew that other woman, the revolutionary student, the minister's sister. I was at Oxford with her, and travelled with her to China on the same boat. She's called Yu Fu-kuei. She's a . . . She's my friend.'

'I thought you said she was dead.'

'No, Lan-hua said that – but she's very much alive, and she's nothing like a revolutionary. She studied English poetry at St Hugh's, and she came back to China – Shanghai – to marry an army officer in the warlord government there. It was he who paid for her university education.'

'Well, I'll be blowed,' said Edmund. 'Did you tell Lan-hua?'

'In her state?'

'Your friend Fu-kuei must have had a change of heart,' said Edmund. 'Met somebody in prison who reformed her and secured her release. Perhaps the officer she's marrying. It's possible. Many of us reject the ideas we held in our youth. If she's marrying a warlord soldier she can't still be a Communist.'

'Edmund,' said Catherine, 'I think she is.'

'That's too contradictory,' said Edmund. 'Did she ever tell you about her beliefs?'

'She never discussed politics. She never appeared interested – but there was always a mystery about her.'

'With her background it's not surprising. She'd hardly confess her past, would she?'

'She nearly did once, on the ship, just before we reached Hong

Kong. She had got me to talk about my experiences in Russia. We were drinking. I told her things I haven't even told you, and she asked me something that puzzled me at the time – whether I had had overtures from the Third International, the Comintern.'

'Had you?'

'No, but I might have had. I'd been in Russia during the revolution, and I left the country at the height of one of the purges. The point is, why did she think I might be a member of the Comintern?'

'She'd been a Communist agitator,' offered Edmund, 'knew how the system worked . . .'

'Yes, but she was small fry, and in China, and from what Lan-hua told me, she and her husband weren't part of any Communist organisation. There wasn't one in China to speak of then. I think she asked me specifically about the Third International because she herself was approached by the Comintern. After her release from prison. Because of her relationship with this officer perhaps. Edmund,' her voice cracked, 'I think they recruited Fu-kuei and that she's come back to China to be a spy. And I'm – I'm the only person who knows about it.'

'Nonsense,' said Edmund. 'Rubbish. It's supposition.'

'But what if I'm right?' she said. 'What am I to do?'

'Nothing. It's none of your business. The affairs of the Yu and Lei families have nothing to do with us. This is just China. Bloody China. My advice is don't get involved. Keep what you know to yourself. Forget about it.'

She let out a deep breath, and smiled. 'You're probably right,' she said. 'Sorry, Edmund, you must imagine I'm a fool. I don't know what I've been thinking lately. There's this. And George. And worry about what'll happen when I meet my father. I don't know where I am.'

'You're tired, that's all,' said Edmund. 'Tired and strained. Anybody would be upset by what went on this evening.'

'Hold me,' she said. She moved across the seat to lean against him. After a moment his left arm came round to support her. 'Now, now, Nurse,' said Edmund, but he allowed her head to rest on his shoulder for the rest of the drive home.

* * *

Old Man Lei and the minister from Shishan were alone, seated on either side of the shrine in the deserted Ancestral Hall. The lanterns still blazed. Occasionally the open door would flash with the light of fireworks. Although the guests had gone, it seemed pointless to deny the children their treat, so Lei Tang and his family were in the garden with some of the servants, who had also been looking forward to this climax of the Mid-autumn Festival. If Old Man Lei heard the explosions and the children's cries of delight, he showed no sign of it.

'Uncle, drink some tea,' said Yu Fu-cheng, softly. 'It will revive your spirits.' He thought that the old man had aged during the course of the evening.

'Why?' his mentor asked. 'In what way did I fail? Why should my children disgrace me so utterly?'

'The times, Uncle,' said Yu Fu-cheng. 'They affect us all in different ways. Your children are no better and no worse than other young people facing the complexities of a new age.'

'If only you were my son, Fu-cheng. Tang has no imagination beyond the daily receipts. And Ming? My pretty Lan-hua? How could she? No, I am proud only of you, Fu-cheng. Only you have not betrayed me.'

Yu Fu-cheng looked dispassionately at the tear-streaked face, the pleading eyes. 'Of course, Uncle, I have always thought of you as my foster-father, and honour you as I do my own – but you are wrong to think unkindly of Lei Tang, who will surely be your support in your old age. You must find it in your heart also to forgive your other children, who have behaved stupidly, in an unfilial fashion – and they will surely regret it when they have come to their senses. Ming and Lan-hua are your flesh and blood, Uncle.'

Old Man Lei banged the arm of his chair with a bony hand. 'I will never forgive them,' he hissed. 'They no longer belong to this family.'

'Uncle, drink some tea,' said Yu Fu-cheng, suppressing a yawn. He was tired, and he had a long journey in the morning.

'Now I will have to loan old Ti the money for his new factory at minimum interest,' whispered the old man, 'even though I will no longer receive what he promised as a marriage portion. It would be shameful if I did not, after we have dishonoured his son.'

'You will find another match for your daughter,' said Yu Fu-cheng. 'I liked that young soldier, but his family is insignificant and provincial.'

'Never!' hissed Old Man Lei. 'She is no longer my daughter.'

'Uncle,' said Yu Fu-cheng, 'you must not disown your daughter. It is not a solution. You would be throwing away a precious pearl. This I know, Uncle.'

'You have never had children.'

Yu Fu-cheng ignored the venom in the old man's voice. 'But I had a sister, Uncle, who also disgraced our family, and my father, no doubt very properly according to the old customs, disinherited her. And what was the result? Pain and grief to her relatives, and a tragedy for her. If only we had helped and supported her when she needed us. But let me tell you, Uncle, the wheel of fortune always turns. None of us can foresee the future. We thought that we had lost her, but what did I discover last week, in an item of official correspondence? She is alive and in Shanghai, and engaged to a rising soldier. I am encouraging my father to reconsider his impetuous decision and, if he allows it, I will seek her out. Then we will ask her forgiveness. Think of that, Uncle. Do you really wish to blight a life, because of a moment's youthful folly, when who knows what is intended by Fate in the future?'

He was pleased to see that the old man had been listening. 'I have not thrown her out of my house,' muttered Lei, 'but I will punish her,' he added.

Yu Fu-cheng waved a hand. 'Oh, by all means. She deserves to be punished. Severely,' he added, for good measure.

'But I will not forgive Lei Ming,' said the banker. 'That he could marry, behind my back, that barbarian, that foreign devil, that fat, ugly whore. With no money to her name, of that you can be sure. That he could stand up in public and announce to people I respect that the Lei family name has been linked to such a monstrous . . .' Words failed him. 'He is no longer any son of mine.'

'Well, it was foolish of him,' said Yu Fu-cheng, 'and he deserves your anger for his disrespect to you, and his singular lack of taste. But again, think of the future. Young men are all too often seduced. Is it so surprising that a boy whom we have sent to study in Hawaii should come back infatuated with American ways and women? But the wheel turns, Uncle. Young men mature. They forget their puppy love and honour the old ways. It has ever been thus. So he has been stupid enough to marry her. He will divorce her when he tires of her, as he surely will, or she will divorce him. In America, from what I read, they make almost a sacrament of divorce. Think of the future, Uncle, and do not make a precipitate decision.'

'No, Fu-cheng, on the matter of Lei Ming, I will not be influenced, even by you. Tonight he disgraced our name, our family, our ancestors. He is no longer a son of mine. And if I continued to support him as he lives with a – with a sea witch, I would be a laughing stock.'

Yu Fu-cheng sighed. 'Drink some tea, Uncle.' He reached inside his pocket, and surreptitiously looked at his watch. It was nearly midnight. 'I respect your decision concerning Lei Ming. I will no longer treat him as if he were your son.'

Old Man Lei leaned back in his chair. Tears ran down his cheeks, as he looked rigidly ahead.

'But, Uncle,' Yu Fu-cheng continued, 'I cannot forget that he was once your son, or the debt of honour I owe you. I will take responsibility for his welfare just a little longer. I have confirmed him as principal of my school in Shishan. I will not go back on my word. I am hiring him not as the son of my old friend and benefactor, but as a teacher in whom I think there is talent. If he satisfies me, he will be guaranteed an income. If not . . .' He left the question hanging. 'Should you reconsider your decision, you will know where to find him.'

The old man sat stiffly in his chair, although Yu Fu-cheng thought he heard a choke. He wondered if he had interpreted the old banker's wishes correctly. At least he was getting two teachers now for the price of one. Lei Ming's wife – the fat woman – could run the English department.

After a while he made his excuses. He had to get up early to catch the train back to Chinchou, and thence to Shishan. On his way to his quarters, he passed a servant and instructed him to carry a blanket to the hall and cover the old man, sitting alone with his ancestors.

4

A Mukden Incident

From the Journal of William Lampsett, Reuters Correspondent, Tientsin, 12 November 1922

Catherine and the Airton family are to go to Mukden, where she expects to find her father. George's mother is insisting he accompanies them. He was complaining about it in the club: he expects to be bored. 'Wish you lot could come along too,' he said. I couldn't resist it and told him that I had been thinking of going to Manchuria. It's true too. God knows, there's story enough there. Chang Tso-lin is rearming after his defeat in the summer. There are border conflicts with the Soviets on the Ussuri river. The Japanese are making menacing new inroads out of their Kwantung colony on the Liaotung Peninsula. The Southern Manchurian Railway, with its attached towns, has effectively became an alternative government, controlling the region's economy. The uneasy cohabitation between Chang and the firebrands within the SMR and the Kwantung Army, who would like to annex the whole of Manchuria to Japan, is under strain. I thought of hundreds of reasons why I should take up George's invitation.

Robby brought me back to reality. He handed me a cocktail when I got home and told me what an ass I'm being. He mocked me, said I'm behaving like a lovelorn schoolboy. He told me Catherine would laugh at me if she knew I was jealous of George. I became angry and said things to him that now I regret. He gave me a strange smile. 'Love's about timing, Willie,' he said. 'Don't worry about George. Trust your Robby. You'll have your chance, but not now. She's got this father thing to work through and isn't interested in anybody at the moment. You be on hand when this quest of hers falls through and she needs somebody to pick up the pieces. Someone boring and avuncular like you, my dear.'

I told him to go to hell, but next morning I phoned up George and told him that pressure of work would keep me in Tientsin.

Far away to the south, a young girl with a red scarf wrapped round her bobbed hair was standing in the crowded Canton railway terminus, wondering what to do. She had no money or clothes. The nice young peasant boy, whom she had come to trust during the arduous journey by bus and sometimes bullock cart from Changsha, where the Tientsin line ended, through Hunan Province to the northern regions of Kwangtung, where at last they reached the newly-built railway line leading to Canton, had last night promised to watch over her things while she slept on her hard-class bunk; this morning he was nowhere to be found and neither was her knapsack. The foul-smelling farmer on the opposite bunk had watched her with amusement, and spat out a gob of tobacco. 'He got off when we stopped at Shao-kuan,' he grunted. Lan-hua had asked shrilly why he hadn't woken her when he saw the boy was stealing her bag. 'None of my business,' he said, and laughed.

She looked over the heads of the crowd at the buildings surrounding the concourse. They were a different shape and architectural style from those of Tientsin. She could not understand the dialect of the people chattering around her. The smells were different. It was as if she had come to another country. She was terrified, and she was hungry. She wanted to go home. She had a sudden vision of her snug room off the courtyard, her *amah* bringing her a hot broth when she was sick. She thought of Ming leaning against the ginkgo tree teasing his little sister affectionately. She wanted to cry.

She felt her breath knocked out of her body. She had been sideswiped by a coolie carrying cloth-wrapped bundles on a bamboo pole. He screamed a torrent of abuse, and something snapped. She shouted back, 'Peasant! Watch where you're going.'

Her anger restored her determination. No, she would never go back. Not after the beating her father had given her. She thought of her pathetic elder brother holding her arms over the bolster as the old man whipped her bare shoulders and back, and the fear on Tang's face before she lost consciousness. She had pleaded to him through the pain to make it stop. Her brother in his cowardice had only pulled her arms tighter.

It had been days before she could move. She had lapsed into a fever, and her *amah* had been worried for her life. 'That your own family could do this to you,' she heard the old woman mutter. Then: 'Why, oh, why didn't you marry that nice boy?'

Lan-hua had raised herself on her elbows, and hissed, 'Never! I no longer have a family! I hate them! I hate them!'

'How dare you say such a thing?' In her agitation the *amah* had slapped her cheek. Lan-hua had made her decision. From that moment on, she began to mend.

She had been a prisoner. Her *amah*, the only person who came to see her, locked the door carefully after she had brought her meals. Lan-hua pretended to have a relapse of her fever, feigning her earlier unconsciousness. One night the old woman had left the door unlocked when she went to her own supper. Lan-hua had leaped out of bed, and stuffed her clothes, with the money she had saved, into her old university knapsack. Creeping along the corridors, avoiding the servants, she had escaped the mansion unnoticed. She had taken a rickshaw to the station and bought a hard-class ticket South.

A hawker loped by. She smelt a delicious fragrance from the wicker containers on his tray. He noticed her eyeing him, and lifted the lid. She saw steaming dumplings and buns. Sadly, she shook her head and mimed that she had no money. He grinned and handed her a *mantou*, then winked and went off, shouting his wares.

This unlooked-for kindness from a stranger was a sign, she told herself, as she bit into the warm bread. She had no idea how she would find the offices of the Kuomintang, or what she would say when she got there – but she would find a way.

The train that carried the Airton family and Catherine into Mukden steamed into a yellow, sulphurous smog, which Dr Airton said was caused by the mines and heavy industry the Japanese had developed on the outskirts of the town. Catherine looked out doubtfully at the dim lamps flickering on the side of the railway track while the carriage clanked over a metal bridge into the modern Japanese cantonment around the station. The Chinese walled city, she was told, was still a mile to the east.

It was a relief to arrive at the luxurious Yamato Inn, a show-piece of the Southern Manchurian Railways Company, the SMR, which, as everybody knew, was the alternative government in the north-east, administering the Japanese railway towns, and control-ling much of Fengtian's and Kirin's industry. The hotel was located in the western wing of the station complex, and the lobby was still ablaze with lights despite the lateness of the hour. Catherine did her best to ignore the bowing manager, in his striped trousers and frock coat, who extended his welcome speech all the way up the oak staircase to their sumptuous rooms on the third floor. He was fulsome about the historical sites in Mukden – the temple in the walled city, the Manchu palace, Nuurhachi's tomb – and how pleased he would be to organise a car and guide . . . He was still talking when Catherine quietly closed the door in his face. She dropped her portmanteau on the thick carpet beside the turned-down bed. It had been a long journey.

She woke late, with a headache she attributed to the sulphur she had breathed on alighting from the train, but when she opened the heavy curtains and looked out over the station concourse, there was no sign of the heavy fog that had greeted them the night before. Above the French mansard-style roofs of the banks and offices, there floated what she imagined at first to be flakes of soot. On closer inspection, she realised they were crows, which had made their nests in the ornamental towers. There were hundreds of them, whirling and spiralling in sinister squadrons in the cold, grey air.

She discovered Edmund and George finishing their breakfast in a cheerful morning room. On her way there she had passed through an important-looking crowd in the lobby, few Europeans, but many Japanese. Bespectacled businessmen in top hats and tails bowed to imposing officers in striped jodhpurs under smart olive tunics bedecked with medals. Most had spurs on their shiny black boots, and some sported gold-tasselled samurai swords that dragged along the carpet behind them. A cluster of Japanese women, dressed in traditional *yukatas* and ornate *obes*, giggled over brochures picked up from the reception desk. In the whole throng, she saw only one Chinese, a distinguished fellow in mandarin robes. Two Japanese businessmen scraped at his heels as he made his stately progress up the staircase.

'This doesn't seem like China,' she murmured, as she slipped into a seat beside George.

'This is Nip Land,' he said, 'ain't it, Edmund, my old Mikado?'

'They'd probably like it to be,' muttered Edmund, lowering his Chinese newspaper. 'Particularly the officers of the Kwantung army, who believe they spilt their blood for Manchuria in the war against Russia.'

'Edmund's going to give us a history lesson now,' whispered George confidentially. 'You'd better order before he gets into his stride. He's trying to shut me up because I started to tell him about my Mukden experience.'

'Oh? What was that?' Catherine poured coffee from the silver pot.

'You'll excuse me if I go back to my newspaper,' said Edmund.

'Go on,' pressed Catherine.

'Well,' began George, 'after you lot had gone to bed, I thought I'd go for a stroll to smoke my cigar. Walked a block, and the fog started licking round me like that yellow dog in the poem. Edmund, what was it you were reading to Catherine on the train? *Arnold Puttock's Love Life* or something?'

'Lord, were you listening? *The Love Song of J. Alfred Prufrock*, by T. S. Eliot,' sighed Edmund, from behind his paper.

'That's the one. I'm not the Philistine I look, you know. Women coming and going with coffee spoons. Jolly good stuff. Anyway, at one point he described smog, didn't he? Compared it to a yellow dog, loitering round the street corner. It was just like that. Yellow murk. Could hardly see your hand in front of your face. Pea-souper.'

'I think Catherine's got the picture,' said Edmund.

'Don't interrupt. I'm describing a profoundly affecting experience. Imagine me, blundering about in the smoke, couldn't find anything open. Well, there was a poky hole-in-the-wall joint run by two bar-girls wearing fur coats because of the cold. Didn't stay there long. Had a beer. Maybe two. Then I became a bit lost. You know how it is.'

'Get on,' said Edmund, who had put down his newspaper, defeated.

'There wasn't anybody on the streets. No traffic. Just big buildings looming on either side. Eerie. And then I heard a noise, a muffled thump-thump-thump, but tinny too, if you can imagine it. I pressed on, cautiously, not exactly rattled – I was too curious. And before I knew it, there he was, under a streetlamp.'

Catherine, who was dabbing marmalade on her toast, nudged him. 'Who?' she asked.

'It was a workman,' said George, 'wearing pyjamas and a cloth cap. He was kneeling all by himself in the middle of the empty street, hammering a long metal rod. God knows why, but he was pretty serious about it. He ignored me. Thump, thump, thump. Or, rather, clang, clang, clang since I was so close to him. On and on like a metronome. Or like Mime in the *Ring Cycle*, forging Siegfried's sword. Wagner, you know.'

'We get the allusion,' said Edmund.

'Well, you must agree it was weird. There we were in our island of dim light in the fog. Him hammering away, me half hypnotised. Not what you see on Pall Mall, is it? Then this other fellow comes out of nowhere on a bicycle, crashes into the metal rod, and goes head over heels, the bicycle wheel crumpling. Uh-oh, I think, now we're for it. But the first chap just keeps banging away as if nothing's happened. The other picks himself up, and gazes at the man with the hammer. Then he picks up the bicycle, the bent wheel over his shoulder, walks off and disappears. Not a word's been said. Clang, clang, clang. The fellow with the hammer hasn't missed a beat.'

'And?' said Catherine.

'Well, he just kept banging away and I came home.'

'Is that it? What's the point?'

'There wasn't any point. Or not one that I could make out. That was what was so rum,' said George. 'I thought I'd better pass it on to you two souls, however, in case I'd missed something of deep significance. Meaningless to the uninitiated, but full of subterranean symbolism for all the blue-stockings and tweedy intellectuals bleary-eyed with the mystical experience. What do you think, Catherine? Have I demonstrated the sensibility of a modern poet?'

'I think you're a blithering idiot,' said Catherine.

'Hear hear,' muttered Edmund.

'How bitter it is to be unappreciated,' said George. 'Hello, is that Cooper's Oxford marmalade? Life's looking up.'

Edmund told her that his parents had already left, to call on their missionary friends, the Gillespies. They would return at lunchtime with whatever news they had gathered about Henry Manners.

'Don't worry, old girl.' George laughed when he saw her expression. 'They'll find him. You know my mother – a female Nimrod. If he's here, she'll track him, if anyone can.'

Catherine felt an odd numbness. Now that the goal of her long journey was nearly in sight, she could not identify the remotest excitement, rather the opposite. If the Airtons returned with no news at all she might be relieved.

It was not that Catherine thought they were on a wild-goose chase. They were reasonably certain, from what the Gillespies had wired, that Henry Manners had returned from Japan, and the doctor had received a clipping of a venomous article Manners must recently have written, since it referred to incidents that had just taken place on the Russian border. The poison of Communism, disguised as nationalism, was spreading through China. The yellow races had their champion . . . The article had ranted on.

It reminded Catherine of speeches the Bolsheviks had made to the soldiers on the eastern front. She was embarrassed that the name at the bottom of such tripe was that of the man she believed was her father.

'"Oh, what a noble mind is here o'erthrown!"' Edward Airton had muttered.

'I don't care,' Catherine had said firmly. 'I want to meet him anyway.'

Nothing much had changed in the month since that awful evening with the Leis. She had still gone occasionally on wild outings with George but recently she had made excuses to stay at home to concentrate on her Chinese lessons. She was also spending more time with Edmund. One day she had taken up his long-standing invitation to visit his hospital, which had impressed her.

She had watched him as he made his rounds. She had become used to his reserved, self-effacing manner, but here she saw another side of him. Clearly the staff worshipped him, and he visibly relaxed in their company, joking familiarly with everyone from gruff Dr Chen down to the young porters. One of the nurses had recently had a baby and out of his pocket he produced a present for her child, a tinkling silver bell. The faces of several patients lit up when he came into the ward. He had time for every one of them, keeping up a bantering conversation as he methodically examined each in turn. One old miner had a suspected hernia and, from the expression on his face as he bit back his pain, she could see that he was terrified. Edmund had charmed him, complimenting him on his length of service in the company, asking his opinion about the new machinery that had recently been installed in the shafts, murmuring appreciatively as the man showed him a photo of his grandchildren; meanwhile, his hands moved over the man's rough skin, as gently as a lover's, probing, feeling, healing.

Later, masked and gloved in the operating room, she had watched those same hands as they made their efficient, economical incisions. Here, Edmund was in his element: decisive, confident, certain, bold, with charismatic authority. She recalled Pavel Alexandrovich as he operated in the broken convent cell, his concentration and command silencing for the anxious nurses the sound of gunfire outside. Edmund had the same self-assurance and calm, and something else: a stillness about him but suffused with hidden energy. Suddenly, she was reminded of the day she had seen him on the beach in Peitaiho. She had been glad of the surgical mask, for she could feel her cheeks flushing.

He had also taken her to Chinese temples and gardens, and once she had accompanied him to the orphanage, which he and his father had privately endowed. Neither had spoken about it, and Edmund had been dismissive of it, but she had been amazed by the devotion of the little children to him, and that he knew all of them by name.

Often they would spend afternoons together, walking by the riverside or in Victoria Park. He would talk of history and literature,

Chinese and Western philosophy. Sometimes he teased her for her extreme anti-Communism, mischievously praising Trotsky and Lenin, then chuckling at her reaction. She could never pin down what he believed. He gave a qualified approval to Sun Yat-sen and the Nationalists, but feared they might be too idealistic ever to become an effective force in Chinese politics. He did not condemn the warlords entirely. 'Some are doing a great deal of good,' he said. 'You were impressed by that minister, Yu Fu-cheng, weren't you, with his social schemes? And then there's Feng Yu-hsiang, the Christian general, who baptised his army with a hose. Can't be anything wrong with him, can there?' She was never sure if he was being serious. An Airton trait, she smiled, but George did not care about anything. She sensed that Edmund's irony covered a smouldering anger at the hopelessness of the common people, but he would say only, 'China? It's always been like that.'

She had always felt comfortable with him, though, and even more so since that night in the car. She found it difficult to put into words. It was not love, she told herself, not anything sensual or physical. Since her stupidity over George – and Andreas! – she had put out of her mind any desire for an affair. It was a special friendship, a steamship interlude, in which she felt no particular anxiety to reach her destination. When she was with him she never thought of her father. Over the passing weeks, she had become uncertain why she was seeking Henry Manners. She could not think what she would say to him, or what she expected of him.

'We have three hours to kill,' said Edmund, when they had finished breakfast. 'Why don't we take up that manager's kind offer and see the sights?'

'I've seen them,' yawned George. 'Fellow said there was a billiard room. Think I'll retire there. Might compose a poem about my mystical experience. How's this for a starter?

> *'In Mukden a man in the fog*
> *Found a girder as big as a log*
> *He banged on the steel*
> *A bike broke its wheel*
> *And the mist curled about like a dog.'*

'I think you're very talented,' said Catherine, pecking him on the cheek, 'but your last line is derivative. Better work on it.'

'That's what makes it literary,' said George, offended. 'It's my homage to Puttock.'

'Goodbye, George,' said Catherine, and linked Edmund's arm. They went into the lobby to look for the manager.

For the elder Airtons it was a morning of bitter-sweet nostalgia. They had taken a rickshaw to their old house in the former International Concession, where their friends had lived since James Gillespie had taken over from Edward as senior surgeon at the Mukden Medical College. The half-gabled porch was as neat as they remembered it. Nellie had been pleased to see that Elspeth had kept up the garden, and although the leaves were browned and floating away in the bitter wind, she could see that her orchard had grown to ripe maturity.

They talked of old times, and friends who had retired or passed away. Edward was full of questions about the college, and Dr Gillespie spoke proudly of their new diagnostic equipment, and the proposal they had just received for the college to be fully incorporated as a faculty of the new university. They chuckled as they remembered their irascible old colleague and co-founder of the college Dr Dugald Christie. 'Do you remember the talking-to he gave Chang Tso-lin during the Great Plague in eleven? What we've seen together, you and I! Boxers, revolutions, wars. When will China ever change, eh? You really should have got a medal in five. Your service on the Port Arthur front went well beyond heroism. You're a living legend, old chap.'

Nellie saw that her husband's face had gone a deep crimson.

'And nobody better deserved the stroke of luck you had when the Kailan Mining Administration offered you a job,' he continued. 'You must have a nice little nest egg to retire on, ha-ha. More than a humble practitioner like me will ever see.'

Edward's eyes pleaded with Nellie to find a way of changing the subject.

Later on, Dr Gillespie drove them to the tall red-brick medical college, which still dominated the riverbank as the Airtons remembered. Nellie noticed tears in her husband's eyes when he saw the

Chinese staff who had gathered in the reception area under a huge red banner that read, 'Welcome Doctor Airton Return.' Many of the doctors were young men whom Edward had trained, and Nellie remembered the matron, who had been a pretty young nurse when she enrolled her, and was now a plump, confident woman in her forties. She proudly introduced her own daughter, who had recently joined as a shy pupil nurse, and Nellie felt the weight of her years.

Edward's inspection of the neat wards was something of a triumphal progress, with the young doctors filing behind him along the airy corridors, eager to show off to their old teacher their knowledge and professionalism. There was a moment of indescribable pathos, when the aged porter, Lao Hsu, long retired, was brought on the arms of two nurses down the corridor, and the two old men embraced.

Edward had tears in his eyes when Gillespie drove them out of the gate, leaving the nurses waving from the steps. Nellie allowed him to slump on the back seat with his memories. It was she, therefore, who raised with Gillespie the subject of Henry Manners.

'I must say,' he said, 'I'm surprised by your interest in him. He's not liked here, you know. Doesn't come to the club at all now. He's rather put himself beyond the pale.'

'Why is that?' asked Nellie.

'They say he's in with the Kempeitai, Japan's military police. You tend to judge a man by the company he keeps. The feeling round here is he's let the side down. He's *persona non grata* at the consulate.'

'I see.'

'Another thing. He's mixed up with those adventurers, like Sutton, who work for Chang Tso-lin at his arsenal. Sutton's not a bad chap. Bluff soldier. Plays a wonderful round of golf with his one arm – but, even so, there's something dubious about him. Of course, these soldiers of fortune do turn up where there are armies to be trained – but it doesn't mean they're the sort of people you'd invite for tea. Certainly not Manners.'

'In that case, it was very good of you, James, to make enquiries about him on our behalf.'

'Well, you and Edward always were saints,' said Gillespie. 'Never ones to cast stones, and quite right too. Far be it from me to . . .' He coughed.

'Have you been successful in finding him? Did you get a message to him that we were coming?' asked Nellie, keeping her tone even.

'I've seen to it that your messages were left at places he might be expected to visit. I haven't received any acknowledgement. Perhaps he doesn't want to be found.'

'It has occurred to me that he may not wish to see us.' Nellie sighed. 'Well, thank you anyway, James.'

Over lunch, in the Japanese restaurant, Nellie told Catherine that they had no definite news, but she stressed that Henry Manners had almost certainly received their messages. He was bound to contact them when he discovered they had arrived, and half believed it as she said it. She was pleasantly surprised by how well Catherine disguised the disappointment she must be feeling, although the girl remained silent, frowning slightly, through the first part of the meal.

The youngsters had decided to spend the afternoon walking in the old Chinese city so, after the meal, Nellie and her husband made their way to their room. Hardly had they settled than there was a loud knock on the door. When she opened it, a haggard, grey-haired man in an old-fashioned frayed blue suit, was standing there, leaning on a stick. For a moment, she stared in confusion at the lined features, the cracked cheeks and the purple pouches under cold, appraising eyes. There was something familiar about him, but she could not immediately place him. It was only when his lips curved into a brilliant, white-toothed smile that she realised who he was. She started, putting a hand to her mouth.

'Aren't you going to ask me in, Nellie?' asked the wreck of the man she had once known as Henry Manners. 'In the circumstances I thought it would be more appropriate if my call was a private one.' She recognised the sardonic tone. Unlike his physical appearance, his voice had not altered in twenty years.

'Henry,' whispered Nellie. She stepped aside, and the tall, slightly bowed figure moved slowly but deliberately into the sitting room. One foot dragged behind him.

'You see my old wound still plays me up,' said Manners. 'Airton, you haven't changed,' he said to Edward, who was standing hesitantly by the desk. His slippers were hidden under the papers he had dropped on to the carpet in his confusion, shocked at the appearance of this ghost from their past.

'Manners, my dear fellow . . .' he began.

'Do you mind if I sit?' asked Manners, and fell into an armchair. 'The leg pains me in cold weather. It's better in the summer. But that goes without saying. Just about anything's better in the summer, isn't it? There, we've dealt with the Englishman's customary preamble about physical ailments and the weather. I prefer the more practical Chinese courtesies, which state that there should be no unnecessary formalities between old friends. If you have some whisky, I'll take one. Otherwise, may I suggest we get on with whatever business you wished to discuss with me?'

Edward and Nellie fumbled with bottle and glass, then slipped into the chairs facing him. For a moment, they gazed at this stranger, who had once been their friend, and who was now observing them in turn, a glint of amusement in his eyes. 'Cheers,' he said, draining the whisky.

'You received our messages?' asked Nellie, breaking the silence which followed.

'Through that idiot Gillespie? I received a dispatch box of them. I even found one of his letters waiting for me in the Happy Cossack Club. Some of the hostesses were quite jealous. They thought it might be a *billet doux*.'

'I see,' said Nellie, as a blush heated her cheeks. 'I'm sorry. To embarrass or inconvenience you was not our intention.'

'No embarrassment at all, Nellie. As you see, I'm here.'

Nellie asked if he had received the letter from his daughter, Catherine.

'The girl who claims to be my daughter? Yes, I received that too.'

'But you didn't reply?' asked Nellie, raising her head. She was calmer now, although what he had said had shocked her.

'No, I didn't,' said Manners. He stared levelly back at her, an insolent curl to his lip.

'I see. May I ask why?'

'I thought it might raise false expectations,' said Manners, languidly. 'Oh, I'm not going to argue paternity issues, although

I've had such problems before now. When a man's led the sort of life I have, there will inevitably be the odd claim – usually a small sum of money settles it – but if this girl has persuaded such good character witnesses as yourselves that she is who she says she is, I'm prepared to give her the benefit of the doubt. Not that that places me under any particular obligation towards her—'

'But she's your daughter,' exclaimed Edward. 'She's Helen Frances's child. Do you think we'd lie to you about that? Would you deny your own flesh and blood?'

Manners ignored him, keeping his eyes on Nellie. 'As we all know, the matter would be hard to prove. Legally, my dear Nellie. In a court of law. You yourself made certain of that when you informed the world that Helen Frances's child was fathered by Tom Cabot. In wedlock, if I remember correctly.'

'You don't have to remind me that I made a terrible mistake,' said Nellie, 'but Catherine has not come to press a suit or claim an inheritance. She just wants to meet the man whom she now knows to be her natural father.'

'I should be touched by that, no doubt. May I ask how she found out? I would have been surprised to hear that Helen Frances had told her. How is Helen Frances by the way? Don't tell me she's here too.'

So he had not heard of Helen Frances's death. As gently as she could Nellie told him of the circumstances, and Catherine's subsequent quest. She could see that the news had affected him, and when he spoke, the insolent drawl had gone. 'I'm sorry,' he said. 'I didn't know.' Did she imagine moisture in his eyes? She could not be sure. His eyes were watery anyway. That, with the red veins on his nose, had caused her already to suspect that Manners was a heavy drinker. It did not take him long to recover. After a moment, he added, in the tones he had used before, 'That's very sad – but it doesn't alter the position in any way that I can see.'

'Have you a heart of stone, Manners?' Edward could not restrain himself. 'Can you imagine what poor Catherine's been through? Her high hopes in coming to find you? She's such a sweet child.'

'Oh, yes, Henry, you'll love her when you see her,' said Nellie.

'I have seen her,' said Manners, coldly. 'I observed her leaving the hotel with two young men. Your sons, I take it? Was the dapper one George? The jockey? I've read about him. You must be proud of him. Didn't he recently win the Tientsin Cup? On China Coast I believe. Good horse.'

'I'm more interested in talking about your daughter,' said Nellie, restraining her exasperation.

'Well,' he said, 'from the brief glimpse I had of her she appeared to be a pretty, spirited little thing. Anybody could see she's Helen Frances's daughter, and it's not only the hair . . . but, as I said, I don't believe I'm under any obligation to her, and I'd rather forgo a closer acquaintance. I hope that doesn't make this a wasted journey for you all.'

'Heavens, man, will you not at least meet her after she's come all this way to see you?' spluttered Edward.

'No, Airton, I don't think I will,' said Manners. 'It's a bit late for sentimental reconciliations. At least, for me.'

'But why, Manners?' Edward was wringing his hands in agitation.

'Calm yourself, Edward,' said Nellie. Her voice was now as stony as Manners's had been earlier. 'Henry will give us his reasons. I assume that's why you've come here?'

'Partly, Nellie,' he said. He was smiling again now. 'Partly to say farewell to my dear old friends before they depart these shores. To wish you *bon voyage*. It's been a long time, Nellie, but I'm glad to see that you are as percipient as ever. As I once told you, I've always respected you. Please don't apologise again for that forgotten social subterfuge of yours. Treat it as an unfortunate malapropism. Cabot? Manners? What's in a name? I know you meant well at the time, and in the end it didn't matter, did it? Helen Frances and I botched things up well enough on our own account without any assistance from you. I assure you, it weighs far heavier on your mind than it does on mine.'

'I saw your letters,' said Nellie. 'Catherine found them in her mother's effects.'

Again, his discomfiture was plain, and there was a long pause, as he took in this information. If it were possible, her mention of the letters seemed to have affected him more than the news of

Helen Frances's death. 'Helen Frances preserved them, did she?' he said softly. 'How very sentimental of her. I'm surprised. Well, it was a long time ago. They mean nothing now.'

'They mean a great deal to Catherine.'

'Then let her keep them.' For a moment there was a note of savagery in his voice, and Nellie saw a flash of penetrating blue in his eyes. He allowed himself to relax. 'I'm not the man who wrote those letters, Nellie, not any more,' he said. 'That man's dead, and I'd rather he remained so. Do you think Catherine would understand if you told her?'

'No, Henry, I don't think she would,' said Nellie.

He closed his eyes for a moment. 'Then tell her what you like,' he said. 'Take her to dinner with that friend of yours, Gillespie, or any of the other fools in the club. They'll put her straight on who her father is today. It's all true, you know, everything you've heard about me. Do I have to go into it for you?'

'No, Henry,' said Nellie, sadly. 'But I don't understand how you've become what you are.'

'There's nothing to understand.' He laughed. 'I've made my bed, and there's no room in it for a daughter. Not one who'll despise me for what I am. Not one who'll remind me . . . Nellie, it's far too late.'

'I don't think she would despise you,' said Nellie. 'She's read your beastly articles, you know.'

He chuckled sourly. 'Yes, they are rather beastly, aren't they? Well, that's what I am today. His Master's Voice. Just a tired old gramophone needle going round the tracks.'

'Do you believe in such drivel, Henry? Are you really full of such hatred?'

'What if I am?' asked Manners.

'Then I'm sorry for you,' said Nellie.

'Doesn't that prove my point?' said Manners, quietly. 'I'm not the father anybody should be looking for. Catherine would pity me at first, then be disappointed and hurt. Maybe not now in the first flush – but certainly over time. And as for me . . . Let's just say that in my present circumstances a daughter would complicate my life and leave it at that.'

'It's not good enough,' said Nellie.

Manners glared at her. 'What gives you the right to judge,' he said, 'after all these years? I've buried my children, Nellie, both of them. There was another. A boy . . .'

'I know,' said Nellie, gently, 'in Japan. Catherine visited his grave . . .'

'Well, she should have left well enough alone,' he said bitterly. 'It doesn't matter. I buried her too. And her mother. Here,' he said, banging the chest of his shiny suit. 'And I'm damned if I'll let you or anybody else resurrect them. Not now. Not after so many damned years. For God's sake, let the dead be!'

'I can't, Henry. Catherine wants her father.'

'But I – don't – want – to be – her – damned – father.' His fists clenched on the linen arm covers of his chair.

Nellie felt a wave of sympathy. She tried to imagine the barren, empty years, and was aware of a tear in the corner of her eye. She watched the grey man in front of her, in his shabby, untended clothes, with his unkempt pepper moustache, and puffy drinker's eyes, and thought of the elegant black-haired figure in dinner dress when she had first met him in Shishan.

He took a deep breath, and gave her a grin. Briefly she saw a reflection of the old Manners. 'Not good enough, either?' he asked.

'You know it isn't,' she said.

'All right,' he said.

'I don't understand,' she said.

'I said all right. If I must, I'll tell you why I can't meet Catherine. Actually, I've already given you the reason, but now I'll elaborate. Only for you, Nellie, because I think you'll understand. I meant what I said when I told you it would complicate my life.'

'Oh, Henry, surely . . .'

'Listen, Nellie,' he spoke urgently, locking his eyes on hers, 'I don't think you can possibly imagine what sort of existence I lead here. My present position would be seriously inconvenienced, compromised, if any of my associates were to suspect that I had a daughter. It would make me vulnerable. I move in a world of unscrupulous people, Nellie, where a man like me cannot afford to be vulnerable. I'm involved – no, better you don't know what I'm involved in. But believe me, please, I could not, and will not, answer for the consequences. For me, and particularly for her.'

'What consequences? I don't understand you.'

'I think you will understand me, Nellie, if you'll only think about it. Remember what I once was. Remember Shishan, your suspicions of me. I'm asking you now to trust me as I never let you then. There, I'm speaking plainer than I ever intended.'

'I've never heard such gibberish,' exploded Edward.

'Edward, be quiet,' snapped Nellie. All this time, her eyes had been fixed on Manners's, and she saw pleading in them. 'Are you implying what I think you are?' asked Nellie, very softly. 'Are you up to your old games?'

Manners did not reply.

'There are other forms of duty—' she began.

'It doesn't work like that,' he interrupted.

Nellie sighed. 'There's nothing I can say that will prevent her looking for you, you know,' she said. 'She has a will of her own.'

'Then it's better she does not find me,' he said, his eyes still on hers. 'And I'm saying that for her sake.'

'And what if she does?'

'Then I'll cut her, in whatever company we find ourselves. Disown her. I won't even recognise her.'

'That would break her heart,' said Nellie.

'Christ Almighty! Is there nothing you can say to dissuade her? Can't you tell her I'm dead?'

'I don't think I can,' said Nellie.

'So be it,' he said. 'I've warned you what I'll do if I'm ever forced to meet her.'

'Your own daughter, man! Your flesh and blood!'

'Edward!' warned Nellie. She turned back to Manners as calmly as she could. 'Is there nothing I can say to persuade you? At least may I give her some hope? That one day circumstances might change? *You* might change? Can I tell her about this conversation?'

'Better not. That would be very dangerous,' said Manners. 'There's nothing you can say. I'm sorry.'

'Then God forgive you, you poor, poor man.'

Edward groaned.

Before Henry Manners left, he asked for, and Nellie gave him, a photograph of Catherine, a studio portrait that had been recently made in Tientsin. When he had gone, Edward railed for some time about the hypocrisy of this incomprehensible request, but Nellie sat silently on the sofa, gazing at the hollow in the cushion on which Henry Manners had so recently sat when he locked his will with hers. Edward was wrong. It had been Henry who had crumpled: he had told her more about himself than she had ever wished to hear.

They didn't reach the walled Chinese city. George, who had acquired a city map, had insisted they walk off their lunch, and that he would guide them there. 'But it's all in Japanese,' said Catherine.

'A map's a map,' said George. 'I've had some military training, you know. Didn't spend the whole war in the mess in Poona. Anyway, I explored this area last night.'

'In the fog?'

'Humour him,' said Edmund.

Inevitably they became lost. When they had walked past the same department store three times, the turbaned Sikh at the door could barely conceal his amusement. 'There must be something wrong with this map,' muttered George. 'Maybe I'm looking at it upside-down.'

'There's something wrong with you, you mean,' said Catherine – but by then Edmund had asked directions.

He led them down a side-street lined on either side by the backs of imposing bank buildings. 'This should take us to the square,' he said, 'and from there we follow the main road east.'

'Hello,' said George. 'I'm beginning to recognise some of these buildings. Look, let's just turn off here for a moment. I want to show you my streetlamp. Where I had my experience last night.'

He disappeared down a narrow alley. Reluctantly, Edmund and Catherine followed. The alley led to another road, and there was indeed a streetlamp, but it was leaning at a sad angle, having been half torn out of the pavement. There was a small crater in the road. The windows of the office building next to it were jagged with broken glass, and the granite facing was pockmarked with holes.

It took them some moments to establish this, because they had to push through a curious crowd of Chinese, who were being held back by helmeted Japanese soldiers wielding bayonets as officials poked in the rubble.

George was delighted. 'Didn't I tell you I'd experienced something strange?' he crowed. 'My, my, that old fellow I saw must have been a bank robber or an anarchist. All the time I was thinking of Mime and Siegfried, I was watching a real-life saboteur! That's what poetic sensibility does for you.'

Edmund had been talking to some bystanders, and had established that a gas main explosion had occurred before dawn and nobody had been hurt. 'Sorry, old boy, it was nothing sinister after all,' he commiserated with his younger brother, gently, but he wore a satisfied smile.

'He was sabotaging the gas mains,' said George.

'Yes, George,' said Catherine. 'Can we go to the walled city now?'

Back on the road they had been following before their diversion, they passed an anonymous building with a large purple awning. A sign read 'The Happy Cossack' and a dusty frame contained faded photographs of scantily dressed women. On the pavement stood a figure who might have been the Happy Cossack himself. He was a giant of a man, broad-shouldered, with an astrakhan busby tilted at a rakish angle on the side of his head, Slavic features and a long, drooping moustache. He wore a narrow-waisted kaftan with wide skirts billowing out below his belt. High spurred boots and a cavalry sabre completed the martial picture.

To Catherine, who was familiar with imperial Russian uniforms, the green epaulettes and the medals pinned over the braided front of his chest indicated a cavalry officer. He was languidly smoking a cigarette, which gave him an air of insouciance, typical of many officers she had known.

'I say, this place looks promising . . .' George said, and the Cossack doorman turned to view this potential customer. As he did so, his pale eyes blazed with what Catherine took to be fury. The next thing she knew, she had been enfolded in a vice-like hug and kisses were being planted on her cheeks, then she felt the moustache brushing her nose, and cracked lips pressed against hers. All the time, the man was trying to shout something but she could make out only 'Shusha, Shusha, Shusha.' In the background she heard an angry bark from Edmund and laughter from George.

Edmund had been all set to come to her rescue, but suddenly the Cossack released her, and held her at arms' length. Tears poured down his cheeks as he finally pronounced the words 'Katusha! Katusha! Our *Rizhi Angelochek*! Do you not remember me?'

Catherine flung her arms round his neck and burst into tears.

'Goodness gracious, Nurse, what are you doing?' Edmund exclaimed. But she had eyes only for Serge, whom she had not seen since the winter of 1916, when she had been a nurse and he the commander of a machine-gun detachment, in their snowy camp at Chertoviche after the retreat to Minsk.

'Serge, is it really you?' she gasped. 'What are you doing here? And why are you wearing that ridiculous moustache?'

The Cossack pulled a dagger from its sheath. 'If the *Rizhi Angelochek* does not like my moustache, I will cut it off, here and now!'

'Oh Serge, you fool – put it away.' She giggled. 'You'll scare my friends.'

'Catherine, are you going to tell us what on earth is going on?' Edmund was looking concerned, and Catherine realised that she and Serge had been talking in Russian. 'Oh, Edmund, let me introduce an old friend.'

Serge had already snapped to attention, clicking his heels. 'Friend to *Rizhi Angelochek* is friend of mine,' he said, with a curt military bow. 'I honour to introduce. Sergei Ilianovich Kovalevsky. Preobrazhensky Regiment. Acting colonel. Retired. And now we go for drink champagne!' he insisted. 'This is celebration. So of course champagne.'

They had initially to watch Serge's flamboyant departure from the nightclub. The owner was a whey-faced, bearded man in a skullcap, who had poked his head through the door to investigate the commotion. Serge pulled him out by his necktie, and upbraided him in Russian. Then he reached into the pockets of his kaftan for a wad of notes, which he thrust into the man's shirt. He stripped himself of busby, belt, sword, spurs and, finally, the kaftan, then hurled them into the owner's outstretched arms. When Serge was down to his vest, striped trousers and boots, the man scurried back into the club. 'See, I resign,' Serge told them. 'Owner no good. Azeri Jew. I tell him, "Next time I come back club, I customer not slave." Maybe this evening, yes? For now, I no money. So you pay champagne. Good? OK?' He clapped Edmund on the back, then linked arms with Catherine and George to lead them to 'good place I know' in another street. Edmund followed patiently behind.

'Aren't you freezing in just your vest?' asked Catherine.

'No, I have Russian's burning heart,' said Serge.

First he took them to a Russian bakery, where he ordered from the fat *babushka* every cake in the shop front, and plenty of cold champagne. They went on to a Russian restaurant, where he ordered *piroshkis*, pickles, *kapusta*, *tvorozhniky* and caviar, bowls of *borscht* and *stalanka*; then delicious lamb dumplings, *chebureki*, a speciality of the house, Kazakh shashlik, chicken *kobleky* and sweetbreads. They washed it down with cranberry juice, vodka and more champagne. Edmund paid. He had tried to make his excuses so that he could join his parents at Gillespie's medical college dinner, but every time he stood up, the big Russian pulled him back into his seat.

All this time Serge and Catherine had been telling each other what had happened to them since they had last met. Catherine attempted to translate, but often the emotion proved too much, and Edmund and George had to wait while they laughed and cried. Serge's story was no more poignant or harrowing than those of many other White Russian refugees who had fled to China since the civil wars. He had fought under Kornilov, commanding an armoured train near the Urals. One by one, his fellow officers had died or gone over to the Reds. He had slowly retreated with the remnants of the White forces to the Russian Far East, and for a year had been a member of a band of monarchist partisans operating behind Bolshevik lines, hiding in the forests near Lake Baikal, making raids on the Trans-Siberian Railway and Red villages. Here he had come across the charismatic cavalry leader, Baron Ungern von Sternberg, and he had joined him when he escaped over the border into Mongolia.

They had all heard of Baron von Sternberg – the mad Estonian convert to Buddhism who believed that he was a reincarnation of Genghis Khan, and of the terrible path he had cut through Mongolia. In 1920 he had sacked the city of Urga, slaughtering every man in the Chinese garrison, heating the merchants in cauldrons over fires to find out where they had hidden their money, raping and butchering their wives and daughters in front of them as they boiled. After that, even the Mongols had abandoned him. Catherine translated sentence by sentence as Serge slowly recounted his horrific tale. 'I was loyal until Urga,' said Serge. 'Then I knew that he was an evil madman, and no longer worthy of respect. By then, after seven years of war, revolution and war again, we Russians no longer knew what was right or wrong. Well, Sternberg taught us.

'To my shame, I did not leave him, not immediately. By then we were fighting the Reds, who had also come into Mongolia. These were our real enemies, and Sternberg, whatever else he was, was a good general, so we followed him, and we were successful enough. At least we killed many Reds. In the autumn we ambushed one of their hospital convoys – no, I won't talk of that, not to you, Katusha, you who were once a nurse ... But it was after what we saw done on that day that a group of us officers decided enough was enough. We hated the Bolsheviks, don't mistake me, but Sternberg treated those people – wounded, nurses, doctors – as no human beings should be treated. Even Bolshevik ones. Many of our own men, shamefully, seemed to enjoy the cruelty as much as he did. To the last, most of our army would have followed him to hell. He opened the door into the dark side of human nature and enticed men in. He turned us into an army of the damned ... Well, not all of us.

'A few of us made our conspiracy against our commanding officer. We found ways to become closer to him, drinking with him, laughing with him, and one night we machine-gunned him in his tent. We thought he was dead. Any other man would have been dead – but he was like Rasputin. We found we could not kill him. No matter how many rounds we fired at him. He came out of the tent, blood running from hundreds of wounds, cursing us. Then we were afraid.

'Katusha, I saw this – this devil, this Antichrist, bleeding from a hundred mortal wounds, climb on to his horse and ride off into the steppe, vowing revenge on us all. I was on my own horse five minutes after he had gone, riding hard in the opposite direction, and eventually I found my way here. To be doorman of a club. Me, Sergei Ilianovich Kovalevsky. That's what he brought me to. Holy Mary, Mother of Jesus. The Reds claim they found him bleeding on the plain, and tried him and put him in front of a firing squad.' He shook his head as if he doubted it. 'Oh, Katusha, I have seen horrors, so many horrors – but that was the worst. That is the one which gives me nightmares today. Enough! Enough of this talk! Champagne!'

Afterwards, Catherine had only a hazy recollection of the rest of the evening. She remembered lurching back along the road to the Happy Cossack Club. They might have been singing the old Russian national anthem. She remembered Serge terrorising the Azeri club owner into giving them a table, and shouting for champagne, more champagne.

A line of half-naked Russian girls was performing some sort of chorus ensemble on the stage. Then a couple in leotards performed a lewd contortionist act. There was Cossack dancing. She also had an impression of Serge hugging a vodka bottle and weeping. It seemed important at the time that she wept too. It was the Russian thing to do.

Much later, Serge suddenly stood up and pointed at a table in the corner, where a large, florid-faced, fair-haired man sat surrounded by beautiful girls. He had a pleasant face, she thought. Lived-in. Attractive. But only one arm. The empty sleeve of his dinner suit was draped over one girl's shoulders. As she gazed at him, Serge strode proudly towards his table and engaged him in conversation. After a moment, the man's good arm lifted off the shoulder of the girl at his other side, and he beckoned Catherine to join them. The next thing she knew she was sitting at the man's table being poured yet another glass of champagne. George and Edmund had come with her.

By then the room was revolving, and it was difficult to concentrate on the conversation, which was all about guns and aeroplanes and armoured trains. The man was a general who commanded a weapons arsenal belonging to the warlord, Chang Tso-lin. How could an Englishman be a general working for a Chinese warlord? She put a hand over one eye to stop the room going round, then recalled that Edmund had told her about an English soldier who had brought Chang Tso-lin a design for an armoured car. Or was it a mortar?

'Excuse me,' she blurted out, 'Are you One-armed Sutton? The mercenary?'

'Do you know, my dear?' The man had a kindly voice. 'I rather believe I am.'

'I'm Catherine,' she said emphatically.

'I'm delighted to meet you,' he replied.

'And I you,' she said. The room had started to revolve again. 'Can you get this room to stop turning round?'

Sutton laughed. 'I'm sorry, my dear. I'm considered to be rather a good engineer but that's beyond my powers, I'm afraid.'

'I didn't mean to ask that question,' said Catherine. 'What I want to know is . . .' What did she want to know? 'Do you know where I can find my father?'

'Alas, I don't think I know who he is,' said Sutton.

'He's Henry Manners,' said Catherine.

This time the man really did laugh. Very loudly. 'The old dog. I know Manners very well indeed, my dear. Who doesn't? But I didn't know he had a daughter. And such a beautiful one at that. Are you sure you meant he was your father, and not a sugar-daddy? That would be more in Manners's line.'

Catherine was surprised to see that George had risen to his feet, and was saying something about an offensive remark that had not been called for. The one-armed man raised his hand. 'Do sit down, old boy. I sincerely apologise. Is she really looking for Manners? I'll tell you what, to make up for my rudeness, why don't I invite all of you to Marshal Chang's parade tomorrow? It'll be a grand show, and Manners will almost certainly be there. It starts at ten. At the Pei Ling arsenal.' He scribbled something on a napkin. 'Here, this'll be good enough. Show it to the guard at the gate and he'll let you in. The four of you. Two Airtons. One Cabot and a

Kovalevsky. Mr Kovalevsky, we can talk further about that armoured train. We're looking for men with experience.'

'I say, this is dashed good of you, General,' said George.

'Well, you're lucky, actually. This morning, after that bomb went off, I thought the whole show might be cancelled.'

'Bomb?' George's voice came out in a squeak. 'Did you say bomb, sir?'

'Yes, some fellow let off a bomb last night in the Japanese Railway Town. Behind the Kempeitai office. It could have been the Nationalists, or perhaps one of Wu Pei-fu's boys. Probably the intention was to make the Japanese think Chang Tso-lin had ordered it, in a clumsy attempt to break good relations and weaken his power base. It was quite sticky for a while, but Chang sent his prime minister to a meeting with the Japanese top brass in the Yamato Hotel this morning and everything was sorted out. Now they're pretending it was a burst gas main. But it shows you what a tricky situation we have in Fengtian . . . I say, are you quite all right, old boy?'

George had slumped back in his seat, a beatific smile on his face.

A look of perplexity appeared on General Sutton's. 'Edmund,' he said, 'I think you might have to take your brother home. And the young lady looks the worse for wear too. Do you want me to get you a car?'

Catherine could not remember afterwards whether she had been taken back in a car or not, but she had woken up in her bed with a dry throat and a thumping headache, and a vague awareness that somebody had arranged for her to meet her father later in the morning.

It was a small enough ceremony, but for Martha it was the culmination of a dream. Well, it was originally Ming's dream, she corrected herself, as she watched him lighting the string of firecrackers that hung over the school door – but she shared it. Their school! She should pinch herself, she thought, remembering her superstitious old grandmother in the Bronx. She could hardly believe such good fortune was hers.

Ming leaped back, laughing, as the taper took fire, and the children screamed with delight when the explosions began. Through the sparks and the flying paper she saw Minister Yu Fu-cheng smiling indulgently. Even his surly father, Old Man Yu, the soy-bean king, who had been persuaded to be a governor, was grinning, and his young wife was clapping.

Martha followed the coil of smoke as it rose into the clear winter sky. Beyond the slate-grey roofs she could see the massive city walls and the sunlight glinting on the tiles of the great gate tower. She was longing to explore the mysterious alleys of this ancient city, Shishan, her new home.

She had had no chance to do so yet, because from the moment they had arrived, she and Ming had been busy making all the preparations to get the tumbledown old building that Minister Yu had allotted them into shape for today's opening. Or, rather, *she* had been busy, scrubbing, cleaning, painting, patching – even wood-working, because the school desks with which they had been provided were in a terrible state. She had hardly seen Ming in the daytime. The minister had had him calling on every family in the town to persuade them to enrol their children, and when he was not doing that, he was paying his respects to the government departments and even the Japanese administration in the SMR cantonment, as the Japanese railway town was known.

Ming could scarcely conceal his delight on his return. Since this Chinese school was clearly being set up in competition to the SMR's, the Japanese mayor had not been happy about it at all. 'But th-that's what it's all about!' Ming had cried as he hugged her. 'This is a Chinese school for the Chinese! Oh, y-you should have seen his s-sour face, but he could only bow and be p-polite because Yu Fu-cheng was with me. Oh, Martha.' He kissed her. 'I'm so h-happy!'

She had pulled him then and there on to the futon in the corner of the staff-room – they had had no time even to think yet about turning the upstairs rooms into their private quarters. She made love to him, caked in plaster and dust as she was, and afterwards she lay with her head on his chest as he expanded excitedly about his great plans. Their plans. If only the folks at home could see her now, she thought. She remembered the stupefaction on the faces of the Hasidic professors in Tientsin when she had told them she was quitting to set up a school of her own with her Chinese husband. She knew that she had burned her bridges with her own society. She didn't care. Ming was her world. She recalled his shy courtship, his tongue-tied formality on that first occasion, after Catherine had left their lesson early because she had a party to go on to, and he had asked Martha to stay, inviting her to eat with Lan-hua and him, and afterwards go to the Chinese opera, and how later they had both been embarrassed by her credulous reaction: 'You mean all those beautiful screeching women are *men*?' How he had been offended, because he had thought she was mocking his culture, and how stunned he had been when she had kissed him, there in the opera stall, and told him, 'You dumb-bat, don't you see? I love your culture. It's opening my mind.' That had been the beginning.

A week later, Lan-hua had mischievously made her excuses – *she* had seen what was going on even before they did – and left them together in a dance hall. They had clumsily waltzed to the discordant music of the Chinese band. 'Are these clowns *trained* to be out of tune?' she had asked him, the fifth time she had trodden on his feet. He had taken this as an excuse to lead her off the floor. She knew how nervous he was, because she had been dancing deliberately close to him. 'Oh, no, you don't,' she had said, and kissed him on the lips. He had tried to pull away, but she had flung her arms round his neck, and one thing had led to another, and by the time he had shyly dropped her off at her lodgings – well, she had thought, as she dreamily made her way up the stairs, her body still tingling with his kisses and the sensation of his hands, there certainly wasn't a cultural barrier any more.

The next morning, early, she had been woken by a banging on her door and on opening it had found three messengers loaded with bouquets of flowers.

They had been careful. Nobody except Lan-hua had suspected their secret. Martha hadn't even told Catherine. Since that day at the races there had been an indefinable cooling in the relationship between the two women. It was not that Catherine had been any less considerate towards her, but Martha had realised that she moved in a different world. Martha would never forgive the rudeness of Catherine's friends to Ming. Ming's cold anger afterwards had taught her a lesson. It was a shame: Catherine had been guiltless – Martha saw no snobbery or prejudice in her – but love meant making a choice, she had realised, and Catherine lived on the other side of the divide. The next weekend Ming had taken her to the Chinese beach at Peitaiho, and in their chalet they had become lovers. Next morning he had asked her to be his wife. They had married in a register office in Chinwangtao, with Lan-hua, who had hurried down when they telephoned her, as the only witness.

Later she had come to understand that whatever the prejudice of westerners towards interracial marriage, it was nothing compared to that of the Chinese. It had made her respect Ming more when she grasped the full extent of the sacrifice he had made for her. Not that it would matter. Nothing – nobody – could stop them. Together they were making a new society, a new world. This school that they were creating was part of it. She had only to look now at the pride on Ming's face as he bade farewell to the minister to know that what they had done was right. He flashed her a smile. She opened the school door, and rang the bell in the hall.

Their assistant, *Hsiao* Hung, had formed the pupils into a crocodile. There was a fumble and a scurry as Martha relieved them of their coats. Ming was already standing at the door of the classroom in his scholar's gown. The crocodile disappeared inside, and a few moments later she could hear Ming's voice as he began his first lesson – with no trace of his stammer. A smiling *Hsiao* Hung, hanging coats on the pegs, caught her eye. Martha mumbled her excuses and hurried into the common room before the assistant had time to see the tears running down her cheeks.

Serge Kovalevsky was dressed in a nondescript charcoal suit when he met them at the gates of the arsenal. He had shaved off his luxuriant moustache and, with his naked face, seemed diminished from the giant figure he had been the day before. They were all suffering from hangovers. A sergeant was waiting for them, and led them through the red-brick buildings of the arsenal, through a gate at the back to a wide, grassy field where a band was playing. He handed them programmes and left them under a clump of elm trees, telling them that General Sutton would join them after the parade.

A miniature grandstand had been set up for the VIPs, and here they saw an imposing array of top hats and morning suits, sashes, medals and uniforms of every colour and description. Catherine recognised the distinguished Chinese gentleman in mandarin robes whom she had seen yesterday in the lobby of their hotel, sitting with other Manchurian officials in the front row. At least half the seats were taken by Japanese. Among the ranks of olive-green uniforms, she noticed a fat, cheery-looking general whom she had nearly bumped into on the way to breakfast. There were several Europeans, defence attachés and consular officials, and not a few ladies, Chinese and Japanese. She peered anxiously, trying to identify anybody who might be Henry Manners, but if he was there she did not recognise him.

'There's another half hour before it starts,' said Edmund. 'Shall we stroll over and have a look at the vehicle park over there? It looks an extraordinarily impressive array of equipment for a warlord's army.'

She glanced to where he was pointing, and saw rows of armoured cars and some miniature tanks, neat lines of cannons and six biplanes being pushed into position on the edge of the field. At first, a guard tried to keep them away, but he snapped to attention when he heard a shout in English.

General Sutton was dressed today in a pale blue Chinese uniform. 'Come on over. Meet my friend, General Chang Hsueh-liang, the marshal's son – or should I say Air Commodore Chang? He's responsible for acquiring these aircraft from France. Had to smuggle in the parts on junks through Ying-k'ou, and we fitted the bombing racks here, but aren't they beauties?'

A slight, fresh-faced man in his early twenties, wearing a white suit, red tie and Panama, was standing next to them. 'Very pleased to meet you,' he said, in American-accented English. 'General Sutton has done an excellent job, but this is so far only a little squadron. We will buy more machines when we can.'

Sutton laughed. 'General Chang is modest,' he said. 'You're looking at China's first air force. And China's first armoured brigade too, for that matter,' he added, pointing at the tanks. 'He may look like a boy, but he's the commander of one of Fengtian's top fighting divisions, and it was his vision to establish this arsenal. Best general I've ever served under. I mean it, sir.'

The young man grinned. 'General Sutton has a silver tongue, and one never knows when he is being humorous. He is our finest salesman, and if I believed everything he told me, my father would be in the presidential palace in Peking tomorrow! I do hope you enjoy our little display. If you will excuse me, I must change into my dress uniform before it begins.'

'I'd better be off too,' said Sutton. 'Enjoy the show. Oh, Miss Cabot, have you found Manners yet? No? Well, he's around. Probably hatching some conspiracy with Taro Hideyoshi and those Kempeitai chums of his. I'll make sure he knows you're here. And, by the way, Kovalevsky, I've talked to young Chang about the train and he's interested. Catch up later. Toot-toot.' He gave the Airton party a last expansive smile and sauntered away in the direction of the grandstand.

'Sounds like you're fixed up,' said Edmund to Serge.

'Maybe,' said Serge gloomily. 'He pay. I mercenary. I fight. Armour train is good. Ah, but sell life for China man? For *Chitai*? It is not Preobrazhensky. Do you remember, Katusha? Fighting for Tsar in 1916? Then, I was Russian officer.' He groaned.

'I remember,' said Catherine. 'But you're still a Russian officer to me.'

He shrugged, then smiled. 'No, I am mercenary, but you are always *Rizhi Angelochek*. Is true. You heal me now.' He picked up her hand and kissed it, then strode off, erect. They followed him back to their allotted position under the trees.

Soon afterwards, the parade began with an echelon of motor-cycles. Then a huge, armour-sided Packard convertible drove slowly across the field to the grandstand bearing Marshal Chang Tso-lin. Catherine had heard several stories about this ex-bandit tyrant over the last few days, and had expected somebody terrible to behold, but he was a tiny little man, with soft eyes and a pencil moustache. She was struck by the strangely delicate gloved hands folded modestly on his lap, and that he was accompanied by three little boys, all in miniature but exact replicas of their grandfa-ther's plumed costume. It might have been a greengrocer and his family, thought Catherine, irreverently, on their way to a fancy-dress party.

It was no greengrocer who stepped out of the car, and walked up the two steps to his seat on the grandstand. The rush of fear that rippled through the ranks of the dignitaries was like a puff of wind through a poppy field. He took his place quietly, gazed indulgently at his grandsons, then settled into an extraordinary stillness, the silence of absolute power, which he maintained for the following hour.

The band had been playing throughout, but now they heard the whine of engines, and observed the planes bounce over the grass and into the air. They flew the length of the field, dwindling to small specks against the grey clouds to the east, then turned and, with a roar, five flew low past the grandstand, rose again and disappeared towards the west. The last plane came in higher, at an angle, towards a large sandbagged target area at the other end of the field. As she watched, something black separated itself from the aircraft, hung momentarily in the air, then plummeted towards a lorry parked among the sandbags. There was an explosion, and the lorry was destroyed. In the silence afterwards she heard polite clapping from the grandstand.

Next, the armoured cars drove in two compact boxes of eight up the field, followed by the matchbox-shaped tanks, then horse-drawn artillery. Finally, six mortars were dragged to the centre of the field, General Sutton striding behind his men.

'See how they play with toys,' said Serge, scornfully.

'Toys they may be, but none of the other warlords is armed like this,' said Edmund. 'Marshal Chang is certainly raising the stakes. I doubt whether the wars of the future will be quite as comical as they have been in the past.'

'No war is comedy, my friend.' Serge put a heavy hand on his shoulder. 'Only general who fight war, maybe, for he is comedy. We soldier men die all the same.'

It was time now for the march-past of the various regional divisions in Chang Tso-lin's army, each commanded by one of the subsidiary warlords in his clique. The first regiment to appear was led by Chang Hsueh-liang, as befitted the marshal's eldest son. He was wearing a modest blue uniform with a simple kepi, but he presented an elegant figure on his spirited black horse. Rows and rows of soldiers, rifles sloped, plodded by. Catherine was amused to see the familiar parasols protruding from their knapsacks.

'This looks more like it,' said George. In a cloud of dust, horsemen were entering the field and positioning themselves in a long line that stretched from the grandstand to the target area. 'I say, they're Mongolians – look at their shaggy hats.'

Edmund was consulting his programme. 'Interesting. Irregular scouts from Shishan.'

There was a wild cry, and the Mongolians charged, sabres and lances thrust forward. They galloped past the grandstand, then halted and wheeled, returning to the centre of the field where they formed into three neat lines. They charged, stopped and, at a shout, in one synchronous motion, they dismounted, bowed and leaped into their saddles again, wheeled and trotted off the field.

George was clapping and cheering. 'What horsemanship!' he cried. 'What fine ponies too. Wouldn't mind taking some back to the track.'

Already, the regular forces from Shishan were marching on to the field. The troops were wearing the same blue uniforms as the ones who had preceded them, but discipline seemed tighter in this brigade: they were marching with a firmer step and in neater lines. They were led by their general, who sat, erect, on a fine white stallion. Catherine and George noticed his scarred cheek at the same moment.

'Catherine, look, there's your beau from the nightclub!' George shouted.

Catherine giggled. 'Lord, so he is. I'd better keep out of sight.'

'But don't you realise? He's the warlord of Shishan. We'll probably meet him there!'

'How do you know *him*?' asked Edmund. 'That's General Lin Fu-po. Bloody good soldier, from all I've heard of him.'

'That name rings a bell,' said George.

'Look! Edmund!' Catherine was now calling. 'There's the young man we met at the Leis. The one Lan-hua didn't want to marry.'

It was indeed Lieutenant Ti. He was leading one of the last

companies, his sabre upright in his gloved hand. As he passed them, he heard Catherine's cry, and his face wobbled in a half-smile as he recognised her. He blushed as red as his cap badge.

'Well, well,' said Edmund. 'What a small world. Minister Yu told me he might offer him a post here, and he's obviously taken it up. Good for him. To serve under Lin Fu-po would be a wonderful opportunity for any ambitious young soldier.'

'Let's try to see him after the parade,' said Catherine.

'We could ask Sutton, I suppose,' said Edmund doubtfully.

In the event they had no opportunity to meet Lieutenant Ti, because something else transpired. The last body of troops had marched past. The armoured Packard returned, and Marshal Chang and his grandchildren were driven off the field. The dignitaries were moving towards a food-and-drink tent that had been pitched under the trees, but Catherine and her party had decided to stay where they were until General Sutton returned for them. Knots of defence attachés and Japanese officers on their way to view the armoured park passed them and Catherine scrutinised each group closely for a man who might fit the image of Henry Manners she had in her mind.

But it was George who recognised the stooping, grey-haired man, leaning on a stick, deep in conversation with two Japanese officers. He ran after him, shouting, 'Mr Manners? It's George Airton. Do you remember me, sir? Little George? I knew you when I was a boy in Shishan!'

The men turned. Catherine had an impression of three cruel faces, two Japanese – and a European, a once-handsome man, with cold, penetrating eyes and a supercilious sneer. Catherine felt faint. George had hailed this man as Henry Manners, but she could see in him no resemblance to the portrait of the man she kept by her bed.

He was speaking: 'George Airton? Yes, I know you. You're quite a star on the racetrack, aren't you?' He turned to his companions and spoke in rapid Japanese.

Catherine saw them nodding, and heard the word 'jockey', which they repeated: 'Ah, champ-i-on jockey, *so desu ka?*'

'We must chat some time,' the man continued. 'I'm sorry, I can't now. We – that is General Taro, Colonel Doihara and I – have some business in Dairen tonight and must shortly catch our train. Give my regards to your parents.'

'Sir, you can't go yet. There's somebody who's come a long way to meet you,' said George, excitement in his voice.

The man's eyebrows rose quizzically.

'Mr Manners,' George was saying triumphantly, 'I'd like to present Miss Catherine Cabot.' As if she were an automaton, or a puppet pulled by strings, Catherine found herself propelled forward. She was aware that she had put out her hand, and that the man had shaken it brusquely. 'Cabot?' he was saying. 'That's a name I haven't heard in a long time. I knew a Cabot once. Tom Cabot. Perhaps you are related?'

Even George looked a little stunned by this last remark. 'Sir,' he said, 'this is Catherine. You remember her surely? Helen Frances's daughter.'

'Oh, yes,' said the man. 'I see the resemblance now. How is your mother?'

Catherine heard herself as if from far away: 'She died. Last year.'

'Oh, I'm sorry to hear it. What a shame,' said the man. Again, he spoke in Japanese, and again there was the hissed *'So desu ka?'*

The older of his two companions, a tall, clean-shaven officer with close-cropped white hair, said, in good English, 'Miss Cabot, I am General Taro Hideyoshi. I once had the pleasure to meet your mother in Shishan when we were all young. You have my deep commiserations.'

'Well, it's sad, but we should be off,' said the man whom George had called Henry Manners, and who showed no sign of recognising her as his daughter.

'Mr Manners,' she said, in as strong a voice as she could muster, 'did you receive my letter?'

'Letter?' he said. 'Were you informing me of Helen Frances's death? That was kind of you. I'll have another look in my papers. I've recently been away.'

'No, it was not about that,' she said. 'Or only partly.'

'I see. What was it about, then?'

'It was – it was about – my father.' Her voice was breaking.

'Tom Cabot? What about him?'

She looked into the face of the stranger, who was contemplating her with scornful unconcern. 'It doesn't matter,' she whispered.

'Catherine.' It was Edmund's worried voice in her ear, but she kept her eyes on Henry Manners, who was shrugging indifferently.

'Well,' he said, 'if it's not important, we'll be on our way. I'm pleased to have met you, Miss Cabot. Goodbye, and goodbye again, George. Good luck in the next cup race.'

The two Japanese bowed, then all three resumed their interrupted conversation as if nothing had happened.

In the far distance she was aware of brown leaves blowing off the trees. There were people in top hats and officers in uniform, milling to and fro, and two young men whom she knew were gesticulating urgently at her with anxious faces. A larger man in a grey suit was mouthing something behind them. She could not hear what they were saying. In the foreground of her vision, as if suspended by invisible wires from the trees, hung a double-sided leather frame containing the portraits of a man and a woman, an officer in uniform and a girl who looked very like herself, old-fashioned studio portraits that must have been made before the turn of the century. As she contemplated them, they seemed to smoke and wrinkle before her eyes. The handsome features distorting, they burned to ash with her quest and her hopes.

When General Sutton reached the grove, only Serge Kovalevsky was waiting for him. 'I'm sorry to be so late,' he said. 'Hell of a bunfight in there, and everybody wanted to hear about the mortars. Where are the others?'

'They go,' said Serge.

'Oh, I'm sorry. I was going to find Manners for them.'

'They meet Manners.'

'Did they? Oh, well, that's a stroke of luck. Are they with him?'

'He go one way, they another. Katusha is very sad. She fainted, then cry on Edmund shoulder. They take her home.'

Sutton chuckled. 'Really? So the old rogue didn't admit to being her father after all?'

'He bastard. I like kill him for making *Rizhi Angelochek* unhappy.'

Sutton laughed. 'You're not the first person who's had that desire, though it's usually the women who have the knives out for him. Bastard he certainly is and no mistake. Poor Miss Cabot. Mind you, I thought the whole thing was pretty damn fishy in the first place. Didn't really see Manners as being the type to own a daughter. Wouldn't recognise one even if he did. Pity, because she seems a nice enough girl. Not the usual run of adventuress. Unwise choice of blackmail target, if that was what she was trying on. Manners is a past master at that sort of thing. Not my business, thank God ... Now, sir, armoured trains. That *is* my business. Straighten your lapels. You, you lucky fellow, have got an appointment with General Chang Hsueh-liang.'

As the two men walked in the direction of the food tent, the band struck up an idiosyncratic rendition of 'The British Grenadiers'.

5

Dem Bones, Dem Bones

From the journal of William Lampsett, Reuters correspondent, Tientsin, 22 November 1922

I have been reading another thundering denunciation of Bolshevism in China by that pro-Japanese hack Manners who has drawn a fantastic picture of espionage masterminded by the small Russian mission in Peking. It is difficult to ascertain the strength of the fledgling Chinese Communist Party. Founded last year, the CCP has apparently held another congress this May in Hangchow, but I cannot for the life of me see that academics and intellectuals like Li Ta-chao and Chen Tu-hsiu can be a threat to anybody. There is hardly any proletariat to speak of in China, except in a few industrial cities like Shanghai and Wuhan. If Comrade Stalin is relying on such weak reeds as these for his revolution, it will be a long time a-coming but, God knows, China is in such a miserable mire of corruption and dissolution that anybody who wishes to do anything about it has my vote. I despair of Sun Yat-sen and his KMT. The local Canton warlord has said, 'Boo,' to him again, and once more he has fled with all his banker friends to Japan. He will be back no doubt but plus ça change.

Yu Fu-kuei thought she had buried her past, but it surprised her one morning in the shape of two letters on her breakfast tray. She adjusted herself against her pillows, sipped her coffee and scanned the lines of characters. If she retained her composure, it was only because she had trained herself to do so.

Who had written about dogs raking up old bones? Was it Webster or Middleton? '*The wolf which is foe to men ... With his nails he'll dig them up again?*' The Jacobean playwrights knew the distorted ironies of the cloaked and mirrored world. Perhaps the mask she wore could withstand any scrutiny. The beauty of masks, she thought, is that they can be worn or discarded at will, and one mask can hide another, and even the bare flesh disguised the skull. The emblem of the mask concealed a whole metaphysics of espionage.

That was what her metaphysically minded mentor from the Comintern had told her. The man she knew as Mr Behrens had spent a whole afternoon lecturing her about disguise. They had leaned over the rails of their ocean liner, watching the seagulls playing in the spray of the giant Atlantic swells. 'Only remember the rules of survival,' he had said.

'But surely we should still have in our minds the greater purpose?' she had asked.

'No,' he said. 'An understanding of purpose is not necessary for you or me. We are the worker ants, who do as we are instructed. The ant does not know what it carries, or why. It fulfils its function, then it dies. Think of its sacrifice, its self-abnegation. It is more beautiful than anything you will find in literature. Accept this, or we stop now.'

'We can hardly stop now. You've told me you're a member of the Comintern. Won't my knowledge of your secret be a threat to you?'

'I have revealed a mask, that is all,' he said. 'You know me as the German, Mr Behrens, with his respectable banker's face. If here on this deck, you were to shout out now, "Come, everyone, listen! Mr Behrens is a spy!" who would believe you? They would see me shaking my head sadly. This poor crazy Chinese woman. And when we arrive in port, after I walk in a dignified fashion down the gangplank, what then? Mr Behrens disappears. What was his real name? You will never know, and I will have forgotten. I am only whom the Party wishes me to be.'

'What if someone from your past recognises you?' she had asked.

'In rare cases you may have to eliminate a person if he or she is a threat,' he said, 'but usually it is not necessary, for such is the strength of the mask. If you wear it confidently enough, that is all anyone will see. You adapt the expression on the mask to the new circumstance, and the disguise is stronger than it was before.'

'What if a friend or family member discovers your secret? Must you eliminate them?'

Mr Behrens had smiled. 'You are forgetting some of my earlier lessons. You no longer have friends. They may destroy you. You have no family. Only the Party. Remember the worker ant. But enough of this philosophy. I was telling you about dead letterboxes and codes. Shall we continue?'

For her it had been easy. She had no family: her father had disinherited her. Her disgrace had been her protection. Confucian society had made her into a non-person. When she and Wang had moved to Shanghai, it had been a further step into anonymity. What remained of the old Fu-kuei had died under torture in prison, and her former identity cremated afterwards. The furnace had consumed her innocence, her self-respect, her pride, her desires, even her capacity to love. Only one part of her stubbornly remained, like charred bones raked along with ashes into the urn: her will, and her intellect; she was a hungry ghost of her former self, existing in her half-resurrected state to perform the tasks set her by the Party.

Like mediums, however, the letters on her breakfast tray were attempting to call her back to life. The coincidence that they had arrived together, with postmarks from two different ends of the country, seemed like a concerted effort from powers beyond the grave.

She read them again, coldly. The first was from her brother, Fu-cheng, who was now a warlord's functionary in her native Shishan. That would explain how he had found her. If there were Yang Yi-liangs working for General Sun Chuan-fang in Shanghai, their equivalents would be employed in the intelligence services of other warlords. She should have thought of that. Perhaps she should have changed her name. It was too late for that now. A pity.

She read emotionlessly as her brother described the joy that the discovery of her present whereabouts had occasioned. He had pleaded with their father, she read, and although the old man had been stubborn at first he had finally wept and relented; he too had nursed a desire all these years to be reunited with his daughter. Her brother looked forward to seeing her shortly when he visited Shanghai on official business. He was eager to meet Major Yang, whose reputation had travelled even as far away as Shishan. He concluded that perhaps the hand of Fate had played a part in this. His ultimate master, Marshal Chang Tso-lin, desired better relationships with other regional generals and, confidentially, he was coming to Shanghai to seek a way of forging closer links with General Sun Chuang-fang. Perhaps Fu-kuei, with her connections, could assist him. Perhaps together they might play a small part in the bringing of peace to their country.

It was evident what her brother wanted. She had always liked and admired him, but she recollected the self-interest behind his every action.

A postscript described a visit he had recently made to the house of their family friends, the Leis. Their sister Fu-hong was well, he wrote, and happily married to Lei Tang. Fu-kuei might be pleased to hear that she had three nephews. He described an unfortunate event that had occurred over dinner, when the daughter of the house, Lan-hua, had astounded everybody by refusing to marry the man her father had chosen. He had gone on to describe the extraordinary announcement by Lei Ming that he had married an American, who was a friend of a red-headed English girl who was staying with the old foreign missionary whom Fu-kuei might remember from Shishan.

Fu-kuei wondered why he had chosen to include this random piece of information. He could not be aware that she knew this 'red-headed English girl', could he? Surely this had to be yet another coincidence? But it disturbed her.

The next letter might have been a sequel to her brother's because it was from Lei Lan-hua. In many ways it was more alarming than Fu-cheng's, because Lan-hua had evidently assumed Fu-kuei was still the revolutionary activist she had been at university. It started with a description of the sorrow Lan-hua had felt when she had heard that Fu-kuei had been imprisoned. She, like everybody else, had thought that she had died 'a martyr to the cause', but now she knew that Fu-kuei had somehow miraculously escaped 'to continue the fight' and was alive, 'the flame of joy' inside her had blazed bright again, 'like the white sun on the Nationalist flag'. She looked forward to the day when Fu-kuei and she could 'stand together on the barricades', as they had once marched together at Tiananmen.

The naïvety of the girl, thought Fu-kuei. Such nonsense could be subject to fatal misinterpretation if this letter fell into the wrong hands.

Lan-hua, she read on, had left her home and, after several melodramatic adventures, had found a job in the propaganda department of the Kuomintang Central Committee in Canton. She now lived in a dormitory with other activists and worked in an office next to that of Dr Sun Yat-sen, whom she referred to as the President. It was the following paragraph that alarmed Fu-kuei.

In my lowly position I know only a little of what is being planned, but we see things and we hear things. I have a friend who is in contact with a certain revolutionary party, which as you know was established in Shanghai last year (were you a founder member?!) and he told me that President Sun has recently received several visitors from Moscow! This morning we received a visit from President Sun himself, accompanied by his chief of staff, Chiang Kai-shek and his vice president, Liao Chung-k'ai. President Sun spent a full minute by my desk! You can imagine how I was inspired in the presence of this great revolutionary. Perhaps it was your example that gave me the courage, but I asked him if in our national struggle we could expect support from the world revolutionary movement. I will never forget his kindly expression as he laid a gentle hand on my shoulder and told me to 'work hard. Have faith. One day we will achieve everything we desire.' He had answered me. His message rings in my ears like the noise of trumpets heralding the fulfilment of everything for which you and I have ever dreamed.

The girl's naïvety was beyond belief, thought Fu-kuei. That the Comintern was seeking links with the Nationalists was no surprise. Two years before Lenin had laid out a strategy in his criticism of 'left-wing' Communism that non-Communist national movements could be supported if they, like the Kuomintang, were anti-imperialist. She doubted whether a vain bourgeois like Sun Yat-sen would ever seriously give them time of day. That was why the Comintern had hidden deep-set agents such as herself in the system, unknown even to the fledgling national Communist groups. She had asked Mr Behrens whether they would be co-operating with the Chinese Communist Party, and he had reacted with as much horror as if she had expressed a desire to join the Catholic Church. 'Do you think world revolution is a game?' he had asked. 'To be entrusted to children?'

If Lan-hua's letter was anything to go by, Mr Behrens's alarm about the CCP was more than justified. What baffled her was how such a flighty girl had heard of her survival and found her address?

She re-examined the envelope, and noticed that another piece of paper was caught inside. A postscript was scrawled on it in large, childish characters:

I forgot to say how I found you again. The answer is – John Soo! He is working here as an engineer, and two weeks ago we met at a dance. I have been seeing him almost every evening. He is such a wise, kind man. He told me all about Oxford and about you. And do you know another extraordinary coincidence? He also told me that you were friends with an English girl called Catherine Cabot. She is a friend of mine too!

This was not just coincidence, thought Fu-kuei. This was an inundation of coincidences, enough to wash away the soil covering a whole graveyard of secrets. Yes, stupidly, she had given Yi-liang's address to John Soo so that he could forward some books to her. Stupid! She had never imagined such consequences.

The weirdest part of it was that both letters had mentioned Catherine Cabot, the one person in the world to whom she had revealed her connection with the Third International. She poured herself another cup of coffee, and ate the *congee* in her bowl. As she did so she began to analyse the implications. Sure enough, using Mr Behrens's methodology, she began to glimpse opportunities behind apparent threats.

First she satisfied herself that neither of these unwelcome correspondents was attempting to blackmail her. Her brother appeared to accept at face value that she was a secret policeman's mistress and was interested only in her connections with the southern warlords. Lan-hua's gushy surmises were based on no evidence. She would, of course, show both letters to Yi-liang. He had probably read them already. She had been trained to assume that nothing received in the open post was secure. If she was monitoring his mail, it made sense to assume that he was monitoring hers.

Lan-hua's letter was actually a gift. Far from inciting suspicions about her, such nonsense could go a long way to allaying doubt. She and Yi-liang could laugh about it. Perhaps they might amuse themselves by composing a curt reply, in which she would tell Lan-hua that she had long ago put aside the naïve idealism of her youth, and now deplored the revolutionary sentiments expressed by her gauche young friend. The girl's hero worship would turn to disappointment and perhaps hatred, and with luck she would never hear from her again. She wondered about John Soo. Never once during her time at Oxford had she revealed to him any interest in politics. If Lan-hua talked to him about this, John Soo might be disappointed in his old university friend but her response would seem credible. Her mask would be strengthened.

Her brother's letter was helpful too. Yi-liang would take a professional's interest in the bait being dangled, and with luck would see an opportunity to advance his own career. If General Sun agreed to adopt an informal diplomatic channel with Marshal Chang Tso-lin, and if she could engineer it so that the meeting took place at her house . . . well, that could be very exciting indeed. It would certainly interest her shadowy masters who communicated with her through the dress shop. She might even have to order another ballgown on the strength of it.

The real problem was Catherine. Ludicrous as it seemed, the English girl had become a threat. She could not fault Mr Behrens's logic. The probability that Catherine was not aware of the significance of what Fu-kuei had told her made her no less dangerous. She had only to mention to Fu-kuei's wily brother that she had once had a conversation with Fu-kuei about the Third International, and his suspicions would immediately be aroused. Fu-kuei could imagine Catherine blurting out the information as a thoughtless joke and with her infectious laugh, 'Do you know, Minister Yu? As you were talking just now about those ghastly Bolsheviks on your borders, I was reminded that I was once asked if I was a Comintern agent! By your own sister! Can you imagine? I don't know what got into her!' Fu-Kuei smiled with affection for her impulsive friend, but was appalled by the malevolent fortune that had acquainted Catherine with her brother and her girlhood companion.

It was no use regretting it or blaming herself. Catherine's innocence was neither here nor there. One of Mr Behrens's less attractive aphorisms had been that history advances on bleeding feet.

No amount of mask juggling could solve this one now. She heard from far away Mr Behrens's voice: 'In rare cases you may have to eliminate a person if he or she is a threat.'

Eliminate Catherine? The idea was absurd. What was Fu-kuei meant to do? Stalk her down a dark alley with a poignard?

She saw her face reflected in the coffee cup, which was trembling in her hands. It resembled a death mask. Empty eyes gazed back at her implacably.

And she knew that all it would take was a simple sentence on a piece of paper left under a carpet. A scrap of information to be processed by wiser heads than hers. One day the newspapers might report a car accident in far-away Tientsin: sententious paragraphs describing 'the tragic loss of a young life, mourned by her many friends', and Fu-kuei would never know if this was not just another sad coincidence. *Remember the worker ant . . . its sacrifice, its self-abnegation . . . more beautiful than anything you will find in your literature.*

She raised the cup to her lips. The coffee was cold. She felt the pot. That also was cold. She reached for the bell to call the *amah*. Her finger rested on the button, in two minds as to whether she should press it or not.

Fu-kuei might have appreciated the irony, had she known that, while she contemplated a death's head in her coffee cup in Shanghai, the subject of her reverie was standing before an actual grave in Shishan several thousand miles to the north. In a memorial garden by a little church that overlooked a medical mission on a hill above a windswept plain, Catherine was gazing sardonically at a headstone that bore her own surname. She was wondering what she would be doing now if she still believed that the man interred below it, Tom Cabot, had been her father.

The garden was neglected and overgrown. The yew trees still marked a sombre ring round the graves, but the metal gate was rusted, hanging on one hinge, and other, more unruly vegetation had been allowed to grow with abandon over, under and around the neat spaces that Nellie Airton had once designed. In the summer this must be a jungle, but winter had already stripped the branches, and the undergrowth had rotted, leaving dry stalks protruding from a thick carpet of leaves.

If Catherine had been Tom Cabot's daughter, she would probably have spent some time tidying his plot. She pictured herself whispering a prayer, as she laid out her flowers to honour him. Rosemary for remembrance? Pansies for thoughts? Fennel, columbine, daisies and violets? She would almost certainly have been proud of him, she decided, this hero of the Boxer rebellion. She would have found comfort here, something to compensate for the bitter loneliness of her vagrant childhood. She might even have left this cemetery a little more at peace with her past.

A gust of wind scattered the dry leaves. It was bitingly cold. The Airtons's missionary friend, Dr Brown, had said that later it might snow.

As she watched Nellie moving among the graves, tidying away the worst of the undergrowth obscuring the stones that marked where her friends lay, Catherine felt a momentary anger that the old woman had insisted she accompany her to this place. Nellie had correctly pointed out that not only Tom Cabot but Helen Frances's father was also buried here. He had apparently been among the first victims of the Boxers. His stone cross was bigger than any of the others. It protruded from the leaf pile like a ziggurat from a lost city. To please Nellie, she had gone through the motions of paying her respects at his grave. She knew that her mother's maiden name had been Delamere. Now she saw through the foliage that her grandfather's first name had been Franklin. That doubled what she knew about him. Her mother had hardly ever mentioned him, as she had rarely mentioned Tom Cabot. They might as well have been strangers, as were all the other martyrs buried here

– Germans, Americans, Italian nuns, several children – a motley collection in a forgotten plot, sad casualties of a senseless war and, for Catherine, just as anonymous as all the hundreds of thousands of other victims of that subsequent, greater war in which she had participated.

Once she would have been moved. Now she did not think she cared.

Looking at her own name carved on a stranger's stone, she suddenly appreciated the true irony of it all. Her quest had not been unsuccessful: it had succeeded only too well. She had sought a real father, and she had found him, and now she knew who she was. Or, rather, what she was. 'Bastard' was a singularly apt term. She was the progeny of a callous adventurer and a weak-minded trollop. Waif she was, and waif she always had been. She was astounded by her capacity for self-deception. Henry Manners's cold rejection, the economy of his contempt, was almost to be admired. It was all that she deserved.

What had she expected? 'I thought you were seeking a father's love,' Edward Airton had once said to her. He had probably been right. How pathetic. How foolish. How credulous. She should be grateful to Henry Manners. He had reminded her of what the world was like. It was not as if she did not already know: three years of bloody warfare, the massacre of her friends, the Russian revolution and a short spell in the Lubyanka had reinforced the lessons of her childhood. Even these gravestones in a Chinese cemetery told the same story. If anybody believed that love could survive in a world such as this, they were blinding themselves to reality.

'Catherine, are you all right?' She heard Nellie's voice from across the garden.

'Yes, Aunt Nellie, perfectly fine, thank you.'

It had taken her a while to recover from the shock. She had remained in her hotel room. The Airtons had been kind. She remembered them coming in and out, sometimes with a tray of food, or a bowl of fruit, and once a box of chocolates, as if she were a hospital patient. 'You must eat, dear,' Nellie had said. 'You must remain strong.' Thankfully, she had had the tact not to say much more than that, and after a while, Catherine had even found some comfort in the presence of the prim, severe woman, sitting in the armchair opposite her, her eyes contemplating Catherine with tender sympathy.

Sometimes during that first day she had sunk into a dream about her childhood. She had become a little girl again, wetting her finger to make the hole in a *shoji* door. There was her beautiful mother with her kindly uncle, but this time they were not arguing, and she was so happy as she watched them smiling and holding hands – but she must have made a sound, because her kindly uncle suddenly turned, and thrust a glowering face right up to the hole in the paper door, sneering at her with venomous hatred and contempt.

After one of these nightmares she had woken to find not Nellie but Edmund sitting in the armchair opposite her. He was reading a newspaper, and smoking his pipe. He was not aware that she was awake, and she watched him for a while. He was frowning, which accentuated the furrow on his forehead. His stillness calmed her. She felt warm, and, surprisingly, content. Almost at peace. She noticed that somebody had placed a blanket over her. The curtains had been closed, and the lamp by her turned-down bed threw a soft light into the room, its pool intersecting with the larger pool of light projected by Edmund's reading lamp.

She examined him curiously, noticing the fine hairs on the back of his hands, the straight nose, the well-shaped lips. She had always thought Edmund had a handsome face but now she saw dignity in the way he held his head, nobility in his high brow. She had an urge to straighten a loose lock that was hanging over his right eye.

Something must have made him conscious that he was being observed because he put down his pipe and newspaper and smiled at her. 'Hello, Catherine,' he said. He uncurled from his armchair and put a palm on her forehead. His hand felt soft and cool. Then he took her wrist and felt her pulse. 'You'll do,' he said. 'Mother thought you might be coming down with a fever, and asked me to sit with you. She and Father had to go out to dinner with the Gillespies.'

'How long have I been asleep?' she asked.

'Oh, hours,' he said. 'Best thing for you. Mother thought of putting you to bed, but we decided not to disturb you. I think you should now, though. Think you can get to sleep again without a draught? I could easily fix one for you.'

Catherine shook her head. She still felt exhausted.

'That's my girl,' he said. 'Listen, I'll slip down the hall to fetch Mother – I think I heard them return – and she can help you undress.'

'Edmund . . .' Suddenly she did not want him to go.

He waited by the door, the kind smile on his face.

'Thank you,' she whispered.

'Poor old thing,' he said. 'How I feel for you.' And he was gone.

The next day when Nellie came into her room with a breakfast tray, she looked surprised that Catherine was up and dressed, sitting in her armchair, where she had been since five. She returned Nellie's greeting coldly. Nellie had asked her whether she was up to coming with them to the Tung Ling, the mausoleum of Nuurhachi, the founder of the Manchu empire – the Gillespies were organising a picnic there today. Catherine had said she would rather remain in her room. Nellie had then suggested that she stay behind to keep her company. She would rather be alone, Catherine had told her. Faced with such hostility, Nellie had left. Catherine had remained where she was for another two hours, contemplating again the scornful face of Henry Manners – but today she felt like scratching it with her fingernails.

The fury inside her made her restless. Towards mid-morning she left her room and strode along the hotel corridors, down the staircase and into the lobby, where she stopped, because she had no idea of what she wanted to do. The manager approached, bowed unctuously in his morning coat, and asked her if she was feeling better today. She glared at him, and he stammered something about young Mr Airton staying behind, and that he was in the billiard room.

'Catherine!' George cried, when she walked in. 'You're up! Good for you, old thing! That's the indomitable spirit!'

Catherine frowned.

'I say,' said George, noticing her expression. He raised his hands in mock surrender. '"Hell hath no fury", eh? Well, that's fine by me, old girl. Wondered when you'd come back hitting. If you need any help in giving what's what to that monster of a father of yours, then St George is your man. Murder most foul. You name it.'

'Pass me one of those cues,' said Catherine.

'That's one weapon, I suppose,' said George, handing over his own. A look of comic concern came over his features. 'Look here, you don't intend to practise by bashing me over the head with that thing, do you?'

Catherine glanced at him with contempt. 'Shut up, George, and lay out the balls.'

He did as he was told, setting the red ball on the seven spot, and positioning a white ball on the D. 'I'm playing English rules. Three balls. That suit you? We can play snooker, if you like. No? All right, you can have the ball with the spot. I'll start with the other, shall I?'

He leaned over the baize and cued his white towards the red. There was a satisfying click. The red ball slewed neatly towards the far left pocket, but bounced off the cushion, coming to rest a few inches away from the white. 'There,' he said. 'I've given you an easy canon to start off with. I'll put your ball in the D now. Aim it at the white and you should hit the red as well.'

Catherine ignored him. Leaving her ball where it was, she moved to the side of the table and sighted her cue on George's ball. She cued it viciously and it hit the red ball, spinning off it and disappearing into the pocket on the right.

'Well done, Catherine,' said George, bemused. 'But you do know you've being using the wrong ball? That happens to be mine you've just pocketed.'

Catherine gave no indication that she had heard him. She was now sighting on the red ball, aiming at the same pocket. She cued hard, but the ball missed, ricocheting round the baize.

'You're not meant to cue the red ball, Catherine,' said George. He was looking a little alarmed.

Again she ignored him. She picked up the red ball, placed it back in its position of the last shot, then slammed it into the pocket. She moved back to the other end of the table, and this time cued her own white ball, which had remained where it was in the D. It rolled the length of the table. Eventually she potted it.

'Very good. That's all the balls gone,' said George, quietly. 'What now? My innings, is it? . . . I see. Not my innings.'

Catherine had taken the three balls back out of the pockets, and rolled each hard across the table. After that she proceeded to pocket them, one after the other. Then, as George watched incredulously, she started the whole process all over again. He put his cue back into the rack. 'If you'll excuse me, old girl, I think I'll leave you to your therapy,' he said. 'You'll find me in the bar.'

Catherine did not look up. She was sighting on the red ball. She clicked it viciously. Like all the others, it bore Henry Manners's face.

By next morning, to all appearances, she had recovered. She had her bags packed early, ready for their departure to Shishan. She no longer felt self-pity or rage, only a cold apathy. It seemed to come from within, starting in the vacuum where she supposed her heart had been, spreading outwards to her limbs. She could function – and even laugh, when she had to, at George's jokes – but she rarely contributed to, and never initiated, a conversation.

It was better once the train ride had started, and she could sit by the window, watching the flat, anonymous farmland flashing by. The remains of haystacks rotting in the millet fields, cottages with matting drying on the roof and corncobs hanging from the windows, thatched drying houses, and lines of peasants on the banks of the irrigation ditches had intrigued her on the previous journey. Today these things hardly registered. They were certainly not enough to distract from the clackety-clack of the wheels that drove away thought.

She had emerged only once from her self-imposed stupor, when she found herself alone with Edmund in the dining-car. The elder Airtons and George had gone back to their sleeping compartments after their meal, and Edmund had remained to smoke his pipe. For a while they had sat facing each other without speaking. Vaguely she was aware that the landscape had changed. Since they had turned north from Chin-chou they had entered a wilder countryside of rolling hills, with fir trees and occasionally a temple or pagoda silhouetted on the skyline.

'We'll be getting to the Black Hills soon. That'll be real forest.'

Edmund had finally broken the silence. She gave no indication that she had heard him. He continued patiently, 'We'll steam through a long tunnel, and follow a river, and then we'll hit the Shishan plain. Fields of millet and soy beans with a monastery in the distance. An old pagoda. Beautiful rich farmland. Poplar and willow trees lining the roads.'

He paused to relight his pipe.

'I remember rather a rustic little station. It may have changed by now, of course. It's fifteen years or so since I was there, but I doubt the Chinese city will be much different. There are great crenellated walls, and gates with portcullises, just like in crusader castles. Inside there are temples and markets. Dust. Smells. People. Everything I love about China. We used to be picked up by a pony cart and clatter up the hill to the old medical mission. For me, on a long leave between school and medical college in Scotland, it was like coming back to my real home. We'd go for long rides in the summer and autumn, and in winter we'd skate on the frozen river.'

He puffed away at his pipe, but his brown eyes watched her closely. After a while he leaned forward, and asked softly, 'How are you, Catherine? Is it still hell?'

'I'm fine,' she answered automatically. Then something in his expression made her add, 'No, Edmund. I'm empty. Lost.'

Edmund nodded. 'It'll take time,' he said.

'Was I wrong? To want to find him? To seek him out?'

'No,' he said.

'He looked at me as if he hated me.'

He took his pipe from his mouth and placed it in the ashtray. He reached across the table and gently took her hands. 'Poor you,' he said. He rubbed her knuckle with his thumb.

She found it soothing. At the same time she felt she wanted to cry. 'He's my father, Edmund. He is, you know. And he knew I was his daughter.'

'I think he did.'

'Then why? Why didn't he accept me?'

'I don't know,' he said. 'Perhaps he wasn't ready for you. Perhaps you weren't ready,' he added.

'I don't understand.'

'I'm not sure if I do,' he said, 'but sometimes things aren't as simple as we imagine, or as they appear on the outside. Not the things that truly matter. I'm sure it's never as easy as just wanting something. There's some sort of understanding involved. A purging maybe. Perhaps there's something you have to go through first, or something he has to do. I'm sorry, I'm not making much sense, am I?' He left off.

She sensed that he was embarrassed. She noticed that, with her own thumb, she had begun to knead his knuckle. Softly. Imperceptibly. 'No, you're not making much sense. Neither are you being very comforting.' She smiled. 'Don't you think that I've been purged enough, one way or another?'

'Yes.' He chuckled. 'When I think what you've gone through in your short life I'm amazed that you've turned out as you have. You're incredible, Catherine. And you don't deserve . . . you certainly didn't deserve . . .' His fingers tightened round hers. 'If only I knew how to turn the clock back, and make it so it never happened.'

'But it did happen. Like everything else happened. I'm sorry,' she said, 'I don't think there is a nice, neat plan in this world. It's not a question of being ready or not ready, understanding or not under-standing. There's nothing to understand, Edmund. No purpose. Just chaos and savagery and cruelty. If there is a God up there He must be cackling His head off. I'm sure He hates us.'

'That's how I felt after Ypres.'

'And what made you change your mind?' she asked. Their fingers were twining round each other, as if they were conducting a sepa-rate conversation. 'Did God come back and tell you this was all part of a plan?'

'No,' he said. 'I never did change my mind. I've never recovered my faith in God, at least not the one my parents believe in. I've never told them, of course. It would upset them. But slowly I did begin to see a purpose of a sort. Even chaos has a logic. Something emerges out of suffering. Courage. Kindness. Love. There is a heroism in just going on. I think one finds dignity and purpose in service to others. Anyway, service is enough to keep one going.'

Their palms were pressed flat against each other.

'It's easy for you,' she said. 'You're a doctor.'

'First class.' He smiled. 'But, Catherine, you were once a nurse. A damned good one, as it happens.'

'Not any more.'

'I don't believe you,' he said.

She felt tears again in her eyes. 'Edmund, I can't,' she said. 'I've tried but I can't. Not after . . . Not after . . . I don't know how to love,' she whispered, clasping his hands tighter.

'I don't believe you,' he said. 'You blaze with passion and laughter and generosity. That's love. I've never known anybody so animated with the sheer joy of life. That's love. What did that Russian keep calling you? He's right, you know. You are an angel. At least, you are for me. Oh, Catherine, you don't need to go looking round the world for some mythical father figure who'll somehow . . . I don't know . . . To tell you the truth, I never really understood what you were looking for. But you don't need him.'

She was weeping now. 'But I need something, Edmund. You don't know how empty it is being me. I need somebody . . .'

Edmund leaned forward and pressed her hands to his lips. 'Catherine, I know this is not the right time, and . . . I'm years older than you are . . . but . . .'

'Oh, Edmund, don't. Don't . . .' But she did not attempt to take her hand away.

'Well, that's a picture out of a book!' George said, behind her. 'Knight comforting damsel in distress. The real *Morte d'Arthur*. But I say, Catherine, this is a bit thick of you, old girl. I thought I was the St George in your life. Ah, well, women's hearts are fickle. Now then, listen. I've been lying on my bunk the last half-hour, swinging like a budgerigar, and very bored, and I was wondering if either of you two would like a game of craps to pass the time. I've got some dice . . .'

She couldn't stand it. She rose unsteadily to her feet and pushed past George towards the sleeping compartment. She was not sure from which of the two brothers she most wanted to escape.

Late in the evening they had arrived in Shishan. It had been like steaming into Mukden again, although this time there was no fog, and the squat buildings of the Japanese cantonment were smaller. Surprisingly, for this time of night, a lot of people were milling about the platform, which was brightly lit by arc lights. And as the train jerked to a halt, above the hiss of the steam, she heard the tinny notes of a brass band. A red banner hung from the roof, and in large white letters she read, 'SMR is proud to welcome famous citizen Dr Airton and family homecoming to Shishan!'

A small reception committee was standing at the end of a red carpet. At another time it might have struck her as comic or surreal, but in her present mood, these bowing, scraping people were just further obstacles she had to pass before she was allowed to go to her hotel room where she hoped to be alone again. She followed the Airton party abstractedly, shaking hands with a dignified Japanese man in a top hat who introduced himself as Mr Tadeki, general manager, Southern Manchurian Railway Corporation, Shishan. He was also apparently the mayor, and he had a wife dressed in traditional clothes, with whom Catherine also shook hands after much bowing. Then she was faced by a fat, grinning young man in military uniform: Captain Fuzumi, commander of the Shishan Railway Garrison. More bows. There were other morning-suited dignitaries along the line, and at the end two or three venerable-looking Chinese merchants, who appeared over-whelmed when they saw Edward and Nellie Airton. There was much weeping and embracing all round.

Edward himself introduced her to one frail old fellow, leaning on a stick. He had white bushy eyebrows, and a face so wrinkled it looked like a cracked eggshell. 'Catherine, this is my old friend Lu Chin-tsai. Your grandfather's partner, dear, at Babbit and Brenner.' Tears were running down the old men's faces.

Nellie had then taken her arm, and introduced her to another merchant, a big, heavy-featured man in his mid-sixties. 'Catherine, this is Yu Hsin-fu, whose son and daughter you met at the Leis' Mid-autumn Festival party in Tientsin a while ago.'

'Delighted,' she had murmured again, only vaguely realising he must be Fu-kuei's father. All she wanted to do was leave. But first there had been speeches, in Japanese, in Chinese, in English. Then Mr Tadeki had given the Airtons a city key, and there had been interminable posing for photographs.

She was aware that an unctuous-looking Englishman was

hovering around all these proceedings, bowing and scraping, rubbing his hands. He had thin strands of yellow hair pasted over his balding crown, a red button nose, red spots on his otherwise pasty cheeks, and he was wearing a dog collar. He had bobbed up to her, blinking and smiling, and told her that he was the Reverend Dr Brown, and he had taken over the mission in Shishan from the Airtons twelve years previously. 'I'm so pleased that you have come,' he told her. 'To have the Airtons and a Cabot back all in one go! What a joyful reunion! Your dear, departed father is so famous, of course, God rest his soul. A tragic martyr's death, but pleasing to the Lord. You must be so proud of him. And of your mother too, of course. Sadly I never met either. Or your grandfather. Of course, he is a martyr too.' He cleared his throat. 'Yes, well, a joyful reunion. Mr Tadeki and I thought that this little welcome would be appropriate.'

'Delighted,' said Catherine again, extending her hand.

Finally it had ended, and she, Edmund and George had been taken to Shishan's smaller version of a Yamato hotel opposite the station, while the elder Airtons were to stay at the mission. They would breakfast together at Dr Brown's home. She had declined to join Edmund and George for a late supper. The latter had given her a flamboyant goodnight embrace at the bottom of the staircase, while Edmund stood uncomfortably to the side.

She had taken his hand, and kissed his cheek. 'Catherine,' he began, 'this afternoon . . .'

'Not tonight. Tomorrow, perhaps. I'm sorry, I'm just too worn down – but thank you,' she said, squeezing his hand. 'Thank you.'

The room was smaller than the one she had had in the Mukden Yamato, but in terms of furnishings exactly equivalent. Just after turning out the lamp she had a vivid image of Edmund's hand holding hers. The sensitive fingers. The golden hairs. But it was not long before a raddled, scornful face made its customary appearance, and when she slept, she experienced the same, searing dreams.

Breakfast with the Browns had been a trial. He had driven them out of the Japanese town into the countryside and up the hill to the mission. Green-tiled roofs glinted in the pale morning sunshine above a red-brick two-storeyed hospital, and on the crest of the hill was a Gothic-looking church. It seemed incongruous in a Chinese pastoral setting but there was a certain Turneresque resonance about this piece of England set against the scudding grey clouds. The Airtons had lived in a small flat at the hospital, but the Browns had built a bungalow on the side of the hill, and in the cramped dining room they had sat down to porridge, ham on buttered toast, and tea. Dr Brown's wife, Lettice, was a frail creature who was bravely coping with a headache. This involved much sighing, fluttering of hands and scurrying about by Dr Brown. Her two girls, Rosemary and Hannah, were wan, thin-faced creatures, and had apparently learned not to speak unless spoken to. Their big eyes followed everything that was going on, but whenever either parent addressed them, Catherine noticed a twitch of alarm.

For most of the meal Dr Brown had conducted a monologue, almost a paean of praise, about the warlord of Shishan, General Lin Fu-po, whom he admired for his enlightenment as a ruler. 'To call him a Lorenzo or a Cosimo may be taking it a little far,' he said smugly, buttering a piece of toast for his wife, 'but in Chinese terms he resembles a Renaissance prince. He has a passionate interest in the welfare of his citizens, and a fervent desire to beautify his city, the Chinese town I mean, and to modernise it so that one day it will equal, probably excel, our not unimpressive little SMR cantonment, which you have seen. This spirit of friendly competition between General Lin and Mr Tadeki, both excellent men, is to be encouraged. Don't you agree, darling?' He handed Lettice her toast. She sighed, and murmured something incomprehensible.

'Of course, sadly,' continued Dr Brown, 'General Lin has been preoccupied recently with these troublesome wars, so his schemes have had little chance to flower, but I have had the honour to be shown some of his plans, and they are very impressive. Very impressive indeed. And he is even interested in religious matters. I have his promise – it has not yet actually transpired – that one day I might be allowed to give a sermon to his troops. You never know. The so-called "Christian warlord", Feng Yu-hsiang, may not be the only one to baptise his soldiers with a hose! Ha-ha! I have my hopes. I have my hopes. Some more tea, dear?' he asked his wife.

It had been a relief when breakfast ended, and Dr Brown left with Edward Airton for a tour of the hospital. It had been arranged for Edmund and George to go riding around the environs of their old home. A horse had been saddled for Catherine too, but she had declined to join them. It was then that Nellie had suggested firmly that she accompany her to the graveyard.

And here she was now, in bitter contemplation of her abortive quest.

'I won't be long, dear,' called Nellie, 'but I must remove these brambles from Septimus's grave. The poor man's been obliterated. I don't know why that idiotic Richard Brown has not seen fit to keep this place in a state of proper preservation.' As she spoke she was tearing out weeds with a violence that Catherine had never associated with her.

'Perhaps he's too busy toadying up to that warlord of his,' continued Nellie, panting with her efforts. 'I happen to know General Lin. He is the most evil man I have ever met, and Richard talks about him as if he were a god. Look at the state of this grave! Did you see those two girls, Catherine? The poor, cowering little mites.'

'Yes, Aunt Nellie.' Catherine had been startled out of her self-absorption. She had rarely heard Nellie speak ill of anybody.

'I cannot abide cruelty or neglect. I always knew that Richard was a fool. He was ever conceited, but I had not imagined he would become so vain, so selfish and so ambitious – and I never suspected him of being a bully. And to his own children! It really is too bad. I blame that weak-minded wife of his as well. What kind of mother can she be?'

Catherine turned, fascinated. She had never seen Nellie in this mood. Nellie was straining at the brambles, her face furrowed with fury. 'Aunt Nellie, would you like some help?' she asked.

'No, dear, you'll scratch your hands – and, anyway, this is doing me good. There! Septimus can see the light again! Poor fellow, he was a dreadful father too, but at least he had the excuse that he was barking mad. And he made up for everything in the end. Richard Brown has no excuse. To think that I spent years of my life attempting to knock some sense into that thick head of his. I should have been concentrating on instilling in him some common decency. Well, that's it. Nothing much more I can do here for these lonely souls. It really is too bad.'

Examining her hands, Nellie walked the length of the now spruced-up headstones to where Catherine was standing. 'Look! I've torn my gloves and cut myself, but it was in a good cause. And I've had a chance to think. This is a good place for that. Catherine, I have a proposal. We won't be able to do much for those two little children in the long term – we'll be leaving Shishan in a couple of days – but we do have this afternoon. The boys will be riding until evening, and Edward's absorbed in the hospital. We had thought of having tea with old Lu Chin-tsai, but we can do that on another day, or Edward can represent me on his own. What you and I are going to do, if you're agreeable, is to give those two little girls the best treat of their lives. Lettice can stew in her vapours for all I care – but we are going to take Rosemary and Hannah for a long walk. They can pick berries, or run around and do what every little girl in the world ought to be allowed to do. And we're going to give them such a dose of good, honest love and affection that it'll warm them for a month.'

Catherine, stunned, nodded in agreement.

It was a glorious afternoon. A pale winter sun broke out of the clouds, restoring colour to the countryside. Hand in hand with the two little girls, they walked down the hill, all the way to the river. At first Rosemary and Hannah were nervous of the two grown-ups who had plucked them away from their lessons but, slowly, they relaxed, when first Nellie, then Catherine told them stories. 'I want you to help me find some secret places,' Nellie said, when they reached the bottom of the orchard. 'I used to know them when my own children were little and living here, and I can describe them to you. But grown-ups don't know how to look for things like children do, so you'll have to tell me when you spot them.' An exciting game began, in which Nellie led them first to an ancient fallen oak tree and told them to look for the magic hole (it was still there as the children discovered, one after the other, when they had crawled through the branches); and to the treasure bush where all the blackberries were; and to the squishy marsh (great fun here with gumboots stuck in the mud); and to the field of fairy mushrooms. Here Catherine saw an enormous toadstool, and picked it, screaming, 'It's mine! It's mine!' and Nellie cried, 'No, it's not!' and the two solemn-eyed little girls watched in amazement as two grownups chased each other round the field, laughing and eventually tripping over in the mud and getting very dirty. Then it was their turn to snatch a fairy mushroom, and soon they were all filthy after a long, tumbling chase, but quite warm.

When they reached the river, Nellie took them to the hidden island of the willow-tree king, where George and his brother had gone fishing, and here Catherine told them stories she had remembered suddenly from her own girlhood in Japan, Austria and Italy.

On the way back, Rosemary and Hannah, now happily holding Catherine's hands, while Nellie walked more sedately behind, skipped and jumped and told her about the little diary they were keeping about the adventures of their dolls. They had to keep it secret because Mummy and Daddy might not like them stealing time from their lessons. Catherine promised not to tell, feeling a great pang of grief and sympathy for them. By then, though, the children were laughing and yelling, vying to outdo each other in impressing the red-haired lady with their inventions. Before they reached the bungalow, they all clustered together for a hug.

They were met by an outraged Dr Brown in the kitchen. Nellie, muddy as she was, shoved him into the pantry before he had the chance to say a word to his children, and there, among the bullybeef tins and the preserves, she talked to him for a good fifteen minutes, as only Nellie knew how. It was a chastened Dr Brown who drove Catherine, Edmund and George back to their hotel an hour or so later.

As she stretched out in her hot bath before dinner, Catherine realised that for more than half a day she had not thought about Henry Manners. And perhaps it was the sensuous caress of the water, or the bubbles on her skin, or the delicious tingling in her fingers and toes as they were immersed in all-embracing heat after a cold afternoon's exertion that helped her decide to put him out of her mind. The happy laughter of the two little girls and the light in their faces lingered in her ears. What a simple thing it had been that Nellie and she had done for them, but what an effect it had had on those repressed children, and how happy it had made them all. Suddenly, she thought of what Edmund had said the day before. 'Service is enough to keep one going.' And, as she lay in the bath, an image of Edmund came to her. The calm, wise smile. The gentleness with which he had lifted her wrist when he checked her pulse. The soft touch of his lips on her knuckle. She remembered the closeness she had always felt towards him. Could there be more to it? she asked herself. Had he really been about to propose to her on the train? As the hot, soapy water caressed her breasts and thighs, it was not a matter of thinking any more, because her body had already decided. As the meniscus of the water tickled her exposed skin, she imagined Edmund's hands spreading over her body, and as she moved the smooth cake of soap down her belly towards a growing heat below, she placed the hot flannel over her face, and opened her lips to taste the wet cloth, dreaming it was her lover's, perhaps her husband's, kiss.

By the time she joined them in the bar, the brothers were in their dinner dress. They were talking to a tall, slightly stooping man, also in dinner dress, with a shock of pepper-grey hair, although she guessed he was only in his early forties. He had an aquiline nose, high cheekbones, humorous, observant eyes, and he wore an old-fashioned pair of *pince-nez*. Edmund introduced him as Professor Ralph Niedemeyer, from Philadelphia. They had met that afternoon, during their ride, when they had stumbled on his archaeological dig.

'What are you digging for?' she asked him, taking a cocktail from George.

Niedemeyer chuckled pleasantly, 'Well, Miss Cabot, it sounds pretentious when I put it so baldly, but I am looking for the origin of mankind.'

'In his Chinese form, I think you said,' murmured Edmund.

'Mankind sounds more impressive,' laughed the professor, 'but there are rather a lot of the Chinese version about, more than any other type of *Homo sapiens sapiens* on the planet, about four hundred million to be exact, so you must admit that it is a big pool to be going on with, but you're right, Dr Airton, I am specifically looking for the lost link that brought Chinese man as he is today to this country.'

'Hasn't he always been here?' asked Catherine.

'Not exactly,' said Niedemeyer, 'but I would hesitate to bother a beautiful young lady with a lot of dry facts, or dry bones, as it may be more appropriate to say.'

'Oh, don't worry about Catherine,' said George. 'She's a boffin. Has a degree from Oxford. That's more than I have. She even understands modern poetry. You know. Coffee spoons and all that. She should be able to handle bones.'

'Coffee spoons?' asked Niedemeyer, raising his eyebrows.

'Yes. Puddock,' explained George.

'I don't think I've ever read anything by Mr Puddock,' said the professor. 'The lady has me at an intellectual disadvantage.' He adjusted his *pince-nez*. 'My apologies for condescending, Miss Cabot. It is rare to see beauty matched by brains. But where to start? Perhaps you have heard of Chou K'ou Tian?'

'Even I know all about Chou K'ou Tian,' said George. 'That's where they discovered Peking Man, isn't it? I thought *he* was the Celestials' ancestor.'

'Unlikely, sir,' said the professor. 'What you call Peking Man is the oldest complete specimen of hominid we have found in China so far, but there's some disagreement in academic circles about how closely he is related to anybody around today. *Sinathropus pekinensis* goes back a very long way, ma'am. He had a low brain case and he was probably a cannibal. His sons were only a slight improvement on the father. By way of Paleolithic finds in the Ordos, we can trace a direct line down to an actual strain of *Homo sapiens*, who lived some twenty-five thousand years ago. And he might have had some justification in calling Peking Man granddad.'

'But the Chinese haven't?' asked Edmund. 'Why not?'

'The modern Chinese is a Mongoloid,' said Niedemeyer. 'The *Homo sapiens* who was discovered in Chou K'ou Tian is not. He was Paleo-caucasoid. He might be an ancestor of the Ainu in Japan at a stretch, but probably he's closer to the likes of us. There was not much difference between his Paleolithic ancestor and the

Mousterian-Aurignacian civilisations of Western Europe in the old stone age.'

'So who are the ancestors of the Chinese?' asked Edmund.

'We just don't know,' said Niedemeyer. 'We have a non-Mongoloid *Homo sapiens* in 25,000 BC, and next time we look there are fully developed Mongoloid societies in 2000 BC, the Yang Shao culture, for example, with their beautiful pots. That's High Neolithic stuff, and these are the boys from whom the Chinese are almost certainly descended. But what I want to discover is: what happened between 25,000 BC and 2000 BC? Where did these Mongoloids come from, and when, and who were they?'

'You must have a theory,' said Catherine. 'It'd be too much of an anti-climax if you didn't.'

'Well, Miss Cabot, I may have better than that.'

'Aha!' exclaimed George. 'He's got him in his trunk! *Hominoidus mongoliensius*!'

The professor laughed. 'Not quite,' he said, 'but let me give you my theory first. If you've followed me so far, you'll know we're looking at the emergence in China, some time between 25,000 BC and, say, about 4000 BC, of a Neolithic strain of hominoid with Mongoloid characteristics. Now, ladies and gentlemen, where else on the planet do we have Mongoloid types?'

'I'll make a guess,' said George. 'Montezuma. No, he was a Mexican. Who was the Inca? I've always thought those South American Indians look Chinese.'

'Idiot,' said Catherine.

'Not at all, ma'am. He's correct. There is a distinct racial resemblance between the Amerindian and the Oriental. They have common Mongoloid characteristics. Look at the epicanthic folds. If my theory is correct, at some time during the Ice Age, a group of Mongoloids crossed the Bering Straits and, if I'm right, conquered and populated the land mass that we know as China today.'

'You mean the Chinese are Americans?' asked George. 'A candidate for the forty-ninth state, perhaps?'

'I wouldn't go that far,' smiled the professor, 'but they and the Amerindians may have common ancestors.'

'And that's why you're digging in Shishan?' asked Edmund. 'Because you think Manchuria must have been on their route?'

'Exactly, sir. There you have my whole theory.'

'You see? I was right,' said George. 'It was Montezuma.'

'Allow me to show you something,' said Niedemeyer. Reaching into the pockets of his dinner jacket he produced an object wrapped in tissue paper. Unfolding it he produced two small bones. He placed them side by side on the bar. 'Now, what do you see? Can you spot any differences between them?'

'Not that I can make out,' said Catherine. 'What are they? Finger bones?'

'Yes, they are, Miss Cabot. Metacarpals, probably from a male hand. And, as you say, there's very little difference between them. However, you may be interested to know that the one on the left was discovered in California ten years ago and belongs to a hominid who lived some time between 12,000 and 10,000 BC. The one on the right was discovered at my dig in Shishan at four thirty this afternoon.'

'Well, I'll be damned,' exclaimed George.

'I am guessing that it dates back to about 8000 BC. If I can find the rest of the body, particularly the skull, I believe we will have our missing link. The true ancestor of the Chinese. I like to think that I will be reuniting a son with his proper father.'

'We'll have none of that, thank you,' said George. 'We've rather done reunions with fathers, I'm afraid.'

Niedemeyer looked puzzled, Edmund caught his breath, but Catherine, after a moment of shock, found herself laughing. It was as if an iceberg in her mind had drifted away.

Professor Niedemeyer declined their invitation to dinner. He said he had to go and meet his Chinese associates. Edmund and he exchanged visiting cards, and Professor Niedemeyer promised to call on him next time he passed through Tientsin. He bowed with old-world courtesy and left.

Both Catherine and George burst into laughter. 'What a nut!' giggled Catherine.

'Amerindians!' hooted George.

'Oh, I don't know,' said Edmund. 'I thought he made sense. I found it fascinating.'

'Do you remember the metacarpals in the tissue paper?' shrieked Catherine. 'Spot the difference!'

'I think you're both being very unkind,' said Edmund. Then his moustache quivered, and he was laughing as loudly as the others.

Catherine jumped off her stool, put her arms round him and kissed his cheek. 'Oh, Edmund.'

'You look on top form again, Nurse.'

'Partly thanks to you, Doctor,' she said, linking her arm with his. 'I've thought a lot about what you said yesterday.'

'All of it?' he asked quietly.

She kissed his lips.

'I say,' said George.

'Come on, let's go in to supper,' she cried. 'I want wine. Lots of it. I want to get really drunk.'

In the hill country north of the Liao Tung peninsula, not far from the borders of Fengtian and Korea, a mail train was making its dimly lighted passage through the night on its way from Dairen to Mukden.

In a first-class sleeping compartment, a shirt-sleeved Henry Manners was playing poker with an equally relaxed General Taro Hideyoshi. At least, the latter had unbuttoned his tunic, and he had certainly accounted for more than half of the contents of the near-empty whisky bottle that stood on the table between them, next to an ashtray already overflowing with cigar stubs.

'You have done well, Henry-san,' the Japanese was saying. 'Those Kwantung Army officers were pleased by your report.'

'I don't know why you needed an Englishman to deliver it,' muttered Manners. 'Your lot provided most of the material – or made it up.'

'It is psychology,' said General Taro. 'It is extraordinary how people are sometimes more inclined to believe things if they appear to come from an impeccable outside source, rather than from their own colleagues. And if, as you suggest, some of the matter may subsequently be discovered to have been . . . exaggerated, then, sadly, the authentic source becomes a tainted one, but the Kempeitai's reputation is unaffected.'

'Chang Tso-lin's military build-up is there for all to see,' said Manners. 'Aren't you painting legs on a snake, as they say?'

'No. The opinion of a noted foreign political commentator, who also happens to have a training function in the Mukden arsenal, is useful and convincing. I do not know if in this case everybody will choose to believe this threat from the warlord – as you know, there are as many factions within the army as within our pacifically minded government in Tokyo – but we will have given them food for thought. It is another grain of sand to add to the growing heap.'

'Chang's no threat to the Japanese,' said Manners. 'He's your client. He needs you to survive. Who will believe he has any intentions against you?'

'There was the bomb that exploded outside our own headquarters,' smiled the general.

'We all know who put it there. Or did you use the Black Dragon Society to do your dirty work for you? We all know the links between the patriotic Young Turks in the army and the Yakuza.'

'Oh, Henry-san, are you beginning to have scruples? It would be sad to think that my old friend is ageing.'

'Are we playing poker or not?' growled Manners.

'I think in our line of work we are always playing poker,' said the general, yawning and stretching his arms. 'When we are not enjoying our lives, sampling wine, food and women – or boys in my case. You especially, my friend, like women. I very much enjoyed your encounter with that red-haired girl the other day.'

'Cabot's daughter? What about her?'

'Is she Cabot's daughter? She does not resemble him. I recall him as an oafish, foolish young man. But she does resemble her mother – who was your mistress. In Shishan and later, if I am to credit the files, in your house in Honshu.'

Manners put down his cards. 'Are you spying on me, Hideyoshi?' he asked coldly.

'Why should I spy on you? We own you,' said the general.

'My private affairs are my own,' said Manners, reaching for his whisky glass.

General Taro laughed. 'The sensibility of a drug-runner! It is touching to see. Your hand is shaking as you hold that glass,

Henry-san. I do worry that you might be getting old. No, I am not spying on you, my friend. I am concerned for you. I am afraid you might be getting careless.'

'How so?' muttered Manners.

'That you failed to recognise your own daughter, perhaps?' suggested the general, quietly.

Manners's hands were still shaking as he put his glass on the table. 'That woman was not my daughter,' he said, his bloodshot eyes rising to look Taro in the face.

The Japanese held his gaze until Manners looked away, then laughed. 'So you say. So you say. Well, my friend, your private affairs are no concern of mine. Shall we continue our game?'

6

A Night at the Opera

From the journal of William Lampsett, Reuters correspondent, Tientsin, 24 November 1922

Catherine must be in Shishan now, the fiefdom of General Lin Fu-po, the man she once insulted in a bar. I wonder if they will meet him and if he will remember her.

He's a brute, like all of them, but one of the few warlords who actually knows his trade. He fought in the Sino-Japanese War of 1895. Was captured and escaped. A Chinese hero. The archives in our bureau are vague about his role in the Boxer affair, but after they were defeated, he had to go into hiding to escape the vengeance of the Russians who'd put a price on his head. For a while he conducted a sort of guerrilla campaign in the Black Hills. Ended up in Mongolia where he did the respectable thing for an out-of-work soldier, and became a bandit. His career has many parallels with that of his master, Chang Tso-lin, who, when the Russo-Japanese war broke out in 1904, used his bandits as irregulars on the side of the Japanese behind the Russian lines. It must have been about that time that Lin got to know Chang. After the war, he appears to have risen up the ladder as one of his trusty lieutenants. His great opportunity came after the revolution of 1911, when Chang sent him to pacify the Shishan area, which was still a hotbed of monarchists – and he ended up becoming the warlord there. Whatever people say about him, he is a brilliant tactician. He managed to capture and hold Jehol in the last war, when all of the rest of the Fengtian forces were being forced back, and made Chang Tso-lin's retreat possible. An interesting, eccentric fellow, who perhaps in other circumstances might have been a force for good in this benighted country.

Catherine wiped away the condensation on the window-pane and, beyond the roofs of the small Japanese rail town, saw a country-side white with frost, but the sun was climbing into a pale blue sky, and the icicles on the eaves were dripping into the puddles on the pavement. All was shining and sparkling, and even though she was shivering, her heart thrilled as she remembered the long kiss she and Edmund had shared at the door of her room last night.

At breakfast they were a little shy with each other. As usual Edmund was reading the Chinese newspapers, but she could see that he was finding it difficult to concentrate, snatching secretive glances at her. When their eyes met, she was amused to see him blush; then realised that the heat in her own cheeks meant she was doing the same. She chuckled. She had not behaved in this way since she was a young girl.

'What's the joke?' George asked, playing with his noodles. This provincial Yamato hotel did not run to an English breakfast.

'Oh, nothing.' Catherine and Edmund spoke together, and blushed again.

George smiled.

After breakfast, wrapped in heavy coats, they ordered two rick-shaws to take them to the Chinese town. Catherine and Edmund took the first and George sat alone in the one behind. The squat rickshaw boys, stripped to their vests despite the cold, chanted a low, monotonous dirge as their cloth-wrapped feet padded along the frozen mud of the road. Their breath hung in the air like puffs of tobacco smoke. Behind them a white cloud of steam from a refu-elling engine hung over the station, and thin grey columns of smoke rose from the town's chimneys.

Soon they were in the countryside. The furrows in the fields were lined with ice, like petrified foam on the crests of a black sea. Tall bare poplars flitted by, while crows made raucous cries as they gath-ered on the bare branches. Catherine and Edmund huddled together on their rocking cradle, the intimacy of the previous evening restored. Edmund kissed her, and she kissed him back.

The walls of Shishan came upon them suddenly. Catherine rose in her seat with a gasp of delight. The ancient battlements and turrets seemed to hang above the plain, like the fortress hill towns on a medieval manuscript. The red moss on the crumbling stonework shone in the mid-morning sunlight like gold tracery. Ahead the dark tunnel yawned under the great crenellated gate tower and Catherine realised that nothing would have changed since her mother first passed under the portcullis more than twenty years before. She knew that this ancient city had played a part in her own heritage, and the very walls seemed to reverberate with the secrets of her past.

The panting rickshawmen pulled up on the timbers of the bridge that crossed the moat in front of the gateway. Soldiers and customs men were examining the loads on peasant carts queuing to enter the city. A young man selling toffee apples was shouting at the top of his voice to drown the cries of a competitor selling pomegranates. Old women in padded jackets and brown headscarves gazed at them curiously. A red-cheeked baby bundled in wrappings on a woman's back bawled in terror at the sight of them. A group of coolies filed by with buckets hanging on bamboo poles. Catherine had seen similar sights before but today she was enchanted.

George came up as Edmund was paying off the rickshaw boys. 'I'm cold as a block of ice and stiff as a board,' he moaned, rubbing his hands. 'Wish I'd had somebody to cuddle with. What do you think of Shishan, Catherine? Suitably exotic? How did old Elroy Flecker put it? While you two have been imitating the proverbial lovebirds I've been mugging up "The Golden Road to Samarkand" in Papa's copy of *Hassan* – I snatched it from his library before we left. "Our camels sniff the evening and are glad,"' he quoted. Theatrically he raised a finger to his nose, and flared his nostrils. 'Mmm, it's not quite "mastic and terebinth and oil and spice" here, though, is it? What you're smelling are the drains – or the open sewers to be exact. Ah, the old Central Asia that I love!'

'The only thing you love is the sound of your own voice,' said Catherine, punching him lightly on the shoulder, 'and I'm not going to be put off by a few bad smells. I've come more than five thousand miles to see this place.'

'Come on,' said Edmund. 'Let's find the market square. There's rather a fine Confucian temple there.'

'And a brothel. It's also where they held the executions if I recall,' said George gaily.

Edmund glared at his brother. 'For God's sake, George,' he whispered, 'have some tact. That was where Catherine's grandfather and Tom Cabot lost their heads.'

'I mention it merely as a feature of the local history, Edmund,' replied George, equably. 'Are we not being antiquarians today?'

'Just have some consideration for her feelings after what she's gone through these last few days,' muttered Edmund. He ran after Catherine, who was striding ahead, giving no sign that she had heard the brothers' exchange. They walked through the great stone gate into the city. The wide street was a shoving, pushing throng of people from every class of society, rushing about their business. Catherine gazed up at the balconies of the houses on either side, from which hung laundry like draped flags, and the ornate shop-fronts with their tracery of flowers and strange beasts carved in delicate wooden panels. They were about half-way down the street – ahead they could see the *pailou* that marked the entrance to the square – when she saw a curio shop, with rows of dusty porcelain vases and umbrella stands, and shelves of bronze statuettes. 'Let's look in here,' she was about to say, when she was startled by a shout from the direction of the gate. The milling crowd began to scatter in apparently aimless panic. A toddler fell over in the mud, and her father ran back to scoop her up. Two boys were pulling a blind storyteller by the sleeve. Catherine was shoved backwards against the front of the shop, squeezed behind a tangle-haired Mongolian artisan and a fat merchant. Edmund was trying to push through the crowd to her side. Somebody had knocked his fedora over his eyes. 'What's happening?' she cried, half alarmed, half amused.

'Don't know,' he called. 'They seem to be clearing the road. See those soldiers with sticks?'

'I wouldn't want to be on the end of one of those *lathies*,' grinned George, whose sleek head had somehow emerged at her shoulder. 'Just look at them slashing away. Like the final furlong of the Ladies' Cup. Some grand panjandrum must be coming.'

As he spoke, they heard the drumming of hoofs, and a squad of wild Mongolian outriders cantered along the now cleared path towards the square. Long rifles bounced on their backs as they rode. Their narrow eyes squinted in their broad faces as they hunched forward in their strange wooden saddles. They looked cruel and alien under their shaggy fur caps, as if they had brought the cold winds of the steppes behind them.

They heard the blare of a klaxon and the sharp retort of exhaust. A green-bonneted Rolls-Royce was approaching from the gate, heading at great speed towards the Yamen, which they could make out by its green tiles on a wooded eminence that rose above the grey rooftops at the far end of the town beyond the *pailous* and the square. Catherine peered over the heads in front of her and felt a frisson of excitement as she identified the figure sitting bolt upright in the back.

General Lin looked every inch the warlord, she thought. He sat in the rigid posture of an emperor on his throne. He wore the padded blue uniform of a private, with no insignia, and a fur cap marked by a single star. His alert posture was that of a battle-hardened soldier and his set jaw reflected the ruthlessness of a conqueror. A leather-gloved hand rested firmly on the pommel of a sabre, which he had positioned upright by his seat. His other hand was raised in a Roman salute. He stared fixedly ahead, his scarred, hawk-like features made more sinister by the black goggles that shielded his eyes. Here was an absolute ruler, returning to his city and his people. But no cheer honoured this Chinese Caesar. In fact, to Catherine, all the bystanders looked cowed. Well, she thought, Aunt Nellie said he was evil. But in Russia she had long ago concluded that any general was more or less wicked: the more avuncular he seemed, the greater the carnage he would cause. At least General Lin looked the murderous part – but Nellie was right: there *was* something unsavoury about him. She remembered the gangsterish figure he had cut in Tientsin. It came to her that it was not apathy but fear he was striking in the breasts of his townsfolk. Yet she was fascinated by him. She had a strange premonition that their paths would cross again, and she remembered, uncomfortably, the words he had used when he had placed the money before her: 'down payment'.

Curiously, she was convinced, however unlikely it seemed, that he had noticed her presence as he drove by. This was nonsense, she told herself, but her sunny mood was shadowed by alarm.

A squadron of regular cavalry armed with carbines clattered past, and there was silence. The dust curled and gradually settled. The soldiers who had been keeping back the crowd shouldered their bayonets, formed into companies and marched off in the direction of the Yamen. Two hawkers resumed the argument they had been having before the soldiers appeared. A dumpling-seller began to shout his wares. A peasant farmer heaved his heavy load of vegetables on to his back. In ones and twos merchants in their brown gowns strolled sedately down the street as if they were unaware of the hurtling mule carts that had materialised from nowhere. The chaotic street life had absorbed the general's passing.

The little European party took a moment to recover, but soon they were on their way again towards the central square. The colourful life of Shishan ebbed and flowed about them, but Catherine could not forget the impression the general had made.

She would have been even more alarmed had she known that, at that very moment, as his motorcade wound up the hill to the Yamen, General Lin was pondering the glimpse of red hair he had seen in the crowd and recalling that, nearly a quarter of a century before and almost at that same spot, he had seen another red-headed girl in an encounter that had changed his life.

At the time he had been a young major riding on a white horse, escorting his mandarin's palanquin towards an execution in the square. The mandarin and he had spotted the red-headed girl at almost the same moment, and the mandarin had been intrigued because the blazing hair of the woman, who happened to be Catherine's mother, had reminded him of a fox-fairy.

This whimsical fancy had led to a chain of unforeseen consequences, involving Helen Frances, Henry Manners and Major Lin. Lin's subsequent enmity with Manners, on account of the fox woman, was one of the reasons why his face was scarred. He had avenged himself for the pistol-whipping Manners had given him by killing the Chinese courtesan whom the other man had stolen from him.

He knew that Ma Na Si – he thought of the Englishman by his Chinese name – was still in Manchuria, employed in Chang Tso-lin's arsenal and therefore under his protection, not to mention that of the Japanese, whom he also served. Lin was in no hurry. And his scar, when he saw it in a mirror, afforded him pleasure: it reminded him of when he had enjoyed the fox-headed woman, Ma Na Si's paramour, on the floor of a brothel as Ma Na Si, tied to a bedpost, looked on. It had been the most singularly gratifying, and certainly the most sensuous, moment of his life.

'George?' she asked. 'Why does your mother hate him so?'

'Who? The general?' They were nearing the *pailou* that led into the square. 'Dashed if I know. I've always thought of him as a bit of a hero. There was this great affair on a train. I remember a soldier with an arrow in his arm, and Major Lin waving his sword with all the banshees out of hell pouring down on him. Thin red line, that sort of thing.'

'But did he do anything terrible?'

'Just about everybody was doing something terrible. We were tied up, shot at, thrown in the bottom of dung carts, sent to a place that looked like a brothel – I remember a horrible old woman with a knife. Couldn't really tell who was helping us and who wasn't. I've got vivid memories but they're all a jumble.'

'Didn't your mother or father ever tell you what happened?'

'Ma and Pa? Never.'

'But surely you remember something about Major Lin?'

'Apart from him being a hero? I do remember being a bit frightened of him when we were besieged in the mission. He'd turn up on his white horse and Jenny and I would hide behind the curtains until he'd gone. Our old cook said he had the evil eye. He can't have been all bad, though. He gave us watermelons once. We chopped them up in the kitchen.'

'That's not much help, George.'

'Sorry, but I was only seven. I'll try to do better next time.' He grinned.

'Is everything a joke for you?' she asked sourly. She pressed closer to Edmund. 'Edmund, do you know why Aunt Nellie dislikes General Lin?' she asked.

'Alas, I wasn't in Shishan. My older sister, Mary, and I were safely at school in Scotland, but George is right. Mother and Father never talk of those days. All I know about Lin is what I've read in the Chinese newspapers. He's a good soldier. I never knew that his history was so entwined with ours. You've actually met him, haven't you? You must tell me about it some time.'

'I don't think I will. I behaved rather disgracefully,' giggled Catherine.

'I can't imagine that.'

'Oh, you know little about what I can get up to,' she murmured.

'I'll vouch for that,' George called over his shoulder. 'You watch her, big brother. She sometimes shocks even me.'

At which point Catherine released Edmund's arm, ran up behind George and kicked him, to the amusement of the Chinese bystanders in front of the temple, which they had just reached.

'You see, Edmund?' cried George, hopping on one foot. 'She has no sense of decency. And certainly no respect for place.' He smiled maliciously. 'You didn't realise, did you, Catherine, that this square is where the famous Shishan massacre took place? That, if I'm not mistaken, was where Tom Cabot and the others were beheaded. About there.' He pointed at a patch of sandy earth in the centre.

'George, stop it,' Edmund snapped.

Catherine, who had been stunned by this information, was staring wildly around her as if she expected to see an oiled executioner emerge with his snickersnee. Instead she saw a quiet open space marked by two *pailous*. Some labourers were sipping tea outside a small dumpling shop at the side facing the temple. In the square an old man and his grandson were flying a kite, and a storyteller was holding another group of children enthralled with a dramatic rendition of one of the ancient Chinese classics. It was the peacefulness of the place that made it so sinister. She had a sudden memory of the overgrown graves on the hill.

'Now,' George went on, 'Mama and Papa – they witnessed it all, you know – must have been watching from somewhere over there.

They were probably hidden in that brothel I was telling you about. It could have been one of those windows above the dumpling shop. So, where we are standing must have been where the mandarin and the officials were, supervising the whole show.'

'Shut up, George,' she cried. She could feel the blood rushing in her cheeks and temples. 'I don't want to hear any more.'

'But it's edifying,' said George. 'You should want to know about your own family history. Look, see that *pailou*. That's where the martyrs came marching in, all loaded with chains, singing hymns until one by one the executioners came to take them away . . .'

'That's enough, George,' said Edmund sternly. 'This is in very bad taste. Come on, Catherine, we'll go into the temple.'

After a while, the darkness and stillness within the candle-lit temple had a calming effect, and slowly Catherine and Edmund regained their spirits as they walked through the great hall hand in hand. It was difficult to maintain a sense of irritation, even with George, when the serene faces of the idols contemplated them with such sublime detachment. The largest was a statue of Confucius, which peered wisely at them out of a smoky alcove behind the main altar. The incense-soaked shrines represented, in typically eclectic muddle, the different faiths that somehow had all been absorbed into the Chinese pantheon. Edmund pointed out Buddhist *bodhisattvas* and Taoist sages, which all, to Catherine, wore the same part-admonitory but infinitely understanding smile. They were being worshipped with impartiality by townsfolk, kneeling on faded cushions, while bored bonzes, yawning on little stools, waited to take their offerings.

When they stepped out again, the square was still peaceful, but Catherine did not wish to linger. George, however, wanted to find the house in which they had hidden during their escape. 'Don't you think it would be interesting to try to get in?' he asked. 'I wonder if it's still a brothel.'

'You can go and find it on your own,' Edmund told him. 'We're going to see if we can get up on to the city walls.'

'I'm not letting you two wander off by yourselves,' said George. 'Don't want you getting lost again, and Mother blaming me.'

Neither reacted to this, for Catherine had seen a familiar figure striking across the square, followed by a knot of laughing children: a plump woman dressed in Chinese clothes, but her stride was that of a confident European or American and the frizzy black hair, part hidden by a headcloth, was unmistakable, as was her loud laugh when she threw a coin into the air behind her for the street urchins.

'Martha!' Catherine cried, and ran after her.

Martha was so startled that she dropped her shopping. 'Catherine? Is that really you?'

They embraced. 'Sister, I'm so pleased to see you. Just look at you in that frock of yours. Long legs and skinny waist. You've come here to show me up, haven't you? Hey! Is that George I see skulking behind you? And Edmund? Hi! Aren't I going to get a hug from you two handsome boys as well? Careful, George, I'm married now.' She giggled as George embraced her enthusiastically. 'Why didn't you let me know you were here?'

Catherine found herself muttering an apology. She felt guilty that she had not enquired into Martha's whereabouts. Her own preoccupations of the last two days had put her friend out of her mind, but there was also the estrangement that had grown between them, and the extraordinary circumstances of their last meeting. 'I wanted to write,' she began, 'but you didn't leave a forwarding address, and I was never allowed into the Lei mansion again, and . . .'

But Martha showed no resentment. 'The Leis wouldn't have known how to find us. Ming doesn't communicate with his family any more. You could have written via Yu Fu-cheng at the city government, I suppose. I've got an address somewhere.' She began to rummage in her large leather satchel.

Suddenly Catherine noticed that she looked exhausted. 'Later, Martha. It's so good to see you again. I'm just glad we've found you. I want to hear all your news.'

Again, Martha appeared to ponder. After a moment, she smiled brightly. 'Hey, how about I show you the school?' She turned, as if the decision had been made.

Catherine sprang after her and took her arm. 'Martha, are you all right?' she whispered.

'Just a bit tired. These last few days, getting the school open, with the bureaucracy and all, I haven't had much sleep one way and another. Ming . . . Well, Ming's a teacher and he tends to leave the more practical things to me.' She shook her head. 'I'll be fine. A cup of coffee will put me right.' Suddenly she chuckled, and Catherine recognised the old mischievous smile. 'Guess I'm being as rude as ever, huh? But I'm pleased to see you, Catherine. I'm really glad you came.'

'You poor old thing,' said Catherine, and embraced her again under the curious glances of passers-by. 'Give Edmund that heavy bag to carry. Let's get you back to your school, and a pot of coffee.'

'I've got some brandy in my flask if that'll help,' offered George. 'I can do St Bernard just as well as St George.'

The school was a converted merchant's house situated in a side-street close to the South Gate. Inside Martha and Ming had whitewashed all the wooden walls, so the corridor that greeted them presented a clean, cheerful appearance. In a small room to the side, little coats and satchels were hanging on pegs. From a classroom down the hall they could hear children's voices chanting their lessons. Martha led them into a room on the left where a large table stood, covered with papers and books, and some high-backed chairs. In a corner was a basin and a small stove. Catherine sat Martha down in one of the chairs and deputed George to make the coffee. It was cold and they had all kept on their overcoats.

This room was also whitewashed, and featureless, except for two garish flags covering one wall. Catherine recognised the official Republican flag, consisting of the red, yellow, blue, white and black bars representing the ethnic mix of China. The other flag she could not identify. It consisted of a blue box that contained a blazing white sun in the left-hand corner of an otherwise crimson background. Flanking the flag were framed photographs of Marshal Chang Tso-lin and Dr Sun Yat-sen.

'You asked for news,' said Martha, as they waited for the coffee. 'Did you hear that Lan-hua escaped to Canton? I got a letter from her . . .' She shuffled among the papers. 'It's here somewhere.'

Catherine and Edmund exchanged a glance. Catherine leaned forward and placed a hand over her friend's. 'Never mind the letter, Martha. We'll see it later,' she said. 'You just rest for a while.'

'Oh, all right.' Martha stifled a yawn. She smiled, and a sly glint came to her eye. 'You know, it's great to have an excuse to sit down. I've got literally hundreds of things to do ... But I thought you'd be pleased to hear about Lan-hua. She's got a job at Nationalist Headquarters. Isn't that great?'

'Terrific,' said Catherine, looking at Edmund.

'Yeah,' yawned Martha. 'It really is.'

'Coffee's up!' George cried.

'I'm going to run out soon,' said Martha. 'It's my only luxury. Bought the beans in Tientsin when I left. You can't get them here except in the SMR town where they cost a fortune.'

'We'll send you some more,' promised Catherine.

Edmund had been examining the photos on the wall and the flags. 'Interesting to see these Kuomintang symbols here,' he said, pointing at the white sun and the portrait of Sun Yat-sen. 'Didn't know Chang Tso-lin and his boys had much respect for the Canton crowd. Does Lin Fu-po approve?'

'This isn't a Fengtian school,' said Martha. 'It's a Chinese school. Ming insisted on that. Anyway, all these warlords pay lip-service to the One China, even if all they're interested in is their own power. More to the point, Ming and I believe in One China. Did I tell you I've applied for Chinese nationality?'

'Martha, you haven't!' cried Catherine. 'You're not giving up your American passport?'

'If I have to,' said Martha. 'This is my life now. With Ming.'

'That's quite a decision to make,' said Edmund. 'I respect you for it – but I'm surprised you can display the Kuomintang flag so openly, especially with their rumoured Soviet connections.'

'It's a free country,' said Martha. 'Anyway, last I heard Chang Tso-lin and Sun Yat-sen were still allies. They may loathe each other but that's the official position. Ming knows what he's doing.'

This time Martha noticed the worried exchange of glances between Catherine and Edmund. 'Are you two thinking poor old Martha's in some kind of jam again? Brother, you couldn't be more wrong. I may be exhausted and unable to put two thoughts clearly together, but I've never felt freer or happier in my life. We're doing things now, Catherine, Ming and me. Oh,' she waved a hand dismissively, 'we only have two classes, about thirty students altogether. We teach the little ones in the morning, and the adolescents in the afternoon, and we don't have enough schoolbooks so I have to spend most of the night copying out tomorrow's lessons – but Ming's a genius in the classroom. He's patient. Inspiring. They love him. In the big picture, it may not be much but it's beautiful, and it's Ming and me, striking a blow against imperialism, colonialism, feudalism – you name it. Catherine, for once I feel I'm contributing to something bigger than myself.'

'Bravo.' George clapped. 'Good for you, Martha old girl. You show 'em!'

'You mentioned that you had to deal with a lot of bureaucracy,' said Edmund, after a pause. 'Don't you have Minister Yu's full support?'

'Oh, yes, and apparently the great general's as well,' said Martha. 'Yu keeps telling us so, but warlords are warlords, and you can't get anything done here except by crossing the palms of the soldiers in the government departments. Permissions for this. Permissions for that. Land use. Fire and safety registration. Telephone. I try not to burden Ming with these problems. He worships Yu Fu-cheng, and I'm sure the minister is quite sincere about his social schemes, but somehow all the money seems to go on Lin's army.'

'We've just seen General Lin making a triumphal entry in his motor-car,' said Catherine.

'Hail the conquering hero, huh? Ming and I don't have much time for General Lin,' said Martha.

'Dr Brown told us he was religious,' said Edmund. 'He had hopes of converting him to Christianity, he said.'

'Dr Brown – if he's a friend of yours, then I'm sorry – is a vicious, small-minded worm. He's been trying to sabotage Ming since we got here,' growled Martha. 'And Lin's a hypocrite. Did you know he closed down all the brothels in the city as part of a moral clean-up, then moved all the girls to the Yamen and his barracks? That was before he set up his daft foundation to synthesise every religion. He has Buddhist monks and Taoist priests at the Yamen, a Mongol shaman, a drunken old Russian Orthodox priest and goodness knows what else. Even I was asked to explain the Torah to some committee!'

'Did you?'

'You must be joking. I wrote back and told them I was trying to become Chinese and learning about the Jade emperor.'

'Was that wise, old thing?' asked Catherine.

'Didn't seem to do any harm.'

'This General Lin sounds quite a card,' chuckled George.

'I think he sounds barmy,' said Catherine, glaring at him.

'If y-you're t-talking about General Lin, y-you're absolutely right. He is m-mad like Mr Hatter in *Alice*.' Lei Ming had entered the room. He wore a plain brown gown, and with his severe black spectacles and newly cropped hair, he seemed taller, more imposing than before. The thin moustache added to the impression of maturity. A red scarf was wrapped round his neck and he was holding an armful of books. He laid them on the table, then kissed Martha's forehead. She clasped his hand. Then he gave them a radiant smile. 'Catherine. Dr Airton. Mr Airton. You are all welcome to the Chinese N-National School of Shishan!'

'I told them you'd take them round,' said Martha.

'W-well, that won't take very long.' He laughed. 'We only have one c-classroom. Is that c-coffee?' He rubbed his mittened hands. 'I apologise it's so c-cold. We can only afford h-heating for the c-classroom. We are typical intellectuals now. We w-warm ourselves on ideas!'

There was a hubbub of laughter and childish chatter from the corridor. 'I'd better help the little ones get their coats,' Martha murmured. Ming put a hand on her shoulder. 'No, *Hsiao* Hung can m-manage,' he said. '*Hsiao* Hung is our assistant. She's a w-wonderful teacher. We are very lucky.'

'Martha says the school is going very well,' said Catherine, brightly.

'Oh, excellently,' said Ming. 'I have just finished a r-report to our patron, M-Minister Yu Fu-cheng, about our first two weeks' activities. He will be very p-pleased. N-next week Martha is starting our first English Literature class. Ch-Charles D-Dickens. G-G-G—'

'*Great Expectations*,' finished Martha. 'Reckon that sums up our position pretty exactly – but we're getting there, aren't we, Ming?'

'We are,' said Ming, proudly. 'With Yu Fu-cheng's support. He is a truly g-great man. Do you know that he is introducing the s-same labour law here that the K-Kuomintang are considering in Canton? We may even get it p-promulgated before they do! And under true Chinese leadership. N-no B-B-Bolshevik influence here. China for China.'

'I notice you have the Nationalist flag on your wall,' said Edmund, pointing with his pipe.

'It's the K-Kuomintang flag,' said Ming. 'They adopted it last year. I am n-not a member of their party and I do not approve of their ties to R-Russia – unlike my sister in C-Canton – but I do believe in the voice of the common people, and m-many of the K-Kuomintang's ambitions are the same as ours. One day we will all march together. I kn-know that is also M-Minister Yu's sincere wish.'

'Is it the wish of Lin Fu-po? Or Chang Tso-lin?' asked Edmund.

'I think there is no c-contradiction,' said Ming. 'N-naturally the generals concern themselves with p-power first and p-people afterwards. B-but that is their function. Yu has General Lin's full support—'

'As long as it doesn't interfere with his getting new guns,' said Martha.

'M-Martha is very tired,' said Ming, giving her a fond smile, 'and does not understand these things as I do. The s-soldiers will step down once the country is reunited. Even m-mad ones like Lin Fu-po. Now,' he said, putting down his coffee cup, 'it would be my p-privilege to show you our school.'

'Fire away,' said George. Ming laughed as he took his arm and steered him into the corridor.

Catherine, Edmund and Martha followed a few steps behind them.

'You're worried that Ming is too damned idealistic for his own good.' Martha sighed. 'I haven't his confidence that Minister Yu is quite as in control of things as he makes out. But I'm not Chinese. So maybe Ming's right and I don't understand.'

'I think you understand things very well,' said Edmund, gravely.

'Yeah? Maybe. There's another thing.' She paused and took Catherine's arm. 'The warlords and the Japanese are as close as sardines.'

'Martha?' asked Catherine gently. 'Are you happy?'

Martha laughed. 'Happy, sister? I told you. I've never been happier in my life. I wouldn't be anywhere else if you offered me the world. No, we're doing something here. I sure as heck don't know how it'll turn out, but it's worth the try. And you know another thing? I'm in love!'

It was shortly after they had returned to the common room, and Ming had introduced them to his assistant, *Hsiao* Hung, a tall, spectacled girl in a red jersey, that there was a loud banging on the door.

'Oh, God,' said Martha. 'Not again! I thought I'd given them all the squeeze they wanted. Ming, you go. Tell them I'm not at home.'

They listened in some alarm to the sharp Chinese exchanges, then heard laughter, and were surprised when Ming came back arm in arm with a blushing Lieutenant Ti Jen-hsing.

They greeted him like a long-lost friend. For his part the young soldier told them excitedly how Minister Yu had given him an introduction that had allowed him to enrol in General Lin Fu-po's division. He reminded Catherine and Edmund that he had seen them at the military review in Mukden, and apologised that he had been too busy with his new duties to seek them out afterwards. He was immensely proud to be part of the modern army that General Lin was creating in Shishan.

Martha was still a little suspicious about why he had come, but Ti only became flustered when she asked what was to be the bill for the school this time. 'My errand has nothing to do with the school,' he told her, blushing, 'although I am very pleased to find my old friends here. I have come with orders for Miss Cabot and her party from my general.'

He became even more embarrassed when he saw their reaction to this remark.

'Orders?' asked Edmund, putting down his pipe. 'What possible orders can you have concerning us?'

'My apologies.' In his confusion Ti had stood rigidly to attention. 'I did not mean orders. I meant an invitation to dine with
General Lin at the celebration at the Yamen this evening. As his
honoured guests.'

'I see,' said Edmund. 'May I ask whether my parents are included
in this invitation?'

'Parents? There was no mention of them. He spoke only of the
red-headed lady and her two companions. I – I guessed that this
might be Miss Cabot, so I volunteered to deliver the summons.'

'Summons?'

'Invitation, I should say,' said Ti.

'I th-think he is t-trying to say that an invitation from General
Lin to the Yamen *is* a summons, Doctor,' said Ming.

'Is that so?' said Edmund. 'Lieutenant, will you please thank the
general but tell him that sadly it is impossible for us to accept his
invitation or his summons. We are already engaged this evening
with my parents, visiting old friends.'

Ti hung his head. 'Your dinner at the house of the merchant,
Yu Hsin-fu, has been cancelled,' he said. 'Both Minister Yu Fu-
cheng and his father have been ordered to join the dinner at the
Yamen.'

'I've never heard anything more preposterous in my life,' Edmund
said, in English.

'Oh, I don't know. I think it sounds rather fun,' said George.

'Catherine, what do you want to do?' asked Edmund. 'This
summons, as he called it, is mainly directed at you. It seems that
George and I are only your companions.'

'I think he wants to realise his down payment.' George chuckled.

'That's what worries me,' said Catherine.

'Don't do it, Catherine,' said Martha, taking her hands. 'Lin's
a nasty piece of work. You don't want to know him, believe me.'

'It's only for dinner,' said George. 'Come on, old girl. St George
will be there to protect you.'

'Have I a choice?' she asked Ti, who avoided her gaze.

'Catherine, you can't refuse an invitation to City Hall. Or not
this one,' said George.

'Mother won't like it,' said Edmund.

'I think we have to accept,' said Catherine. 'Anyway,' she added hollowly, 'as George says, it might be fun.'

Ti's visit had cast a pall on the subsequent conversation. Both Martha and Lei Ming found it difficult to conceal their disapproval that Catherine had accepted the warlord's invitation. Catherine had the suspicion that, despite their obvious happiness, the underlying tensions in Shishan were causing them problems, and that they did not always see eye to eye. At one point Edmund expressed surprise that Ti had known they were to dine with the Yus that evening, and Martha told him that Shishan was full of Lin's spies: nothing happened in the city that the Yamen did not hear about. 'Y-you don't know that, Martha,' Ming had started, but Martha snapped, 'Come on, Ming. See things as they are. He's a warlord, for God's sake. This is a police state.'

It had been a relief when *Hsiao* Hung reminded Ming that the older students would soon be arriving for afternoon classes.

'You should rest, old thing,' said Catherine, as they made ready to leave.

'Yeah, some day,' said Martha.

'We'll come and see you before we go,' said Catherine.

Just after they had stepped into the street, Martha rushed out and took Catherine's hands one last time. 'Sister, you be careful tonight. I don't trust any of these people. Look after yourself, okay?' She hugged her quickly, and hopped back into her house, but Catherine had seen the tears on her cheeks.

They arrived at the Yamen at dusk. The sharp wind snapped at their overcoats as they stepped out of the Model T Ford in which Lieutenant Ti had brought them. The chauffeur drove off to park among a collection of vehicles lined against the high stone walls.

Clearly, other guests had arrived before them, but they lingered to take in the view. A wedge of geese flew across the pale orange globe sinking into the shadows of the Black Hills far to the west. There were no birds flying above the grove of dark pines that ringed this outer courtyard. As their eyes adjusted to the twilight, they made out, under the gloomy shade of the branches, the shapes of parked armoured cars, the squat gun barrels pointed menacingly towards them. Sentries in huge padded greatcoats, wearing fur caps with batwing side flaps, stood rigidly to attention by the brass-studded red doors, bayonets fixed to their rifles. They had passed similarly attired troops of soldiers, marching in neat companies, along the winding length of the road, which stretched up from the barbed-wired gate that separated the town from the general's headquarters. The Yamen was apparently no longer the traditional mansion of a Chinese magistrate, but an armed camp.

They had to bend their heads as they were ushered through a small portal in the right-hand flap of the heavy doors, which remained locked and barred. More bayonet-wielding sentries stood on the other side, and a corporal sitting at a desk checked their names against a sheet of paper. As they waited, they heard the echo of boots on paving stones reverberating round the portico that ringed a large open courtyard, in which shadowy lines of soldiers in full kit were at attention while a sergeant inspected them. On the other side of the square, Catherine noticed a tall, narrow structure, whose shape was strangely familiar. With a cold shock she realised what it was, just as George blurted, 'Good Lord! It's a guillotine!'

Ti led them across the square and up some stone steps, which mounted to a platform on which stood a shadowy ceremonial hall. Catherine was reminded of the Lei mansion, but the Yamen was constructed on a larger scale. This building perhaps also contained offices, but as soon as they had passed through the great doors, they found that its traditional interior had been altered. A whitewashed concrete corridor illuminated by a single, fly-encrusted lightbulb led through to the next courtyard beyond. Sentries stood at attention by the doors on either side, and saluted as Ti passed.

The next courtyard was like the first, but empty and dark. The flagstones were in a terrible state of repair, and Catherine nearly tripped on a tuft of grass. As she supported herself on Edmund's arm she looked up and saw flitting black shapes against the violet sky. Bats.

There was another flight of steps and another platform, but the hall here was heavily padlocked. Ti led them through a circular 'moon gate' and along a dark alley to the side. The light was fading fast, but in the third courtyard, Catherine could make out the shapes of what appeared to be scores of crouching figures. She could hear the tinkle of hammers against stone, and what sounded like the drag of chains. A standing figure was fiddling with something. There was a spark and the sudden glare of a hurricane lamp, then the figures were revealed as ragged men in thin, padded jackets, with manacles on their ankles. Ti explained, 'These are all condemned men, but General Lin is enlightened, and allows them to expiate their crimes through hard labour.'

'Glad he told us that,' muttered George. 'Otherwise we might have felt sorry for the poor sods.' Catherine felt Edmund's hand tighten on hers.

They followed Ti through another moon gate into a smaller side courtyard, lit by red lanterns hanging from the leafless branches of some willow trees. A large two-storey building loomed before them, ablaze with lights. 'This is the opera and banqueting hall,' said Ti. 'I will leave you here.'

'Will you be taking us home later?' asked Edmund.

'I think so,' said the lieutenant, frowning. 'I haven't had my orders yet.' He saluted and left.

The hall was divided into two halves. The side they were in was a huge open auditorium. Above them they could see the dark beams that supported the ceiling. The space itself was dominated by a jutting stage. The proscenium was exquisitely carved with birds, leaves and flowers. Dragons and phoenixes wound round golden pillars under a curlicued Chinese roof. The stage was empty, except for three musicians who sat rather sombrely on a dais at the rear. On a bench before them were a huge drum, a pair of large cymbals and a flute.

In front of the stage were several small tables, on which had been laid out earthenware cups and pots of tea. The benches around them were already full of an extraordinary collection of people, some of whom Catherine recognised. She saw Minister Yu Fu-cheng. At the same time he noticed her and gave her a benevolent grin, with a wave of his fan. His heavy-browed father, sitting beside him, also nodded at them. She was surprised to see, at a table near the front, the American paleontologist whom they had met the night before, Professor Niedemeyer. With him was the Japanese commandant, Captain Fuzumi, who waved. Dr Brown, wearing his dog-collar, his black coat and his sanctimonious smile, was at the same table. His unexpected presence made her wonder if Edward and Nellie Airton were also there, but she could not see them. Instead she was amazed to recognise, at the same table as a red-nosed and grey-bearded Russian Orthodox priest, the young Buddhist *rinpoche*, whom she had last seen on the train when she and Martha had first travelled to Tientsin. As before, he was accompanied by his acolytes, kneeling behind him and telling their beads. Their eyes met, and for a moment his face lit in a radiant smile, then sank back into sullen somnolence at a look of reproach from one of his priestly guardians.

As a corporal ushered them to an empty table in the front row, she heard a burst of high-pitched laughter, and saw nine or ten women, with fans and painted faces, in a gallery on the other side of the room directly facing the stage. Most were Chinese, chattering animatedly among themselves, but there were at least two Europeans. One, in a skimpy purple dress that revealed her broad shoulders and deep cleavage, was a striking red-head. She was resting her chin on the back of her hand and looking thoroughly bored.

'I say, look at them.' George was grinning from ear to ear. 'A warlord's harem.'

Catherine, however, had recalled what the prostitute, Svetlana, had told her in the Starlight club: 'Funny, he only ever chooses natural red-heads like you.' This made her realise that the one person she had expected to see in the hall was not there.

'We're obviously in for a show of some kind,' said Edmund, 'but it looks as if we have some time before it starts. I'm going over to pay my respects to Minister Yu.'

'I'll come with you,' she said.

Minister Yu and his father had already stood up to meet them. She allowed Edmund to do the talking. The minister was as charming and courteous as he had been at the Lei mansion, but as she observed him she noted that the twinkle in his eye, which had been so noticeable, had gone. The little man looked tired, almost careworn, and there was a pallor to his skin. He asked Edmund if he had met his father, Yu Hsin-fu.

'At the station,' said the old man, gruffly. 'We should all have been having dinner at my house tonight.'

'But we are having dinner together, Father,' said his son, smoothly.

'Not at my house, and not with the *daifu*. I was looking forward to seeing my old friend Ai Er Tun. I spent good money on the dinner, you know. Abalone. Bear's paw. I've a good mind to give this jumped-up bandit of yours a piece of my mind. And he only sent a corporal to tell me. Where's the respect in that?'

'Father,' said Yu Fu-cheng, 'remember where you are, and don't talk so loudly.'

'I'm not afraid of him,' said the old man, truculently.

'I think we'd better get back to our seats,' said Edmund, tactfully. Yu Fu-cheng gave him a grateful smile.

Brown was by their table, talking to George. 'Ah,' he sighed, 'so you know my friend the minister? Goodness gracious, you've become very well connected all of a sudden. To be honest I was surprised to see you here at all. As it was, I only got my own invitation very late in the afternoon.'

'My parents weren't invited?' asked Edmund.

'Well, the strange thing is that they were, and that surprised me as well, until I thought that General Lin must have heard about the little ceremony we put on at the station for them and realised they were VIPs. Or perhaps it was a token of respect for the guests in my house – but they refused to come! I told them that that was hardly polite. General Lin is, after all, the warlord. It amazes me that they did not wish to meet the man after everything I have told them about him.'

'Staggering,' said George.

'Yes, that was what I thought,' said Brown. 'But they are advanced in years now . . .'

'Methuselahs,' said George.

'Indeed,' said Brown, looking at him warily. 'Excuse me, I ought to get back to my seat.'

As he spoke the lights in the hall went out, and a furious drumming and ringing of cymbals swelled up from the stage, quite drowning the clatter as Dr Brown stumbled over a stool, knocking the Russian Orthodox priest off his seat. The lights on the stage blazed, and Catherine gasped at the sight of twenty little boys cartwheeling and tumbling and leaping to extraordinary heights in a kaleidoscope of colour and movement. Their faces were painted red and white, and their actions were simian. In between their acrobatics they crouched on all fours and sniffed the air. Then she recognised the figure of the Monkey King, who leaped on to the stage to a great shout of '*Hao!*' from the audience, and stood on one foot, one hand cocked to his ear, the other holding a magic wand. 'This is from "Monkey Stealing the Heavenly Peaches".' She heard Edmund's voice through the din.

'It's marvellous,' she shouted back.

'Wait till they start singing,' called George. 'It's hideous.'

'What?'

'Hideous,' shouted George – but there was no singing, at least not in this act. The action on the stage reached an intensity of impossible movement and ended as dramatically as it had begun. The stage was extinguished in blackness.

'*Hao! Hao!*' the audience cheered. Catherine clapped as enthusiastically as the rest.

When the lights went on again, they saw a tableau of gods and goddesses, clustered round a majestic central figure of a woman dressed entirely in white. Her mask-like face was painted cream and peach pink, with blue eyelids rising to phoenix-tail eyebrows. Her piled-up hair gleamed with jewels and ivory combs, and enormous strings of pearls hung from either side of her head, yet Catherine did not see beauty so much as hardness in the thin vermilion lips and red-rimmed eyes that seemed to stare at her with a fixed intensity. 'Here we go,' she heard George mutter.

'It's "The Sky Goddess Scatters Flowers",' whispered Edmund.

'Oh, God, whoever said this was going to be fun?' said George.

'You did,' Catherine whispered.

'Hush,' said Edmund. Following some slow clangs from the cymbals, the flautist played a haunting tune, and the woman in white began to sing.

To Catherine it was incomprehensible. The woman's entire repertory seemed to consist of the repeated word '*yi*' in impossibly high notes, occasionally lilting, occasionally rising, sometimes reaching peaks of which she had not thought a human voice capable, and which the woman held for long seconds, until the audience thundered its approval with a loud '*Hao!*' and banged on their tables. The '*yi*' sessions were punctuated by clanging cymbals, which was the signal for the woman to swirl her long sleeves and make elegant gestures with her hands. Various tutelary spirits and sages appeared from time to time, sang their pieces, also in incredibly high notes, and went off again to a clanging of cymbals, while the Sky Goddess presumably blessed them. The scene climaxed with the whole array of gods and goddesses singing '*yi*' and, after a final solo from the goddess, which reached an ear-splitting shriek, a net opened above and the whole stage was enveloped in petals. The lights were extinguished to a roar of '*Hao!*' and a thumping of tables that lasted a good minute. When the lights went on again the Sky Goddess stood alone on the stage.

She remained immobile until the shouting ceased. The hard eyes seemed to stare directly at Catherine, who was conscious that her table in the front row was part illuminated. When there was silence, the goddess gave a curt bow, flicked her sleeve over her arm and walked towards the wings with a very masculine step – but that did not surprise Catherine, for under the harsh lights she had noticed that the makeup on one side of the woman's face was smudged, revealing the outline of a livid red scar.

The Sky Goddess who had performed for them was General Lin.

He joined them shortly after they had sat down at a large table in a small banqueting room in the other half of the hall. Only the chief guests had been invited here: the officers, who comprised the bulk of the audience, were eating in the main dining room next door.

General Lin must have entered by one of the panels in the wooden back wall, because he seemed to materialise at the head of the table, immediately silencing all conversation. Behind him loomed the big, black-bearded bodyguard whom Catherine remembered had been with him in the nightclub. Next to him was the short man with whom she had danced, but today he wore a plain black gown rather than a white suit. The three figures remained standing in the nervous silence while Lin's cold eyes surveyed his guests. Like his factotum, he was wearing a simple black gown. There was only a hint of makeup rimming his eyes, and a touch of powder on one brow. Catherine, in the chair on his immediate right, had the profile of the good side of his face. The young *rinpoche*, in the seat of honour on his left, had the benefit of the scar.

In the shocked silence, Catherine heard the loud ticking of the grandfather clock in a corner of the room. It was the only piece of furniture besides the table and chairs, and the only decoration, except for a Buddhist painting of Nirvana on one of the side walls that faced a Russian icon of the Virgin. She looked at her fellow guests seated round the table: they were gazing up at their host with a variety of expressions. Edmund and Professor Niedemeyer, seated opposite her, were contemplating him with polite curiosity; Captain Fuzumi smiled with nonchalant unconcern; George's face quivered with barely suppressed amusement. On the faces of the others, however, she saw varying degrees of alarm, even fear. The Russian priest's mouth hung open; Yu Hsin-fu stared moodily at his plate; the young *rinpoche* was blinking in what appeared to be a mixture of wonder and horror; a Taoist priest appeared frozen; and the fixed smile and bulbous eyes of Dr Brown resembled the startled expression of a landed cod. The general's twisted lips lifted in a scornful sneer.

Minister Yu Fu-cheng, seated in the co-host's position opposite General Lin, broke the silence. Rising to his feet and taking his glass of *gaoliang* wine, he proposed a toast to the exquisite performance they had witnessed on the stage. The others stumbled to their feet to add their praises. 'Magnificent. Sheer perfection of art and form,' Catherine heard Brown's reedy voice, echoed by a rumbling '*Horosho! Horosho!*' from the Russian priest, and '*Hao!*' from Yu Fu-cheng's father.

General Lin slowly raised his own glass, and held it in front of his face. He turned to Catherine, and waited while she, too, picked up her glass. She saw the livid scar and the bead-like eye examining her. 'You are all welcome,' he said, in a surprisingly soft tone. '*Ganbei!*'

She winced as she swallowed the acid, sour-tasting spirit, noticing as she did so that the general did not touch the liquor but handed his glass to the bearded bodyguard, who drained it on his master's behalf. 'Be seated,' said Lin, in the same soft tone. '*Bie kechi*. Don't be formal.' He coiled elegantly into his chair, with some of the grace he had used in his female impersonation. The bodyguard and the short man pulled up stools behind him. Soldiers appeared with dishes of cold meat, which they placed in front of all the guests, except for the *rinpoche*, who received a plate of vegetables. He gazed longingly at the duck and pork as he lifted a strand of spinach to his lips. Since General Lin gave no indication that he wished to converse, they ate in silence.

The cold meat finished, the soldiers replaced the plates with bowls of pink prawns. General Lin raised his glass of *gaoliang*, and on his signal everybody drained theirs, except the *rinpoche*, who was excused – he was now looking sadly at a plate of sweet potatoes, which he had been given instead of the prawns. Again, the general handed his own glass to his bodyguard. He did not touch his food.

The third course was mushrooms, so for once the *rinpoche* could partake. General Lin did not touch his portion. Nor did he join the third toast he forced on the assembly. The only sounds in the room were the ticking of the clock, and the slurping of the Russian priest and Yu Fu-cheng's father.

It was during the fourth course, while his guests were struggling with large steaks, sizzling on heated iron platters, that he addressed Edmund: 'You are the old *daifu*'s son,' he said. 'Perhaps I knew you when you were a little boy.'

'No, General, you're thinking of my brother, who is sitting over there. George was in Shishan then.'

George, his mouth full of steak, grinned amiably. Swallowing, he quickly drank some tea, and said, 'You were kind enough to give us some melons once, sir. Never forgotten it.'

The general contemplated him. 'I remember that you and your sister acted bravely, considering your age at the time,' he said.

'Where are your parents? I had hoped to see my old friends again tonight.'

'Ah, General,' said Dr Brown, 'perhaps I can explain. We all received your kind invitations. An honour, General, as I explained to Dr and Mrs Airton, my houseguests. I did my best – my very best – to convince . . .'

General Lin lifted one hand fractionally off the table and Dr Brown quailed under his withering stare. Lin turned to the elder son. 'I am disappointed not to see them,' he said. 'You will tell them, however, that I understand . . . their indisposition. You will pass on to them my respects.'

He raised his glass for another *ganbei*. Catherine drank with the others, but her cheeks had flushed with the strong liquor. Meanwhile, General Lin had begun to address Yu Fu-cheng. 'I have seen your report on the labour law,' he said. 'I will give you my comments when you have returned from your business in Shanghai. I am pleased that you have brought your father tonight, another of my old friends. *Lao* Yu,' he addressed the old man familiarly, 'have you considered the proposal I gave you concerning cash crops?'

Yu Hsin-fu raised his heavy eyebrows, his face reddening. 'I have considered it, General, but my business is soy beans.'

'You will remain the Soy-bean King,' said General Lin. 'Is that not what they call you? My Japanese advisers are only suggesting that you convert a few of your fields to this new crop, which in cash returns will bring you greater profits. Is that not what your colleagues are proposing, Captain Fuzumi?' Fuzumi gave a broad grin, and bowed his head.

'I am not an opium farmer,' grunted the old man.

'But you are a loyal citizen of China and Shishan,' said General Lin. 'These are times of war and it behoves our merchant classes to maximise their profits so in turn your son can maximise the taxes he returns to me. I am here to defend your interests, in token of which I require your support. Perhaps my proposal was not clear in its details. Fu-cheng, you will take it on yourself to explain it to your father. So that he understands.'

The minister had quietly placed a restraining hand on his father's

thigh. 'We are grateful as always for your kindness and consideration, General,' he said.

Lin nodded, and raised his glass for a fifth toast. More dishes
came, and more toasts. Lin turned his attention to Professor
Niedemeyer, who for the next half-hour explained his theories about
the origins of Chinese civilisation. The little man in the black gown
whispered a translation into the general's ear. When Professor
Niedemeyer had finished, Lin told him he would look forward to
seeing his results, and raised his glass again. By now Catherine,
having drained her eighth glass, was feeling queasy.

'You will talk among yourselves,' she heard Lin saying. 'This is
a convivial occasion.' Rather stiltedly, low conversations began
around the table, urged on by Yu Fu-cheng. It was then that she
heard the factotum's voice in her ear. 'General Lin has asked if you
remember meeting him before?' he said, in fluent Russian. He
mistook her surprise for incomprehension and repeated the question in English.

She turned to the general, who was looking at her with his twisted
smile. 'Tell him . . . No, I'll tell him in Chinese.' She struggled for
the words. 'At club you not dance with me. Only give tea.'

Lin raised his eyebrows. 'You left the table before I invited you to
dance,' he said. 'Even though I paid you. You owe me, young lady.'

'You like dance now?' said Catherine, giving him what she hoped
was a haughty look. She immediately regretted her temerity, but the
drink had raised a devil and she realised she could not stop now.
The general was observing her with new interest.

'One day we may dance,' he said. 'Tonight I will recall only part
of your debt. A down payment from you this time.'

'And what you want me do?' asked Catherine.

Lin pointed at her glass. 'Three drinks,' he said. 'It will be your
penalty for rejecting me.'

'Easy,' said Catherine, lifting her glass. Lin picked up his own
and passed it to the bearded man. 'No,' said Catherine, putting
down her glass.

'You refuse to drink with me?' he asked.

'No – but I drink, you drink,' said Catherine. 'You,' she said,
pointing at him.

She saw his eyes narrow, and wondered if she had gone too far. Another part of her was aware that the table was now silent and everybody was watching them. She had given him a public challenge.

'*Xing.*' He shrugged and gestured to the soldier to bring him a new glass.

When it was brimming, she raised hers. '*Ganbei,*' she said, and watched him drain his, then followed suit. General Lin gestured for the soldier to refill the glasses. They drank again. Then repeated the process once more. She saw with satisfaction that General Lin's cheeks had reddened. Her head, on the other hand, suddenly felt clearer. The *rinpoche* was gazing at her in open-mouthed admiration.

'Talk among yourselves,' Lin snapped at Yu Fu-cheng, who did his best to force a murmur among the guests.

Lin was not smiling when he turned to her again. She forced herself to hold his gaze. 'Are we equal now, General?' she asked.

'No, I paid for more than three drinks,' he said. 'You owe me still.'

'We leave tomorrow,' she said. 'You must come long way find me again for dance.'

He nodded slowly. 'We will dance,' he said. 'Perhaps I will invite you here again for a proper family reunion. When all debts can be repaid.'

'I don't understand.'

'No?' She heard him sniffing repeatedly, and realised this was his laugh. She felt that he was playing with her. 'What you mean family reunion?'

He was sniffing more noisily. Suddenly he stopped and leaned forward so that his face was close to hers. She could not look away from the red cicatrice, which broke the line of his eyebrow and snarled his lips. 'I know you are the fox woman's daughter,' he said. 'You have the same texture of hair and colour in your eyes, and your limbs are as well shaped.' She had the uncomfortable feeling that she was naked to his knowing gaze. 'I know also who is your father.'

She suddenly felt frightened. 'My father, mother dead,' she whispered.

'Not your father,' he said, running a finger down the line of his scar. 'You have my word. One day we will have a reunion – and then we will dance.'

Abruptly he turned away from her, and faced the rest of the table. He had only to raise his hand for the talking to stop. He lifted his glass. 'It is no longer early,' he said. 'I have only recently returned to my duties in Shishan and there is much to be done. Fu-cheng, you may see your father home, but then you will return to my offices. I have some instructions concerning your trip to Shanghai. For you others, I thank you for joining me tonight. I drink to your health.'

He drained his glass, stood up, bowed curtly and left by the panel through which he had come, followed by the bearded bodyguard and the little man in black.

Catherine was struggling to comprehend his enigmatic last remarks: 'Family reunion?' It did not make sense – but she had little time to think about this before George was by her chair, clapping her on the back. 'My goodness, Catherine, you have a nerve. You humiliated him.'

'Yes, well done,' said Edmund, kissing her cheek. 'Not, perhaps, the wisest course of action to beard a warlord in his own den, but wonderful to see it happen. How are you feeling?' he asked.

'She's tootled. What do you think?' said George.

'Oh dear.' Edmund looked embarrassed. 'Niedemeyer here found some more bones today, and offered to take me to his house to show me. I'd thought you might like to come along too, but if you're not feeling up to it . . . Niedemeyer, we might have to make it another day. Catherine's not . . .'

'It's no matter at all,' said Niedemeyer. 'I'll surely be coming through Tientsin soon.'

Catherine shook her head. 'No, Edmund. You go with Professor Niedemeyer. I'll go back with George and wait for you.'

There was a confused flurry of farewells. Except for the *rinpoche*, who had been whisked away by his acolytes, the other guests were, like her, rather the worse for drink. They managed to avoid Dr Brown, whom they subsequently discovered was in the courtyard being sick, and followed Lieutenant Ti back through the dark

Yamen. The walk cleared Catherine's head, and she found the drive through the city, the wind freezing her face, exhilarating. By the time they reached the Japanese town and their hotel, both she and George were ready for another drink at the bar.

A Chinese jazz band was playing and some of the Japanese tourists were dancing, but George and Catherine found a quiet table. They were both intoxicated by their encounter with the warlord, and giggled together over his operatic performance.

'Talk about Fu Manchu,' laughed Catherine. 'Did you hear him laying into poor Minister Yu and his father?'

'Sinister bugger every way you look at him. My God, you were brave to take him on like that.'

Catherine laughed harshly. 'I was, wasn't I?' she said, and George kissed her.

'Oops, sorry,' he said, drawing back. 'Forgot. You and Edmund are all chummy now. You're off limits to the likes of me, aren't you? Bad St George.'

Catherine took his hand. 'Oh, George,' she said.

'Is it the real thing, old girl?' asked George, tenderly. 'Is it love? Wedding bells? All that?'

'I don't know,' said Catherine, suddenly feeling very sober. 'It might be. I never thought I could love anybody but . . .'

'It's funny how things turn out,' said George. 'Lose a father, find a husband, all within a couple of days. I lost a mare once, in a poker game with Andreas and some others. A winner too, won the Robert Hart trophy on her. Felt like my racing days were over when I woke next morning and remembered what I'd done. But a few days after that I got offered China Coast. Fate, I suppose, has its silver lining from time to time. Didn't work out all that well for the fellow I lost the mare to. She tripped on the training track and broke her leg. Had to be put down. There you go. Guess in the end I'm one who's lucky at cards after all. That means, I suppose, I should be content to be unlucky in love.'

'Oh, George, you'll find someone,' she said. 'It would never have worked out for you and me. You knew that. We're too alike,' she said. 'Wild. Irresponsible.'

'You're probably right,' he said, 'but it did cross my mind.'

'You never did anything about it,' she said, 'even when I threw myself at you.'

'I'm shy,' said George. 'One of nature's innocents.'

'You?' she said, and giggled. 'We had some good times together, though, didn't we? Do you remember the rickshaw race?'

'I was merely being St George pulling my lady-love to victory. It was you sitting in the back who did it,' said George.

'It was Andreas falling over and breaking his leg,' said Catherine.

'That too,' said George.

She laughed. She felt comfortable sitting beside him sipping her martini. 'Are you very upset?' she whispered, pressing her lips softly against his ear. 'Jealous?'

'Me? Jealous?' He looked as if he would make another witticism, then his shoulders slumped. 'Do you want me to be honest, Catherine? I think I'm devastated with jealousy. Sometimes you don't know what you've had until you've lost it. I was pretty beastly to you this morning in the square. That was probably part of it . . . But am I unhappy for you and Edmund? Certainly not. Always knew he was the better man . . . And I'll get over it. That's St George, you see. Overriding disaster with a smile on my face. I'll give you an example. This morning I found I'd lost one of my cufflinks. Did you hear a squeak from me?'

She did not laugh, but snuggled closer. 'He's not the better man,' she whispered. 'Nobody could be more generous than you.'

'What might have been, eh?' said George.

'Oh, George.' She looked up at him and he kissed her lips. She found herself responding.

It was George who pulled away. 'Now, now, Miss Cabot. Finish your drink, and let's get you to the dance-floor. Clear your head before Edmund comes back and claims his own.'

The band was performing a tango. George lampooned the movements, burlesquing the great Latin lover. Catherine giggled and played along. She let the music take her, enjoying the abandon and the knowledge that George's strong arms would catch her. The music changed to a slow waltz. They danced formally at first, George again lampooning the steps, but after a while she nestled against him, resting her head on his shoulder. She felt the strength of his trim body, and remembered the smell that had once so excited her. The music wafted around them. She felt George's arms close round her back. They rocked together, and time passed.

Eventually, she felt George lift his head, as if something had caught his attention.

'What's the matter?' she murmured, resenting the disturbance to her comfort.

'Oh, nothing.' His cheek touched hers again. 'You know, Catherine, I really am happy for you,' she heard him whisper.

'George,' she found herself whispering back. 'Oh, George.' And she sought his lips again. One last time, she told herself. He moved his head down to hers.

Then looked up, and stiffened. Confused, she turned in the direction in which he was staring – and saw Edmund's face at the edge of the dance-floor, the clenched lips, the frown, the hurt in his eyes, before suddenly he turned away.

'Oh, God, George.' In a violent motion she twisted out of his arms. Her shoe caught against his foot, and the strap broke. It delayed her as, hopping, she tried to leave the floor. She kicked it off and released the other.

By the time she reached the lobby, Edmund was nowhere to be seen. She ran up the stairs, along the corridor to his room and banged on the door, calling his name and telling him it was all a mistake, that she loved him – but the door remained closed.

George straightened his bow-tie. He ordered another martini from the bar, and produced a cigar, which he lit with care. He sat on a bar-stool, his foot beating to the rhythm of the band. After a while he began to whistle along. Anybody observing him would have considered that this was a man without a care in the world.

7

The Last Emperor

From the journal of William Lampsett, Reuters correspondent, Tientsin, 2 May 1923

Chang Tso-lin is building up a powerful army. Junks and freighters daily break the feeble blockade of the Powers. He now has three squadrons of Breguet fighter aircraft, double the number of tanks and armoured cars, and at least three armoured trains. His ambition is naked for all to see. It is said that in the friezes in his outer yamen *the flowers and fruit patterns reveal hidden dragons. Another carving shows a tiger with a ball in its claws – the Tiger of the North stretching his power over the globe.*

His enemy, Marshall Wu Pei-fu, sits secure in the capital city, controlling the financial resources of the heartland provinces, and believes he is unassailable. A moderate Confucian, a poet and a scholar, he, too, loves his symbolism. As he keeps a token emperor in a deserted palace, so it is said he has a chess set open on a table next to his desk, but he never touches it. His pieces are living men and he thinks he has already worked out the gambit that will bring his adversary to checkmate.

But Chang Tso-lin is a gambler rather than a chess player, and invariably wins when he plays the tiles. He knows what Wu Pei-fu does not, that fortune is a blind servant, more easily deceived than deceiving. Human weakness once identified is more potent than an army's strength. Such is the bandit's wisdom.

Fu-kuei stood by the sideboard preparing a fresh pot of tea for the three men sitting at her dining-table. She was only half listening to what they were saying. While they discussed bonds and guarantees, fluctuating rates of exchange, and formulae to calculate accumulated interest, she was contemplating her lover, Yang Yi-liang, who was leaning back in his chair, one booted leg crossed over the other, a cigarette in one hand, the other cushioning the back of his head. His lips were curved in a sardonic smile, and his half-closed eyes observed with humour and detachment the exquisite pressure that her brother was imposing on Lei Tang. He was entirely confident, relaxed and very handsome. The soft light from the chandeliers had smoothed away the care lines on his skin, and to Fu-kuei he appeared as youthful as when she had first met him.

It was strange, she thought. She no longer thought of him as an enemy, and her hatred of him had died away. At one time, she remembered, it had been only that hatred which had kept her going. When she thought of the system that had violated her, she had given it his face. His innocence and apparent kindness were inconsequential. He wore the uniform. He commanded the prison. Even his generosity had represented a weakness she could exploit.

At first she had thought only of revenge. On that night, so long ago, when she was still a prisoner, but released into his care, she had crept down the corridor of his apartment, concealing a kitchen knife in her sleeve.

It had been the cause that saved her, and him. It had brought her back from the brink. As she stood over his sleeping body, the knife raised in her hands, it had seemed that a voice outside herself had told her he would be more useful to her alive. And she herself, it persuaded her, would have to remain alive if she was still to serve the cause. Murdering him might bring her a form of sensual gratification, but she would not long survive her revenge. She had an obligation, it reminded her: during those nights and days of torture in her cell, although her body had been broken, shamed and defiled, the cause had retained a purity and purpose – her only purpose. Clinging to that idea had kept her alive, and sane, even if at times she did not know what that meant any more. Her willpower had been reduced to the cause. They were actually one.

It had not been easy. The point of the knife had wavered above his chin. From her violated depths, she felt the urge to plunge it into his throat. Willpower had restrained her, and the cause indicated what she had to do. She had taken off her clothes, and crept into his bed. His embraces had been no more repulsive than the attentions of the gaolers who had abused her for five weeks. Indeed, there had even been an intellectual satisfaction in making the moves that first fooled, and later made him believe there was mutual love between them. At the time she had no idea how she would exploit her advantage beyond securing her release. A cold part of herself watched with detachment and some surprise as her body responded instinctively to his endearments, and her words spoke a passion that she certainly did not feel. Could it be so easy?

She had discovered later that her emotions, although buried, had not been unaffected. When the ship had pulled away from the Shanghai dock, she had collapsed into a paroxysm of sobs; it was as if a floodgate had been opened and a white wave of anger, guilt, sorrow, disgust, above all relief, had smashed away her defences. Even so, as she cried by the ship rail, the cold part of her had observed Yang Yi-liang also weeping on the shore, and realised that he must be thinking that, if she was sobbing, she loved him and did not want them to be parted. Even in breaking down she had strengthened her cover.

Later on, during the voyage, Mr Behrens had taken her vaguely formed ideas and shaped them in the context of world revolution. She had confessed what she had done, and he had congratulated her. 'You have learned through your torture what it takes sometimes years to teach. If we were to speak in philosophical terms you have already reached that point of oneness which is the sage's Nirvana, and in us creates the detachment that makes for a successful operative. When the Idea and the Will are one, and the desires of the body are but *maya* . . . Congratulations, Miss Yu. I am delighted for you. Maintain that distancing of what you do from what you are, and you will be invulnerable. I tell you, so often in a honey operation, such as the one we intend for you with this man Yang, the seducer is seduced. Why? Because the target is good, he is kind, he is virtuous, he is attractive. It is pathetic, is it not? So many roubles of training lost to a single orgasm, or even the gift of a bonbon or bouquet! Mankind is frail – but not you, I think, Miss Yu.'

As she looked at Yi-liang now, she wondered. All through her time at Oxford, even when she received his cheques, she had preserved her detachment – indeed, her dislike. She had told herself that a man who could be used in such a way deserved scorn. On her return to Shanghai, she had resumed the pretence of love, and it had been as easy as before.

So, what had changed?

She poured the boiling water from the Thermos into the pot, and as she did so she heard Lei Tang's whine. 'But the loan you require consists of more than the total assets of our bank. How can we give surety for such a sum?'

'Lei Tang, Lei Tang,' Fu-cheng murmured, his eyes twinkling behind his spectacles. 'Why do you worry so? The surety you give your syndicate will be back-to-backed with government guarantees, and the personal guarantees of Marshals Chang Tso-lin and Sun Chuang-fang. What could be more reliable?'

Lei Tang bowed his head, and Fu-cheng continued: 'The Manchurian provinces are the richest in China, and the Yangtse delta provinces controlled by General Sun are the most fertile. The revenues he secures from taxes on manufacturing and enterprise in Shanghai on top of that are enormous. Isn't that so, Major Yang?'

She saw Yi-liang grin, as he lit a new cigarette elegantly with his Zippo lighter. 'Oh, assuredly,' he said.

Fu-kuei smiled. Certainly of one thing she was sure. Over the last year, she had developed a respect for Yi-liang's professional competence. She had also come to admire his style. She knew how ruthless he could be, and how dangerous his intelligence network was to her own cause, but he bore his responsibilities lightly. She knew of the various crises that had occurred from time to time in his professional life, but he resolved them with detachment and charm. It had never been more so than during his negotiations with her brother over the last few months. That General Sun Chuang-fang had taken up the offer dangled in Fu-cheng's letter to her had not been unexpected, but it had surprised her that he had delegated such an important matter entirely to Yi-liang, and that they were both prepared to countenance her continuing involvement as the go-between with her brother. In fact her presence, she saw, had helped: every meeting with her brother could be disguised as a family gathering.

There had been no conflict with her duties to her other masters. The orders she had found in the dress shop merely told her to do all she could to encourage this alliance, and to report the details. It would be in the revolution's interests for the northern warlords to fight each other.

So, over the several meetings in her house, and once on an apparent pleasure excursion to Soochow, when Fu-cheng had had a quiet meeting with Sun Chuan-fang in the upper storey of a teahouse by the lake, the details of the alliance between the Fengtian and Kiangsu factions were worked out. There had been little disagreement over the military preparations (although Fu-kuei suspected that her outline of the various battalion strengths on either side was certainly what interested her other masters most), but there had been a major argument about the post-war settlement, particularly on the matter of which warlord would ultimately control the rich province of Shantung. Neither Yi-liang nor her brother could make a decision on this, and it had taken several references back to their respective warlords, but Fu-kuei had enjoyed the confrontation between her brother's wheedling plausibility and Yi-liang's insouciance. In the end Yi-liang had proved the better poker player, for Fu-cheng, with a chuckle and a flap of his little hands, had conceded Shantung in exchange for Henan for Chang Tso-lin. Yi-liang, his eyes shining with humour under a theatrical frown, had slapped the table and agreed. All that remained was to negotiate the financial settlement, the incentive for General Sun, and Fu-kuei had been staggered by the amount of Mexican silver dollars that Yi-liang had quietly asked for.

Another bargaining session began, and ultimately Yi-liang had knocked six million dollars off his demand in exchange for joint control of Henan, which he had deftly returned to the table. Fu-cheng, his legs dangling from his chair, had shaken his head from side to side and told his sister that she had found not only a champion of soldiers to be her lover, but also a champion of horse-traders – and then he had clasped Yi-liang's hand. It was all agreed, except for the details of the payment, and the incidental matter of where the money would come from, which was why poor Lei Tang had come to be squeezed between them this evening. He was now taking refuge in his abacus.

'We have accepted your exorbitant interest rates,' said Fu-cheng, kindly. 'Your bank will make a fortune. I will personally tell your father how skilfully you have negotiated. He will be proud of you.'

'It is the risk,' whispered Lei Tang miserably. 'As I understand it you are planning a war.'

'There may be a war,' said Fu-cheng, 'and if there is you will achieve even better returns. And were we not talking about a governorship of the central bank for your father? Just think of the prestige and opportunity. Major, can you not see young Lei here one day taking up the position of finance minister in a unified China?'

'He has all the right qualities,' murmured Yi-liang.

Fu-kuei put the lid back on the pot, leaving a few moments for the leaves to settle.

There was an irony here, she decided. When she had been under obligation to Yi-liang, it had not been difficult to hate or despise him. Once she had begun to spy on him, it had been as if their relationship had equalised. Extraordinarily, it had created a complicity between them. They were partners. He supplied the information. She passed it on – and every time she betrayed him she felt closer to him. Once Fu-cheng's letter had arrived, and Yi-liang had drawn her into the negotiations, they had become partners in fact. Her other masters even sanctioned it. They laughed together every time he scored a point against her brother. She had instinctively taken Yi-liang's side. She began to enjoy the game she was playing and, imperceptibly, her respect and affection for him had grown. More than that, she began to notice his physical presence when he was in the room. And at night she found she was no longer pretending anything.

As she moved her palm to feel the temperature of the teapot, she remembered how, the night before, she had nestled against him under the blankets, to escape the icy wind that rattled the windows and haunted her dreams. The warmth in his belly and thighs had gradually suffused her own, creating a heat within that caused her to cling to him the more. In his sleep, his protective arms had curled round her shoulders and, responding to her lips on his nipple when she pressed her head urgently against his chest, his hands had moved slowly down her sides, cupping her breasts, rounding her thighs, lifting her behind, settling her on his hardness, in oh-so-gentle a rhythm. Their heat had melded in a liquid fire below, while their tongues and lips twisted and sucked in the private pavilion of her hair, which had fallen in silken folds over his face, enclosing them in a personal world of touch and texture, moisture and smell, where intellect, dialectic and complexity were expelled. Afterwards he had kissed her chin, her nose, her eyes, her lips, then his tongue had kneaded her ear, and not a word had been spoken, before his hot breath had settled back into regular sighs, and his hand on her sex had slipped on to the sheet. After a while she, too, heard the night rattle no more.

She shivered at the memory. She was afraid – because she knew these feelings. She had experienced them before, with her husband Wang Yi. Then she had thought of them as love.

It was with a start that she focused back on the dining room.

'No,' Lei Tang was murmuring, his face twisted with discomfort and fear. 'My father would never agree. If anything went wrong, our bank would face ruin. Perhaps for half the sum . . .'

'My friend, my friend. Cousin,' smiled Fu-cheng, 'do you think that I, who owe everything to your family, would be capable of suggesting anything that would not be to your ultimate profit? This is an undreamed-of opportunity we are offering you. Where is your patriotism?'

'I can't,' whimpered Lei Tang.

It must be time soon, thought Fu-kuei, for her brother and Yi-liang to produce the trump card, which until now they had kept concealed. Quietly, she moved to the table and replenished their glasses of tea. She sat down, folding her hands on her lap. Yi-liang smiled at her.

Could she really have lost her self control to the extent that she was falling in love with him? Could she be capable of such a major lapse in discipline?

A cold chill down her spine reminded her that it was not the first time. There was still the issue of Catherine to be resolved.

She had not reported Catherine to her masters. Although she knew she was flouting procedure, she had decided to wait for positive proof that Catherine had betrayed her, unwittingly or otherwise. Rereading Lan-hua's letter she had realised that Catherine had not spoken to her about Fu-kuei and would be unlikely even to meet her again, since Lan-hua was in Canton and Catherine was in the north. Fu-cheng was the greater danger anyway: he had plans to come to Shanghai. She had decided to probe him after he arrived to establish how well he knew Catherine, whom after all he had only mentioned in an aside in his letter. After their first reunion, and the tears she had guessed they had both manufactured, she had steered the subject to his letter, asking for more details about the scandals in the Lei household, enquiring who were these foreigners whom he had mentioned. 'Who was the red-headed girl?' she asked archly.

Her heart had leaped into her mouth when he had answered dismissively, 'The fiancée, I think, of one of Ai Er Tun *Daifu*'s sons. A rather difficult young woman, I would imagine, although I have never directly spoken to her. She was rude to General Lin when they were recently in Shishan. I doubt we'll be inviting her again! Why do you ask?' His eyes had twinkled.

'Oh,' she had answered slyly, 'I was curious that you had mentioned a woman in one of your letters.'

'Why shouldn't I mention a woman?' He had grinned. 'I will marry one day – but not a foreign fox like her!'

'You marry, dear brother?' She had laughed. 'You are a monk without the saffron robes.' He had responded in kind, and the subject had dissolved in sibling banter, while inside she was almost faint with relief. He had not spoken to her! He did not want to see her again! Catherine was reprieved!

Fu-kuei had relaxed after that – but she knew she was justifying a lapse of duty. She had allowed personal feelings to come in the way of her work.

And now she was allowing herself to fall into an even more dangerous trap. Behrens again! He always had an answer to everything: *So often in a honey operation . . . the seducer is seduced.* She would control herself.

But as Yi-liang leaned forward for the kill, his boyish smile was so attractive. 'You have mentioned before that the Lei family is patriotic,' he said quietly.

'Indeed. They are a byword for the old Confucian virtues,' said Fu-cheng.

'How interesting,' said Yi-liang. 'And the children – they also have these Confucian virtues?'

'Of course,' said Fu-cheng. 'Especially Lei Tang here.' He gave him an affectionate smile.

Yi-liang reached into the pocket of his tunic for a report, which he spread over the table, checking details as he spoke. 'Yet his sister works for the propaganda department of the Kuomintang in Canton, and has known affiliations with the Chinese Communist Party. On January the twenty-second she attended a talk given by CCP Committee member, Li Ta-chao. Two nights later she was seen at a rally organised by the CCP to protest against the foreign concession at Shameen Island, a demonstration incidentally condemned by the Kuomintang propaganda department for which she works . . . Need I go on?'

Lei Tang sat silent, his face drained of colour.

Fu-cheng waved a hand. 'My dear Major Yang, I know this girl. She is young and misguided. She has gone to Canton entirely against the wishes of her father . . .'

'She has a brother, Lei Ming,' Yi-liang continued inexorably, 'whom it appears that you, Minister, have taken under your wing – but after his return from university in the United States he wrote two articles for left-wing magazines expressing extreme socialist views. I have the clippings here . . .'

'Yes, yes, I know. I have read them,' sighed Fu-cheng. 'I have talked to the boy often about this, and I am encouraged that he has amended his views.'

'I'm sure he has,' said Yi-liang. 'And no doubt the girl in Canton is also a harmless young thing – but it provokes questions about the Lei banking family, which raises such non-conformist children.'

Fu-cheng lifted his eyebrows in nicely feigned horror. 'You are not suggesting . . .'

Lei Tang's voice was a croak: 'My father has disinherited them.'

'That is easy to claim, but more difficult to prove,' said Yi-liang. 'It would be most unfortunate if Marshal Wu Pei-fu, who presently holds jurisdiction over Tientsin, were to receive a report like this. Even more so if he were to hear that the Lei Bank had been negotiating with his enemies . . .'

Fu-cheng shook his head. 'Major Yang, that is a shocking idea. It is in poor taste and, besides, unnecessary to make such threats, for Lei Tang, I am sure, has already been reconsidering his position, and I am certain that we are near agreement. Are we not, Lei Tang?' Lei Tang was sitting with his mouth open, shaking. Fu-kuei wondered if tears were glistening in his shadowed eyes. 'Mr Lei, have some more tea,' she offered, in her most placatory tone.

There were times during that snow-flurried winter and dust-choked spring when if Catherine had known her assassination was being debated in her friend's mind she might have welcomed such an easy way out of her problems. Not since that day in the forest glade when she had discovered her friends' murdered bodies and herself adrift on the tide of revolution had she found herself so rudderless, confused, or abandoned – and when she attempted to pull herself together and find a way forward, she discovered that her thoughts had no more pattern than the snowflakes or the yellow sandstorms swirling outside the window in Meadows Road.

Edmund had not been angry. He had been formal and distant. There had been no opportunity to talk to him before they left Shishan. Their last day there had been a numb round of visits to friends of the elder Airtons. Somehow she had found the words when she was spoken to but her awareness was centred on Edmund, at the other side of the table, or walking ahead with his parents, calm, considerate, speaking his beautiful Chinese, polite, unapproachable. Nellie had taken her on a short walk through the snow with Dr Brown's children, but her heart was not in the games; again, somehow, she pretended. She had not feigned the tears when finally they hugged and their thin arms clung round her neck, but she did not know if she was crying for her, for them, or for them all. There had been no grand farewell at the station that evening; only a surly, chastened Dr Brown had seen them off. At the last minute she had remembered Martha, and telephoned the school. She had told *Hsiao* Hung their departure time, but Martha had not been on the platform. Catherine had been relieved. At the end of dinner, she had found herself alone with Edmund, again in the familiar surroundings of a dining-car, although this time they were not disturbed by George, who, tactfully for once, had retired to his bunk with his parents.

She apologised. She begged his forgiveness. She explained that kissing George had meant nothing. It had been a mistake. She had been drunk. She told him that she loved him. Edmund had listened to her, with calm attentiveness, smoking his pipe. 'I don't think that's the point,' he had said quietly.

'The point? What do you mean?' she had blustered. 'I love you.'

He had sighed, and put down his pipe. 'Oh, Catherine,' he said. 'There's nothing to forgive. You're you, and I love you for it.'

'Well, then,' she had insisted, trying to reach his hands, which he pulled away.

'It wasn't the kiss,' he said. 'I know it meant nothing. That was just George being mischievous. I think he's jealous. Oh, dammit, you can kiss whomever you like and I won't care. Nothing you can do will ever make me feel any different towards you.'

Tears were running down her cheeks. 'Then what? I don't understand.'

He frowned. 'It's not you,' he said finally, 'it's me.' He sighed. 'I walked last night, Catherine. In the snow. I don't know where I went. When the dawn came up I found myself miles away, deep in the countryside, and had to find a carter to bring me back to the hotel. And all the time I was thinking. Mainly of you. How much I loved you. The life you exude. The joy, the naturalness, the exuberance. It was all those things, not the kiss, that impressed me on the dance-floor. I was there for some time, watching you. I think George saw me before he kissed you. Maybe he wanted to queer my pitch. It didn't matter, because I knew already it wouldn't work between us. No, don't say anything, let me finish.

'I'm twelve years older than you. That may not be important. Some marriages work at twice that age difference – but it's something I'm conscious of. Maybe I also feel a heel for pressing my attentions on you in your moment of weakness. When you were down because of your father. I think you believe you love me. Now. But you were looking for a father and I'm an older shoulder who can give you support . . .'

'Edmund, that's not what I feel!' she cried. 'That's insulting, and patronising.'

'You may be right,' he said, bowing his head. He seemed to be struggling for words. 'Actually, none of that's important,' he said, lifting his head. 'You see, I – I don't think it would be fair to you. I'm not right for you. I saw you dancing, laughing with George. I'm a stick in the mud. I'm old. Not in years perhaps, but inside. You'd tire of me, I know it – and I couldn't bear that. We do have things in common. The war. Nurse. Doctor. But what does that come down to? We share a wound. That's not something to build a marriage on, a life together. Slowly, I would fill your world with shadow, when you were born to live in the light. I won't do that to you.'

'If we're hurt can't we heal each other?'

'No,' he answered quietly. 'No, I don't think so. I – I haven't the confidence in myself.'

She had begged. She had pleaded. She had become angry. She had cried. The white-capped Chinese dining attendants, polishing the glasses, had grinned to hide their embarrassment. Edmund had been adamant. Finally, he had told her that he was too tired and confused to say any more. Let them talk again when they reached Tientsin.

They had not talked again in Tientsin. Shortly after arriving back at Meadows Road, Edmund had packed his small rucksack with his clothes and left for Tangshan, where he had stayed for six weeks. Meanwhile Fate, not satisfied with what it had done to Catherine already, had delivered its *coup de foudre*. Waiting for her on the side table of the Airtons's hall had been a letter from her solicitors, whom she had left to deal with the issues of her mother's estate. It was a brief, businesslike note, telling her the debts were such that they could only be settled by drawing on what remained of her mother's earlier legacy from the Cabots, who, the lawyers had discovered, had changed their wills before their death in the influenza epidemic of '17. There had been a lot of complicated explanation, but the message was simple enough: she was penniless.

She had stood in the hall and laughed her harsh laugh, shocking poor Nellie and Edward Airton. In the space of a fortnight, she had lost her father, her lover and now her income. She was waif indeed.

Of course the Airtons had been kind. They were always kind. Nellie had told her that, as far as they were concerned, Catherine was part of the family. She could stay on at Meadows Road, certainly until they departed for England, and if she wanted she could accompany them back on the voyage – they would pay her passage, they would be delighted to have her company. At home they would help her challenge this ludicrous decision of the courts. Catherine had assented. She had no other idea of what she wanted to do.

For the first two weeks she had moped in her room, watching the snow falling outside the window. Edmund would return. It had been such a silly misunderstanding, she told herself. He had been hurt and would recover. He had said he loved her. She was so confident that she even recovered some of her cheerfulness . . .

Edmund did not return. The third week she had been irritated and impatient. The fourth week she was angry. The fifth week she despaired. By the sixth she was showing signs of a fever, which had developed into something approaching pneumonia by the seventh. That had perhaps been a good thing, she decided later. She could not have faced the Christmas festivities. Lying in bed, she was spared the good cheer, or most of it. At one point they all came up to see her in their paper hats – Edward and Nellie, George, his sister Jenny and her husband, Lionel Charters. Jenny had been full of her husband's promotion to run the Maritime Customs Service in Nanking, and Catherine had smiled wanly as she chattered on, wishing they would go away. She had wondered where Edmund was. He appeared later, alone, without a paper hat, looking as easy and relaxed as he always did, giving her a sad but not unaffectionate smile.

'Hello, Nurse,' he said. 'Happy Christmas.'

She had had the strength to turn away her head. She did not want him to see her tears.

After a while he had left, saying he would come again when she was feeling better. He didn't, and she was relieved.

Before the end of the year she had recovered enough to get out of bed. She waited until the day after she had heard that Edmund had returned to Tangshan. Then she surprised everybody by coming down for supper, fully dressed and made-up. George beamed with pleasure and said something rude, and she responded in kind. Nellie and Edward Airton looked on in wonder as the drink and wit flowed. After the old couple had gone to bed, Catherine stayed on for a nightcap. George brought his drink and cigar over to her sofa, and sat down beside her. 'Well, you've made a resurrection and a half,' he said, 'but I'm glad to see you in the land of the living again.'

She looked at him coldly. 'You owe me,' she said.

'What have I done now?' he expostulated.

'You knew Edmund was watching when you kissed me on the dance-floor.'

He became very still. 'I seem to recall you responded enthusiastically.'

Abruptly, she rose to her feet and walked to the door.

'Oh dear,' she heard him drawl. 'Am I to be punished?'

She paused, then turned and gave him a long, frosty look. 'Yes, George,' she answered. 'I think you are.' Before she turned to go, she added, 'You might leave your bedroom door ajar tonight. That'd be a start.'

Their first love-making had been mechanical. George had no technique. He had been sitting stiffly in his purple pyjamas on the side of the bed when she came in, his feet pushed into his leather slippers as if willing them to be glued to the floor. His gaucheness and nervousness surprised her. He had reminded her of the bashful chorister from Brasenose she had seduced as a dare during her second year at Oxford. She had regretted it afterwards because she felt she had hurt the boy, who had fallen in love with her. It had been against her rules. She had no such qualms about George. She dealt with him brusquely, lifting her nightdress over her head and pushing him backwards on the bed. Roughly she opened his buttons and smoothed her hands down his chest and belly, appreciating the firm flesh and tight muscle in a detached way, as she did the rounded strength of his arms. She ignored the alarm in his eyes as she undid the cord at his waist. He was not hard, so she made him so, using her fingers and her tongue. Then she lowered herself on top of him and rode him till he sighed. She could feel him come, and slacken, but she tightened herself and kept him inside her. He groaned and smiled, and she saw his lips forming to say something. 'Don't you utter a bloody word,' she panted venomously. He looked confused. After a moment, gingerly, he moved his hands to touch her breasts. 'Yes, you can do that,' she said.

Eventually he hardened again. He lifted himself and embraced her, kissing her shoulders, her chest, her neck. She allowed him to roll her underneath him, and he pounded vigorously, enthusiastically above her until he had climaxed again. He gave a great exhalation, and flopped on to his back beside her. 'My God, Catherine! Why ever didn't we do that before?' he had cried, then propped himself on one elbow to look down at her. She felt him lift a sticky strand of hair from her forehead. 'Goodness, you're crying.'

'I'll get over it,' she had said dully. She lifted her legs off the bed, put on her nightdress and left, feeling George's bewildered gaze on her.

After that she had visited his bedroom infrequently, spacing the intervals to tantalise him, keep him guessing and in thrall, but she insisted that every evening he take her out on the town. The night following her seduction of him, if such it could be called, had been the great New Year ball at the Gordon Hall. She had gone dressed to kill. She did not dance with George, but she did with everybody else – Willie Lampsett, Robby and stranger after stranger. The men flocked round her. She laughed and flirted. The ladies looked disdainfully at her and, no doubt, whispered about her in the dressing room. Occasionally she had observed George, at the side of the dance-floor, cigar in his mouth, eyes shining with admiration, smiling proprietorially. She drank with abandon – only champagne. In the early hours of the morning, when first light was already illuminating the stained-glass and mullioned windows, she had pulled George off a sofa, instructing him to take her home. Her head was as clear as if she had just doused herself under a cold shower.

The next night she insisted George give her dinner at the Astor House Hotel. On the dance-floor she had cut away the partner of a mousy American girl wearing a pearl necklace that did not suit her, leaving her to the attentions of George while she flirted with the girl's delighted fiancé until the bar closed. George, who had gathered the rules of the game, patiently and good-humouredly regaled the girl with the most racy and shocking tales he could invent. However, when he attempted to share the joke with Catherine on the drive back to their house, she ignored him.

Occasionally Catherine and George would go out with Willie Lampsett and Robby on their rampages as they had done before, but more and more Catherine's interest was on the wider social scene in Tientsin. George, as a personable raconteur and champion jockey, was much in demand, not only with the younger set but also among the *taipans* of the big hongs who enjoyed his irreverence and wit. Hostesses began to realise, however, and it was not to their liking, that an invitation to George had to include Catherine Cabot, or he would politely refuse. Their menfolk relished Catherine's company. She was guaranteed to shock in some way or other, challenging over the dinner-table even the most senior members of the community on their social responsibilities, their ignorance of Chinese politics, or anything else that came into her head. With her intellect (and the ideas she had picked up from Edmund during their long walks before Shishan) she could usually argue her corner convincingly, with a sharp, railing humour that, far from irritating the old men, flattered them. Their wives would see this for the flirtation it was and frown. At dances with the younger men – the junior cadres from Jardine's or Swire's and other hongs – her flirtations were more obvious, and there were several broken hearts as she played off one against another. On these occasions, George would always be in the background, smiling indulgently, smoking his cigar, ready to take her home when she wanted to leave. He appeared to relish the game. By not reacting to her disdain of him, he was raising the stakes.

In the daytime, while George was at the China Railways, Catherine would be on her own. She had refused all of Nellie's invitations to join her in her charity work with the women's guild or her bridge sessions with other missionary wives, and after a while, Nellie had stopped asking her. She saw little of Catherine, who would sleep late, and sit for most of the day in her room where she thought of ... nothing. Sometimes, when she was home, Nellie would knock and bring her a cup of tea. 'Are you all right, dear?' she would always ask, looking at her keenly with her piercing eyes, and every time Catherine would answer, 'Yes, I'm fine,' or, to justify the long hours she spent in her room, 'Just a little tired.' Nellie would leave. At five Catherine would bathe and dress for the evening.

One night, as Catherine was leaving him after her perfunctory love-making, George told her he would stick the course. 'I'm not going to lose, you know. Only the brave deserve the fair, and all that.'

'You really think there's anything to win?' she had said, as she slipped out of the door.

Towards the end of February, the farewell parties for the Airtons began. Catherine was naturally included in the invitations. What she said to some of the missionaries, about atheism, about rice Christians, no doubt shocked Nellie and Edward, but they, too, seemed to grasp that some game was being played inside Catherine's soul, and remained quiet. On these occasions George would listen and smile. Only Edmund could not hide his pain, which made Catherine smile.

A couple of weeks before the Airtons's departure, over dinner at the Astor House Hotel, George lit his cigar while she drank her coffee, and grinned at her. 'Are you going to keep this up until the boat goes?'

Catherine gave him a sour look but did not reply.

'You really intend to go back to Britain with Ma and Pa?'

'Have I a choice?' she said.

'You have several, actually.'

'And what are they?'

'You could jack it all in somewhere in the Indian Ocean – you could make it rather dramatic. Break a few hearts first. Have the purser at daggers drawn with the first officer or whomever you decide to seduce. End it all with a bit of scandalous behaviour at one of the on-board parties, then disappear into the blustery waves. They'd talk about it all the way to Suez, maybe even Gibraltar.'

'You're being serious, aren't you? What makes you say that?' she said, looking at him keenly. 'Do I seem the suicidal type?'

'You put on a pretty good impression of hating the world. And yourself,' said George. 'That's what it's all about, isn't it? But you're not self-pitying. You're decisive enough, and you have a sense of style. I can see you putting on a last grand show.' He puffed happily at his cigar.

'And what are my other choices? If I don't decide to – jack it in?'

'Well, you can head back with Ma and Pa. Make their lives a misery for a while. Go the round of the solicitors to discover there isn't any way you can get your money back, and take up a job as a typist on some rainy London high street. That's an option, I suppose.'

'You see me becoming a typist?'

'There are other professions for attractive women with no money. You'd start at the top end, no doubt, but it's a slippery slope.'

She laughed. 'Marriage? Children? Some respectable husband? That's not an option, I suppose?'

'No, Catherine,' said George. 'You're too proud, and too honest, to live a lie.'

'So what does my adviser suggest? Besides leaping off a boat in the Indian Ocean.'

'Stay here,' he said. 'With me.'

She put down her coffee cup, and stared at him. He was nonchalantly blowing out a cloud of smoke. 'Over the last few weeks have I not made perfectly clear what I think of you?' she asked icily.

'Perfectly,' he said. 'That's why I'm proposing to you.'

'You think I'd marry you?'

'Yes,' he said. 'I think it'd be rather fun, don't you? I'm due months of leave, and I can extend it anyway. We can have a damned good honeymoon. After the racing season, of course. I want to run China Coast a few more times.'

Catherine, for once, had been stunned into silence.

'Think about it,' he said, 'while you're breaking some other poor sod's heart on the dance-floor tonight in your attempt to punish me. Here's something to concentrate your mind. Treat it as an engagement token, if you like. Or just a gift from George. You should wear it in any case. It matches both the colour of your hair and your delicious anger.' He flipped open the lid of a small velvet-covered box. It contained an enormous ruby ring. 'If the worst comes to the worst,' he added, stubbing out his cigar, 'you can pawn it. It may buy you a month or so to decide whether you want to become a typist or take up an older profession.'

Eventually she agreed. She imposed many conditions. A truce was declared. She no longer visited his room at night. In return she flirted less and less with others on her evenings out with him. Usually they dined together, danced quietly or sat with their cock-tails and returned to Meadows Road early.

One evening, together, they met Nellie and Edward Airton in the latter's study, and announced their engagement. Nellie exchanged a long glance with her husband, who appeared to hunch in his chair. 'It's not what I expected,' she said, after a while. 'Catherine, are you serious about this?'

'Of course I am, Aunt Nellie,' said Catherine.

'You love my son?'

'We're made for each other,' said Catherine.

'Then there's nothing I can say,' said Nellie.

'You could try "congratulations",' said George, cheerfully.

'I hope so. Oh, I hope so,' said Nellie. 'Here, you'd better both give me a kiss,' she said, and sniffed back her tears.

The Airtons departed on schedule, leaving their house in Meadows Road to George and Catherine as a wedding gift, on the stipulation that Edmund could have a room there if he needed one. Jenny, who had come up to Tientsin with her children for her parents' departure, elected to stay on in the house, on the excuse that she would be helping to prepare for the wedding, but really, on Nellie's insistence, to act as chaperone. Nellie did not wish tongues to wag which they would if George and Catherine lived alone there for the three months before their marriage. In the event, George moved in with Willie Lampsett, so Catherine and Jenny were left to their own devices. They lived separate lives. Jenny had her friends among the Tientsin wives. Catherine rediscovered her former interest in learning Chinese. She and George went out in the evenings as usual.

Two days before the wedding, Edmund returned from Tangshan, and took his old room in the house. He was kindly and affectionate with Catherine, congratulating her on her engagement to his younger brother. She was pained to see that he was sincere. They had dinner alone together. Willie and Robby were giving George a stag night, and Jenny was out with her friends. Silver glinted in the dark-panelled dining room as *Lao* Tang served them with a formality that had not changed since the elder Airtons's departure. At first they ate silently.

'Well, Nurse,' Edmund said finally, putting down his knife and fork, 'it's all worked out for the best.'

'You think so?' she said.

He sighed. 'Yes, I do,' he said.

'You don't have any regrets?' she asked.

He was still for a long moment. 'Better to say I don't,' he said.

'How noble you are.' She excused herself shortly afterwards and lay on her bed. She heard Jenny return, a murmur of conversation between her and her brother before they went to their bedrooms. Then there were only the noises of the night. She waited a long time.

His door slipped open easily. The room was washed in pale blue moonlight. He had the windows and curtains open, and she felt a chill breeze touch her skin as, in a movement that was now familiar to her, she lifted her nightdress over her head. Edmund's room was similar to George's, but in Edmund's there was a tall, standing mirror. In its reflection she could see her white body and his head against the pillow. The picture she saw was Pre-Raphaelite: the noble features of the sleeping knight, beside him the temptress, with ivory limbs, waves of russet hair hanging modestly over her breasts and, most striking to her, the sad, solemn visage of the betrayed and betraying maiden, dark shadows under the eyes and slightly parted lips, expressing a sorrow and yearning that surprised her when she recognised it was herself.

'Edmund,' she said, in a hard, clear voice, which shattered the atmosphere.

His eyes flicked open. He saw her and turned away his head. 'Catherine!' he cried. 'What are you thinking of?'

'Look at me,' she said. 'Look at me, Edmund.'

She saw his features, cracked half in horror, half in fascination. She waited, secure in her power over him. His eyes strained to keep themselves on her face but, with satisfaction, she saw them lower, towards her breasts, towards the alluring dark region below, and up again. She saw his lips quiver, in desperation, in fear, and his eyes plead wildly. She leaned forward slowly so that strands of her hair brushed his face. She put a finger to his lips, and whispered, 'Hush, it's all right.' She lifted the sheet and slipped in beside him, enclosing his rigid body in her arms, pressing herself against him. She moved her lips to his. They resisted. She felt him trying to turn away. 'Sssh,' she breathed, and kissed him softly. It did not take him long to respond, as she had known he would.

She kept her lips on his, sliding her tongue along his teeth, finding the tip of his own. She felt his hands run the length of her arms and settle on her back. Keeping the kiss, she let her hands move inside his pyjamas. She pulled the cotton cord, and touched him below. She felt him shudder. There was no need to excite him as she had to with George. She ran a finger along his length, then enfolded him in her palm, stroking his arousal, feeling it grow. He broke away. 'We can't do this, Catherine,' he whispered, but as he spoke she felt his fingers on her breast.

'We can, my darling. We are,' she murmured, nuzzling his chest, aware that his touch on her nipple was lighting fires in her. She settled on her back, allowing him to lead. His lips and tongue moved over her body, exploring her nipple, the curve of her breast, her belly, the hollows of her hips; his moustache ruffled the down on her thighs, and mingled with the coarser hairs of her triangle. Her body arched as she felt the soft, wet touch in her cleft. She groaned and pulled him to her, fumbling with her fingers to guide him, and then he was inside her, filling her. 'Oh, Edmund' – she wanted to say, 'my darling,' but she could only gasp as he possessed her.

'Oh, God, oh, God,' she heard him cry. 'We mustn't. We shouldn't,' but he intensified the rhythm of his thrusts. She gripped his legs with her heels, her nails gouged his back, her head rocked from side to side, and she saw his face grimace, as if with unbearable pain, as he arched his back above her, and then he groaned and she groaned, and he fell on her body panting. And after that he wept. 'What have I done? What have I done?'

'You've fucked your brother's fiancée, Edmund,' she said coldly. 'What do you think?'

'Forgive me. Forgive me.'

'For cheating your brother, or abandoning me?' she asked. 'Bit late in either case, isn't it?' But even as she spoke she brushed away the flop of hair that had fallen over his forehead. It was something she had always wanted to do. 'You'll get over it,' she said. 'I have. Anyway, now you know what you'll be missing.'

She left him lying face down, sobbing.

'Oh, by the way,' she added sweetly, 'I wouldn't worry about our precious age difference. You performed rather well. One of the better fucks I've had recently.'

As she passed the mirror, her nightgown over her shoulder, she had one last look at her reflection. She saw a lithe body, a maenad on a Greek vase wearing a cruel smile. As she stepped into the corridor, a door opened and Jenny's face peered out, her hair in curlers, her face masked in white cream. She looked like a clown from Chinese opera, especially when her eyes widened in shock.

Catherine, naked, sauntered down the corridor towards her, and pressed her face close to the startled eyes. 'You won't say anything about this to anybody, dear Jenny, will you? It would be such a shame to spoil the wedding, which you've prepared so beautifully. Goodnight, darling,' she added, and kissed the white cheek.

Chuckling, she made her away back along the corridor to her room, her nightgown dragging behind her along the carpet, like a hunter's trophy.

Next day, after a magnificent ceremony at the Catholic cathedral (George had dutifully gone through the lessons with Father Molinari and converted to the true faith), followed by a memorable reception at the Jockey Club, an event that merited two full columns and a photograph in the *Peking and Tientsin Times*, with Willie Lampsett as best man, Mrs Jenny Charters as matron-of-honour, and her children as bridesmaids and pages, George Airton and Catherine Cabot were married. Some people noticed that George's elder brother slipped away before the reception. He was not on the pier, later that afternoon, when the newly married couple were seen off on a liner for the first leg of their year-long, round-the-world cruise.

That autumn, Borodin arrived in Canton.

Lei Lan-hua and her colleagues in the propaganda department were among the first to see him. They clustered by the window that overlooked the garden that separated their office building from the Presidential Palace, and gazed with awe at the two great figures strolling deep in conversation across the lawn. They made a striking contrast: President Sun, in his Chinese gown, exuded a frail dignity; the Russian, in his pearl grey commissar's tunic, embodied strength and purpose. Lan-hua was captivated. She saw a well-set, lank-haired man with a pale face and a heavy moustache. His white features were lined with care. His eyes were deeply shadowed, but they shone with intelligence and resolution, and there was authority in his gestures. When he raised his finger to express a point, he inspired confidence. She felt a tingle in her spine: she was looking at history in the making. Moscow had been true to its word. It had sent its adviser, Lenin's personal emissary. The international revolution had come to China.

Over the next month, the offices and corridors buzzed with rumour. The long-promised Northern Expedition, to rid the country of the warlords, was at hand. Arms and funds would come in Borodin's wake. General Chiang Kai-shek had gone to Moscow to negotiate the details. Meanwhile Borodin, an experienced Russian activist, who had formed Communist parties in countries as far away as Mexico and England, would remodel the Kuomintang on revolutionary lines. There were counter-rumours. The more reactionary elements within the Kuomintang had become alarmed when, at a reception, Borodin had equated President Sun's Three Principles – People's Rights, People's Nation and People's Livelihood – with the principles of the Bolshevik revolution: Democracy, Nationalism and Socialism. The idea of socialism had scared the wealthy businessmen and arch conservatives who made up the right wing of the party, and they were attempting to persuade President Sun that Borodin, far from coming to assist nationalism in China, had the subversive intention of setting up a Communist state. There seemed to be deadlock, and Lan-hua and her friends were worried when President Sun's meetings with Borodin became less frequent.

By November, the city was in turmoil. The local warlord, Chen Ch'iung-ming, hearing of the arrival of the Soviet advisers, had decided to march on Canton to drive out President Sun and the Kuomintang for good – and with only three hundred professional troops and their general away in Moscow, the president and other government officials were planning flight to Japan.

When she met her friend John Soo one evening for dumplings, even he, who had such confidence in the revolution, was depressed. As usual, he was well informed. He told her that at a meeting of the Central Executive Committee of the Kuomintang that day, the defeatism had been alarming. 'But what about the Russian support?' she had asked. 'Surely Borodin can do something?'

'Borodin is just one man,' he said, 'and a foreigner. Even the Communist Party here are divided about him. Some of them don't want a revolution to be led by Moscow. They might be happy to see him fail.'

'No,' she said, 'that's impossible.'

'We'll see,' he said, in the calm, wise way she so admired. 'Borodin's speaking to the committee tomorrow. Let's see what happens. There are some good people among the Nationalists. Liao Ch'ung-kai is steady, and as Sun's vice president his views carry some weight.'

She heard about Borodin's speech afterwards. He had spoken with cold, controlled anger as he told them they were blind to the one asset that they, and only they in the whole country, had. 'The unity and strength of the people,' he thundered. 'You think a puny warlord can stand up to the mobilised will of the masses? If you had listened to me we would already have ten thousand workers at the front.' And he had proceeded to outline, in impressive detail, how volunteer militias should be formed, how the city should be barricaded and defended. 'I promise you, the workers of this province will flock to your colours if you offer them reform, and if this bandit's army were twice the size they will drive it away!' He had finished speaking to a shout of applause.

Two nights later, Lan-hua had found herself, with her hair tucked into a forage cap and a heavy rifle in her hands, beside John Soo, in a hastily dug slit trench on the bank of the river. The dark mass of the city could be seen downstream, and moonlight made rippling patterns on the black stream. Occasionally a sampan or a junk would glide by, the creak of its rudder distinct against the lapping sound of the water. They were waiting for the sky to explode with gunfire and shells. She had never been more terrified in her life; or – and this was strange – so content to be where she was. She could not remember such excitement in the mere fact of being alive. She heard the flutter of a night bird in the trees behind her, and started; at the same time she saw John Soo smiling at her behind his glasses, and she smiled back. The long night passed in his comradeship, and later, when the most beautiful dawn she had ever seen in her life streaked the waters and cloud with stunning streamers of red and gold, she had hugged him out of sheer spontaneity and joy that they had survived.

The very fact that the Nationalists had resisted was enough to scare off the warlord's army. Chen Chiung-ming had outnumbered the rag-tag defenders by ten to one, but warlord armies on the whole did not like fighting, and certainly feared determination.

After the Nationalist victory, Borodin's influence was assured. He was careful to give all the credit to President Sun Yat-sen. During the Nationalist congress in January, when all his recommendations to restructure the party were adopted, he kept a low profile, allowing President Sun Yat-sen and Vice President Liao Chung-kai to make the speeches. After that, he remained in the background. Although he and his wife, Fanya, were usually to be seen somewhere at the rear of the rostrum whenever there was a public pronouncement, he rarely spoke.

However, Lan-hua saw him almost every day, in the garden below her window, talking animatedly to President Sun or to other leaders of the Party. He had been given his own offices in a house behind the president's. One day, Lan-hua was ordered to report there. She had been chosen, because of her knowledge of English, to be a junior interpreter. To her delight, she found that the work involved much more than interpretation or translation: she was one of a small team working on a new constitution for China. In her office she also had a chance to see who came to visit the Russian adviser, and after a while, she was no longer surprised to recognise among the callers many whom she had thought most reactionary in the party. The ambitious, it was clear, had come to appreciate that the quickest path to the president was through the offices of Mikhail Borodin.

General Chiang Kai-shek returned from Moscow and he also came to call. He was a proud, conservative young soldier, but even he seemed affected by Borodin's easy charm. Once Lan-hua interpreted for him in Borodin's study. He and his military adviser, a gruff, hard man called General Galen, were showing Borodin the plans for the new Whampoa military arsenal, which would be built on a confluence of the Pearl river and provide training for the army that would one day sweep to the north. General Chiang's deputy as commandant of the new arsenal, was also there. Colonel Chou En-lai, she was thrilled to hear, was a senior member of the CCP. It had been Borodin's achievement that Chinese Communists were now in alliance with the Kuomintang.

The only time she allowed herself to break away from her work was when John Soo was in town. She looked forward to his infrequent leaves from the arsenal. As a CCP member and an engineer trained at Oxford University, he had been recruited by Chou En-lai to work in the artillery section, where he was much occupied in designing new guns and batteries. She knew this was important work, and told herself that she did not resent the fact that she saw him so seldom. It had been drummed into her by the Party disciplinary section during their study sessions that personal lives must be secondary to political work, and she accepted this – but that could not prevent her counting the days until his next leave. Her colleagues had, of course, noticed her excitement when such a day came near, and teased her mercilessly. She disliked it, and sometimes went so far as to lose her temper with them. John Soo was a good friend, she told them. He was her political mentor, older than she was. Shouldn't activists use their connections with older comrades to broaden their political experience? But even as she said it she blushed, remembering that night on the river and their embrace afterwards.

Of course she had never truly believed that someone as important as John Soo could be attracted to her. Or not in that way. He was invariably reserved and proper. He was certainly not like some of the senior officials she had heard about, who used their rank to trap the affections of their junior colleagues. It had been a great scandal when one of the secretaries in the office had been found to be pregnant by one of the deputy ministers; Mr Borodin had had to hush the whole thing up. Not that John Soo was so senior, and she – well, she was certainly not a giddy girl like the disgraced secretary: she had a trusted position, if a junior one, in the Praesidium. John (she loved the way he used a foreign name; it marked his commitment to internationalism) also took his responsibilities seriously. That was why she respected him. He was like an elder brother or an older cousin. They had common friends, Catherine and Fukuei, and that was a link – of sorts.

But sometimes she caught herself wishing their embrace on the river had meant more than just shared elation after a military victory, and dreamed that one day he might see something else in her other than that she was a bright young activist who appreciated his counsel and wisdom. He was so handsome, so self-assured.

But on the precious occasions that she did meet him, for a meal or a visit to the cinema, he invariably discussed politics, and she would listen dutifully. Of course it thrilled her. The military wing was the vanguard of the struggle. Her eyes would glisten as he expanded excitedly on General Galen's brilliance, and the speed with which a professional military establishment was being created. By the end of the year, he told her, General Galen would be ready to launch his first campaign to mop up the warlords in Kwangtung and Kwangsi Provinces. She had hardly been able to contain her excitement. John was an insider. He knew what he was talking about – but how much more excited she might have been if he had only noticed the new blouse she had worn for him under her uniform, and the shiny buckles she had attached to her shoes.

One night they went to see the latest film by the great American comedian, *Charlee*. It had been funny, especially the scene where the tramp was hanging on a building tottering on the edge of a cliff. John Soo had laughed and laughed, and the mood of hilarity had lasted into the restaurant afterwards. Eventually he had become more serious, but there was a twinkle behind his spectacles when he told her he had some good news.

'What?' she cried. 'Has there been a decision about the Northern Expedition?'

He laughed. 'We must learn to walk first,' he said. 'Soon,' he added, when he saw her pout. 'In two years, maybe three. No, nothing as dramatic as that, but for me it's almost as exciting. We are to leave for our first manoeuvres. It's official. It will be a training exercise, but if it goes as well as expected, Commandant Chiang and General Galen might bring forward the first real attack on Chen Chiung-ming to the autumn.'

'Oh,' she said, deflated. 'How long will you be gone?'

'No more than a month. Six weeks at the most.'

'Six weeks!'

A look of concern flickered over his honest features. He reached across the table and grasped her hand. 'Oh, Lan-hua,' he said, 'it's not that long before we'll see each other again.' He blushed and pulled back his hand. 'I'm sorry,' he muttered. 'That was forward of me.'

'I'm pleased by your news,' said Lan-hua, her own cheeks burning. 'This is a significant step forward towards our revolutionary goal.'

John Soo's face fell.

'What's the matter?' she said, alarmed.

'Nothing,' he said. 'I apologise. I mistook your reaction earlier. Stupid of me. I – I had thought you were indicating that you might miss me.'

She could hardly believe what she had heard, but next moment tears were bubbling in her eyes. 'Oh, I will miss you,' she said. 'I will. I will.'

'And I you,' he said, clutching her hands again. 'I have the tenderest of feelings towards you, Lan-hua. My dearest – comrade,' he added quickly.

Neither had known quite what to say after that – but they held hands until it was time for her to take the bus back to her dormitory.

Later, lying on her bunk, she had had to squeeze her eyes shut to control her leaping imagination. This was the most thrilling place and time to be alive. Anything was possible. She had never been so happy. And she was in love.

From the journal of William Lampsett, Reuters correspondent, Shanhaikuan Front, 15 July 1924

It's a relief to be on campaign again. I've been slowly going out of my mind during the last year in Tientsin. I don't know what was worse – watching George's successful wooing of Catherine in the early part of last year, or the absence of either of them while they took their honeymoon. I gather from Robby they're back now but, like a coward, I'm using the war as an excuse to delay our reunion a little longer.

I'm exhausted. We've been from pillar to post today. Nobody knows what's going on, though it appears that Chang Tso-lin's advance has been halted. With all his tanks, armoured trains and aircraft, the common wisdom was that he would have swept Wu Pei-fu's army before him and broken through the funnel of mountains and sea. God knows how Marshal Wu managed to mobilise an astonishing half-million men to meet him.

The opening formalities indicated that this would be another warlord comedy. Wu's fleet of ships anchored in the Po-hai Gulf and bombarded the approaching army with high-grade explosive shells. Chang's Breguets flew off to challenge them, and after a few bombs had exploded in the sea, Wu's navy steamed round a promontory to bombard somewhere else. Little damage was done by either side – but to correspondents as seasoned as Woodward and me, this use of modern weaponry augured things to come. And we've been vindicated. Over the last few weeks, a new standard of bloodiness has developed in warlord fighting. We've had ample opportunity to observe the toll in the makeshift dressing stations.

Nevertheless we've had to revise our opinion of the north-eastern threat. It's apparently been the same in the southern theatre, where Wu's forces have quickly contained the half-hearted attacks by Sun Chuang-fang across the Yangtse. In addition, the well-disciplined troops of Marshal Wu's ally, the 'Christian general' Feng Yu-hsiang, have mobilised in his stronghold in Shansi and are now threatening a circular movement along the length of the Wall to drive into Chang Tso-lin's western flank. The continued optimism, therefore, of Chang Tso-lin and his Japanese advisers appears baffling.

It is true, of course, that a division commanded by General Lin Fu-po, whom many consider to be the most effective commander in the north-eastern army, has hurriedly moved to Jehol to counter Feng, but the prevailing opinion is that this is too little too late.

Lieutenant Ti Jen-hsing found himself in command of a company of crack soldiers assigned to protect Chang Tso-lin's Englishman, the one-armed General Sutton, who had chosen to accompany Lin's forces. A hundred miles to the west of Shanhaikuan, they were hunched in their positions in the rocky hills, which folded upwards, like frozen waves, to the ridge on whose winding eminence they could make out, in the velvet light before dawn, the turrets of the Great Wall. This, relatively, was one of the more accessible parts of the Wall. Ku Pei K'ou was the pass through which Genghis Khan had entered China centuries earlier. He had had the benefit of treachery to smooth his passage: a bribed enemy had opened the gates. The forces attacking today expected no such assistance. From the movements on the battlements they could see that it was strongly defended. The medieval builders had designed their defences well. The zigzags, spurs and abutments, at almost any angle, offered the defenders clear lines for enfilading fire. Ti knew they had field cannon and machine-guns. Looking at the bamboo ladders, which his men were twining into shape, he wondered whether any would even reach the Wall. Through the gloom, he peered at the steep, rocky slope over which they would have to attack. He noticed that his hands were shaking. Disgusted with himself, he clutched the pommel of his sabre. His throat and tongue were parched. He knew it was not thirst but fear. He willed himself to light a cigarette and tried to appear nonchalant as he smoked it in his gloved hand.

Behind him he heard the clink of metal. The Englishman was siting his mortars among the shadowy outcrops, whistling some strange foreign tune. Ti knew the plan of attack. It was simple. The mortars would clear the Wall of its defenders, forcing them to retire into the turrets. His men would advance with the ladders. They would then storm the turrets individually. Once the Wall was breached, General Lin's men would leave part of their force to guard it against General Feng's approach. The others would march on an undefended Peking, at one stroke ending the war. It seemed mad to him, but Lin appeared happy to go along with the Englishman's eccentric ideas. What worried him now, however, was that his starting position was half a mile away from the Wall. He had a respect for mortars but none he knew of had the accuracy and range to hit a target so distant. Through an interpreter, he had pointed this out to the Englishman, and the latter had laughed, tapped his red nose, and muttered something about 'the Sutton patent'. Ti realised, with a sinking heart, that he could do nothing about it. His life was in the hands of Fate. Let me not be wounded, he breathed a silent prayer, let me not be wounded. If I am to die, let it be quick.

Pink light had begun to seep over the eastern horizon, and the tops of the hills were transforming from grey to emerald green. He looked at his watch, as other officers along the lines of the hill were doing. It was time to advance. The calculation was that the enemy would not observe the movement through the shadowy undergrowth until they were close enough to make their final assault. By then the sun would be up and the mortars should be in operation.

He cleared his throat and blew lightly on his whistle. He had to make a mental effort to take that first step away from the protection of the boulder, but in a moment his boots were crunching on the pebbles, and he was slithering down the slope into the darkness of the valley that they had to traverse before mounting the next hill leading to the Wall. In the gloom he sensed, rather than saw, the movement of the men around him, and he heard the muffled curses as the ladders caught in the creepers. He imagined the other companies, a thousand men all told, doing the same. He felt a sudden pride, then anxiety lest his own company or behaviour disgraced the division. That would not happen, he told himself. It was difficult going, and that was a relief because, after a while, he concentrated only on the business of finding a way through the tangled growth. A branch whipped into his face, drawing blood, and he cursed aloud. Curiously, this amused him, and soon he was elated. The sweet smell of the vegetation mixed with the delicious breeze of morning, and the sweat and exertion were exhilarating. With a shock he realised he was leading his men into battle. It was what he had always dreamed of. He became impatient, wanting only to reach the summit and his destiny.

The branches thinned as they climbed. Suddenly, above them, close enough almost to touch, shining pink in the morning light, was the Wall. He could make out each crumbling stone, each broken parapet, with photographer's clarity. And he saw the heads of the enemy outlined above it, and their rifles. As he looked, there was a shout. They had been observed. He saw a scramble as rifles were sighted. He heard the crack and echo of their shots, and a rustling in the leaves above him. He pulled his sword from his scabbard, and stood upright. The words came to him instinctively 'Sha-a-a! Ki-i-ill,' A part of him knew that the mortars had not fired. He did not care. His sword was in his hand and the enemy was ahead. He charged.

And almost immediately he reeled back, stunned, as the top of the Wall mushroomed in flames, flying dust and masonry. The air whistled and shrieked, as shell after shell fell in an elegant and leisurely traverse along the parapet. He could not believe the accuracy. For a moment he stared in fascination, then yelled at his men to follow him. Within minutes they had reached the side of the Wall and positioned their ladders. There seemed to be no opposition. The mortar barrage, like a creeping, fiery slug, had skipped the tower on their right, and was now progressing along the next length of the Wall, where other companies were already moving forward with their ladders.

He gripped the light bamboo, and pulled himself upwards. It was a race with the sergeant who was climbing the ladder next to him as to who would be first on the Wall. Ti vaulted the parapet and landed on the slippery stones at a crouch, his sword stretched out ready to deal with any enemy. Then he saw why the pavings were slippery. He was standing in a pool of blood. Unrecognisable human parts and uniforms lay around him. He looked about wildly. He heard a whimper and saw a boy hunched in an abutment, his scared eyes pleading as he clutched his wounded arm. Ti screamed, '*Shaa!*' and sliced his sabre through the boy's neck. He held his sword above his head, admiring the sunlight glinting on the blade, and the clean red rivulet running down to the hilt. Casually, he noticed the masonry of the parapet flicking and chipping at his side. Somebody was firing at him. Up some steps he saw the turret, and the rifles protruding from the door. '*Shaa!*' he yelled, and took the steps two at a time. He sensed the sergeant and his men following him. Before he reached the door, men were tumbling out, holding out their open palms, pulling at their armbands. He had killed two before he understood that they were surrendering. Then he ordered his men to halt, but it was a minute more before the bayoneting ceased.

Leaving his men to deal with what prisoners remained, he clambered up the ladder to the roof of the turret. He blinked in the sunlight, and had to shade his eyes to take in the beauty of the scene he saw around him, green hills folding in waves to the horizon, and the Wall winding in impossible spurs to the height of the mountains. He leaned against the parapet, breathing heavily. The plan had worked. The way to Peking was open. He had fought his first battle, and won his first victory.

A rather stale one, as it turned out.

From the journal of William Lampsett, Reuters correspondent, Chinwangtao, 29 July 1924

It's clear now why Chang Tso-lin and his Japanese advisers were optimistic. They had deliberately sent General Lin westwards, not to fight the Christian general, but to combine forces with him.

It was the usual round of Chinese shadow-boxing and treachery. It appears that, earlier in the year, a large sum of money was loaned to Marshal Chang by the SMR and various Japanese banks and this was, in due course, secretly transferred to Feng Yu-hsiang in Sian.

Pocketing his bribe, Feng and his men marched south, singing 'Onward Christian Soldiers' as they trudged over the passes – and attacked their unsuspecting commander in the rear. Naturally, it was a rout. It had all been planned months in advance.

Feng has taken Peking unopposed and is now waiting Marshal Chang's arrival so they can decide between them who will constitute the new government. Wu's puppet president, Cao Kun, has already fled to the safety of the foreign concession in Peking. Nobody knows where Wu Pei-fu is. Outwitted and outflanked, he is believed to have sought safety on one of his battleships. Meanwhile his troops have exchanged their armbands for those of the Fengtian clique, and joined their erstwhile enemy. Marshal Chang is marching south to the Yangtse, occupying Shantung and several other provinces along the way.

Peking, 20 August 1924

I've just had the honour, if such you can call it, of interviewing the man of the hour, Feng Yu-hsiang, in the stately mansion he's commandeered in the capital. His men conduct church services in empty palaces, and Feng indulges his egalitarian eccentricities. The foreign diplomats paying court to the new regime are, no doubt, surprised that they are received by a burly general dressed in the uniform of a peasant private. The whole country has been shocked by his announcement that the abdicated emperor and his court are to be ejected from the Forbidden City. In due course, 'Henry' Pu Yi, will be put on a train to Tientsin. He will be a curious sight for the foreigners dining at the Astor House Hotel.

For the moment it is divide and rule. Feng strengthens himself round Peking and Chang Tso-lin is consolidating his power in the south. He has already installed one of his ex-bandit cronies, the so-called Dog General, Chang Tsung-chang, as warlord of Shantung. The gossip here is that when his ally, the Kiangsu warlord, Sun Chuang-fang, reminded him of a certain deal by which he should have been given Shantung for his services, Marshal Chang expressed no knowledge that such a deal had taken place. There were no serious repercussions, except it is to be noted that shortly afterwards a well-known Tientsin banking house collapsed. One can only speculate.

*   *   *

Lieutenant Ti, stationed for several months on the stretch of Wall he had captured, rapidly became bored with the scenery and wondered, in the light of the political events that had transpired, why the battle had ever taken place. Eventually he decided that it must have been an indulgence on the part of Marshal Chang Tso-lin towards his English armourer to give him a chance to demonstrate the effectiveness of his 'Sutton patent mortar'.

In September he was allowed to rejoin the rest of General Lin's troops, who were encamped among the old Ch'ing dynasty tombs to the east of Peking. Officially they were liaising with the Christian general's forces. In fact, most of the men suspected that they were there to keep watch on them in the event of treachery. Boredom on the Wall was replaced by the boredom of garrison duty, albeit in picturesque, if spooky, surroundings. The yellow roofs and walls of the emperors' tombs were forbidding places, and many of the men feared that the ghosts of such powerful men, not to say gods, would take unkindly to being disturbed by modern soldiery.

They became even more alarmed when one day a convoy of Feng's soldiers came to the valley. They were not armed, but they had specific instructions. Lieutenant Ti received an order from General Lin to accompany them and report to him if anything unto-ward occurred. He followed them into the locked tomb of the Ch'ien Lung emperor, through the deserted halls, to the large burial mound at the back. When they began to dig into the mound, he used his field telephone to call Lin's headquarters. So it was that Lin was also there when, after several hours of digging and some dyna-miting, Feng's men broke into the sealed burial chamber, and together they made their way down the clammy steps to the under-ground palace, its every wall covered with Buddhist script and carv-ings of tutelary spirits.

Ti had never seen such treasure but what awed him most was the sight of the emperor himself and his empress lying in state in their marble coffins. The flesh had rotted away and the bare skulls gazed up at the vaulted ceiling. Covering them were magnificent blue robes emblazoned with golden dragons. Their hats had fallen aside to reveal the tangled coils of their queues. It was the glimpse of grey hair, of one of the greatest emperors China had ever known, that suddenly filled Ti with terror. Lin, however, seemed unaffected by the sacrilege. There was a strange glint in his eyes, and his face was fixed in such concentration that he appeared to be grimacing. Ti had the weird feeling that the expression in his eyes was hunger.

They watched as Feng's men efficiently secreted the jewellery and ornaments in their knapsacks. One came towards them hesitantly, holding a tortoiseshell comb, studded with jade and gold. Did they wish to take a souvenir? he appeared to be asking. Lin shook his head curtly. His eyes were devouring the emperor.

The men had a sack for him. After lifting away the brocade, they swept the bones into the jute folds. A thigh bone fell onto the floor. With a quick movement Lin picked it up. He examined it closely. 'What are you going to do with the bones?' he asked sharply.

'We're going to take them outside the tomb, photograph ourselves with them, then scatter them. Those are our orders, sir,' said the sergeant in charge.

'You won't mind if I keep this?' Lin's tone was such that it was a statement more than a question.

'By all means, sir,' said the sergeant. 'We can't give you a skull, I'm afraid. We've orders to smash those.'

'This will do,' said Lin, tearing off a piece of the brocade to wrap the bone.

They walked in silence back to Lin's car. Ti had still not recovered from his shock, but felt he ought to say something. How often did a junior soldier get a chance to talk to a general?

'Sad day for China, sir,' he said. 'Ch'ien Lung, I mean. It seems a shame.'

Lin turned to look at him. Ti quailed under the hard eyes and the ferocious scar.

'You're the officer who was first on the Wall, aren't you?' Lin said coldly. 'Sutton told me about you. You did well. I will promote you to captain,' he added. 'Report to my headquarters this evening.'

'Yes, sir.' Ti saluted, and held the gesture as the staff car drove away in a cloud of dust past the red imperial walls and the yellow tiled towers.

8

Broken Mansions

From the journal of William Lampsett, Reuters correspondent, Peking, 20 September 1925

I am fed up with covering this International Tariff Conference in Peking, while a war is going on near Tientsin, which I'm missing.

What a farce! It makes me ashamed to be a Westerner. As if accords signed in Washington promising the dismantling of extra-territoriality in the concessions could make a ha'pence of difference to the warlords. It's like a delegation of chickens sent to regulate a fox-run.

Panic, of course, ensued among the dignitaries when they heard that, while they were talking, a war had broken out between Chang Tso-lin and Feng Yu-hsiang. The great plenipotentiaries fell over themselves trying to get tickets on the armoured train that would apparently break through the Young Marshal's lines and get them safely to the coast. I watched the so-called international train set off from Peking station. Every flag of every nation fanned across the front of the engine; detachments of embassy guards bristled with bayonets on the foot rails; I suppose they wanted to demonstrate the dignity and prestige of the Powers. Well, it didn't work; the train turned back at the first sound of gunfire, before it had gone two miles outside the city.

It's meat to us pressmen. I heard tonight, though, that Feng Yu-hsiang has played his master card, suborning Chang's sidekick, Kuo Sung-lien, to turn his divisions on his master. Tomorrow morning I'm going to try to get over the hills to Manchuria to see if I can be there for the débâcle.

* * *

By the time that Edmund had finished at the convent, it was already late in the afternoon. He had a two-hour walk ahead of him along the ridge to his own hospital. Mother Pia had offered him her sedan chair because the sky was darkening for rain, but Edmund did not like to be carried on other men's shoulders, and after the young novice's death, he welcomed the rough wind on his face and the exertion that the climb up a steep hill offered. Cold rain might even drive away some of his anger against the waste and stupidity of it all, he thought.

The convent nestled on a shelf ringed by bare granite cliffs that rose to a clump of woodland separating two rocky peaks. The path descended to a wooden bridge over a fast stream that tumbled from a waterfall deep in the gorge. Standing on the slippery planks, the clatter of water in his ears, Edmund looked up at the buildings that hung above the mist and spray. The plain grey brick structures, with their black-tiled roofs, were as bleak as any of the villages that could be found in these remote fastnesses of the Yanshan range. Only the whitewashed wall that ringed the grounds, and the stone bell-tower that had been modelled on an Italian campanile and stood next to the squat brick chapel, indicated that this was a dwelling for foreigners. Edmund had a sudden memory of the medieval hilltop villages he had seen in the Marches on a walking tour of the Apennines in his student days, and dark castles that brooded over precipitous gorges. Transported to China, these Gothic European appendages created a scene as gloomy as the haze of pine trees dripping in silent shadow on the hillside.

He was surprised by how much the death of a stranger had affected him. The girl had been only twenty-three. If the convent had called him five days ago – even two days ago – he would have been able to save her life and perhaps her arm, but they had applied peasant poultices to the cut caused by a rusty scythe. When the arm had blackened with gangrene, they had taken her not to his hospital in which, thanks to Niedemeyer, there was a dispensary full of modern medicines and antiseptics but instead to their draughty chapel, where for three days and nights the twenty nuns – three ancient Italians, one young Montenegrin and sixteen Chinese peasant women – had knelt in a circle and prayed for . . . what?

Her life? Her soul? By the time Edmund had been summoned, the black rot had reached the girl's shoulder and she was dying. Half conscious, burning, delirious, she was pleading in local dialect for both the Virgin Mary and Kuan-yin to save her. The other nuns crossed themselves each time she mentioned the Chinese goddess. Edmund wondered if the sisters had brought the sick girl to the chapel for exorcism – he would not have put it past them. He had a vision of the white faces of the young orphans crouched in the rear pews; this dying novice had once been a little girl like them, taken from her village to serve Jesus. He had brusquely ordered all of the children and nuns except Mother Pia and the young Montenegrin, Sister Ursula, out of the chapel. With their help he had performed an amputation at the shoulder. Sister Ursula administered the anaesthetic. When it was done, Edmund had the convent porters bring a litter and carry the girl to her cell. He had sat with her until she had woken.

He had had no high hopes. She had been too weakened by her illness and this latest shock to have much chance of survival. Still, he had witnessed miracles in the trenches, and she came from sturdy northern peasant stock. Often life and death depended on willpower and sheer bloody-mindedness: he found himself willing her to live. She lay still, gazing blankly at the white ceiling. Edmund could not tell whether she was aware that she had lost her right arm. He pressed her other hand between the palms of his own. The wet brown eyes in the plain face turned questioningly towards him; for a moment they responded to his smile, then flickered with panic. She tried to speak but all that came out was a sound like the bark of a small terrier. Edmund became aware that the convent's bell was tolling vespers. He sensed the life going out of his patient. Sister Ursula rushed forward and began to mutter the last rites. When the bell ceased ringing, he closed the eyes.

'So she was taken away,' Mother Pia had said later, as he was preparing to leave. 'Let us pray she found the peace that she did not have in her short life. It is God's will.' Somehow he had retained his politeness, and shaken her hand as she bade him farewell by the barred convent doors – the porters gawping as they crouched under an elm tree with their pipes. 'So much to do,' she said, shaking her white cowl. 'One of those wastrels will have to go to the girl's village and tell her parents, who will no doubt want compensation, even though they were willing to abandon their girl-child during the great starvation. You know that we had to buy half of our young nuns? It was the only way to save their lives. You would have thought they would be grateful that we are preserving their daughters from superstition and bringing them up in the service of God, but they always want more.'

Superstition! thought Edmund, acidly. It was superstition that had killed her.

'Well, thank you, Dottore. Do not take it to heart that you have failed. We can none of us understand God's purpose.'

You should have called me sooner, he thought of saying – but instead he told her about the rumours he had heard: that Chang Tso-lin had fallen out with General Feng Yu-hsiang and war had broken out again; that armies might be moving in this direction. Either side would wish to control the important pass at Shanhaikuan, and the ridge above the convent would be on an army's line of march.

'We do not fear warlords,' smiled Mother Pia. 'In any case General Feng is a Christian. Or so they say.'

'It may not be General Feng who comes by,' said Edmund. 'Mother Pia, many of these soldiers are just bandits in uniform. Your convent is not protected.'

'Yes, yes, we are poor defenceless women. We have been so for the thirty years since this convent was founded. These are not Boxers, dear Dottore. We will not be harmed.'

'In my hospital we have plenty of spare rooms, and we would welcome your nuns.'

'I do not think that my nuns will be safer in your establishment than here. Are not your patients soldiers and bandits themselves? Thank you, Dottore, sincerely thank you – but we are fortunate to have a stronger Protector, He to whose service we have devoted our lives.'

'Well, the offer's there,' said Edmund, lamely. He turned to go.

'Trust in God,' said the nun. 'Sometimes I grieve for you, Dottore, that you will not allow God into your heart.'

Edmund bit back the angry retort that formed in his mind. He nodded and raised a hand in farewell. 'If I hear any news I'll let you know,' he said.

Stupidity and superstition! The whispers and gurgles of the water tumbling over the stones beneath him seemed to mock him with derisory laughter. He clenched and unclenched his fists in impotent fury, then realised how ludicrously he was behaving. He shouldn't be angry with the old nun. She was right: he had failed, as he had failed in almost everything else he had tried to achieve recently. There was no point in dwelling on it. Settling his rucksack on his back he set off up the gorge, his old army boots falling into the comforting rhythm of the march. It was a two-mile tramp up the hill in the other direction by the winding path, but he knew of a goat trail that would bring him to his road in half an hour. Soon he was pulling at branches to keep his balance as he made the almost perpendicular ascent to the ridge.

He was panting for breath when he reached the coll. He rested his hands on his knees, luxuriating in the wind that flapped his clothes and pulled at his fedora, the sweat now chilled on his forehead. He squinted into the gale to get his bearings. Grass and grit, blown up by the gusts, stung his cheeks. Here three paths met. One ran deep into the Yanshan, to remote villages so off the beaten track that it was said their inhabitants had still not heard that there was no longer an emperor on the Dragon Throne. In their shrines they worshipped mythical beasts, part horse, part snake, part cow, their animist beliefs predating Confucianism or even Taoism. Edmund had once spent a weekend exploring the dense pine forests and gloomy gorges on one of the butterfly-hunting trips in which he occasionally indulged, and been appalled by the poverty of the half-clad peasants, with their stone tools, who watched him furtively from the darkness of their tumbled huts, or scurried away at his approach. Wryly, he smiled. This was a dark, benighted part of the world. He was glad, for once, that his own route led in the opposite direction, along the ridge path to the coast and civilisation.

It was an easy enough walk. The ridge stretched like a causeway; on either side the peaks and foothills lapped like lines of frozen waves to the horizon. On one of the further ranges to the south,

Edmund could sometimes make out, on a clear day, the turrets of the Great Wall. Usually, these anonymous hills, disappearing in a misty haze that merged indistinguishably with the pale sky, gave him the impression of an immense ocean – but today banks of black cloud lowered in the north, like the rising smoke of a far-away battle. Here and there, searchlights of weak sunshine broke through the advancing shadow, highlighting the ridge-lines with electric clarity, picking out the woodland on the black slopes in a ghastly emerald green. It was as if the closing storm was drawing in and concentrating the remaining light, corralling the wind around the ridge top so it swirled in ever-anxious gusts, shaking the lemon-coloured grass in different directions, and humming about his ears.

Edmund quickened his pace, suddenly claustrophobic in the heavy atmosphere. One hell of a thunderstorm was brewing. He did not want to be exposed on the ridge when the lightning came.

Nobody understood why he had suddenly given up his lucrative position at the Kailan Mining Administration – certainly not Jenny, who wrote stern letters from Nanking, telling him he must pull himself together and take up this job or that, offering the help of her husband, who was now one of the grandest customs officials in China, and 'can open any door you like'. Not even his parents. He knew that he had disappointed his father, and the cheerful letters from his mother describing their new life in Edinburgh, with his elder, unmarried sister Mary, barely disguised her underlying puzzlement and concern. George never put pen to paper, but Edmund was aware that the eccentricity of 'the elder bro'' was a subject of ribaldry among Tientsin's fast racing set; not that he cared about that, or anything else George thought or did. He could go to the devil as far as Edmund was concerned, he and his wife . . .

Let him not think of Catherine . . .

He had more than enough to worry about at his hospital in making ends meet. Niedemeyer had been a brick, providing medicines and initial funding, but he was a businessman as well as a philanthropist and expected that Edmund should make his little enterprise pay. Edmund now dreaded the monthly letter from Chicago, asking after the market garden, and the orchards his walking patients tended, querying the price of apples and aubergines, the quality of pots, pans, kettles and farming tools that the more crippled patients manufactured in the workshop. Edmund could not blame him. After all, it had been the vision of a self-sustaining commune that he himself had initially sold to the American.

They had met accidentally outside the Gordon Hall. Edmund had not worked for several months, and the carelessness of his dress and his unshaven appearance had shocked Niedemeyer. The international concession in Tientsin was then an armed camp: British soldiers had established barricades on the main thoroughfares and the women and children had been evacuated to the coast. It was not that the Chinese armies during the Second Fengtian-Chihli War, as they called the conflagration that had taken place last year, had any intention of encroaching on the foreign domain, but the hypothetical danger had added spice to a dreary summer. For the young men in the town it had all been a lark, and George and his friends in the volunteer militia had proudly swaggered in their old Great War uniforms, taken out of mothballs.

Edmund had ignored them, spending his days in his flat, reading or walking aimlessly along the Bund, as he had done every day since his 'retirement'. Occasionally, he pulled himself together (as Jenny demanded) and thought of how he might rebuild his broken life, but no job appealed. The thought of involvement in the community, of talking every day to people who knew *her*, or who asked him about George and his racing triumphs, appalled him. That was why he had left the Kailan Mining Administration in the first place although he would probably have been dismissed anyway. In the six months after his brother's wedding, his moroseness and acerbity had caused offence; his visits to the mining works at Tangshan had almost ceased; his assistant had taken on more and more of his workload; and he had made mistakes, once prescribing the wrong medicine to a society patient, thankfully with no ill effects beyond a rash that had kept her away from the St Andrew's ball. After that his private practice had suffered, and he had been shaken out of his self-absorption at the thought of what other, more lethal medicine he might have prescribed in his absentmindedness. Shortly after that he had handed in his resignation, which was quietly accepted.

That night, for the first time in his life, alone in his flat, he had drunk himself into oblivion.

Niedemeyer had taken him in hand. In the bar of the Astor House Hotel he had given him two Manhattans in quick succession. Then he had refused him any more alcohol, and filled him with coffee while he proceeded to unburden himself of what was on his own mind, for Neidemeyer – although one might never have guessed it from his elegant and fastidious demeanour – had been very upset. He was more than upset, he told Edmund, 'I am exceedingly vexed. I might even say that I am enraged. If I was a lion, sir, I would be tearing at this table with my claws.' Edmund had been intrigued.

It had all started, Niedemeyer told him, when one morning he had been denied access to his dig. He had been forcibly expelled by a cordon of bayonet-wielding soldiers. He had gone to Minister Yu Fu-cheng to protest – he knew that General Lin was away at the wars – and the minister had shown him an order, signed by the general, not only closing the excavation but confiscating everything he had discovered there, including the now nearly complete skeleton of '*Homo proto-mongoliensis*,' as well as the pots and shards that, he told Edmund proudly, revealed a flourishing, previously undiscovered, civilisation. 'They even raided my house. A life's work, sir, snatched away by thieves in uniform.' On Minister Yu's advice he had taken the matter to Mukden. 'They told me I was a freebooter, sir. They said that I, Ralph Greevey Niedemeyer the Second, was attempting to steal treasures belonging to the Chinese nation. I told them I was a respectable scientist, and that I had a permit to conduct my excavations – granted by General Lin. And they asked me to prove it. Well, I couldn't, because they had stolen my permit along with my other papers, and all my notes and findings. And when I told them about the importance of my bones to history, to science, they did not believe me. That villainous Lin, or one of his acolytes, had sent a report to Mukden claiming I had not been conducting a paleontological dig at all. They said I'd been treasure-seeking in the grounds of a temple. That, as you know, is a barefaced lie. But I realised then that it was a conspiracy – by the whole government – to steal my bones.'

'Vexing, indeed,' murmured Edmund, disguising a smile.

Niedemeyer chuckled. 'Yes, I can see the comical side. Although it was galling, I assure you, to be disbelieved by even our own consul general. I'm not dismayed. I know that one day scientifically I will be vindicated, when my finds make it into the light of day. And they will. Although what General Lin wants with them now baffles me, to be sure . . . No, that's not what enraged me. It was what I saw afterwards that disturbed me.'

'And what was that?' asked Edmund.

'War, sir, and the effects of it,' said Niedemeyer, simply. 'A most degrading spectacle.'

'It's certainly that,' said Edmund, raising his eyebrows at this unexpected turn in the conversation.

'It struck me that I've been selfish, living in an ivory tower and blinding myself to the misery that is everyday life for people in this country. Now I have woken up and I am prepared to put academe behind me. I am living in the twentieth century, sir. They deported me, you know, out of the Manchurian provinces. I'd made too much of a nuisance of myself. That was a week ago. They wanted me to take a boat from Newchwang back to the States, and I said, "The hell I will, I'm coming to Tientsin where I have business." So I asked the hotel to book me on a train – but there wasn't one running. That was the first time I even focused on the fact that a war was on. Stupid, you might say, but I was in a cussed mood, and not to be thwarted, so I hired a car to bring me here. Spent a fortune in bribes, but this fellow agreed to drive me through the war zone.'

Edmund tried to picture Niedemeyer in his Homburg and velvet-lined coat sitting in the back of a car driving through a battlefield.

Niedemeyer noticed his incredulity. 'Oh, I was in little danger. The show was more or less over, Fengtian forces triumphant and marching south. I'm not saying it wasn't a rough ride. We were shot at once or twice. Reckon the boys were being boisterous. But the driver just stepped on the gas, and we got through the checkpoints. That was the exhilarating part. Most of the time we were bogged down in lines of trucks – and columns of refugees,' he added. 'Displaced persons. That, I believe, is the modern term for the victims of cruelty that would have been familiar in the time of the pharaohs. Old men, women, children carrying everything they owned on their backs. Starving. Every village and hamlet we passed burned to the ground. Looted. Crops destroyed.' He shook his head.

'What did you expect?' asked Edmund. 'That's war.'

'Expect? I don't know. As I told you, I'd chosen to live my life in an ivory tower.' Niedemeyer was wiping his spectacles, which had misted. 'I missed the Great War, you see. Spent it teaching in Philadelphia.'

'You were lucky,' said Edmund.

'It was the callousness of it all,' continued Niedemeyer. 'I'm not talking about the fighting. You expect that to be nasty. Even I know what modern weapons can do – my family used to make them – but the cruelty of this war didn't appear to be directed against the enemy. It was the innocent who seemed to be suffering. The weak, the defenceless . . . I thought, Why am I spending my life trying to recover the history of our past when modern humanity lives and behaves no better than brutes? Where have we come, in all these thousands of years? I saw one old man by the side of the road with a pig. Soldiers jumped off a truck to take it from him. It was all he had. He resisted and they shot him. That happened ten feet away from where I was sitting in my limousine.'

'That's China,' said Edmund, marvelling at his friend's naïvety.

'It's not good enough to say that, Dr Airton. It's our common humanity at issue here. I cannot drive by, see a man murdered for protecting the last thing he owns, and be unmoved. I cannot drive by a field hospital and see the wounded dying by the roadside untended – under the hoofs of officers who ride by laughing – and not wish to do something about it. I was the one who felt evil, defiled, because I didn't do anything about it. I don't know what to do now, and I guess I'm – ashamed.'

'What could you have done?' Edmund started to say, but the recollection of something Niedemeyer had said earlier made him freeze. 'Wounded untended, did you say?'

'Yes, it was a butcher's yard,' said Niedemeyer. 'And not just one. Near Shanhaikuan I saw . . .'

Edmund was only half listening. He had the sudden, sharp memory of a train siding in Chinwangtao, wounded men lying where they had been thrown on to the tracks – and of an English girl leaping from a second-class compartment. 'If you have the money in your family that you say you have, Niedemeyer,' he had interrupted the American, 'I'll tell you what you can do – what *we* can do.'

He had outlined then and there a plan to establish a rehabilitation community – non-religious, non-denominational – in the mountain areas where the battles had been fought that could treat the wounded from either army without prejudice or politics; that would gather the maimed and broken, bring them back to health, then give them land to farm. They would establish a haven for men who did not wish to join another army or make recourse to banditry, create an island of sanity in a war-torn land, a commune of the healed . . .

He felt the first heavy drops of rain patter on his fedora. The wind howled in his ears.

Nobody had believed they could do it, but Niedemeyer, his appetite whetted by his confrontation with bureaucracy over the bones, had proved a master of negotiation with the generals. Of course, at the end of the day, his money had talked. Edmund thought of what Mother Pia had said to him about buying girls for her convent. Had they not done the same when it came to finding wounded soldiers for the hospital? Was charity in this country just a matter of purchase? Rice Christians. Rice soldiers. But he had work to do again, and for months he had lost himself in his daily chores – and there were times when he felt that the patients in his charge were grateful, that his vision was being achieved. There were times when he went whole days without thinking of Catherine . . .

A fir tree flashed white in front of him; he counted the seconds to the rumble that followed. Through the rain and the darkness to the north, he saw a silhouette of mountains against a sheet of flickering light, then darkness again as the sky cracked around him. It was like the artillery bombardment at Ypres before the big push. It had rained that night too, and all the following day, when the broken remains of the attack were brought to the field hospitals behind the lines . . . In the next flash, he made out a crop of rocks just off the track to the right. He might find shelter there. He began to run.

Shelter? Was that what he was looking for? Escape? As he edged himself between two large boulders, hunching his shoulders to avoid the icy trickle of water that dripped from the mossy overhang between his scarf and his neck, he admitted that he was fooling himself. There was no escape from Catherine. That vision of her had given him the idea to set up his hospital. Not the real Catherine, perhaps, but the one he had loved – the lost girl seeking a father, seeking, like him, a meaning in a world that had none; bravely defying any odds to help strangers because it was the right thing to do; defying the establishment with her unconventionality; uncompromising in her hunger for life . . . Now he wondered whether such a person had ever existed.

The real Catherine greeted him every time he opened a newspaper. He knew he would be happier if he did not read the society columns and the gossip sections but he could not help himself. There she was, in the *Peking and Tientsin Times* or the *Tientsin Tatler*. Sometimes there was a photograph of her at a ball, wearing a helmet of feathers at a charity bazaar, or leading in George's horse after one of his victories on the track. That picture particularly irritated him: Catherine all scarves and silk, a hat like a bathing bonnet on her head, her mouth open in an inane laugh, and George, in jockey's colours, looking down smugly and possessively from his horse. More recently, she had been photographed with the Chinese empress in the strange court of exile that had been established for Emperor Pu Yi in the Japanese concession. Catherine had been appointed a 'companion' of the court in some spurious honours list, she and the wife of the *taipan* of Butterfield and Swire . . .

In photos with other women, Catherine wore the latest fashions with such unconscious ease that even the prettiest seemed dowdy in comparison. She would stand as demurely as the others, but the flamboyant cut of her dress, the grace of her posture, the coquettish turn of her head undermined any formality that the photographer was trying to create. On other occasions she appeared deliberately to burlesque it. She would stand half turned to the camera, eyes wide with innocence or amusement, one hand resting casually on her hip, the other curled inwards, pointing her cigarette holder at such an angle that it seemed to invite a study of her *décolletage*. Edmund, who examined every photograph with a magnifying-glass, could never decide if her mischief was artless or designed, but he noted the glances of disapproval from worthy matrons, the envy in the eyes of younger women.

More frequently she was photographed with men. These pictures upset him for a different reason, but he cut them out with masochistic relish, forcing himself to study them until he felt he had curbed his anger and jealousy. Then he put them in a drawer with the others, and did not look at them again, but he thought about them – even now, sitting under a rock in a thunderstorm. A recent photo in the *Peking and Tientsin Times*, reporting on a trophy match at the golf club, showed Catherine, dressed outrageously in male plus-fours, laughing coquettishly among a group of Jardine's griffins, one of whom was standing intimately behind her, his arms stretched over hers as he demonstrated how she should make her stroke. His chin was half hidden in the hair that fell over her shoulder. Edmund remembered the smell of that little hollow in her neck. He had nuzzled it during their lovemaking . . .

He knew this was the way to madness . . .

Of course there was no mention in the newspapers of Mrs Airton's rumoured affairs. Edmund heard about those during his visits to Chinwangtao to buy supplies. He remembered his first visit, shortly after he had established his hospital. He had managed to find a room in the yacht club because the small hotel was undergoing repair. In the bar he had met a chandlery salesman, who was swapping war stories with a petty officer from one of the American naval vessels anchored in the harbour. When Edmund had introduced himself, the salesman had lifted his frothy moustache from his tankard and burst into uproarious laughter. 'Airton, did you say? You're a brave man to be sporting that name in these parts.' When Edmund had asked rather frostily what he meant, the man had winked at the American, who chuckled and said, 'Englishwoman who came aboard our ship during the evacuation. She was a red-head so they called her the Scarlet Lady, but it was her scandalous behaviour that earned her the epithet.'

'Or the colour of her hair below-decks.' The salesman sniggered. 'Isn't that what you said?'

'Could be,' smiled the sailor. 'Reckon you need to ask our offi-cers to get the answer on that one. By all accounts they got a look-see. You really called Airton? Hope you ain't related – or married to her!' He slapped the bar. 'You'd be wearing one hell of a pair of green horns by now if you were.'

'I see.' Edmund heard a roaring in his ears. 'This woman's name was Airton, then?'

'Yup. Mrs Airton, that was her name. Beautiful woman, even if she was a bad 'un. I saw her piped up the gangplank. Danced up like a skittish colt. Wasn't a man on board who didn't have the hots for her, and that was before she even stepped on deck – captain gave her the honour to spite you Brits. Apparently she'd refused refuge on one of the Royal Navy vessels with all the other wives from Tientsin. Said she wasn't partial to British officers because they had beards.' He winked at the salesman. 'Must have had some good reason to grace us Yankees with her favours. My, my, I don't know if half the stories were true, but we heard the music, the parties, and the stew-ards said she had them all by the heartstrings – or by the balls, more like – even the old captain. By the end of the Emergency, when the warlords had finished their fighting, the officers were fighting each other over her. Duels. Broken hearts. Love tokens. Intrigues. You've never seen such shenanigans. It was like one of the old romances.'

'An adult romance,' added the salesman, with a leer.

'You can say that again,' said the sailor. 'I ain't an officer, but I know women, and I know whores.'

That was when Edmund had left the bar. He could hear the laughter behind him, and the American calling, 'Hey, Mister, where're you going? Hey, you weren't married to her, were you?' It was worse during the summer season when the fashionable in Tientsin decamped to the beach at Peitaiho. Edmund knew that if he drove ten miles down the coast he would find Catherine and her friends at the China Railways bungalow.

The thunderstorm had passed. To the north he could make out breaks of pale light in the clouds. The rain had settled into a steady downpour. The gusts of wind were no longer violent. Edmund stretched his legs and looked at his watch. Ten minutes past four. He should make it back to the hospital before dusk.

As he clambered to his feet, his thoughts were still on Catherine. He had last seen her after the Lei funeral, eight months before . . .

Edmund had been surprised to receive the invitation. He did not know the Lei family well, although his father had been a good friend of their relatives, the Yus, in Shishan. He imagined that he had been invited to represent his parents, as he had done once before. It was not a convenient time to leave the hospital – an epidemic of typhus had spread in one of the wards, but his two Chinese doctors were good men: the middle-aged Dr Chen, and the fiery young Dr Wu had worked with him at the Kailan Mining Administration; if they had stayed in Tientsin, they could have earned plenty of money; it was part loyalty to Edmund, and part idealism, that had made them volunteer to join him in his Waste Land, as he termed it; and they had proved themselves over the many months they had worked with him, helping him turn abandoned farmhouses and barns into clean wards and surgeries, recruiting nurses and training convalescent patients to become orderlies. Dr Wu, who was of peasant origin, had been the moving force behind the establishment of the farm, negotiating to buy the land, supervising the planting of fields and orchards. Edmund had taken the train to Tientsin, checking into the Yamato hotel in the Japanese concession, because he thought he would be unlikely to meet anybody he knew there.

At the appointed hour, he stepped out of his taxi at the Lei mansion. A servant met him outside the gate, but did not offer to accompany him, indicating that he should walk through the first two courtyards to the main hall. Edmund was surprised by the impression of dreary neglect. The first courtyard, which he had remembered as being so active with servants running about the business of a great household, was deserted. The rooms to the side were padlocked. Moss hung from the roof tiles, and the paint on the pillars was streaked with grime where it had not peeled. As he passed through the corridor separating the offices in the first hall, he observed that the shelves were no longer lined with ornaments, and that piles of unopened documents lay in disorder on the tables and desks. In the garden beyond, his shoes crunched on fallen leaves.

The two great ginkgo trees were leafless for it was winter – but the air of dereliction that permeated the place had nothing to do with the season: the atmosphere was that of a house waiting for the receivers. Perhaps that was the case, he thought. He remembered hearing that the Lei Bank had made unwise loans during the Fengtian-Chihli war, and that the family had fallen on hard times. He had not grasped the extent of the catastrophe that had befallen them; the desolation of the house convinced him they had been bankrupted.

He lifted the heavy curtains of the main hall and felt a sense of *déjà vu*. It was as brightly lit as it had been for the Mid-autumn Festival three years before. The family were seated formally on the chairs. Lei Tang was erect on his father's seat. He looked stunned, his features taut with incredulity; one of his hands quivered where it rested on the side of his chair. The faces of his grandmother and his wife, Yu Fu-hong, flanking him on either side, were also rigid masks, although occasionally Fu-hong would cast a protective glance at her husband, as if checking that he had not broken down into indecorous emotion. The minister from Shishan, Yu Fu-cheng, was wearing an expensive silk gown, white as was appropriate for mourning, his dangling brogues tapping the chair leg, and his alert eyes flitting about behind his spectacles. When he saw Edmund his face broke into a radiant smile, which rapidly transformed into a funereal frown.

On the left, with Lei Tang's children were Lei Lan-hua and Lei Ming, she in a modest cream cheongsam, and he in a white suit. Lan-hua did not appear to have changed, but Ming's moustache and the care lines on his forehead were more pronounced than when Edmund had last seen him; in contrast to his distraught elder brother, he had an aspect of responsibility and maturity. Edmund was surprised to see the younger brother and sister in the mansion. The death of their father must have occasioned a family reconciliation. Edmund exchanged a friendly nod with them as he moved towards the coffin. He noticed three young women on the other side of the hall, one weeping silently. He presumed that these were the dead banker's concubines.

The soul of Lei Chuan-hsi may have departed, but his physical presence still dominated the room. High up on the family altar, in a large gold picture frame, embedded in the flower arrangements, a photograph of him in his younger days gazed down severely at his family. He was frowning slightly, as if calculating the cost of the funeral arrangements that had been made on his behalf. Certainly these had been prodigious. Layers of white chrysanthemums cascaded from the top of the altar, over the table and on to the floor, with burning incense holders, garish paintings of the Buddha and Kuan-yin, offerings of fruits and wines, a box of Johnnie Walker, sides of barbecued pork and beef, a steamed mandarin fish, dumplings, pastries, roast ducks and chickens, a wedding cake, piles of ghost money and papier-mâché models of a palanquin, servants, a Chinese bed, a radio, a motor car – all the luxuries that Old Man Lei would require on his onward journey. In the centre of the hall was his coffin, an ornate sandalwood affair; Edmund could smell the fragrance of the wood above the incense. A bonze had been hired to chant prayers for the departed. Edmund could see his bald pate bobbing on the other side of the box. The drone of his rising and falling '*om mani padme hum*' were at first the only sounds in the hall, but as Edmund bent over the coffin, he became aware of other sounds emanating from outside: muffled trumpets and drums, and a strange wailing echo composed of many male and female voices. Professional mourners, he supposed, and the band for the procession.

It was a shock to see the white, waxy features of the old man. Coins had been placed on his eyes, but this was not the face of a man at peace. No amount of undertaking cosmetic had been able to release the rictus of the mouth and jaw, or the furrowing of the brows; this was the face of a man who had died in pain. He'd had a heart-attack, a massive one, Edmund concluded. The stretched skin and sunken cheeks told another story. In the three years since Edmund had seen him, Lei had all but wasted away.

Edmund bowed three times and stepped away. He became aware that Ming was standing beside him. 'Thank you, Dr Airton, for coming. It's so very g-good to see you again,' he said.

'I wish it had been in less sad circumstances,' said Edmund. 'I'm so very sorry.'

'Come,' said Ming. 'The other mourners are drinking t-tea in a side room. They've paid their respects. Lan-hua and I will take you there. We're not needed here. The formal parts of the proceedings are n-nearly over. The p-procession will start soon.'

He realised that the room to which Ming was leading him was the same chamber in which he had attended that grisly banquet when the family had broken apart, which seemed inauspicious. Edmund inclined his head towards Tang and his grandmother. The old woman smiled politely but Tang, in his self-absorption, did not seem to notice him. As Ming lifted the hangings, Edmund saw that the room was full of old men in traditional Chinese dress, seated round the walls, conversing quietly. Lan-hua came up behind them.

'Hello, Edmund,' she said. She touched Ming's sleeve. 'Second Brother, let's not go in there. I couldn't bear it. It's all the capitalists in Tientsin, and they've only come to gloat over our misfortune. Anyway, I need some fresh air.'

Edmund followed the brother and sister down a corridor that led into the third courtyard. This, like the others, was a picture of neglect. Junk was piled in what had once been a neat garden – a sofa, a rusty stove, a stringless lute, broken toys. One corner of the courtyard had been dug up, and sticks in the soil indicated that vegetables had been planted there; in a large wicker cage, the height of the wall, he could make out the hunched feathers of pigeons on bamboo rails.

'Tang s-spends most of his day now talking to his p-pigeons,' said Ming. 'Fu-hong does all the work. As you've noticed we've had to lay off nearly all the s-servants.'

The three, wrapped in overcoats and scarves, hands in pockets against the cold, walked silently up the path and back again.

'The bank?' asked Edmund, after a while. 'There's no chance ...'

'N-none. Our c-credit was over-extended even before Tang decided to f-finance the warlords. I never realised how much we had b-borrowed ourselves. All those s-sympathetic mourners in the waiting room were quick to c-call in our d-debts. Lan-hua's right. Now they've come to g-gloat. Fu-hong's sold most of our valuables. If you w-went inside you'd see most of the r-rooms are stripped, even Grandmother's. Self-effacing little Fu-hong's become the tyrant of the household. A g-good thing too, in m-my view. Tang's a b-broken man.'

'He's desolate about Father's death,' said Lan-hua.

'Yes,' acknowledged Ming. 'He loved Father. P-poor Elder Brother. He's got no one to lean on now.'

'What will he do?' asked Edmund.

'Sell the mansion probably,' said Ming.

'It's as bad as that?' asked Edmund, shocked.

'"Slippers to s-slippers in three,"' said Ming, harshly. 'Isn't that the way of the w-world?'

'The capitalist world,' said Lan-hua, quietly. 'Though I never thought it would happen so quickly.'

They walked on in silence, Ming and Lan-hua absorbed in their own thoughts.

'This funeral,' said Edmund. 'I heard the band getting ready outside. It looks as if it's going to be very . . . lavish.'

'How can we afford it?' smiled Ming. 'We can't – b-but you know how important f-face is to us Chinese. At least, Tang seems to think so. He must have b-borrowed the m-money.'

'Yu Fu-cheng may have contributed,' said Lan-hua. 'He owes everything to Father.'

'You th-think so?' said Ming, bitterly. 'It's my understanding he was the one who p-persuaded Tang to make the loans that broke us. I don't think we need that s-sort of gratitude.'

'I thought you hero-worshipped him,' said Lan-hua. 'What about your own gratitude? He set you up in that school.'

'I've g-got to know him b-better,' said Ming. 'He c-can't help us. Not really. He's scared of General Lin like everybody else. He b-blows with the wind. Martha and I have to rely on ourselves. Every day's a st-struggle. That's why I had to leave her in Shishan. We have no B-Borodins to help us up there, you know.' Lan-hua frowned. 'I'm afraid Mr Borodin has problems enough of his own in Canton,' she said. 'Since President Sun died earlier this year, he has had to struggle against Chiang Kai-shek and the rightists in the Kuomintang.'

Ming laughed. 'Are you losing confidence in the r-revolution, Little Sister?'

Lan-hua bristled. Then, noticing the smile on his face, she punched her brother playfully. 'Don't tease me, Ming,' she said. 'Nothing can stop it. One day we will be strong enough to take the revolution north and then there will be no more warlords to worry about. My friend John Soo who works at the Whampoa arsenal, says—'

'Oh! John Soo!' laughed Ming. 'Is *that* the name of your C-Communist lover?'

This time the punch was a hard one. 'He's not my lover,' she said firmly, her cheeks reddening. 'He's a – a very good friend. And a dedicated revolutionary. He's my – my teacher,' she added. 'A better one than you.' And she kicked him.

As he watched them tussle, Edmund found himself laughing too – but he was interested in what Lan-hua had been saying. 'Do you really believe Chiang Kai-shek's forces are capable of launching a Northern Expedition?' he asked. 'They've been talking about it for years. You really think your armies will be strong enough to take on Chang Tso-lin?'

'One day,' said Lan-hua, panting after her exertions.

'W-why not?' said Ming. 'Can't you see? My little sister has h-history on her side!'

'I'm not going to talk to you,' said Lan-hua, 'or any more about politics. Not to anybody as dialectically handicapped as you've obviously become in your provincial town, Second Brother.' She turned to Edmund. 'Tell me about yourself. What are you doing now? How's Catherine? She married your brother, didn't she? I was hoping they'd come with you. I think Elder Brother invited them. I told him to.'

Edmund felt a chill in his spine that had nothing to do with the cold. 'I wasn't aware . . .' he mumbled.

'I'd have liked to see her,' said Lan-hua. 'We were all such good friends once, but I imagine she's very busy. She's become quite the society lady, hasn't she? Or so they say.' She peered at him inquisitively.

'Apparently she has,' said Edmund. 'I rarely see her now.'

He was relieved when Fu-hong came hobbling into the courtyard, looking sternly at her brother- and sister-in-law. 'Come on, you two,' she snapped. 'What are you doing idling about here? It's time for the procession. You're still family, you know. You should be more supportive. Your brother's wasting so much money we might as well do things properly.' Lan-hua and Ming looked at each other, eyebrows raised, but they meekly obeyed the imperious summons.

There were white hoods and cloaks for all the mourners. Edmund, feeling only a little foolish, took his place among the eminent businessmen, similarly draped, who had come to offer their condolences – or gloat, as Lan-hua had said. There were bankers, merchants and city officials. They treated the foreigner in their midst with exquisite politeness. One or two ceremoniously offered him their name cards; Edmund recognised some illustrious names. They were to march behind the family, who would follow the coffin, carried in a palanquin. The procession was to be led by the band, dressed in shabby tinsel uniforms. Immediately behind them were the Buddhist priests, chanting prayers. At the rear was a donkey cart on which was placed an enormous drum. Behind that milled the untidy rabble of some forty professional mourners – men and women – dressed in ragged hoods and aprons made of sacking. As the band was preparing its brass instruments in a cacophony of squeaks and wails, they practised their howls of grief. Edmund wondered about the delay, until he saw that Tang, Ming and Lan-hua were still occupied with burning the ghost money and the paper offerings in a brazier set up outside the gates. Red flame and black ashes fluttered in the cold breeze.

Eventually they set off down the main street in the Chinese part of the city. What with the screams and howls of the mourners, the booming of the big drum, the chanting of the priests and the discordant fanfare of the band, not to mention the frequent blare of horns from passing lorries and ringing of bicycle bells by trishaw taxis, Edmund at first found it difficult to distinguish any particular strain in the wall of noise that stunned his ears, although he had the impression that the brass band was trying to play 'When The Saints Go Marching In'. As he became more accustomed to it he made out 'Swanee River' and 'Alexander's Ragtime Band'. It seemed an inappropriate choice of repertoire, but nobody seemed to care.

Excited children were running along beside the procession. Women leaning on balconies were enjoying the spectacle. The businessmen were carrying on a conversation about the markets, shouting at the top of their voices to make themselves heard. Ahead, he could see the family. Lanhua and Ming had their heads down in their cowls, as if they wished to hide from what was going on around them.

It was about an hour's walk to the graveyard, which was situated on a hillock that overlooked a shantytown on the outskirts of the city. The mourners and the band had obviously been paid well, thought Edmund. They did not cease their cacophony through the long march. Nor did the noise abate as the procession filed through the *pailou* at the entrance, and up one of the paths that led through the mausoleums. They did not have a long way to go. Lei Chuan-hsi's tomb was at one of the lowest levels. Nor was it as grand as some of the other tomb palaces. It consisted of a simple curved wall, made of concrete, set waist-high in the slope, and two steps to a small platform in which there was a gaping rectangular hole the size of the coffin that was to be placed inside it. In the wall there had been fixed a plaque with Lei's name in large characters and the same photograph that had looked down on them in the ancestral hall. Several strings of red firecrackers hung forlornly from a trestle above the grave. Edmund overheard a businessman mutter, 'That shows you how poor they are. They squander money on a showy funeral and bring him to a pauper's grave.'

The noise did not abate during the burial ceremony; and the chanting Buddhist priests had again to compete with the banging of the drum and the sporadic eruption of the band. The coffin was finally lowered into the ground to the accompaniment of Buddhist prayers, a final enthusiastic burst of wailing, and an out-of-tune rendition of 'Auld Lang Syne', drowned in the explosions of fire-crackers.

In sombre silence, in contrast to the exuberance earlier, the mourners, hired and invited, the band, the priests, the palanquin-carriers, the drummer and his cart descended the hill, leaving only the family standing by the grave. Edmund noticed that Tang was still in his shell-shocked state; now Ming supported their grand-mother, who had fallen to her knees, sobbing, when the first sod of earth had thumped on to the coffin lid. He was wondering whether he, too, should leave, allowing the family some privacy for their grief, when he heard a motor-car pull up, and the incongruous bray of English voices carried on the wind: 'I say,' a young man called, 'do you think we've missed the show?'

'We wouldn't have, Reggie, if you hadn't lost the way,' came those oh-so-familiar husky tones. 'Come on, somebody's still up there.'

Edmund turned, and saw, striding up the path, a vision of lithe limbs in chiffon and silk under an open cashmere coat, a silver and tortoiseshell band failing to restrain the blowing red mane, green eyes crinkled against the wind, soft red lips half open as if she were about to call out: Catherine, as fresh and enticing as the day he had first seen her. Behind her, walking at a slower pace, were two young men, dressed in leather coats and goggles, one taking off heavy driving gloves. They seemed a little abashed by the sight of a Chinese funeral party.

Catherine walked straight to Lan-hua and hugged her fiercely. 'Darling,' she murmured, 'what a beastly, beastly thing. I'm so, so sorry. Your poor father.'

The Lei family were staring at her as if she was an apparition. Lan-hua looked disconcerted, and Ming went pink when Catherine hugged him too. 'And he wasn't very old, was he? Such a sad thing. I'm so, so sorry we're late. It's Reggie's fault. He really has no sense of direction. He and Tom are just a pair of blithering idiots when they get behind the wheel. But they've been angels for all that. I wouldn't have known how to get here without them. You don't mind that I've brought them along, do you? I promise they'll be well behaved.'

She turned to survey the rest of the family. When she saw the grandmother, she clasped her hands in prayer-like fashion before her face, and bowed in the pantomime manner of Aladdin to Wanky-poo. Clumsily, her two squires attempted the same. Edmund wished that the white funeral hood could cover him completely.

Then he heard her giggle, and her face was directly in front of him. Her long neck rose from her pearls, and a wisp of red hair blew on her brow. Those challenging eyes crinkled now with merriment –

or irony, even ridicule. 'Edmund, is that really you?' he heard. 'Goodness, you do look the hermit in that silly cowl! You're no Friar Tuck, though, are you? You're thin as a rake. My ghostly confessor, perhaps?' And he heard one of the young men behind her snort, thinking she had made a joke.

'But it's so delicious to see you again,' she continued. He felt the light touch of her arms as she embraced him, the moist press of her lips on his cheek, and a brush of her hair on his eyes. He smelt the familiar scent. 'It's been ages,' she said. 'You should come and see us, you know. George and I miss you terribly.'

He felt the blood pounding behind his forehead. He did not know whether it was anger, shame or desire – but he pushed her away roughly. 'Catherine, this is a funeral,' he whispered urgently – angrily, 'not a cocktail party. Show some respect for this family's feelings, and their customs.'

Her cheeks flushed, but she controlled herself and, hand on her hips, turned to one of her young men. There was a dangerous light in her eyes. 'Tom, did I ever introduce you to my brother-in-law, Dr Edmund Airton? He's my conscience, you know. Like Jiminy Cricket. He thinks I'm behaving inappropriately.'

She turned to Ming, who like the rest of his family, had not uttered a word. She took his limp hand. 'Ming, I'm sorry if I've embarrassed you and your family. I didn't mean to. That's the way I am, I suppose. But I know what it means to lose a father.' Here she glanced coldly at Edmund. 'I know . . . yes, I know the anguish that you are all going through. And you, Lan-hua, Tang, and all the rest of your family have my deepest and sincerest sympathies. And my love.'

Her voice stumbled on these last words, and Edmund was shocked – appalled – to see tears well in her eyes, and slide down her cheeks. As he watched, Lan-hua also burst into tears, ran forward and threw her arms round Catherine to sob convulsively on her shoulder. Catherine's other arm reached out, and included Ming in the embrace. Lei Tang, Fu-hong and the grandmother had bowed their heads stiffly, obviously moved. The three concubines were weeping openly, while Minister Yu Fu-cheng smiled beside them.

Edmund stared in disbelief. For a moment, Catherine's haggard face lifted, mascara smudged, and her eyes met his. He could not make out the message she was trying to convey, and it did not matter because now he would not believe anything this consummate actress told him.

He could not bear it any longer. He bowed to Lei Tang and the grandmother, pushed past Reggie and Tom and strode down the path, pulling off the white cowl and gown as he went.

Now that the storm was over and the rain had temporarily stopped, a pale light filtered through the overcast sky. Edmund tramped along the ridge path, making good time, as the hills stretched away on either side of him.

The mountain ridges to the south were converging with his, and on his right he could make out, quite clearly now, the black sentinel towers of the Wall. A mile or so ahead the road would climb through thick woods to a rocky promontory, then wind down the precipitous cliffs, the ruined segments of the Wall tumbling beside it towards Shanhaikuan and Pohai Bay. The setting sun would be lighting the crests behind him by the time he started his descent, and the valley and the shoreline would be hazy in the dusk, but still he looked forward, as he always did, to the magnificent view far over the ocean. On a cloudy day like today the water would glimmer, like dull, beaten steel, to the horizon. From there it would be only a twenty-minute walk to his hospital, built on a spur of one of the lower slopes. *Lao* Chang, the porter, would have the lanterns lit, and he might have time for a whisky on the veranda of his bungalow before night obliterated the view.

It would be good to relax in the solitude of his Spartan home. After supper, he might open his gramophone, and play soothing music, Mahler or Mozart, or read something light, like Boswell's *Life of Samuel Johnson*. Johnson's magisterial aphorisms were always comforting: the curmudgeonly anatomy of mankind's weaknesses and foibles; the confident belief that spiritual peace can be found in the philosophical acceptance of life's limitations. Alas, there was no such order in Edmund's universe. He lived in an age where the beneficent effects of progress had come home to roost.

It had been Newton's light that had hung over the trenches, in the tracer, in the whiz-bangs, in the gas-clouds. It was the likes of Edmund, in his inadequate field hospital, who had had to patch up the victims of mankind's clever inventions. It was what he was still doing, on the other side of the world.

Above the wind he heard the noise of a motor, peered behind him and saw the pale lamps of a car bouncing and slithering along the mud towards him. He stopped, amazed. How could a car – a Model T Ford by the looks of it – have got up here? It slid to a stop on the grass verge, and a tall, thin man in fedora and trench coat, a pipe clenched in his teeth, stepped out and hailed him in English: 'I say, is this the road to Jehol?'

'No, it's not. You're miles off. This path leads to Shanhaikuan. Who are you? What are you doing up here?'

'Bugger! I suspected I was lost, but hadn't realised I was as lost as that,' said the man. Then, remembering his manners, he responded to Edmund's question, stretching out his hand in greeting. 'I'm Lampsett, Willie Lampsett, Reuters,' he said. 'Been driving overland from Peking these last couple of days. Trying to keep off the major roads because I don't want to be stopped by Feng Yu-hsiang's boys. Trying to get to Manchuria, actually, to cover the *coup d'état*.'

'Manchuria? *Coup d'état*?'

'Yes, hadn't you heard? One of Chang Tso-lin's generals, Kuo Sung-lien, has decided to topple him. News we got's about a week old, but it seems he's reached the Liao river, driving everything before him. Only Lin Fu-po's division was standing in his way. It may all be over by now. Unless the Japanese came in on Chang's side – but I don't see that happening. One warlord's as good as another to them.' He paused for breath. 'By the way, if you don't mind me asking, who are you? Didn't expect to meet an Englishman taking a constitutional in this wild neck of the woods.'

'My name's Airton.' Edmund's mind was racing, trying to make sense of what the journalist had told him. 'I live close by here,' he added.

'I know who you are, then. You're George's brother, the doctor. You run a hospital for war wounded or some such. Edmund, isn't it? He told me about you. Thought once of doing a guns-toploughshares piece on your commune, but never got round to it. Stroke of luck for me, though. Mind if I camp the night with you? I'll be even more in your debt if you can spare me a hot bath and a bite of supper.'

'It's a pretty steep path down the mountainside,' said Edmund, doubtfully. 'More a mule track than a road.'

'A mule track would be luxury after what I've been through these last couple of days.' Lampsett banged the bonnet affectionately. 'Sturdy beasts, these Model Ts. Isn't science wonderful? Come on, hop in.'

Twenty minutes later, they were bouncing down the mountain-side, Lampsett hooting as he wrenched the wheel round the bends, and Edmund hanging on to the strap with all his strength to prevent his head banging against the roof, promising himself that the next time the rear wheel spun over a bottomless crevasse, he would leap out, however undignified. He might have done so, had he not suddenly discovered that he was enjoying himself and, even stranger, did not care what happened to them. Soon he was laughing and yelling as loudly as his driver. When the car screeched to a halt in a cloud of dust in the hospital courtyard. Edmund and Lampsett were leaning back in their seats, their muddy faces streaked with tears of laughter.

'I told you,' Lampsett managed after some helpless moments.

'Told me what?' panted Edmund.

'That we could rely on science,' gasped Lampsett. 'Isn't it good to be alive? Now, where's that hot bath you promised me? Wait!' he added, turning in his seat to riffle in the litter of papers, suit-cases, tin cans, jam-jars, binocular cases, revolver holsters, rugs, maps, sleeping-bags, boots and sweaters jumbled in the back. 'First things first. I've got just the thing, if it hasn't smashed. Yes,' he cried, brandishing a dark brown bottle. 'Lagavulin! A twelve-year Islay! I promised myself I'd open it at the first sight of civilisation. You qualify, my dear doctor, in every way.'

They opened the Lagavulin during dinner, after Edmund's house servant, a one-eyed soldier from Anhwei, had served the fried chicken and vegetables that was the only dish he knew how to make.

When they had met for a beer on the veranda, both men had shown a degree of shyness. Dinner dress imposed its own formality, and the memory of their hilarious adventure, now it was over, was faintly embarrassing. Edmund was surprised to see that the sober individual who had emerged from his bath bore little resemblance to the madcap motorist he had met on the mountainside.

He was a little disconcerted, also, to observe that there was a hard, cynical quality about the man. He looked older too. It was as if his boyish enthusiasm had been washed off with the mud of his journey. Hard, watchful eyes stared from thin, ascetic features, missing nothing. The Lagavulin was a good icebreaker, but it took both men some time to relax.

Over dinner, when Lampsett described the political situation, he did so seriously, with clipped precision and acid asides. He told Edmund about the Tariff Conference and the treachery of Chang Tso-lin's subordinate that had brought him over the mountains. 'Feng Yu-hsiang's played his master card,' he said, 'suborning Kuo Sung-lien. It may work too – it's on the cards the rebels *will* get rid of Chang Tso-lin – but then we'll have an even more dangerous state of affairs. A power vacuum, because odds are the other warlords up there will have no truck with Kuo, and set up their own independent fiefdoms again. The Japanese will move to protect their railway kingdom, and poor old China will be in a worse state than before.'

Lampsett gave a harsh laugh, then stopped. Edmund was surprised to see the hard eyes soften. 'Do you know why I came out here, Airton?' he asked. 'It's because I believed that the future of humanity lies in this country. You'd have thought that, after the war, we'd have learned something, but look how we've managed to cock things up since. Look at Russia, and Germany. Bolshevism? Weimar? Look at Britain trying to cope with an antiquated empire. Each in their own way, they're still caught up in the tired toils of bankrupt nineteenth-century idealism. America, the great hope of free nations, has withdrawn in on itself, preaching non-intervention as if it was a virtue. China's a mess now too, but you have to look beyond that to its potential. Only yesterday it was a feudal country. Only fourteen years ago an emperor sat on a throne, and now it's a republic.

A flawed one, torn apart by all sorts of conflicting forces it doesn't understand, but what a great experiment! What a turbulent primal soup! There's Communism. There's nationalism. There are ideas we've never heard of, all boiling in the pot. And four hundred million people, Airton, who are only now waking up. All this warlordism, this chaos, doesn't matter. The Chang Tso-lins, the Sun Yat-sens are ephemeral. But something new is happening here, and that's why it's the story I've chosen to cover. Who knows how it will end?'

He smiled shyly. Edmund refilled his glass. 'Seems you're a bit of a poet, Lampsett, as well as being a mad motorist.'

'My motoring's better than my poetry,' he said.

They took their tumblers and the bottle, and reclined on Edmund's sofas. Somehow the conversation moved to the Great War and they found themselves exchanging reminiscences. They had both served in Flanders. Edmund found that Willie – they had mutually agreed to use Christian names – had been wounded, leading an attack at the third battle of Ypres, and in all probability had been treated at Edmund's field hospital. 'You were probably the one who stitched me up,' he said.

'That was one of the appalling things about that slaughter,' said Edmund. 'The anonymity of suffering. I don't remember people. I remember wounds.'

'I was a head wound,' said Willie. 'Trepanned. Here.' He showed the scar under his thin hair.

'I did a lot of trepanning that day,' said Edmund. 'Plenty of amputations too. It was a butcher's yard.'

'"What passing bells for those who die as cattle", eh?' sighed Willie, closing his eyes, his tumbler on his chest.

'Is that Owen you're quoting? You said you were a poet.'

'No, you did – although now you mention it I do write the occasional verse. Never been published. I see from those books on your shelf that you're partial to poetry too. Is that *The Waste Land*? I like Eliot. Apparently so does your brother George. He keeps quoting *Prufrock*.'

'Do you know George well?' asked Edmund.

'He's a good friend,' said Willie Lampsett. 'As is Catherine.' He took a sip of his whisky. 'He's a lucky man, George: lucky on the racetrack, lucky in love. It seems unfair, doesn't it?' There was a long, uncomfortable silence. 'You're not married?' he asked.

'No,' said Edmund.

'Nor am I.'

'Not found the right girl?'

'Right girl's not interested in me,' said Willie. 'Or, rather, she's married to somebody else. What's your story?'

'I don't have one,' said Edmund.

'Everybody's got a story, old boy,' said Willie. 'But you're right, it's usually wiser to keep such things to yourself. God, this whisky's gone to my head.'

They talked desultorily for a while.

'You mentioned Catherine,' said Edmund. It was now nearly midnight and there had been a long pause in their conversation, in which they had both been drinking steadily. 'I've seen a lot about her in the newspapers.'

'You don't want to believe everything you read in the newspapers.'

'You should know?'

'Yes.' Willie gave one of his harsh laughs. 'I should know.' He leaned over and picked up the now nearly empty bottle. 'World's been very cruel to Catherine,' he said, slopping the remains of the whisky into Edmund's glass and his own. His words were a little slurred. 'She seems to make enemies despite herself. It's jealousy or envy, I suppose.'

'From what I hear, Catherine's capable of being pretty cruel in return,' said Edmund, bitterly. What was he saying? The Lagavulin must have gone to his head too.

But Willie was laughing. 'Oh, she stands up for herself. No doubt about that,' he said. 'That's what's wonderful about her. I've never met anybody with so much spirit or courage. There's a wild side to her too, but it's only ever in fun. She's not cruel. Wherever did you get that idea? I can't think of a kinder, more generous soul on the planet. And she's loyal to her friends. There's nobody like her. Have you seen the way she lights up a room? Conversation stops. Heads turn . . .'

'Loyal to her husband?' Edmund could not prevent himself. There was a devil in him.

'What do you mean, old boy?' Willie was blinking at him in confusion. 'Loyal to George? Of course she is. Why ever would she not be? Oh,' he said, 'you're talking about her supposed affairs.'

'There are rumours,' said Edmund. 'I hear of them even here, and I've seen her with her young admirers.'

Willie tried to sit up, but sank back on the sofa. 'God, I'm pissed,' he said. 'It must be exhaustion. I'm usually good with liquor.' He laughed. 'Do you know? The last person who said such a thing to me about Catherine – it was in a bar in . . . I can't remember what bar it was in – anyway, I hit him so hard he fell over and broke a table. I'd do the same to you if I was sober, even if you are called Airton and you're her brother-in-law, and even if I am enjoying your excellent hospitality . . . I've never heard such bloody balls . . .' He yawned. 'Admirers? Of course she has admirers. Everybody *admires* her. *I* admire her. But anybody who dares to say . . .' He drifted off.

Edmund sat there for a moment, holding his empty glass. He picked up the bottle. After a time he noticed that it, too, was empty. He remembered he had half a case of Bell's in his wardrobe. 'Willie! Wake up! Willie! I want to get to the bottom of this. Wake up! I'm getting another bottle.'

'Did I tell you how she lights up a room?' murmured Willie.

When Edmund staggered back with the new bottle, Willie was snoring. He swayed above him for a moment, then turned, brought a blanket from his bedroom and draped it over the prone figure. He turned off the lamp. The moonlight coming through the veranda windows lit the way to his single bed, on which he collapsed, without bothering to take off his clothes. He had caught a glimpse of silver on the sea, beyond the lawn, far below, and thought of the warships at anchor in the bay. He recalled snatches of Willie's conversation. He thought about Willie's animated defence of Catherine. Suddenly one of his earlier remarks came vividly to mind: 'Right girl's not interested in me . . . or, rather, she's married to somebody else.' He began to laugh. So that was it! Willie Lampsett was in love with Catherine too! Poor sucker! he thought. Poor tragic sucker! Join the bloody club. But soon his laughter faded into snores, which were deeper than Willie's snorts from the next room, and after a few minutes, the two men's breathing was reverberating in unconscious harmony, while outside a fresh wind whispered in from the sea, blowing clouds across the moon and darkening the mountaintops.

'Edmund! Get up!'

He heard Willie's urgent voice through his headache. He opened one eye. Pale light was coming through the window. 'What time is it?' he mumbled.

'Just after five. You'd better come quickly. There's an army outside. They're looting your hospital and I think they're arresting your doctors. Tell me – it may be important – what was the name of the general who released his patients to you?'

'Army? Looting my hospital, did you say?' Edmund, head pounding, sat up in bed. He felt a constriction round his throat, and realised it was his bow-tie.

'They're Fengtian troops, Chang Tso-lin's,' Willie explained quickly. Edmund was scrabbling on the floor for his shoes. 'They've been streaming up that mountain path since three. I was woken by trucks. When it was light enough, I looked down from your garden with my binoculars. I reckon more than three divisions are heading down the coast road. I also spotted a column of tanks. It's a big force, all right, and coming out of Manchuria. That can only mean one thing. Kuo Sung-lien's coup failed. The Japs must have come in on Chang Tso-lin's side after all. And now he's come south to deal with Feng. His men are bloody angry, and at the moment they're taking it out on your hospital staff. They're accusing them of harbouring Kuo Sung-lien's men. That's why I asked you whose division you got your patients from.'

'They come from all kinds of divisions and armies,' panted Edmund, as Willie followed him up the path leading to the hospital. 'And I don't know what generals Niedemeyer was dealing with. What does it matter anyway? We're non-political,' he shouted in frustration.

'You'd better tell that to the officer who's haranguing your doctors.'

In the courtyard soldiers were standing on the loading bay of the main hospital, a converted barn, hurling down boxes of medicines that others were loading into the back of lorries. Two men were trying to lift one of the operating tables through a downstairs window. Another was hacking at the bricks and window-frames with his bayonet to create a bigger space. The patients had already been carried out of the building, and were lying in the flowerbed outside the office hut, groaning, as they waved their stumps or sought to retie their bandages. The fitter patients, the farm workers, cooks and porters, were standing in two ragged lines, with their heads bowed, or gazing sullenly at the soldiers who guarded them with bayonets. Beside Willie's battered Model T, its ransacked contents scattered over the paving stones, four young privates were posing for a corporal with a box camera; they might have been tycoons standing proudly by a Lagonda. In the centre of the square stood Dr Chen, still wearing his pyjamas, and Dr Wu, who had a stethoscope hanging over his white coat (he had been on night duty); three scared nurses were weeping openly behind them. A young officer was yelling and waving a revolver. As Edmund watched, he slapped Dr Chen hard across the face with his gloved hand.

Edmund started forward in rage, although he felt Willie's restraining hand on his arm. He strode briskly across the square and caught the officer's wrist as it was raised to strike again. 'Stop it! What do you mean by this?' he shouted, then froze, as the officer's angry face turned to him. 'Ti Jen-hsing!' he whispered, before the butt of a rifle was slammed hard against the back of his head.

Lying on his back on the paving stones, he knew he should lift his arms to try to prevent the beating he was receiving. Vaguely he was aware that Willie was pinioned in the arms of a private while another soldier thumped him in the stomach. Above him he saw the sallow features of the corporal who was about to strike him again, and wondered inconsequentially what had become of the man's box camera. Then he blacked out.

When he woke Mother Pia's wrinkled face was smiling down at him. He seemed still to be in the courtyard, although the hospital building was a shell, and black coils of smoke were curling from its broken timbers. He turned his head and saw nuns moving among the amputees and the maimed, who were still stretched out in the flowerbed. He tried to move and found that one leg and an arm were in splints and bandages.

'Oh, Dottore, so you have decided to rejoin the living. I am so pleased,' Mother Pia said. 'God's ways are very strange. Yesterday you offered us your protection, and today it seems we must look after you.'

'What time is it?' he muttered. Then he remembered everything that had happened, and whispered urgently, 'Dr Chen, Dr Wu, are they all right?'

Willie's voice spoke: 'You've been out cold most of the day, old boy.' He came into view. He had a bandage round his head, but seemed otherwise unaffected. He was holding a cup and saucer. 'These nuns have just arrived. Somehow they heard what had happened here and are taking control. They've done a better job of binding you up than I managed earlier but, then, for a long while I thought you were dead.'

'Dr Chen? Dr Wu? The patients?' Edmund pleaded.

'Your staff have gone to join the wars, old chap. Conscripted into General Lin Fu-po's regiment, along with anybody else here who could walk, and the nurses, of course. They'll be all right. Looks like you and I were the only battle casualties. Afraid you've lost your hospital, though, and everything in it. Burned to the ground because it had harboured traitors.'

'They'll be all right, you said?'

'I would think so,' said Willie. 'Better than being shot, which is what might have happened to them. Lin Fu-po himself came by in a staff car; he drove in, observed the burning buildings for a minute or two, and left with that savage young captain. Cold, sinister fellow – but it seems it'll be people like him who are going to be the powers that be for a while to come.'

'Hush, Mr Lampsett,' murmured Mother Pia. 'No politics, please. The *dottore* must rest.'

Edmund closed his eyes.

'What do you think Airton'll do now?' he heard Willie ask the nun.

'Oh, God will find something for him to do,' she said brightly. 'You'll see. The *dottore* never believes me, but I tell him always, God has a purpose, even when we are too blind to see what it is.'

9

Lovers and Daughters

From the journal of William Lampsett, Reuters correspondent, Shanghai, 28 May 1925

This weekend students from Shanghai University are planning a march through the international concession to protest at the foreign police force's aid to the Japanese. Tension has been brewing in the city ever since Japanese factory foremen shot striking cotton workers ten days ago. The co-ordination of strikes has been unprecedented, as has been the unity in the slogans and demands. Some suspect the fell hand of the CCP.

Due notice has been given of the students' proposed route and nobody is expecting it to be anything but a peaceful show – although we can probably expect a few exemplary arrests and broken heads. But I fully intend to march with them. I might be able to meet some of the principal activists and discover if this really is a movement organised by the CCP.

Shanghai, 31 May 1925

I was with the peaceful protestors when, about three thirty in the afternoon, the chanting column reached the Wing On department store and a cordon of constables tried to steer the demonstration back along Nanking Road. Some hooligans who had attached themselves to our march stoned them and the crowd forced its way through, but near the Louza police station, we were stopped again by a thin line of armed Chinese and Sikh policemen. I heard their commander, a nobody called Inspector Everson (I've met him), shout a warning, but it was in English and had no impact on the crowd. Then the policemen panicked and fired. I saw a boy in front of me collapse, a patch of crimson spreading over his white shirt, but by then I was running for my life.

It was only four volleys and, as I discovered later, only three students were killed outright; five more died later of wounds. If this were British India, probably not much more would be heard about it – on a scale of massacres, this is no Amritsar – but in China, in the heart of a Treaty Port, in a city already radicalised after a century's humiliation at foreign hands, it is enough. The general strike has spread to the rest of the country, an anti-British boycott stretches from Canton to Tientsin. All classes sing the anti-imperialist anthem – warlords, capitalists, workers, bourgeois, intellectuals – but it is the labour leaders and the CCP who have come into their own. I am probably still reacting to what I saw, but a part of me wants to say, Bravo to them! Bravo to the May 30th Movement, as it is now called! It is about time the worm turned. I share their anger, and feel positively subversive.

That Sunday, Fu-kuei and Yi-liang spent a quiet day on the lake in nearby Hangchow. When they arrived back on a late train, they discovered that Shanghai had been transformed. A loudspeaker was blaring patriotic slogans. Strangers were hugging each other in the station concourse, weeping on each other's shoulders. A student in a Chinese gown was haranguing a small crowd. Yi-liang made his way to a newspaper stand and bought a late edition of the *Ming Po*. He scrutinised it, frowned, and silently passed it to Fu-kuei, who found her own eyes misting with tears, and anger, when she read about the massacre.

'What will happen?' she asked Yi-liang late that night, when they arrived, exhausted, at their home.

'General strike, I expect,' he said, pouring himself a drink. 'It's no longer a matter of arresting Bolshevik agitators. They're martyrs now. It plays into Kuomintang hands, of course. And even the warlords will have to come in behind what they'll probably call a patriotic movement against imperialism. It's strange how things turn out, isn't it? All it needed was one stupid English policeman. He's done in three minutes what Sun Yat-sen failed to achieve in a lifetime. I wouldn't be surprised if they're carving a statue of him in Moscow as we speak. We might as well toast him. He's made my life easier for the next few months. Nobody will be interested in arresting insurgents for a while. Here.' He gave Fu-kuei a glass. 'To Inspector Everson,' he said.

'No, to China,' said Fu-kuei, her eyes gleaming, her chest suddenly constricted by an uncontrollable rush of pride.

The next two months were intoxicating. There were protest marches in all the Treaty Ports, in major and even minor cities. Intellectuals and writers wrote stirring denunciations of imperialism, which were printed in newspapers and journals, and copied on to red posters in marketplaces and town squares for all to read. Workers in other cities joined the general strike, and the boycott on foreign, particularly British, goods was universal. One day, Fu-kuei and Yi-liang had themselves driven to the docks where they saw the mountains of cotton, rice, silks and other export goods mouldering under the hot sun; stevedores wearing strikers' armbands stood guard to make sure nobody came near; the gantries and cranes were idle, and the cargo ships rusted on the pier. As they watched, a large limousine pulled up on the dock: four Englishmen in white cotton suits stepped out; one had been driving – all the chauffeurs, all the servants, even the *amahs* had joined the strike. The four men, hands on their hips, looked sadly at their fortunes rotting away. Fu-kuei recognised one as the *taipan* of a big trading house: she had seen his photograph in the newspapers and knew he was on the municipal council, he stood there silently, shaking his big head. She squeezed Yi-liang's arm, unable to conceal her elation, and even Yi-liang smiled.

Over the summer Fu-kuei read the newspapers each day and marvelled: the strike leaders, young CCP activists who until that time had lived furtively in underground cells, were sitting at the same tables as the capitalists who had feared and reviled them. With the Chinese Chamber of Commerce, the merchant guilds, Kuomintang representatives and representatives of the warlords, they were drafting in committee a set of demands, an ultimatum in fact, to be given to the foreign-controlled municipal council. For once she had nothing to report to her masters, because Yi-liang had nothing to report to his: everything that was happening was there for all to see in the newspapers.

She continued to visit Barkowitz's shop. For weeks, she would turn the flap in the carpet and find no messages. One day in early July, however, there was a slip of paper. On it was written a simple instruction: 'Find means to infiltrate CCP/strike leadership and report attitudes/plans allowing us to gauge level of support. You may pass on Major Y's information to give credibility/cover, but do not – repeat *do not* – reveal your other connections.' She was thrilled. She felt she had wings.

By next morning she had worked out a plan. It seemed to her that she should do as much as possible in the open, because she knew that, even though his warlord was now ostensibly supporting the strikers, Yi-liang would not have relaxed his vigilance on the CCP. So when he came home for lunch she was at her most kittenish. 'Yi-liang, we can't sit idly by and do nothing while all these great events are happening in our country.'

'I'm not sitting idly by,' he said.

'You aren't but I am.'

'Well, what do you want to do?' He smiled. 'You can hardly go on strike, because you don't have a job. And I can't imagine you want to boycott your favourite Lipton's tea.'

'I'm being serious.' She pouted. 'I want to work in one of the soup kitchens for the striking workers.'

He exploded with laughter. 'You in all your jewellery?'

'Why not?' she said. 'Madame Liao and her daughter are working in one. And so's May Ho. Why can't I?'

'Anything for the revolution,' he agreed eventually. 'I'll see if I can get you a place in one of the more fashionable soup kitchens.'

'No, I don't want your help. I want to do this all by myself. It's my contribution.'

He shook his head, and weakly waved goodbye as he went chuckling out of the door.

She had already done her research and that afternoon she was driven in Yi-liang's Rolls-Royce to one of the steelyards near Woosung, which she knew that strike leaders sometimes visited.

She had chosen to wear her most expensive mink coat and a string of large pearls. She wore a diamond ring on her finger and gold bangles glinted on her wrists. As she had expected, they laughed at her when she entered the canteen. Two young men dressed in student's uniform looked at her suspiciously from a table where they were eating noodles.

Haughtily she surveyed the room. 'This floor is filthy,' she said. 'Look at those slops. It's unhygienic.'

'Oh, I'm sorry,' leered a fat cook, through the laughter. 'We don't have any *amahs* to tidy up after us here, you know. Staffing's so difficult these days. You may not have heard in your mansion, but there's this most inconvenient general strike going on.'

'Yes, I know,' she said. 'I've come to join you. There's a sign on your gate asking for volunteers. I'm a volunteer.'

She noticed that even the two students were smiling. She slipped off her coat and threw it on to one of the benches. She walked to the corner of the room where she had seen a bucket and mop. 'Where's the tap?' she asked the cook. 'You have water, don't you?' She was aware of the stares as she filled the bucket, and ignored the renewed laughter as she began to scrub the floor. She felt herself perspiring under her cheongsam; the silk would probably be stained – all the better, she thought, and carried on scrubbing. By the time she had covered half the floor, the laughter had stopped; by the time she was sweeping the water and the slops out of the door into the yard, she had won their respect.

She leaned on the mop and surveyed the room. One of the scullions was holding a wok he had been scouring and was staring at her with his mouth open.

'Since May the thirtieth there are no rich or poor, exploiters or exploited,' she said quietly. 'Here.' She pulled off her ring and flung it into the wok. It tinkled as it spun to the bottom. She followed it with her gold bangles. 'These'll get in the way of my work,' she said. 'Why don't you sell them and buy more food for the strikers?'

'What about your pearls?' somebody called.

'But I like my pearls.' She smiled, fingering them, and this time they were laughing with her.

When the striking workers arrived for their meal, she was behind the big soup tureen, ladling the broth.

One of the two students sidled up to her when the meal was over and they were tidying up. 'Who are you?' he asked.

'I'm a patriotic Chinese,' she answered, continuing to pile the bowls.

'We see that. You've also given us your name, but who are you really?'

'You mean what do I do when I'm not serving soup?' She looked him directly in the eyes. 'I'm the mistress of Major Yang Yi-liang, head of counter-intelligence for General Sun Chuan-fang. Does that answer your question?'

She watched him as he backed away. He and his companion scuttled out of the canteen. She smiled, and put another bowl on the stack.

After that it all followed predictably. For two days nothing happened. She supposed that they were checking to see if she really was Major Yang's mistress. On the third day she saw a young man in a Western suit reading a newspaper at one of the tables and observing her surreptitiously. She ignored him. On the fourth day he had a companion, a thicker set man with a crew-cut who chain-smoked. She remembered she seen his photo in the newspapers: he was one of the CCP leaders, a factory worker who had instigated one of the first strikes against the Japanese. Once the strikers had finished their meal, he came up to her, 'Why are you doing this?' He asked her.

'To serve my country,' she said. 'And the masses.'

'The masses?' he repeated, raising a heavy eyebrow. 'Do you know who I am?' he asked.

'Yes,' she said.

'Is there anything you want to say to me?'

'I'd like to help,' she said.

'By serving soup?'

She scrutinised his coarse features, her own expression impassive. Then, glancing to left and right to ensure that nobody was observing them, she reached through the slit of her cheongsam and retrieved the crumpled piece of paper she had tucked into her girdle. His heavy paw closed on her palm.

'Goodbye,' she said. 'I sincerely hope that the great movement you have started here is successful.'

When she withdrew her hand, the paper, on which were summarised details of Yang Yi-liang's CCP suspects, had been taken away.

It took another week. She waited patiently, serving the soup. Then the young man in the Western suit returned and took his accustomed place with his newspaper. Again she ignored him. As he was leaving, he bumped into her, as if by accident. 'Sorry, sorry, so clumsy,' he apologised. She noticed laughing eyes. In her hand she had a piece of paper with the name of a park in the French concession and a time the following morning to meet.

She had told the driver to take her to King and Fook, a jewellery shop located on Avenue Marshal Foch that she visited regularly. As they passed the entrance to the park she asked him to stop the car. She felt faint, she said, and wanted a few minutes of fresh air. No, there was no need for him to accompany her. She saw the young man on a bench, absorbed in his newspaper. She sat down beside him and made to adjust the strap on her shoe. Out of the corner of her eye, she saw that he was grinning at her. 'We decided to trust you,' he said.

'Thank you,' she replied.

'We had no idea they knew so much about us. Your lover is impressive.'

'Thank you,' she said again. 'I think so.'

'But you're betraying him?'

'We are both seeking to help China, he in his way, I in mine,' she replied.

'"One bed, two dreams."' He quoted the proverb. 'Is that possible? Do you love him?'

'That is no business of yours,' she said.

He laughed. 'My name's Chin Hong-chi,' he said. 'I'm to be your contact.'

They met several times over the next few weeks, choosing a different rendezvous each time, in department stores, tea-rooms, Victoria Park, once in a cinema. He never came to the steelworks canteen, where she continued to work in the evenings, though sporadically now. There was no need to any longer. She had made her contact. Yi-liang had been amused: 'I thought the novelty would wear off,' he said, when she had found excuses not to go for four nights in a row.

The first meetings with Chin had been brusque and businesslike. He handed her a list of the information he and his colleagues required; she provided what answers she could. On her visits to Barkowitz's dress shop, Fu-kuei would report the times and places of her assignations and the questions she had received; usually she would receive questions in return about the strike. As she got to know Chin better, he became forthcoming. She soon learned that he was an idealist, believing in revolution with a simple, almost innocent passion that reminded her of her days with Wang Yi. Like Wang, he came from a peasant background, but he was clever, had worked hard and won a scholarship in engineering at Shanghai University. She found herself warming to him, on occasions exhibiting almost maternal care, although he was not much younger than she; one chilly day she caught herself upbraiding him because he was not wearing a sweater.

She never had to interrogate him: he was so excited about what was happening. He was eager to tell her the latest triumphs in the strike, the course of negotiations with the foreign imperialists, the contacts they were making with other cities throughout China. When she was with him, she felt stirrings within of the innocent, idealistic part of herself that she thought had died. At first, when the strike was going so well, it seemed that everything she had once believed in was attainable. She and Chin would find themselves building cloud castles of optimism about the future; sometimes, however, back in her bed, with Yi-liang sleeping beside her, she would recall those conversations, and remember that she and Wang had believed they could right the world. Then she feared for the strike and the movement. And for Chin.

Sometimes she was disturbed by her feelings for the young man. She told herself that he was just a contact, a revolutionary comrade, even – but more and more his mischievous humour, his intelligence, his teasing good looks, the sheer pleasure and relaxation of being in his company penetrated her defences, and she found herself thinking of him with the affection and pride of an older sister for a favourite younger brother. And there was his resemblance to Wang. That disturbed her in a way she could not quite fathom. Sometimes, when she realised that she was in danger of dropping her guard, she would be severe or formal with him – but he would raise his eyebrows and parody her in a way that made her helpless with laughter. She told herself it did not matter. It was all part of the intoxication that everybody was feeling today, it was the May 30th spirit – but then she would be alarmed again, and ponder for long hours in the solitude of her bedroom. She felt that in some indefinable way she was losing control of herself. She was certainly not falling in love with him. That was a ludicrous idea and, anyway, she was satisfied sexually – more than satisfied – with Yi-liang. It was something else that worried her, something much more dangerous: emotion was affecting her work – it was as if the frozen persona she had tried to create was melting.

One day Chin met her with an expression as dark as death. He was not interested in the information she had for him. 'We're betrayed,' he said. 'The whole cause is betrayed. The Chamber of Commerce has tricked us. The International concession will be run as before, except there will be token Chinese on the council, capitalists, running dogs. They're talking of calling off the strike and the boycott.'

'Will you let that happen?' she asked.

'No, of course we won't. We'll fight on. We have to.' He turned a pathetic face towards her. Her heart ached in sympathy. 'But I'm not sure if we can do it on our own,' he said, his face falling into his hands. 'The rightists are taking over the unions.'

Self-consciously at first she put an arm round him. 'It'll be all right,' she murmured, as if comforting a child. 'It'll be all right.' It had seemed natural afterwards for him to lean his head on her shoulder while he sobbed like a little boy. She had smoothed the hair on his wet forehead, and quickly kissed his cheek. She had hurried home much disturbed. That evening, when Yi-liang came to bed, she made love to him with urgent, hungry abandon.

Chin had been right. The strike was running out of momentum. First one factory, then another went back to work, agreeing to token reforms and meaningless pay rises, meeting not half the conditions they had originally demanded. The CCP activists were now being frozen out of the negotiations with the municipal council. The Chamber of Commerce and the merchants' guilds gave a banquet for leading foreign businessmen. The head of the Chinese Chamber and the president of the council were photographed shaking hands, grinning at the camera, as if they had been announcing a successful business merger. The May 30th spirit was fading away.

A few days later, Fu-kuei was about to leave her house for an assignation with Chin. She was surprised to see Yi-liang standing in the hall. 'You're back early,' she said.

'I missed you,' he said. He had a strange smile. 'It's the fifth anniversary of the day we met.'

'Is it?' She had no idea.

'Yes, it is,' he said. 'I thought we would celebrate.' He produced from behind his back two bottles of champagne.

'Now?' she said. 'It's three in the afternoon.'

'Now,' he said. 'Why not?'

'I have an appointment,' she said.

'What? with a hairdresser? Or your dressmaker? Consider it cancelled. You now have an appointment with me. Upstairs,' he added, with a sly smile.

'Upstairs?' she repeated – but something in his expression made her laugh. 'What's got into you?' she asked, as he bowed her up the stairs.

'What's got into me? A devil, perhaps,' he said, as he followed her. 'Yes, a fiery devil. And a sudden desire to see you naked, defenceless, in front of me. You probably weren't expecting to be ravished this afternoon, but you'd better prepare for it.'

She giggled. There was always a fall-back rendezvous. She would see Chin tomorrow. No harm done. And this afternoon – though she could not understand what had got into him – she would enjoy whatever Yi-liang had in mind.

They made passionate love. Yi-liang, for all his fiery devils, was more than usually gentle and tender, and she responded in kind. They drank the first bottle of champagne in bed. The next he poured over her breasts and belly. They did not bother to get up when the servants called them to supper.

Next day when she turned up at the new rendezvous, Chin was not there. She waited half an hour, then left. That night she read about his capture in the evening paper. Though he was not named, she knew it must be him. The report merely stated that the foreign police in the international concession had arrested an 'insurgent and saboteur' in a department store. He had been handed over to the Chinese authorities and was being questioned by the military police, who were 'assisting' the local police force with their enquiries. She knew what methods they would be using.

Next day she saw on Yi-liang's desk a list of activists who had been secretly tried and shot at the gendarmerie in Chapei. Chin's name was third from the end.

Why? She paced the carpet in her room, thinking again and again over the circumstances of his capture. She had to keep thinking, she told herself. She had to be rational, objective – everything that Mr Behrens had ever trained her to be because otherwise, she knew, she would break into hysterics. All she wanted to do was curl into a ball and weep – but if she did that she would be giving in. All the past years would be wasted. She owed it to the cause, to her beliefs, to the very meaning of the struggle to keep going. She owed it to Chin. Now, more than ever before, she needed her self-control. She must think. Think. How had this happened?

Chin had been arrested in the tea-room of the Sincere department store. That was where she would have been meeting him had not Yi-liang returned home unexpectedly. Was it coincidence? Or had someone revealed the details of the rendezvous? But who would know? How had Yi-liang discovered it? She was sure now that he had been behind the arrest. Why else had he come home if not to prevent her also being arrested?

The only people who had known the details of the rendezvous were Chin and herself. She stopped pacing, and stood frozen on the carpet. No, that was not true. She had been to Barkowitz's shop two days before, and she had submitted her routine contact report.

And she had noted the time and place of her next meeting. Her masters also knew.

But why would they betray her contact? There was no possible motive. Chin's arrest would mean that the CCP would never trust her again. They would assume that she had been Yi-liang's pawn all along.

Unless they wanted to make an unbridgeable gulf between her and the CCP. The CCP in Shanghai, unlike the branch in Canton led by Borodin, was not taking direction from Moscow. Perhaps her masters had begun to doubt her loyalty, fearing that if she became too close to the local Chinese party, she would not be so easily controlled. Had they suspected somehow her tender feelings for the young man? She had to reach for the bedpost to support herself. Had Chin been sacrificed as a means to preserve her true role, not as a vanguard of Chinese revolution but as a foreign agent? It was unthinkable.

She heard a timid knock, and the *amah*'s face came round the door. 'Master is downstairs,' the old woman said. 'He wants you to get dressed and come down.'

'Tell him I'm not feeling very well,' said Fu-kuei. She experienced a rush of revulsion at the thought of him.

'*Tai-tai*, he was insistent,' said the *amah*.

'Very well,' sighed Fu-kuei. 'What does he want? He's never here at this time of day.'

'I don't know, *tai-tai*. He was very impatient.'

When she came down, Yi-liang was waiting. He was dressed in his army greatcoat, and polished boots. He was leaning against the wall, frowning and slapping his cap against his knee – but he smiled when he saw her. 'There you are,' he said. 'Get your coat. We're going for a drive.'

'Where to?' she asked. She felt empty in the pit of her stomach. She wondered whether she, like Chin, was about to be arrested and whether she would soon be in a cell in the gendarmerie.

'Oh, nowhere in particular,' he said. The chauffeur was waiting by the door of the Rolls-Royce. 'I thought I'd take you shopping,' he said, as he followed her in. 'Didn't I interrupt one of your shopping expeditions the other day?'

He gave the driver an address in the French concession. Fu-kuei leaned back against the seat and closed her eyes. So he knew. 'When did you find out?' she asked quietly.

Yi-liang turned to her with an innocent smile. 'Find out what?' he asked. 'Oh, the address of your dressmaker? You told me yourself – long ago – and, anyway, I see all the bills. What a wardrobe you must possess now. There's nothing else I need to know, is there? I've always assumed there's been absolute openness and trust between us. Am I wrong?'

He began to whistle the tune of one of Shanghai's current popular songs. Fu-kuei closed her eyes again. She could tell, from the sway of the car and the traffic sounds outside, the direction in which they were heading.

They parked opposite Barkowitz's shop. Yi-liang was looking at her with an amused expression.

'What do you want me to do?' she asked dully.

'Go shopping,' he answered cheerfully, and made to open the car door. He paused. 'Hold on,' he said. 'That's strange. Who are those people? They don't look the usual types who'd have business at a ladies' establishment.'

She saw that a lorry had stopped on the other side of the road. Out of the back jumped three or four men, ruffians in workers' trousers and vests. Two were holding revolvers, and another an iron bar. As she watched, the man with the iron bar smashed the front of Barkowitz's window display. The men with the revolvers went inside. She heard the tinkle of the doorbell.

'I think they must be gangsters,' said Yi-liang, conversationally. 'Green Gang, perhaps? Or Red Gang? They look intent on robbery, don't you think? Or perhaps your Mr Barkowitz hasn't being paying his protection money. What a shame that the foreign concessions are not in my jurisdiction. The lawlessness these days is deplorable.'

Almost distantly she heard the sound of gunshots inside the store. The doorbell tinkled again, and she saw Mr Barkowitz's female assistant staggering out of the shop clutching her arm, which was bleeding. One of the gunmen followed her and fired into the back of her head. She slumped untidily behind the lamppost.

A moment later, his companions came out of the store. Two had dresses and bolts of cloth in their arms. The other appeared to be holding a cashbox. They threw them into the back of the lorry and leaped aboard. The engine roared as it drove away. Passers-by were frozen on either side of the street staring. Fu-kuei saw a woman in a fur coat leading a poodle; she appeared to be screaming but Fu-kuei heard no sounds: it seemed that she was watching a reel of a silent film. As she watched she saw yellow flames licking the curtains of the window display. One of the mannequins began to melt.

'Dear, dear,' said Yi-liang. 'What a nuisance. It appears, my love, that you will need to find a new dressmaker. Are you still in the mood for shopping, or shall I ask the driver to take us home?'

That night Yi-liang did not at first attempt to make love to her. He lay on the bed as stiffly as she. A pool of moonlight lay between them.

'I've been very stupid,' she said.

'Have you, my darling?' He rested himself on his elbow and observed her.

'It was the excitement of the May Thirtieth Movement,' she said. 'I was reminded of . . .'

'The follies of your youth?' he asked lightly. He leaned over and kissed her forehead. 'I understand, you know,' he said.

'Will you forgive me?'

He laughed and folded her into his strong arms. 'Of course.' He kissed her eyes, which were welling with tears.

She wept silently, while he made love to her. She knew that, from now on, she would be under permanent surveillance. That would be the condition for his continued protection.

'You don't know what it's like to live day by day with a man you love, and find that not an ounce of affection is returned.'

Catherine, wearing only panties and a camisole, was standing in front of the long mirror in her bedroom, pressing a frock to herself. She turned to the man smoking in an armchair behind her, one green tartan sock resting on his knickerbockered knee, his yellow polka-dot bow-tie clashing with his red face and carroty hair. 'Stop moaning, Robby,' she replied, 'and give me your serious opinion. Is it to be the pink dress or the lilac?'

'Neither colour suits you, darling. You should wear green to match your sparkling eyes. Mind you, both of those rags are so flimsy it hardly matters. If it's an impression of nakedness you're attempting, you might as well go out as you are. Your pert bottom peeking out of those frilly knickers looks delicious, at least from where I'm sitting.'

'I thought you weren't interested in female bottoms.'

'Yours happens to be a very boyish one, my dear,' said Robby, blowing a smoke-ring. 'Anyway, it's extremely unkind of you not to pay any attention to the outpourings of my heart, when I'm always there to cheer you up after your own tattered love affairs.'

'What rot, Robby! What affairs? And when have I ever confided in you?'

'Ooh, what a cold, cruel creature you are. Your flirtations, then. Your teasing little pranks. Your peccadilloes with poor, innocent young boys. You can pull the wool over Georgy's eyes but not Uncle Robby's. I swear the other day I heard little Reginald Whatever-his-name-is from Jardine's weeping in the men's lavatory in the Astor when you and that new Russian jockey fancy of yours were behaving outrageously on the veranda.'

'I was humouring Igor. He was drunk,' murmured Catherine, reaching for another dress. 'Anyway, we only kissed.'

'Only kissed!' snorted Robby. 'The thing I most detest about you, my darling, is your hypocrisy. And your heartlessness. No, I see there's no point in discussing love with you. There's no sensitivity in you. You wouldn't even begin to understand if I were to explain my plight.'

'I think I'll wear the white one,' Catherine decided. 'How does it look?'

Robby waved dismissively. Catherine pulled the fringed white frock over her head, straightened it and pirouetted in front of the mirror. She sat down at her makeup table. 'All right,' she said, reaching for her lipstick, 'so you're in love with Willie. Or are you talking about one of the houseboys?'

'Please,' sighed Robby.

'Well, have you told him?'

'You must be joking,' said Robby. 'He's a conservative Englishman. He'd throw me out of the house.'

'You never know,' giggled Catherine. 'Cold fish that he is, how do you know he isn't repressing a similar devotion to you? He's put up with you as his houseguest for three years.'

'I amuse him,' said Robby, miserably. 'That's all. We were at school together. Served in the trenches. There's a bond, I suppose. Oh, yes, he's concerned for me. Tries to hide the bottles, that sort of thing. Lectures me sometimes. But he has no idea what I feel for him. You see, Catherine, sadly he's not remotely queer. That's the long and the short of it, I'm afraid.'

'Well, why doesn't he get a girlfriend, then, to put you out of your misery?' she asked, dabbing her eyelids.

'You mean you don't know?' Catherine could see in the mirror that Robby was half smiling, but there was a sad, hangdog look in his eyes. She turned on her stool, curious. 'You're right in one respect,' he said. 'Willie is repressing his emotions, but they're not for me. Have you really never noticed? Well, I'll tell you. He's madly, passionately in love. Keeps a photo in a silver frame on his bedside table. I die of jealousy every time I see it.'

'What? Has he some English rose in the home counties?' Catherine turned back to her mirror. 'A childhood sweetheart?'

'No, my dear Catherine. He's in love with you, my darling. Always has been, ever since he's known you.'

Catherine put her false eyelashes back on the table. 'This is your idea of a joke, I take it?' she said.

'I wish it was,' said Robby. 'He pines for you, like Lancelot for Guinevere, and as hopelessly.'

'Lancelot did not pine hopelessly for Guinevere,' said Catherine. 'That was what all the trouble was about.' She applied a row of eyelashes. 'Well, he's never ever given any sign of it,' she said. 'I thought he rather disapproved of me.'

'He wouldn't, would he?' said Robby. 'Willie's one of your old-fashioned Christian gentlemen. All steely eye, and hard resolve, while big heart beats silently in the manly breast. As I told you, I find him irresistible.'

'You do talk rot, Robby. Willie's George's best friend. They're out together duck-shooting as we speak.'

'Isn't that my point?' said Robby. 'Willie's far too honourable to think of dallying with somebody else's wife. Let alone a friend's. Although George is hardly anybody's idea of an ideal husband.'

'Now, now,' said Catherine, applying rouge to her cheeks. 'You're straying into forbidden territory.'

'Am I?' murmured Robby. 'Separate bedrooms? Separate lives? You hardly see each other. George is up shooting before dawn, or exercising his ponies, while you never see the light of day before noon. At weekends he plays golf. In the evenings he's at the club. Last summer he abandoned you at Peitaiho – well, you and all your little friends. Do you ever exchange a word? Never at the parties I see you at together. Both you and he are always busy entertaining somebody else.'

Robby put out his cigarette stub in the ashtray and lit another. Catherine was making up her eyebrows, ostentatiously ignoring him.

'Oh, yes, you're the dutiful wife when he wants you to be. You go with him to balls and you support him when he's racing. You hang on his arm and flatter the *taipans* for him. You allow him to show you off. I'm sure that appeals to his vanity. He owns the perfect, beautiful wife, doesn't he? Well, not so perfect, are you? There is also that whiff of a reputation about you. All those adoring young bucks in your train that he appears to tolerate so good-humouredly. The outrageous stories about you that are never quite substantiated. Does he encourage them? Does it bring a flavour of mystique to your glamour? "Good old George," they say, no doubt, at the club. "Equable George. He's got a wild one there – but look how unruffled he is. He'll tame her if anyone can." As if you were one of the Mongolian mares he rides on the track.'

'Is there a reason for your offensiveness,' Catherine murmured, 'or do you have a particularly bad hangover today?'

'You know very well that I only have hangovers when I haven't been drinking. No, I'm intrigued, my dear, by the improbable success that you and George have made of your marriage. For it is successful, is it not? And highly original that happiness can be based on infidelity! It could perhaps be the subject of a French farce. For it rebounds to his credit, does it not? Is it a game the two of you play? Because, for all the talk, you're discreet. Did she? Didn't she? Whisper, whisper, and then in you both come, all white scarves and sequins, arm in arm, and the whole assembly bows at your feet. Even the ladies vie to have you on their charity committees. Lady Innocence. The queen of society.'

'Have you finished?' asked Catherine quietly.

'No, I'm just getting started,' said Robby. 'My interest, you see, is in what happens backstage, when the actors and actresses have taken off their greasepaint and the lights are down. I know about clowns. I am one – a good one, as it happens – and I am all too aware that it is only a tragedian who can carry off comedy well. What binds you to George? It isn't his private fortune. He hasn't got one. Even with his prize money from the track, his income as a relatively junior railway employee can only be modest. Goodness knows how he maintains his lavish style, but it is you who have made him the toast of society. Oh, I see the calculation there. Handsome George is incapable of love – for women and, alas, also for men – but he knows the value of a good buttonhole. Yet why should you choose to be his buttonhole? That is what I ponder. Because you're rather trapped, aren't you, in George's gilt cage, for all the dashing naval officers with whom he allows you to play? When I met you I recognised a free spirit, and even then I thought that our little Tientsin world, with its children's games, was confining. Yet you flower here, like a tired orchid in a little pot. I wonder why.'

Catherine was putting on her earrings. 'I don't think you wonder anything, Robby. You're too shallow to be curious. You're building up to something particularly bitchy because you're feeling bilious today.'

'No, I am merely thwarted in love, and a little jealous, yes, that my dear Willie chooses to love you, though you pretend not to be interested when I tell you. And I'm intrigued. Because I sense a dark little secret, and I can't make out what it is.'

Catherine showed him her profile. 'There. How do I look?' she asked.

'Too much rouge,' said Robby. 'Fresh peaches and cream. You look like a blushing bride, which, for a vamp like you, is thoroughly inappropriate.'

'Thank you. I'll take that as a compliment and leave my face as it is.' She began to brush her hair.

'That George is complacent I understand,' continued Robby. 'It's your behaviour I find strange. For, Catherine, you can't play the innocent with me. It's not just a question of where there's smoke. Remember, I was at Peitaiho too last summer . . .'

'Robby, has anybody told you that you're a bore?'

'Frequently. It's part of my charm. Now, come on, Catherine, I know you took lovers: you weren't that discreet. But I know something else too. You loathed yourself for doing so.'

'Oh, really?' said Catherine.

'Well, look at the vapid types you surround yourself with. I understand you, Catherine. You're not somebody to be satisfied with an empty brain and a fine torso. That's my line of country, not yours. You're slumming, Catherine, and I wonder why. I saw you at breakfast, that time George came down for the weekend. Nobody can disguise his or her true character at breakfast. Certainly not you, with your expressive eyes. I saw the pain in them, and the hatred in them, when they flashed at one or other of your *beaux amoureux*, grunting over their bacon or giggling over the kedgeree. And I saw another thing. George's smug smile.'

'Robby.' It was a warning growl.

'And I thought, Am I missing something? Is George the amiable cuckold he seems? Or is there a bit of the Svengali here? Is it for his pleasure rather than yours? Does he watch? I wondered . . .'

The silver hairbrush sailed through the air, missed Robby's head by a fraction, and smashed a vase on the shelf.

'Damn, I liked that pot,' said Catherine, quietly. She stood up, and walked over to Robby, who gazed up at her nervously. She studied him severely, then ruffled his hair. 'Come on,' she said. 'I've had enough of your spiteful nonsense. Let's go downstairs and you can teach me that new dance step.'

Both turned as they heard a knock at the door.

'*Jinlai!*' called Catherine in Chinese.

Lao Tang's white head appeared round the door. His enigmatic expression revealed no surprise that there was a man in Missy's bedroom. '*You keren zai louxia,*' he told her. 'There's a guest downstairs.'

'*Shei?* Who?' asked Catherine in surprise. 'I wasn't expecting anybody this afternoon.'

'*Wo buzhidao. Shi yige laoren. Waiguoren.* I don't know. An old man. A foreigner,' said *Lao* Tang, superciliously. He offered Catherine a silver tray, on which lay a visiting card. 'Douglas Pritchett, Counsellor, British Embassy, Peking,' she read. 'I haven't the faintest idea,' she said, to Robby's raised eyebrows.

'Does he want to see Master?' she asked.

'No, Missy,' said *Lao* Tang. 'Only you.'

'How very peculiar,' murmured Catherine.

Robby and she descended the staircase together and, on entering the sitting room, saw a bald man whom Catherine judged to be in his mid-fifties sitting stiffly on the sofa. He had a worn, lined face, and a heavy grey moustache, which hid his lips and seemed to press down on his chin so it almost disappeared into his collar. He was examining his fob watch, which he had taken out of the tweed waistcoat of his old-fashioned suit. On the sofa at either side of him he had neatly placed his Homburg and fawn gloves. His frayed leather briefcase rested on his knees. At their approach, he rather fussily repocketed his watch and, with some effort, rose to his feet.

'Mr Pritchett?' Catherine enquired.

'Ah, Mrs Airton, how kind of you to see me. And, ah, Mr Airton,' he added, nodding to Robby.

Robby laughed. 'Sorry, you have the wrong man. I'm Berry, Robby Berry. Friend of the family.' He threw himself into an armchair, pulled out his cigarette case, and casually lit up. Belatedly remembering his manners, he offered the case to Mr Pritchett. 'Do have one. They're Turkish. With gold filters.'

Pritchett looked uncomfortable. 'Thank you,' he said, 'but I don't indulge. My, ah, apologies. I assumed . . .'

'Oh, I don't mind,' said Robby breezily. 'It's almost flattering to be mistaken for George.'

The Emperor's Bones

'Do sit down, Mr Pritchett,' said Catherine, settling herself on a chair. '*Lao* Tang will bring some coffee.'

'That's very kind,' said Pritchett, resuming his former seat. Catherine gave him a radiant smile, raising her eyebrows interrogatively.

'You are naturally wondering why I have called on you so – ah – unexpectedly,' Pritchett responded. 'I have been in Tientsin on business and am shortly to return to Peking. Unfortunately my train leaves in less than two hours but I took the opportunity . . .' He paused, embarrassed. 'Mrs Airton, the matter that I wished to discuss with you is – ah – of a private nature. If this is an inconvenient time . . .'

Catherine leaned over and smacked Robby's knickerbockers. 'Off you go, Robby. We're about to have a grown-up conversation.'

'Charming,' said Robby, irritably stubbing out his cigarette in the ashtray. He bowed to Pritchett and went out, brushing haughtily past *Lao* Tang.

'I do apologise for Mr Berry,' said Catherine. 'He's an artist,' she explained. 'He makes cocktails. Now, what is this private matter?' she asked, after *Lao* Tang had poured the coffee, and slipped quietly out of the room.

'Forgive me,' said Pritchett, 'if I request that this conversation remains private between the two of us.'

'That depends on what you wish to talk about,' said Catherine, frowning.

'I understand. I'm being presumptuous. Let me leave it to your own judgement, then, when you have heard what I have to say.'

'You are being very mysterious, Mr Pritchett,' said Catherine.

His moustache fluttered in what might have been a smile, but the sad expression in his eyes did not change. 'I am afraid that mystery is part of my profession, Mrs Airton. In the embassy it is my role to handle and analyse – ah – secret matters. I should not be telling you this. To the world I am merely a senior administrator, responsible for economic reports. However, I am asking you to trust me, so I feel it behoves me to be honest with you from the start.'

'You're telling me you're a spy?' asked Catherine bluntly.

Again the moustache fluttered. 'Well, something like that,' he

317

said. 'It may surprise you, Mrs Airton, to know that this is not the first time we have met, although you will certainly have no recollection of the previous occasion since you were only an infant at the time. I once met your mother and your present parents-in-law in Peking after their remarkable escape from the Boxers.'

'You knew my mother? Helen Frances?' Catherine's voice rose in surprise. This was not what she had expected.

'I did, although my business at the time was more in connection with your father.'

'Tom Cabot? What possible business could you have had with him? Anyway, he was killed. By the Boxers.'

Pritchett coughed. 'Mrs Airton, I think you know that your natural father was not Mr Cabot. Indeed, I believe that you have already visited Manchuria to see Henry Manners.'

Catherine flushed. She stood up, knocking over the small table and her coffee cup. 'You said you were presumptuous, Mr Pritchett. Indeed you are. How dare you insinuate that I . . . ?'

Pritchett raised his eyes to stare directly into hers. The sad expression was gone, and Catherine found herself confronted by two hard stones. 'That you are illegitimate, Mrs Airton? A moment ago you told Mr Berry that we were to have a grown-up conversation. You know that I am telling you nothing of which you were not aware. And I do not think, from what I hear about you, that you care much about society's opprobrium. Nor do I, frankly. There are far more urgent matters to discuss. Can we at least start by being candid with each other on what we both know to be fact?'

'I should throw you out of my house,' said Catherine, resuming her seat after a long, angry pause. 'Henry Manners is not my father. I do not accept that as a fact. Yes, since you have obviously been spying on me, I don't deny that I once had a foolish hope, based on a misunderstanding of some of my mother's letters, and I did go to Manchuria to seek him out. But he made it clear to me, hatefully so, that I am no daughter of his. He is a detestable man, loathsome, and if you are a friend of his, I pity you. Now, is that candid enough for you? If you have a train to catch, you should go.'

Pritchett remained motionless on the sofa. 'Did it never occur to you, Mrs Airton, that he may have had a reason for rejecting you in the way he did? To protect you, perhaps?

'What are you insinuating now? That he is a spy too? And if I became involved I would be mixed up in spying as well? What a silly idea. If he's anything, he's some sort of toady or agent of the Japanese. In fact, he's despicable, and I wouldn't even want a father like him. May he rot, for all I care! I never want to see or hear of him again.'

Pritchett sighed. His eyes had regained their sad softness. 'Oh, Mrs Airton, Catherine, I do understand. Did Edward or Nellie Airton never talk to you about him? I'm sure they did. They knew him as well as I did, or better. Did they never tell you that he was once a fine, proud man?'

'Yes, and that he's fallen into a dark side. I've heard all that cant. All right, he was my natural father. Does that satisfy you? But what business is it of yours?' She felt tears behind her eyes. 'What bloody business is it of yours?' she said quietly. 'What gives you the right to enter my sitting room and interrogate me about my father?'

'Perhaps I wish to make amends,' said Pritchett.

'Oh, God, not you too! You and Nellie Airton! Thank you, I don't need any amends. If my life's a mess then I alone am responsible for it.'

'It's not to you I owe them,' he said. 'I was hoping that I could ask for your help – no, please hear me out. I told you what my business is. I should tell you also that Henry Manners was my best agent, oh, since long before you were born. I won't go into details. I am not allowed to. Suffice to say, your father did valuable work for his country during the Boxer times, the Russo-Japanese war, in the Great War and afterwards. He was a hero. I'd like you to know that. But sometimes in my profession one has to ask terrible things of people. Agents are forced to do things, pretend to be things, which – which after a while make a tax on their souls. I am sorry if that sounds pretentious, but I fear it is literally so. We have agents, double agents, triple agents, conspiracies within conspiracies, masks within masks, and a man can only pretend so much, even the best of them. After a while it is difficult to distinguish what is shadow and what is reality. One forgets where one's loyalties lie.'

'I really am not interested,' said Catherine, fumbling for a ciga-rette.

'I will only take a little more of your time. Please, Catherine, Mrs Airton, I think you of all people understand the world we currently live in. I know of your service in Russia during the war, and the revolution . . .'

'God, is there anything you don't know?'

'Please. Alliances have changed dramatically in the last decade, and old certainties have been stood on their head. Bolshevism threatens us all, but there are other threats, which in my world we must somehow adapt against as best we can. There are rogue factions in the Japanese military, in Manchuria, for example, who wish to overthrow everything that our civilised nations are striving for. Semi-criminal brotherhoods like the Black Dragon Society have support within the army, the SMR and the intelligence agencies. And they are becoming more powerful, meddling already in Chinese politics. We saw an instance in the last civil war, when the Kwantung army, against orders from Tokyo, intervened to save Chang Tso-lin. That is a dangerous precedent.'

'Didn't you say you had a train to catch? This really has nothing to do with me.'

'But it has something to do with your father. You see, I sent him to Manchuria, at a time when we were in alliance with Japan. I asked him to become close to these military factions, to help them. Well, he was all too successful, and now he's involved in everything they do. Some of their activities are criminal. He has put himself in terrible danger.'

'If you're so worried about him, why don't you order him to leave? He's your precious agent.'

'For several years he has not been, my dear. I told you that some-times the pretence can become reality. I am afraid that your father has now thoroughly identified with the other side. It is a long time since we – ah – closed the books on him. He has become a dead agent. That is the rather unfortunate term. He no longer works for me or the British government. He is beyond our protection. There is nothing I can do to warn him. Rather, he would not listen to me even if I could.'

'Mr Pritchett, why have you come to me? I told you I'm not interested in anything to do with Henry Manners.'

'You are his daughter. I was hoping you might find a way to reach him.' Pritchett's shoulders slumped. 'If you were visiting Dairen where he lives . . . I thought . . . I hoped . . . that he might listen to you. Perhaps it was a foolish whim.'

'Mr Pritchett.' Catherine walked over to where he sat and looked into his eyes. 'You may know many secrets, but obviously you know nothing about human nature. When I saw my father, in Mukden, I was as close to him as this. And do you know what he did? He sneered at me. He might as well have spat in my eye. Do you think that that is a loving relationship between a father and a daughter? Do you really think he will listen to me? Or that I now care what danger he is in?' She reached down beside him and picked up his hat, then his gloves. After he had stood up, she handed them to him. 'Please leave now, Mr Pritchett. Catch your train. Go back to your secret world. I do not think that you ever need come here again. And forgive me if I don't see you to the door.'

'Mrs Airton, I beg you, consider.'

'Mr Pritchett, I did not invite you to my house. And now I am asking you to leave it. Do you really wish me to call *Lao* Tang?'

'Mrs Airton, your father has many enemies. It is not only he who is potentially in danger. His associates are very ruthless men, and if they knew that he had a daughter—'

'*Lao* Tang!' she called. '*Kwaidian. Keren yao zoule.*'

'All right, Mrs Airton, I'm leaving. But you have my card. Cable me. Telephone me if ever—'

'Mr Pritchett, goodbye,' said Catherine, firmly.

He bowed his head and left, escorted by a hovering *Lao* Tang to the door. *Lao* Tang closed it gently after him, then turned to Catherine. '*Wangbadan zoule!*' he announced happily. 'The turtle's egg has left.'

Despite her trembling limbs, Catherine could not help laughing at the old muleteer's obscenity. She returned to the sitting room and slumped into the armchair that Robby had vacated. *Lao* Tang had followed her. 'Gin toni', Missy?' he asked. 'Plenty on-da-rocksu?'

'Yes, *Lao* Tang,' she murmured. 'That would be lovely.'

She sat there, holding the glass. Outside the window, the trees in Nellie's garden were blowing wildly in the November wind – but Catherine's mind was far away, recalling that military parade in Mukden, and how her life had almost ended when her father, flanked by two Japanese officers, had turned his back on her and walked away.

'What possible right . . . ?' she murmured. She wished that the odious little man would return: she would pull those ridiculous moustaches off his face.

She thought of his last words, and became livid with fury. She tipped the glass to her mouth and the ice tinkled against her teeth. The man was trying to blackmail her. Or threaten her. The bloody nerve . . .

'It doesn't matter,' said a voice deep inside her. 'Calm yourself, Catherine, forget it. It's the past. Forget it.' She forced herself to put her shaking hands on the chair's armrests, and to breathe deeply, as she had trained herself to do.

Eventually her outrage subsided, and the picture of Manners's hideous features, which had reassembled from her subconscious while Pritchett had been talking, became less distinct. It took an effort of will, but over the months and years Catherine had indeed trained herself to forget. That was how she had survived. The trick was not to think. To concentrate on her dresses, her schedule, her parties, her flirtations. Robby had talked about theatre. Well, that was what it was: she was a trouper. And it worked: the most insurmountable problems went away. Time passed. Just act, Catherine. That was all she had to do.

George had taught her. It had taken a while. At first, during their long honeymoon on the liner and after, Catherine had been depressed. For all she knew of George and despite all the reasons why she was marrying him, she had somehow believed that their wedding would make a difference. After all, she had burned her boats. She had drawn a line under the past. That night with Edmund had been her last gift to a lost love, a savage expiation, but as she had closed the door on Edmund's bedroom, she had felt emptied inside, and wept a little when she returned to her own bed, but she had slept well afterwards: no dreams came to haunt her. In the morning she had been ready to face the wedding and a new life. She had enjoyed the service. She saw Edmund's white face in the pews and felt nothing; she was relieved when he failed to attend the reception. George's speech had been hilarious, and that evening, in their spacious cabin, the matrimonial suite, she had made as passionate love to her new husband as she had to his brother the night before. And that first night he had responded, diligently, and afterwards she had been dreamily content, until he got out of bed, washed, put on his purple pyjamas, then got back in, perfunctorily kissed her cheek and slept. She had convinced herself that he was tired, and was careful not to touch him in case she disturbed his rest.

In the morning he had been charming, amusing, showering the bed with flowers that he had ordered with the breakfast tray, and she had enjoyed his whimsicality with possessive affection. They had gone up to the sun deck, and she had laughed as he drew waspish little word portraits of their fellow passengers. She had nestled against his arm, while he strolled proudly, smoking his cigar. She had never been happier. The sun shone on a choppy sea. Great white clouds rolled on the horizon. She was married to George, and George was using all he had to delight her, to entertain her. As the prow cut through the waves, and seagulls swirled aside in the ship's passing, she saw the prospect of their weeks alone together, stretching ahead.

At luncheon, on the captain's table, George had been equally entertaining, but his witticisms had been directed for the pleasure of the other passengers. That evening the purser had organised a get-together ball. 'Please let's not go,' she had begged. 'Let's just be alone.'

'But, darling, it'll be fun,' said George. He had supervised her dressing like a couturier. 'I want you to be gorgeous to impress them all.' In the event, he had spent most of the party in the bar, sidetracked into a game of bridge; Catherine, who had been dressed as gorgeously as he had desired, had danced with strangers. At three in the morning when they returned to their cabin, George had been too tired to make love. He apologised. The following night he did not apologise. When Catherine nestled into his back, twisting her legs with his, he had gently disengaged himself.

After a week, whenever she heard, 'Darling, it'll be fun,' she had wanted to scream. 'I want to be with you,' she told him, over and over again.

'But, darling, you are with me,' he always replied. 'You make me so proud.'

'It's just like our courtship, when you had me go out and dance with others. But that was a sick game.'

'What nonsense. I love watching you dance,' he would say. 'Anyway, you always come back to me.'

Smoking a cigarette, sipping her second gin and tonic, she remembered one of Robby's remarks as she had been dressing that afternoon, something about George and his mares on the track. Robby was a perceptive little beast, she decided, even though he was not as clever as he thought he was. Now she thought about it, she supposed that George had been training her. Coaxing her. Wheedling her to do what he wanted. *He understands his horses, talks to them, never uses a whip.* Wasn't that what they always said? Well, after a while, she had learned to jump through his hoops. It was pleasanter that way. It was easier than resisting him. And sometimes, yes, it was fun.

They had crossed the Pacific and travelled through America and Europe, always in company, with George the life and soul of the party, and Catherine his beautiful consort. They had sailed slowly between tropical islands; they had lived like nocturnal animals, coming out at dusk to dance on the deck, or to drink coconut cocktails by the roaring fire of a Hawaiian *luao*. They had disembarked in San Francisco and moved from one glittering city to another. They haunted nightclubs, cabarets and desert casinos, carried between anonymous nightspots in hired limousines and across the continent in a wash of bootleg champagne in their Pullman compartment, where George would tell jokes to the ladies among their fellow passengers and Catherine would flirt with their husbands. In Kentucky they had attended the races, where George, whose reputation had travelled before him, came into his own. In New York, and later in Paris, he led Catherine through the dress shops, buying for the evenings to come. There were more parties on the steamer to Le Havre, more cities and more parties. They had attended racing balls in Fontainebleau. They had drunk until dawn in smoky bars in Pigalle and the Reepersbahn, where transvestites danced the tango with sailors on the cigarette-strewn floor. Catherine had danced with them, and George smoked his cigar, watching from the side. And then, finally, there was the passage back to China on a P&O liner. By then Catherine knew the score. In their cabin they had separate bunks.

They had spent only two frosty days in Edinburgh with George's parents. Nellie had asked her repeatedly whether she was happy, and she had replied each time that she was, deliriously so. She had held George's arm when they strolled together in the castle, and sat on the arm of his chair when his father and he returned to the sitting room after their port.

It was not even a matter for discussion that they should have separate rooms when, after nearly a year, they returned to Meadows Road.

And it was not a bad life, Catherine thought, as she put her empty glass on the table. George gave her a free rein, except when he needed her to accompany him to one of his society events. She enjoyed her reputation. It amused her sometimes to think how shocked everybody would be if they knew how few lovers she really had. She was careful, as always, not to break hearts – but she liked the company of her young admirers, vapid though Robby said they were. They were a diversion, and they kept her from thinking about the useless life she lived – from thinking at all.

Sometimes, like now, the past would return to haunt her: she would meet a White Russian who would talk of the war, or she would hear news of Edmund – he had been severely injured in some dreadful warlord incident up in that mountain hideaway of his. Willie had told her about that: for some reason he had been there when it happened Now Edmund was setting up another hospital with that American friend of his. For a while, after Willie had told her, she had been upset, as she had been when she had seen Edmund at that awful Chinese funeral and he had been so cruel – but life went on.

And she supposed that she had found peace, of sorts. Like George, she entertained. She provided spice in this boring expatriate society. She served. The thought made her chuckle. Edmund once said to her that service was the meaning of life or some such idealistic cant.

Well, she was not going to be hurt again. That horrible Mr Pritchett had tried to blackmail her into entering the world again. Never. Thank God for George. He had taught her how to have fun.

And yet, sometimes, it seemed so empty . . .

'Come on, Catherine,' she said aloud, stubbing out her cigarette in the ashtray. 'You have things to do.' She moved over to George's gramophone. She flipped through her record collection until she found the one she was looking for, and adjusted the needle on the turntable. Never mind that Robby was not there to teach her the new steps; she would work them out herself. That would show him. Soon she was lost in the New Orleans beat. She had thrown off her shoes, and her stockinged feet moved across the carpet.

Bloody little man Pritchett, she thought. Obnoxious Robby, with his sly innuendos. Oh, yes, he was perceptive, irritatingly so. But allowing George to be a voyeur as she cuckolded him? She hadn't sunk that low.

The music came to a close, and she put the record on again.

What else had he said? That Willie was in love with her. What nonsense! But as she danced, she thought of the last time Willie had come to the house. He had called in for tea, during a brief return to Tientsin between those incomprehensible warlord conflicts that he covered for his bureau, and he had been rather silent and withdrawn, gazing at her with that severe expression as she poured milk into his cup. Was it true that he kept a photograph of her by his bedside? Robby would say anything for effect, but he did not often joke about Willie, whom he probably really did love, poor man. Why had he told her? Did he seriously think that she would enter into a love affair with Willie? She liked Willie. He was one of the few friends – the only one, really – with whom she never had to pretend. But a love affair with him?

That would be dangerous, Catherine.

She heard the warning. Or was it a challenge?

The sound of the needle clicking at the end of the track brought her back to herself. 'Bloody Robby,' she said aloud. 'What stupid nonsense.' And she laughed, unconvincingly. 'Don't even think of it,' she told herself. 'Not in your wildest imagination.'

She had never thought of Willie in a romantic manner, even when she was single. He had always just been there. Watchful. Dependable. He had seemed so much more grown-up than the rest of them. He was the only one who took his job seriously. Unlike the others, he had an interest in China, although he never bored them with it. She had danced with him a hundred times, and enjoyed it: he moved elegantly, and knew the steps. He was never intimate so she felt comfortable, almost safe, in his arms, as if he were her unconscious chaperon. There was a correctness and consideration about him that she had always found reassuring. He had a dry wit and teased her affectionately, but never attempted to hurt her as the others did. He was the only one who stood up to George, and held his own; that was perhaps why George respected him. It was natural that he should choose him as his best man. Catherine had simply taken him for granted. He was as solid a fixture of her Tientsin life as the Gordon Hall.

Did she find him attractive? On the surface he was cold and stiff. Those thin lips and the high, smooth forehead; the fine, receding hair, the pale pupils; his lightly freckled skin; his long, ascetic nose and don-like precision. She had a brief vision of Edmund's lived-in features, the brown depths in his eyes, his trim, muscular body, his beautiful hands, the grace with which he moved – she snapped that shutter closed as soon as it opened. No, Willie wasn't traditionally handsome, but there was an intensity in him, a passion that sometimes revealed itself when he talked to her.

If it was true that Willie loved her, as Robby had told her this afternoon, why hadn't he done anything about it? The record had ended again. Mechanically she lifted the needle back to the beginning.

How could she be contemplating an affair with a friend? They already had a relationship. And if, under whatever unconceivable circumstance they were to enter into such a thing, and George discovered it, he really would be hurt. Willie was his best friend. He might wink at her other affairs: he knew they didn't threaten him. But there would be no play about an affair with Willie on either side, his or hers. On the other hand, she suddenly thought maliciously, serve George bloody well right. Robby had called him a Svengali. He thought he controlled her every move. She would get her own back with this. It would raise the stakes in whatever sick game they had agreed tacitly to play together.

Robby would help, she thought. He would find vicarious pleasure in that, especially because of the way he felt about Willie. The only place they could meet would be Willie's house. She couldn't risk anything here. If she visited him one afternoon, instead of him calling on her ... If she could arrange it with Robby that the servants were out of the way ... She knew what dress she would wear ... and what she would have on underneath ...

'Oh, come on, Catherine, control yourself,' she said aloud. 'You've only had two drinks.' Willie was a friend. She loved him as a friend.

This had gone too far.

'Dammit,' she said softly. She switched off the gramophone, went to the door and called for *Lao* Tang to bring her another gin and tonic. She looked at her watch: two dreary hours to fill before she had to dress for tonight's party at the Aglerns. Tonight would be no different from any other. She would bathe, put on her face, pick up the dress George would have chosen beforehand. At the stroke of seven, he would be in the hall in his dinner dress, waiting patiently for her to come down. He would compliment her on how she looked, and say something witty, and she would laugh politely for the benefit of the servants. They would set their smiles, and step out to the chauffeured car. And they would have fun. Another long night of interminable fun ...

10

The End of an Affair

From the journal of William Lampsett, Reuters correspondent, Tientsin, 23 April 1926

China has never been in such crisis. In Canton, Chiang Kai-shek has been squabbling with Borodin since the right-wing coup in March, but it would be foolish to think this will stop the Northern Expedition. Neither politician can afford to break the alliance between the nationalists and Communists, the so-called United Front, and both left and right wings of the Party are committed to Sun Yat-sen's old dream to unify the country. General Chiang is seeking a rubber stamp from the Kuomintang Congress for his military plans. His armies are ready to march.

Meanwhile, the warlords are belatedly reading the runes. Chang Tso-lin's divisions are streaming down from Manchuria to strengthen Sun Chuang-fang in Kiangsu and Wu Pei-fu in Henan. And I write – nothing. Nothing of this. The Baron in London presses me every day. I must go to Peking to interview Chang Tso-lin. I must go to Canton to interview Borodin, but I make lame excuses to stay in Tientsin.

Those arms, those eyes, that hair beguile me in a tangled net . . .

The Yu family villa nestled two miles or so north-east of Shishan in a pine grove on the south side of a hill. It was a pleasant walk through spring countryside to get there, and the converted farmhouse, in which the old muleteer and soy-bean tycoon lived with his new wife, was attractive in its simplicity. The walls of the city shone in the distance, and the rolling fields of the great estate spread to the horizon.

For all that, Martha had come to dread this monthly luncheon, though Ming insisted they always went. Over the last year Old Man Yu had become intolerable. Each enormous course turned into a fulmination against the general political situation in Manchuria, the new taxes, General Lin, and against his own son, Minister Yu Fu-cheng. The latter, remarkably, was the only one who ever kept his composure, silently choosing the more delicate morsels with his chopsticks, his bright eyes twinkling behind his spectacles as his father's tirades thundered over his head. For Martha, it was a matter of controlling her boredom. It was tougher for Ming. Old Man Yu invariably made him match toasts with him in his terrible *gaoliang* wine. Since Ming was too polite to refuse, and he had no head for spirits, his face would flush with an allergy, and he would be sick for two days afterwards – which meant Martha had to take over his classes.

It was not as if they lacked problems of their own. She knew that Ming, although he rarely spoke of it, was desperately worried about his family in Tientsin. His elder brother had been inept in the matter of selling the mansion: the family had received not half of its true value. It was disgraceful that the buyer, a rich textile manufacturer, a former client whose initial business had only been made possible by Lei Bank funds, had cheated his former benefactors. Doubly so when one remembered that the late Lei Chuan-hsi had thought so highly of this man that he had offered the hand of his only daughter to the latter's son. Ming and Martha had been stunned when they learned that the buyer was none other than the father of the young soldier they had met at the banquet on the night that she and Ming had walked out of the family home. Occasionally she saw Captain Ti, as he was now, at the head of his company, marching through the town; he had prospered mightily in General Lin's employ – a position he would never have received had it not been for Lei patronage. He was certainly no longer the blushing boy who had charmed them when they first came to Shishan: he swaggered like the rest of Lin's hardened soldiers, or slouched insolently on his horse. He snubbed them as inferiors, staring haughtily over their heads as he rode by. Perhaps he was getting his own back for Lan-hua's rejection.

Not that Martha cared: she was concerned only for her husband. Ming had recently come back from visiting his brother in Tientsin. 'They're living in a h-hovel,' he had told her. 'Tang can't seem to find work. His wife is making what little money they earn, s-sewing for one of the c-clothes merchants. She even has G-Grandmother helping her.' When she examined the accounts, Martha saw that Ming had been surreptitiously sending money every month to his family, which they could not afford.

The school was not going well, partly because of the exorbitant taxes General Lin had been imposing on the shopkeepers in Shishan: Martha and Ming had had to lower their fees, since the inhabitants of Shishan, in their straitened circumstances, daily threatened to withdraw their children. There were other pressures. The odious missionary, Richard Brown, had last month filed a complaint to Minister Yu, apparently encouraged by the authorities in the Japanese railway town. He had accused Ming of teaching an inferior form of English and using radical, subversive texts. Martha had had to spend a morning in the minister's office, explaining that Charles Dickens's *Hard Times*, and George Eliot's *Silas Marner* were not socialist manifestos, and that the translation of *Fathers and Sons* was not a Bolshevik tract simply because it had been written by a Russian. Minister Yu, to his credit, had dismissed the complaint, but he had clearly been irritated, and Martha suspected that he, too, was under pressure.

And then there was the intimidation. Twice now stones thrown in the night had shattered their windows and they had had to buy expensive shutters. Three weeks ago in the marketplace their assistant, *Hsiao* Hung, had been jostled and threatened; they had complained to the military authorities but had been told that the acts of hooligans were not their business. Last week, Martha's cat had been discovered disembowelled on their doorstep, its blood smeared over the lintels. Hooligans again, said the authorities. Martha had urged Ming many times to take down his Kuomintang flags, because it was an obvious provocation to their enemies, but he had always stubbornly refused.

Now she was not in the mood to listen to Old Man Yu's rants about the state of his soy beans – but she remained silent, as was expected of her. Over the years Martha had studied how to be a good Chinese wife. She had even learned to speak the language. At least the old man's mutton was good, she comforted herself, and his pork. Martha had long ago put aside her Jewish sensibilities. They lived on short fare at the school.

Old Man Yu's third wife, a short, red-cheeked peasant girl of half his age, brought in a large pan of chillies floating among transparent noodles in a brown sauce, a Shishan speciality, and filled up each bowl.

'Come on, husband, eat up,' she said. 'If you're going to be so unreasonably angry, you might as well fuel yourself with some hot spices!'

'What do you mean, unreasonable?' he growled. 'Ask that useless son of mine over there if I'm being unreasonable.' He pointed at Yu Fu-cheng. 'He's breaking his own father with his taxes. Not to mention all the other poor tradesmen who are trying to make a living in this benighted town.'

'This is delicious,' said the minister to his stepmother, who was younger than he was. She beamed with pleasure.

'You're not going to avoid my question by toadying to my wife.' Old Man Yu thumped the table so the bowls shook. 'You're the finance minister. You tell me. How is an honest merchant to survive when he's being squeezed of everything he earns?'

Yu Fu-cheng laughed and leaned back in his chair. 'Well, Father, I grant that we have increased taxes, but they are not so exorbitant if you consider all the factors involved. This is a wealthy part of the country, and the political situation is complicated. With the Nationalists' activities in the south, it is not inconceivable that there will be another war.'

'Listen, boy, what do I care about wars in other parts of China? As a young man I came to the north-east, over the Wall, to these wild lands – and you don't know how rough they were in those days – to avoid China's wars. Everything I own, I built up for myself, with no help from any government. We had to rely on ourselves. Oh, yes, we paid our dues to the black societies, but they protected a man who was prepared to work for his living. We all helped each other, and that was how I prospered, and how you got your precious education.' He paused, looking sheepishly at his guest. 'All right, Ming, your late father helped as well – but he also profited from my success. That's what business is about. Mutual help. Feeding from the same trough. Not these days. I work, and Lin takes my money. Stinking turtle's egg! He even tells me what crops to plant! He appropriates the whole harvest, paying me a pittance, and then he splits the profits – which are a hundred-fold – with the Japanese! *Tamade!* He doesn't even use my transport company!'

'Now, now, Father, we shouldn't be getting into that.' Martha was surprised to see that the usually amiable Yu Fu-cheng was frowning. 'You know you're talking about only a small portion of your estates. It hardly affects your soy-bean income.'

'Oh, doesn't it?' the old man growled, his face reddening. 'I'll have you know that by special order of the Yamen, I am required – required – from last week to plant half my land with opium poppies. More than half. Some arrogant shit of a captain brought the order round, with a squad of soldiers, terrorising my poor wife so she had to hide in the kitchen. Don't tell me you don't know anything about that. Or doesn't the general inform his finance minister of his depredations?'

Yu Fu-cheng's shoulders slumped. His fat lips curled downwards. For a moment his two plump hands fluttered by his sides. 'I really do not think we should go into this, Father. These are short-term expedients, due to the coming war.'

'Extortion, I call it. I agreed with you before, when it was a small crop on hilly ground – not good for the soy bean – and I thought, Yes, General Lin is putting pressure on my son, and we all have to pay the odd bribe. So I planted the muck and kept quiet about it. But every year the yield's had to increase, hasn't it? And now this. It'll break me. It wouldn't matter if I could be in charge of selling the stuff, or involved in the processing, not that I like the idea – I've never touched drugs, even in my early days – but no. Lin takes the profit, leaving me barely enough to cover the labour costs. He and his Japanese middle men. Greedy bastards. I think it's a disgrace for China. And I'm not even a patriot.'

Suddenly Martha was alarmed. She had been watching her

husband, who had until now been amused by the bickering between father and son, but his face was pale. She touched his sleeve. Ming shook her away.

Old Man Yu was thundering on at his son. 'And you, you hypocrite, with all your modern ideas! Fat lot of good it is having a son as an official if he doesn't help his own family. You're no better than an accountant for a gang of opium-runners.'

Slowly Ming rose to his feet, his napkin dropping to the floor. His hands were trembling.

Old Man Yu looked up and shook his grizzled head. 'Now come on, Ming, sit down,' he muttered. 'We were only discussing a matter of business. It's not so important.'

'Is this true?' asked Ming, quietly. 'Minister Yu, is this true?'

Yu Fu-cheng put down his chopsticks, his face grimmer than Martha had ever seen it. He nodded. 'Yes, it's true.'

'That the f-finances of Shishan are based on the p-proceeds of opium-smuggling?'

'Well, it's not exactly smuggling,' said Yu Fu-cheng. 'The cultivation of poppies is legal, as is the opium trade within certain limitations. And it's not true that we rely on the proceeds of opium. As I said, this is a rich region and our taxes—'

'B-but a large p-proportion of y-your finances comes from opium, traded through the Japanese? W-where does it go? To enc-enc-encourage addiction in the ci-cities and the countryside? To add to the m-misery of the Chinese people?'

'I believe that the Japanese trade most of their opium in the south. Not, as far as I know, in areas controlled by Fengtian forces.'

'And you app-approve of this?'

Old Man Yu was looking very uncomfortable. 'Now Ming, my boy, whatever I said earlier, in business you have to be hard-headed and I dare say—'

Yu Fu-cheng silenced him with a wave of his hand. 'Father, with respect, I think you've said enough.' He leaned back in his chair, and observed his interlocutor. 'Your high-mindedness does you credit, Ming, and it is excusable in one so young and idealistic. You have the virtuous qualities needed for a teacher. I'm afraid that outside the classroom life is never as clear-cut. Please do sit down.

Your height, as much as your moral outrage, is dizzying me. Thank you. Drink some tea,' he added. 'It will calm you.'

Quietly Martha took Ming's hand. It was still trembling.

'For a moment look outside Shishan to the wider picture,' said the minister. 'At the moment two large forces are balanced to confront each other. In the North, our Marshal Chang Tso-lin controls much territory. He is playing for high stakes, the unity of China – but his strength depends on alliances with local warlords. He needs to control them, and that requires money. He is now preparing for perhaps the greatest threat that he has yet faced. What was once a comic government in Canton has become a powerful one under this new General Chiang Kai-shek, who receives assistance from the Bolsheviks. We have long laughed at the idea of a Northern Expedition, but now it looks as if it will become a reality. There will be no buying off the Kuomintang. It will be a bitter war, like none we have yet seen, so our marshal's armies need to be strengthened, and that also requires money. In a time of peace, with the rich resources that we possess, taxation is more than enough to fill a government's coffers – but we are not at peace. We are forced to consider other alternatives. Opium brings higher profits than soy beans.'

'So you do approve,' said Ming.

'That is not at issue. As you know, I have made enormous efforts to improve the economy of Shishan, as Prime Minister Wang in Mukden has done for Fengtian as a whole. And we could be prosperous and self-supporting, were we not in a situation of almost permanent warfare. Please try to be a realist. Do you think that my father's estates are the only ones to be planted with poppies? I assure you that I have done all in my power to reduce the impositions on him. Such is filial duty. But have you travelled in the countryside? In other provinces? You will find that the whole of Manchuria is a blowing poppy field.'

'And the f-farmers who grow it b-benefit from the c-crops? I think not,' said Ming.

For a moment, Yu Fu-cheng hung his head. 'No, there is tremendous suffering,' he said. 'Much farmland that should still be used for growing food is being converted to poppy. We are facing shortages, and there is hunger. It is regrettable. There are some – some warlords who are not as scrupulous as my own, and I fear they grow for their own profit rather than to fit out their armies.'

'You're saying that General Lin is sc-scrupulous? Wh-what about the m-money he is spending on his big m-museum, or m-mausoleum, or whatever it is, behind the town? Where does he get the m-money for that?'

'He is more scrupulous than some others,' said Yu Fu-cheng, quietly. 'Or I choose to believe so.'

'As far as I am concerned, anybody who d-deals with the Japanese to feed p-poison to the Chinese people is a t-traitor. And if you are assisting them, so are you.'

Minister Yu's cheeks reddened. His eyes narrowed behind his glasses. 'Oh, you naïve boy,' he said softly. 'Do you think we like dealing with the Japanese? Do you know how powerful they are? Our marshal is in an impossible position. He is tied to them. Without them he would have been destroyed by Kuo Sung-lien. Probably he would have been destroyed by Wu Pei-fu in earlier wars. But do you think he does not know what are their ultimate aims? Listen, boy, in their colony in Dairen is the Kwantung army. It is probably stronger than Chang Tso-lin's combined forces. They don't listen to their weak government in Tokyo. They still believe that Manchuria belongs to them by right of conquest, after their war with the Russians. Under the military-controlled SMR, which is actually a *de facto* government, their secret police are doing everything in their power to undermine China. There is a bureau run by a certain General Taro. Working for him is a man called Doihara, as evil a fox as ever walked this earth. He runs a drug ring throughout the country, with the sole object of sapping Chinese strength. He even has foreigners working for him. They employ an Englishman who writes propaganda to persuade the foreign powers that Japan is harmless, but this same Englishman organises the drugs into the foreign concessions. And there are many, many Chinese who are their creatures. Do you think that Marshal Chang and our General Lin do not know what they're up to? But we are not yet strong. When China is unified, then perhaps we can take them on, but now we must compromise with them, even in their drug-running activities.'

'It is d-despicable,' said Ming. 'It d-disgusts me. I think you are finding excuses to c-cloak the activities of our own warlords, who are cynically robbing the country for their own profit. Lin is one of the w-worst. And you are his slave.'

Martha tensed, but Yu Fu-cheng leaned back in his chair and laughed.

'Oh, how I envy you,' he said. 'You're so sure of yourself, aren't you? Ah, yes, youth, and its charming certainties.' His eyes narrowed again. 'And you, who live such a life of virtuous, uncompromising rectitude, did it ever occur to you where the subsidies that keep your school in existence come from? Do you believe that in my counting-house I have a pile of clean money that I reserve for your unsullied institution? My dear, dear Ming, has it not occurred to you that if it were not for opium money, and my protection, there would not even be a school in Shishan?'

Ming stood up and thumped the table with his fists. 'I do not need your subsidies. I reject your help. From now on we will run the school on our own.'

'And how long will that be? The Japanese are already demanding that your school be closed. Do you think General Lin is impressed that you hang Nationalist flags in your classroom? Why do you think that hooligans are allowed to break your windows and kill your cat? Don't you know that in this town nothing happens without the tacit approval of the military? Oh, Lei Ming, you are lucky that I am a man who knows how to compromise. You may consider me corrupt, but it is only my corruption that stands between you and almost certain destruction.'

'Oh, stop it,' moaned Old Man Yu. 'I had meant this lunch to be such a pleasant occasion.'

'You have only yourself to blame,' said his wife, slapping his head affectionately. 'You and your temper. And look, none of you has eaten my noodles and I have two more courses.'

'We m-must go. I am sorry,' said Ming sullenly. Martha stood up and took his arm.

'Oh, don't,' whined Old Man Yu, but Ming, head held high, had already left the room.

'Ma Ta.' Martha heard Yu Fu-cheng address her. She paused in the doorway. 'Please encourage your husband to think over what I have said. You understand what a dangerous situation we are all in. You are not as naïve as he is.'

She nodded.

'Ma Ta,' said Yu Fu-cheng, 'I will do all that I can to help you. Please try to understand me. In ancient days, an honest official, when faced with choices from which his conscience recoiled, might have had the luxury of resigning and be honoured for it, at least by posterity. I fear, however, that today such an indulgence on my part would lead to no good, and perhaps more harm – for me as well as for others. It is the times.'

She nodded again, and followed Ming into Old Man Yu's yard.

There was no reasoning with Ming all that day, or the next. She tried to persuade him that the drug issue was not in their power to control; it would be suicidal to abandon Minister Yu's help on a point of principle. They were doing good in the school, for Shishan and China, and it was more important that they keep going, even if they had to compromise. As she said this, it struck her how much she had changed in the four years that she had been in the country: the brash Bronx girl who had arrived on the steamer would never have given in to intimidation. 'I love you, Ming,' she told him. 'I know you're right to hate it. I hate it. But we must use our heads now, however much our hearts are breaking. There are some battles we just can't fight.'

She had been struck to the depths of her soul when Ming, his face contorted, had turned on her: 'What do you care? You're a foreigner. What do you understand about China?' and 'You're like all the others. You patronise us. You lecture us on how things should be. You say you want us to be like your United States – but it's hypocrisy, like everything you foreigners bring to us. What you say and what you do are different. You're happy for us to remain corrupt and backward, so you can show how superior you are.' She had fled, sobbing, out of their common room, and later Ming had come to her, where she sat at one of the desks in the classroom, and put his arm round her as he apologised – but he was adamant about his principle.

She knew that it was too serious a matter to leave alone. She steeled herself to argue with him, however painful. When he finished a class, she would be waiting for him. 'Ming, we have to talk about this.' He would throw his books on the table, turning his back to her. 'Money's money. We need it or we'll go under. You know that. What if it is opium proceeds? Then we're turning bad money into good. It's what we're doing here that is important.'

After two days of this she got through to him; with tears streaking from beneath his spectacles into his moustache, he muttered, 'You're right. Of course you're right.'

She threw her arms round him. 'Oh, Ming, how I love you,' she whispered.

'I'm not taking down the flags,' he said. 'I w-won't take down the flags.'

Martha smiled at his stern expression. 'Okay, Ming, that's all right, you keep the flags,' she said, and buried her head in his breast.

She realised, even then, that this was not the end of it. Yu Fu-cheng had made clear that their real problem lay with the Japanese. From the very beginning, when they had taken in pupils from the Japanese school in the railway cantonment, they had faced cold hostility. Although she had persuaded Ming to tone down his Nationalist curriculum, the very fact that it was a Chinese school, run by Chinese for Chinese, had been a patriotic challenge, a defiance of Japanese imperialism. Never had the Japanese articulated this, but their continual obstruction, the recent threats to which the school had been subjected, albeit from anonymous sources, convinced Martha that the problem would not go away. And she knew that, ultimately, if it came to a choice between their school and the Japanese, Lin's military necessity would make him side with the latter. After the lunch at the Yus, she no longer had much confidence in the minister's ability to protect them indefinitely. For the next few weeks, she thought long and hard. She hated compromise as much as Ming did, but the survival of everything they had striven for was at stake. She saw no alternative. She had to talk to the Japanese.

She did not tell Ming. She knew he would have prevented her. She had little idea anyway of what she would say to the SMR administrator. She believed there had to be a compromise, a middle ground. Perhaps there could be a discussion on a shared curriculum, more co-operation between the two schools. She had once met Tadeki Honjo, the Japanese mayor. He had seemed a decent man, a man who might listen. Or so she told herself.

So that she did not arrive flustered, she spent money on a rickshaw to take her the two miles to the Japanese railway town. The neat brick and stone buildings, with their Western porticoes and roofs, were a shock after more than a year in a traditional Chinese city. From the windows of the hotel, she heard jazz music: the band was rehearsing. Shop windows glittered with luxuries. Japanese men and women were strolling down the wide pavements, the gentlemen in dark suits and the ladies in kimonos. As she passed them, they bowed politely. She had a sudden strange impression that she had been spirited into a chocolate-box drawing of Manhattan in the nineteenth century, where everything was made pretty and unreal. It took her a while to get her bearings, but soon she saw the granite headquarters of the SMR, with the Japanese sentries standing outside. The bespectacled clerk inside could not have been kinder. He asked her to wait while he went to see if Mr Tadeki was available. Soon she was climbing a marble staircase behind him, and ushered into a small office, where Mr Tadeki sat behind a large desk. As she entered, he stood up, bowed and waved her courteously to a plush leather seat.

It was a laborious interview. He spoke no Chinese and she no Japanese, so he called in a young secretary to translate. The formalities were endless. They discussed the weather, he described the new station extension, the painting and gold-leaf work being done on the Shinto temple to which the SMR had subscribed; he told her that he had heard wonderful things about her school.

Restraining herself, Martha tried to match courtesy with courtesy. Eventually she lost patience. 'Please, can you tell Mr Tadeki that I have come to discuss the serious problems that exist between us,' she told the interpreter.

There was an exchange in Japanese. She was alarmed to see that Mr Tadeki's bland smile did not alter. 'Mr Tadeki says he is not aware of any problems,' the interpreter told her. 'The SMR supports learning institutions of any kind, and he compliments you on the good work that you are doing in Shishan.'

'Oh, come on,' said Martha. 'Mr Tadeki must be aware that there have been complaints against us, certainly inspired by Japanese distrust and misunderstanding of our intentions. I've come here to see if there cannot be some form of collaboration between the Japanese school and our own. In the curriculum, for example. We might discuss examination practice or other common goals. There should be no politics in education,' she added, for good measure.

There was another long exchange. 'Mr Tadeki says that he is not aware of any complaints,' she was told, 'but he supports collaboration between educational establishments. He says he is no expert on educational matters, but he doubts that there can be much in common between the curricula of Chinese and Japanese schools. However, he asks if you have considered the field of sports. Mr Tadeki was once a champion basketball player.' As the interpreter said this, Mr Tadeki grinned and bowed. 'The SMR might consider sponsoring a basketball match one day between the pupils of the two schools. Mr Tadeki would be happy to take the role of referee.'

Martha's cheeks flushed. She felt she was being mocked. 'Please tell Mr Tadeki that I have come here in all sincerity and with absolute seriousness,' she said.

The smile did not shift. 'Mr Tadeki is also being serious. He believes that basketball encourages healthy minds in healthy bodies. He believes that this is a fundamental precept of modern education. His good friend Mr Brown has told him that this is also encouraged in Anglo-Saxon colleges, so Mrs Lei as a foreigner may be familiar with the idea. He would be more than willing to speak to the principal of the Japanese school about arranging a match.'

Martha knew then that she was being presented with a stone wall. She tried again to explain her position, but she could not bring herself to beg. Mr Tadeki was still happily talking about basketball when she got up to leave. He and the interpreter both stood courteously to bow her out.

At the top of the staircase, she saw two military officers. Their backs were turned to her, but she noticed that while one was sprucely attired in the olive-green uniform of the Japanese Imperial Army, complete with hanging sword, the other was dressed in the ill-fitting pale blue uniform of Lin's Shishan forces. The two men were obviously on the best of terms. The Japanese had one gloved arm round the other's shoulders and both were laughing at some joke. When they became conscious of her presence, they turned and she recognised Captain Fuzumi of the SMR Railway Guard. The other was Captain Ti Jen-hsing. Fuzumi's round features broke into a pleasant smile, and he bowed deeply. Ti nodded curtly. He wrinkled his nose as if he had suddenly become aware of a bad smell. Having acknowledged her, his eyes remained fixed above her shoulder as he stepped aside to let her pass.

She did not know what prompted it. Perhaps it was desperation after her disappointment with Tadeki, but the unfriendly face was familiar at least, and Ti must have access to Lin.

'Captain Ti,' she addressed him, 'for old times' sake, please can I have a word?' She noticed that Fuzumi's features had become wreathed in another smile as his little eyes twinkled from one to the other. The idea that she had some business with his colleague appeared to amuse him. Ti stared at her coldly.

'We are in great trouble at our school. I am sure that it is a misunderstanding, but I do need to talk to somebody. Mr Tadeki is no help. If I could have an audience with General Lin . . .'

'Lei *Tai-tai*. Mrs Lei,' Ti spoke sarcastically, 'I am a soldier, not an educationalist. Your problems are not my concern, but since you have mentioned old times' sake, let me give you a word of advice. You are a foreigner, so perhaps you do not understand the situation in our country, but your husband is Chinese. He should not meddle in matters that are inappropriate. Tell him to curb his politics, and concentrate on being a teacher. Above all, let him check his tongue.'

Martha stepped back as if she had been struck. Ice inched down her spine.

'And another thing,' he added. 'Don't think that your connection with Yu Fu-cheng can always help you. His star is declining in Shishan. I say this to you out of friendship. There are new, dangerous forces about to be released in China. General Lin will soon be marching south to meet them. I do not think he will wish to leave any problems behind him when he goes.'

Abruptly he turned his back on her and walked down the

corridor, his boots clicking on the marble. Fuzumi, still smiling good-naturedly, gave her another deep bow, then followed his friend. She heard their laughter echoing round the walls, as they disappeared from sight.

She leaned against the wall for support, breathing heavily. Her chest felt tight. She had to rest for a few moments before she had the strength to go down the stairs. At the bottom, Mr Tadeki's clerk was waiting for her, smiling behind his glasses, ready to usher her politely into the street.

Her attempt at seduction had not only failed: it had been humiliating. It had been as bad in its way as the degrading episode in Andreas's flat – she shuddered at the memory – although Willie, of course, unlike the Austrian, who had thankfully disappeared from Tientsin three years ago, had behaved in a gentlemanly fashion throughout. Nevertheless, for nearly a month afterwards, she had blushed when she looked at herself in the mirror, hardly believing what she had done, how gauchely she had behaved. When she remembered how trampishly she had dressed, she nearly died of mortification. Willie must have imagined that she had taken leave of her senses. Oh, God, had she really slouched on his sofa, cast bedroom eyes at him, then kicked off her shoes, like a parody of a sultry Clara Bow, or a predatory Swanson? The most excruciating part of it was that he had pretended it was a practical joke, asking her if Robby and George were hiding in the wings ready to surprise the adulterers. When he had seen the blush of shame on her face, the angry tears of mortification in her eyes, he had kindly offered her a handkerchief. Then he had had the tact to leave her alone to compose herself, pretending he had an urgent cable to send. She had let herself out of his bungalow quietly before he returned.

It surprised her, therefore, when one afternoon shortly after Christmas, *Lao* Tang came to her room to tell her that Mr Lampsett had called to see her. She was alone, recovering from a cold she had contracted after her humiliation. George had left the previous day for the New Year racing in Shanghai, eager to run China Coast against the southern champions. Ordinarily he would have insisted that Catherine accompany him to gild his glory, but in this instance her red eyes and pale complexion had convinced him she would not be able to cut the dash for the admiring Shanghai throng as impressively as his other, four-legged, mare. Cautiously she descended the stairs, wondering what she might possibly say to his best friend whom she had offended.

It was even more of a surprise that Willie, waiting in the sitting room, was holding a bouquet. 'Happy Christmas, Catherine,' he greeted her. 'I've come to apologise.'

'Apologise?' she said. 'Shouldn't it be the other way round?'

'No,' he said. 'I behaved in a cowardly fashion. You were obviously unhappy, and had come round to see me to talk to me about something that – that was concerning you and I chose to mock you. I've been feeling guilty about it ever since. I suppose I felt awkward, as George's friend. I forgot that I'm your friend too.'

Catherine stared at him for a moment, then let out a peal of laughter. She tripped forward and kissed him on both cheeks. 'You idiot.' She giggled. 'Well, we're both idiots. Happy Christmas. Come on,' she said, taking his hand, 'sit down on the sofa and tell me what you've been up to these last weeks. *Lao* Tang will bring tea.'

The rest of the afternoon passed in delightful banter. Catherine had never seen Willie so boyish and relaxed. It was as if the embarrassment had deepened their friendship. They discussed mutual acquaintances, laughing at the pomposity of some of Tientsin's senior citizens. They talked about Robby and his extravagance. For the first time, Willie admitted that he knew of Robby's deviancy, but that he had always protected him and always would; he was alarmed about his alcoholism but there seemed little he could do about it. 'He's deeply unhappy, and this is his way of hiding it,' he said. 'It's hard for – for somebody like him in our society.'

Catherine looked at him sympathetically. 'You know why he's unhappy?' she said.

Willie nodded sadly. 'I do. But he's never said anything. Better that way.' It seemed natural that she should take his hand to comfort him.

Shortly after six he told her that he should leave. 'Stay for dinner,' she said. '*Lao* Tang will cook something.'

He smiled. 'No. Better I go. Are – are you sure about tomorrow?'

'Of course,' she said. 'It's not as if I had any other plans.'

Next morning, at ten, he was waiting outside her house in the Buick he had bought to replace his burned-out Model T. Catherine was in a blue suede overcoat; it was ankle length and narrow-waisted, fur-lined and trimmed. With it she wore an astrakhan hat. 'You look like Anna Karenina,' he said, as she got in beside him.

'And who are you? Prince Vronsky?' she asked. He looked at her contemplatively with his pale eyes, then put the motor in gear.

They drove out of the city to the duck marshes beyond Taku.

'Usually I come here with George in his private rail carriage,' he told her. 'We set off before dawn, and the cook roasts the birds we've shot and we have them for breakfast on the way back – but what I like about this place is not the shooting but the wildness,' he said, as they walked along one of the windswept banks. 'I some-times drive here by myself, especially in the winter. Don't you think these cold, clear December days have a painter's light to them? Pastel. Almost Mediterranean. It gives the desolation an air of grandeur. Look.' He pointed at a covey of ducks rising against the pale blue sky. 'Aren't they beautiful? I'm glad I don't have a gun today. I have to cover enough killing in my work.'

He began to speak about his job, the long weeks he spent following armies on campaign, the complicated warlord politics. 'I know there's not ten people back home who are interested,' he said. 'We think we're inoculated against wars after our own four-year horror, and who cares if one general with an unpronounceable name on the other side of the world slaughters a village belonging to another? But I think it's important, Catherine. God knows what human suffering is going to be unleashed if this Northern Expedition really gets off the ground.' He paused, and looked at her shyly. 'Sorry. I shouldn't be burdening you with my preoccupa-tions.'

'No, don't stop,' she said, taking his hand. 'I want to know what's happening in China. I've been hiding myself from reality these last few years.'

He chuckled softly. 'You and every other resident of these Treaty Ports.'

They walked through the ochre and white landscape hand in

hand. Willie talked and Catherine listened. After a while, she clung to his arm, and snuggled closer to him. It might have been to seek protection against the wind. Later, he put an arm round her waist.

They were watching a fisherman, who had carved a hole in the frozen swamp water and was squatting, hunched in his padded jacket, holding a long rod. He was a solitary figure against the ice, which, in this part of the marshes, stretched to a blank horizon. 'Catherine?' murmured Willie. 'Tell me about your marriage. Is George cruel to you?'

'No.' She sighed. 'Let's not talk about him.'

'His manner towards you is . . . cold,' he said. 'Sometimes I think he treats you like an ornament.'

'Have you been talking to Robby?'

'No,' he said. 'I'm a reporter. It's what I've observed.'

'I'm sure we're no different from most married couples.' She attempted a laugh. 'We take each other for granted sometimes.'

'I cannot imagine how anyone could take somebody like you for granted,' he said. Again, she attempted a laugh, then leaned towards him and kissed his cheek. 'Thank you,' she said, and then she did laugh. The sound tinkled in the silence. 'Your face is freezing,' she whispered. 'I'm shivering.'

'Let's get back to the car,' he said. 'There's a rug in the back. To put over your knees,' he added quickly.

'Of course,' she said.

For most of the drive home they were silent. They stopped once to let some sheep cross the road. She turned to look at him and found he was contemplating her. 'You wanted to say . . . ?' he asked.

'No, nothing,' she replied. 'I thought that you . . . ?'

'No,' he said, and they both smiled.

'Are you warm enough?' he asked her.

'Fine,' she said. 'I have the blanket. Are you?'

'I'm fine, fine,' he answered, and, for no reason, it was funny, and they laughed aloud.

When she was getting out of the car at Meadows Road, thanking him rather formally for the pleasant excursion, he interrupted clumsily, and asked if she would join him for dinner. 'I thought, with George away, and since it's the New Year holiday, and neither of us . . .'

'I'd love to,' said Catherine.

'Of course if you're tired,' he continued, 'but the Astor has a good roast this season. I don't mean to . . .'

'I'd love to,' repeated Catherine. She leaned into the car and kissed him quickly on the lips. 'Pick me up at seven,' she said, and ran up the path to the front door that *Lao* Tang, with his almost supernatural sense of timing, had already opened for her.

Having dinner with Willie at the Astor House Hotel was like old times although, in this winter season, they were one of only a few couples eating there. They both ordered the roast and Willie chose a good Margaux. Over dinner they reverted to the carefree humour that had characterised those evenings when she had first arrived in Tientsin, before her marriage. Willie had hilarious stories to tell of the municipality's indecision during the last war, and later, during the trade boycott, mimicking various illustrious councillors so maliciously that Catherine's laughter pealed round the silent dining room and, as in the old days, heads turned in disapproval. Over the second bottle she described the panic of the women who had been evacuated to the coast during the 1924 Emergency, and how she had watched from the pier, waiting her turn to be taken in the lifeboats to the British destroyers anchored offshore. Even over the sound of the wind and the rain she could hear the screams as burly matelots lifted one matron after another in slings up to the decks. 'I wasn't sure if they were scared for their lives or because they thought they'd never see their luggage again.' She giggled. 'The prospect of being locked up with that zoo for weeks appalled me. So, when I saw a jeep-load of American officers, I went up to them and threw myself into the protective arms of Uncle Sam. I had a marvellous time, but you should have seen the faces of those women crowded on the top decks as I drove away!'

'You're amazing,' said Willie, shaking his head.

'No, I'm not.'

'I think you are,' he said.

'Come on, Willie, take me somewhere to dance. This place is dead. Take me somewhere with a band. Take me to the Starlight.'

'Is that appropriate?' asked Willie, smiling.

'Of course it is. We're reliving old times, aren't we? That's where we met that terrible warlord. Do you know? I bumped into him again in Shishan, and he said I owed him a dance!'

'I bumped into him again too,' said Willie. 'and it wasn't dancing he was interested in. But all right, come on.'

The Olgas and Svetlanas greeted Catherine like an old friend and Willie ordered champagne for them all, but after a short time he and Catherine left them at the table to go on to the dance-floor. The Russian girls nudged each other, and exchanged knowing looks. At first, Willie attempted to dance correctly, but Catherine put her arms round his neck and pressed her body to his. For a time they swayed together, to the slow pulse of the cornet; when the tune changed to ragtime, they still swayed, out of time with the music but neither cared. When they finally kissed, they were oblivious to the cheers and laughter that erupted from their table; nor were they aware of the row when the *mama-san* tried to make the Olgas and Svetlanas dance with Chinese clients, an attempt the girls defeated by ordering two new bottles of champagne on Willie's account.

'You know, we can't do this,' murmured Willie, his lips moving down to nibble Catherine's neck.

'I know,' whispered Catherine. 'Don't stop.'

'George is my friend,' he said.

'You're right, my darling,' said Catherine, seeking his mouth.

'I should take you home right now,' he said, 'before we . . . before we . . .' This time it was he who kissed her, and it was a long time later that they left the dance-floor. Still arm in arm, they bought another bottle of champagne for the girls, paid and stepped into the cold night air.

'I'm going to drive you straight home,' said Willie, on the pavement. 'This is all wrong.'

'Yes, you must,' said Catherine, but it was to Willie's bungalow that they drove, and it was long after dawn that he roused her, and even then they could not resist making love once more, before they tiptoed past Robby's room and out to the car. Their goodbye was formal, though, when they arrived at Meadows Road, because *Lao Tang* was waiting as usual by the open door. 'Missy have velly good party.' He beamed, ushering her into the hall, then asked her if she would like breakfast before or after she had rested.

Later, in her bath, she felt dreamily content, luxuriating in the memories of the night, of Willie's shyness and how she had guided him. It had been so gentle, so innocent, so exploratory. She sat up in the bath, feeling the coldness of the air on her wet body. My God, she wasn't falling in love, was she?

When George returned from Shanghai, Catherine felt for the first time in her marriage that she had something to hide.

Lei Lan-hua was working late in the secretariat, translating a speech for Mr Borodin. He had come to her desk personally to ask her if she would perform this chore. That was typical of his kindness and consideration. How she admired him.

She recalled how he had sat casually on a stool next to her, smoked his pipe and contemplated her with his big brown eyes. 'But you look tired,' he had said, after he had thanked her. 'A young person shouldn't devote all of her time to the Party. Promise me that when you have finished you will rest. What's become of that handsome young engineer who works at Whampoa?'

She had blushed and asked him how he could possibly know about John Soo.

'There are many things I know.' He winked, pulling at his heavy moustache.

She explained that John Soo was away with the Second Division, fighting the southern warlords. 'Ah, then you have chosen a hero to be your lover,' he said. 'But he's the one to envy, I think.'

She had told him rather priggishly that John Soo was only a comrade and a good friend, and Mr Borodin had tapped out his pipe ash on the window-sill and given her a mischievous smile before plodding back, with that slow, tired tread of his, to his office.

She was translating a passage now about the Northern Expedition that rumour among her colleagues said would be the main subject discussed at the congress. 'The Northern Expedition must be our goal,' she read Mr Borodin's neat script, 'and we must never be deterred from its eventual realisation. But is our Party truly united? The vision of a great Northern Expedition attracts us now with compelling force – but are we ready? Is our political foundation solid? I share your dream, comrades, but I urge caution, and above all patience, lest our dream proves itself to be but a chimera . . .'

Lan-hua had to look up 'chimera' in the dictionary, and was startled to read that it meant 'a figment of the imagination, a wild and unrealisable plan'. Was that really what Mr Borodin meant to say? That the Northern Expedition was unrealisable?

Despite her loyalty to him, her faith in his wisdom, she felt a twinge of despair. How long would they have to wait? Like all her friends here, she had been buoyed up over the last exciting months by the almost daily bulletins about their victories over the southern warlords. She was immensely proud to think that John Soo was in the vanguard of those offensives. Yet all these campaigns were only groundwork for the greater one to come.

She yawned and stretched. She was tired. She was tempted to leave the rest of the translation to the morning. Perhaps then she would view Mr Borodin's argument in a clearer light. She knew that she should not question her superiors.

She became aware that her tunic felt sticky on her body. It was still spring, but the weather in Canton was already humid. She wondered if the water in her dormitory would still be hot. Outside her window she heard cicadas clattering in the plane trees, and beyond them the sounds of the city, the occasional whine of a motor-car, the hooting of a barge on the river. From a room above her she heard the click of mah-jongg tiles, and laughter. She leaned lazily against the back of her chair, letting the heat and the comforting night noises wash over her.

She was startled awake by a clatter against the window-pane. Then she heard a faint call: 'Lan-hua! It's me.'

Controlling her excitement, she lifted her head cautiously over the sill. The lamplight reflected on his round spectacles and under one arm he held a parcel. He was waving and smiling. 'John Soo!' she screamed. 'You're back!' She hurtled down the concrete stairs, and out of the door. John Soo was standing with his arms stretched wide and she threw herself at him. He caught her and twirled her round so her feet left the ground. 'You're back!' she cried.

He laughed as he put her down. He picked up the parcel. 'It's a jacket from Nanning,' he said. 'Spoils of war. No, I'm joking. I bought it, but it's red silk – the colour you like. I hope it fits.'

'Oh, you're back,' she murmured breathlessly. 'You must tell me everything. Everything. You're so thin. Didn't you have anything to eat when you were fighting?'

'We were on campaign rations,' he said proudly. 'Look,' he said, eyes gleaming, 'what are you doing this evening? I've paid my respects to my parents and now I want to take you dancing. In your new jacket. I want to celebrate this wonderful day. With you, Lan-hua.'

'What's there to celebrate?' She giggled. 'Just you coming home? Is that all?'

'Well, aren't you pleased?' he asked, abashed, then saw the teasing in her eyes. 'All right,' he said. 'Let's go and celebrate something really important. Haven't you heard? We've defeated all our local enemies, and now it's decided. The Northern Expedition is on.'

Lan-hua's shoulders slumped. She remembered what she had just been reading in Mr Borodin's speech. 'I don't think it is,' she said. 'Or not yet. The congress has to pass it, and not everybody supports it.'

'Oh,' he laughed, 'you're only saying that because you spend your time with politicians. I've been with the army. I know their mood. And the mood of our generals. We're not going to let any politician stop us now. We're invincible!' he shouted at the top of his voice. 'The revolution's started! By summer we'll be in Peking! And I'm in love!'

She was blushing and giggling. 'I think you must be drunk,' she said.

'Only with happiness.'

'And who are you in love with? Some dumpy Kwangsi peasant girl you met on campaign?'

'I'll tell you when we go dancing,' he said, and shouted again at the treetops: 'When we go *dancing*!'

His mood was infectious. She found herself running beside him, still holding his hand, out of the secretariat courtyard, all the way along the path to the gate of the compound. A bus was pulling in to the stop. They leaped aboard and sat together near the back. Lan-hua was only momentarily surprised when John Soo put an arm round her shoulders – he had never been so forward before. They got off near the riverbank. He led her to a small restaurant in an alley, famous for its smoked duck. As they ate, he told her story after story about his campaigns. He was irrepressible, and so funny. At times she was crying tears of laughter. 'I forgot!' he said suddenly. 'We're meant to be celebrating. Here!' he called the waiter. 'Rice wine. A pot. Your best Shaohsing!'

'I don't drink,' protested Lan-hua.

'You do tonight,' he said. 'To the Northern Expedition! *Ganbei!*'

And, of course, she did drink, cup after cup. Strangely, however, the wine did not make them more boisterous. By the end of the meal, their mood was serious. They decided not to go dancing. Instead they walked by the riverbank. A cool breeze blew from the water. Through the darkness they saw the swinging lights of barges moving downstream.

After an hour, they had left behind them the buildings of the city and were in the countryside. It was a moonless night, and the Milky Way shone above them. In a bamboo grove, on the outskirts of a farm, John Soo took off his tunic, laid it on the grass and they lay down together looking at the stars through the leaves. Afterwards, neither could remember who had made the first move.

Somehow Catherine maintained the act. She accompanied George to his dinners and parties. When his horse won a race, she was always there to lead it in, and was the life and soul of the celebrations afterwards. George had become even more the gallant, at least in public. He was revelling in his reputation as the hero of the track. On one occasion, after he had been awarded his prize, he had kissed his wife passionately in front of the stewards, bending her backwards like Rudolph Valentino, then taken a bottle from a waiter and drained the bubbly from her shoe. On that occasion, Willie had also been there. They had been photographed for the newspaper, George still in his jockey's colours, his arms round his wife and his best friend, as Catherine held the cup apparently ecstatically in both hands. Willie, too, had been smiling, though she could only guess at what feelings burned within him.

They met when they could, in the daytime because her evenings were usually for George. She would ask George's driver to take her to a department store, or the Astor House Hotel, pretending she was shopping or had a luncheon appointment with friends, and tell him to collect her some hours later. Then she would slip out of the back entrance, and take a rickshaw to Willie's bungalow.

In the past she had developed similar ruses with her other lovers and the stolen hours in cheap Chinese hotels had been amusing. With Willie it was different, dangerous. She would wear dark glasses and a scarf, even though she knew that this was ridiculous. In the past, her lack of concern had been her protection. Once in a rickshaw she had stopped at an intersection beside a Rolls-Royce filled with acquaintances from the Women's Institute; she had leaned out of the cab and waved to them, then giggled on the way to her assignation. Now she was convinced that anybody could see her guilt.

The strain was also telling on Willie. In the first few weeks after they had begun their affair, they would fall into each other's arms, tear off their clothes and feed hungrily on each other until the alarm rang on the bedside clock that Willie had set punctiliously for the time she had to leave. In the early days, they often ignored it, giggling as they made fanciful excuses as to why she would be late for her driver, and inevitably, deliciously, words would give way to the urgent rhythm of their desire. In those days the illicitness and danger of what they were doing had been part of the excitement. But this abandon had not lasted long. As time went on, Willie insisted that they get up when the alarm went, and paced nervously back and forth as she dressed hurriedly.

Irrationally, she began to hate Robby, although she knew there was nothing to blame him for – in fact, it was the opposite, because he was the guardian of their secret. More than once, lying in bed, they had heard the doorbell ring and lain there, hearts in their mouths, while they heard Robby making cheerful excuses to whoever had called as to why Willie was not around. Robby had been sweet about it from the beginning when, hand in hand, they had sat on the sofa and told him what had happened. Robby had roared with laughter, and told them, 'Mum's the word. You can rely on Uncle Rob.' But he was always there, always there . . .

Once, after they had made love, they had heard Robby whistling in the next room. 'Hasn't he anything better to do?' she had snapped. Willie, as usual, had lain silent, the agonised expression that she had come to dread on his face. 'It's as if we're some sort of perverse threesome,' she had continued, and Willie had sighed, and told her it was difficult for Robby. 'It's difficult for me too,' she had said.

'Look,' he had told her some days later, 'tomorrow, let's not meet here. Why don't I take you for lunch? We haven't talked for ages.'

'You want to meet in public?' she said.

'Why not?' he said. 'I sometimes think we've become paranoid. I'm a family friend. I used to call on you for tea, and nobody thought anything of it.'

'I thought you preferred doing something else with me?'

The agonised expression again. 'Oh, Catherine. Of course I do, but love's — love's not just . . .'

'Fucking?' she prompted, and giggled.

'I hate this secrecy. This deception. I look back to that day I took you to the marshes, and we talked and talked. I felt so free that day.'

'Robby won't be pleased if we fail to turn up for one of our assignations,' she murmured.

'Fuck Robby,' he said, and she was surprised to see his thin white shoulders shaking with tension. 'Fuck George. Fuck everybody.'

'No,' she said softly, 'fuck me.' And after a while, clumsily – he was no great lover – he had settled himself over her waiting body, and time passed gently until it was time for her to go.

They could not meet next day – Catherine had a charity function at lunchtime – so two days later she met him in the Astor House Hotel. 'Willie!' she called across the lobby. 'Willie! It's been simply ages!' She ran up to him, hugged and kissed him on both cheeks.

'Do we have to go through this charade?' he whispered.

'Of course.' She laughed loudly for the benefit of whoever was listening, and took his arm. 'Now, come on, take me immediately to our table. I want to hear all your news.'

When they were seated – 'Give us your quietest table,' she had told the smiling *maître d'hôtel*, her voice echoing round the dining room. 'I have an assignation with this lovely man. He's been avoiding me for simply months and now I've got him, he's going to tell me all his secrets' – Willie sat uncomfortably until they had ordered.

'Come on, Willie,' she said irritably. 'It's all right now. We can speak *en clair*.'

'This sham is everything I detest,' he said. 'It's not what I wanted.'

'Darling, we're adulterers meeting in public. There is a form, you know.' She puffed at a cigarette. 'If I'd known you wanted to quarrel I wouldn't have come. Oh, God, there's your agonised look again. Do at least try to remember there's a gallery to play to.'

'Catherine, I can't do this,' he said. 'I may as well come out with it. I'm going away. Tomorrow,' he added. 'To Canton.'

'I see,' she said. 'To get away from me?'

'No, of course not.' He looked shifty. 'I have to go to Canton for the bureau. I've been neglecting my work, and too much is happening. I've been cobbling other bureaux' material together, but it won't do. Yesterday the Kuomintang congress approved General Chiang Kai-shek's plans for the Northern Expedition. That means civil war, Catherine, a bloody great conflict that'll probably envelop all China. The bureau wants me to interview Chiang Kai-shek, Borodin, Galen – anybody I can. Then they want me back in Peking to find out what Chang Tso-lin is going to do about it. I could tell you right now. He'll mobilise. He's already established his alliances – all the warlords have common cause. Even his old enemy, Wu Pei-fu, has pledged allegiance to the Peking government. It could be Armageddon, Catherine. I have to go.'

Catherine had reached out her hand and clasped his. 'Do you think I'd try to stop you?' she whispered. 'Of course you have to go. I wouldn't stand in the way of your professional duty. It's who you are.'

'I may be not be back for weeks,' he said. He seemed to be struggling for words.

'I know,' she said. 'It doesn't matter.'

'I – I wanted to tell you that I thought it might be a good thing,' he stumbled, 'for us both.'

'I'm not sure I understand you,' she said.

'Oh, Catherine, are you really enjoying this sort of life? The cheating? The betrayal?'

She was taken aback. 'No,' she said, 'but it's part and parcel of having an affair. I'm not certain what else we can do in the circumstances. Surely the important thing is finding ways to be together.'

'Are we really together, Catherine? Hiding like rats from the world?'

Their faces were only inches apart across the table. Catherine was peering intently into his pale eyes. 'Oh, God, Willie, what have I got you into?' she said softly. 'You want to go, don't you? For the war, of course, but also to get away from me.'

'Soup, Madame Airton,' announced the *maître d*'. 'Cream of asparagus for you, and lobster consommé for Monsieur. *Bon appétit*.'

They waited silently until he had gone.

'Sometimes I feel as if I'm being torn apart,' said Willie. 'It's not that I don't love you. You're my life now, and I can't stand it that every evening you go back to him.'

'I don't have to,' said Catherine quietly. 'I could leave him.'

Willie stared at her. 'Don't joke, Catherine,' he said.

'What makes you think I'm joking?' she said.

'It wouldn't work,' he said.

'Why do you say that?' she asked, lifting her spoon and tasting her soup.

'I couldn't support you on a journalist's salary,' said Willie, 'not in the style you're used to, and we'd – we'd be pariahs here.'

'Is that so important to you?' she asked. 'We could go somewhere else. Build a life on another continent. Find a tropical island. But China's your big story, isn't it? It seems you must make a choice, then, between China and me. It's not that complicated, you know.' She paused. 'Are you going to eat your soup? You should. The waiters will think it very odd if you don't.' She smiled. 'Actually, you don't really have to make that choice. You can have your wars, and you can have me whenever you come back from them. I'm quite content to be your piece on the side. I'd have thought most men would be quite happy to be in a position to eat their cake and have it.'

'Catherine, I love you,' he said.

'So you say, Willie – but if you do, you must be manly about it. Take me as I am and accept that you're cheating on your friend. Or stand up to George, and take me as your mistress in the open. Or your wife, if that makes you feel better about it. I'm sure George would give me a divorce. But don't moan and dither about what a hard time you're having.' She put down her spoon. 'Actually, it would be good if you did go to your precious wars. It might concentrate your mind and perhaps then you will decide what you want from me.'

'Catherine, I can't believe you can be so cruel. I was hoping we could discuss this.'

'There isn't anything to discuss. You brought me here to say goodbye. Now you've said it. I hope you'll change your mind and I'll be here when you return, but now I've lost my appetite. I'll let you come up with the story for the restaurant and all these gawking onlookers. It'll give you a bit of practice, perhaps, in how to manage a lie.'

She stood up. Willie raised a hand as if to detain her, but she turned her back on him. As she passed the *maître d'* she gave him a dazzling smile. 'The soup was delicious,' she said. She allowed a waiter to help her into her coat, and strode briskly across the lobby, through the swing door and down the steps. She hailed a rickshaw and told him to take her to Meadows Road. It was a slow journey through crowded traffic. Even so she retained her composure, as she did when *Lao* Tang met her at the door. It was only when she reached her bedroom that she fell face down on her bed and cried.

Willie phoned, apologising, saying he had delayed his departure by two days. They agreed to meet at his bungalow the following afternoon. Their lovemaking was tender and she did not slip away when, towards evening, they got up. She insisted on helping him pack for his journey. Afterwards they went to the sitting room, where Robby was ready with his cocktails. She stayed for dinner. It was like old times, although it was Robby who kept the conversation going. When the servant brought in the coffee, Robby excused himself, leaving her and Willie on the sofa holding hands. Now they were alone together, there seemed little to say.

When she returned to Meadows Road, she found George in the dining room, pasting newspaper stories about himself into an album. 'You're back late, my dearest,' he said. 'A lover?'

'You can be so crude, darling,' she answered, pretending to yawn. 'Actually, I was with your friends, Willie and Robby, whom you don't bother with now you're so grand. Still, I was half expecting you'd be there. Robby was giving a farewell party for Willie, now he's off to the wars.'

'Well, just as long as you're enjoying yourself, old thing. You won't forget tomorrow's do at the Maynards', will you?'

'Do I ever?' she said, turning towards the stairs.

'That's my love,' murmured George, riffling through his clippings.

It had been a cold, miserable spring in Shanghai, but this Sunday the sun was shining. Yi-liang suggested a walk along the Bund. Fu-kuei acquiesced, as she always did to his suggestions, and together they strolled among the holiday crowds. The merchant edifices of the Bund towered behind them; from the Soochow creek they could hear shouts from the barges and sampans. Occasionally the air rumbled with the hoot of a freighter, warning the smaller craft on the Whangpoo to get out of the way. She sensed the stirring of a great city alive with activity; it was a contrast to the life of silence she had become used to at home. Since the day he had taken her to watch Barkowitz's murder, she had become little more than his spaniel, with certain house privileges. His study door was permanently locked to her, and access to his Rolls-Royce now required his permission in advance. Perhaps this excursion was fitting; Major Yang was walking his dog. On the surface nothing had changed between them – Yi-liang was as courteous and considerate as he had ever been, and at night he was more than loving. But Fu-kuei knew the rules of the kennel. She thought back to those days when he had first released her from prison to the confines of his flat; she had been freer then, her gaoler less assiduous, the regime less severe.

The irony was that during their evenings alone he would talk to her about his work, Chinese politics, his private opinion (this was always perceptive and original, certainly not influenced by establishment dogma) and sometimes even his ambitions, which were remarkably modest. Fu-kuei thought it ironic that now she was even better informed than she had been before she was denied access to his secret sources.

He was under no illusions about the threat that the Northern Expedition posed to his warlords, and he saw Shanghai as the key. 'A Communist rising in this city will ensure a Bolshevik government in Peking within five years,' he said. 'And they're coming. CCP leaders. Organisers, not demagogues, experienced men, trained in Whampoa and the Kwangtung wars. They're hiding in the international concessions, making their preparations. I heard one report that Chou En-lai, who was Chiang Kai-shek's deputy in the Military Academy, is in Shanghai already.'

They became aware of a clamour beside the towpath. An old hawker was shouting and gesticulating at them. His toes were congealed in a twisted stump; each rib could be seen in a bare torso and one eye was jellied with pus. He had a rough board and stool, and tins of shoe cream lay on the paving. 'High-born, *xiansheng*,' he whined at Yi-liang, 'Let me clean your boots. Honour me with your mercy.'

'Come on,' said Yi-liang, steering Fu-kuei away.

But she had seen the agony in the remaining eye, and the despair with which the grey head sank on to its skeletal shoulders. 'He's starving, Yi-liang,' she said. 'Let us give him something.'

'Give one beggar a coin and you'll have hundreds clamouring round you like pigeons,' he said. 'What have they been trained to say now? "No mama, no papa, no whisky-soda!"' He snorted derisively. 'It's a syndicate, Fu-kuei. They maim themselves deliberately.'

'Oh, please, Yi-liang.' She pulled his arm. She had always avoided beggars before, but now she felt that this man was trapped in a prison from which he could never escape. Not unlike herself.

Yi-liang was laughing. 'Oh, have it your own way, you silly thing. Get your shoes cleaned if it makes you feel better – but I'm not hanging around to watch you. Join me when you've finished. I'll be in the tea-room of the Cathay across the road.' And he walked off, hands in his pockets. As she stretched out her shoe, the old man clasped his hands in thanks. '*Do xie, do xie, xiansheng*! Heaven praise the first-born.'

Thankfully it did not take long. Fu-kuei reached in her purse and gave him some cash. He clasped her hands, bobbing his head in thanks. When he released her, she was holding a thin slip of paper in her palm. She froze. The old man began to whine at another customer. Surreptitiously she read the note: 'Colombian Coffee. Sincere Department Store. Any Friday. 10 a.m.' It might have been an advertisement, but scrawled on the back were two faded pencil marks: 'For one person'.

She felt dizzy. The slip of rice paper, caught on an air current, floated upwards like thistledown, and disappeared over the embankment into the Whangpoo.

She was her quiet self again when she joined Yi-liang in the Cathay Hotel, but her mind was churning. She was being reactivated. Somebody wanted her to spy again. But who? And for whom?

Lao Tang woke her. 'Telephone, Missy. Mr Lampsett,' he said.

She grabbed her dressing-gown from its hook, ran down the stairs to the hall and picked up the receiver. 'Willie!' she cried. 'Willie! Where are you?'

'In Tientsin.' A tinny voice strained through the crackle. 'I arrived this morning . . . this morning.'

'I heard you, my darling,' she said. 'That's marvellous. When can I see you?'

'I leave for Peking this afternoon. I only have three hours.'

'You must come here,' she shouted. It was a terrible line.

'Are you sure?'

'Yes, yes, darling. Come as soon as you can.'

'All right. I'll be there in . . .' She could not distinguish what he said.

'I adore you,' she called.

'Yes. I love you too. Listen, darling. About what you said. In the restaurant . . .'

'I can't hear you.'

'What you said in the restaurant, about the deception, and you leaving George. I've . . . I've been thinking about it . . . and . . .'

'Oh, darling . . . oh, darling.' She could hardly contain her emotion.

'Anyway, I've decided, I think you're right . . .' His voice broke up in the whistle and whine.

'Tell me when you get here. Hurry. I've been yearning for you,' she shouted.

'What?'

'Just come, darling, come, as soon as—'

The line went dead.

She ran up the stairs to her bedroom. She pulled open drawers and scrabbled abstractedly through her smalls. She could not determine which dress to wear. Frocks and hangers piled on the unmade bed. Eventually she was in front of her dressing-table mirror. She fumbled for her lipstick, but had hardly started to apply it before she heard the doorbell ring. She slipped on whatever shoes she could find and ran down the stairs, beating *Lao* Tang to the front door. Yes, it really was Willie, in his fedora and trenchcoat. She threw her arms round him, and kissed his lips. She wouldn't let him go. She pulled him past the startled *Lao* Tang to the sitting room, and when they were on the sofa she kissed him again.

'Steady, Catherine,' murmured Willie, all too aware of *Lao* Tang standing at the door, the *amah* peering behind him.

'Morning coffee, Missy?' asked *Lao* Tang, with aplomb.

'Yes, coffee, tea, anything,' cried Catherine. 'Oh, Willie, I can't believe it. You're here. You don't know how I've missed you. It's been weeks. I've nearly died.'

'Well, I've missed you too, darling,' said Willie, still looking a little stunned.

'I want to hear everything you've been doing since you've been away,' said Catherine, breathlessly. 'Oh, I can't bear that you have to go away again.'

'I'm sorry too, darling, but I need to interview Chang Tso-lin,' said Willie. 'It's on, you know. The movement north has started. As I left Canton, troops were marching through the street. I was lucky to catch one of the last steamers. They—' But his words were extinguished by her kiss, which this time he returned with passion.

'Come,' she said, standing up and pulling at his arm. Her face was hot and flushed.

'Catherine, is this wise? The coffee—'

'Bugger the coffee.'

She almost dragged him up the stairs. In her bedroom, the *amah* was hanging the clothes that had been abandoned on the bed. She took one look at Catherine, dropped the clothes and scurried out. Catherine kicked the door closed behind her. She hopped towards the bed, dropping her shoes as she went, and pulled the sheet, the blankets and the remaining dresses on to the floor. 'Oh, Willie, we've so little time.'

'Catherine, I'm not sure we should be doing this,' he muttered. 'It's George's bedroom.'

'It's not. It's mine,' she said, pulling her dress over her head. 'Come on, Willie. Do I have to undress you?'

He began to pull feebly at his tie.

'Oh, you idiot. You sweet idiot,' Catherine laughed, 'let me.' She was already naked.

'My God, you're beautiful,' he whispered.

She pressed herself against him and kissed him, her fingers unbuttoning his trousers. 'No, don't stop kissing me,' she breathed, as she helped him pull off his jacket, his waistcoat, then hurriedly undid his collar and shirt. She sensed his excitement against her stomach and he began to pressure her towards the bed. 'No, I want you naked,' she whispered. 'Here, sit down.' In one movement she pulled off his trousers and pants, then his garters and socks. He looked up at her nervously, his hands over his erection. 'You fool, you fool, you dear fool,' she cried, and threw her arms round his neck, her weight pushing him backwards. 'Oh, God, Willie, it's been so long, so long.' They rolled for a while on the bed. 'No,' she panted. 'I want you now. Here.' Desperately she groped for a pillow and shoved it under her bottom. She raised her knees to her breasts, settling her haunches, laying herself open for him. 'Oh, Willie, yes. Please. Now.' Next minute, she felt him inside her. He was straining on his outstretched arms. Her nails were scratching the back of his thighs. As she shook her head from side to side, gasping, squealing, she saw his contorted features as he laboured above her. 'Oh, yes.

Oh, yes,' she panted. 'No, deeper, deeper.' He was panting heavily, wheezing a little and uttering a faint 'Oh, oh, oh' through his clenched teeth.

It was then that the languid voice interrupted them. 'Well, well, I never expected to see such a sensational enactment of French *théâtre vivant* in my own house. Bravo. Last time I watched anything as lively was during a chi-chi cabaret show in Lahore, where the climax was an act with a snake. Perhaps you have something like that in store for an encore?'

It was Willie who moved first. Whimpering with shock and shame, he scrabbled by the side of the bed for something to cover himself. All he could find was a red silk frock, which he crumpled into a ball and pressed to his crotch. Catherine moved more deliberately. Ignoring George's mocking laughter, she pulled up the sheet and cast it over Willie's legs and her own.

'Please don't stop what you're doing on my account,' said George, reaching into his breast pocket for a cigar. 'I thought it would be you, Willie. Spotted your car outside. Couldn't be sure a moment ago, though, when all I could see were a pair of wriggling buttocks – there's a certain anonymity about naked bums. Confuses a fellow.'

'How long are you going to stand there and gloat?' asked Catherine. 'Now you've surprised us, don't you think you'd better just leave?'

'Oh, I'm not gloating, old girl,' said George, lighting the cigar. 'You know me.' Puff, puff. 'Life and soul and all that. Always happy when other people are enjoying themselves. Especially when it's my wife and my oldest chum. What is this, Willie? Some sort of rest and recreation between the wars? Do hope Catherine's as obliging as you require.'

'Don't let him do this, Willie,' hissed Catherine. 'He's baiting you. Stand up to him.'

George laughed. 'Don't think that'd be a good idea, old dear. That frock of yours he's clutching to his cock looks pretty flimsy, and he's obviously a bit shy. Don't see why, of course. From what I saw, he appears to be most adequately hung. Nice display, old boy. Tip-top. But, then, Catherine, you're an old hand at this sort of thing, aren't you? Always knew how to choose a fellow with the parts in the right place. You should be flattered, Willie, my old *frère*. Catherine usually likes her bucks to be younger in the tooth than you or I. Cradle-snatching's her line.'

With growing anger and disgust, Catherine punched Willie's arm. 'Tell him, Willie. Tell him you're taking me away with you. Tell him what you told me on the phone.' But Willie hung his head. His pale eyes gazed at the shadow of his knees under the sheet. He looked as if he was about to cry.

'Well,' said George, puffing at his cigar, 'seems like you two have a lover's tiff on your hands and I'm *de trop*. I'll get out of your hair, shall I? There'll be brandy downstairs for anyone who needs it. Nothing like brandy to bring balm to the troubled soul.' He turned to go, but peeped back in again with a broad smile. 'Thought while I was up here I'd help choose your dress for the ball tonight, Catherine – but it's probably not the right time, old girl, is it? No, it can probably wait till after you've got your present guest off your hands.' They heard his laughter fading down the stairs.

For a long moment afterwards, the two sat stiffly under the sheet. Slowly Willie raised his head. His eyes were imploring. 'Catherine,' he said.

'Get out,' she whispered.

'Catherine!'

'Get out,' she said. 'Go.'

'I love you,' he said. 'I do.'

'Just go,' she said.

She rolled on to her side, and curled up with a pillow clutched to her chest. She heard him shuffling with his clothes. Eventually she heard the click of the door handle. She heard a last plaintive 'Catherine, I love you', then the door clicked shut, and there was silence.

It was perhaps an hour later that she became aware of a hesitant knock on the door. 'Go away,' she sobbed – but *Lao* Tang came in anyway, with a cup of tea on a tray. 'Ah, Missy,' he said gently, putting it down on her side table, 'you drink hot tea. All rest, never mind.'

'Oh, *Lao* Tang,' she whispered, pressing her face into her pillow, 'what am I going to do?'

'You think something nice say Master. Say you velly solly. Then by'm'by other Master come back. Always 'nother day.'

She made a sound that might have been a laugh. 'I wish it was so simple,' she whispered. 'Thank you, *Lao* Tang, for being a friend.'

'You all right, Missy? Sure? *Lao* Tang go now. You need anything, you call.'

Later, she roused herself, dressed carefully and went downstairs. George was in the living room. She heard the tinkle of a glass and a decanter. She went in and sat down in the armchair by the fireplace.

'Well, you look spruce,' said George. 'Fancy a G and T?'

She took the glass he offered.

'I don't think much of your knight in shining armour,' said George, conversationally. 'Didn't exactly stand by you in the lists, did he?'

'I'm leaving you, George,' said Catherine.

'Are you, old girl? And where do you intend to go?'

'I don't know yet.'

'Money?' asked George, casually. 'Or is dear Willie going to provide? He didn't seem all that keen to take up your invitation an hour or so ago. Or did I misread the runes?'

'I thought you might do the decent thing,' said Catherine, 'and divorce me. There's usually a settlement of some kind. I don't need much.'

George laughed. 'Now, why on earth would I want to divorce you?'

'I've given you cause.'

'My dear girl, as if I'd let a little thing like that get in the way of a perfect relationship! No, Catherine, I've got used to having you on my arm. And it may be rather vain of me, but I think I suit you as well as you suit me.'

She sipped her gin and tonic. 'I'll find a way,' she said.

'Goodness, is that the time?' said George. 'You and I had better buck up if we're going to be ready for the ball tonight. Cheer up, old love. Where's my trouper?'

* * *

It was a letter from her sister-in-law, Jenny, that gave Catherine the idea: Jenny was in touch with Edmund, and kept them informed of his movements. Catherine had heard that his and Niedemeyer's second hospital for veterans had not got off the ground, but with the imminent prospect of the Northern Expedition they had concocted a new scheme: to establish a field hospital somewhere in the Yangtse area where everybody presumed the real fighting would take place. Jenny had mentioned that Edmund was back in Tientsin. It did not take Catherine long to find out where his office was located. When she called, he was sitting behind his desk.

'Catherine!' he said, standing up nervously. He did not offer her his hand.

'I won't beat about the bush,' she said. 'I've come because I've heard you're looking for nurses. You won't find one better than me.'

He stared at her, then laughed. 'What makes you think I'd employ you?' he asked. 'If you were the last person in the world, I wouldn't want to work with you. Haven't you ruined enough people's lives? Anyway, it isn't going to be a party down there. There's no fashionable social circuit in a civil war.'

'Good, you despise me,' she said, looking him in the eyes. 'I see that as a recommendation, because I have no high estimation of you either. With emotion out of the way, there's room for a professional relationship. Whatever else you think about me, you know I'm a good nurse, as I know you're a good doctor.'

'Doctor. Nurse,' he said sarcastically. 'Haven't we both outgrown that little fantasy of ours?'

'I have. I don't know about you.'

Edmund sat down. He gazed at her for a moment with what might have been a wry smile. 'One thing that hasn't changed about you is your nerve,' he said. 'What does George think about this idea of yours? He's happy about it, is he?'

'I don't give a damn what he thinks,' she said.

'I see. So poor George is going to be another broken heart you leave behind you?'

'That's none of your business, Edmund,' said Catherine. 'I'm offering you my services as a nurse, not as a sister-in-law, or as a former lover for that matter.'

Edmund was silent for some minutes. 'I do need experienced nurses,' he said. 'What terms are you expecting?'

'Any terms you like,' she said.

'I'll tell you one I'll insist on. You serve under my authority, and you do anything I damn well tell you to do. Without questioning me. It bloody well will be Doctor, Nurse, from now on, Catherine, with all the discipline you'd expect in a top London hospital. Otherwise you'll be out on your ear.'

'Sounds reasonable to me,' said Catherine. 'Well, Doctor, when do we set off?'

'Next week. You came to me just in time. Will you be ready?'

'I'm ready now,' said Catherine.

Lan-hua, along with the rest of her propaganda division, had been sent forward up the lines to one of the liberated villages. Their task was to paste posters explaining to the peasants the aims and philosophies of the Northern Expedition that had so triumphantly set off from Canton three weeks before. Mr Borodin had given her leave to return to her old unit for the duration of the campaign. She was only sorry because she believed it would not last long. The Kuomintang armies were sweeping all before them. They received a hero's welcome in every village. All along the road they were cheered by children waving the Kuomintang flag. She and her teammates had joked that they were preaching to the already converted.

Still, she enjoyed her new job. Now, in a circle of admiring children, she was pasting on the wall of a temple a poster she had painted herself. It was of a young woman – who looked unusually like her – wearing a military tunic, rifle on her back, pointing her outstretched arm at cowering capitalists and imperialists, who were fleeing before her righteous indignation. She heard the rumble of military vehicles approaching. Another column of trucks on the way to the front. As soon as they heard the new sound, the fickle children ran away laughing and screaming. She smiled, fixed the last corner of the poster to the wall and followed them.

The box-like vehicles rumbled past. Soldiers were straddling the bonnets and hanging off the struts that held the canvas covers. As one passed her, she was vaguely aware that a soldier had opened the door of the cab and jumped on to the road. She saw him pushing his way through the throng, but it was only when he was close to her that she recognised him. 'John Soo!' she screamed, and threw herself into his open arms. 'What are you doing here?'

'I've come to check your artwork.' He wiped the dust from his spectacles.

'No, seriously.' She squeezed his waist.

'A river ahead requires a pontoon bridge,' he said. 'Actually I must go immediately – but I need to do something first,' he said.

'What?'

'This,' he said, and kissed her full on the lips.

'You can't,' she squealed. 'People are watching!'

'I don't care, we're doing away with feudalism and the old ideas, Lan-hua. We're building a new world.' He kissed her again. And she kissed him back. The crowd cheered. Even the old men and women, some of whom still had bound feet. The ground beneath them shook as the lorries trundled on their way to the front. The Kuomintang flag flapped loudly on the roof of the headman's house, shaken by the same wind that was blowing their whole army onward and forward. As she gave way to her lover's embrace, Lan-hua realised that the old standards no longer applied. This was more than a war to liberate the country of its tyrannous warlords. This was the beginning of a new Chinese revolution.

PART TWO

The Northern Expedition
1926–1928

11

The Worker's Paradise

Extracted from a report by William Lampsett, Reuters correspondent, Nanking, 12 December 1926

If the warlords had united early, they might have defeated the small Nationalist force that marched optimistically out of Canton on 6 June, but Wu Pei-fu in Hunan refused the aid offered by Chang Tso-lin. He was routed and by September the triple city of Wuhan on the Yangtse had fallen to the Kuomintang.

Each victory of the Nationalists increased the size of its army, because in time-honoured tradition, defeated warlord troops changed armbands and joined the ranks of their vanquishers. In addition, many minor warlords made accommodation with the Kuomintang, bringing their forces and their territories under Chiang Kai-shek's command.

Leaving his subordinate, General Tang Sheng-chi, to continue the war with Wu Pei-fu over the Yangtse into Hepeh, Chiang Kai-shek, taking his main force, crossed over the mountains to Kiangsi Province to confront the eastern warlord, Sun Chuan-fang, but as Chiang's troops began a bloody siege of the city of Nanchang, it became clear that the provisional government left behind in Wuhan was coming under the control of left-wing/CCP elements of the Kuomintang. When Borodin and other Marxist leaders arrived in Wuhan at the end of the year, the first signs of a Nationalist/Communist split became manifest, but neither Borodin nor Chiang at this stage was willing to acknowledge

a collapse of the United Front, as their alliance is called.
Borodin's strength increased when the workers of Wuhan
drove the foreigners out of their concession in Hankow, and
later the Kuomintang foreign minister, Eugene Chen, negoti-
ated with the British for the formal return of this Treaty Port,
a startling precedent that made the foreign powers take the
Northern Expedition seriously for the first time.

On the eastern front Sun was no more successful than Wu
Pei-fu in stopping the Nationalist advance. In desperation, he
called on other warlords' help. Chang Tso-lin was declared
generalissimo of a new alliance, the 'Anminchun', and ordered
his subordinate, Chang Tsung-chang, the rapacious Shantung
warlord, known as the Dog General, to send troops to support
Sun in Kiangsu. It was vital that the Nationalists were
defeated before they took Shanghai.

They ate their first Western breakfast in months. Then, reluctantly
leaving the small but comfortable German hotel, and fearing the
worst, Catherine and Edmund joined the knots of people hurrying
along the four-mile boulevard that stretched the length of Hankow's
waterfront in the direction of the British concession. As they walked
in the clammy heat past the neat provincial villas and iron-railed
gardens in the French quarter, the faded tea godowns, nightclubs
and opium dens in the Russian concession, the imposing American
and British consulates, and finally the granite-fronted offices in the
business district, they became aware of a rumble, like far-away
thunder. At first it was barely perceptible under the familiar creak-
ings and cries of the rickshaw-pullers and carts, but as proximity
and volume grew, they recognised the sound for what it was.
Artillery. So it had started. Near the great clock tower of the
Customs Building, they found a vantage-point and, with a sinking
feeling of inevitability, watched the furious battle that was taking
place in the Chinese city of Wuchang a mile away across the Yangtse.

Their view was obscured by the steamers anchored at the wooden
piers that stretched out into the swirling yellow waters, and beyond
them by the screen of destroyers and light cruisers, nearly a half-
mile of sleek metal-clads anchored in mid-stream, summoned to

protect the interests of the foreigners threatened by the armies of the Northern Expedition, which all now feared were about to invest the triple city of Wuhan. This huge port, dominating the central reaches of the Yangtse, controlled the major rail line to the north; if the Nationalists took it, it would have far-reaching implications not only for the outcome of the civil war, but also for trade. For the first time, the foreign powers were preparing to intervene. The vessels' decks were cleared for action; their guns were trained on the opposite bank. Catherine could make out in the clear morning sunlight the Red Ensign of the Royal Navy, the Stars and Stripes of the US Yangtse Flotilla and, further upstream, the Red Sun fluttering on the high masts of the Japanese Imperial Fleet.

Her attention, however, was focused on the crenellated walls of the old city that tumbled picturesquely to the waterside on the further shore. The last remnants of the warlord army left by Marshal Wu Pei-fu after his retreat across the river were besieged there, and for the last two months it had been her home.

The thunder of cannon fire rolled over the water as each army pounded the other. Occasionally red bursts of flame would rise from within the walls, and columns of black smoke would wisp up to merge with the cloud that hung over the town. Catherine could imagine only too easily the devastation this bombardment was causing in the narrow streets. She mentally co-ordinated each explosion with the map inside her head. As usual the civilian quarters were suffering. Those fires in the west could only be the cotton warehouses burning in the market area where she used to buy fruit. She imagined familiar faces running in fear.

The smoke was as dense as the smog over the industrial city of Hanyang, on the northern bank of the Yangtse. Separated from Hankow by a southern-flowing tributary that joined the larger river here, it was in Hanyang, the third city of Wuhan, with its big arsenal and huge, belching steelworks, that Marshal Wu was now rallying his army to prevent Nationalist forces crossing into the north. It had been to Hanyang that Catherine and the rest of the hospital staff had retreated the day before.

She and Edmund had left the nurses there the previous night, crossing by ferry into the foreign concessions. They needed to make contact by telegraph with Niedemeyer to ensure a continuing supply of medicines. They also hoped to find out from the foreign community a clearer picture of what was happening than they could elicit from the propaganda of Wu Pei-fu's forces.

The news was not good. It was rumoured that one of Chiang Kai-shek's divisions had already made its way upstream across the Yangtse and was advancing to besiege the two northern river ports. There were fears that the whole triple metropolis would be surrounded, in which case Marshal Wu's army would be trapped or, as Edmund had heard the doom-merchants in the club speculate the previous evening, Marshal Wu would abandon Hanyang and Hankow to their fate, and retreat north up the rail line to make a defensive position in the high mountains that separated Hupeh Province from Henan. Either eventuality would be disastrous for the foreigners in the international concessions, despite the navies that had come to protect them. The Kuomintang, it was said, were no better than Bolsheviks. Their property, and perhaps even their lives, would be at risk. Although Edmund believed that this was alarmist Catherine, after her experiences in Russia, was inclined to agree.

Yet standing beneath the acacia trees on the Bund, with the magisterial colonnades of the banks and office buildings in the British concession shining in the sunlight, the bystanders were exhibiting a curious sense of detachment from the war going on around them. The foreign concessions might be threatened, but they had not yet lost their smug sense of superiority and their imperious air of permanence. In the street behind them, coolies shuffled by under their heavy loads of brick tea and building materials, watched by imposing Sikh policemen. Rickshaw-pullers and chauffeurs waited quietly in the shade for their masters, who were now observing a battle through their binoculars with the same insouciance as they might have watched a cup race at one of the two racetracks north of the city.

Catherine, in her rumpled nurse's uniform, looked around her with scorn at the neat white suits, ducks and blazers, topees and boaters of the privileged classes. The women wore frocks and flowered straw hats. The men murmured knowledgeably and pointed their canes. She would not have been surprised to learn that a bookie's stall had been set up under the trees to provide odds on the opposing armies. George would be in his element here, she thought ruefully. Soon they would all become bored of the battle, and retire to the Recreation Club for tiffin. They would not be as relaxed, she decided, if they had spent the last month south of the river in a field hospital. This was no longer one of the comic operas of competing warlords to which they were all accustomed. This was modern twentieth-century butchery, as bad as anything she had witnessed on the eastern front.

A flash of silver in the sky above the besieged city caught her eye, and even at that distance she was able to make out three aeroplanes swooping for a bombing run. They banked away, leaving explosions in their wake.

'So Stalin has kept his promise. He has given the Nationalists aircraft,' said Edmund, lowering his binoculars. 'Those poor people in the city.'

'We should still be there,' said Catherine. 'It was disgraceful abandoning them.'

'In war you have to make choices,' said Edmund. 'If we'd stayed in Wuchang we'd have been cut off from Niedemeyer's supplies. You've been in retreats before. You know the score.'

Catherine recalled the incomprehension and fear in the eyes of her Chinese nurses when she had told them yesterday morning that they were to evacuate the hospital, taking with them only the walking wounded. She had delivered Edmund's orders to the staff in the stern, uncompromising tone of command that she had adopted over the previous two months, brooking no dissension. She could sense their resentment and anger, and was reminded of her and Marya's quarrels with Mamasha so long ago.

She did her job with cold efficiency, not because she cared about the lives she was helping to save, but because the hard work allowed her respite from thinking about her own wretched life. There were times when her calm amazed even her. Six weeks before, when their hospital had been overwhelmed with wounded pouring in from the first battles beyond the lakes south of Wuhan, Edmund and his two Chinese surgeons had worked day and night at the operating-tables.

She had bullied and shamed the raw, untrained nurses through their shifts, sparing neither them nor herself, insisting on high standards of cleanliness and tidiness in temperatures that sometimes reached more than a hundred degrees. When one of her young charges, P'ei Yuan-ling, had fainted at the sight of an appalling abdominal injury, she had been there to take over. For three days, she had given the girl responsibility for stacking and burying amputated limbs. Now Sister P'ei was one of her most hardened assistants. Today she was satisfied that her small team was as professional as it could be in the circumstances.

Besides supervising the nurses and the wards, Catherine oversaw the kitchens, the laundry and the accounts. Once a fortnight she went to the harbour to receive Niedemeyer's consignment of medicine, which always involved stand-offs with corrupt customs officials whom Catherine had learned to outface. Her experiences with junior officials had stood her in good stead when she was forced to seek the aid of higher authorities. When it became clear that there was no room in their compound for any more wounded, Catherine had marched past the bewildered guards into Marshal Wu's headquarters. She had been shown into the general's presence. His initial anger and alarm at her intrusion had given way to amusement, and he had instructed his adjutant to give the terrifying foreign woman what she wanted.

She had returned to the hospital with a guard of bayonet-wielding soldiers who had quickly cleared the adjoining houses of their occupants. She had not spared a thought for the feelings of the dejected householders she was evicting. She needed the space their homes provided. She rarely gave a thought to anybody's feelings, as long as the job was done. She was unforgiving when any of the nurses' tender sentiments for the convalescent soldiers got in the way of their work. She knew this was hypocritical, remembering vaguely her own feelings for wounded Russian soldiers during the Great War, but she did not care: these were broken Chinese bodies that she had to mend. If she thought about them as human beings at all, she despised them. About the only thing in the favour of these warlord soldiers was that they were fighting Bolsheviks, whom she saw as the enemy. That made it simple for her: one side she despised, the other side she hated – almost as much as she hated and despised herself. Not that she thought about it very much. She did not have time to think.

It surprised her, therefore, when one day Edmund, who had been watching her progress through one of the wards, told her that he would not know what to do without her; he could see in the patients' eyes that they worshipped her, because there was more healing power in her calm and efficiency than in his scalpel. He had been right to hire her. 'You need to get some sleep, Doctor,' she said curtly, and carried on with her duties. Intimacy with him was the last thing she wanted. He had set her terms of employment and she respected him as a doctor. That was all. She rarely thought of the feelings she had once harboured for him. Those belonged to another woman in another age.

As she watched the smoke over Wuchang, she felt shamed and humiliated. Of course Edmund had made a sensible decision. Before they had left they had handed over their hospital to the Red Swastika, the Buddhist equivalent of the Red Cross – but that to her was a mark of failure.

The evacuation had turned rapidly into a nightmare. Their departure had been orderly enough. Edmund had negotiated with the military authorities to provide mule carts for the patients and their supplies, and an armed escort. But she had not been prepared for the horror and panic they had found at the docks. Wu Pei-fu had commandeered every launch and sampan for his retreating men, but a vast crowd of terrified citizens was being held back by bayonet-wielding soldiers. As Catherine and her company of nurses were steered through the throng, she saw bundles of coloured clothing scattered on the red flagstones: dead men, women and babies. Edmund was shouting and arguing with a port official, who was thumbing his forms, shaking his head. The captain of their escort pulled out his revolver and pointed it at the man's temple. The official shrugged, and pointed towards a coal barge, moving towards the docks from mid-river. Somehow they got their mule carts to the river's edge, and then there was another shouted argument with a company of Hunanese infantrymen who had also seen the barge. With a rattle, rifles were cocked, and it was only when Edmund moved between the escort and the angry soldiers, shouting there was room on the barge for all, that they stood down.

Catherine had sat huddled with the crying nurses in the bow as the barge moved off. There were sickening thumps as drowned bodies of soldiers and civilians hit the side. Soon they were passing through the line of moored battleships towards safety on the other shore.

'Good Lord, I think they intend to make an assault from the river,' exclaimed Edmund, peering through his binoculars. 'They must be mad. Here, have a look.'

It took a few moments for Catherine to focus the lens on the great grey walls. She saw the ridge of the battlements wreathed in white smoke, and occasional jets of red fire from the old cannons, then lowered the binoculars to view the muddy flats of the river-bank, and started. A flotilla of sampans was trying to land. The yellow water chopping around them was erupting in spouts and fountains. Ant-like figures were running towards the city from boats that had already beached. None was getting near the walls. They appeared to be rushing forward, then disappearing into the ground. There was something surreal about the murderous fight taking place in dumb show. The only sound above the distant murmur of shelling, which had been continuous since they arrived, was the applause of the bystanders around them. Disgusted, she handed the binoculars back to Edmund.

'That'll teach the Bolshies,' chortled a fat, heavily moustached man next to them. 'Bravo the warlords.'

The woman beside him, waving her opera glasses in the wrong direction, was giggling, 'What's happening? I can't see.'

There was pain in Edmund's weary features. 'They're still coming on. What unbelievable bravery, Catherine. What unspeakable, useless gallantry.'

'Can we go?' she asked.

He sighed. 'Yes, we ought to get back to the nurses. They'll have seen the fighting and be scared. Anyway, we need to find a house to set up a new hospital.'

They were silent as they walked out of the British concession towards the ferry pier for the crossing to Hanyang. They had to push their way through great crowds of refugees from the Chinese city who, frightened by the renewed fighting, were seeking protection in the foreign concession on the Hankow side. One young man was straining under the weight of a grandfather clock, anxiously watched by his grey-haired father. An old woman, separated from her family, was shouting her daughter's name. They had no difficulty in finding a seat on the ferry to the Chinese side. The boat was almost empty of townspeople. 'They obviously see the writing on the wall,' observed Edmund.

'Wuchang seems to be putting up a good fight,' said Catherine.

'It's only a matter of time. You saw the Nationalists throwing themselves against the walls. I've never seen such spirit in a Chinese army. This is something new, Catherine.'

Catherine reached in her pockets for her cigarettes. As the ferry approached the dock, she saw crowds pushing and heaving on the other pier, more refugees attempting futilely to escape the inevitable. 'I take it we're to prepare for another retreat then?' she asked coldly. 'Now you've decided the Bolsheviks are going to win.'

'Niedemeyer thinks we should stay here,' said Edmund.

'Whatever happens?'

'Whatever happens,' said Edmund.

'So now we're to provide medical services to the Reds?'

'We will treat any wounded man who comes to our door,' said Edmund. 'Do you have a problem with that, Nurse?'

'No, Doctor,' said Catherine, treating him to an icy smile. 'I've dealt with Bolsheviks before. I know what the bastards are like. Do you?'

Edmund opened his mouth to retort, but at that moment, the ferry bumped against the stanchions on the other bank. She followed him as he forced his way through the throng that crowded forward as soon as the metal gangplank hit the wharf.

For the next ten days she was occupied with establishing the new hospital. After some consideration, Edmund and Niedemeyer had decided that it would be better to set it in an old courtyard house located just outside the foreign concessions on the Hankow side of the tributary. There, they thought, it would be easier to claim neutrality, and, in the worst case, their closeness to the international city gave them a better chance of protection. Catherine busied herself with the administration, while Edmund and the two Chinese doctors secured supplies. They could still hear the thunder of the guns from the Wuchang siege, especially in the stillness of the hot nights, then others beyond Hanyang, where Wu Pei-fu was holding off the Eighth Division of the Nationalist Army, which had indeed crossed the Yangtse upstream. First a trickle, then a stream of wounded were ferried to their hospital. Catherine and her staff were soon back in their old routine.

During one night of violence, Edmund armed the walking wounded to protect the gates from looters. Catherine watched from the roof as undisciplined soldiers from Wu Pei-fu's armies smashed shops, forced their way into private houses and loaded valuables and food onto the mule carts that were already streaming away from the doomed city. One house on the other side of the street was set ablaze; and in the flickering light, Catherine watched the soldiers stumble beneath their loads. A young girl was dragged screaming from her door towards a cart while a corporal beat back her imploring parents with the butt of his revolver.

Despairing, Catherine realised there was nothing she could do.

It was a relief when day dawned, but with it came the news that the general whom Wu Pei-fu had charged with Hanyang's defence had opened the gates to the enemy. The twin cities on the northern bank of the Yangtse were in Nationalist hands.

At noon, from the roof, Catherine and Edmund saw the first companies of Kuomintang soldiers marching down their street. A young woman with a megaphone was shouting to the scared inhabitants that the National Revolutionary Army had liberated their city. Behind her two strong young men carried banners: one was the Nationalist flag, the other the hammer and sickle.

Lan-hua had been one of the first activists to enter liberated Hanyang. Her brigade leader had posted instructions that propagandists should wait for confirmation that the enemy forces had been pacified, but she and several of her colleagues were having none of it. They were the vanguard of the revolution: it was their duty to be the first to bring the message of liberation to the oppressed workers. With the complicity of a company sergeant, whom they had bribed with cigarettes from the political-supplies department, she and her friends had smuggled themselves into the back of a truck and driven the fifty miles east from the Yangtse crossing point at Yochow to the Hanyang front. Two days in a wet slit trench under heavy shellfire, suffering the danger of imminent extinction and the amused glances of General Tang Sheng-chi's hardened veterans when she flinched at an explosion, had dampened her enthusiasm, not to mention the glimpses of bodies torn apart by machine-gun fire – but all that had been forgotten on the glorious morning when she heard that the enemy had fled. She had unfolded the red flag from her knapsack, tied it to the rifle of a fallen comrade and followed the soldiers into the city.

At first she had been depressed by the silence in the deserted streets, the scared passers-by who ran away from her. This was not the triumphant welcome that had greeted her in the villages on the march from Hunan. As she threaded her way through the empty thoroughfares, she had become more and more disappointed and perplexed, until she had come across a large factory complex from whose gates hung large posters proclaiming a strike. The streets were thronged with artisans in blue and grey overalls, cheering the incoming troops.

Now, two months later, she saw herself as a hardened revolutionary. The furnace of summer had cooled to a mild autumn, but the ardour they had brought with them intensified, and every factory in the city had joined the general strike. Lan-hua had been appointed an adviser to the propaganda section of the Hupeh General Labour Union, and it was her duty to see that each factory had access to printed material and posters. Shyly at first, but growing in confidence, she had learned to harangue reluctant workers, who in their pig-bristle godowns or sugar mills, steelyards and rice-packing halls were initially scared to risk their livelihoods in industrial action. Her allies were the arsenal workers and the heroic railway unionists, who had been the first to strike against the warlords and been bloodily suppressed in the previous year.

She knew that activists like herself were being criticised by the more right-wing members of the Kuomintang, who had arrived with the army, and she had blazing rows with an official of the Interim Economic Committee who urged her not to provoke the anger of the Chinese bourgeoisie in the city, whose factories were also being affected by the slowdown. It was the imperialists, of course, who were her prime target. That first month had been glorious. She knew that actions like hers were damaging the economic power of the enemy. One day she and her friends had hired a sampan and bobbed the length of the Hankow waterfront, looking into the concessions. The esplanade was deserted, but for a few soldiers and Indian policemen. There were no coolies pulling loads, no office workers going in and out of the tall buildings. Freighters rusted on the wharfs, hatches closed, and the cranes stood idle. Opposite the Hong Kong and Shanghai Bank, they saw a European businessman gazing forlornly at the river. 'Perhaps he's contemplating suicide,' one of her colleagues had suggested, 'or trying to calculate how much money he's lost!' They had screamed mocking slogans at him through their megaphone and cheered when he walked away, as if they had secured another small victory.

Occasionally, visiting factories near the railway station, Lan-hua had seen truckloads of wounded men returning from the front. There were not enough hospitals in Hanyang so many were being treated in the foreign-run hospitals in Hankow. That disturbed her. She did not like to think of National Revolutionary Army soldiers in the hands of foreigners.

John Soo was attached to the 4th Division under the personal command of Chiang Kai-shek. After the resistance in Wuchang had been squashed, Generalissimo Chiang had moved across the mountains with the main army to challenge the eastern warlord, General Sun Chuan-fang. Sometimes Lan-hua received news of the fighting in Kiangsi. Three times already she had heard reports that the provincial capital, Nanchang, had fallen, yet the battles outside its walls still seemed to be going on. She was worried about John, who had not written to her for weeks. As a good revolutionary, she tried to put personal feelings out of her mind, but sleepless in her bunk at night, anxiety nagged her.

The big question was: when would Borodin come? Weeks ago it had been reported that the main government in Canton would move to Wuhan. She knew that Mr Borodin and his wife, Fanya, with Madame Sun Yat-sen, Eugene Chen and some of the more radical leaders of the Kuomintang had left Canton, and must now be struggling along the route that the army had taken to get here. She knew that the revolution needed a leader to take control. Recently her arguments with the right-wingers had been more vituperative, and behind the scenes these scabs, as she thought of them, had been negotiating with the Chamber of Commerce, even with some of the foreign firms, to settle the strikes. Already, the managers of several striking plants had agreed to pay the higher wages demanded, and the workers returned to their lathes. When Borodin came, she told herself, he would make things right. But where was he?

A hand was pulling at her blanket. Instantly she was wide-awake. It was *Lao* Han, the burly worker from the arsenal whom she had met on her first day in Hanyang. He had lifted her and her flag on to his and his comrades' shoulders. Since that day, he had been her most loyal supporter.

'Quickly, sister, get your clothes on. Something's up.'

'What?' she cried, pulling the blanket to her chin.

'We're marching on the concessions. I've got a sampan near the ferry. Hurry.'

She was immediately on her feet. 'Their guns?' she asked, as they ran through the twilight. 'Their navies?'

'*Tamade!* Who cares? We're thousands. Didn't you want the workers to rise up? Now it's happening.'

It was exhilarating to be on the choppy river in the dawn light, blood-red foam on the oily water reflecting the first rays of the rising sun. In the gloom she saw the shadows of the ferries and the other sampans on either side, all crowded with workers, heading for the Hankow terminal that loomed ahead.

It took her a moment to steady herself on the other shore; she felt the solid paving stones under her cotton shoes, but she was dizzy from the rocking of the boat. Nobody spoke, but she sensed from the rank smell and the heavy breathing that hundreds of male bodies were gathering around her in the dark shadow of the warehouses. The tension, the fear, the excitement made a physical bond.

Following *Lao* Han, she began to run. Impelled by the motion around her, it was as if her separate personality had become sublimated in a common purpose. The greyness around her now revealed heads, blue caps, wrinkled, leathery skin, and shining eyes fixed resolutely forward. The alley opened into the Bund. Blinking in the dazzling light, she saw the beaten gold of the river, the silhouettes of the trees against the glare, the shining white edifice of the Taikoo offices. She heard her own shrill voice echoing in the sudden masculine roar that thundered around her '*Ba gong! Ba gong!* Strike! Strike! Strike!' Then the cries rose and died, and the heaving column shuddered to a halt.

A line of sandbags barricaded the road in front of them, not fifty feet away. Lan-hua, in the front rank of the workers, saw the set English faces, shadowed by their soup-plate helmets, calmly sighting along their levelled rifles. In the silence she heard a metallic click and rattle, and noticed the machine-guns mounted at either end of the barricade. The squat barrels were pointing directly at her head. Unconsciously, like every one of her companions, she took a step backwards.

She felt frozen, unable to move a limb. From one of the warships in the river came the long-drawn-out hoot of a siren. It tore the silence, disorienting her. The stillness was even more oppressive when the noise died. She saw an officer climb the barricade. He wore baggy shorts and white socks that came to his knees. He stood silently observing them, arms folded.

Suddenly at a sound from their left all eyes turned. An *amah*, wearing baggy black trousers and a white tunic, was pulling a large perambulator into the street from a small garden. She was waving a rattle and cooing endearments at the foreign baby inside. She swung the pram round and, still gazing at the child, began to propel it towards the riverbank. Suddenly she stopped, and stared from side to side. Lan-hua saw the colour drain from her face. With a loud 'Aiiaayah!' she pushed the pram back in the direction she had come.

It was as if a spell had been broken. The ranks of workers burst into harsh laughter. There were catcalls of 'Foreign lackey!' As the *amah* scuttled back to safety, a worker threw the first stone at the soldiers. A hail of projectiles followed it. *Lao* Han beside her pulled out of his pockets two bricks and handed one to Lan-hua. As she hurled it forward, feebly, with both hands, the British officer scrambled down behind the barricade. Lan-hua recalled the May 30th incident in Shanghai, which had been the last time the British had fired on an unarmed crowd, and was chilled.

She was shaken by a shattering burst of noise, then felt a tug at her arm and saw *Lao* Han's mouth shouting some silent warning. She dropped to her knees beside him, and put her hands over her ears to shut out the sound. I'm dead, she thought. I can't escape. Oh, why does it have to end like this? The noise went on and on, a wall of white sound inside her brain. Her muscles tensed as she waited for the blows into her body that would end her life.

Her ears were still humming in the sudden silence when *Lao* Han pulled her to her feet. She looked around her, befuddled. People were running – but not away from the firing: they were running towards the barricade. 'Come on, sister,' she heard. 'You're not hurt. They fired over our heads to scare us.' She peered ahead. Sandbags were flying into the air, tossed aside by workers. 'The soldiers?' she muttered.

'Cowards,' said Han. 'They're running away. Come on! Where are your banners? I'm going to fly one from the top of that bank building.'

And together they entered the British concession, proudly, through the gap that had been made in the barricade. Lan-hua stared curiously at the British soldiers who were standing in formation to the side, ready to protect themselves, bayonets fixed on their rifles, but otherwise taking no action to prevent the hordes of workers running into the town. The officer who had stood on top of the barricade was watching them flood past with a wry smile. He looked a little like her friend, Edmund Airton, who had come to her father's funeral. She stopped in front of him. 'You let us pass,' she said, in English, 'though you had guns.'

'Better than an article in the Sunday papers about another Chinese massacre perpetrated by villainous British troops, don't you think, madam?' He bowed politely. 'Oh,' he added, 'since you speak such excellent English, I would be enormously grateful if you could persuade your colleagues not to take too many liberties with our property and buildings. Somebody will only have to repair them again.' He pointed down the road to where a swarm of workers were climbing the bars that protected the ground-floor windows of one of the banks, while another knot hammered on the great teak doors with a bench they had uprooted from the esplanade. 'And by the way,' he added pleasantly, 'if any of you considers laying hands on our civilians with violent intentions, please think again. We are still armed, as you can see, and I doubt whether our powerful friends in their boats on the water would be any more amused than we would be. Good day, madam. I wish you an enjoyable stay in Hankow.'

'What's he saying?' asked *Lao* Han suspiciously.

'That he hopes we won't hurt anybody,' said Lan-hua.

The burly arsenal worker lifted his chin in the officer's face. 'Imperialist blood-sucker!' he shouted. 'You'll get what you deserve.'

The officer wiped spittle from his cheek. 'You have charming friends, madam,' he said.

Lan-hua looked at him coldly. 'What you said about the buildings, Captain,' her cheeks were flushed with a mixture of indignation and exhilaration, 'they're not yours. They're ours. They belong to China. To the people. My advice to you is to take all your citizens and yourselves on to your ships – and go away.'

As she turned on her heel, it seemed that she was floating on air. Her defiance of the British officer intoxicated her: she had struck her own personal blow for the revolution, humbling the enemy in his pride.

That night, lying on a couch in an occupied office building, her comrades snoring around her on the Persian carpets, she could not sleep. Her mind whirled with the events of the day. She recalled the shout of triumph when the great doors of the Hong Kong and Shanghai Bank were finally flung open; the sudden respectful hush of the workers who had burst into the gloom of the huge hall, gazing in wonder at the tall marble pillars and the ironwork filigree on the windows; the cold anger on the faces of the Englishmen, whom they ignored as they crowded into the luxurious apartments on the top floors; their scramble on to the roof, where *Lao* Han, true to his word, had raised the red flag . . . And later, around noon, she had stood in the press of chanting revolutionaries jeering as the once-imperious British – men, women and terrified children – filed in line to one of the piers, clutching their belongings, while sailors waited in launches to evacuate them to their ships. There was an expression on their faces that had thrilled her to the pit of her stomach: it was the expression she had drawn on the cringing imperialists in her posters: hatred, shame, fear, defeat.

Over the next few days tension mounted. The revolution had won a victory – its vanguard occupied the British concession – but the outcome was uncertain. Representatives of the right wing of the Kuomintang came to 'negotiate' with the General Labour Union, arguing that it was dangerous to antagonise the Powers further before the Northern Expedition had won its goals, and the Interim Economic Committee was even arguing that the office buildings should be given back to the big firms, if only temporarily, so that the trade on which the city depended could be allowed to continue.

Lan-hua and her small group of activists kept themselves busy, printing exclamatory posters and optimistic broadsheets, while a lookout, crouching by the big bay window, kept a wary eye on the naval activities on the river. On the fourth night there was a storm. Lan-hua heard the thunderclaps, saw the white bursts of lightning illuminating the room and for long seconds imagined that the naval bombardment that they feared had begun.

They woke to a wet, misty morning, and the news that Borodin had arrived in Wuhan.

It was like a whisper of spring.

The whole city came out to greet him. Vast crowds flocked to the arsenal in Hanyang where he made his first address. They mobbed the ferry piers on either side of the tributary hoping to catch a glimpse of the great man as he crossed on a motor launch. In the captured British concession, they gathered in their thousands on the Bund and filled the square in front of the Customs Building where, from a second-floor balcony, Borodin, flanked by General Tang, Madame Sun, Eugene Chen and other leaders, stood with his arm outstretched, saluting the revolution.

Lan-hua, standing proudly at the back of the balcony with the rest of Borodin's staff, saw before her a sea of rapturous faces: artisans, labourers, clerical workers, peasants, soldiers, the proletariat in all its variety but today individually indistinguishable, united in solidarity and joy in victory. Tears in her eyes, Lan-hua felt she saw below her the future of her country. Even the bourgeoisie had come to support the Nationalist government: gathered in their brown mandarin's gowns round a banner that announced in huge golden characters their congratulations on the victories of the Northern Expedition, they too were cheering. Lan-hua suddenly thought that if she were to die at that moment, her life would have been fulfilled and worthwhile.

Five hundred miles to the north, Captain Ti Jen-hsing had brought his company back to camp after an exercise in the hills. He was tired and looked forward to an hour in the hot tub that his orderly was preparing for him. His men had performed well over the heavy route march through two days of continuous rain and, as a reward, he had staged a surprise night attack on a small, unsuspecting village. Each house had been invested silently and efficiently before its occupants had had time to hide their food and valuables. The soldiers had therefore feasted on pig and goat, and afterwards entertained themselves with the farmers' daughters (Ti knew when to turn a blind eye to standing orders).

He had written his report for Colonel Yen, and was confident that his men satisfied all of General Lin's rigorous criteria for toughness, endurance and an ability to live off the land. Besides ephemeral loot, his raid on the village, until now spared the depredations of warlord armies because of its inaccessibility, had yielded seven fit young men, whom he had press-ganged to serve as porters for the march south.

Whenever, if ever, that would be . . .

It had been nearly three months now that General Lin's division had been kicking its heels in a flyblown camp by the Yellow river near Loyang. Prolonged inactivity and boredom had strained friendships, and the only escape from argument had been gruelling exercises set with increasing frequency by the general. Most galling of all was the news from the front. Neither Wu Pei-fu nor Sun

Chuan-fang had been able to hold back the Nationalists, whose western divisions had taken Wuhan, Nanchang and Kiukiang, and whose eastern division had marched almost without resistance up the coast from Fukien, and was now in the south of Chekiang, pushing towards Hangchow. Ti and his men had nothing but scorn for their warlord allies that had allowed themselves to be so cravenly beaten. They would show them, they told themselves. Chang Tso-lin had but to give the word, and the White Russian armoured trains would roll down from Shantung breathing fire and destruction from their nine-inch guns, Lin's and other crack divisions would march down into the flatlands scouring all in their path and there would not be a Bolshevik or a whining Nationalist left standing.

Yet the order never came.

And the rain kept falling.

Ti sighed. He had done everything he could do. His company would be ready when the time came. He picked up his report. He'd deliver it before he had his bath. He made his way across the threshing floor-cum-market square towards the only substantial farmhouse in the village. Colonel Yen and his adjutants had long ago commandeered it as a temporary divisional headquarters, and although they had been there for three months, it retained its air of ramshackle impermanence. The other buildings in the occupied village had fallen into an even more advanced state of dilapidation, the original inhabitants having joined the starving refugees streaming across China. Their huts were now being used by officers who preferred a roof and rats to a damp tent, or as stables, stores and canteens for the commissariat. At the end of the street, a barn had been turned into a brothel, listlessly served by the only inhabitants of the village still remaining, the girls who had been sold voluntarily or involuntarily by their parents before they were evicted. Peasants with daughters to sell were the lucky ones: they received cash; for any other goods, payment was by promissory token inscribed with the head of Generalissimo Chang Tso-lin. They were not entirely useless: Ti's men had found that they made good cigarette paper.

There was only one building in the village into which Ti had never been and he glanced at its curved roofs and pillars as he walked across the square: the small Taoist temple that Lin had taken over as his private quarters. There the general had remained, throughout the autumn, leaving only occasionally to visit the nearby Buddhist caves at Lungmen on the Yi river. Sometimes accompanied by his red-haired Russian mistress, he would spend the whole day contemplating the ancient carvings. Ti had once been in charge of his escort. The general had spent the day high on the cliff face in a grotto in which a statue of Kuan-yin had been carved out of the rock. He had emerged as the sun was setting; his features strangely pale so that the scar appeared more livid than usual on his cheek. He had given Ti one order before he settled into the back of his car. 'You will remember the location of this cave, Captain,' he said, 'so that you can instruct an engineering platoon to come tomorrow to remove the statue within. It is then to be shipped to the Yamen in Shishan. Are you clear?'

'Yes, General.' Ti had snapped to attention. He had spent the next two days in the dreary gorge, supervising what proved to be a highly complicated task, but somehow the statue was extricated from its plinth at the minor cost of one crushed coolie. It had been packed and sent off under guard, and Ti, who was not a superstitious man, was glad to be rid of it. The assignment had reminded him of the day he had spent with the general in the Ch'ien Lung emperor's tomb.

He had not dwelled long on the matter. Everybody knew that Lin Fu-po was strange. Rumours circulated among the troops that the general spent his days in his dark temple contemplating human bones. On evening inspections, Ti had heard the men muttering round their campfires about how he had laid out a skeleton piece by piece in front of the altar of one of the inner sanctuaries of the temple, and performed strange rites. He had no idea where this tale had originated. Colonel Yen, who was the only officer regularly to visit the general, said he had seen no sign of a skeleton – although he would put nothing past the mad turtle's egg. It was Yen's habit to be rude about his commander, although never in his presence when he cringed like everybody else. 'But why ask me?' he would growl. 'I only ever see him in his outer office, don't I? I'm a full colonel but he treats me like a flunkey. Only that black-bearded brute of a bodyguard has access to his inner sanctum. And the pale foreign whore he keeps. How would I know what they all get up to? Maybe it's black magic or devil conjuring. More likely he's just a greedy bastard, like all these warlords. They all want to be emperors. Our madman is stocking up on imperial relics. They say that tomb he's building for himself outside Shishan is full of statues and treasure. He's a magpie. A lunatic collector. Frankly I don't care. If the men believe he's using a corpse to put spells on the Bolsheviks, they'll fight all the harder, won't they? Now come on, who's joining me for a game of mah-jongg?'

Ti despised Yen, but on this matter he agreed with him. Lin's sinister manner invoked fear in his men – he himself felt nervous in his presence – but they all knew that there was no better battle-field commander in the Fengtian army. He rarely wasted lives in his plans of attack, and up to now had a solid record of victory.

Ti lifted the felt hanging that muffled the draught and went into Headquarters. A young adjutant, who was sitting at the desk by a coal stove, told him that Colonel Yen was busy. He could hear grunts and scuffles from the next room. 'Interviewing peasant informers, is he?' asked Ti. 'How old is this one, and where did he manage to catch her? Never mind,' he said, taking pity on the boy's embar-rassment. 'Give him this report when he's finished. I'm going to the bath house.'

As he lowered his half-frozen limbs into the scalding water, his toes tingled. It was as if the pain was helping him rediscover forgotten parts of his body. He let the heat seep into his every pore, and gradually the ache in his thighs and shoulders eased away in a timeless half-sleep where images of the last few days jumbled in his mind and mixed with memories of his home, girls he had slept with and girls he had not. Lei Lan-hua's face came to mind, the proud girl who had jilted him – but he had never forgotten the pearly teeth, the cherry lips, the sloping eyebrows, the fringe of hair on a wide brow . . . Well, she had had her come-uppance, as had the rest of her family. Now that his father owned their mansion . . .

'Captain Ti!' It was the adjutant from Headquarters.

'What is it?' he snapped, irritated.

'General Lin wants to see you. Urgently,' the young man replied. His wide eyes registered alarm.

Ti also was alarmed, although he tried to keep his features impassive. 'Do you know what it's about?' He attempted to put a casual note into his question, as he got out and began to dry himself.

'No, Captain. Colonel Yen said only that you had to go immediately.'

When he presented himself at the temple, he was glad of only one thing: that he was in his clean dress uniform. If he was to be cashiered, or worse, he would at least accept his fate in a soldierly manner. It was unprecedented that the general would demand to see a junior officer, and it did not bode well. He racked his brains to think what he might have done. Had he let his scorn for Yen show too openly? Had the man fabricated some charge?

Lin's bodyguard was waiting for him in the courtyard, and Ti followed him through the first hall. He felt rather than saw the great statues of the four Guardian deities with their massive swords and maces on either side. A lantern was burning in the window of one of the monks' rooms at the side of the next courtyard. Ti was relieved. He had imagined that his audience with Lin might be in the main hall under the great statues of the gods, with perhaps, if the rumours were true, the bones of a skeleton laid on the altar. The bodyguard lifted a hanging and ushered him into a small room, cleared of any furniture except for a desk and a camp bed. Behind the desk sat General Lin, in a simple private's tunic, his head bent over some papers.

'Are you interested in politics, Captain?' The shaven head remained bowed over the papers. 'Do you have Nationalist sympathies?'

'No, General,' said Ti, startled. 'I am loyal to Fengtian.'

'Yet you carry with you literature that might be described as revolutionary.'

'No, General, I – it is a lie.'

Lin looked up, then reached down by his side and laid a satchel on the table. Ti recognised it as his own. Two volumes slipped out on to the table, Lu Hsun's latest essays, and Pa Chin's *Youth*. 'And these?' questioned the soft voice.

Ti felt the blood draining from his head. 'They're just stories, General. I enjoy reading. I happened to pick them up.'

The eyes bored into his own.

'I do not support the Kuomintang, General,' he said. 'I am not a Communist.'

Lin's eyes continued to search his face. 'No, I don't think you are,' he said. 'Nor, as a matter of fact, are these writers, although they are over-clever idealists. Colonel Yen has shown his ignorance by drawing this matter to my attention. Do you know why he has reported you to me?'

'No, General.'

'Have you been insubordinate?'

'No, General.'

'But you do not respect him. You need not answer.' He picked up a sheet of paper. 'I have just been reading your report on your exercise. You did well. Tell me, Captain, why are we fighting this war?'

'To unify China, sir, and defeat the Bolshevik menace.'

'Yes, I know the slogans. Nothing more?'

Ti could not think how to reply. Did the general want the truth? That a warlord army fought only for loot. That it hardly mattered, in this devastated China, who fought whom since every faction wanted one thing only: power and control of the economy. That, for a man like Ti, a life in the army promised a career leading to riches, honour, promotion and a step above the life of a humble provincial merchant like his father . . . He was sure Lin was testing him, and that this interview was of supreme importance to his future, but he could not understand what was at issue.

'To restore our traditional Chinese values,' he attempted, and momentarily closed his eyes, as a drop of sweat trickled from under his cap band.

He heard a low, hissing chuckle, opened his eyes and saw that Lin was smiling. 'You lie very well, Captain,' said the general. 'And in your attempt to flatter me, you have spoken more truth than you understand. Yes, we are fighting to restore our traditional values, but what are they? Can you answer me that?'

Ti bowed his head. 'No, sir,' he muttered.

'What distinguishes a human being from an animal, Captain?'

'His intelligence? Rationality?'

'A wolf can be cunning, a dog shows fidelity, and even a tigress will sacrifice herself for her cubs. Sometimes an animal can display more intelligence and rationality than a human – but only man has a soul, Captain. Virtue. What the sages called *jen*. And when man lives in harmony with himself, society is harmonious, and there will be order in earth and heaven. Do you believe that, Captain?'

'It must be as you say, sir.'

'Oh, it is, Captain, it is – or was thousands of years ago when our ancestors created civilisation, but things have deteriorated since then and now we are in a period of *luan,* of chaos. Do you know why we are fighting, Captain? It is to regain the stolen soul of our country. Our *jen*. Out of this destruction will come a new beginning – as you say, the restoration of our ancient values. It is time for our ancestors to return.'

Again, Ti heard the hissing laugh, although Lin was on his feet now, with his back to him, looking at a picture of the Buddha on the wall.

The general turned, the lopsided smile still on his face. 'Of course you do not understand a word of what I am saying, but you are an educated man and one day you will. The first step is, in any case, to defeat the enemy – the Bolsheviks and the others. You may be pleased to hear that I received orders this evening.' He picked up a telegram from the desk. 'Our division is to report to Marshal Chang Tsung-chang, the warlord of Shantung, in Tsinan. From there we will advance south in support of General Sun Chuan-fang, who has at last requested help. Our own Marshal Chang Tso-lin, with his son, Chang Hsueh-liang, will advance in the centre to support Wu Pei-fu. Our combined forces have a new name, the Anminchun, the Army for the Pacification of the People. It is appropriate, no?

'You will now return to Headquarters to wake Colonel Yen from his drunken slumbers and order him here. Take your satchel with its subversive books, and also these.' He passed over a small silk purse. 'Inside you will find stars to sew on your tunic. You are from this moment promoted to major, with an increase in pay of ten taels a month. Know that I will be watching your career with interest. If you do well and are loyal, I will reward you further.

These are testing times, and sometimes I will make special demands. Do you understand, Major?'

Ti's thoughts were swirling. 'Yes, General. Thank you, General,' he managed.

'Good. Then we have an understanding,' said Lin. He returned to his desk and lowered his eyes to his papers. Already he seemed oblivious of Ti, despite the click of his boots and his full salute. Followed by the black-bearded bodyguard who had materialised at his elbow, Ti left the temple.

He did not know whether to feel astonished at his promotion, or thankful that he had escaped from the general's presence unscathed. He walked unsteadily to the headquarters hut and passed on Lin's order to the adjutant that Colonel Yen should report immediately. He did not feel like retiring to his tent so took the path beyond the village and climbed to a bamboo grove that overlooked the camp. It had stopped raining, but he could hear the trickle of water in the leaves, still dripping from earlier showers, and the mud was soggy beneath his boots. Among the trees, Ti thought that he had entered a darkness within a darkness, but as he stood there the black night clouds rolled away, and for a moment he saw the moon and several faint stars – and thought of what else Lin had said: they had orders to march. They would be going to war at last. As this realisation struck him, he heard faint cheers from below. Yen must have passed on the news, he thought. The cheering grew louder, competing with the eerie call of a night bird in the woods.

But Ti could not share entirely in the elation. Lin's other words had come to mind: 'I will make special demands' and 'We have an understanding.' As if to reassure himself, Ti felt in his pockets and his fingers touched the sharp edges of the stars inside the silk purse. Part of him felt he deserved this promotion, but he also had more than a suspicion that it was not just for merit. The general had chosen him for a purpose he did not yet understand. That mad conversation about souls and ancestors had had in it something of the nature of a pact. Standing in the darkness of the bamboo grove, the clouds hiding the moon again, the newly appointed Major Ti realised he was shivering – and it was not because of the cold.

* * *

As a cold December day was breaking, Lan-hua was lying in John Soo's arms on a narrow bed in a rented room at a cheap hotel. Grey light was spreading through the window and outside she could hear the first sounds of morning – the chant of a beancurd-seller, the creak of a rickshaw, a hoot from the river. John murmured in his sleep. She feared it was another of his nightmares.

She had been shocked by his appearance that first morning when he appeared outside her dormitory, his satchel over his shoulders, unkempt after a four-day boat journey up the river from Kiukiang. His hair was flecked with grey and deep lines were carved in his cheeks and forehead. His eyes, although they smiled at her, seemed to be concentrating on something far away. After their first fierce embrace, when she had felt that her chest was being crushed, he had lapsed into a sort of wooden passivity. He let her take him by the hand as she almost dragged him to Borodin's offices so that she could apply for three days' leave. When she came out, leave granted, he was leaning against the wall as she had left him, his head bowed, gazing at the pavement. She had taken him to a dumpling shop and fed him. 'You're so beautiful,' he said. 'All the time, that's what kept me going, thinking about how beautiful you are.' She asked him to tell her of his experiences, the siege of Nanchang, the eastern campaign. 'Not today,' he said quietly, and would not be drawn.

Instead she had regaled him with stories of her own triumphs and he had listened attentively, nodding, smiling when she became excited, but she had been disappointed: she had so longed to share these moments with him, and now she had, she sensed at best remote approval, at worst polite interest. She had wanted to cry out to him, 'Where is your passion? Your revolutionary fervour?' but the pain in his face stopped her. 'John,' she said, taking his hands in hers, 'what happened in Nanchang?'

He had bowed his head, and when he looked up, he said, 'Like you, we won a great victory.'

'That's cause for celebration.' She squeezed his hand. 'Yet you look so unhappy.'

'I'm sorry,' he said. 'I'm very tired.'

She had taken him to the hotel, and they had lain down together on the narrow bed. There was an unfamiliar tension in his body, a tautness in his limbs. Again his arms crushed her to him, and he held her as if he would never let go. 'I can't breathe,' she murmured, and only then had he relaxed a little. She was astounded that his cheeks were contorted as if he was trying to hold back inconsolable grief. 'What's wrong?' she whispered, smoothing his hair.

'I'm sorry, so sorry,' he muttered. 'I – I can't control my happiness. All these months, these terrible months, I've dreamed of you . . . In the worst moments, I've thought of you . . .'

She had kissed his lips, the salt tears on his eyes, his nose, his cheeks. Lips on lips she had fumbled with his trousers, kicking off her own, and when they came together it was with a violence she had not known before. She felt him come well before she was ready, but he continued to thrust inside her until she told him gently to stop. Then she had felt a long shudder run the length of his body, and she had held him shaking in her arms until he slept. He did not wake for fourteen hours, but it was not a quiet sleep. He mumbled and shook, and once he shouted something about heads and walls, sitting up in the bed and pointing a shaking finger. Sweat poured down his forehead, his legs, his arms, and dampened the front of his vest.

She woke to find him leaning on one elbow, his round spectacles on the end of his nose, looking down at her. 'You're back,' she murmured sleepily.

'Yes.' He smiled. 'I'm back.' This time when they made love, it was as tender as she had remembered from before, and afterwards they both slept dreamlessly.

'You don't have to tell me what you went through,' she said later, as they ate *congee* in a small restaurant. 'It must have been terrible. You were talking in your sleep last night – about heads on walls.'

She saw John pale.

'Is that a memory of an experience you had?' she asked.

'Yes,' he said. 'One I try to forget in my waking moments.'

'Can you make yourself forget?' she asked.

Silently, he shook his head.

'Please tell me,' she said. 'Share it with me. Whatever it is. Perhaps you'll feel better after you tell me.'

He gazed at her long and hard, considering. Then he leaned

forward over the table and began to speak, in a low monotone, his eyes turned away from her.

They had made a night march and caught the garrison by surprise. John and his engineers had waited on a hillside while picked troops boarded the vehicles that he had spent the previous day repainting in the colours and markings of the enemy. It was a daring plan. If all went well, the enemy would unsuspectingly open the gates of the city for the convoy, and Nanchang would be invested before it realised it was being attacked. He watched, heart thumping, as the lorries disappeared into the darkness. For the next hour he chain-smoked as he listened to the tramp of the rest of the column marching down the road to join the battle.

Near dawn they heard the first shots. Over the shadowy mass of the city walls he saw the arc of tracer bullets and occasionally he heard the thump of a grenade. There was a long silence, which lasted well after the sky paled with first light. In the distance he could make out the river and the mountains. He saw the general hunched in his camp chair, hugging a mug of tea, while his aides peered through their binoculars. Then he heard the cheers. A flag was waving above the city gateway. It was the Nationalist flag.

They entered the city in triumph. There were few signs of the short, bloody fighting that had taken place. Whatever defence had been mounted had crumbled quickly. The surprised garrison had surrendered after the gateway and the walls had been secured. It was rumoured that the enemy commander had been caught in his bed when Nationalist soldiers overran the Yamen.

John was in the central square when his general declared Nanchang to be a liberated city. Crowds were cheering. University students were embracing the soldiers. Citizens were pressing dumplings and pastries into their hands.

John found that he was being mobbed. A short girl, with a fashionable bobbed haircut, pinned a camellia flower to his tunic, then threw her arms round him and kissed him, blushing afterwards at her daring, but she did not release his hand. 'Is this – is this the revolution?' she cried. 'Are the warlords gone?'

'Yes,' he said. 'Yes.' He looked down into her shining eyes, and saw a resemblance to Lan-hua. He kissed her. He could not resist. A moment later, he had been pulled away by a knot of young men in student uniforms, who lifted him on to their shoulders. He still had the impression of the girl's warm lips on his own, and thought of Lan-hua, wishing she could be there. This was revolution as it was meant to be.

It did not last. The rest of the army failed to reinforce them. In the afternoon, Sun Chuan-fang's troops counter-attacked from the river. There was bloody hand-to-hand fighting as the Nationalists, outnumbered, retreated street by street. John had blurred impressions of shouting, screams, panic, chaos, and men falling around him as he followed in the jostling, disorganised crowd that was streaming to the city gate. He was lucky to find a hold on one of the trucks that made it back to the lines and safety. Half the column that had entered the city that morning had been killed or captured.

Wearily they prepared for the enemy's advance. John spent the night supervising the digging of trenches. He was so exhausted that he could hardly think. As dawn broke, he was standing to with a rifle, his head resting on the parapet, waiting for the inevitable attack, which he knew he was unlikely to survive – but by mid-morning the rest of the army had arrived, and he was allowed to rest.

The army settled down for a long siege.

Within the city, as they subsequently discovered, the warlords had been conducting reprisals on the townsfolk who had come out in support of the Nationalists. The punishment was particularly severe for the students, many of whom were executed as fifth columnists. Two days after the failed attack, the first heads were mounted on the walls. Many young women's were among them. Any girl with bobbed hair was automatically considered to be a revolutionary. One of the heads displayed on the wall, John saw, had belonged to the young girl who had kissed him.

In the end, he had been grateful for the kites. After a week of pecking, there was no resemblance to anybody any more. John had finally been unable to distinguish male heads from female, or what had been the style of their hair.

* * *

'Lan-hua, I hope you can understand why I kissed that girl,' he said, in the silence that followed his story. 'She could only have been twenty, and she was full of life. Like you, Lan-hua. Please forgive me . . . Later I saw them – the birds – pulling out the string of her eyes. When I dream, I dream it is happening to you.'

Lan-hua had already dropped her spoon, and had clapped her hands to her mouth. 'That's horrible,' she whispered.

'War is horrible,' he said. 'It's not glorious, even if you are fighting for a good cause. It doesn't ennoble you. It does the opposite. For the last two months I have been living in a muddy hole in the ground. Like an animal. And to survive I have developed the instincts of an animal. When I hear a shell I know instinctively if it is one of ours or one of theirs, and I duck or I run. Sometimes I just cower and moan. I think with my nose now. I smell fear. I smell death. I sense movement in the dark. When all is noise, and the ground is shaking, there is no rational mind, no John Soo with his Oxford Ph.D. John Soo is nothing but a quivering wire of nerve and flesh, stinking with terror, willing extinction of the world just as long as he is untouched.'

'I don't believe you, John. That's not you.'

'Believe me. One battle, one moment in a battle, is a lifetime. And in that long moment of eternity you see yourself for what you really are. And afterwards it is difficult to live with yourself. We spent two months in front of those walls, under those grinning heads, trying to take back the city. I was there for every one of their useless attacks. I'm a bridge-builder, with some knowledge from Whampoa days of gun emplacements – so they put me in charge of siege works and mines. Well, they had nobody else. I was the only qualified engineer on hand . . .'

John never discovered who had come up with the idea that they could dig their way under the city walls and blow them up. He knew little of mines and sapping, but a simple grasp of geology was enough to tell him that first they needed to shore up the river-bank. He tried to point out to his superiors the foolishness of digging holes on an alluvial plain in the rainy season when the river was rising, but nobody listened. Orders were orders.

One night the river flooded and a hundred of his men were drowned underground; fifty more were machine-gunned, caught in the moonlight when they climbed out of the filling trenches.

John had been spared witnessing this disaster. Two nights earlier he had been moved behind the lines with malarial fever. As he discovered afterwards, he had been doubly fortunate: his assistant, a nice young boy from Kweilin, had survived the drowning so he had been shot for sabotage. That had tidied up the matter as far as the general staff was concerned.

When John was on his feet again, a week later, he found he had been given a hundred more coolies to replace the ones who had died. He received orders to dig new mines as if nothing had happened. He told them they should shoot him, too, since it had been he who had designed the original trenches, but his superiors laughed and told him they had found the culprit. They advised him to rest a while longer because he had clearly not got over his fever. They were no longer interested in mines by then anyway, their heavy guns having finally arrived from Hunan; it had taken some time because they had had to be dragged over the mountains.

The guns made little difference. They did some damage to the walls – but they weren't attacking just walls: they were attacking trenches and machine-gun posts. The men ran forward in waves over the muddy ground with no possible cover or protection. Sometimes they came very close before they fell, or were blown to pieces, or just disappeared. Day after day, John watched from his bunker, shaken by shells. At night he was not spared, because the events he had witnessed in the day entered the fabric of his dreams.

'There's one recurring dream,' he told Lan-hua, 'in which I am sent on to the battlefield after the attack to gather up the heads and limbs and guts and hearts and testicles scattered in the mud, and it's my job to sew them back together again, to make new men out of these body parts. And the monsters I make jeer at me and jostle me, and complain that I've given A's leg to B, and B's head to C, and C unpicks his insides again because he is looking for his heart.'

'Oh, John, I don't know what to say.' Lan-hua was confused. She had never heard anybody speak like this before. She clutched instinctively to her certainties. 'But – but you won a victory. Over the militarists. For the revolution. It was a sacrifice. A noble one.'

John Soo's eyes widened, then he laughed, a harsh bark. 'Sacrifice? Fourteen thousand Cantonese boys dead in front of a gate that was eventually opened by bribery. By payment of gold to one of General Sun's corrupt subordinates. Yes, it was a victory, a great victory.'

'This cynicism is horrible,' she said.

He took some time to reply. 'I'm not cynical really,' he said eventually. 'I think I still believe, deep down, that what we are doing is right. I guess I'm just tired.'

'Oh, John,' she said, 'you mustn't be dispirited. Let me take you now to what was the British concession. Let me show you how we've made it part of free China. You'll see our flags flying over the roofs of their banks and offices. It will prove to you that what we're doing is worthwhile. You will see for yourself how we've defeated imperialism.'

'All right.' He smiled.

Even then, she had been alarmed. Perhaps it was the mild irony in his voice, the slightly patronising overtone.

She had taken him to the Bund, and proudly pointed out to him where the barricade had been, where the foreigners had fled to their boats. She pulled him to the other side of the boulevard so that he could look up to see the Kuomintang flag hanging from the mast of the Customs Building. John had smiled, but said nothing. A column of strikers – steelworkers from one of the Japanese mills – was marching down the centre of the road. They were raising their fists in unison, chanting slogans. They carried big red poster banners, and flags bearing the hammer and sickle. Lan-hua cheered as they went past, and experienced a moment of irritation that John did not join in.

That night, she had taken him to a duck restaurant like the one they used to frequent in Canton – and there they had had their first argument.

Lan-hua had forced it. Later she realised it had resulted from the frustration that had been building in her all day, ever since breakfast when John Soo had told her about his experiences in Nanchang.

This new battle-worn John Soo frightened her. Her heart had gone out to him when he had described the horrors of the battle-field but she had felt embarrassed and confused too. Of course she knew that battle was frightening – she herself had been under fire – but John's reaction had been unexpected, subtle, subjective, human . . . and weak. Soldiers were meant to show courage, to face the worst in a spirit of self-sacrifice, fired by the revolutionary spirit. She did not question his courage, but the manner in which he had described the heroic struggles before Nanchang – that was what Mr Borodin had said they had been – had been critical, questioning, personal, and that horrible story about the girl, her eyes . . . She did not want to think about it.

John had changed. When she looked at him now, careworn, tired, it was still the smiling, calm, affectionate face she remembered and loved, but something was missing: there was no longer that fire of enthusiasm in his eyes. She missed the strength of purpose, wisdom and steadiness that had marked him out from all the other men she had known. She still felt an urge to touch him, to run her hands down his cheeks, to nestle her head against his chest and find shelter there. He was her lover . . . but was he still her comrade? Lan-hua felt a sudden premonition and fear. She knew that she had to bring John back to the revolution – to the shared dream that had brought them together. It had been John's conviction that had inspired her, his certainty – but now he was wavering. She sensed a gulf opening between them.

'John?' she had asked him, over the stripped duck bones and empty plates. 'Would you like to meet Mr Borodin while you are here? I can probably arrange it, although he is very busy.'

He had smiled. 'I know you admire him, Lan-hua,' he said, 'but no, I'd rather spend my time with just you.'

'Oh, John, please.' She grasped his hands. 'He is so wise and kind. I know you're troubled by what you've seen, all those horrible things that have happened. He will be able to explain them for you, put them into perspective . . .'

'No, darling. I've had enough perspective to keep me going for a long while.'

His reply had startled her. 'But you admire him? Don't you?'

'Of course I respect him – but I question what he is doing here. Do we have to discuss politics, dearest? I'm so happy now, just being with you. Away from war and pressure. We have so short a time together. Can't we forget this horrible world with its politicians and generals?'

'I don't understand you, John. You've been strange ever since you arrived – and don't tell me you're tired again. Didn't I show you what we've achieved here? How we've liberated Hankow? Didn't I tell you how Mr Borodin intends to reorganise all the unions into a national force? Can you imagine my joy in working with him? To be at the very centre of the revolution?'

John's laugh had stabbed her heart. 'Lan-hua, he's a Russian. He reports to Stalin.'

She could not believe he had said that. He must have seen the pain in her expression because he spoke gently, squeezing her hand. 'Lan-hua, open your eyes. It's Chiang Kai-shek who leads the Northern Expedition, not Borodin. This is a Chinese struggle. Don't you see that a left-wing government supported by the Soviets in Wuhan threatens to break the United Front?'

She pulled her hand away. 'Mr Borodin created the alliance between the Communists and Nationalists. He would die to protect it.'

'For the moment, dearest. The Communists are not strong enough on their own in this country so he has to work with the Kuomintang. But the bulk of the support for the Kuomintang comes from the bourgeoisie, not the Communists. Generalissimo Chiang must consider their interests too. Do you think they're happy with what's going on here?'

'I don't see why not,' said Lan-hua. 'You saw yourself how we drove out the British.'

'I saw the river stacked with foreign gunboats, the Japanese concession untouched and full of soldiers. The British may have given up paper sovereignty but they still own the buildings and their businesses. The condition for their withdrawal was that normal trade would resume. But your Mr Borodin hasn't been able to bring the strikers to heel. Face it, Lan-hua. There's anarchy here. And now the foreign powers are enforcing a blockade on the river to bring what they see as a Communist dictatorship to heel. They're even stopping medical supplies. Food is running out. Your Mr Borodin will have to deal with starvation soon enough, and then who will your labour unions turn on? Really, dearest, you must look beyond the rallies and the slogans and see the situation for what it is.'

He had crossed over from his side of the table to lift her to her feet. 'Please, no quarrels,' he whispered, as he put his arm round her waist. 'Not these three days.' She had let the warmth of his body absorb her anger, and after a while her protests had become mere pouts of her lips for his kisses to smooth away. Walking back to their hotel, her head resting on his breast, she had persuaded herself that it was wrong to let politics come between them. She would love him and look after him; her body would absorb his pain and give him rest, and in the morning he would be his old self, free of his disillusion.

Now, twenty-four hours later, it was the dawn of their last day together. In a few hours John would have to go to the pier where a sampan would be waiting to carry him down the Yangtse back to the army. Yesterday had passed in uncomfortable silence. They had been to a movie in the afternoon. It was an American comedy. Buster Keaton was performing interminable stunts on a steam train. She had seen the flitting grey images but she had not been able to make sense of them or to understand why everybody else was laughing. John, too, had been silent. For a while they held hands, then put them back in their laps.

Over dinner she had tried one last time to reach him. 'John, you are still a Communist? You do still believe?'

'Is it really so important?' he had asked.

'It is to me.'

'I'm sorry, Lan-hua, I can't answer you. I don't know what I believe now. Communism. Nationalism. They're just words. I will continue to fight for Chiang Kai-shek. The militarists who are against us seem morally more despicable than we are, so I'll do my part. Sorry, Lan-hua, that's not what you wanted to hear.'

'I don't understand why you've changed,' she said.

His face contorted, but he pulled himself together and smiled affectionately, his eyes warm behind his spectacles. 'Lan-hua, I fervently hope and pray that you will never be in a situation, like I have been, that might cause you to change. You asked me what I believe. Well, not much, as I told you – but there is one thing. I love you. Stay as you are, Lan-hua. Stay the idealist, the revolutionary. Let me remember you as you are today.'

'Oh, John . . .'

'Listen, my love,' he said, 'it's late. If we go back to our hotel now, I can get my things and be gone before your dormitory curfew or before we have to pay for another night. I can sleep on the boat and stay on it till it leaves in the morning. Better we part as friends now than quarrel and spoil the memory of what may be our last time together.'

She had nodded bravely. She had kept her composure until John had packed his toothbrush and his laundry into his knapsack and was ready to leave. Then she had sat on the bed and howled, and one thing had led to another, and now it was morning.

Looking down at John's sleeping head, she felt suddenly that she was seeing it for the first time. In his sleep, the lines on his broad forehead, so prominent when he was talking to her, seemed to have smoothed away, and she saw other marks on his soft brown skin that she had not noticed before: a tiny scar on his chin, a mole under his ear. She followed the fine line of his eyebrows, admired his nose against the pillow, his sensuous lips and an almost perfect set of teeth. She had always thought of him as older than herself, mature, but now he looked like a boy. How little she knew this man, and how presumptuous and selfish she had been these last three days, she thought. What had this face seen? What had that mind, turning now in its nightmares, experienced? He had told her but she had not listened. She had condemned him, and for what? For suffering? For struggling to find his own meaning in a chaos she could not even imagine? For seeing the world as it was and not as she wanted it to be? While she was spouting lines from the Party school, like the teacher's pet proclaiming a lesson.

She found herself shaking him, pulling at his arms. He woke and smiled. 'Darling, what is it?' he asked.

'I don't want you to go,' she sobbed.

'Oh, dearest,' he said, and put his arms round her shaking shoulders.

She watched the little sampan until it was out of sight. It took a little time to negotiate its way through the moored boats anchored in the tributary, and John, in a ridiculous straw hat, waved from the prow until perhaps he could no longer distinguish her any more among the throng on the Hanyang dockside, but he remained where he was, a tall, solitary figure against the grey water. She continued to wave until the sampan rounded the bend at the confluence with the Yangtse, where it disappeared, taken by the strong current. Afterwards, on the ferry back to Hankow, she sat alone, sometimes splashed by spray when the prow sank into a furrow of the waves. She barely noticed. She was lost in her own misery. She had convinced herself that she and John would never meet again. Her thoughts veered between regret for the missed opportunities during his all too brief furlough, fear for his safety in the campaigns to come, and fear for herself, without her one true friend in a city that had lost all attraction and excitement.

12

The River Flows East

F rom the journal of William Lampsett, Reuters correspondent, Wuhu, 19 February 1927

It won't be easy for the Nationalists. The terrible and debauched Shantung warlord Chang Tsung-chang, he of the mutton-chop whiskers and red epileptic face, once Marshal Chang Tso-lin's fellow bandit, then his deputy, now his independent ally, has already crossed the Yangtse with his troops and his armoured trains. He typifies the brutality of the warlords. The left-wing newspapers caricature him as the Dog General because of his gargantuan appetites, sexual as well as culinary. He publicly boasts of his three 'don't knows' – how much money he has in his coffers, how many soldiers he has in his army, how many women he has in his harem. This rapacious overlord has looted his province with the thoroughness of a plague of locusts, ordering his collectors to tax the bark on trees when told that the granaries were exhausted. He is the sadistic disciplinarian who once tied the commanders of his artillery units to the muzzles of their cannon when they complained of the quality of their ammunition, and blew their bodies over a shooting range for the edification of a group of visiting military attachés. He is pillaging the villages of the ally whom he has come to assist. For all his brutal eccentricities, few doubt his ability and his ruthlessness, and the formidable punishment that his hard-bitten mercenaries will deal out to the Nationalists who cross his path. And moving down from the north to support him are the well-armed forces from Fengtian, who in numbers and matériel exceed those of the

National Revolutionary Army. The battle for Shanghai will be savage.

Following her encounter with the beggar on the Bund, Fu-kuei had spent three days working out a subterfuge to escape Yi-liang's chaperons and visit the coffee shop in the Sincere department store. On her arrival there she had felt a fool: it had indeed been a Colombian coffee promotion. She had sipped her coffee slowly, and after an hour had left. It was as she was going down in the lift that a young European man had pushed past her when the iron grille opened on the haberdashery floor. She was jostled against the attendant and the lift shook. 'Very sorry, lady, I was in a hurry,' said the man.

She had a glimpse of red cheeks and brown piggy eyes under a fedora. The accent was lower-middle-class English. He leaned down to pick something up from the floor. 'Here, I made you drop this,' he said roughly, and disappeared. He had stuffed a handkerchief, not her own, into her palm.

She got out at the next floor and hid in the ladies'. In the cubicle she unwrapped the handkerchief. Inside she found a folded piece of rice paper on which were written her instructions: she had immediately recognised the style, the secret password and the code. After she had deciphered the text, she had smiled at the sardonic postscript, which might have been written by Mr Behrens himself. 'Blessed are the meek for they shall inherit the earth.' She swallowed it, then felt a rush of pleasure warm her cheeks. She had been gathered back into the fold.

The message had outlined a complicated arrangement of signals and fail-safes, and new tradecraft that depended on beggars as go-betweens. At first she had been sceptical, but then she saw the cleverness. Her masters obviously knew that she was unlikely ever to be out of surveillance. Beggars, the most omnipresent yet invisible section of any community, would in theory be able to approach her wherever she went, causing irritation to anybody who happened to be with her, but no suspicion – especially if she began to give generously to the ragged throngs that clustered outside the public places Yi-liang allowed her to visit. In time she might be asked for specific pieces of information, but for the moment she should do nothing but practise this new tradecraft. Fu-kuei thought it surprising that the Comintern should be in a position to employ Shanghainese beggars, but she knew that the Party's resources were far-reaching, and for a woman like her to hand out alms would not be out of character. Shanghai society women were always experimenting with new religions and charities.

As the weeks went by, Fu-kuei became marked out as a charity stool-pigeon, much to Yi-liang's disgust, although he only shrugged and shook his head indulgently at her new enthusiasm. Several times she heard the password spoken by somebody in a crowd, and blank pieces of paper were passed expertly into her gloved hand.

That had been more than seven months ago, and now her trade-craft had become routine.

These days, smog hung heavily over the metropolis, as if the brooding January sky was allying with the warlords to suppress the tension and expectation that threatened daily to erupt into rebellion in the factories and tenements. Since the heady days of the May 30th Movement the labour unions had been forced underground, but as Fu-kuei reported to her masters, secret cells were proliferating, and the trained revolutionaries who had infiltrated the city from the south – always keeping a step ahead of her lover's raids on their hideouts – were preparing a vast, armed insurrection.

In the last few months, she had found ways to re-establish her contacts with the CCP, at a low level but close enough to hear rumours of the great stratagems being conceived. The Party in Shanghai had determined that this time there would be no alliance with right-wing interests. It was their intention to hand over to Chiang Kai-shek the *fait accompli* of an already-existing soviet in China's most populous city. The workers were already radicalised. Warlord control was weakening. The time was ripe for a rising.

And the head of Marshal Sun's counter-intelligence, her lover, Major Yang Yi-liang, was actively assisting behind the scenes.

It had all begun with what she thought of as his 'midnight confessions', the first of which had occurred only a month or so after her reactivation as a spy. They had made love, he passionately, she pretending, as it had always been since his murder of Barkowitz.

Afterwards he had begun to taunt her with the information that his agents had received intelligence of an arms shipment to be delivered to Communist activists aboard a Russian freighter, giving her times, location and even details of how they were planning their ambush. At first, distrusting coincidence, she suspected that he had discovered the renewal of her spying activities and was laying a trap – so for the next two weeks she had worn the silver brooch on her dress that signalled she was under surveillance, and had not passed on the information. In due course he had told her of the raid's success, how twenty crates of rifles had been impounded, arrests made and one Soviet diplomat quietly expelled from the consulate general. When she had congratulated him, he had looked at her strangely. 'Yes, I'm doing my job,' he said, 'but sometimes I don't see the point of it any more.'

She had thought little more about it. If he had been checking on her, she was reasonably certain that she had allayed his suspicions. But what had been odd was that his 'midnight confessions' continued – with increasing regularity. He told her about another raid soon to take place, this time against a secret Communist cell. Again, she did nothing. Some nights later, he told her that the house had been surrounded and several students and workers had been arrested; only the ringleaders, the professional revolutionaries whom he had sought to capture, had escaped. He did not think they had been warned. He attributed it to bad luck. She had said nothing. He had looked at her severely, then said, 'I wasn't sorry they escaped. Sometimes I question whether I'm in the right job.'

That had been when she suspected that there might be more to this than mere indiscretion. She had felt a thrill in her stomach. Was this some form of overture to her? However, she kept her voice casual when she asked what he meant.

'I don't know,' he said. 'Never mind. I'm just tired. Talking nonsense.'

After a few more 'midnight confessions' she was more certain. For whatever reason, he was experiencing a crisis of loyalty to his warlords. One night he told her about the fate of the people he rounded up for interrogation. 'We have become more and more brutal, Fu-kuei. I'm ashamed. Once I hand them over, these poor idealists – that's all they are – are tortured, starved, sometimes executed, and we are hated because of it. I once believed I was protecting the country from revolution, but more and more, when I see the corruption, the greed of the warlords I serve, I think I'm nothing but a thug protecting some gangster's cartel. I tell myself I'm a soldier, doing my duty. I'm good at what I do, but sometimes, when I've delivered some poor frightened nineteen-year-old girl into the hands of a brute at the gendarmerie, who I know is going to rape her, I think ... Never mind what I think. I shouldn't be discussing this with you.'

She was still suspicious. This was too good to be true – but she could hear no insincerity in his voice. She wanted to believe him, even if she knew it was dangerous. 'You know you can always talk to me,' she had murmured, putting her arms round him and holding his head to her breast. 'Whatever our differences, you know I love you.'

'Sometimes I wonder how different we really are,' he had said.

'What's happened?' she asked cautiously. 'It isn't like you to complain. Is your position being undermined at work? Is it politics?'

He laughed. 'My position? I couldn't be riding higher in my General's estimation. I'm the good, reliable retainer. I'm even becoming the trusted confidant, and that means I'm having to wink at more and more abuses and cruelties. Now that war's approaching with the Nationalists, you'd have thought we'd be focusing all our efforts on strengthening our armies. Not a bit of it. I spent the whole of last week organising the transfer of General Sun's private bullion on board armed freighters so it could be shipped to a bank in Hong Kong, out of harm's way.'

'Are you honestly surprised?' she had asked quietly.

'No,' sighed her lover. 'But I don't like having to send a schoolboy to execution for a stupid belief that justice exists in the world. Do you know what we're planning now? You won't believe this latest stupidity ...'

She had listened carefully. Next day, coming out of the Cathay Hotel after her weekly hairdressing appointment, she had extracted her purse, full of cash, from her bag. Seven or eight beggars clustered round her on the steps, and before the Sikh doorman had a chance to drive them away, one had given the password. This time the dollar note she passed over had enfolded a piece of paper with lines of neat code inscribed on it. A week later, a message congratulated her on the accuracy and usefulness of her report, and contained her first orders: 'In view Northern Expedition's entry Wuhan, imperative gauge Shanghai CCP support for United Front plus real capability for solidarity strikes or rising. Contact using any means. Hide links with us, but use Major Y's information for credibility.' Her heart had sunk. She had received an instruction exactly like this during the May 30th Movement. It had led to disaster and tragedy: the death of Chin Hong-chi; the murder of Barkowitz and his innocent assistant . . . Not a day had passed when she had not thought of Chin, and of that body crumpling under the lamppost . . .

She had been uncertain at first about what to do. Yi-liang's surveillance could make it hard for her to make contact with the CCP, even if she could think of a way to find them and win their trust again. Then she had thought of the 'midnight conversations' . . .

'We're going to lose this war,' Yi-liang had told her one night. It was shortly after that terrible week in early November when a wave of demonstrations had spontaneously erupted in some of the workers' districts in sympathy with the events in Wuhan. Warlord troops, reinforced by contingents from Fengtian forces, had fired on unarmed crowds. Yi-liang had locked Fu-kuei into the house 'for your protection'. When he returned, three days later, he was ashen and exhausted. He had drunk nearly a full bottle of whisky in his study but had been unable to sleep. Fu-kuei lay nervously beside him. Eventually she plucked up the courage to ask, 'Are you going to tell me what happened?'

'Haven't you heard?' His voice was slurred from the alcohol. 'We restored law and order.'

She remained silent, waiting. The glow from the electric heater cast a red light over his haggard features.

'We didn't just fire on them – the women, the children,' he continued. 'Not those northern boys. Our allies. No, that wasn't enough for them. They went through the streets afterwards. Gangs of them with swords. Anybody they didn't like the look of they cut off their head, then and there, in the middle of the road, and went on their way, leaving the old women gawping and dropping their vegetables. The streets became very quiet after that.'

'They killed innocent bystanders?' Fu-kuei was horrified.

'Probably. They weren't CCP,' said Yi-liang. 'Counter-intelligence wasn't even consulted. Terror's the thing nowadays.' After that, neither of them could sleep. They lay side by side looking at the flickering reflections on the ceiling, waiting for the dawn. A few days later, he said, 'Face it, they're outgunning us on every front. Their troops, unlike ours, have discipline, and a cause they believe in. They'll take Shanghai. It's only a matter of time. Then they'll be after my head – in revenge for so many of their men that I have put away.'

She felt her heart pounding. The opportunity had come. She might never again have a better opening. She steeled herself – and whispered the words she had prepared: 'You could make yourself useful to them first. Somebody with your knowledge, and skill.'

He stiffened beside her. 'Go on,' he said.

'Chiang Kai-shek might be grateful for the assistance of General Sun's counter-intelligence chief,' she said.

'You mean I should betray my general? Spy on him? I could never do that.'

'Couldn't you? You haven't been speaking very highly of him lately.' She paused. 'Even the Nationalists will have need of an experienced counter-intelligence officer when they take Shanghai.'

He lay silently for a long while. 'I won't deny that I haven't been thinking something along those lines.'

'I could help you,' she said.

'How would you do that?' he asked. 'I see. Through your Russian friends – is that it? That really would be a betrayal, wouldn't it? Is that what it's about? Have they contacted you again?' With a violent motion, he turned in the bed. The next moment she felt his hands round her throat. Panicking, she felt the blood rushing in her ears. There was an unbearable pain in her larynx. She could not breathe. 'You want me to be a traitor to my country. Become a foreign agent, is that it?' he shouted. 'Is that it?' Her eyes clouded with a red mist.

She struggled, pulling feebly at his wrists, and he relaxed his fingers. 'No,' she choked, and began to cough. 'No. I couldn't . . . even if I wanted to . . . You saw to that . . . when you murdered Barkowitz. That's . . . over.' She felt hot tears on her cheeks.

'I'm sorry, my dearest, I'm sorry,' she heard. 'I had to be sure.' And she allowed herself to rock in his strong embrace.

Later they had made a plan. She told him in some detail how she had worked for the CCP in the past. 'You found out all that.' He whistled admiringly. 'I knew you had wheedled something off my desk, but never so much as that!' With his help, she told him, she could do so again. She would report on Major Yang's activities, but this time it would be even more valuable information because he would give it to her himself. He could also tell her how to make contact; with his sources, he probably already knew as much about the CCP organisation as they did themselves. Naturally, they would not believe her at first. It would be dangerous. They might even detain her until the veracity of her information could be proved – but if she could persuade them that the head of Counter-intelligence was really prepared to help them, they would gratefully use his assistance. She would remain the channel of communication. Meanwhile, he would make contact with the right wing of the Party in Nanchang, offering them information about General Sun's military preparations. That would cover his position with both sides of the United Front. He could be a key help when it came to an insurrection of the workers, who would rise when the army was approaching. 'Will that happen?' he asked, raising his eyebrows.

'You told me it would,' she said.

'So I did,' he answered. 'Well,' he leaned his head back against his folded arms, 'you and I are to become traitors. Who would have thought it?'

'Not traitors,' she said. 'Patriots. For China.'

'All right,' he said. 'For China. And ourselves.'

The first step was easy. With his knowledge, she had taken his Rolls-Royce to a house in the French concession, where, he had told her, lived a go-between he had been watching for some time in the hope that it would lead to the capture of bigger fish. She had told the startled man that his cover as a trade representative was blown and recommended that he should disappear – but before he did he would perhaps like to pass on to whomever it concerned that the police knew about a secret meeting that was to be held in a warehouse in Chapei that night, as well as the name of the informer who had told Major Yang of it. She explained who she was, then said where she would be drinking tea the following Tuesday afternoon if any of his friends would like to take the matter further. As a token of good faith, she had passed on copies of counter-intelligence documents that she thought might be of interest. Yi-liang had told her later that the raid had taken place and the warehouse was deserted; the informer's body had been found in the Soochow creek.

She waited in the teahouse but nobody approached her. She was not dismayed. She knew these things took time. Loudly, she told the waitress on departure that she would return the following day, and the next. She had the satisfaction of seeing a man at a corner table briefly lower his newspaper.

Even then Yi-liang tried to dissuade her. When she returned home she found him pacing the carpet. 'Thank heaven,' he cried, embracing her. 'You're all right.'

'What did you expect?' she said.

'I don't like it. I should be the one approaching them. It's too dangerous. These are ruthless people and they might—'

'We discussed all this, Yi-liang,' she said. 'They would never trust you. I must be the go-between. Yes, I'm a little scared, I know the risks – but, Yi-liang, what we're doing . . . it's for China. And for us.' She kissed his forehead. 'Anyway, it's too late now to change our minds. Don't worry. I'll be all right.' She laughed. 'Didn't you say I was a good agent?'

'Oh, I hope so, Fu-kuei. But if they touch a hair on your head . . .'

On the third day she waited, again without any approach. She left the teahouse and walked in the direction of the alley in which Yi-liang's Rolls-Royce was parked. She heard the roar of a motor and the screech of tyres. She saw a black sedan and men leaping out of the doors. She had barely time to notice they were masked before her arms were pinioned and a handkerchief was pressed over her mouth and nose. She smelt cloying fumes. By the time they threw her into the boot, she was unconscious.

When she woke, she was tied to a chair. It was freezing cold, and she felt nauseous. She sensed empty space in the darkness around her. She must be in some warehouse or hangar. From somewhere far away she heard the buzz of machinery – a chainsaw, perhaps. She smelt wood and resin, and, closer, the sour aroma of garlic. She heard breathing. She was not alone. 'Hello,' she called. Her voice echoed. There was no reply. Only heavy breathing, and a harsh cough. She saw a flicker of light and the glow of a cigarette. 'Listen,' she said, 'I want a glass of water. I'm parched.'

Silence.

'You won't be able to interrogate me if I'm too thirsty to speak,' she said.

'What makes you think we're going to interrogate you?' It was a rough, but not unfriendly voice.

'Because I have information for you and you'd be stupid not to. Anyway, if you were going to kill me, you'd have done so already.'

She heard a chuckle and the murmur of low voices. 'You're a brave one, aren't you?' came the original voice. She felt a tug of pain as her head was pulled backwards by the hair, then the cold drip of water on her lips. She gulped gratefully. 'Thank you,' she said.

'We know about you,' said the voice. 'You betrayed us in 'twenty-five.'

'I never betrayed you,' she said.

'You think we'll believe you and your lover-boy a second time?'

'Major Yang was not involved in 'twenty-five,' she said. 'I stole information from him. This time it's different. He wants to help you.'

'Why should he do that?'

'Because he thinks the warlords will lose,' said Fu-kuei.

'And why do you want to help us?'

'Because I believe it's best for China. So does he, actually, but you don't have to believe that.'

'I don't believe anything you say. If you spied on him and he found out, why's he still keeping you as a mistress?'

'He loves me,' she answered. Her explanation was greeted by barks of laughter. 'Why don't you try me?' she said. 'I've given you some information already. It was accurate, wasn't it? You took it seriously enough to eliminate the informer whose name Major Yang gave you. Ask me anything you like, and I'll try to answer you.'

'No one doubts your lover's knowledge,' said the voice. 'You gave us accurate information before. We're not going to swallow that bait again.'

'Kill her.' It was another, reedier voice. 'We've wasted enough time.'

'You heard the boss,' said the first voice. 'Why shouldn't we kill you and have done with it?'

'Because, if you do, Major Yang will hunt you down,' said Fu-kuei. 'That may not particularly alarm you. No doubt you think that all your safe-houses and cells will protect you. They might or they might not – but one thing's for sure. You'll have lost any opportunity to have an insider in the warlord's camp to help your insurrection.'

'Or betray our plans to lover-boy's secret police.'

'You'll never know, will you,' said Fu-kuei, 'if you kill me?'

Someone slapped her hard in the face. The blow was strong enough to knock her and her chair over. Her head banged on the concrete floor. Roughly she was pulled up again. Her cheek was stinging and she felt a trickle of blood on her chin.

'Still so confident?' said the voice.

'Yes,' she said, through the ringing in her head. 'I'm telling the truth. Listen, what have you to lose? I know you're suspicious of us. You have every right to be. I would be if I were you. Give us a test to prove our good faith.'

'A test?' the voice mocked.

'Get Major Yang to do something for you. You have me as a hostage. You can drop me into the Soochow creek if he fails.'

'And what sort of test do you propose?'

'Can't you work that out for yourself?' she said.

They left her in the darkness – with the terror it had taken all her will-power to hide.

She had no way of calculating how long she remained alone in the warehouse. Every anxious moment was an eternity. The buzzing of the saw had long ceased. All she heard was the slow drip of a tap into a pail. It was like the thump of a kettledrum beating her towards her execution. The whole idea seemed foolish now. She had heard the scepticism in her interrogator's voice. Why should he believe her? She imagined Yi-liang pacing his carpet and felt overwhelming regret.

Her hands were pulled roughly, then suddenly released as her bonds were cut. Her fingers tingled painfully as the blood began to flow into them. Then she was blinking as a flashlight was pointed into her face. The beam lowered and in the pool of light she saw a hand thrusting a piece of paper and a pen towards her. 'Sign at the bottom of the page,' said the voice.

'What is it? It's blank,' she said.

'It won't be when your lover-boy gets it. It'll contain our demands – for his test.' The voice broke into a cough. 'This smoking will kill me one day,' he muttered. 'Your end will be quicker if Major Yang doesn't play ball.'

They blindfolded her and retied her hands. She felt a gust of sleet on her face as she was pushed into the open air. Then they entered another building, where she was pulled along clanging corridors, and down some steps into a basement. She was thrust into a small room and stumbled against a metal bed. 'There's a chamber pot somewhere in here,' said the voice. 'There's also some food on the sideboard and a pitcher of water.' They released her hands and slammed the door. She tugged away the blindfold but the room was as dark as the warehouse had been.

The cold, exacerbated by the damp, chilled her from within and without. The floor was covered in water from some broken pipe. Within five minutes of her arrival her teeth were chattering and her limbs were shaking. She found an old blanket folded at the foot of the bed, but she had to wring out the moisture before she could use it, and the clinging fabric only made her colder. She hunched inside it, nevertheless, hoping that the relative warmth of her body might dry it out. It had some effect. Eventually her teeth stopped chattering. She still felt wet and cold, but found she could tolerate it.

Thankfully they had left her her watch. The pale phosphorescence on its dial provided the only source of light, and after hours had passed, she could recognise the fractional gradations of shade that distinguished the walls, the low-slung bed, the sideboard and the bucket. The moving objects, the rats and insects, she could identify by the scurrying sound they made. Her hearing had become honed for want of any other sensory stimulation.

But as her physical situation stabilised, she found herself prey to a worse ordeal: the vicious spiral of her own despair. Alone in the dark, there was nothing to stop her imagination, tantalised by fear, undermining whatever will remained to her.

A rat brushed her ankle. Afterwards she felt grateful, even though at the time her revulsion and rage propelled her from the bed to scrabble on the wet floor in an attempt to catch it. She wanted to swing it by its tail and smash it against the wall. It had been a purely animal reaction, and utterly ridiculous, because how could she possibly have a chance of catching a rat in its own element? But after she had flailed, yelled and sworn, her fury subsided, and some objective part of her saw how comically she was behaving. She began to laugh, despairingly at first, but it broke the spell. She was soaked, she stank after her half-immersion in the filthy puddles on the floor, and her teeth were chattering with cold, but she felt alive. Alive – and angry.

Three days later they came for her. They gagged her, blindfolded her and pushed her back along the corridors. They threw her into the boot of a car. After hours' driving, she heard the boot click open. She had already resigned herself to being executed – but after they had pulled her out, they left her lying in a ditch and drove away.

Eventually, by rubbing her bonds on a sharp stone, she managed to untie herself. From the silhouette of factory chimneys, she established that she was in a field near Woosung.

When she reached home, Yi-liang hugged her, with tears of relief running down his face. Later, she asked him what he had done to convince them, and he showed her a newspaper account of a mysterious breakout in a military prison and the escape of several political prisoners. 'Two guards killed!' she gasped.

Yi-liang shrugged. 'Sometimes you have to show how serious you are prepared to be,' he said.

That had been two months ago.

In the reflection of the jeweller's window, she saw a figure loom up beside her. She recognised the coarse features and the crew-cut. It was the labour leader whom Chin Hong-chi had once brought to the canteen to vet her. She felt a flush of elation: he had a high position in the CCP. She also knew from Yi-liang, the price on his head. She was getting closer to the top. 'We meet again,' she murmured, still gazing at the jewellery in the window.

'They told me you'd moved on from serving soup,' he grunted.

She recognised his voice. She had heard it in the warehouse – he was her interrogator. She felt a rush of hatred and anger, then controlled herself. He had been doing his job as she had been doing hers. By referring to the soup kitchen, he was implying that they had not met since. If that was how he wanted to play it, that was fine with her. 'We do what we can,' she said.

'Some of us think you and your boyfriend can do a little more.' He flipped a half-smoked cigarette on to the pavement. 'Pick that up when I'm gone. Drop your handbag on it or something. Some friends of mine want to meet you. You'll find an address and a time on the paper. Don't take too long or it'll burn away.'

He hawked loudly and slouched off down the street.

Half an hour later, Fu-kuei was in the back of the Rolls-Royce. If the chauffeur had looked into his rear-view mirror, he might have noticed an uncharacteristic expression of contentment on her usually sombre features.

It took Catherine several false starts, a considerable bribe to the black-marketeers, and interminable negotiation in a waterfront teahouse with an assortment of rogues who might have come out of a Fu Manchu thriller by Sax Rohmer, but eventually she and Edmund found themselves in a sampan with a lean old man wearing an eyepatch; he was apparently the captain of a motorised junk. He was smoking a cigarette backwards, with the burning end in his mouth, so as not to waste any of the nicotine and tar, and scowling at them with his one good eye. He seemed about as miserable at the prospect of taking a foreign woman downriver as Edmund was in letting her go. Even at this late stage, sitting on the greasy bench beside her, he was trying to dissuade her.

It was a relief when they reached the junk, a high-pooped affair with semi-rotting timbers, its mast flying an assortment of washing. A row of red-chapped faces gazed blankly down at them from the deck. Catherine counted two women, one old, the other young, and eight children, from early teens to toddler. The sampan shook as a muscular young man jumped down, holding a rope. Flashing Catherine a cheery smile, he snatched her suitcase out of her lap and threw it up to be caught by another man, older than himself and clearly his brother. Then he offered her his hand.

'Catherine, are you sure you know what you're doing?' said Edmund. 'It's not too late to change your mind.'

'Stop fussing. You need the medicines, don't you? I'll be back in less than a month. Mind you keep up discipline while I'm away.' She grabbed the proffered arm, then the rope, and a moment later she was on deck. She smiled at the women and children. One of the little ones screamed and hid behind his mother. The old man and his son scrambled up behind her. She leaned over the rail and looked down for the last time at the sampan, bobbing precariously in the rushing yellow current. Edmund was standing forlornly near the tiller woman. 'Sit down, for God's sake,' she cried. 'You'll fall in the water and then there'll be no bloody point in my going.' Her words were drowned in the clatter of the junk's diesel engine. The sampan began to drift behind them. Edmund was shouting something.

'What?' she called.

'I care for you.'

She thought she must have misheard. She opened her mouth to utter a scornful rejoinder, then felt a moment of weakness, apprehension, regret. The dangerous implications of the adventure she was embarking on momentarily dismayed her. 'Look after yourself, Edmund,' she shouted, but the sampan had already floated away.

She wore her nurse's uniform through the British blockade, and browbeat the surprised tars who stopped the junk into taking her to see the captain of their destroyer. As she expected, her show of authority distracted them from searching the hold – the junk was lying low in the water and she had assumed that her new hosts would prefer their cargo to remain undisturbed.

It was a bonus that she happened to know the destroyer captain from shipboard parties at Peitaiho, and he was sympathetic enough when she explained her intentions not only to let her through the boom but also to detail a launch to accompany her for a day to protect her from pirates near the infamous Lion Rock downstream. 'After that, you're on your own, I'm afraid. You should be all right if you travel at night, but beware warlord gunboats, which still control the river at various points. They're an untrustworthy crowd, bandits every one of them, even if they do wear a sort of uniform. And don't, for God's sake, think of going near the south shore till you reach Nanking – it's crawling with Bolsheviks. Oh, sorry, I forgot,' he corrected himself. 'You're pally with the Bolos, aren't you? That's who the medicine's for, isn't it?' She gave him a withering look, and he laughed. 'Don't worry, politics aren't my concern, thank God. And if a captain can't bend the rules for an old friend, what's the point of him? Anyway, that's it. No more lectures. If I remember correctly, Mrs Airton, you're one to go your own way whatever anybody tells you – and I'm damned sure you're capable of looking after yourself.'

The family on the junk had been suspicious of her when she had first come on board but the expert way in which Catherine had forestalled a search on their vessel, not to mention the face given them by a naval escort purring along the water behind them, made them reassess their passenger's standing. By lunchtime they were all great friends – although Catherine found their accent impenetrable.

They were even more impressed when, that evening, as the launch veered away upstream, all the barbarian sailors stood on deck and saluted. Even the surly old paterfamilias at the junk's tiller returned a silver-toothed smile, while his two lithe sons climbed the rigging and cheered; the women and children waved until the launch disappeared into the descending twilight. As the family chattered excitedly over the box of bully beef that the sailors had swung over before departing, Catherine stared at the now empty horizon, where even the shoreline had become indistinct. Soon the only light visible was the orange reflection of the mast lamp breaking into fragments on the waves, and later, far above her head, the first stars twinkling in the arching cathedral dome of the night sky.

She felt a tug on her arm, looked down, and made out a shadowy bundle of clothes from which a pair of serious brown eyes frowned up at her. She lifted the child and went below to the large cabin where dinner was waiting.

At first it was like a glorious holiday. At dawn on the first morning, they caught up with a fleet of merchant junks and, with safety in numbers, the captain felt confident enough to travel by day. Catherine sat high up on the poop, playing with the children, or attempting to talk to the women. She had established that the elder lady was the captain's wife, and the younger the wife of the middle-aged son, who had fathered the children tumbling over the deck. There was also an ancient grandmother on board, but she remained below decks in her closed-off quarters, where there was a shrine to Ma Tzu, the Sea Mother, who gave special protection to fishermen. They had turned off the engine to conserve fuel, and a brisk wind shook the huge rectangular sail on its bamboo struts. The only sounds were natural ones, the creak of wood and the splash of waves.

Catherine had changed into Chinese peasant costume, with a scarf covering her red hair and a thick padded jacket to keep out the cold. Pale sunshine occasionally broke through the grey clouds, and then she delighted in the sight of the brown sails all around her.

Sometimes she dozed, and in her half-sleep images of the hospital returned – the terrible wounds being treated in the lamplight, the crowded wards, the screaming crowds that came almost daily to demonstrate outside their gates, and Edmund's face, frowning in concentration over his scalpel, nodding in concern when she made her reports, joking calmly with the nurses after some more than usually frightening incident. Once, caught outside in the street, he had been forced to stand for hours as a mob pelted him with mud and vegetables, grimly outfacing his tormentors until with grudging respect they slipped away . . . She would shake herself awake after these dreams, and for a moment feel disoriented, surprised by the inexplicable silence and the wind on her face.

Most strange, and welcome, was the absence of background clamour, the jangling medley of roaring voices, loudspeakers, cries of pain and marching feet from which she could never normally escape ... The junks, gliding past her in their beauty, conjured a peace she had almost forgotten existed – swans on the Cherwell, the creak of oars on the Isis, an exhibition of Chinese scroll paintings that Edmund had once taken her to see in her early days in Tientsin ... And when one of the children appeared beside her, grinning mischievously, her eyes misted over with temporary gratitude.

This idyll lasted two days. At noon on the third day all the junks pulled down their sails. Soon little boats were bobbing between them, and after a while, the elder brother made his way up to the poop to report to his father. 'Warships,' Catherine understood, fifteen miles further down the river. 'British?' she asked. 'Foreign?'

'Sun Chuan-fang,' the old man mouthed slowly, to make her understand that they belonged to the warlords. His two sons shrugged their shoulders, then went forward to cook some rice.

An hour later, when the women began to raise their washing on the mast line, Catherine realised that the junk's skipper intended them to stay where they were. She climbed the steps to the poop to remonstrate with the old man, who sulkily avoided looking at her, gazing off with his one eye towards the blank shore. The younger brother, grinning, performed a pantomime of a hanging. 'You mean it would be dangerous?' she asked. He nodded happily. 'I've paid you for the danger,' she said. She reached in her pocket for some cash, pointed to it, and repeated: 'Danger. I – you – already pay.' All three men contemplated the deck as if they wanted her to disappear. She saw that it was useless to argue.

She paused for a long moment as she made up her mind, then went below to look for her suitcase. She was conscious of the old grandmother examining her with curiosity. She flung open the lid and fumbled among her clothes, slammed it shut and returned to the deck. When she confronted the three men again she held a diamond ring in her palm. It was her last keepsake of her mother, Helen Frances.

Father and sons examined it appraisingly.

'This is worth more than your damned junk,' she said. 'I'll give it to you when we reach Nanking – but only if we leave now.'

The three men whispered together in their strange dialect. Then the youngest went forward, and disappeared into the hold. She waited, palm outstretched, wondering what she would do if they refused. It did not look promising.

She heard the sound of bare feet behind her, turned and saw the younger brother return. He was holding a rifle in each hand, with another slung over his back, and what appeared to be bandoliers hung over his shoulders. Her stomach went cold.

'Night-time,' the old man muttered. 'Wait till night-time.'

The younger man passed her, grinning. He threw one of the rifles at his brother, who caught it; the other he laid at his father's feet. He twirled the third expertly like a baton, then, amazingly, offered the butt to her. 'Danger,' he snorted, and bit his thumb. All three men were smiling now.

Slowly, she nodded, and pocketed her ring. 'Good,' she said. 'Night-time. That's fine.'

They slipped away shortly after dark, travelling for the first few miles under the putter of the engine. The women and children were below. Catherine was crouched amidships with a British army issue .303, leaning against one of the rice sacks that the brothers had spent the afternoon bringing up from the hold. At least she knew now what contraband they were carrying. The brothers had piled the heavy bags along both sides of the junk, heaped up at the prow and around the poop, and Catherine had the whimsical notion that their boat resembled a medieval warship like those she had seen in illuminated manuscripts. She was doubtful that the rice bags would be very effective in the event that a modern warship fired on them, but they were better than nothing. She had ceased to be surprised by anything that came up from below: beside her on the deck was a coalscuttle German helmet from the Great War – the others were already wearing theirs – and at the front of the boat the younger brother was sitting behind what appeared to be an ancient Gatling gun.

At an order from the old man, all lights on the junk were doused, and shortly afterwards he cut the engine. Expertly steered by the older brother, the junk drifted downstream, pushed by the fast current. Catherine felt a weird sense of disembodiment and she thought of the danger that lay ahead. Occasionally, the captain barked an order to one of his sons, or the younger man at the prow would shout a warning to his elder brother of driftwood in the water, and these brief reminders of human companionship were welcome, because she had rarely felt so alone. She had a vision of Edmund, frowning at her with concern, shaking his head perhaps at her foolishness . . . She had been so beastly to him these last few months. She had been sarcastic, unforgiving, cold. Yet he had never said an unkind word to her. How she wished he was beside her now . . .

She was startled out of her reverie by the sudden clatter of metal and grinding machinery, and a blaze of lights that dazzled her. The deck heaved, rolling her against the mast, and the junk rocked violently on a swell. She was conscious of something huge passing upstream. Lifting her head over the rice parapet she saw the gigantic side of a freighter. In the reflected glare of its electric lights she saw the elder brother and father on the poop deck, both straining on the tiller, and the younger brother standing on top of his rice sacks laughing and slapping his knees. By the time she had calmed her jangled nerves, the freighter was dwindling into the night. She had read a name as it passed: *Kobe Maru*. Typical, she thought. Catherine Airton arms herself for battle, then gets sunk in a collision with a Japanese freighter. What sort of clowns had she hired?

It must have been two or three hours later that she was woken from a fitful doze by a rough shake of her shoulder. The shadowy figure of the elder brother was kneeling beside her. He seemed to be pressing a finger to his lips and pointing ahead. As she peered into the impenetrable blackness he returned to his post. She groped for the helmet and placed it on her head, tightening the strap. It was heavy and scratched her skull. She searched for her rifle, and panicked when she could not find it. For two minutes she crawled over the deck, eventually discovering it against the doors that led below. Panting, she returned to her position against the rice wall. With trembling fingers, she reached into her pocket for a cartridge and slipped back the bolt. There was a flutter in the pit of her stomach, and a fire of nervous energy in her limbs. She knew the feeling: she had experienced it before during a brief fling with a naval aviator at Peitaiho, when he had offered to take her on an illicit flight in his biplane. It was exhilaration. Excitement. Anticipation. Cautiously, she lifted her head over the rice-bag wall.

At first she could see nothing and wondered if it was another false alarm. Then, far ahead, she was surprised to make out a faint phosphorescence like moonlight on the water – but there was no moon on that overcast night. She shivered involuntarily. The river must be narrower here, she thought, because the junk was drifting faster, the wash susurrating on the prow like wastewater trickling down a drain. The creak of the bending mast and straining timbers sounded equally loud, threatening to give them away. By now she had recognised those pale pools of colour for what they were. A search-lamp was playing over the water, and as they drifted closer, she saw anchor lights, and the dim orange glow from port-holes. When she strained her eyes she was able to distinguish the leaden shadow of the ships' superstructures, the sharp cut of the bows, the humps of the gun turrets and, oddly, white shapes fluttering like bats around the masts – underwear being blown in the wind – which dashed her last hopes that these might after all be friendly foreign naval vessels. Over the sound of the waves and the timbers, she recognised the unmistakable metallic noise of bolts being clicked on her companions' rifles, and the rattle of the ammunition belt being adjusted to the Gatling. The old man was now at the helm, steering through the blackness that cloaked the southern shore.

With horrified fascination Catherine watched the first gunship looming up towards them. It was as if the course of time had slowed, but suddenly the vessel was dead parallel. Its metal flanks inched past in a ghastly slow motion. Thankfully its search-lamp was pooling the water safely to port, but Catherine, who could see the activity on board – a sailor smoking by a rail, another on watch by the prow – could hardly believe their own invisibility. The few seconds it took to pass were like eternity. Yet they remained unobserved. Catherine gasped and realised she had held her breath for more than a minute. Soon they were bearing down on the second ship, anchored about a hundred yards further downstream.

This time, also, they were in luck. The search-lamp was playing across the water on the other side. Catherine, scanning the decks, saw no movement aboard. They passed the bows, the forward guns, the control tower. When they were amidships, she caught a burst of music and singing from an open cabin window. They were approaching the stern now. Only a few more yards and they would be past. Already she began to experience the elation, the intoxication of triumph . . .

A flash of light blinded her with almost physical force, and she lurched backwards behind the rice bags. The whole junk was illuminated with photographic clarity. Blinking, she saw the elder brother on the poop, shading his eyes. His father, behind him at the tiller, was staring grimly ahead, his chiselled features outlined starkly in the glare. Then, the gunship sounded its klaxon. She saw the arcs of orange flame before she heard the gunfire. The younger brother was churning the handle of his Gatling. His brother and father were firing their rifles. It was as if the sky had unleashed a clatter of tropical rain. She heard bullets thudding into the rice bags, the hornet hiss of projectiles passing over her head; then two loud cracks, a high-pitched whine and a roar. A fountain of icy water cascaded over her shoulders. Fumbling with her heavy rifle, blinded by spray, Catherine felt the bag give way and found herself sliding downwards in a slither of wet rice grains that clogged her lips and nostrils. Inadvertently her finger curled on the trigger and the shock of the report threw her backwards against the mast. She found herself lying not uncomfortably on her back, watching the firework display above, waiting for the shell that would blow apart their frail craft.

Then, suddenly, mysteriously, as if a curtain had descended on a play, everything was as pitch black as before. The brother at the prow yelled something indecipherable, half in triumph, half in pain. A fraction of a second later the clatter at the side of the boat ceased, and the thunder of the guns faded until the vague rumble was as inconsequential as a faraway storm. She heard the diesel stutter into life, and felt the wind on her face again.

A few minutes later the elder brother came forward with a lamp, grinning from ear to ear. He gestured to her to follow him. Their feet crunching over a carpet of rice and loose chips of wood, they made their way to the prow, and there she saw what had caused his apparent hilarity. The younger brother, clutching his left leg, was reclining in a chaos of fallen rice sacks, out of which the Gatling barrel protruded, feathered with rice fluff. Her nurse's eye immediately saw that a bullet had passed straight through his calf.

The elder brother's merriment had been caused by concern. In the years she had spent in China, especially the last few months, Catherine had learned that what foreigners took for callousness was often no more than an attempt to disguise fear. She imagined that her companions were all as shaken as she was by their narrow escape. She hardly dared imagine what would have happened had not a lucky burst from the Gatling gun knocked out the search-lamp just before the younger brother had been wounded. She cleaned and bandaged his leg and assured his father and brother that no bones were broken or arteries cut and that the hero would walk again. After he had been carried below to the wailing attentions of the women, she sat on the poop with the other two men to share the foul-tasting *gaoliang* wine that the elder brother had produced from the hold, and experienced a night of almost abandoned gaiety. By morning, the skirmish with warlord gunboats had become a battle of epic proportions, and the old man was blinking roguishly at her with his one good eye.

In the grey dawn light, the battered junk puttered into a side stream where the reed-covered banks offered a degree of safety from prying eyes. The elder brother staggered below, returned with some quilts, and the three lay where they were on the untidy poop, their heads resting on perforated rice sacks. For a while, Catherine was unable to sleep and gazed up at the great white canopy of the sky. She saw the ragged V of wild geese flying to the south, listened to the lap of water on the gunwales, and smelt the vegetable fragrance of the creek. She found herself wondering at the scale and variety of this vast country, with its contrasts of brutality and tranquillity, its depths of squalor and the almost perfect beauty in the most unexpected places. As her eyes closed, it occurred to her how insensitive she had been, how arrogant, how blind – and it baffled her that she had passed half of her life without truly appreciating how wonderful it was merely to be alive.

The rest of the voyage passed without undue incident. They travelled at night, sleeping through the day. One afternoon, anchored in a canal, they found themselves surrounded by long skiffs from which fishermen cast their nets. The delicate coils would lift and settle on the surface, the silk shimmering like the wings of insects making their way slowly across a summer pond. On another day they watched a cormorant fisherman. Carefully he placed the bird in the water; there was a flurry of splashes, and the long black neck emerged with a silver fish in its beak. Catherine believed, on those occasions, that she had been wafted back into an eternal China, unaffected by the centuries of wars and turmoil.

It was a strange contrast: the balmy days and the nervous nights. When they crept by the Nationalist-occupied port of Kiukiang, they were as tense as they had been on the night that they had run the gauntlet of the gunboats. They could see the watchfires on top of the high, medieval walls that rose out of the river, and were convinced that they would at any moment be stopped by one of the small patrol craft drifting silently near the docks; in the event they glided by unobserved. Three nights later they passed the border between Kiangsi and Kiangsu provinces, and a day after that the peace of the river was disturbed by the far-off noise of battle. At night the line of the southern shore glimmered with sheets of fire that resembled lightning on the horizon. Catherine and her companions watched silently, keeping their own thoughts. When the noise of battle passed behind them, the younger brother became merry again and sometimes the silence of the night passages would be livened by his deep-throated chanting of ancient songs. Like the sough of the wind and the splash of the waves, the great sky and the endless horizon, these were in harmony with the timeless traditional rhythms of the river, ever transmuting, never changing. It seemed impossible to imagine that such a journey could end.

When, one day, the old captain told her that they had reached the last stretch of their voyage, Catherine was overwhelmed by a sense of melancholy and regret.

That evening, before they set off, they had a feast below with the women and children. The old man's wife cried and clung to Catherine's arm throughout the meal. Catherine brought out presents for the children – pencils, crayons, wooden toys – that Edmund had had the forethought to send with her. She chose articles of her own spare clothing for the women, and for each man she had a penknife made of Sheffield steel.

As dawn was breaking, they anchored at Hsiakwan, the port of Nanking, where Catherine saw a fluttering Union Jack on the stern of a British destroyer moored mid-river. Half a mile away loomed the massive walls of the city but, looking at the waterfront, which was not dissimilar to the ferry pier at Hanyang, she had the strange feeling that she had arrived back where she had started.

Two hours later she was standing on the deck with her suitcase, surrounded by the whole family, even the grandmother, who had insisted that she, her chair and her blankets be carried above for the departure of their honoured guest. Catherine felt reluctant to leave them: the bustling city intimidated her, challenging her with her own reawakened responsibilities. She felt like a child about to be packed off to school again after the summer holidays. She had one final piece of business to attend to, her last gesture of gratitude, and she wanted to hold off the moment for as long as she could.

Eventually there were no more courtesies to extend, no more hands to shake, no more children to hug. She took the father and brothers aside, then reached into her pocket for the diamond ring. 'Thank you,' she whispered, and pressed it into the captain's hands.

All three laughed. With some consternation, she saw the younger brother take the ring from his father, and limp towards the small mirror attached to the mast to ward off evil spirits. With some force, he scratched the surface with the edge of the ring. Then he drew Catherine by the arm to the mirror. There was no mark on the glass. He showed her the ring where one side of the diamond appeared to have disintegrated. Then he reached into the pocket of his filthy jacket and pulled out a piece of folded black cloth. He unrolled it, and she caught the sparkle of gemstones. He picked out a diamond at random and drew it across the mirror. The thin scratch was unmistakable. Now all three men and even the women were grinning at her.

Her ears burning, Catherine understood. 'You knew all along it was a fake stone! But why did you agree to fight the warships?'

The old man took her hand, his one eye twinkling as brightly as the stones. 'You – already – help – us.' He mouthed each word, as he always did, assuming that, as a foreigner, she was incapable of understanding otherwise. 'You – stop – British sailors – searching boat. We – owe – you,' he said. 'Now – friends in Shanghai – Communists – get – guns. No problem.'

'Guns?' she exclaimed. 'I thought you were smuggling rice.'

'Rice and guns,' smiled the elder brother.

The whole family was laughing, she could not tell whether at her naïvety or at the fact that her cheeks were now the colour of her hair – and then she was laughing with them. Typical, she was thinking. Oh, Helen Frances, you leave your daughter an only heirloom, and it's fake! And, Catherine, you risked your life to bring arms to the Bolsheviks!

Laughing and crying, she hugged each member of the family in turn, from the youngest to the oldest, and walked down the gangplank on to the dock, with a feeling of lightness in her heart.

Major Ti Jen-hsing and his men were standing shoulder deep in the freezing water of a canal. Their faces were pressed into the oozy mud bank, the black water behind them rippled like a lava flow with the reverberation of explosions, and their whole universe shook with volcanoes of violence, fire and noise. Ti lost more than twenty men that night, some killed by shellfire, others from exposure or by drowning. He exhorted and encouraged the shivering line to sing to keep awake; but many of the new intake, stretched beyond endurance, closed their eyes, drifted into dreams and slipped quietly under the icy surface. Their bodies floated behind their comrades like shadowy driftwood, rolling and turning when a shell burst close, or bumping gently against each other in a swell. When, shortly before dawn, a lull in the bombardment allowed the numbed survivors to charge over the lip of the bank and across the fields, Ti lost a dozen more to machine-gun fire before they reached the entrenched enemy position. The barrage in the night had fallen indiscriminately on both armies, and the defenders were as battered and shell-shocked as their attackers. Resistance was token and most held up their hands in surrender. But neither Ti nor any of his soldiers was in a mood for mercy and they bayoneted every man.

That had been a relatively minor skirmish. General Lin's division had crossed the river with the rest of Chang Tsung-chang's Shantung forces two months before. Ti, exhausted, filthy and cold, had forgotten the number of fierce engagements they had fought since then. He loathed this canal-crossed countryside, with its sucking mud, its stench of manure and corruption, so unlike the dry northern arable plains where he had trained. Nor had there been any of the rich pickings his men had anticipated – if anything, these impoverished hamlets in the estuary lands offered less than the villages in the north. In peace they had been taxed into destitution and at the approach of armies most families had loaded any valuables they had left on to their sampans and disappeared among the maze of waterways. So Ti's soldiers, expecting to live off the land, were hungry too. Unlike the warlord forces, the National Revolutionary Army had an efficient commissariat. Ti's men no longer counted success in terms of how many of their enemy they killed or captured, but in how many knapsacks of provisions they picked up from the field.

A week after their trial in the canal, Lin's division had advanced to a position on a low ridge, facing the army of a minor Kiangsu warlord who had gone over to the Nationalists' side. For once there were no canals to cross, but the no man's land was even more formidable because of that: a slope of dried-out barley field rolled half a mile down to a stream and a clump of woodland in which the enemy forces were dug in. If Lin, as expected, gave the order to attack, they would face withering fire before they came near the enemy. The only cover between was a walled Christian monastery. Ti, looking through his binoculars, saw white flags fluttering from the church steeple and the roofs of the various buildings. The roofs would offer good vantage-points to site machine-gun posts or mortar batteries, he thought. He calculated how long it would take his companies to run the distance, and scanned the slope for any folds or contours that might offer protection. He saw none. He would lose half of his men before they reached the monastery walls. There would then be a further three hundred yards and the stream to cross before they reached the enemy – and since he would be at the head of the charge, he would be one of the first to fall.

He shrugged. Up to now he had been fortunate. He could not expect his luck to last for ever. He thought that perhaps he should write a letter to his father. If it was found on his body after the battle, someone might deliver it. But what was the point? He had nothing to say. It was noon: a pale sun was in the sky and there was grass, not mud, to lie on; the rich colours of wood and earth glowing in the clear winter light gave the illusion of warmth. It would be another hour before Colonel Yen's deputation returned.

It would be good, he thought, if the colonel's negotiations were successful. On the whole he would prefer to live out another day. He knew that Lin did not like to waste his forces without advantage – not that that cold fish cared if his men lived or died.

He had earlier watched Yen's progress through his binoculars until he disappeared under the shade of the trees. The officer's face had been anxious when he had taken his place in the motorbike sidecar, clutching his little white flag of truce. Ti could understand why: a flag of truce was usually effective only until you were within range of enemy machine-gun fire. Yen had received a direct order from Lin. Faced with the certainty of execution by firing squad if he did not go, he had adopted the less risky course – and his gamble seemed to have paid off. The enemy were clearly prepared to listen to what Lin had to offer.

Ti was not optimistic that Lin's bribe would be accepted. War had changed since the days of his first campaign, when he had naïvely believed that payment of a bribe was dishonourable. Today settlement of a dispute by such means seemed like a civilised courtesy from another age.

Perhaps it was only Ti who had changed. He, too, had once thought he represented the ideals of a modern China. No more . . . He had long ago burned the books in his knapsack as fuel to keep out the cold. He had learned to kill, loot and steal to survive; he was an automaton who obeyed orders; he believed in nothing, except that he hated the enemy, and the enemy was anybody who stood between him and his most basic desires – the soldier who attempted to deny him life, the farmer who sought to hide his food supply, the village girl who struggled when Ti wanted satisfaction between her legs. He lay back in the grass, chewing a dry stalk of barley.

He was woken by cheers. He sat up, rubbed his eyes and reached for his binoculars. The motorbike, with Yen in the sidecar, was returning up the slope, and beside it, on a well-groomed horse, a cadaverous man with general's epaulettes on his shoulders and a plumed kepi on his head. A corporal rode behind him holding aloft a torn Nationalist flag. Switching the glasses to the wood-line, Ti observed knots of bedraggled soldiers spilling out into the sunlight. Many had tied white flags to their rifles; others, weaponless, were waving their arms in the air, presumably cheering. Many of his own men had left their positions and were running down the slope. A more disciplined cluster was marching behind General Lin, who was riding slowly down the hill to meet his surrendering opponent. Ti felt a flush of pride, and in a moment he was on his feet cheering as well.

The surrender was perfunctory. The two generals saluted. The corporal with the flag passed it to his warlord, who presented it to Lin, who passed it to his black-bearded bodyguard. The two generals then turned their horses up the slope, and made their way to Lin's tent.

Ti walked down to observe the fraternisation going on in the valley. The brown earth of the millet fields was scattered with discarded Nationalist armbands. It was already difficult, from uniforms alone, to distinguish which soldiers had originally belonged to which army. They sat in circles on the ground sharing liquor and tobacco, but there seemed little of what either side really wanted, which was food. This warlord's army seemed not to have benefited from Nationalist logistics, and was as starved as their own. As he walked among the men, Ti heard complaints, jocular at first but becoming more bitter: avoiding slaughter was all very well, but what a soldier really wanted was loot. A large truculent sergeant accosted him: 'Major, when are we to get the order?'

'What order?' snapped Ti.

The man pointed an unsteady finger in the direction of the monastery, darkly silhouetted against the pink of the evening. 'To take that, of course. They say its stores are stacked with grain. They're rich, these foreign devils. And my friend here,' he put his arm round a corporal from the other army, 'tells me that the place is full of refugees, with their pigs, and their chickens . . .' He paused meaningfully. 'And their women.'

'Christian women?' Ti pretended to laugh with them. 'Looking to be converted, are you, Sergeant? I'd be careful of that lot. Might put a spell on you. Shrivel your frog with all their prayers and singing.' He clapped him on the back and moved on, worried. If there was one order that was sacrosanct, it was that foreigners should not be molested and that their property should remain untouched. General Lin had lectured all his officers on the dangers of provoking the foreign powers into entering the civil war, and would never condone the sacking of a religious house for loot and plunder. The men were angry, though. Discipline was slipping. Ti wondered whether he should report the matter to Colonel Yen – but he had passed the man earlier: he had been sitting in a circle with some of the warlord's officers getting as drunk as the men. He shrugged.

During the night, he woke to find the black beard of Lin's body-guard almost brushing his cheek as he squatted above him. 'Come, Major,' he whispered. 'The general wants you.'

Lin was waiting by his tent. A black cape hung to his ankles. He wore his forage cap low over his eyes. His scarred face appeared skeletal in the flickering shadows of the fire. The bodyguard re-appeared leading three horses. Nobody spoke. They rode over the ridge and down into the valley in the ghostly blue moonlight. They had to pick their way past the scores of drunken bodies scattered over the field; to Ti it looked more like the aftermath of a battle than an orgy. When they reached the walls of the monastery, they dismounted. The bodyguard kicked awake one of the sleeping soldiers and ordered him to guard the horses. They entered the courtyard through the remains of a timber gate that must have been blown open by an explosive.

A huge fire was burning in the centre of the yard, which was packed with men staggering about in various states of intoxication and undress. Some soldiers were roasting pig carcasses on long spits. Others were squatting on the flagstones, tearing at the flesh of chickens, the fat running down their chins. Two men were fumbling through the steps of a peasant dance to the accompaniment of an out-of-tune flute and the banging of makeshift drums.

To the side of the square Ti saw a pile of prone figures, who seemed to have passed out on top of each other. Then he noticed the staring, fixed eyes, and realised they were not soldiers: they were in farmers' clothes and were of all ages – he saw the gnarled features of old men, and the smooth faces of boys. They had been bayoneted or shot. One of the bodies was clothed in a brown robe; the prominent nose and neat beard showed he had been a foreign priest.

At the far end of the courtyard, he made out long, shuffling queues of soldiers. Some were chatting quietly among themselves; others smoked or dozed on their feet. Occasionally a man would come away, fumbling with his trousers. Then Ti saw the thin female shanks, knees bent upwards towards their bellies. He counted nine or ten peasant women, being methodically raped.

General Lin showed no reaction, except to pull his forage cap further forward over his face. The three made their way unnoticed to a door in the side of the building. On the way, the bodyguard snatched a smouldering branch from the fire and a bottle of wine from the hands of a drunken soldier. He soaked the branch in the liquor and produced a slow-burning flame. The dim light cast by this makeshift torch was enough for Ti to perceive a line of doors at regular intervals along the whitewashed corridor, each opening into what appeared to be a monk's cell. The bodyguard kicked them open one by one.

In the first they found a group of officers taking turns with two girls, whom Ti assumed were either prettier or younger than the women outside. They did not notice their general in the shadows but shouted drunkenly at Ti, 'Find your own. These are ours.'

They passed on.

The second cell was empty.

In the third they discovered a European priest nailed to the wall with bayonets through his wrists and ankles. He was moaning. At a nod from Lin, the bodyguard handed the torch to Ti and went inside. He came out a moment later, cleaning his knife blade with a towel.

Lin must have caught the shocked expression on Ti's face. 'You did not expect me to be merciful, perhaps?' he murmured. 'It was sacrilegious of our men to inflict such torture on the man, though the imagination in their method surprises me.'

They found Yen in a large cell, brightly illuminated by candles. He was in bed with a shaven-headed European woman, quite young, who was whimpering beneath him as his heavy haunches thumped up and down above her spreadeagled legs. Above them, a small icon of the Virgin Mary gazed down sadly. Another, older, woman, also naked, was gagged and tied to a chair; her head, which had been shaved less recently, was covered with a light brown fuzz, matching the colour, thought Ti, of her fixed eyes, now turned wildly towards these new intruders.

The evidence of Yen's violence was all over the room. Scattered over the floor were torn black robes, ripped white cowls and two crucifixes that had clearly been torn off the nuns' necks, because the strings had broken and beads had rolled over the stone floor. The body of a white-bearded priest lay behind the door; he had been shot between the eyes.

Lin coughed. Yen leaped off the woman, startled, and stood to attention, clutching a sheet to his crotch. The girl curled into a ball and cried. 'General,' he stuttered, 'my apologies. I had not known that you were coming. These – these nuns—'

'Yes, Colonel, what about them?' asked Lin, coldly.

'Well, General, I – I didn't mean to monopolise them. If you were interested, I could – I could – have them cleaned up, bathed and—'

'No, Colonel, I do not share your tastes . . . but you are off duty and may do as you like with your free hours. Was this the abbot?' He kicked the sandals lightly with his boot.

'I presume so, General. He – he tried to resist arrest, and—'

'He tried to protect those nuns from you. It is a pity, because I would have liked to talk to him. Where can I find the chapel?'

'I – I think it is through the door at the end of the corridor, on the other side of another small courtyard . . . General, if I can be of help in any way—'

'No, I have no further need of you. You may carry on.'

Ti could contain himself no longer. 'General, I must protest. Your standing orders – these are foreigners—'

'In good time, Major. In good time.'

They crossed the second courtyard and entered the dark chapel. Lin waited while his bodyguard moved round the room lighting the candles on the altar and on the pillars. Then he progressed round the walls and paused in front of the centrepiece of the altar, which was a portrait of the Madonna and Child. 'This has no particular artistic value, but look closely,' he murmured. 'Is it not interesting, the resemblance of this Mary goddess to the Buddhist saint, Kuan-yin? The expression is benevolent, calm and compassionate. Even the colour of her cloak, blue, representing the ocean that surrounds the world, is the same as in many portraits of Kuan-yin. Does it not strike you as coincidental that two religions, separated by centuries and distance, appear to worship the same spirit? Do you not sometimes wonder, Major, if there is not one religion behind them all? The ancients' worship of the Earth Mother was universal. You are silent, Major. Does what I say not interest you?'

'It is fascinating, General,' said Ti, 'but I am only a soldier and not used to thinking of such things.' He could not quite believe that after the sights they had just witnessed they were calmly discussing paintings.

'You should,' said Lin. 'There is nothing more important to understand than our origins, particularly in these days of chaos.' He moved on to study the paintings in the alcoves behind the pillars. 'Ah, Major, come and look at this one,' he said. 'This I had not expected to see.'

It was a small oil of a woman, wearing a loose green robe and red cloak. She had full, pouting lips, pink cheeks, and a frank, knowing expression under half-raised eyebrows. What impressed Ti was the long auburn hair flowing over her shoulders. It reminded him of somebody, a foreign woman he had once met, but in his tiredness and anxiety he could not think whom.

'This is a copy, Major, of a famous painting by an Italian master.

The original is a fresco in a church in Italy, but I once came upon a reproduction in a book. This is the Magdalene, one of the less respectable Christian saints. The interesting thing about her is that she was a prostitute. It is interesting, is it not, that the Christians should venerate such a woman? You are an educated man, Major. No doubt you are aware that the earliest religions were fertility cults that probably originated in the worship of the female sexual organs. Were you also aware that another term for priestess was "Holy Whore", and that coupling with her was considered a form of communion with the Earth Mother?' He lightly ran his finger over the tresses of the Magdalene's hair. 'Yes, I would be pleased to add this painting to my collection, more so because I once had dealings – intimate, unforgettable dealings – with a woman whose looks uncannily resembled the prostitute saint portrayed here. Curiously, her daughter resembles her even more.'

Ti was losing patience. 'That is very interesting, General, but what has it to do with the situation in the monastery?'

Lin threw back his head and laughed, a high-pitched, sinister squeal. 'You might say everything, Major. What have we been observing tonight in the courtyard and in the cells if not a form of fertility ceremony? But I am teasing you, Major, and you are right to remind me of my duty.'

'General, if it was discovered that our troops have perpetrated an atrocity against foreigners, there will be a diplomatic incident.'

'Then we must make sure no one hears of it – at least, not that we perpetrated it.'

'I do not understand you, General,' Ti said.

Again, Lin laughed. 'I was right to keep my eye on you. You are conscientious, and you think of the bigger picture.' He observed Ti closely, a twisted smile on his disfigured lip. 'I appreciate your concern, Major, but for the moment we are to do nothing.'

'Nothing?'

'I would not wish to interrupt the hard-earned and well-deserved recreations of my men. Let them enjoy themselves at least for this night. In a while, you will ride back with me to the camp – unless you yourself are interested in participating in the entertainments offered here . . . No? . . . I am pleased to hear it . . . Tomorrow morning you will return here with two armed companies. Those soldiers and officers foolish enough to be found here you will arrest. You will arrest Colonel Yen whether he is here or not.'

'Colonel Yen?'

'As you have reminded me, Colonel Yen has disobeyed standing instructions. He will be shot. You may punish ordinary soldiers as you like. I suggest something notional, a light pack drill, perhaps. Officers will be decimated, however. You may choose which ones you shoot. You will spare the competent ones, naturally. Be careful to include officers from our own side as well as from among our new allies. We must be seen to be fair. When you have cleared the monastery of our men and, more importantly, of any grain or provisions, you will burn it to the ground.'

Ti's mind was reeling. 'What about the women? And any foreign monks or nuns who are still alive?'

'I don't expect any of them to be alive, Major. This is to be a tidying-up operation. I expect you to be finished by mid-morning at the latest. Then you will form our divisions – theirs and ours – into companies and we will begin our retreat to Nanking.'

'Retreat?' Ti was outraged. 'But we have been winning every engagement.'

'*We* have, Major. My colleague, the Dog General, has been less capable. The Nationalists are advancing on all fronts. It is a shame, but such are the fortunes of war. It may not be obvious but we are in danger of being surrounded. I am glad that our division has been reinforced. The new intake will serve as useful cannon fodder to cover our retreat.'

'General, they have their own warlord.'

'Ah, yes, but sadly, in my tent tonight, he ate something that disagreed with him. My bodyguard found it necessary to bury him. Putrefaction follows quickly on food poisoning. Naturally there is no necessity to inform his troops of his demise. They will hear that he has left them with my gold and their share of the booty. I imagine they will be upset, but perhaps that will make them all the more willing to serve a newer, fairer master. Now, are there any questions, Major?'

Ti's head was swirling with the implications of what Lin had told him. 'Just one,' he muttered. 'You said we are not to be blamed for this atrocity. How will we hide it?'

'The Nationalist flag that was surrendered to us, Major. Leave it on the smoking ruins. I am sure the world will draw the right conclusions. Any more questions?'

'Colonel Yen, sir. If he is to be shot tomorrow, who will replace him?'

'Why, you will,' said the General. 'As soon as he is buried you will take his commission. Congratulations, Major – or should I say Colonel?'

Lin nodded dismissively and turned back to the painting, which his black-bearded bodyguard was removing carefully from the wall.

As Ti rode away under the moonlight over the field of corpses (as he feared many might become if they slept outside on a cold night), his tired mind was still trying to make sense of what he had seen and heard. Twelve hours ago he had been expecting certain death. Now he was to become a colonel. He would have to slit a few peasant throats and shoot some of his fellow officers first – that was a mildly repulsive prospect – but he appreciated the clarity of his general's plan. He would have no compunction about shooting Colonel Yen and, now he thought about it, one or two other officers who did not pull their weight. No, he had no objection to his orders. Perhaps he should write to his father after all, he thought suddenly. The old man would be proud to know that his son had earned another promotion.

Far away from any war, in the northern city of Dairen, a tall figure in a Homburg and astrakhan-collared overcoat was tapping his way along a snow-dusted street. The grand European buildings, built by the Tsarists to adorn their Manchurian showpiece, a warm water port on Pohai Bay, showed signs of ageing. In the cold north the most Olympian façade became blackened quickly by soot, and in the twenty years since the city had become the capital of Japan's Kwantung colony, the once proud city had lost some of its grandeur. Over the doors of the St Petersburg-style cafés, cloth hangings advertised the *sashimi* to be found within. Along the wide boulevards where once dandified officers had promenaded with their ladies in carriages and barouches, a padding rickshaw boy would pull a matron in her kimono, a Japanese settler would trot by on his straw *zori*, farm produce bundled on his back, or a banker and an officer would pass the time of day. Not that Henry Manners noticed his surroundings. He was irritated, preoccupied and wishing he had had a drink before he set out. He had been summoned to see General Taro Hideyoshi at the headquarters of the military police, the Kempeitai, and he did not know why.

As usual he was kept waiting on a bench in one of the white-washed corridors. It was all part of the regular humiliation, which was why he hated coming here. The seat was slung too low for the comfort of his long legs, and it was painful, with his old war wound, both to sit down and get up. When Manners showed his disdain or, in the early days, raged at the delay, the guards merely sniggered behind a veil of forced politeness. Nowadays he waited patiently, reading his newspaper and pointedly ignoring the chained criminals under bayonet guard who were sometimes placed on the bench beside him, as he did the prostitutes and informers, and the arrogant officers clicking their boots and scraping their sword scabbards on the marble floor as they strutted by. This time he was kept waiting for three-quarters of an hour. He had forgotten his newspaper, and was therefore in a foul mood when Taro's orderly bowed before him, telling him that the general was pleased to see him now.

As usual, when he entered the elegant office with its *shoji* wall, its calligraphy scrolls, the ancient suit of polished red armour topped with a devil-masked, antlered helmet, and the gold-tasselled samurai swords, General Taro was all smiles and apologies. 'Henry-san, I have kept you waiting again. I am so sorry but, you understand, we are exceptionally busy these days and so many unexpected emergencies arise . . .'

It was an old formula and, as usual, Manners saw no point in expostulating. 'Hideyoshi, pleased to see you too, old boy,' he grunted.

The general ushered him into a low-slung chair. 'You will have whisky as usual?'

Manners, as always, accepted. 'Well, Hideyoshi, what can I do for you this time?' he asked, his temper somewhat restored by the prospect of a drink. 'Problems with the drug shipments again?'

'No, Henry-san.' Taro observed him from his elevation behind his desk. 'The recent shipments of opium have passed through smoothly. It was clever of you to find an Englishman in the China Railways to help us, even if he is expensive.'

'He lives beyond his means. That's why we can rely on him.'

'As you, too, live beyond your means, Henry-san. Or do you share a little in the cornucopia of riches the long-suffering Japanese administration provides?'

'If you mean, am I taking a cut, of course I bloody am. And not as much as some of the stooges in your employ.'

The general threw back his white-cropped head and laughed. 'You have always been such a forthright man. That is why I enjoy working with you. May I ask you a personal question? How is your family?'

'My woman? Haruko? She's fine. Why do you ask?'

'No, your daughter, Henry-san. How is she?'

'That old chestnut? As I keep telling you, I don't have a damned daughter.' He glowered over his empty glass, hoping the general would offer him another drink.

Taro pushed over the bottle with an elegant, gloved finger. 'No? Really? Not a red-headed English nurse, who now works for the Communists in Wuhan, and who, in a great scandal, left her husband – also, coincidentally, an official of the China Railways?'

'I don't know what the bloody hell you're talking about.'

'She must be leading a dangerous life now. War is so uncertain, as is revolution. The most violent elements of the criminal under-world tend to gather in such chaotic circumstances – assassins, extortionists. It is impossible to imagine all the ways a person can come to harm, even an innocent young nurse . . . If you were her father, I would have thought you would be concerned for her.'

'Well, I'm not, am I? So whatever threat you're building up to on that score won't cut any ice. Listen, if you're worried about my loyalty, just go ahead and tell me.' With a shaking hand, he poured himself another shot of whisky.

'Oh, I am not worried about your loyalty. But let me tell you a story, Henry-san. A fiction, if you like, as old men such as you and I will sometimes make up over our drinks. Let us say that living in Mukden or Dairen is another old man whose life has led him into strange paths. He is very lonely, this man, and perhaps he hates what he has to do for a living. But one day into his sad life comes a beautiful young woman, whom he realises to his shock is his natural daughter from a previous existence – no, don't interrupt, Henry-san. I am not talking about you. This is only a story about a lonely old man who suddenly finds his daughter again after many years. At first he is naturally very happy to see her, proud of her good looks and accomplishments. Then he begins to worry. His life is so complicated, even shameful, that he does not wish to involve her in it. Perhaps, too, he is a little concerned, because he has many enemies who might one day, if they knew he had a daughter, punish him by punishing her. So, very sadly, he denies he is her father and she goes away.'

'You're barking up the wrong tree, Hideyoshi.'

'As I said, this is only a story. Where were we? Yes, this poor young girl returns to – where? Shall we say Tientsin? She is heart-broken. She has no other family, and the old man discovers, because he keeps a close eye on what happens to her, that she has no source of income. How can he look after her? How to make amends for his cruel rejection? He is clever, this old man – oh, yes, Henry-san, this old man is very clever, and subtle, and he knows how to please many masters and satisfy many objects all at the same time. He happens to be looking for help in his profes-sional work. Let us say he needs a railway official to wink at various dubious packages he intends to smuggle into Tientsin for his employers. And by good fortune he finds such an official, whose lifestyle is not commensurate with his means, and who would be very happy to do small services for our old man in exchange for the vast riches he promises in return. Such windfalls can easily be passed off as gambling triumphs for, by another coincidence, this official happens to be a sportsman – let us say a jockey. Nobody will ever suspect that his newly found wealth does not come from the racetrack. He is extremely pleased to assist the old man – but the old man is not one to give favours for nothing. He sets this young official a condition: he must marry his daughter, and keep her in the style to which she is accustomed. That is no problem for the young man, for the style to which she is accustomed is the same as his own and, anyway, the girl is beautiful. He is a personable young man, and plausible in his wooing. He is assiduous and patient, because he knows the advantages that he will attain if she accepts his hand. The long and the short of it is that the daughter falls in love with him. They have a grand wedding. Everybody is happy, the old man, his employers, his daughter and the railway official.'

'Very interesting,' said Manners. 'And utter balls.'

'Is it, Henry-san? I have noticed that you never told me the name of this railway official to whom each month we channel through you such an exorbitant sum. Not that I care particularly, as long as the job is done, but is there any reason why you should be so concerned to protect his identity?'

Manners gave a barking laugh. 'A journalist always protects his sources. Especially from ruthless bastards like you, Hideyoshi.'

Taro laughed with him. 'All right, let us leave aside the telling of stories and get down to business. As it happens, it is as a journalist that I have called you here today. I have a job for you.'

'Oh, yes? And what do your friends in the Kokuryukai want me to write about this time? More lies about the Bolsheviks?'

'No lies, Henry-san.' He twirled the globe by his desk and pointed to China. 'See the situation today. Warlords in the north, Nationalists in the south – but they are in disarray. Generalissimo Chiang leads the right wing in Nanking, and there is a break-away Communist government under Borodin in Wuhan. Stalemate, which is all well and good. But, Henry-san, the former "Christian general", Feng Yu-hsiang, now in Moscow's pay, is fighting his way eastwards to reinforce Borodin. If he joins him, then the Communists will have as powerful an army as that of Chiang Kai-shek. The generalissimo will have no choice but to pass leadership of the whole Northern Expedition to Borodin. Can you imagine? A Bolshevik government controlling half of China – under a Russian! It is unthinkable, is it not, Henry-san?'

'Yes, I see that it would be vexing for the Japanese imperium.

So, you want me to write another ranting editorial about the Bolshevik menace, is that it?'

'That would be superfluous. Already the editorials of all the foreign newspapers are as vituperative as you have ever been.'

'So what *do* you want from me?'

'We have no contact with Borodin. It would be useful to know what he is thinking, but it is difficult for Japanese these days to travel easily to Wuhan. It is relatively simple for foreign correspondents of the Western press to be given passes through the war zones. Well, Henry-san, you are an accredited foreign correspondent.'

'No,' growled Manners. 'Not on your life. It's a daft idea. With my reputation as a Bolo-basher, Borodin wouldn't see me.'

'Oh, I think he would. That such an enemy of the Communists should travel all the way to Wuhan to interview him would intrigue him – especially since he will know of your connections with imperial Japan. Don't be modest, Henry-san. You are a celebrity.'

'I'm too old to be risking my neck in any damned war. I'm retired. Find somebody else.' Manners poured himself more whisky.

The general sighed. 'I must return to my story, Henry-san, because I did not finish it. I'm afraid it did not have the happy ending I implied. You see, however clever the old man had been, he had not anticipated one thing – that his daughter would tire of her railway-official husband and run away with his brother to Wuhan. Of course, as far as the old man's employers were concerned, there should have been no problem, because the official was still greedy for his money and would continue to provide his little services. No doubt at first the official was even pleased to be rid of a troublesome wife whom he had never really desired – but the arrangement, as far as the old man was concerned, was not satisfactory at all. Without "the family tie" there would be nothing to prevent this young man feeling free to renege on his former agreement, or even to give his allegiance elsewhere – perhaps directly to the old man's employers, Henry-san, who might decide they no longer required the services of an expensive middle man. And as for the daughter, well, if any ruthless character wished the old man ill, what then? His daughter would be entirely out of reach of his protection . . .

Alas, that is as far as my story has got to. I have not thought of an ending yet, Henry-san. Can you help me?'

'Catherine Airton is not my daughter,' he said weakly. 'I've told you a hundred times.'

'Yes, Henry-san, most convincingly. I have been talking about an anonymous old man. I would like to think that he would weigh his options carefully, and perhaps decide that his best course would be in future to work even more industriously for his employers, knowing that, in their generosity, they would certainly give him protection for years to come, and also guarantee the safety of his daughter. What do you think of that ending, Henry-san? Does it satisfy you?'

'You're a bastard, Hideyoshi,' he muttered. 'Yes. Yes, I suppose so.'

'I did not hear you.'

'"Yes," I said. All right, I've changed my mind. I'll do your bloody interview with Borodin.'

'Oh,' the general clapped his gloved hands, 'that is excellent. I am very pleased to hear it. It should not be a difficult task for you. You are an experienced man. All we want is for you to size up the situation and report, and if there should be a problem, to deal with it, as only you know how.'

'The Kempeitai's responsible only for internal security. This has a Kokuryukai stamp, like the drug-running. It's Black Dragon Society business, isn't it? You want me to assassinate him, don't you?'

'I expect you to use your usual resourcefulness,' said Taro. 'Oh, I see that your glass is empty. How inhospitable of me. You are naughty, Henry-san. You have allowed me to become so absorbed in the pleasure of my story-telling that I have forgotten the basic courtesies. In fact, so much have I enjoyed our conversation today that I may break my usual rule and share with you a glass . . . to wish you *bon voyage*, Henry-san, and *bonne chance*.'

13

Nanking Purgatory

From the journal of William Lampsett, Reuters correspondent, Tientsin, 25 March 1927

There is something obscene about coming back to Tientsin. The disinterest goes beyond callousness. All Robby was interested in was showing me his new cocktails.

I am still stunned by the events of the last week, the disgusting scenes as the Dog General's army retreated from Nanking. I suppose I should have stayed to cover the Nationalists' arrival. Then I could have scooped whatever atrocity is supposed to have happened there – but I am surfeited by war and its inhumanities. What I saw was atrocity enough.

For a whole day I watched the Shantung mercenaries streaming through the city gates in the direction of Hsiakwan and the docks. They had taken to the ancient art of pillage with the enthusiasm of newly hatched locusts. During the afternoon they ransacked the department stores. Taiping Road took on the appearance of a Mardi Gras, as brightly coloured frocks and silk nighties, leopardskin coats and sables, broad bolts of satin and worsteds fluttered like pennants from the loosely tied bundles above the looters' heads. Other soldiers had stripped the mechanical- and electrical-goods floors, and staggered beneath ceiling fans, clocks, Singer sewing-machines, refrigeration boxes, a lawnmower, phonograph players and polished cherrywood wireless cabinets. What are they going to do with them? And what will be the fate of the two boxes of croquet hoops and mallets I saw carried on the broad shoulders of a sturdy, bearded sergeant?

The Dog General made sure he was among the first to get away. Settled against the upholstery of an open limousine, its boot piled with trunks and hat boxes, two of his mistresses, one Russian, one Chinese, their necks dripping with pearls, nestled against his beribboned chest. He was shouting and laughing; one white-gauntleted hand poured champagne into the glasses of his cronies sitting opposite him, while the other tapped ash off a big cigar. This was while a column of impressed porters, most without shoes, trudged silently by on the other side of the road.

Eventually I became sick of the dreary progress of mule carts and donkey panniers loaded with the worldly goods of ordinary citizens, stolen from their homes. The victims as usual were the poor.

Catherine was in limbo. The telegraph lines had been cut shortly after she had arrived in Nanking. She assumed that her message had got through to Niedemeyer but she had no way of knowing whether he had found a means of passing it on to Edmund. Last night the retreating warlord forces had blown up the city's generating station and the waterworks. Catherine, sitting in her dark hotel room, the candles extinguished so as not to draw the attention of any drunken looter who might take it into his head to practise his marksmanship at a profile in a lighted window, watched the fires spreading from the Ho Ping Men Gate section, and tried to calculate how many times in her life she had found herself caught up in the débâcle of a defeated army.

As she had anticipated, Jenny Charters had not been remotely amused by her unexpected appearance a fortnight before in Chinese peasant costume, still less when Catherine had explained the reason why she had come to Nanking. Grudgingly, she had shown her to the guest bedroom. When Catherine had come downstairs in a clean frock, Jenny had been somewhat mollified, but it had been a stilted conversation as they sat opposite each other in the drawing room sipping coffee. Jenny prattled on about life in Nanking until Catherine's mind numbed with the tedium. She realised, however, from Jenny's covert glances at the clock on the mantelpiece and the fear in her eyes when Catherine seemed about to bring up any of the taboo subjects – Edmund, George, her marriage – that this mindless chatter was merely her sister-in-law's attempt to hold the fort until her husband returned for tiffin. Jenny, she reminded herself, was of the school that firmly believed 'the man knows best' and would follow her husband's lead on how to deal with a wayward sister-in-law. She wondered if she would regale her women friends with the story of how courageously she had handled her morning's ordeal all alone with her scandalous relative.

Catherine had forgotten that she was a scarlet woman. Somehow, during the seven turbulent months in which she had been running a field hospital, coping with the daily realities of death and survival in a world of warfare, destruction and suffering, it had slipped her mind how important sexual morality was in the larger scheme of things.

Naturally, Lionel had been gravely polite, as befitted the dignity of a mandarin in the Maritime Customs Service. After he had handed his hat, his gloves, his overcoat and his cane to the servant, acknowledged his three children, who had lined up dutifully to greet him, and kissed his wife, he had given Catherine a magnanimous handshake and even gone as far as to peck her on the cheek. Tiffin was a formal occasion in the Charters household, as everything was, and clearly the rules that nothing of moment should be spoken of in front of children and servants applied, so it was another tedious hour before they retired for more coffee in the drawing room. Lionel listened attentively as Catherine explained her predicament, and Jenny sat demurely on the sofa, her hands folded in her lap, apparently studying the flower arrangement in a corner of the room.

'Mmm,' was his considered comment, when she had finished.

'Does that mean you'll help us?' asked Catherine, breaking the long silence that followed.

'I'm sorry, Catherine,' he sighed, 'but I don't see what I can do.'

'Then I'm sorry if I did not explain myself clearly enough. I'm right, aren't I, that freighters of various nationalities travel up the river with permits to pass the naval blockade? I saw one or two on my way down here. My understanding was that their cargos are authorised by the Maritime Customs Service. By you, Lionel.'

'That's correct.'

'Well, with your influence, it would not be difficult, surely, to arrange for regular shipments of medicines to be carried on these vessels and later unloaded in Wuhan for the use of our hospital?'

'I regret that what you are proposing would be tantamount to the smuggling of contraband, Catherine. Technically, you see, your hospital is operating under the auspices of what my masters in Peking would consider an illegal government. Under the present national emergency, what you are suggesting could only be interpreted as an attempt to aid and abet the enemy. My hands are tied, my dear.'

'What twaddle, Lionel!' Catherine exploded. 'Edmund and I have nothing to do with the Bolsheviks. We spend half of our time trying to prevent them closing us down. We wouldn't be aiding and abetting anybody except wounded men who would die if we didn't help them. In the name of charity, please reconsider.'

'It might be easier if you were connected with an international organisation, the Red Cross or the Red Swastika, for example . . .'

'The Red Swastika are corrupt and disorganised, and they see us as competition. Anyway, they aren't getting any supplies in either.'

Lionel shrugged. 'Perhaps if you applied to your socialist friends in Canton. Through this Borodin or whatever his name is . . .'

'I beg your pardon, what do you mean, my "socialist friends"?'

'Aren't you and Edmund socialists? I thought that was the whole point of your quixotic crusade. To bring on the revolution, or whatever Utopia you believe in. Isn't that one of the reasons why you ran away together?'

Catherine was lost for words. Lionel calmly sipped his coffee. It was Jenny who broke the silence: 'George was heartbroken, Catherine. All of us were shocked. We hardly knew how to tell Mother and Father. Catherine, how could you do it? With George's own brother!'

'Do what, Jenny?'

'Elope,' squealed Jenny. She pulled a handkerchief from her sleeve, then dabbed her eyes. 'For so many years . . . After that night, when I saw you . . . I saw you . . . coming out of Edmund's room. All those years, I'd hoped that . . . I tried to forget, but . . .'

With quiet dignity Lionel got up, sat by his wife on the sofa and put an arm round her. 'I hadn't intended to raise this matter, Catherine,' he said, in the portentous tones he might have used to admonish an errant official, 'but I cannot blame Jenny for expressing her feelings. Of course, what you choose to do with your private lives is nobody's business but your own, but you should be aware of the anxiety and distress that your selfishness, and Edmund's, has caused within our family. Can you imagine how difficult it has been for us to explain to our children their uncle and aunt's behaviour?'

'That Uncle Edmund and Aunty Catherine are lovers, you mean?'

'Well, they're young still, so we haven't exactly put it in those terms,' said Lionel primly.

'How prurient you both are. You told them that we've gone away on holiday together, perhaps?'

'It's hardly a humorous matter,' sniffed Lionel. 'Can you deny it?'

'That Edmund and I are living in sin?' She laughed, but suddenly she had an image of Edmund's compassionate face as he unwrapped the bandages on a stomach wound to find a writhing mass of worms where the intestines should have been. She recalled the angry faces of her nurses when she had ordered them to remove a terminally ill patient from his bed in the ward to make way for another patient who had a better chance of survival, and the reproving looks she received when the new arrival had died in the night, while the man they had moved to the squalid dying room lived on for three more days. She remembered how Edmund had held her back when an officer and a squad of soldiers had come to their hospital with a warrant and arrested three recovering soldiers. 'Let them go, Catherine, there's nothing we can do,' Edmund had whispered, as the porters loaded the men on to stretchers and carried them away.

She collected herself, and looked Lionel in the eye. 'You have no idea what sins Edmund and I commit every day of our lives,' she said coldly. 'But you're right. My private life, and Edmund's, is none of your business. I've come here to ask for your help to bring medicine to wounded soldiers.'

'Nationalist soldiers. Bolsheviks.'

'Wounded men, Lionel, deserving of compassion, whatever their politics. Most don't have any politics, anyway. They're conscripted peasants, dying for something they don't understand. I don't care what you think of Edmund and me. Just consider the tragedy that has overtaken this country and what you might do to help. For God's sake, Jenny, Edmund's your brother and he's pleading for your support. So am I.'

For a second, as Lionel reddened, Catherine believed she had got through to him. But he had worked himself into a rage.

'You have a lot of nerve, Catherine, coming uninvited to our home and lecturing us. I don't think you have grasped my position here. Your Communist friends have already forced their way into two British concessions along the river. The situation in Nanking is already delicate. It is neutrality alone that protects us. Do you think I would abandon my responsibilities and jeopardise the safety of my family for a bunch of Bolsheviks?'

'I'm not asking you to jeopardise anything, Lionel. I'm just hoping you might show a modicum of humanity. Will anybody think the less of you if you used your influence to put some medical supplies on a ship?'

'I won't contravene an internationally agreed embargo, and that's my final word as an official of the Maritime Customs Service – but since, my dear, you are also presuming to hector me about humanity, let me tell you something else. I wouldn't help you or Edmund even if I could. What I don't think you realise, living in your world of immorality and naïve idealism, is that civilisation itself is in the balance today. This isn't a simple battle between warlords and Nationalists. The very values and order of our society are being threatened by godlessness and chaos.'

'This is you being neutral, is it? Or are you about to begin a peroration on the White Man's Burden?'

'You can be as sarcastic as you like, but yes. I and people like me – of the same breed as you, Catherine, may I remind you – are indeed devoting our lives to the service of humanity—'

'Service? Do you even know what that word means?'

Lionel sighed. 'It would be profitless to argue further. Anyway, some of us have responsibilities and standards to maintain, thank

God, and I am late for the office. We can talk again after dinner. Perhaps by then you will have decided what you want to do with yourself. I doubt you will be able to return to Hankow. If you wanted to go on to Shanghai I could possibly help you find a berth on a steamer. There are still one or two running. From there my advice would be to return to Tientsin.'

'With my tail between my legs?' She laughed harshly. 'No, Lionel, I shall find a way to return to Hankow with or without your help – and with my medicines. I thank you for your hospitality, and yours, Jenny, but I won't trouble you further. I assume there is a hotel in the city that might overlook my Bolshevik and immoral credentials?'

Tears of outrage were running down Jenny's plump cheeks. 'Well, Catherine, I don't know. I think you're being jolly ungrateful. We take you into our family, a penniless adventuress. Ma and Pa treat you like a daughter. You break their hearts, and George's, who is kind enough to marry you . . . I . . . I just don't know . . .'

'No, I don't think you ever will. Don't ask the servants to bring down my bag. We Bolsheviks believe in equality, you know.'

Lionel, ever the gentleman, rose when she did, then enquired if she had intended to ask him for money. She looked at him with such scorn that he had to drop his eyes.

A few moments later she was in a rickshaw on the way to the Garden Hotel. The first thing she did when she reached her room was to tear off her frock and sink into a hot bath, her second of the day, then put on her spare nurse's uniform. She had felt more soiled after her morning with the Charters than during her whole voyage on the junk.

As she lay soaking in the water, her anger cooling while the heat soothed her limbs, she wondered what Edmund would say when he found out what a mess she had made of her mission. Probably nothing. He would give her one of his sad smiles and thank her for trying. He would think the best of her, and Lionel. He would make excuses for them both. Well, damn Edmund. It was because of the passivity in him that he needed her. It was why they worked so well together – because she would never admit defeat. She was *yang* to his *yin*, or was it the other way round? Damn Lionel. Damn all of them. She would find her own way of getting the medicines.

Was she being unfair? Edmund was a realist, as she wasn't. In their professional relationship, she relied on his strength, knowledge and common sense as much as he relied on her determination, ruthlessness and perversity. It was always Edmund who held the bigger picture, viewing the land like a hunt master while she was his foxhound snapping with her sharp teeth. That the world should think they were lovers! Absurd!

Yet lying in the bath, the warmth of the water embracing her, she recalled that night before her wedding: the flop of hair, the startled eyes, his skin in the moonlight . . . She had looked down on him with the scorn of her disappointment and hurt . . . but he had not allowed her to consummate her triumph. Instead he had possessed her and she had felt a giving inside herself. It had taken her all the effort of her conscious mind to remember that she was there to punish this weakling who had rejected her. She had forced herself to utter words to cut him, hurt him – and had ended up hurting herself. She had become her own Fury, in an endless wandering through a purgatory without love.

It was stupid to rake up these memories. They hardly mattered now. Both she and Edmund had moved on. She did not need anybody to help her with the burden of life that it was her punishment to bear. She had even taken a perverse satisfaction in the fact that she no longer desired anything in her pathetic, unwanted existence. One day it would all end, and the unfortunate accident of chemicals that had made her the unpleasant creature she was would dissolve and there would be no Catherine, only nothingness, an oblivion deeper than sleep.

She sometimes envied the dead. In the hospital ward, after a futile struggle to preserve a spark of life in a doomed patient, she had closed the staring eyes, and wished that she could end her own struggle so easily. She knew it was only pride, that most stubborn of all her flaws, that prevented her finishing it all with a potion from Edmund's pharmacy, but that would be against the rules she had set herself.

What was the matter with her? Why was she raking old coals? She knew what it was. Life had been calling her; its voice had been carried on the calm of a Yangtse morning, in the beauty of the wind and the stars, in the easy-going companionship offered by the junk crew. The fisherfolk casting their nets had caught her in their toils, the laughing children rolling on the deck had absorbed her into their simple, sensual world, the cheery younger son rippling effortlessly to the top of the mast and hallooing from the yardarm had thrilled her with the sheer joy of his physical congruence with nature around him. She had had a holiday from the war and, more than that, from anything that made a demand on her. Suddenly she remembered a vision from a distant past – Kirghiz faces, offering forgiveness, acceptance, hope and absolution in the freedom of the steppes. Hope. Alluring, ephemeral and insubstantial as the wind in the grasslands; flashing, like a butterfly in sunlight, just beyond the reach of her fingers; something that, despite all her efforts, she had never been able to catch.

So she wouldn't waste any more time trying now, she decided, reaching for her towel. Her holiday was over. 'Come on, Catherine,' she said aloud. 'You have a job to do. Back to the rack.' And later, examining herself in the mirror, armoured in her neat nurse's uniform: 'You're not going to fail. You haven't before and you won't now.'

But every door was closed. Lionel had seen to that. The British consul refused to see her. The managers of the shipping offices shook their heads apologetically. The wharf men jeered. The young American doctor in the Kulou missionary hospital, who was happy to accept Niedemeyer's promissory note for the medicines, told her that he might be able to help her find a sampan to take her upriver. There were some converts among the boat people, he said. When he returned to her hotel, he was angry. 'Who is this guy Charters? What have you done to rile him? The word's out about a British nurse who's to be avoided like the plague. Even the smuggling gangs are saying it's bad joss, and enforcers are posted on every pier. Looks like a sizeable amount of money's been paid by somebody to buy them off.' Even then she had refused to be defeated. She had sent a telegraph to Niedemeyer in Chicago asking if he could find a way to help through diplomatic channels. But that had been four days before the retreating warlord army invested the city . . . and now Catherine had lost all communication with the outside world. All she could do was wait for the Nationalists to take Nanking, and trust that a new regime might be more amenable to her pleas. Her experience in Wuhan did not fill her with much confidence.

She sat in her darkened room, sardonically watching the retreat. The sun had long set but an ant trail of pillage continued past her window, illuminated only by the reflection of the burning buildings that cast a dull orange glow over the night sky. It was perhaps inevitable. If they had looted foreign department stores, what was there to stop them looting a foreign hospital?

Towards midnight a procession of twenty mule carts trotted by, whipped on by a more disciplined section of soldiers than most that had passed her way. They were northerners by their height. The mule train was preceded by a column of riflemen marching in step, led by a general, hunched on his horse, caped and wearing a private's forage cap. Another butcher escaping with his spoils. The fires in the suburbs had died down a little, and it was difficult to distinguish much in the gloom, but several of the men in the mule train were carrying burning torches and she could see the red crosses on the boxes loaded on the carts. There was no doubt from where these had been looted. In a flare of one of the torches the words 'Kulou Hospital' were stencilled on the side of a cart. The procession carrying her medicines disappeared into the dark void at the end of the road.

After a while, she left her seat by the window and lay down fully clothed on her bed. She smoked a cigarette, one of her last. She saw the end burn red in the blackness and waved it from side to side. The jagged flight of dim light reminded her of a night on the junk when she and the children had watched fireflies playing over the water. Distantly, she heard the whisper of a faraway bombardment. The sound lapped against her consciousness like the slap of waves on the side of a boat at anchor.

The meeting took place in a small room at the top of a tenement building. The single bulb that hung on a long wire from the clapboard ceiling cast only a dim light but even so Fu-kuei felt dazzled when the blindfolds and the sacking hoods were roughly pulled from her head and Yi-liang's. Hunched opposite her across the narrow table was the crew-cut labour leader. Behind him, their faces indistinct in the shadows, sat three or four others. Occasionally a blue film of smoke from their cigarettes floated into the pool of light cast by the bulb.

Nervously she cast a glance at Yi-liang, who was leaning back against his chair with his arms folded. The white civilian suit he had chosen to wear was unrumpled, a smile curved his lips, and his eyebrows were raised in half-questioning, half-sardonic amusement. Fu-kuei, admiring his handsome profile, felt a rush of sudden pride. For a moment it dampened her fear. She could hardly believe that such nonchalance could be assumed even though he had told her he would be playing a part. 'We must show that we are not to be intimidated,' he had said, as they walked to the assignation. 'It's like poker. If they think we aren't confident, they won't believe a word we say. Are you sure you want to do this, Fu-kuei? A slip may cost us our lives.' She had told him she was not afraid – but that had been before they put the hoods on them, before she had seen the expressions of the armed guards who now stood behind them, covering them with their pistols. She had been expecting hostility – but nothing like this.

'Cigarette?' grunted the crew-cut man, lighting one for himself and pushing the pack across the table. Yi-liang ignored it.

'Well,' continued the man, 'I never thought I'd be sitting face to face with you, unless it was in one of your torture cells.'

'That's where we may all end up if things go wrong – or if we're betrayed,' murmured Yi-liang. 'How do I know I can trust you?'

The crew-cut man gave a throaty laugh. 'I might ask you the same thing,' he said.

'We know where we both stand, then, don't we?' said Yi-liang. 'Are your friends over there going to come out of the shadows?'

'Comrade Lee can speak for us perfectly adequately,' said a cultivated voice from behind a cloud of smoke.

'That's a Chekiang accent,' said Yi-liang. 'Are you Chou En-lai?'

'It doesn't matter who he is,' grunted Lee. 'As the man said, you talk to me and I talk to you, or those hoods and blindfolds are back on you in a flash and you're out of here. And not to your comfortable little home either. Into the canal with a bullet in the back of your head. There's plenty of us who would be happy to do you that favour. That's where you may end up anyway if you don't satisfy us this evening.'

Yi-liang remained still, regarding Lee with a level stare. 'I don't think so,' he said. 'You need me, or I wouldn't be here. And as you know from the papers that Fu-kuei has given you, I have quite enough information about your organisation to ensure that my department will find you. They will certainly look in my safe if I go missing, and you can be sure I have left clear instructions. They may not catch every one of you but it will put an end to your uprising.' His voice hardened. 'Shall we stop comparing the size of our cocks and at least pretend we can do business with one another?'

Fu-kuei tensed as she heard an angry murmur behind her, and the metallic click of a revolver being primed. Lee's eyes had narrowed as Yi-liang threatened him. For a long moment he and Yi-liang glared at each other, then Lee's shoulders relaxed, and he lit a cigarette. 'Keep it calm, Major,' he said. 'Those boys behind you are just itching to pull the trigger. They've lost friends and comrades because of you. You don't know on what a slender thread your life is hanging.' He turned in his chair. Smoke drifted across the room. Eventually, an elegant hand waved from the shadows, presumably instructing Lee to proceed. From the shuffles behind her, Fu-kuei sensed that their guards had also stood down – though she continued to feel a prickle at the back of her neck, conscious of the guns still pointing at them.

'All right, then,' said Lee. 'Tell us what you know about this uprising we're meant to be planning.'

Yi-liang sighed. 'More games? Have it your own way. Where do you want me to start?'

Lee coughed. 'Wherever you like,' he managed. 'As long as it's to the point.'

'Let's begin with the big picture, shall we? Chiang Kai-shek's eastern forces are less than twenty-five miles away to the south. They could theoretically come in to Shanghai at any time they like . . .'

Fu-kuei listened as Yi-liang cogently summarised the military and political situation. The cigarette smoke coiled out of the shadows as he spoke, but none of his sceptical interlocutors gave any indication that they either agreed or disagreed with the points he made. She felt that he and she were on trial, and she dreaded what the final sentence would be.

But Yi-liang was as relaxed as if he were conversing with guests in his own parlour – rather slow-witted guests to whom everything needed to be explained. He sounded bored as he went patiently over the logic of recent events that had brought the city to its crisis, and his manner was offhand when he came to what Fu-kuei knew was the meat of his argument: why the CCP should strike, and strike now. Briskly he outlined the balance of forces arrayed against them: warlords, Nationalists, foreign troops that had come to re-inforce the concessions. He was casual as he reeled off information that he could only have acquired through his secret sources. Now he was outlining the reasons why it was imperative that the CCP must make their insurrection before the warlords left Shanghai, so that the incoming Nationalists would be presented with a *fait accompli*. It would take precise timing, he told them. They must wait until the warlords had begun their evacuation but before the vanguard of the National Revolutionary Army arrived to take their place. 'It won't be easy for you,' he said, 'because the Dog General's men will still be commanding the key garrisons and police stations, and you know how ruthless they can be.' He paused. 'Frankly, from the information I have on your strength and the support you can draw on, I wouldn't give any odds on your success. You'll get a mob on the street that'll turn into a rabble when they send in their Shantung professionals, and your militia – well – against the Dog General's regulars . . . ?'

He left the question hanging. Fu-kuei hardly dared breathe. She knew that the critical point had arrived, and from the intake of breath from the men in the shadows and, more ominously, the shuffle of the guards behind her, it was evident that everyone else present did too. The tension in the room was almost palpable.

Yi-liang gauged his moment. 'That's where I come in,' he said quietly. 'With my knowledge of their dispositions I can give you the upper hand.'

In the silence afterwards Lee turned to his superiors. There was a long pause, in which Fu-kuei felt that her heart had stopped beating. They didn't believe him, she told herself. They don't trust us. Then, when she had all but given way to despair, the hand in the shadows waved languidly at Lee to proceed. Her fingers unclenched. She began to breathe normally again.

'All right,' Lee was saying. He was speaking in the same hectoring tones as before, but Fu-kuei felt that some invisible barrier had lifted. 'Assume what you say is correct, and somehow we can turn the odds in our favour, what's Chiang Kai-shek going to be doing while we mount our insurrection? Just stand by and let us take the prize out of his hand?'

Yi-liang's expression was almost playful. 'He *wants* you to rise up,' he said. 'He thinks the warlords will destroy you. He sees himself as the fisherman in the proverb who comes across the crane's beak locked with the crab's claws. He benefits from the struggle between the bird and the crab, and snatches both. The generalissimo's being clever. He thinks he has you in a trap.'

'And are we in a trap?'

'Not necessarily. It's why we're talking, isn't it?'

'So let's take it we're successful,' said Lee. 'We storm the key points in the city. Why doesn't Chiang just come in and crush us afterwards? Our militias might be able to see off a few departing warlords – all right, with your help,' his lips curled as he made this grudging acknowledgement, 'but they wouldn't be strong enough to take on the whole Kuomintang army.'

'He wouldn't dare try,' said Yi-liang. 'If he even attempts to bring in the army against the workers of Shanghai that'll be the end of the Northern Expedition. His own troops would turn on him. Remember, Chiang's pledged to uphold the United Front. You and I might know the real score, that you Communists and the right wing of the Party are at each other's throats, but the ordinary people don't. They think the CCP and the Kuomintang are one and the same. If you have control of the city, Chiang will have no choice but to recognise you, and that'll be the end of his political career. Borodin, or whoever is in control of the CCP, will take over the Kuomintang – and the Chinese revolution. That's the stake you're playing for – and that's why you need somebody inside the warlord camp who'll help you seize control of the city before Chiang arrives.'

He picked up his untouched tea and drained the cup. The only sound in the room was convulsive coughing from Lee.

'And you're that man?' It was the cultivated voice that had spoken earlier.

'Have you anybody else?'

One of the men in the shadows dragged his chair into the light. He had a crop of untidy hair and a long, pleasant face distinguished by heavy black eyebrows above humorous eyes; his chin was grey with afternoon shadow. There was an elegance and economy in his movements that Fu-kuei found attractive. She judged he was about the same age as Yi-liang. In fact, there was a languorous similarity about the two powerful young men who now contemplated each other across the table.

'I thought I was only to have the privilege of conversing with Comrade Lee,' said her lover.

'Comrade Lee seems to have been overcome by a fit of coughing. Smoking is a terrible habit,' smiled the other, lighting a new cigarette from the stub of his old one. His face suddenly transformed into a serious frown, and the eyes became penetrating under the creased eyebrows. 'That was a perceptive analysis, Major Yang, but wrong in one particular. This is the Chinese Communist Party. We don't take our orders from Mr Borodin or any Russian. And another thing. The CCP is also committed to the United Front. If we should mount an insurrection against our common warlord enemy, it will not be for reasons of inter-party wrangling, but because we are committed – as I sincerely hope that the generalissimo is committed – to the Chinese revolution.'

'Slogans?' murmured Yi-liang. 'But you still intend to seize power.'

The man's face relaxed into its charming smile. 'Yes, Major Yang, if we can, we will seize power.'

'Then I suggest we get on and plan your insurrection.'

Fu-kuei passed the next two hours in almost dream-like elation as she watched the maps spread out on the table, and Yi-liang's pencil scratching out details of the defences of each police station in Shanghai's main industrial districts: Hongkew, Yangtse-poo, Chapei, Woosung, Nantao and Pootung. Her eyes stung as an ever denser cloud of cigarette smoke coiled and curled above the heads of the three men peering over the diagrams, calculation and concern in their faces as they worked out tactics of attack. She experienced a thrill of excitement when a snort of approval or an occasional shared smile indicated a moment of understanding, or the resolution of a difficulty. She listened with awe as Yi-liang rattled off numbers – of guns, men, armoured cars, machine-gun posts, auxiliary reserves. He answered their questions with expert assurance, occasionally raising his own: 'How many armed militia did you say you could spare to cross the creek here? . . . That's not enough . . . Well, if you haven't enough rifles to arm so many workers, we'll have to get you some more, won't we? You make sure of the men, I'll make sure you get the guns . . . How? I don't know yet, probably from the Woosung arsenal. Fu-kuei will pass you the message . . .' Every time he said it her heart thumped with pride.

She saw the revolution she had dreamed about unfolding in front of her eyes.

'You will need the workers to come out first,' Yi-liang was saying. 'but the warlords won't take that lying down. You saw how they dealt with strikes before.'

'And no doubt they will use the same barbaric methods again,' said the saturnine man. 'Beheadings in the streets and heads carried on poles in the crowded thoroughfares inspire outrage as much as fear. It is sad that so many innocent people will have to be sacrificed, but their example will inspire others. I hope, incidentally, Major, that once the strike begins, you on your part will not feel it necessary to restrain your warlord colleagues . . .'

'It is flattering that you think I could,' said Yi-liang, 'but I won't blow my cover prematurely. Not until the insurrection. You'll get your sacrifices.'

Fu-kuei was shocked at the ruthless turn in the discussion – although intellectually she saw its logic – and its inevitability. That had been one of Mr Behrens's favourite terms. She had not thought of him for a long time – perhaps she would no longer have to. All the disparate forces that had pulled her life in different directions were now moving in one unstoppable flow. She felt confident that she was working now for what she had always wanted, the Chinese revolution alone. These men were the instruments to achieve it – and she would help. She felt a rush of joy, pride, liberation from the murk in which she had struggled for so many years.

The conversation had turned to the gangs. 'They're a powerful force too,' said Yi-liang. 'Do you have any contacts with them?'

'The Green Gang? The Red Gang? You must be joking,' said Lee. 'They're criminals in the pay of the capitalists. They oppress the people more than the warlords do.'

'You don't want them against you, though,' said Yi-liang. 'They can field a lot of well-armed, disciplined men. They're linked to Chiang Kai-shek too. Their leader, Pock-marked Huang, who poses as chief of police in the French concession, knew him when he was a younger man. Some say he even inducted him into his gang.'

'I remind you, Major,' the saturnine man interrupted, 'Generalissimo Chiang is not our enemy – but I see that the gangs could be a threat. What do you propose?'

'Leave them to me,' said Yi-liang. 'I've used them before. They can be handled.'

'Very well. No doubt you will inform us how in due course.'

Fu-kuei looked at her lover with surprise and renewed respect. He seemed god-like tonight, displaying absolute mastery. She knew, of course, of his connections with the gangs: he had hired thugs to burn Barkowitz's store but, she realised, even then he had been ruthless in pursuit of what he had perceived as his duty, or of what he believed was right. She had never felt that he was anything but honourable, even though she had detested his cause – but now his cause was hers. And it came to her that she had been the instrument of Yi-liang's conversion, on their own private road to Damascus.

The men were standing. The conference was over. The two CCP rank and file – longshoremen by the look of them – who had brought them here had come back into the room and were waiting with the hoods and masks. The armed guards who had covered them during the early part of the meeting were sheepish now. One was even grinning shyly at her. She heard those words again from her lover: 'Fu-kuei will pass you the message.'

'Yes, Major,' said the black-browed man, whom she was now convinced was Chou. 'It would not be appropriate for you and I to have direct contact again. Madame Yu will continue to deal with Comrade Lee through the channels they have established. I have, however, one further question before you go.'

Yi-liang paused, and for the first time that evening seemed to tense.

'Major, you are a man of great ability, but you are not a revolutionary. Rather the opposite, more's the pity. Why are you helping us against the warlords?'

Fu-kuei felt the atmosphere in the room become still, as though a collective breath was being held.

Yi-liang turned. 'It's simple, isn't it? You're going to win.'

'Is that all?' The man had moved to their side of the table and his penetrating eyes were searching Yi-liang's face.

'You're going to need people like me when you've achieved your revolution. You don't want an idealist to keep order afterwards. You'll need somebody practical. When it comes down to it, ideology has a habit of getting in the way of what needs to be done.'

The man kept his eyes on Yi-liang's face. Fu-kuei was surprised to see a bead of sweat forming on her lover's temple. 'We'll see,' murmured the man. Then, he tapped Yi-liang on the back. 'But first we need to win, don't we?' he said cheerfully. 'If we do, then whatever your motives are, you will have played a part, and the people will be grateful. As will I. Goodnight, and I apologise for the inconvenience of our security requirements. Enemies can become friends but, sadly, it is usual that full trust only follows later. I hope, for all our sakes, that you pass your test when it comes, Major.'

Catherine was woken by the chill of the dawn. Limbs aching, she moved to the window, conscious of the silence after the mayhem of the night before. The stucco facings on the banks and offices opposite her shone a faint pink in the sun's first rays and at first there was no indication that anything was out of the ordinary. Above the dull grey roofs she could see mist rising from the trees on the mountainside beyond the city walls. The shops further down the road were boarded, but that was not unusual at this time in the morning. She expected in a few minutes to see the watchmen who had sat out the weary night in the halls of the office buildings gathering by a stall at the entrance to the alley for their breakfast of *doujiang* and *youtiao*. Her ears strained for the sounds of the dumpling-sellers who would usually begin around now to chant their wares as they moved down the street with their pushcarts. In a while, if it was a normal day, rickshaws would pass by, dropping off the clerks who came early to collect the telegrams. She looked below to where the sweepers would be brushing the road in front of the hotel.

There were no sweepers. No rickshaws. No dumpling-sellers. The entrance to the alley was empty. There were no watchmen. A bank's heavy door was hanging on its hinges. Paper was fluttering on the pillared steps and eddying like autumn leaves over the pavement. With a shock, Catherine saw they were bank bills and specie notes. The sack of the day before had not been a bad dream. The looters of the warlord army had gone and the city lay numb, the streets deserted, waiting for the next shock.

She remembered the Red Cross medicine boxes, tokens of her failure, disappearing into the gloom, and anxiety seized her: if the hospital had been sacked, what had happened to the doctors and nurses – the young American physician, Terry Donovan? He would be all right, she told herself. The warlords might be after plunder but they would not dare harm a foreigner. Even the Bolsheviks in Hankow had restricted themselves to taunts and intimidation; they had not laid hands on Catherine or Edmund, or any of the foreign residents, as far as she knew. But she was worried. She would go to Kulou Hospital right away, she decided, to offer consolation to her friends and see if they required any help with their patients.

Monsieur Delarge, the Belgian general manager, was hunched unshaven in his shirtsleeves over the reception desk in the empty lobby. 'Madame, where are you going?' he called, as she strode past. 'It will be dangerous outside. The Nationalist army, even now they are entering the city and, believe me, they will be worse than the animals who have just left.'

'I'll be fine, Adolphe,' called Catherine, cheerily, and pushed through the revolving door.

Pulling her cape round her against the cold, she walked briskly down the middle of the empty road. The hospital was not far, a few blocks to the south-east near the Drum Tower. She took a short-cut up an alley. Without the usual crowds the city seemed alien. There was not a soul about. Occasionally she observed signs of looting, and in the ashes of one burned-out restaurant she saw a disconsolate family, a grandmother, an old man, two babies, sitting silently on a blackened roof beam. She passed on.

When she came across an unfamiliar *pailou* by an intersection, she realised she was lost. She stood at the crossroads, uncertain of which way to go. Then, for the first time, she observed movement. There were some figures a few hundred yards away. They appeared to be coolies, squatting with their backs to a mansion wall, while others were loading goods on to a wagon. She hurried towards them, thrilled by this sign of normal life. When she got closer, she saw they were not coolies but soldiers, in the brown uniforms of the Nationalist army. And the bundles they were throwing into the cart were bound prisoners – merchants by their costume. She froze. For a long moment she stared at them and they at her.

She wanted to turn back the way she had come, but she knew that was not possible. Two of the soldiers had unslung their rifles, and another, with corporal's stripes, was shouting something at her. There was nothing else for it. 'Come on, Catherine. You've brow-beaten a general. You can deal with a few soldiers.' She clung to the thought that they wouldn't hurt a foreigner – they wouldn't dare. She adopted the haughtiest expression she could muster, then the ward sister stepped forward confidently, in all her imposing authority – at least, that was how she hoped it would appear.

'Please let me pass,' she said quietly, in fluent Mandarin. 'As you can see from my uniform I am a nurse, and I'm on my way to the hospital.'

The soldiers stared at her uncomprehendingly, then laughed, shouting at each other in a southern dialect she could not under-stand. The men guarding the prisoners had come up behind her; she could see jeering hostility in their eyes. The corporal, a shorter, fatter man than the others, was scowling at her. She made a move forward. He blocked her. The scowl turned into a grin. She felt fingers tugging her hair at the back of her headdress. Angry, shocked, she flapped them away. The soldiers around her laughed again.

Then she recognised '*hong mao*', red hair. She tried to calm herself. They've never seen a red-head before and they're curious. Keep cool, Catherine, and you'll be all right. She pretended to laugh with them, unpinned a strand of her hair and said, '*Hong toufa. Zai Yingguo hen pubian.* Yes, red hair, in England it's quite common. See, I am English. *Wo shi Yinguoren.*' She repeated it, hoping they would understand the implication: that it was dangerous for them to harm a foreign national. They only laughed the more.

She felt herself jerked to the side. One of the soldiers, a boy, had pulled her cape. She was immediately jerked to the other side as another tugged at it. She found herself turned like a top and struggled to retain her foothold. The clasp broke and the cape came away in their hands. She stumbled, lost her balance and grazed her palms on the paving. On her hands and knees she found herself staring in disbelief at the corporal's puttees and boots. She looked up wildly and saw his sneer – and a hungry look in his narrowing eyes. None of them was laughing now. Oh, my God. They want to rape me. She jumped to her feet. Although she was aware that she had lost any shred of authority, she could still put on the voice that had intimidated her nurses. 'You will let me pass. Immediately.' The corporal's answer was to reach out both hands and press them over her breasts. His lips curled in a sly, questioning smile. She spat full in his eyes.

His blow knocked her backwards. She felt a stinging pain in her cheek and her vision blurred. Rough hands grabbed her arms, her hips, her legs. She was being lifted. She screamed, trying to kick and scratch, but their grip was too tight and it was only her body that jerked and arched in their grasp. Her headdress had been pulled off, and the corporal was running his hands through the long tresses of her hair as if he was weighing a bolt of silk. She jerked her head to bite his fingers, but they were too far away.

She felt a sudden cold brush of air on her legs. One of the soldiers had pulled up her skirt, and was tugging at the garters that held up her stockings. She jerked her knees and this time made contact. He staggered away holding his nose. The others laughed.

They had dropped her on to a pile of wet coal sacks, stacked against the side of a house. She was pinioned with a soldier holding either arm. Others were pulling off her shoes, unrolling her stockings. She was naked from the waist down, at their mercy. A man put his hand on her crotch, ruffling the hair. There was another cry of 'Hong mao,' and a peal of louder, harsher laughter.

The soldiers were pushing forward the boy who had first pulled her cape. He was blushing as he fumbled with his belt. She heard the other soldiers chanting, 'Hoong nyang! Hoong nyang!' What was that? Bridegroom? Bride? Suddenly she felt absolutely calm, almost disembodied, as if she was watching a show performed by somebody else; she saw her kicking feet, as if from a great distance. The other soldiers were pulling down the boy's trousers. My God, she thought. This is really happening. It was probably one of the last things Marya saw before she died. She was aware of the boy's face close to her own, the apologetic look in his eyes. He doesn't know what to do, the calm part of her said. He's a virgin. Scared. Well, damn him. So he should be. Damn them all. She strained her neck forward and fixed her teeth in his cheek. She felt her head pulled away, with the boy's flesh and blood in her mouth.

There were angry shouts. She heard the scuffle and rattle of rifles. She saw the muzzle of a gun pointed directly at her temple and instinctively closed her eyes. So this was how it was to end. Well, she was ready. She heard a loud, reverberating crack, as if the sky was tearing, and a roar that filled the space around her, not an unpleasant sound; it had a purring monotony that reminded her of the junk's diesel turning the propellers through the Yangtse's yellow waters. At first she was surprised – relieved, anyway, that there had been no pain – but then she wanted to cry in her disappointment: she was still thinking, feeling; she was still aware. Oh, it was unfair.

It had been a bad day for John Soo, although that was not unexpected or unusual; these days, every day was bad, and had been for the month since he had returned to Kiukiang from leave in Hankow. His thoughts had been of Lan-hua, as he had trudged up the steep bank from the dock to headquarters. An angry adjutant had reprimanded him for being late back from his furlough, then read him a report that somebody had written belatedly about the attack on Nanchang, blaming him and his team of engineers for their failure to mine the city walls. 'We can't punish you because we've already blamed your dead assistant,' the man had said sourly, 'but you're being transferred to the logistics department of General Chien Chung's sixth Corps, who are now somewhere east of here, attacking Kiangsu. Don't ask me where. Nobody has any idea where the front is now. You'll have to find it.'

John had tried to protest. He was an engineer, a bridge-builder. What role could he possibly play in a logistics department? Anyway, General Chien Chung was little better than a warlord, commanding undisciplined Hunanese soldiers. He couldn't even speak their dialect. 'If you complain any more, I'll put you on a charge,' said the adjutant. 'Now get out. You've had your orders.'

It had taken three days to find transport east; four more in the back of a truck, his back jarred on the bad road over the mountains; and another two before he found General Chien's headquarters on a hillside above Wuhu. His reception had been frosty: nobody had heard that he was coming, or was interested in finding out why. The head of the logistics department had gone for an inspection down the lines. He had to wait in the muddy camp, seeking shelter for three nights from pouring rain under the wheels of parked trucks because nobody had a tent for him.

The food in the canteen was execrable: animal innards floating in a red, spicy soup. The Hunanese, chattering in their incomprehensible dialect, loved it, and slurped it up as if it were noodles. Eventually his new boss, a Colonel Loong, had returned. At least he spoke Mandarin. He examined John's papers in the tent that served as his office, rubbed tiger balm on his bald temples, and sighed. 'It's typical, isn't it? I ask for an interpreter and they send me an overqualified Whampoa engineer. Do you speak any English?'

'Of course,' said John, wondering what relevance this had to anything. 'I studied at Oxford University.'

'Spare us! A scholar as well! Well, I suppose it takes all sorts to make a revolution. You might as well start right away. The turtle's egg's been sitting in his tent for a week without being able to talk to anybody. He's in as foul a mood as you obviously are, so you should get on together.' He thumbed through the papers in his drawer. 'Here it is. This is what we need. Try to get a good price for us.' He handed John three sheets of rice paper, on which was inked a list of letters and numbers. He looked at it blankly. Colonel Loong rolled his eyes theatrically. 'Oh, heavens, you don't know what I'm talking about, do you? Don't say it. They didn't tell you what your job is. God only knows how they intend to run the country if we manage to win this war.'

'No, Colonel, I don't know what my job is, who the turtle's egg is, or what this list is that I'm to bargain a good price for. Or why I'm here, for that matter. I'm a bridge-builder, not an interpreter or a merchant.'

Colonel Loong leaned back in his chair and laughed. 'Well, Lieutenant Bridge-builder, you're both those things now. That's a list of the weapons we want to buy. The turtle's egg is an Austrian arms merchant who'll supply them. You're the go-between. Is that clear enough? Ask what he's charging, and the delivery dates, then come back to me and I'll find out what our budget is, if anybody in HQ has even thought of budgets yet, which I doubt. I don't know how I ended up with this job. I was a clerk in a tea company. Oh, and by the way, you should be more senior. It'll make the foreign devil believe he's dealing with somebody important. What would you like to be? A captain? A major? Come on, it'll mean more pay, and it'll entitle you to a tent. I'll make you a major. Field promotion subject to confirmation. Get these stars sewn on that shabby tunic of yours. And, please, bring me back a good price.'

That had been a fortnight ago. John had been grateful to be given quarters, but he hated being an arms-dealer, and he loathed the bestial, corrupt von Henning, with whom he had been closeted in a grimy tent for nearly a week, negotiating the contract. The man was arrogant, overbearing, rude, prejudiced, everything that John Soo detested. For all John's new rank, von Henning treated him like a servant, demanding tobacco, or alcohol, which he drank through the day, apparently with no effect on his red-faced constitution; in the evenings he insisted John drink with him 'to show good faith'. Then von Henning would clap him on the back and say, 'Enough business. Pleasure now.' Pleasure, John realised, consisted in demands for women. John complained to Colonel Loong, who ordered him to go to the captain in charge of the men's brothel. Thus the newly promoted Major John Soo discovered that his duties consisted of pimping as well as arms dealing.

It was some time before he had gathered that the commissions he negotiated were not only for Andreas von Henning but were to be shared with his high command, including Colonel Loong – although nothing was ever said.

Eventually, negotiations over, paper signed, he had driven the man to an airstrip, which had been levelled out of a dry paddy-field especially for the purpose, and watched him leave in a biplane to Shanghai. He had never felt more pleased in his life to see the back of somebody – but it had only been a week's respite. The fighting had reached the outskirts of Nanking, which was expected to fall any day and he was ordered to go in with the advance troops and wait there for the freighter that von Henning had said would carry the arms. Payment would be delivered on receipt.

So, in a convoy of two jeeps – Colonel Loong had detailed a squad of soldiers to accompany him – he had set off from Wuhu in the early hours of that morning. After a six-hour drive, he had arrived on the outskirts of Nanking as dawn was breaking. The light revealed little evidence of fighting. It appeared that General Chien had allowed the warlord troops to retreat unopposed, but everywhere he looked he saw evidence of looting: burned farmhouses, slaughtered animals, a miserable line of refugees filing along the side of the roads with the little that remained to them. John had seen the methods employed by the enemy before, but it still disgusted him.

When he had set off months ago with the 4th Corps from Canton, he had been proud to belong to a new sort of army, one that did not ravage the countryside, one that paid for its porterage, as well as for any item of food or assistance it required from the peasants and townsfolk they were liberating from the feudalism of the past.

He had been shocked therefore, shortly after driving through the city gates, to see soldiers of his own army, the Hunanese 6th Corps, behaving with the same rapaciousness as the warlords. When he had seen a group of riflemen coming out of a warehouse with bags of sugar on their backs, he had been tempted to halt his jeep and arrest them. He might even have tried, but he saw an officer he had met at Wuhu, a Cantonese like himself, leaning against the wall, observing the scene. He hailed him from his car. 'Captain Wong, what's happening? Shouldn't you be stopping this?'

His friend had sauntered over. '*Lao* Soo, it's good to see you. Yes, it is disgusting, isn't it? But we have orders not to do anything about it.'

'What?'

'Don't ask. Apparently it comes from High Command. Colonel Tseng told me himself. We're to give the troops a day "to restore order in the city by any means". That apparently applies to the foreign imperialists' quarters of the city as well. Especially the foreigners' quarters,' he added, in a low voice.

'That's mad.' John Soo could hardly believe what he was hearing. 'Dangerous, even. There are foreign gunboats on the river. Anyway, we're the National Revolutionary Army. We don't do things this way.'

Captain Wong shrugged.

John Soo had driven on. He saw a shopkeeper dragged out of his shop and slapped across the face. He saw a line of men carrying crates of liquor out of a restaurant. In another street he saw soldiers driving the inhabitants from their houses at gunpoint and forcing them to kneel in the road. His initial horror and anger was turning into a burning sense of shame. He had not joined the army to countenance this. A military policeman blew a whistle and raised his hand to stop his jeep. John's first thought had been to round on the man and tell him he should be doing something more useful than traffic duty, but he controlled himself as the man told him he should divert into the one of the side-streets because soon General Chien would be driving up the main street formally to take possession of the city.

Inevitably John and his two jeeps became lost in the maze of lanes. The looting was even going on here as stray knots of soldiers wandered from home to home. Then they turned a corner and John saw a sight that caused his disgust to boil over into action. There, on a coal stack against a wall, a group of soldiers were raping a woman. One had his trousers down and was being pushed by his companions over a prone body, of which John could see only the bare, kicking legs. He saw something else, a piece of black clothing, perhaps a cloak, lying in the middle of the road and on it a red cross. He could not believe it. The brutes were raping a nurse.

He accelerated towards them and slammed on the brakes. Leaving the engine running, he leaped out, pulling his revolver from his holster. He hoped his men were following him. He raised his gun above his head and fired. The shot echoed down the alleys. The soldiers turned. Several were holding rifles at the ready and John saw the barrels turned towards him – but they did not fire. His men had also levelled their rifles. It was a stand-off.

Ignoring the guns ranged at him, he walked towards a fat corporal and slashed his pistol across his face, leaving a bleeding gash. The man whimpered and fell to his knees. The guns of his companions lowered. For a moment they looked at each other with scared eyes, then one ran and the others followed. John kicked the corporal to his feet, and he followed his running men. The whole incident had taken less than a minute and not a word had been spoken.

John turned his attention to the woman, who was lying immodestly but quietly on a pile of coal sacks. He saw flowing red hair, and realised, with alarm, that she was a foreigner. Her skirt was over her face. John knelt beside her and pulled it down to cover her exposed lower body. She was lying so still that he thought he had arrived too late. Blood spattered her face. He leaned over her to ascertain if she was breathing. Then, with a shock, he recognised her. She was Yu Fu-kuei's friend, Lan-hua's friend. It was too much of a coincidence. 'Catherine,' he whispered, 'are you alive?'

The familiar green eyes opened and blinked.

'It depends on your definition. I don't think so,' she replied, in a remarkably composed voice. She frowned. 'I know you, don't I? You're John Soo. The last time I saw you was on the Cherwell.

I didn't know you were dead too. God! Trust my luck to end up in a Chinese heaven! Have you been appointed my bloody guardian angel or something?'

Well, thought John Soo, wryly, this wasn't the reaction he had expected when he had just saved her from rape and worse, but she was still the acerbic Catherine Cabot he remembered.

Her first reaction was to take out her anger on her rescuer. She knew it was unfair. Hopping on the road, pulling on her torn stockings, she raged at him about the indiscipline of his army, the brutality of the Bolsheviks, the terrible state of a country where a woman couldn't walk along a street without being attacked by gangs of ruffians that he and his like were no doubt proud to command. He was no better than all the other bloody warlords and militarists and thieves and looters, who were a plague on humanity and a ruin of civilisation, and he was obviously a total idiot who hadn't learned a thing from Oxford . . .

At which point, with her shoes back on, and some of her dignity restored, she realised she sounded like Lionel Charters. She astounded the bewildered John Soo by bursting out laughing, and confused him even further by throwing her arms round him and kissing him on both cheeks. 'Thank you, you dear man, for saving me,' she cried. 'Forget all that nonsense I've been raving. I had to get it off my chest. It's been building up for some time. I suppose attempted rape has that effect on a girl. I'm not really myself yet . . . John! What are you doing here?'

'Catherine, are you sure you're all right? Can I take you somewhere to rest? Would you like a blanket, or – or a cup of tea or something?'

'So you've picked up some English habits after all. Where on earth in this ruined city do you propose to find me a cup of tea? No, I'm fine. Really I am. Shocked, I suppose, but they didn't hurt me. Not really. Just a slap or two. Would have been much worse if you hadn't come along. Once I get that horrible man's blood off my face I'll be good as new. Really.'

And she did feel fine. Better than fine. The blood was coursing through her veins as if she had just run a cross-country marathon.

The dingy street around her – every faded brick – shone with the clarity of detail that a short-sighted person might perceive after his oculist had given him a new pair of spectacles: a sparrow was chirping in the garden over the mansion wall; the familiar scent of the Chinese city – a mixture of dung and drains and woodsmoke – smelt sweet in her nostrils. Her hands and feet tingled with life and energy. Was this the feeling of somebody who has come back from the dead? She became aware that John was apologising to her. 'I cannot say how ashamed I am,' he was intoning. 'It appals me to think that soldiers from the National Revolutionary Army could be capable of such an atrocity.'

She kissed him again. 'John, it's not you who's to blame. You've always been a decent sort of a chap. Every army has its bad hats. Criminals. You'll catch this lot and punish them. I hate some of the things that the Kuomintang stands for, and the political activists you're working for, but I know you're not as bad as the warlords. Even in Wuhan I saw the discipline of your troops. This must have been an aberration . . .' She saw his agonised expression. 'What, John?'

His shoulders slumped. 'I don't think this time it was an aberration, Catherine. Those Hunanese are under orders to hurt foreigners.'

'Don't be silly. That would be folly.'

'I couldn't believe it until I saw what had happened to you, but an officer told me the troops have been instructed to "restore order in the foreign quarters". This is not the army I knew.'

For a moment, Catherine tried to make sense of what he had just said. Then she grabbed John's hand. She felt unnaturally calm. 'Jenny. Lionel. The children. I must go to them. John, will you help me? My relatives. They'll be in danger.'

He took no convincing. A few minutes later, the two jeeps were speeding, horns blaring, in the direction of Nanking University and the foreigners' villas. With squealing tyres they turned through wide-open gates into the Charters's driveway – and saw soldiers on the front lawn. Two were straining under the weight of one of Jenny's favourite antique chests. Through the open french windows, Catherine could make out others moving inside. The blood that had been raging inside her seemed to stop flowing, and she felt a great coldness. They had arrived too late. She knew it, with all the certainty of Fate. She was unable to move.

John, however, had the energy of a madman. Pistol in hand, he was shouting orders at his men and running towards the open doors. As she watched, she saw the soldiers on the lawn drop their load and put their hands in the air, while one of John's riflemen covered them. The others had followed him inside. She heard the sound of two shots fired in rapid succession. There was a long, dreadful delay when nothing happened. Eventually four or five men filed out of the house, their hands on their heads. One had a wound in his leg. John's soldiers made them join the others on the lawn, where they crouched under the muzzles of the rifles. Two of the men were not wearing trousers. 'Oh, God. Jenny,' she whispered.

Five minutes later, John came out of the house and walked to the jeep, his face stern. 'Catherine, you'd better come inside,' he said.

'Are they . . . are they . . . ?' She could not bring herself to say the words.

'It's just better if you come inside.'

The sitting room, where only a few days previously she had sat and sipped coffee, was a wreck of smashed furniture. Her foot crunched on something hard. Vaguely, she was aware that it was a cup from Jenny's best tea-set, which now lay in fragments on the skewed Persian carpet. Incongruously, in a window alcove, a side table stood erect, with one of Jenny's flower arrangements, set beautifully in a Ming vase. A framed photograph stood beside it of Lionel and his smiling family. She saw John pointing at a sofa that had been knocked to its side, and she heard a whimper from behind it. 'Better that a woman looks after her,' said John, quietly. 'I'll leave you. One of my men heard a noise from upstairs. Foreign voices. It's probably your brother-in-law and the children. I'll go now and—'

'No-o-o!' They heard the screech from behind the sofa. Catherine saw a tousled head emerge. The eyes were two bruised patches, and the mouth was swollen and disfigured. It looked like the face of a clown whose makeup had streaked. But it was Jenny. The thick lips were slurring words more like grunts than human speech. 'No – I don't – I don't want – them – to see – me – like – this.'

'Oh, Jenny, my poor Jenny.' Catherine moved slowly towards her so as not to alarm her. 'John,' she said urgently, over her shoulder, 'go to them. See if they're all right but on no account let them come down here. Not till I call you. If any of them are hurt let me know and I'll be up when I'm finished here.' She heard the click of his boots on the parquet floor, fading towards the stairs. 'Jenny, it's Catherine. Yes, Catherine. You remember Catherine. You're going to be all right,' she murmured. 'I'm coming round the side of the sofa. Now, don't be scared. All those men have gone and it's just me. I'm a nurse, so you can trust me. It's only me.'

She had to make an effort to keep her soothing smile in place when she saw her sister-in-law, hunched, naked, rocking, arms clenched round her knees, flinching away from her as she approached. She knelt beside her, whispering, 'My sweet girl,' and 'It's all right now.' Only when she felt that Jenny had become used to her presence did she put her arms round her and hug the battered face to her cheek, stroking the matted hair and repeating her endearments. She felt the tense body begin to relax, then shake violently again.

'Lionel – Lionel . . . If he – if he – knew – what those – men . . .'

'Sssh, dearest, try not to think of it.'

'No – Catherine – you – don't – know – him. He would – he would – leave me.' The last words came out in a wail.

'It's not your fault, darling,' Catherine whispered, as tears of anger pricked her eyes. Yes, Lionel probably would leave his wife if he knew that she had been soiled, as he would perceive it. Worse, he might keep up the marriage for form's sake, but make Jenny's life a living torment. 'Jenny, darling, he won't find out – not that you've been raped. I won't let him. But first you have to help me. I have to examine you to see how badly they hurt you, and then get you washed and dressed again, so no one will ever know. No one. Ever. It'll be our secret. Yours and mine. Now, can you do that for me? Let me take you to the bathroom. Come on, darling. I know how brave you are. Will you do that for me? Please. For Catherine, who loves you? Come on, now, there's my brave Jenny.'

And slowly, treating her as tenderly as the hurt child she had become, Catherine brought her back to a semblance of her former self. She soaped away the filth with a sponge, and treated the wounds on Jenny's face with mercurichrome that she found in the bathroom cupboard. She checked Jenny's body and found that, besides the ravishment, she had not been injured. The scratches on her breasts and thighs would heal. No doubt Jenny would find a way to conceal them from Lionel.

She wanted to go upstairs to bring down clean clothes, but Jenny resisted. 'No – no – I must put on the old clothes. He mustn't suspect.'

'All right, darling,' said Catherine. 'Let me gather them up for you. I don't think they're too badly torn.'

Catherine raised the sofa to its upright position, and settled her there. 'Can I get you anything? Brandy? A cup of tea? Are you sure you're ready?'

'Yes, I want to see my babies,' sniffed Jenny. 'They must have been so scared. Catherine? You promised. You'll never tell?'

Catherine promised, and called John to bring the others down. She heard the thunder of feet on the stairs. Tom, Bunny and Esther ran weeping into the room and into their mother's arms. Lionel followed in his shirtsleeves. Catherine could tell from his livid complexion that he was furious. She had already heard him yelling at John: 'Who the hell do you think you are, keeping us locked up like prisoners? I'm going to report you to your general.' When he saw Catherine, he began to shake. 'You? I might have known you'd be mixed up with these Bolsheviks. Well, you and your looter friends have certainly wrecked our house. Now, where's my wife? Oh, my God. My God . . .' He froze, when he saw the bruises on Jenny's face.

'I'm all right, Lionel. They didn't really hurt me,' she pleaded, in a voice that was nearly as strong as normal, and made a brave, pathetic attempt at a smile.

Lionel was standing rigidly, clenching and unclenching his fists. He had lost all his composure and looked what he was: a frightened man. 'Jenny?' he whispered. 'Jenny, what did they do to you? Did they . . . did they . . .'

The bruised slits of Jenny's eyes opened wide in fear.

'What do you think they did to her, Lionel?' Catherine stepped in. 'Can't you see for yourself? While you were locked safely upstairs, several brutes of looters – you can see them outside on the lawn – were torturing your wife to try to make her reveal where you keep your jewels and money. That's what they were after, and she bravely resisted them. You can thank your stars that Major Soo came by and stopped them doing anything worse. I've treated the bruises on her face. They'll heal. Mercifully they did nothing else to her. You should be damned proud of Jenny. I am.'

'Oh,' muttered Lionel, looking embarrassed, and – hatefully – relieved. 'Then I suppose I owe you my thanks, Catherine. You too, Major Soo.' He cleared his throat. 'But it's still an outrage. An outrage!' he shouted. 'And you can be damned sure I will make a formal complaint as I told you, Major – although of course I will say good words about you.'

'If I were you, Mr Charters,' said John smoothly, 'I would be more concerned about getting your family to safety. The town is very dangerous, and there are lawless elements about. One of my men has just found out that several foreigners are gathering at a house in the northern suburbs. It's apparently on a high bluff where the city walls directly overlook the river and your navy vessels. Am I right in thinking that it belongs to the Standard Oil Company?'

'Yes, you're referring to Lion Hill,' acknowledged Lionel. 'But isn't that a bit panicky? Can't your much vaunted Nationalist Revolutionary Army keep order?'

'I'm sure it will impose order in time,' said John, 'but in the meanwhile, you have seen for yourself what happened here. My man has also told me that several foreigners have already regrettably lost their lives – a Dr Williams when a mob stormed the university, the German harbour master, the Japanese consul and others. Your own British consulate was attacked, and your consul wounded. I believe he has been taken to the Standard Oil house. I suggest that you follow.'

'My God! The British consul wounded? This is outrageous!' But he argued no longer. He did, however, keep up a mutter of abuse, in the back of John's jeep with his family, as they drove through the poorer sections of the town and up the wooded hill that led to the bluff. Smoke from several burned-out mansions showed that this exclusive residential area had not escaped looting. 'Is this the new liberal China we've all heard about? Are these the famous principles of Sun Yat-sen? You know damned well the only organisation in this country that works is the Maritime Customs Service and now your bully boys are smashing that . . .' John ignored him to concentrate on his driving.

The other jeep, minus two soldiers who had been detailed to look after the prisoners, followed behind, and Catherine took comfort from that, because, ominously, as they neared their destination, they saw lines of soldiers marching up the road in the same direction.

Clearly John had had the same thought. In Mandarin, he muttered to Catherine, in the front seat beside him, 'Your refuge may not be as secure as it sounds. I'll have to leave you there, though. I'll try to make it to General Chien's headquarters to see if I can argue some sense into somebody – but I confess I'm not optimistic. Still, you'll be with the others. There may be a certain safety in numbers.'

'You've done enough already, John,' said Catherine. 'Do you know why we're being attacked like this?'

'I can't imagine. It's against everything we stand for. I can only think it's some faction within the Kuomintang that wants to embarrass Chiang Kai-shek.'

'Poor John,' murmured Catherine, briefly putting a hand on his.

'What's that he said?' came Lionel's hectoring voice in the back.

Catherine turned and gave him a sweet smile. 'Major Soo was remarking that the weather is pleasant for this time of year.'

When they reached the Standard Oil compound, various Europeans, all armed with hunting rifles or pistols, surrounded the jeeps. The Charters family were greeted like heroes. 'My God, old boy, we feared you were a goner,' said one luxuriantly moustached man, his pinstriped suit swathed in bandoliers. 'Lord, what's happened to Jenny?'

'My wife's a heroine, that's what,' said Lionel. 'I'll tell you all about it inside. Don't worry about these chaps,' he continued, waving at the soldiers. 'They're friendlies.'

'Glad some of them are. Trust you to arrive with a military escort, Lionel. Good show.'

Lionel turned to John Soo. 'Well, Major, my thanks again. I'm glad there's at least one white man among the Bolshevik hooligans in your slovenly army. If I can, I'll put in a good word for you when order's restored.'

John turned a cold stare on him. 'Mr Charters, I am not a white man. I am a Chinese, occupied in liberating my country from imperialists like you. And there are no so-called Bolsheviks in this corps. We are probably all bourgeois, as you are – but that doesn't make me any less your enemy. Your days of exploitation are over, Mr Charters, and I am saying that on behalf of the Chinese people. I apologise that you have been a victim of unreformed and criminal elements, but I promise you, they do not represent the Chinese people, who will evict you one day in a legal and responsible manner, when a unified and properly constituted government has overturned all your unequal treaties.' With that he turned his back on the spluttering Lionel and walked to where Catherine was standing on her own.

'Well done, John.' She smiled. 'That told him.'

'I believe it, Catherine,' he said quietly. 'Despite everything that has happened I still believe in our revolution. I have to.'

'I know you do,' she said. 'We probably stand on different political sides, but I respect you none the less.'

He laughed. 'And I you. I know now why Fu-kuei and my Lan-hua have spoken so highly of you. You are a courageous woman.'

'Your Lan-hua?'

'Yes.' He smiled bashfully. 'She and I hope one day to be married, if we survive this madness.'

'Oh, John,' she said. 'I'm so pleased for both of you.'

'I meant to tell you about it earlier, but there has been no time.'

'We'll meet again,' she said.

'I hope so.' They smiled at each other, friends. 'Oh, by the way,' he said, reaching into his pocket for a crumpled scrap of paper. 'Talking of old friends, I don't know if you're still in touch with Fu-kuei. Anyway I've written down her address in Shanghai for you. If things work out well today I imagine all you foreigners will be evacuated there. She's living with a senior man in the secret police, and might be useful to you. Say hello to her for me if you see her. Sorry, Catherine, I must go.'

Not caring if anybody saw her, she kissed his cheek. 'Goodbye, John. Good luck. Thank you for saving my life, and Jenny's.'

'It was my duty.'

She watched the two jeeps drive down the hill, then turned wearily, preparing herself to rejoin her race and breed.

A day and a bit later she found herself crouched under a blanket on the deck of a British destroyer, steaming down the Yangtse under the stars. Around her she saw the silhouettes of her fellow refugees, sharing the sailors' rum and noisily regaling them with their heroic exploits during the siege of the Standard Oil redoubt: of the firing from loopholes while the women and children huddled in an inner room; of the brave American oilman who had lowered himself down the city wall on a rope under enemy fire and commandeered a sampan to take him to one of the destroyers; of the joy, the relief, when the naval guns opened fire and bombarded the city, causing the Bolshevik soldiers to run like the craven cowards they were; of the hair-raising scramble down a rope-ladder in the dark, women and children first, the lowering of the wounded on stretchers, the stumble behind an oil lantern on the steep cliff path, and the elation when the shadowy figures on the beach turned out to be boat parties of British tars . . .

Catherine could not remember much about it. She had spent all of her time with the wounded, including the British consul, whose stomach wound she had treated with only the memory of Edmund's operations to go by (the naval surgeon on board the destroyer had told her afterwards that she had done a 'damned good job for an amateur' and 'I wouldn't have believed it but the fellow will probably live. Well done, Nurse!'). She had also done her best to comfort two female American missionaries who, despite the scepticism of most of the foreign community, led by Lionel, had been raped, and were hysterical because of it. In fact, for the twelve hours or so in which the house had been besieged, Catherine had been kept so busy ministering to the demands of wailing women, once slapping the cheek of a consular wife when the woman's hysteria threatened to get out of hand, that she was hardly aware of any shooting. No wounded had come her way, so either the defenders had been extraordinarily fortunate or the attacking Hunanese soldiers had been half-hearted – but she kept these heretical thoughts to herself. She was ignored, even ostracised, on the destroyer. She could only assume that Lionel had spread the word about her supposed Bolshevik sympathies. She didn't care. She didn't want to be with these alien people anyway. She certainly did not want to go to Shanghai, but she had had no choice: she could hardly have abandoned the wounded consul and the others in her care, and once she was on board the destroyer there was no way back to land. So she would go to Shanghai and see if she could find a way upriver to Edmund and Wuhan after that. In Shanghai she would almost certainly find her medicines. Niedemeyer would fix that for her.

She must have dozed, because she woke with a start at a tug on her shoulder. It was Jenny. 'Catherine, I can't stay here long,' she whispered. 'Lionel might find out I've been with you, and – oh, I'm sorry, Catherine. I know I'm weak and selfish, but I had to thank you. I'll never forget what you did. Ever.' Stifling a sob, she hurried away.

Poor Jenny, she thought. Had she really done the right thing in helping her to conceal the terrible abuse inflicted on her? Catherine had been affected enough, she knew, by her own near escape from a similar fate. But she was strong, and used to life dealing its hand of unutterable horrors. She believed she was resilient enough to take anything that a malign fortune might throw at her. Jenny's recovery amazed her. She had seen her walking arm in arm with Lionel on the deck, pathetically bearing her heroine's scars, even managing to look happy. As did Lionel, who was basking in the glory of his wife's reputation. Anyway, she thought cynically, when a whole country was in the process of being raped, did one woman's misfortune really matter?

She knew in the depths of her lonely heart that it did immeasurably. She thought of the Donne quotation that Fu-kuei had once recited to her, on that other boat journey so long ago. 'No man is an island, entire of itself; every man is a piece of the continent, a part of the main.' It was true: there was no escape into individual oblivion, or away from the grinding responsibility of service to one's fellow creatures. Hurt to one was hurt to all, and Catherine, however much she struggled, was caught in the fishermen's net. She may not like the other fish gasping beside her – the English parasites like Lionel, for example, attempting to live a lotus existence in a country in its death throes – but she knew that her fate was interconnected with theirs, and beyond them to John Soo, Yu Fu-kuei and Lei Lan-hua, and everybody else around her struggling to make sense of this nightmare world.

The dark river swirled by, as the destroyer drove its inexorable course downstream to the confluence of the Yangtse and the sea. Occasionally the raging waters revealed themselves in the faint wash of a wave, or a splash of foam, caught momentarily in one of the ship's lights before rolling away like a tormented soul returning to its lake of pitch. Watching one of these waves hold itself, totter, then fall back into the darkness, Catherine thought that it might have stood for any one of the wretched creatures condemned, like her, to spend their brief time on the planet; protesting for a moment their unhappy lot, submerging again into their habitual misery; each soul a bubble in the river of an aching humanity, swirling together in living disharmony, flowing maniacally towards a black ocean, that, for all she knew, stretched to an eternal horizon of despair.

14

Shanghai *Götterdämmerung*

From the journal of William Lampsett, Reuters correspondent, Tientsin, 9 April 1927

The unexpected success of the Communists' insurrection in Shanghai poses a problem for Chiang. Theoretically they are still his allies, but if he recognises the People's Commune, it will be tantamount to acknowledging the leadership of Borodin and the left wing of the party in Wuhan. He is under pressure from his bourgeois supporters and foreigners alike to eliminate them, but he dares not send in his troops for fear of alienating the ordinary people who, in most part, have supported the insurrection, believing Chiang's own rhetoric about the United Front.

He is now giving a remarkable demonstration of Chinese prevarication and fence-sitting. When he arrived in the International Concession, he was fêted by the scared capitalists, but on the same day he started negotiating with the Communists, and has already publicly agreed to some of their demands. He is on the horns of a dilemma. His numerous forces gathered outside Shanghai are easily strong enough to overwhelm the Communist militias, but it would be political suicide for him to attempt it. He is damned if he does and doomed if he doesn't. This is the crisis of the Northern Expedition.

Sitting on a bench in a small park in Chapei, Fu-kuei absorbed the colours and freshness of a sunny spring afternoon, allowing her concentration to wander and her limbs to relax. It was the first time in more than a month that she had devoted any time to mere

488

sensual pleasure; yet today she did not feel she was shirking any duty or responsibility. She sat contentedly, enjoying the soft touch of the breeze on her cheek and the inconsequential twitter of the birds in the trees. She was vaguely aware of how exhausted she was. During the tense weeks of the general strike she had hardly slept, hardly eaten; she had lived from moment to moment on adrenalin and nerves. Never in her life had she experienced such heights of elation and triumph, such depths of fear and occasional despair, sometimes all within the space of a few chaotic hours. It had been a carousel ride of excitement and tension – and now it was nearly over.

Her memories blurred into fractured impressions of anxious journeys through warlord-patrolled streets, the noise and chaos of mass demonstrations and late-night meetings in candle-lit rooms. She had spent hours with Comrade Lee, reporting troop disposi- tions, changes in police routines, trying to remember exactly what Yi-liang had told her in their hurried exchanges over breakfast or a snatched dinner. He was so occupied in his official role that he hardly ever found time to come home – their own meetings had taken the form of secret assignations – but when he was with her he had always been calm, gentle, assured, a rock in the swirling foam of the crises lashing round them. He would listen patiently to Comrade Lee's questions, ask some of his own, and it was rare that he could not give her an answer on the spot. He would certainly have it the next day, along with information, neatly written on rice paper so that if necessary she could swallow it, covering points that Comrade Lee had not thought to ask, as well as new ideas of his own, suggestions, warnings of raids. It seemed on occasions that it was not the CCP but Yi-liang who was masterminding the insur- rection. Admittedly she had adjusted that impression on the few occasions when she had had the privilege to brief Chou En-lai, and glimpsed a larger picture of history in the making. Then she had felt a rush of awe, humility and pride, and gratitude that she had been given a small part to play.

There had also been incidents she wished she could forget, such as the frightening occasion when, caught in the middle of a demon- stration of cotton-mill workers, she had been pushed towards a barricade, where warlord soldiers were waiting for them. She had run for her life when they opened fire. The images of falling bodies and women trampled in the rush would remain with her for the rest of her days. It had been a massacre. More horrific still had been the aftermath when, huddled in a doorway, she had watched the executioners saunter by with their broadswords. Before her eyes, they had pulled a student from a doorway further along the street, riffled though the pockets of his gown, found a pamphlet and beheaded him on the spot. She had never known that there could be so much blood in a human body; she had stared, appalled, at the fountain gushing from its neck. The bespectacled head, some yards off, seemed to glare at her accusingly. She had remembered then her lover's conversation with Chou about the inevitability of sacrifice, and shuddered; she had to remind herself that such horrors served the cause, and justified it. Sacrifice was part of the plan. This, like the other atrocities being committed by the warlords, had been tinder for the insurrection to come.

There had been a terrible two days when the general strike had faltered under the repression. Comrade Lee had been preoccupied, when she had arrived at the assignation with Yi-liang's latest information, good news, incidentally, that the Shantung troops were drawing up their plans to leave because Chiang Kai-shek's troops were expected on the outskirts of the city in four days. 'Four days?' Lee had grunted. 'It might as well be an eternity. We should have struck when the iron was hot, when we had the masses.' He had told her that the Central Committee was debating whether to bring forward the insurrection, or even to cancel it.

She had returned home miserable.

Then Yi-liang had shown his true mettle. 'Here,' he had said. 'Give me that rice paper and a pen. Get this to Chou En-lai. I will personally guarantee that the workers will be out on the streets again tomorrow in greater numbers than before.' He had sealed the letter, then hurriedly left the house.

The next morning it had been reported that, during the night, White Russian mercenaries attached to the Shantung forces had driven through the streets of Chapei in jeeps mounted with machineguns and fired indiscriminately at the homes on either side of the road. Many men, women and children had been killed. Immediately, the General Workers' Union had called for a mass demonstration to be held that afternoon. The strike was on again in full force.

Fu-kuei had not been sure whether it was a coincidence or whether Yi-liang had planned it, but it had done the trick. When she saw Comrade Lee that night, he had been his usual, coughing self. 'Tell your lover,' he had wheezed, hawking into a filthy handkerchief, 'that the Central Committee has agreed we go ahead as scheduled. Three nights from now. Make sure he's ready.'

Three more feverish, chaotic days of anticipation: there had been almost open warfare between the warlord forces and the enraged populace. The repression had been even bloodier than before, but Yi-liang had reported that the trains departing from the station were full of retreating troops and an endless stream of boats from Woosung and other dockyards, as the northern army began its retreat. When the day came, he had been exceptionally tender. They had made love, which they had not had time to do for weeks – and he had begged her, this day only, to stay at home. 'Look,' he had said, when she protested, 'your job's done, and mine really begins tonight. I won't be able to do it if I have to worry about you.' She had kissed him, and agreed.

Through the night she had sat at her open bedroom window chain-smoking, although it was a habit in which she did not usually indulge. Around midnight she had heard the first explosion, and later, the sound of sporadic gunfire, at first from far away, and then all around. About three a.m. it was very close, and she had known that the local police station three blocks from her house was under attack. She was so familiar with the plans of the station that she felt she could picture the assault. She had wanted to put on her clothes, rush out and join them, but she had restrained herself, remembering her promise. The silence that descended at about five in the morning had almost stretched her frayed nerves to breaking point.

When the dawn came it had been beautiful, with purple streaks of cirrus floating across a lilac sky. She had been convinced that such beauty could only be a mocking sign that the insurrection had failed.

At eight, Yi-liang had returned, tired, dishevelled, his face set in a grim frown. 'Oh, no, Yi-liang?' she had half sobbed.

Then he had given her the schoolboy grin she loved. 'Comrade Fu-kuei,' he said, 'consider yourself a leading citizen of the People's Commune of Shanghai!' She had thrown herself across the room, forced him on to the un-slept-in bed, and for the next two hours devoured him.

At noon, they had driven together through the streets. From many of the houses hung Kuomintang banners or makeshift red flags. Yi-liang had prepared a hammer-and-sickle pennant to fly on the bonnet of his Rolls-Royce. She had watched it flapping and cracking in front of her, and had hardly been able to keep the tears from her eyes, especially when the ordinary men and women of Chapei and Yangtse-poo, her comrades, for whom she had struggled and conspired for so many years, broke into cheers as they passed. After their triumphal tour of a free city, they had driven to the Commercial Press Building that the CCP Central Committee were in the process of establishing as their official headquarters, now that they had been able to come out into the open for the first time.

Fu-kuei had expected to find a mood of elation and celebration, and had been surprised by the businesslike, almost sombre atmosphere. Men and women she did not know were in the process of storing files in cabinets, speaking urgently on the telephone, poring over maps, or rushing in with memos. It might have been a war room rather than the offices of a new, confident government.

Eventually, they had found Comrade Lee in an untidy office, full of unpacked boxes, on the second floor. He, too, had been growling and coughing into a telephone. A grey film of soot from his overflowing ashtray already covered his desk. 'Well, Comrade Major,' he had greeted them when he put the phone down, 'how does it feel now that you've formally become a turncoat? Still happy to be on the winning side?'

'I'm satisfied enough with a job well done.'

'It's not over yet. We've the Kuomintang to deal with now. Their first troops have entered the city. There've already been some incidents when they encountered our militia on the barricades. We'll be impossibly outnumbered if things go the wrong way.'

Fu-kuei's heart had sunk.

But Yi-liang had answered with assurance, 'Yes, but you have politics on your side now. And the masses. Chiang has to acknowledge that you control the city, and the workforce. That's the reality and the Kuomintang will have no choice but to accept it.'

'Let's hope so. I don't like the fact that Chiang's chosen the International Concession to make his official entry. That gives all the wrong signals, especially as every merchant and banker is flocking to the pier to meet him.'

'I think he's made a shrewd move,' Yi-liang had replied coolly. 'The foreigners are incensed by the atrocities in Nanking. They'll be even more worried now they've got a Communist government across the Soochow creek. And they're powerful, with thousands of troops in the city already and more who can be brought in by ship. Chiang's making a gesture that he's no threat to them, that's all. It's in our interests for the moment to keep the Powers neutral. Don't worry. He'll come cap in hand when he's set his own house in order. As I said, he's got no choice.'

Lee had fumbled for another cigarette. 'I'd love to debate with you, Major, but I'm busy.' He had paused, coughed and added grudgingly, 'Look, don't think we're ungrateful. You've done a good job for us, but now's not the right time for us to be seen dealing with a former secret policeman. You've done what you could for us. We'll stay in touch through Comrade Yu. We may need information from you on the old security arrangements in the city. She's welcome to drop by when she wants. She's less conspicuous than you are – as long as she refrains from wearing her mink.' He had uttered a coarse laugh, which disintegrated into one of his coughing fits.

Yi-liang had looked hurt. 'So now I'm no longer useful I'm to be discarded? Is that it, Comrade?'

Lee had looked at him coldly. 'What did you expect? A medal? A few weeks ago you were clapping us in prison. Don't worry, you'll get your reward. Chou En-lai promised you a job, didn't he? You're the sort of practical man we need, aren't you? Be patient for a while. Wait till we set up a working government. Then we'll find something useful for you to do.'

And they had been dismissed.

That had been nearly a fortnight ago. Fu-kuei now felt even sorrier for Yi-liang. He had sunk into apathy. When she tried to engage him in conversation about the latest rumours, or news of the negotiations with the Kuomintang, he would shrug or grunt, change the subject or maintain a sour silence. She knew he had taken to going for long walks in his civilian clothes; otherwise, she presumed, he just lazed about their home. When she returned in the evening after one of her long days, he would be either slumped in a chair in the sitting room, a book open but obviously unread on his knee, or sitting in his study at his empty desk. He never asked what she had been doing. Now he no longer had a job, his authority and energy seemed to have drained away.

Sometimes she felt she should be spending more time with him, but the revolution of which she was now a part had become too absorbing. She had taken up Comrade Lee's invitation to 'drop by' the Commercial Press Building; each time he had received her warmly, almost affectionately, and on her fourth visit in as many days he had taken her down to the office floor below, and given her a desk. She did only menial secretarial tasks, taking dictation and copying out memos in her neat hand, and often there was nothing for her to do at all, but she drank in the tense atmosphere of comradeship under stress, and shared the fears when it emerged that Chiang Kai-shek appeared to have struck a deal with the capitalists, and the elation when he accepted yet another demand from the Central Committee of the CCP.

It was frustrating that she could not spend all of her time with her new companions, but her old masters were still pressing her for information. She saw no harm in providing what they wanted, although she did find it distasteful to spy on her friends. She comforted herself that soon there would be no need for secrets of any kind.

Today she had lunched in a hotel in Hongkew, and when she had come out a crippled beggar woman had approached her with the password. She had dutifully exchanged the latest information for a new list of questions – the usual requests about the new Party organisation and the composition of the militias. Crossing a small park on her way home, she noticed the beautiful white blossom on the cherry trees, and with no other pressing engagements, she had succumbed to the temptation to enjoy a few moments of this gorgeous spring day.

Now, in almost shamefully delicious torpor, she was experiencing an emotion that was strange and new; she wondered if it was happiness.

Idly she watched some old couples waltzing to a tinny gramophone under the trees. Further away, another group was practising a slow-moving form of martial arts involving complicated manoeuvres with gold-tasselled swords. For a while she was charmed to witness these signs of ordinary life, so far removed from the politics that now occupied all her waking hours – yet in a way this ancient *kung fu* art form that she was observing was no less disciplined or dedicated, she thought, than the Party discipline she had come to respect in her comrades and friends. It took no less devotion from these old men and women to move their bodies so gracefully, all in perfect time with their teacher. How wonderful life was, she allowed herself to think simplistically. What a wonderful world she and others were creating for ordinary people like these.

Her reverie was interrupted by the thump of a heavy body beside her on the bench. It was a European in grubby artisan's clothes; he had what appeared to be a sailor's pom-pom hat drawn low over his eyes and he smelt of alcohol. An impoverished White Russian, she decided. She was a little annoyed that her solitude had been disturbed, and was thinking of moving to another bench . . . She started when she heard the grave, familiar voice.

'Well, well, my clever, scholarly little Miss Yu Fu-kuei! Now a real revolutionary at last! How have you been enjoying the world of action? You see, I followed you this morning from the Commercial Press Building, and I know that you have been accepted into the heart of the CCP. Bravo. Were you there with rifle and flag on the night of the barricades? I must confess I'm impressed that my *protégée* has done so well for herself.'

'Mr Behrens!' she gasped.

'No, no, I am not Mr Behrens any more. That pompous fellow disappeared long ago. The world knows me now as humble

Sailor Savarin, a stoker on the steamship *Krupskaya* that docked in Shanghai some weeks ago. Isn't life full of surprises? And how the wheel of fortune turns! Once you knew a prosperous businessman who travelled first class. Now a drunken mariner from the lower decks comes to take his place! Do you remember my lectures on the importance of the mask? I suspect that the student now has lessons for the teacher. It has been so many years, Fu-kuei. Allow me an unforgivable moment of self-indulgence to tell you how proud I have become, observing your progress and celebrating your triumph.'

He contemplated her kindly. 'Who would have believed it?' he continued, while she stared at him in amazement. 'Do you know? Two years ago, when your lover discovered your secret and did such unspeakable things to our mutual friend Mr Barkowitz, we had all feared that you were "blown", or worse. We mourned you. Yet you survived. How, I wonder? And not only did you survive – to fight another day – you turned your lover to your own way of thinking so that he betrayed his own cause. You have displayed resourcefulness beyond my wildest expectations, my dear. You are like the proverbial phoenix rising from the ashes. What a shame that it was at such cost. Poor Mr Barkowitz. Such a gentle, earnest fellow, and so dedicated to our cause. I recruited him, you know, as I did you, and all the others who, unlike you, were not so fortunate to escape the retribution that followed the break-up of our little organisation. Is he still alive, I wonder? In what prison does the sad, broken fellow eke out his lonely days?'

At first, Fu-kuei had thought she was suffering some hallucination, that the ghost of her mentor, with whom she had had so many internal conversations over the years, had somehow materialised from some recess of her mind, but the man beside her was flesh and blood – he reeked of it – and though the red, vodka-soaked features appeared coarser than she remembered, the pedantic, ironic voice was unmistakably that of Mr Behrens. But something he had said puzzled her.

'But Mr Barkowitz is dead. He was shot when his shop was attacked. I was there.'

Mr Behrens chuckled. 'No, no. Your Major Yang is not a

murderer. He is a secret policeman, a professional, my dear, as I attempted to train you to be. It is information that he desires, not gratuitous slaughter. I have reliable reports that Barkowitz was seen in the back of a car, driven by those gangsters whom your lover likes to employ. He was deposited at the Central Gendarmerie, where we presume he was tortured to reveal everything he knew about our operation. That was why we had to close down the network. It was most inconvenient for us. It is also why you have not heard from us for such a very long while.'

An alarm bell was ringing dully in her confused mind. 'But we have been in touch,' she muttered.

'It is charming of you to say so, and of course, my dear, you have been in my thoughts too – but I am talking of a more professional relationship than the mere reveries of professor and student. Yes, Miss Yu, now that the situation in Shanghai is so very different and promising, and now your policeman lover has been neutralised, it is perhaps time for us to invite you to rejoin the wider struggle. Your position with the CCP could not make you better placed. Our masters are extremely concerned that the United Front, which as you know Comrade Stalin has made the lynchpin of his China policy, is under stress. Some of your new comrades are perhaps a little parochial in their intentions and believe they can conduct a revolution all on their own . . .'

'You are asking me to spy on the CCP?' She had some difficulty keeping her voice calm. 'To begin spying again?' she added, hoping he would contradict her.

'Well, yes, I suppose I am. Only at first on certain elements within the CCP, bad elements or unenlightened ones, since I am predisposed to be generous. It might appear distasteful to you if you think of it as reporting on the activities of your friends, but I recollect that we once agreed that in our business we should have no friends. It is so much easier that way. I am sure you also remember the lesson of the worker ant that I taught you, and our respective positions in the grand design . . . Of course we will need to adopt a completely new system of tradecraft. Alas, there is no Mr Barkowitz to help us any more – but I have some ideas.'

'You're – you're not satisfied with the beggars?' She had to ask, to make sure, but she had a sinking feeling, guessing already what his reaction would be.

'Beggars? What an extraordinary question. Why are you suddenly talking to me about beggars? What have they to do with anything?'

And she knew – but she did not want to believe it. Her thoughts racing, she tried to play for time, until she had worked out what she would do. 'It's nothing. Sorry. Tell me – tell me about the new tradecraft.'

But Mr Behrens was staring at her intently under his bushy eyebrows. 'No, Miss Yu, you tell me about beggars. There is something significant here that I should know about. You should not keep secrets from your old teacher, you know. That would not be appropriate at all.'

She could not think what to say. Mr Behrens's eyes had hardened as they bored into hers. She remembered how she had always thought of him as a Svengali, with powers over her mind. Even now she wanted to unburden herself, confess, tell him everything, seek his absolution – but at the same time she knew how dangerous that would be. With an effort she turned away her head. She was panting slightly.

'Beggars? Why beggars?' she heard him murmuring beside her. 'There are syndicates of beggars in this city, under the control of the gangs. The gangs? Oh, yes.' She heard a low, cold chuckle. 'Oh, yes. How subtle, yet so obvious. Of course he would be able to secure the services of the beggars' guilds. As go-betweens, no doubt?'

She clung desperately to the view of the waltzing couples under the trees and the troop of martial artists exercising with their swords. They represented normal life, removed from all horror, all complexity, all betrayal.

'Oh, my poor Fu-kuei.' Mr Behrens was sighing. 'How I feel for you. If only you had paid more attention to what I had taught you. Of course, I should have realised. He is clever, your lover, so very clever. And he must have made dear Mr Barkowitz sing like a bird. All our codes, all our passwords. But why did you not suspect? Didn't I tell you that after a ring is blown, we never use the same tradecraft again? I feel so immensely sorry for you. Such a clever sting that it fooled even you. Or are your eyes clouded by love, my sweet? Or romanticism? For the revolution you so, so desire? Oh, gracious, what a mess. Tell me, how long has this been going on? Six months? A year? Clearly this new factor changes the situation.'

'Less than a year,' she whispered. She turned a pleading look at Mr Behrens, who was watching her with gentle, sympathetic eyes.

'And what have you been telling the brave Major Yang, your lover, all the time that you thought he was helping the CCP? Oh, no. Are those tears in your eyes? Oh, my love, my poor love. Don't worry. No harm has been done that cannot be rectified. It is never too late. There is no mess that cannot be tidied. But I have to think. What to do?' He smiled. 'There will be an answer in the book of rules. There always is. That is the beauty of it, the inevitability of the grand design. It is what I taught you. There is always a procedure available, a solution to be found, even for the most unanticipated problem.'

He leaned back against the bench and appeared to relax; a smile curved his lips. When he turned to face her again, a tender, almost loving look radiated his features. Gone was the raddled seaman. It was the Mr Behrens of old. Gently, he extended his left arm round her shoulders. Instinctively she leaned against him, seeking his comfort, his wisdom, his forgiveness, abandoning her will to his authority, because it seemed the easiest thing to do. Slowly he turned his body, so that his kind eyes were close to hers. The ironic smile she remembered played on his lips. He looked so wise, so assured, so calm . . .

'You see, I have found the answer,' he whispered. 'I told you there was no need to worry.'

With a sudden movement he shook his right arm. She felt a prick of pain on her throat. It was as if she had woken from a trance. Her mind raced. There was nobody she could call on to help. Nobody observing them would notice anything unusual; they might consider that here were two lovers in an embrace; the knife pressed to her throat would be invisible. She would be dead before she opened her mouth to call. She felt a cold, detached calm as she looked into the tender eyes that appeared almost apologetic for what their bearer had decided to do. Inevitability, he had said. She understood. She knew the code by which Mr Behrens lived. She had made it her own. There was only the cause, for which any and every sacrifice must be made. And with the knife to her throat, she discovered that she believed in it, with all her intellect and deep within her soul. It was inevitable. It had always been inevitable. The sheer impersonal simplicity of it was awesome. She knew what Mr Behrens had to do, and what she had to do – if he would only give her time.

'My dearest Fu-kuei, I am so proud of you,' he was whispering. 'You, of all my agents, were the most brilliant. I had such high hopes for you – but we are all prisoners of the rules. And you have created a mess that I can tidy in only one way. It is regrettable and it hurts me, but I hope you understand and will forgive me. Goodbye, my most loyal agent.'

She saw his eyes narrow. It was time. She fired through the pocket of her coat the little Beretta that Yi-liang had given to her for her protection during the general strike. The wry smile on Mr Behrens's lips remained curled where it was, but there was a momentary confusion in his eyes before they settled into a pained, recriminating stare that followed the heavy body that slowly sank on top of hers. She waited in the darkness of his coat, her mind and body numb, the scent of stale alcohol reeking in her nostrils. Her neck was stinging. The knife had cut her as he fell, but only a harmless nick. She would not bleed to death under the body of the man whose own blood she imagined was mingling with hers.

She waited for the old folk doing their exercises in the park to come up to them. They must have heard the sharp report of the gun and be curious, but nobody came, and when she shoved Mr Behrens a little to the side, she observed that the swordsmen and - women were still engaged in their ancient choreography, while the dancing couples performed a foxtrot from a newer, harsher century. Nobody was paying attention to the unlikely lovers locked in an embrace on a park bench: a foreign man with, presumably, his Chinese whore. The peace of the park was undisturbed.

She had killed a man. She had killed her mentor. She felt no remorse, only lassitude. She wondered if his departed shade would be proud of what she had done. The prize student, who had trumped her master. With sudden revulsion, she wriggled, and pushed away the heavy weight. He slumped back against the bench, his head hanging forward under the ridiculous pom-pom. He looked his latest disguise, a drunken Russian sailor, sleeping off a debauch. Quickly she lifted his arm settled it, with the knife, inside his jacket. Thankfully, little blood had penetrated the thick serge of his donkey jacket.

She looked down and saw the blood staining the front of her coat, felt the wet warmth on her neck. It couldn't be helped. It was only a short walk to her house. Luckily her coat was dark so the blood would not be immediately apparent. If she walked quickly, perhaps nobody would notice her. If they did, well, in these violent days, they would probably turn away their heads. She hurried past the martial artists and out of the park.

She tried not to think, concentrating only on her fast steps clicking along the pavement. *One, two. One, two.* She knew now that she had been a pawn in her lover's game, but she could not understand what his intentions had been. What they still were, she corrected herself, for they must even now be directed against the CCP, or she would not still be passing messages. She had to stop him. She had to warn Chou En-lai. But first she must find out what it was about. In her pocket, next to the revolver, was a list of questions about the CCP's security arrangements. Of course, only an enemy would want information like that. She had been stupid. The man she loved had betrayed her – but what was his motive? Why had he helped them, if he was at the same time using her against them? If not for Yi-liang, the insurrection might have failed.

She let herself quietly into the sitting room. Yi-liang was asleep on the sofa, snoring. With the Beretta in her hand, she stood above his prone body, contemplating him, the handsome features, the trim perfection of his figure in the loose white cotton of his suit – this snake who had betrayed her and, more importantly, the cause for which she lived. Mr Behrens had said that he was not a murderer, that he was a professional who only dealt in information. Well, she knew he was a murderer: he had murdered her hopes, her trust, her love. She looked down at the small gun in her hand. She had already used it to kill one man she had respected today. It would be so easy to press the trigger again, to execute one she despised. No, she restrained her anger. She, too, was a professional. She, too, needed information. More than the tragedy of her shattered life hung in the balance today.

'Wake up.' She prodded him viciously with the gun, then stepped back a pace so that she could cover him.

He was instantly alert. His eyebrows raised a fraction when he saw her. His lips, however, curved in a slow, easy smile. 'Fu-kuei,' he said, 'you're covered with blood. What on earth have you been doing? You've obviously found out my little secret or you wouldn't be pointing that thing at me. Well, it was only a matter of time, I suppose.'

'Why?' she asked coldly.

He covered his mouth to hide a yawn. 'Why? I told your new hero, Chou En-lai, I like to be on the winning side. That's partly it, I suppose. We all have to get by, and you must admit we have become used to a rather grand lifestyle – but please don't think I'm prompted purely by reasons of career. Like you, I have some shreds of idealism. I like to think I'm doing what's best for China. And I found myself in a position where I could be useful. And make you useful while I was about it.'

'You've betrayed me. Lied to me. Used me. You betrayed Sun Chuan-fang. I know you are planning to betray the CCP.'

'Oh, come on, Fu-kuei, who's betrayed whom? You're an agent of a foreign power – or you thought you were. That you were working for me doesn't excuse the fact that you were spying on the people you're to help. Nobody forced you, you know. That day on the Bund when a beggar first approached you, you could have come to me and told me. In fact, I was sitting in the tea-room at the Cathay hoping you would. Face it. You and I are very similar. That's why we make a perfect match. I must say you were very thorough. I wish all my agents were as industrious as you.'

'Please don't try to charm me, Yi-liang. It won't work. Not any more. I want to know what use you plan to make of the information I have been supplying to you.'

'Isn't it obvious? I've been using you to verify all the data we have on the strength and locations of the CCP militia so we can destroy them when the time comes. You've been extremely helpful.'

'I still don't understand, Yi-liang. If you are the enemy of the CCP, why were you so helpful to them in their insurrection?'

'I would have thought that was obvious too. To destroy your enemies you must first bring them out into the open. That particularly applies to an underground organisation like the CCP. Chiang now has them where he wants them. He knows exactly who they are, and where they are, and it will be comparatively easy for us to deal with them. It would have been more difficult if they were still hiding in their underground cells. You've done us a great service, Fu-kuei. You've helped us draw them out.'

'So you work for Chiang Kai-shek?'

'Since before the beginning of the Northern Expedition. I wasn't lying to you when I told you that I had become disillusioned with the warlords. The Kuomintang offers us the best chance of a decent government, and I'm proud to serve them. The fact that they've promised me my old job, and a promotion, doesn't hurt either. So there you are. Now you have it all.'

'No, Yi-liang, that's not all.' She was amazed by how calm she was, as she tried to absorb the enormity of what he had just told her. 'You haven't told me when and how you intend to destroy the CCP.'

Yi-liang gave his boyish grin. She hated him for it. 'I'm hardly likely to tell you that while you have a pistol pointed at me, am I?'

'You'd better,' she said. 'Or I'll shoot you like the dog you are.'

His grin did not falter. 'I think you're so angry with me that you just might at that.' Casually, he rested both arms on the back of the sofa. 'Well,' he smiled, 'you're not giving me much choice, are you? Where would you intend to shoot me, by the way? I hope you're accurate.'

Despite herself she glanced at the barrel of the revolver. She judged it was pointing directly at his heart. 'Oh, you can be sure I'll be—' Her head was knocked backwards by the pillow he hurled at her face. She fired, and felt his powerful frame knocking into her. The back of her head cracked on something hard, and for some seconds a mist blinded her. When she had recovered enough to move again, she realised she was lying with her head against the grate. Yi-liang was standing over her, her pistol in one hand, the other pressed to his shoulder, which was welling blood. As she watched, dazed and despairing, she saw him edge to the open door, and heard him shout something.

A few moments later two soldiers in brown uniforms came into the room. 'Here,' he said, handing over the Beretta. 'One of you'd better cover her with this while the other has a look at my wound. Bind it up, would you? She's only grazed the skin. Don't worry. This has been a lovers' tiff. I won't be pressing charges, and I'd be grateful if you fellows don't mention anything about it – heavens, how a tigress can scratch, eh?' She heard them laugh, before she slipped into unconsciousness.

She woke to find herself lying on her bed. Her head was pounding. She put up a hand and touched the bandage round her temples. She became aware of the smell of cigarette smoke, and saw Yi-liang, now wearing his old uniform, his arm in a sling, slouched in the armchair. 'What time is it?' she muttered.

'It's not yet midnight. You've been out for a few hours. Nasty bang to your head, I'm afraid. Sorry about that, but the doctor said you'd be all right. I had to wipe all that blood off you before I called him. He gave you an injection to make you sleep . . . What have you been up to today? It wasn't just your blood on your clothes. You haven't been shooting Russian sailors in parks, have you? That's the sensation of the neighbourhood this evening. Don't worry – nobody's connected it with you. They're looking for a prostitute, it seems.'

'I'm going to stop you, you know,' she said dully. 'Somehow I'm going to warn the CCP.'

'You can try by all means,' he said, 'but you'll find it difficult to get out of this room. Tomorrow morning I'm having security bars put on all the windows. With murders in the local park we can't be too careful, can we? And Corporals Chen and Wang have agreed to take turns to sit outside your door. I've persuaded them that until you've calmed down about my affair with a flower-girl, you're a danger to me and yourself. They're most understanding. Sorry, my love, I'm afraid you know too much now. Don't think Comrade Lee or any of your other friends will come looking for you. I've already sent a message to the Commercial Press about your unfortunate fall. I'll pop in to see you when I can but I'm likely to be busy for the next day or so. Yes, it won't be long now. Sorry.'

'I'll stop you,' she muttered. 'I'll find a way.'

She saw him advance towards her with a syringe. 'The doctor said I was to inject you again if you woke. Better anyway you sleep. You can plan your escape in the morning.'

'I'll find a way,' she repeated, before she lost consciousness again.

After the destroyer, anchoring in the Huangpu, had delivered her and her fellow refugees into the arms of a reception committee of concerned citizens, complete with a military band, reporters and a host of voyeurs eager to see the victims of an atrocity, Catherine escaped in a rickshaw to the Park Hotel.

It did not take her long to realise, however, that in Shanghai she would encounter the same difficulties she had faced after her arrival in Nanking. If anything it was worse, because the international concession was a city under siege. There were soldiers, sandbagged machine-gun posts and roadblocks on almost every street. The atmosphere was one of barely restrained hysteria.

In the dining room at her hotel on the first evening she had overheard a group of traders at a neighbouring table loudly denouncing the members of the municipal council for not showing more resolve. She listened with mounting incredulity to their hysterical accounts of the atrocities that were supposed to have been committed by Nationalist troops in Hankow, Kiukiang and Nanking – from missionaries being flayed alive and hung on crosses on the Hankow Bund to the slaughter of men, women and children as they were forced to swim out to the naval vessels through treacherous currents and a hail of gunfire. 'That load of refugees who arrived today from Nanking,' said one thick-set young man. 'they're keeping it hush-hush, but I have it on good authority that there was not a woman among them who wasn't gang-raped. In front of their husbands and children. And their servants,' he added, for good measure, as he puffed his cigar. 'And the poor souls who were left behind after the evacuation from Hankow, I hear they were all rounded up and forced into military brothels.'

'Good God,' said one of his companions, a straw-haired boy whose features were vaguely familiar. 'Are you sure about that? I think I might know one of them – Catherine Airton. Ever heard of her? Made a big splash in the social set in Tientsin when I was posted there a year or so back. Married to the fellow who owns China Coast. Luscious red-head. She and I, well . . . a chap shouldn't tell. Anyway, that's by the by. What I wanted to say was I'm pretty sure she was in Hankow, and she didn't come down with the other refugees because I checked . . . My God, she was pretty wild, but she didn't deserve that fate.'

Catherine had not been able to contain herself. She remembered the young man now: he had been one of the griffins at Butterfield and Swire, who had once had to be helped home, worse for drink, after one of her parties. Leaving her coffee untouched, she swept over to their table and kissed him on both cheeks, to his blushing embarrassment. 'Toby!' she cried. 'How marvellous to see you! Do introduce me to your friends. Remember me? I'm Catherine Airton. Just down from Hankow and Nanking, you know, for a bit of a rest from the gang-rape and the brothels and all the other things the Bolshies like to get up to.'

That had not helped her. The next evening, after she had spent a fruitless day being politely rejected at shipping offices and the British consulate, a diary columnist was waiting for her in the hotel lobby. Although he was obviously after atrocity stories, she agreed to the interview, thinking she might be able to highlight the problem she was facing in getting medical supplies to Edmund's hospital in Hankow. When pressed, she told him truthfully that she knew of no personal attacks on foreigners in Hankow. As for Nanking, she said that there had been incidences of outrage against some women and a little melodrama as they made their escape, but she expressed John Soo's view that what had occurred there was not characteristic of the National Revolutionary Army, which in her observation was a remarkably disciplined and well-behaved force. The next day the *North China Herald* published an article, headlined '*Society Hostess Becomes Bolshevik Sympathiser: Tender Loving Care Provided To Red Soldiers; Nanking Outrage was "exaggerated", claims Mrs George Airton of Tientsin.*'

She discovered this when a plump-faced matron, ample bosom heaving with indignation, flung a newspaper angrily on to her table at breakfast. 'If I were you, Mrs Airton, I would be ashamed of myself,' she declared, glaring through her lorgnettes. 'In my view you are a disgrace to your country and your race. My husband and I are of half a mind to move out of this hotel rather than share it with the likes of you.'

She stared out of her window on to the racetrack below her, the park in the centre filled with tents belonging to the Bedfordshires who had been rushed in for the city's protection. 'Well done, Catherine,' she murmured to herself. 'Lionel couldn't have done a better job. You've cooked your own goose now.'

She had intended to visit an acquaintance in the Maritime Customs Service that morning, hoping that, with his help, she could counter Lionel's obstruction, but she saw little point now. She looked down her list of shipowning companies: Swires, Jardines, Dodwells. She knew that none would give her the time of day, not after this public character assassination. She had one chance. The previous afternoon, at the telegraph office, she had managed to get a trunk call through to Professor Niedemeyer's home in Chicago. He had no news of Edmund but he had been busy in the meanwhile, he assured her. Having assumed that after the Nanking Outrage Catherine would come to Shanghai, he had already purchased a supply of medicines, which were waiting for her in a warehouse on the Quai de France. He had not yet been able to organise passage, but he gave her the address of the agent of an American shipping line owned by a Harvard alumnus friend of his, saying he would cable an introduction. He had told her to be in good heart: he believed in the essential kindness of humanity. There was little evidence of that here, she thought bitterly, but she would try his friend's company. The Americans were not generally as priggish as the British.

This one was worse. When she arrived at his office on the Bund, he let her through the door, but the *North China Herald* was lying open on his desk. Mr Joseph Huckleberry, it emerged, was a lay preacher of the Unitarian Church, and Catherine was subjected to a half-hour sermon on the godlessness of the Bolsheviks. He would not break the embargo for her, despite the instructions he had received from his head office, but, if she were of a mind to repent her folly, he would be happy to introduce her to his Church. Catherine thanked him for his courtesy and left.

For the rest of that day and the next she stubbornly visited every company on her list; then she tried the smaller agencies, even a Bolivian one, although as far as she was aware that country did not have a sea-coast. The dark, comfortable-looking young man she found there took her into his cubbyhole of an office and was surprisingly helpful. '*Si*,' he kept saying, playing with his rings or brushing a comb through his hair. '*No problema. No es problema.*' But it turned out that there were two very big *problemas*: one, his company did not have any ships on the Yangtse, and two, if he was going to help her, the service he expected from her in return was perfectly clear.

Even then she did not give up, although she was becoming desperate. There were still the Chinese companies. Until now she had avoided them because she thought that dealing with them would be fraught with politics: most Chinese shipowners would presumably be more anti-Communist even than the Europeans. She got a list from an eager young man in the offices of the Chinese Chamber of Commerce whom she assumed was not a reader of the *North China Herald*.

Back at the hotel, it dawned on her that she had left Edmund more than a month ago without a single result to show for it. She felt a rush of guilt, mixed with longing: she should be by his side. She was failing him on what had turned out to be a fool's errand. When she had left, there had barely been enough in their store of bandages and lint to last another few weeks, and as for the morphine . . . She saw in her mind his sad, forgiving eyes and wanted suddenly, urgently, to brush back the flop of hair from his forehead, to stroke his brow . . .

A large couple emerged from the elevator, noses in the air as they pushed by. The man grunted, 'Bolshevik bloody do-gooders.'

She felt the crush of despair, but pulled herself together and stepped into the lift beside the cheery, white-uniformed attendant. The elevator's ping when it passed each floor was like a bell tolling her failure.

She entered her dark, empty room, and lay down on the bed. She hadn't the energy or the inclination to examine yet another list of shipping offices, to plan another route to tramp, to face the disappointments of yet another futile day. If only somebody, anybody, would help her.

Then she remembered that John Soo had given her Yu Fu-kuei's address. He had said that she was living with a secret policeman, who might be able to help. It seemed desperately unlikely. She had not thought of her exquisite, tiny, self-contained friend for years. She remembered saying goodbye on the gangplank in Hong Kong harbour after some quarrel or argument. There had been a coldness between them, some worry of hers that Fu-kuei might be a Communist agent. Ridiculous – but she had believed it for years and that was why she had never contacted her. It was so long ago . . . but she remembered how friendly they had been at Oxford, and how intimate they had become on the ship, how she had told Fu-kuei about her terrible experiences in Russia. Fu-kuei had pressed her hand and looked into her eyes with such warm sympathy. Oh, it would be good to see her again, she thought.

Why shouldn't she? She had the address. It was somewhere in Chapei and should not be difficult to find. It was late afternoon: why should she not hire a taxi and go there now? She justified her sudden desire to see her friend by persuading herself it was even her duty to do so. John Soo had said that Fu-kuei's policeman friend was well connected. Perhaps he would help her with one of the Chinese shipping companies. There could be no harm in asking. She had to try every channel available . . .

But she knew that was only an excuse. She wanted to see Fu-kuei. That was all. A friendly face: just one person in this callous, cruel city who would not reject her. For the first time in her life, proud Catherine was at the end of her tether, and wanted a shoulder to cry on.

There had been no means of escape. Yi-liang had been thorough. The windows were barred. Her door was locked on the outside. One of the two corporals was always on guard. It was they who brought in her trays of food. When the servant came in the morning to make the bed and clean the room, either Corporal Wang or Corporal Chen was with her, making sure that she did not say a word or pass a message. She spent the day pacing the Tientsin carpet. She had no idea of what was happening outside. The corporals treated her with courtesy, but they were obviously under instructions not to talk to her. On the afternoon of the second day, her self-control broke, and she screamed and banged on the door. She was ignored.

For long hours she sat at the window and gazed into the empty courtyard through the bars. She would see Yi-liang, in his uniform, leave early in his Rolls-Royce. Sometimes a servant would cross the yard, or a tradesman would deliver food. Each time the corporal who was not guarding her door was there. Yi-liang had obviously warned them that she might try to drop a message or call out to stray visitors. He himself returned late at night. She would wait for the sound of his boots on the landing. The key would click. He would enter her room with his affectionate smile, and ask her gently how she was. Was her head still painful? Would she like to see the doctor again? She would refuse to look at him, and after a while, he would go away, and the key would click in the lock.

Shortly before noon on the fourth day, the Rolls-Royce returned, followed by a black Buick. Yi-liang stepped out, along with two Kuomintang officers in their brown uniforms, and a suited man wearing dark glasses under his fedora. They all seemed on excellent terms. Out of the Buick stepped a European in the uniform of the international concession's police force. She started in shock. It was the red-faced young man who had passed the message to her in a handkerchief in the lift at the Sincere department store. Her cheeks flushed with shame and anger. Below her window, Yi-liang was introducing the Englishman to the other men. They all laughed at something the Englishman said. Yi-liang clapped him on the back, and steered him and the others inside. They disappeared from view.

Fu-kuei sank back against her chair, as a wave of hopelessness flooded through her. She had no doubt that Yi-liang had invited these men to plan the coup against the CCP. It must be imminent. She could hear voices from the dining room below her room. If only she could find a means to overhear. There must be a way to warn her comrades. There *must*.

Desperately she pulled the window latch. She could open it a fraction, before it bumped against the bars. If they had left the window open below, perhaps she could make out what they were saying . . . The voices were drowned in the louder buzz of the city. She slammed the window shut. What about the fireplace? Perhaps a clear sound might come up through the flue. She knelt in the grate and wriggled her upper body inside the chimney. She coughed when she dislodged some soot. Eventually she withdrew. She had heard nothing but the sigh of the wind. She tried to recall Mr Behrens's lessons about surveillance techniques. He had said something about an upturned glass on floorboards. She grabbed the glass of water from her untouched lunch tray and drained it, heaved aside the Tientsin carpet, lay flat on the floorboards, her ear pressed to the base of the upended glass. Nothing. It was useless.

As she lay pathetically on the floor, hair matted with soot, the sheer foolishness of her situation struck her. She began to sob, with regret, anger, mortification, appreciating just how useless she had been all along. She had believed she could make a difference, but she had been a child playing a dangerous adult game that she had never understood. For all Mr Behrens's teaching and her later experience, she was really no better than the simple idealist who, with Wang Yi, had played with fire and been burned – only now, she thought bitterly, she deserved to be punished, because she should have known better.

The hours passed. She cleaned herself in the bathroom, then put on fresh clothes. She sat by the window and watched the chauffeurs smoking by the limousines. After a while, the murmur of voices died away. Yi-liang and the others must have finished their lunch and gone either to the sitting room or the study.

She was startled by the sound of running motors. Were the guests leaving? She looked out of the window and saw the Rolls-Royce and the Buick still parked where they were. A convoy of three more cars was purring in through the gate – two black Lincolns and another Buick. There were burly-looking men in padded jackets on the running-boards carrying machine-guns or pistols. As the cars drove through the gates they leaped off and spaced themselves round the yard, covering all angles of fire. The third car stopped in the gateway, blocking any entry or exit, and four more men got out, similarly armed. Bodyguards.

The first two cars had crunched to a stop by the door. She saw below her the heads of Yi-liang and the Englishman, stepping forward to greet their visitors. She recognised the occupants of the Lincolns as soon as they stepped out: a large, overbearing man in the uniform of the French concession police, and a tall, elegant man with a bald head, dressed in a long Chinese gown. Yes, she knew them. Everybody in Shanghai knew them. These were Huang Ching-yung and Tu Yueh-sheng – Pock-marked Huang and Big Ears Tu – the acknowledged heads of the Red Gang and the Green Gang, who between them controlled all the criminal syndicates in the city.

She was sickened to see Yi-liang bowing and bobbing in front of them, and the condescension with which the gangsters acknowledged such servility as their due.

Fu-kuei left the window and sat on the edge of the bed. It was all clear to her now. She should have guessed long ago. She should have remembered the fate of Barkowitz. Mr Behrens had said something about those gangsters 'whom your lover likes to employ'. He would use the gangs, of course he would, as he had used the beggars who were so many and so ubiquitous that they would never be noticed. Who could tell a gangster from an ordinary artisan? They wore the same clothes; they ate in the same restaurants. They were like bacteria in the water system, invisible. There were thousands of them – certainly they outnumbered the CCP militia.

She sat on the bed, contemplating the rumpled carpet and the final, hurtful irony. Yu Fu-kuei, the secret agent, who had never known the significance of the information that she had so patiently gathered for her masters, was now possessed of all the information she needed to make a difference, prevent a disaster, if she could only pass it on – but, with all her knowledge, she was impotent. The pawn, plodding across the chessboard for others, had been queened, but she was more powerless than ever before. It was worse than that: she was condemned, with all the information in her hand to prevent it, to watch passively a tragedy unfold, knowing that she, as a pawn, had already unwittingly contributed to the success of her enemies' schemes.

The gangsters did not stay long, which told her that the plans were already in place. She heard the engines starting. Listlessly she stood by the window and watched one car after another leave the yard, the bodyguards leaping back on to the running-boards with their guns. The Englishman departed in his Buick. The Kuomintang officers and the man with the sunglasses took the Rolls-Royce. Yi-liang stood for a while in the empty yard contemplating the dust of their departure. Then, head bowed, he returned to the house. Briefly he glanced up at her window. His face was set and melancholic. With sudden intuition, she knew that tonight was the night.

She heard his heavy steps come up the stairs, and click along the landing towards the spare room he now used. She heard the steps return. There was an exchange with Corporal Wang outside. The key was inserted and turned in the lock. She turned to face him. She did not move from the window. Yi-liang was wearing his cap; he had his revolver holster on his belt and his lanyards over his neat tunic. His face was sombre as he observed her.

'Are you going to execute me?' she asked. 'Will I be the first of the Communists you murder tonight?'

'Of course not. I love you,' he said. 'I would never let you come to any harm.'

'Really?' she answered scornfully. 'Well, I hate you.' She stressed every word.

Pain twitched his features. He sighed. 'I know,' he said. 'I sometimes think you have always hated me – deep inside.'

'I've always hated what you stood for,' she said. 'But you're wrong. I did come to love you, until you betrayed me. I'd always believed you were honourable.'

He nodded slowly. 'Yes,' he said, after a long moment. 'I can see why you think me contemptible now. I'm sorry. I had to use you, Fu-kuei. If there had been another way . . . No, there's no point in going into what's already happened, or in apologies.' His shoulders slumped. 'I have to go. The car will be back for me soon. I'm taking Corporal Chen with me, and dismissing the servants. They'll be better off with their families tonight. I'm sorry you must remain in your room. After tomorrow it won't matter any more. Corporal Wang will be outside your door if you need anything, and I'll be back when I can.'

'After spending a night murdering my friends? What makes you think I would care if you return or not? You'd be better off shooting me now. Why don't you? We won't be able to go back, you know, to how things were. Once you let me out of this room you won't ever see me again – and if I can hurt you, I will.'

Again, he nodded silently, that same look of pain brushing his face. He turned to go, and paused. When he faced her there was an angry glint in his eye, and his voice quivered when he spoke. 'Do you remember, Fu-kuei, that you once signed a document saying that you abjured communism? Before you went to Oxford? That was probably the happiest day of my life. You see, I believed you. All right, you can say I was naïve, but love makes you so. Can you imagine how I felt – it was some time during the May 30th episode – when a routine raid on a Communist cell revealed a list of agents and informers, and one of the names on it was yours? Of course I concealed the evidence from my colleagues, but I followed it up on my own, and sure enough I found out a pattern in your movements that eventually led me to a Comintern spy-ring. And I discovered that the woman I had been living with, sleeping with, the woman I had loved for all those years, had been spying on me. Don't talk to me of betrayal, Fu-kuei.'

'So you paid me back in my own coin, is that it? And what you're going to do tonight – is that also part of your revenge for being cheated by a woman?'

'No, Fu-kuei, it's not like that.' He took a deep breath. When he spoke it was in the same soft tones that he had used before. 'I'm not saying it wasn't hard for me. After I discovered what you had done, there were times I was so angry I could have . . . Never mind, I was cruel enough to you as it was, but after a while I forgave you. Or, rather, I realised that I loved you so much I didn't care what you had done or what you believed in because I didn't want to lose you. I put our happiness – my happiness, if you like – before my professionalism. We can get by, I thought. Maybe one day you could come to love me. If not . . . Well, I was protecting you. That was something. I lived in a corrupt system, serving warlords. I did my job, but I tried to preserve our private little world . . .

'That was before the Northern Expedition, which changed everything. Then we were all compelled to face issues a bit larger than our own private circumstances, and every one of us had to decide where we stood, what sort of China we were prepared to tolerate. And I realised, despite my love for you, maybe even because of it, that I was not prepared to give over my country to the Communists. I knew what I had to do. I did it. I involved you because you were in a unique position to help me. I hope to finish it off tonight, and I'm not ashamed of what I'm doing – however contemptible you believe my actions to be, Fu-kuei – because I believe it's right for China. Even if I risk losing you.'

They were both silent. He stood by the door, she by the window, an unbridgeable gulf between them. For a moment, as he had been speaking, she had glimpsed the man she had loved, the old, honourable Yi-liang whom she had believed in. He gave her a sad smile. 'I have to go.'

She felt something break inside her – and a wild, desperate hope. Sobbing, she threw herself across the room. She tripped on the carpet and fell on her knees at his feet. She clutched his boots, the serge of his trousers. 'Please, Yi-liang, please,' she moaned. She had lost all sense of dignity, of pride. She saw only the terrible thing that was about to happen, which she must prevent at all costs, even if it meant abasing herself. She would do anything – anything – just so this man, who said he loved her, would stop what he was about to do. 'Please, please, please,' she begged. 'If you do love me, stop them, please stop them . . .' She raised her tear-streaked face and saw the pain in his eyes as he tried to lift her up. 'You can. It's not too late . . .'

'Fu-kuei,' he said gently, 'don't do this. There's nothing I can do now to stop it, even if I wanted to. You know that.'

'Oh, please,' she cried, struggling out of his hands, clinging to his boots. 'You met them. Chou. And Lee. They're decent people. Please save them. Oh, please.'

'I can't,' he said firmly, as he tried to move away. 'It's out of my hands now.'

'No,' she wailed. 'Save some. Save one. Oh, please, save Chou. If you love me, Yi-liang, please, you have to do something! You have to! You have to . . .'

In the end he had to push her brutally away. She tried to reach again for his boot but with a curt 'I'm sorry, it's too late,' he left the room, leaving her lying on the floor in her misery. The lock clicked. The quick tap of his boots faded away along the landing and down the stairs. She pulled herself off the floor and ran to the window. 'Please,' she screamed, but he got into the back of the Rolls-Royce and closed the door. The car turned and moved out of the gate. She clutched the bars, trying to shake them, screaming for him to stop. But he was gone.

It was more difficult than Catherine had anticipated. At the entrance to the iron bridge that crossed the Soochow creek, British soldiers manning a barbed-wire barricade stopped her taxi. 'Sorry, miss, there's to be no traffic across the creek after five p.m. Don't ask me why. It's new orders we've just received.' Catherine pointed to her nurse's uniform, and in her hectoring ward-sister's tone told them that she urgently needed to take penicillin to a hospital in Hongkew.

Eventually they relented: 'Considering it's five off five and strictly, the curfew's not started – but you can't take the car, miss. You'll have to find transport the other side.' A soldier opened the barricade for her and she walked across the empty bridge, her shoes ringing on the metal. There was none of the busy sampan traffic that usually clogged the creek.

She managed to find a rickshaw outside the German consulate. The ancient rickshaw boy was reluctant to take her at first. Despite his broad Shanghainese dialect, she gathered that there were road-blocks on all the streets bordering the Chinese section of the city. Eventually, when she agreed to pay a triple fare, he consented to take her as far as the barricade at North Sichuan Road, the dividing line between the International Concession and the Chapei district. There she was forced to make up another story before the American marines guarding the barricade agreed to let her pass. She was surprised by the touching concern they showed for her safety. A corporal asked if she wanted an escort to accompany her to the hospital she had invented: 'Nobody knows what this is about, Sister, but all of us have a feeling something's brewing in the city tonight. I'm not sure I like the idea of a woman walking by herself in the Commie sector, especially one so goddamned pretty as you are.'

She flashed him her most engaging smile. 'What a charming compliment, Corporal – but nobody will bother a nurse going about her business.' She left them shaking their heads and walked resolutely through the barricade, stepping briskly in case they changed their minds.

It was all very puzzling. At first, as she walked up North Sichuan Road past the jewellers, who were putting up their shutters for the night, there did not appear to be anything unusual, just fewer people about than she would have expected on a weekday evening. She saw the Kuomintang and hammer-and-sickle flags hanging from some balconies and wondered if the Bolsheviks who had taken over the city were imposing a curfew, but the restaurants and teahouses were open, although the clientele were predominantly artisans swilling strong liquor. She supposed they were strikers from the factories, which she had heard were still closed. 'Revolutionary thugs,' she muttered. She consulted her map and, in the absence of rickshaws, began to walk briskly.

As she threaded through the side-streets, she noticed more and more artisans lounging in little knots, spitting on the pavement or squatting round a chessboard. There was something sinister about them, the way they watched her. They appeared tense, as if they were waiting for something to happen. She remembered the American corporal's warning, and told herself it was nonsense – but she hurried her pace.

She came into a wider avenue where there was a large building festooned with red flags – obviously, she thought disdainfully, some sort of Party headquarters of the new regime. The young men and bob-haired women laughing on the steps reminded her of a university campus. Probably they were students; it was always the students who were the first to succumb to idealistic nonsense – before they were corrupted by the machine. For all that, she was pleased to see them. Unlike the sinister artisans, they appeared to be normal, ordinary people.

It was a brief respite. When she walked into the next side-street, she was subjected again to menacing stares from thuggish men hovering in doorways and outside teahouses. She could feel a brooding evil in the air. She had no idea who they were – only that she wanted to get away from them.

The light faded and the narrow streets became darker, and suddenly she knew of whom they reminded her. They had the bovine malevolence and the lazy menace of the hard men employed by the Cheka. She shivered as she recalled the Lubyanka, and the cruel, stupid guards who lounged with their guns in the dim, dank corridors, watching coldly the innocents herded past. She saw again the hateful face of the man who had interrogated her and afterwards his smug smile when he had first made her strip . . . her helplessness . . . how she had tried to smile through her disgust and fear while he kissed her and pawed her body . . .

Since then she had adopted a hard self-sufficiency, determined that nobody would ever hurt her again, but she knew, deep inside, it was a sham. She was weak and despicable; in the moment of her trial she had allowed herself to succumb, betraying her Moscow friends in the confession that had not been extorted unwillingly – on the contrary, she had been eager to sign, after only eleven days in the cells, so that she could save her own worthless life . . .

Why are you thinking about this, Catherine? she asked herself. Why drag it all up again? She had thought she had buried these hateful memories. Was it because she was about to visit Fu-kuei, the only person to whom she had ever confessed what she had done? Was she feeling guilty that she had ignored her friend for so many years, because of her hatred of the Bolsheviks, believing that Fu-kuei was one of them?

She heard a gobbet of spit hit the pavement behind her. One of the thuggish shadows was standing in her path. She pushed past him, and heard coarse laughter behind her. She hurried on.

At last she came out into the open and found herself facing a small park. Recovering her nerve, she consulted her map again and saw that it would provide a shortcut to Fu-kuei's house. In the twilight she saw men and women practising their *tai-chi*. She allowed herself a wry smile. She had probably been imagining things, allowing her depression after so many days' failure to get the better of her and lead her into morbid self-indulgent fantasies.

On the other side of the park there were neat little residential streets of walled, European-style houses: obviously a prosperous suburb. Catherine was pleased for Fu-kuei: her lover must be wealthy. The roads between the rows of houses were semi-deserted, but there were no thuggish men about. Catherine began to relax. As she got closer to her destination, excitement mounted: soon she would see her old friend again. What would she look like? What would they say to each other? God, after all this she'd better be there: wouldn't it be just Catherine's luck to discover that Fu-kuei was not at home?

It was almost dark now and she had to use the torch in her satchel to identify the street names. There it was: Yangtse West Road, Second Alley. A street of big houses, comfortable orange light shining in the windows. She swung the torch beam over each number as she passed. Number sixteen. Number seventeen. This was it. A wide-open gate led into a courtyard, and there, silhouetted against the pale mauve sky, was a large two-storey house. The disappointment came like a hammer blow. Not a light was on. Nobody was at home. She wanted to cry.

She walked into the yard, her shoes crunching on the pebbles, and stared at the blank gabled edifice. It was as quiet as a tomb. For a long moment she stood there, the torch casting a pool of light on the ground. She thought of the long walk she would have to make back to the barricade – past those terrible, threatening men. She imagined the mocking look the American corporal would give her when she asked to be allowed through. But there was no point in hanging around.

She would leave a note. Fu-kuei might telephone her. Her trip might yet be worthwhile. She fumbled with the torch and groped in her satchel for a pad and a pencil. She blinked as the torch swung its glare on her face, and heard a call: 'Catherine!'

She started. The house was as blank as before, and there was nobody in the yard. She heard the plaintive cry again. 'Catherine!' The sound had come from the direction of the house. She swung her torch over the façade and saw a flash of white in one of the second-storey windows. A pale, haggard face was gazing down at her. Two white-knuckled hands were clutching the bars. 'Fu-kuei?' she called hesitantly. 'Is it you?'

'Come closer.' The voice was hoarse, almost a whisper. 'We mustn't be heard.'

'Darling, is that you?' Catherine kept her voice as low as she could. This apparition of her friend horrified her. 'Fu-kuei, what's happened to you?'

'Catherine, I'm a prisoner. You must find a way to release me.' The whispered voice was urgent. 'There's a guard – only one, but you have to be careful. He probably won't be armed but he has a key hanging from his belt.' Catherine thought she must be dreaming. A prisoner? A guard? Fu-kuei a prisoner in her own house? It was bizarre. 'It's all right, darling. Don't worry,' she called back. 'What do you want me to do?'

'Get him to the door,' said Fu-kuei. 'Then . . .' Her face cracked with despair. 'Oh, I don't know, but you have to find a way.'

'All right, Fu-kuei, don't worry. Leave it to me.' She spoke confidently but she had no idea what she was going to do. She clicked off the torch. It was heavy enough. It might serve. Are you serious, Catherine? Are you really considering battery? This was lunatic. 'Fu-kuei,' she whispered, 'what's the name of your policeman friend?'

'Yang Yi-liang,' came the disembodied voice. 'Major Yang – but Catherine, he's the one who—'

'Never mind, darling, leave it to me.' You're mad, Catherine, an internal voice told her. She didn't even have a plan. Don't do it, the voice urged. Call the police. But she couldn't do that: this Major Yang, who was imprisoning Fu-kuei, *was* the police. Before she had time to change her mind, she rang the doorbell. It clanged in the empty house. She rang it again. Good, she thought. Lights are going on. She heard the thump of steps coming to the door. She closed her eyes to nerve herself.

A short man in uniform was silhouetted against the light of the hall. He had a pleasant, honest face, and was smiling inquisitively. A bunch of keys hung by a hook from his belt. '*Shei?* Who is it?' he asked.

She stepped forward into the light, and saw his features change with astonishment. '*Waiguoren!*' he muttered. 'A foreigner! What's this?'

'Good evening,' Catherine greeted him, in her best Mandarin. 'I've come from the hospital to give medicines to your patient. A Major Yang told our doctor it was urgent. Have I the right place?' She smiled sweetly. 'This is Major Yang's house? Yes? Are you Major Yang by any chance?'

The soldier looked thunderstruck, as she had hoped. 'No, I'm not,' he said. 'This is his house but you can't—'

'Good,' said Catherine, putting a firm foot forward into the doorway. Instinctively the man stepped back, and she was across the threshold. 'If you'll just show me where the patient is,' she said, keeping up the momentum.

He recovered and tried to block her way. 'I have no authorisation. You can't come in here.'

'Oh, my God!' She gave a piercing scream, staring over his shoulder. He turned and she hit him on the back of the head with the torch. It shattered. The bulb and glass separated from the handle and the batteries flew across the room.

The man was staggering, holding his head. Before he had time to recover, she slipped in beside him, pushed him with all her strength and grabbed for the keys. He tripped and tottered out into the porch, falling head over heels down the steps. She slammed the door after him, slid into place the chain and two bolts, then turned the key. She leaned against it, heaving for breath.

A moment later the man outside was trying the handle, shouting and banging on the door. She did not have much time. She ran up the stairs, screaming Fu-kuei's name, and heard a sound behind a door. After several attempts she found the right key to open it, and almost lost her balance when her friend embraced her.

'Listen, darling, there's no time for that now,' she panted. 'That man – he's outside and trying to get in. We've got to deal with him somehow.'

Frantically she ran back down the stairs with Fu-kuei behind her. 'He can't break those bars on the windows. Where will he try to get in?' Fu-kuei was probably in shock, she thought. Her friend's soft eyes were staring at her bemusedly.

'The – the kitchen?' Fu-kuei offered. 'A strong man should be able to break down that door.'

'Good,' said Catherine. 'We've got to let him in, then hit him with something heavy enough to knock him out. Can you think of anything that will do it?'

'Yi-liang's golf clubs,' said Fu-kuei. 'They're in this cupboard here.' She opened it and they collected one each.

'God, we don't want to kill him,' said Catherine, looking at the sharp edge of the club in her hand – but she had no time to think of anything else. The corporal was battering at the kitchen door. Catherine motioned Fu-kuei to one side of it and she stood on the other. The wood of one of the panels was already cracking. It gave way. A hand reached in and groped for the key. Catherine tensed. The key turned, the door opened and the man stepped cautiously into the dark kitchen. She saw a knife in his hand. With a grunt, Fu-kuei slashed down with her golfing iron, but he sensed the movement and ducked. The iron hit him only on the shoulder. He howled with anger and lifted his knife. Fu-kuei backed away, and Catherine swung her club, hitting him neatly on the side of the head. He let out a long breath and dropped to his knees, then fell forward on his face.

'Is he dead?' whispered Fu-kuei.

Catherine examined him. Thank God, he was only stunned. There was a lot of blood, but it was not a serious wound. 'Fu-kuei, quickly, get me some rope.' She chuckled. 'Looks like I learned something useful in all those bloody golf tournaments in Peitaiho after all.'

It was only after the two women had tied the groaning man to a chair in the sitting room, and after she had staunched the bleeding and bound up his head, that Catherine relaxed, ready to hug her friend and ask her what the hell this was all about. But now Fu-kuei was impatient. She struggled out of Catherine's arms. 'I have to go. Immediately. I may already be too late. The gangsters—'

'Gangsters?' cried Catherine. 'What have gangsters got to do with you, Fu-kuei?' Then she remembered the thugs she had seen on her way. She felt a chill in her spine. Something was going on in the city and her friend was involved. This was all much more complex than the domestic tyranny she had imagined.

'It's too complicated to explain, Catherine. And there's no time. Yi-liang is planning to use them tonight to attack the Communists. I must warn them before it's too late, or there'll be a massacre.'

Catherine froze. 'Then you *are* a Bolshevik,' she whispered. 'My God, all this time I was right. You're one of them.'

'Catherine, there's no time for that now.'

Catherine's mind was whirling. 'Good God, you've been spying on your policeman lover, haven't you? All this time. And he's found out and locked you up. Because you've discovered his plans to deal with the Reds. Oh, Christ, Fu-kuei! What the hell have you made me do? If your lover's getting rid of the Communists, I'm on his side.'

Cold anger crept through her. She had damned near killed a man tonight. She had done it for her friend, who, it turned out, was a Communist spy. She had been tricked into helping a criminal. 'Fu-kuei, if you plan to warn the Communists,' she said softly, 'I'm not sure that I'm prepared to let you go.'

Fu-kuei's brow furrowed. 'Catherine, you can't stop me. This is Chinese politics. It has nothing to do with you.'

The picture of the yelling protestors outside her hospital flashed through her mind, the flags, the rallies; the hatred on their faces as they spat at Edmund when he quietly confronted them in the street. She saw the legs of her friends under their blankets after Bolshevik deserters had murdered them in a quiet glade. She saw the face of her tormentor in the Cheka . . . 'Oh, yes, it does, Fu-kuei,' she said softly. 'More than you could possibly imagine. If I can stop you warning those bastards I will.'

Suddenly Fu-kuei became very still. Catherine saw the soft eyes harden, then flick towards the poker in the grate. Catherine reacted instinctively. They ran towards it together and reached it at the same time. For several minutes they struggled to wrest it from each other's grip. Then, with amazing strength for such a small person, Fu-kuei pushed her. Catherine's head hit the mantelpiece. Dazed, she thrust away her antagonist. Fu-kuei's eyes were glittering. She spat across the poker, clutched between them in a feral grasp.

And, in a moment of stark clarity, Catherine saw what she was doing. Had her stupid hatred brought her so low that she was engaged in a death grip with her friend? Yes, she loathed the Bolsheviks and everything about them. If there was any way to destroy them, she would support it. In her mind, they were brutes, like the Chinese gangsters she had seen in the streets today – but Fu-kuei had said it was those gangsters who would be unleashed tonight. Suddenly she recalled the bright young students she had noticed on the steps of the Party offices this evening. They were young Chinese boys and girls – like Lan-hua, or John Soo, or even Fu-kuei – guilty only of idealism. They were ordinary young human beings with life and hope ahead of them – and they were the people whom the gangsters would murder. They would probably do worse to them first. Catherine knew what such animals could do: they had done it to Marya and Olga; they had done it to her. And was Catherine, who was a nurse for God's sake, with a responsibility to save lives, trying to stop her only remaining friend preventing this atrocity because of her own selfish desire for revenge? What on earth was she thinking?

She was ashamed. She let go of the poker and Fu-kuei fell backwards, a look of surprise on her face when she found the weapon uncontested in her hands.

Catherine observed her. 'You should see yourself,' she said calmly. 'Go ahead and hit me with that thing, if you have to. My God, Fu-kuei, that it should come to this.'

Fu-kuei raised the poker and Catherine glared at her, challenging her to strike. She did not care any more. 'Go on,' she said. 'I don't give a damn.'

Fu-kuei's face crumpled. The poker fell from her hands and she was weeping, her tiny body shaking with great, shuddering sobs.

Catherine continued to observe her dispassionately. She felt empty of any feeling. She heard a sound beside her and remembered the wounded corporal, who must have been watching this scene and thinking that both women were stark raving mad. Catherine began to giggle. 'You'd be right,' she said. 'We are mad. The whole damned planet is mad.' She knelt down beside her friend and pressed the wet face to her own. 'All right, darling,' she whispered. 'I'm still your Catherine, and you're my Fu-kuei, and both of us are a pair of idiots. Don't worry. You'll be yourself again in a minute. You poor thing! Look at you! I've never seen anybody in such a state. You're worse than I am. Come on, don't cry.'

'Catherine,' Fu-kuei sobbed, 'I'm so sorry. I know you hate the Communists after what they did to you . . . but . . . it's not the same. It really isn't. These are innocent people . . . and the gangsters will . . . murder them, Catherine. They're my friends. I must . . . try to save them . . . even though I think I'm already too late.'

'It's all right, Fu-kuei. It's all right. Listen, darling, just tell me so I know. Who's using these gangsters to do their dirty work to get rid of the Communists? Is it the Nationalists?'

'It's everybody.' Yu Fu-kuei was still sniffing, but Catherine was glad to see that the hysterics were subsiding. 'Even the foreign concessions are in on the conspiracy. I saw an English policeman with Yi-liang today, in this house, planning it, with the gangsters.'

'The English have done a deal with the gangsters?' Catherine took a deep breath. She remembered the barricades and the strange new orders that had so confused the soldiers. Suddenly she felt disgusted. 'You really want to do this? You know how dangerous it might be. The gangs are already on the streets. I saw them. You may be right, too, that it's too late.'

'I have to try. Don't you see?'

Catherine stood up, and gazed for a moment at the empty fire-place. 'People shouldn't go around murdering each other whoever they are,' she muttered. She turned back to Fu-kuei. 'You really think you can stop this? That if I let you go, you can make a differ-ence?'

'I don't know,' said Fu-kuei, in a small voice.

Shaking her head at her own foolishness, Catherine discovered she had made another decision. 'All right,' she said firmly. 'We'll go and warn the bloody Communists together. Yes, I'm coming with you.' She laughed. 'I've been so hopeless at everything else I've tried that I might as well help the damned Bolsheviks for a change. As it is, everybody in Shanghai thinks I *am* a Bolshevik, so nobody would be surprised. Come on, up you get. This wasn't quite the reunion I'd imagined, but . . . what do you expect when you have two such hopeless cases as you and me? I suppose that's what makes us friends.'

Ten minutes later the two women were riding towards the park on the corporals' bicycles, which they had found in the garage. It was as they were proceeding down a shady avenue that they heard the first shots.

It would be remembered as a night that fear descended on the city, and more so because few understood what was going on. Afterwards many Shanghai citizens would say they had had a presentiment that something was about to happen, as if they had become aware of a shadow descending on the streets, or sensed in the air the tension of an approaching thunderstorm. There had been no official curfew but many shopkeepers closed early and went home to their families. Others, seeing in their neighbourhoods the presence of menacing strangers, decided that tonight they would close the shutters and stay indoors. The night was not long advanced before it became clear that those presentiments had been right.

Most residents of the Chinese quarters of Shanghai – the lucky ones – remained in their homes, but there were few who slept, huddling instead under their quilts, or squatting by their charcoal stoves, straining their ears in the intervals between gunfire. Sometimes it would be far away, sometimes in the near neighbourhood; sometimes in their own street, sometimes next door. Through the tenement walls they would hear shouts in rough voices, the clang of the tailboard of a truck being closed, the scream or the protest of an unfortunate victim being taken away to his or her fate. The silent listeners would only relax when they heard the gunning of the motor echoing in the deserted street, and the diminishing roar of the vehicle as it drove away.

Despite the gunfire, most of the killings that took place that night were done in the traditional manner, with cold steel – for the members of the Green and Red Gangs were conservative by inclination: their induction into the societies had consisted of ceremonies and blood-brotherhood rites that dated back to an ancient past, and their preferred weapons, when they could use them, were hatchets, knives and swords. When they were not accompanied by a punctilious Kuomintang intelligence officer or military policeman, who insisted that those captured be interrogated rather than executed, they tended to favour beheading as their chosen means of dispatch. Lists of Communist Party members in their districts had been circulated so they knew which house to raid and which young activist or student leader to pull away from the hands of his or her parents, and take into the street, where the strongest of their number would be waiting with a tasselled execution sword. They would leave the hacked bodies lying in blood, and go on to the next address. When there was any uncertainty, there was a sure rule of thumb: any young man they found in a long scholar's gown, or any young woman with bobbed hair was almost certainly a Communist, and was treated accordingly.

It was particularly enjoyable for those who had been chosen to do their work in the International and French concessions. The French concession was the preserve of the Red Gang where everything was easy because Pock-marked Huang was head of the police force there, but those Green Gang members who had been allocated targets in the International Concession would remember for the rest of their lives the freedom of the city that they had been given that night. They felt like kings when the sullen British soldiers, whom in ordinary circumstances they would have avoided like the devil, lifted the barricades to let their trucks pass. Of course, the soldiers had been given instructions, as had all the policemen in the city, to ignore them, and they could go about their business with impunity, as if they were cloaked in invisibility.

Into the middle of an empty Nanking Road, where in the daytime proud Englishmen went shopping with their wives, or under the skyscrapers that bordered Bubbling Well Road and the racecourse, they would drag their moaning victims, and behead them, then and there, with their broadswords, while foreign policemen watched in fascinated horror, or turned away, and high up in the lighted windows they would see curtains closed hurriedly. They would play games. After cutting a female CCP activist on the breasts and thighs so that she squealed, they would allow her to crawl, bleeding, to the feet of the foreigners, begging for their protection – then bring her back, screaming, and cut off her head, while the foreigners averted their eyes. Of course, these entertainments were reserved for the lowly rank and file. The more senior CCP members were loaded into the trucks for execution later in the Lung-hua prison, which had been especially reserved for the purpose.

The Party headquarter buildings, scattered around the city, were more difficult nuts to crack because armed militia guarded them. A concerted rush from the shadows had been enough to overpower some of the smaller ones, such as the Fuchow Guild in Nantou and the police station in Pootung. At the Huchow Guild in Chapei, a pitched battle between the pickets and the gangsters had been going on for about half an hour before a column of military jeeps drove up, hooters blaring. Major Yang Yi-liang was in the leading vehicle and shouted through a loud-hailer for both sides to disarm. Scores of heavily armed Kuomintang troops leaped out of the vehicles and levelled their rifles at the gangsters. Yang supervised his men as they forced the thugs to kneel, binding their hands behind their backs; then, with only two soldiers, he walked boldly to the door of the Guild. He met Comrade Lee at the door. The customary cigarette was in his mouth but Yang was more aware of the two pistols in his hands.

'Well, well, it's our old friend the turncoat major,' Comrade Lee growled. 'What tricks are you playing now?'

'No tricks. As you see, I've disarmed your attackers. I've just come from Military Governor Pai's headquarters with instructions to protect you. More troops will be coming in soon to help you put down this counter-coup. The bankers are so desperate they're using the gangs. Didn't I warn you about them?'

'So you're with the Kuomintang now, are you? And you expect me to trust you?'

'You wouldn't employ me, would you? You should count yourself damned lucky that you have me still to help you. Who do you think alerted the garrison?'

'All right, you'd better come in. I'll let the Labour Union leaders decide if you're telling the truth. Your weapons first, please, and those of your two men.'

And it had all been very easy, because when the tea and cakes were served in the boardroom, Yang told a most plausible story.

He informed the assembled leaders that it would be some hours yet before all the troops could be mobilised, and meanwhile the Commercial Press Building was under heavy attack. He would like the help of the General Labour Union's militia to help him disarm the gangsters there. He passed over a letter from General Pai Ch'ung-hsi, who was commanding in the generalissimo's temporary absence in Nanking, authorising every assistance to be given to the CCP to pacify criminal elements in the city.

Half an hour later, followed by a column of armed workers, Yang stepped back into the street, and three hundred gangsters burst out of the alleys. They hacked the stunned militia to pieces with their swords, then rushed the still open doors. It was over very quickly. When Yang went back inside, he noticed that Comrade Lee still had a cigarette in his mouth, although his head was separated from his body. In the room where Yang had recently enjoyed tea and cakes, the leaders of the General Labour Union were being stripped before their cold journey in the back of a truck to Lung-hua.

The siege of the main Party headquarters had proved more difficult. The battle for the Commercial Press Building lasted all through the night and well into the early hours of the morning. Few activists were still alive when the gangster force stormed the doors in the dawn light. Again, Major Yang supervised the arrest of the leaders, including the saturnine Chou En-lai. He made some rather hurried arrangements; then, exhausted and no longer able to contain his revulsion for the methods that he had so successfully employed, he decided to return home for a bath.

While these events took place, Catherine and Fu-kuei were kneeling with about a hundred other bound men and women in the workshop of a castings factory.

They had been captured as they cycled down a narrow alley they had hoped would lead to the back of the Party headquarters building. It had been dark, and they could hear firing ahead. Catherine had been making a lame joke in an attempt to lighten their tension, something about what their respective Oxford colleges would think of a pair of their alumni being found on a Bolshevik barricade – when suddenly they were dazzled by headlights.

Before they had time to react their arms were pinioned by rough hands, and they had been dragged off their bicycles. Someone with a flashlight had cast a beam in their faces. '*Tamade!* It's a foreigner. Some kind of nurse,' they had heard a pleasant young voice cry. Another deeper, but equally cultivated voice had answered from the darkness, 'The other one looks like a Red. Probably the foreign woman is Comintern. Throw them both in the back.'

They landed heavily on the slippery metal floor of a truck, already half full of prisoners. Strong hands had helped them to their feet, as the vehicle lurched into the main street, and they had become aware of the sad, set faces of young men and women, many in student clothes. One pig-tailed girl had been crouching on the floor, crying. Another, with bobbed hair, was shivering in the arms of her lover or husband, who was mumbling words of comfort.

'Are we in the hands of one of the gangs?' Fu-kuei had asked a grim-faced young man beside her, who looked angry rather than scared.

'I don't think so,' he said. 'They appear to be some sort of young capitalists' militia. They've been stopping at houses and dragging us out of our beds. Not that there's any difference between them and the gangs,' he added. 'They're just as vicious.'

'Why don't you escape? Jump off the tailboard?' asked Catherine, who had been thinking that she would do just that.

'Look behind us,' he answered, and they had observed that a jeep was following them, manned by several smart-looking young men, some in eccentric uniform, all tags, shining boots and halyards, others in white suits. One, wearing a boater and a silk Chinese gown, was pointing a heavy machine-gun directly at them. 'Some tried earlier,' said the young man. 'They killed them, then shot some of the others who hadn't jumped. Didn't you notice the blood on the floor?'

It had been about then that they passed their first execution. Both Catherine and Fu-kuei's eyes had been drawn by a flurry of movement at the side of the road, as shadowy figures pulled a young man into the street. They had watched with horror as a big man raised a sword. Mercifully the jeep coming behind them had blocked their view. They had not long been spared, though. Several times during the nightmare journey, they were jolted when their truck veered to avoid the hacked remains of corpses in the road.

Eventually they had driven through factory gates. Young men in similar attire to those in the jeep, all heavily armed, had been waiting for them. They had been kicked and herded towards the workshop, and told at gunpoint to kneel on the concrete floor beside many others who were already crouched there with their heads bowed to the ground. They had noticed that the prisoners' bound hands were bleeding: their wrists had been tied together with barbed wire. Soon, Catherine and Fu-kuei had felt the pain in their own wrists, but hardly noticed it because they had seen what else was happening in the workshop.

A gaping red furnace was casting its hot light into the room, and two young men were stoking it from a pile of coal. Behind a table set to the side sat three others, dressed, extraordinarily, in British-style uniforms, complete with polished Sam Brownes. The one in the middle was a huge, broad-faced man in his late twenties, with red cheeks, handsome in his way, but the wide slit of his mouth was set in a permanent sneer. He seemed to be in command, for all the others deferred to him. Catherine, of course, had no idea who he was, but Fu-kuei knew: his photograph was a regular feature in the society columns of the Shanghai newspapers. He was Tommy Hsu, the eldest son of a cotton millionaire, whose father had given him a chain of cinemas on his twenty-first birthday. He was never seen without a glamorous actress or singer on his arm, and his parties were the talk of the town. Tonight he was conducting some sort of kangaroo court.

Shortly after they had entered, they had seen three of the militia drag one of the kneeling students to stand before the table, where Hsu proceeded to interrogate him. In front of him were stacks of paper containing lists of names, and what appeared to be dossiers that he would sometimes check. He barked the questions or, rather, statements because he seemed to know everything about the young man whom he was accusing of being a Communist. The trial did not last long. There was a whispered consultation between the judges, and then Hsu boomed, 'Guilty! Take him away!'

The three militiamen lifted the student, one holding him by the arms, the other by the middle, the third by the legs, and hurled him headlong into the furnace. The two stokers slammed the door, and the cavernous hall was filled with shadow. Catherine and Fu-kuei were frozen in shock and incredulity. They heard a communal whimper of fear and a ripple of shudders down the line of kneeling people beside them. Then the young man with whom they had been talking in the truck wriggled to his feet, and yelled, 'Murdering capitalist bastards!'

'Who spoke?' Tommy Hsu was on his feet and coming round the side of the table, reaching for his holster. In one movement he pulled out his pistol and shot the young man in the head. The body slumped, gurgling blood.

'Now, that was a confession!' the big man was shouting. 'Who else wants to confess?' He walked angrily down the line waving his pistol. 'All right! Let's get back to proper procedures. We've a long night ahead of us.'

When the two stokers had judged that the body was satisfactorily incinerated, they reopened the furnace door and threw in more coal. Another whimpering victim was brought before the tribunal – a young girl this time. 'Guilty!' Hsu pronounced. She, too, was carried, screaming and kicking, to the furnace.

Militiamen armed with pistols walked up and down between the lines, making sure that there was no communication between their prisoners. Once, Catherine heard a man whispering to his neighbour. The guards heard too, and pistol-whipped him until he was unconscious. On another occasion, a girl – the one with pig-tails who had been crying in the truck – stumbled to her feet and ran screaming towards the door. She was shot dead before she had gone ten yards. Catherine and Fu-kuei edged closer together, until they could feel the warmth of each other's body.

The trials and executions continued through the night. Most of the victims were so stunned that they walked to the tribunal without resistance. When it came to the turn of the lovers whom Catherine had seen in the truck, the girl screamed and whimpered, turning her head backwards desperately to her young man, calling his name – but he looked away, tears running down his cheeks. She was quickly dispatched, and he followed her into the furnace ten minutes later.

Catherine managed to persuade herself that the death she would soon face, although horrible in every way, would be quick. No human body could stand a millisecond of such heat before the heart stopped. It would be a quick stroke, not the burning, that killed her. Or she prayed it would be. She thought over the events of her life and saw irony in the way it would end. Recently she had thought of her useless life as a hell on earth; well, she was witnessing hell tonight, in a detail that not even Hieronymus Bosch could have imagined. She took comfort that there would be extinction after a brief shock, and finally, for her, peace.

She was sad that Fu-kuei would suffer with her, and wished now that she had continued that stupid struggle with the poker. On the other hand, if it was to end like this, she was glad she had found her friend again. Hours into the morning, when she saw the high windows of the workshop lighten – few prisoners remained now – she noticed that the guards had relaxed their vigilance and were gathered by the door to smoke. She risked a quick whisper: 'Fu-kuei, I'm so glad we're together.' The guards did not hear her, but neither did Fu-kuei. Her white face was staring rigidly at the floor. Catherine wished that she could hug her.

The furnace door clanged. It had been the Russian sailor, the only other foreigner in their group. Catherine had not been paying attention to his trial. Presumably he had been found guilty of being a Comintern member, as she would be. Perhaps he was one, she thought. It was so typical that she would be condemned under the wrong colours, but it was not inappropriate: one way or another she had been flying false colours most of her life.

She judged that there were only about three or four more in line before it would be Fu-kuei's turn. She was glad Fu-kuei would go first. It would be painful for her to watch Catherine's execution. Catherine saw that dawn had indeed broken. White light was mixing with the hideous yellow glow of the furnace. She wondered what sort of day it would be. She hoped it would be a bright, clear morning – but then she heard the clatter of rain on the roof.

Suddenly she thought of Edmund. Theirs was such a complicated relationship. It would have been interesting to see how it would have worked out. She smiled, thinking of how angry he would be with her that she had got herself into such a jam.

There were only two more before them now. She saw Fu-kuei's sad eyes contemplating her. 'I'm so sorry,' she heard her whisper.

'Don't be. We're together, darling. That's everything, really.'

Oh, God, had she whispered too loudly? She heard the click of boots behind her. Well done, Catherine, you're to be pistol-whipped now.

But the boots paused, and clicked past her. She saw a young man, wearing blue military uniform, striding up to the tribunal. Well, she thought, here's the real thing. This one isn't a playboy in fancy dress. Idly, she watched as the man flung a piece of paper before the three judges, and heard voices raised in a loud argument. She saw the man turn and point towards Fu-kuei and her. Then the big bastard who had been presiding over the court shrugged and waved his hand in acquiescence. The man in the blue uniform turned, with an eager look on his face, and walked towards them. He was a handsome fellow, she noticed inconsequentially. She did not know why but she felt a sudden rush of hope.

It was a cold day so the servants had lit a fire in the grate. Catherine sat on the sofa opposite Fu-kuei in the armchair. Neither said much. What was there to say?

Eventually, after the clock had struck nine, Yi-liang returned, tired and haggard, and sank into the other armchair.

Nobody spoke. After a while he pulled himself up and threw a log into the dying fire. He turned towards Catherine and attempted a smile. 'Corporal Wang sends you his regards – mingled with a few curses – from hospital,' he said. 'That was a mighty blow you gave him.'

'I'm sorry. I had to do it,' said Catherine.

'Don't apologise. You were resourceful and brave. You both were,' he added uncomfortably. 'And Corporal Wang's a hard-headed old soldier. He'll recover.'

Catherine did not reply.

He stood irresolutely by the fire. 'I've arranged the transport you wanted up to Wuhan. It wasn't difficult,' he said. 'You leave in three days.'

'Thank you,' she said.

'The least I could do,' he muttered wearily. He went back to his chair. 'The workers came out in demonstration,' he said suddenly, 'in Chapei and Woosung. The Kuomintang troops fired on them. It was terrible. Worse than anything the warlords ever did.'

Neither of the women said anything, but now that he had started, Yi-liang seemed desperate to unburden himself. 'Chiang came back in the afternoon. He had a big reception from the bankers and the Chamber of Commerce. There's a military curfew over the city now, and a lot of new proclamations. The General Labour Union's been formally abolished, to be replaced by a body to be organised by Tu Yueh-sheng. The gangsters are to control the city's labour, it seems.'

Still, neither woman spoke. One of Yi-liang's knees was twitching, and haunted eyes stared out of a gaunt, stretched face. 'Oh, by the way, Fu-kuei,' he said, after a long silence, 'I meant to tell you earlier but in the horror of what had happened to both of you I forgot. Chou En-lai is safe. He got away. At least I managed that.'

'Thank you,' said Fu-kuei dully.

'It was the least I could do.'

The three sat in silence. The fire burned in the grate.

15

The Captains and the Kings Depart

From the journal of William Lampsett, Reuters correspondent, Nanking, 28 July 1927

The United Front is done for. It's now a civil war within a civil war, as the bourgeois Nationalists under Chiang Kai-shek face off against the Communist Nationalists gathered round Borodin in Wuhan. The unlikely kingmaker appears to be the chameleon of the warlords, General Feng Yu-hsiang, once mocked as the Christian General who baptised his troops with a hose, now suddenly transformed into the Red General, Stalin's man, with Stalin's money and Stalin's matériel, advancing with sizeable forces from the West. Up to now he's betrayed every faction he's ever allied with. Will he support Borodin as expected, in which case the Communists will have the upper hand? Or will he be as false as ever to his colours and do a deal with Chiang Kai-shek, in which case Borodin might as well pack his bags and go home?

Two weeks after the pacification of Shanghai, Generalissimo Chiang Kai-shek, his war chest now replenished with huge contributions from the city's grateful merchants, ordered his troops to deploy across the Yangtse. They faced bitter resistance from the warlord forces that had rallied after their defeat – the remnants of Sun Chuang-fang's depleted troops had been reinforced by the main strength of the Fengtian army – but reasonably reliable reports came through to Nanking that the Nationalists had captured the important transport hub of Hsuchow.

John Soo, kicking his heels in the new Kuomintang capital had to content himself with the rumours that dripped down from Headquarters. He had learned to be sceptical. Despite the apparent victories, the political picture was appalling. He feared that if the situation deteriorated into a triple civil war, as each side of the Kuomintang tore at each other's throats while the warlords attacked them both, the advantage would be on the side of Chang Tso-lin, and he would be caught on the side of the losing army. If Chiang Kai-shek gained the upper hand over Borodin and recovered Wuhan, it might be even worse. Lan-hua, with her bobbed hair and Communist sympathies, could easily suffer the same fate as the thousands of other young men and women who had already been murdered in the right-wing Kuomintang purges that had taken place not only in Shanghai, but in all the other cities that the Kuomintang had taken. The idea that Lan-hua might fall into the hands of the brutish northerners, in the event of a warlord victory, was enough to make him sweat in his bed with fear.

But there was nothing he could do about it. If the worst came to the worst, he determined, he would desert, go to Wuhan, and rescue her or persuade her to leave, but it was not a decision to be taken lightly. For all his new cynicism, John still hoped that the Nationalists would triumph as a united force. So he bided his time, waiting on events as they unfolded.

The nature of his job did nothing to lift his spirits. Colonel Loong had expressed immense satisfaction at the success of the first arms deal and had authorised John to negotiate another. Yet again he had found himself secluded for weeks in the odious company of Andreas von Henning. If anything, the negotiations had been worse than on the first occasion, for in a city, even one as ransacked as Nanking, there was no shortage of the entertainments that the arms-dealer desired. The Garden Hotel might have become a little run-down after the murder of the previous European management during the Nanking Outrage, but lower standards meant greater tolerance of the prostitutes and cabaret girls with whom the Austrian liked to keep company.

On one occasion, as John had unrolled his drawings to discuss the specifications of the new mortars, a Russian prostitute had wandered, stark naked and yawning, out of the bedroom. Von Henning had called her over and made her sit on his knee, while he continued to peer through his cigar smoke at John's papers. When the girl had become bored, her hands had strayed to von Henning's thighs, and he had responded, kissing her shoulder and running his hands over her breasts. John, blushing, had asked if they wanted to be left in private, but the Austrian had murmured, 'No, go on, Soo. Continue with what you were saying.' Later, John had sat for fifteen minutes listening to their noisy lovemaking through the half-closed door. When von Henning came out, buckling his belt, he had laughed at John's furious expression. 'Soo, my friend, such a long face! Listen, why don't you try her? I'll treat you. What the hell? She's cheap. Cunt like a mouse's arsehole.' At which point, John had gathered his papers and left the room to the sound of the Austrian's mocking laughter. But von Henning had complained later to Colonel Loong, and John had received an official reprimand for his discourtesy to their guest. After that he had had no escape from the late-night carousing in cabarets, the drinking, and all the other indignities that von Henning now delighted to inflict on him.

Eventually, agreement of a kind had been made. This time Loong had insisted on conducting the final negotiation alone with von Henning in his headquarters. No doubt they were refining the commissions. By that stage John had not cared. He had been counting the minutes to the man's departure the following day.

Two weeks later, von Henning had returned. Again John had been delegated to accompany him on his debaucheries, but it had been Loong who went down to the docks with the Austrian to receive the cargo when the rusty tramp steamer arrived.

John Soo had smelt a rat: why had the idle colonel taken such pains to see this particular cargo stored in person when he had a flunkey to do it for him? That evening, von Henning had found the woman he wanted early, and John, for once excused a debauch until dawn, found himself free shortly before midnight, only a little the worse for drink. Even so, it was probably this slight intoxication that emboldened him to check the cargo.

He took a rickshaw to his semi-deserted headquarters, and annoyed the dozing corporal at the desk by ordering him to secure a jeep with two armed riflemen as escorts. The unorthodox requisition would certainly get him into trouble next day – but he had a premonition that these soldiers would be needed.

It took them less than half an hour to drive out of the city gates and down to the docks at Hsiakwan. He had no trouble getting access to the warehouse: his rank and the riflemen were enough to intimidate the guard at the gate of the compound. The sergeant in charge was quickly rousted from his bed, and with a clang the heavy metal doors were swung open, the electric lights turned on. The piles of crates stacked in three neat layers on the concrete floor were easy to identify; they had been deliberately stored separately from the other matériel. He ordered the sergeant and the two riflemen to open the boxes on the top layer, then climbed up to look, and felt the first twinge of doubt. He saw rows of neatly packed Winchester repeaters, all oiled and to the specification that had been ordered. He told the men to carry one box down so it could be emptied on to the floor. They did so, and revealed layers of rifles to the bottom. He ordered a second to be emptied. It was the same.

He wondered whether he had made a fool of himself, but nevertheless ordered the men to bring down a box from the second layer. It, too, appeared to contain rifles. The sergeant was openly grinning. 'Would you like me to bring down another box, sir?' he asked politely. 'Perhaps that one will contain what you're looking for.'

'No,' he said curtly. 'Empty this one.'

All three grinning now, they removed the top layer of rifles, but before they had laid them on the floor they were staring at John open-mouthed. Beneath the rifles were stacked rows of small gunny bags. 'Give me your bayonet,' John ordered one of the men. He pressed the point into one of the bags, and when he withdrew it, he lifted the blade and examined the black, treacly substance that stained it. He put it to his lips. 'Sergeant,' he said quietly, 'open the rest of the boxes.'

When he was satisfied that the rest of the crates also contained opium, he ordered the sergeant to lock the warehouse and post a guard outside. He got back into the jeep with the two riflemen and ordered the driver to take them back to Nanking. As they neared the Garden Hotel he checked his revolver and made sure it was loaded.

He opened the door to von Henning's suite with the key he had demanded from the night porter and, with the riflemen, moved silently through the dark sitting room. They could hear grunts and squeals from the bedroom. John pulled out his revolver, took a deep breath and opened the door. He switched on the light, heard a scream and saw the flash of a naked bottom as the Chinese girl who was riding von Henning leaped to the side of the bed and pulled the sheet to cover herself. Von Henning, exposed in all his hairy virility, lazily raised his head from the pillow. His eyes narrowed as he recognised John. 'So, finally, young Soo, you have decided to share in my pleasures . . .' A smile was spreading over his red features. Then he noticed the gun.

'Get dressed,' snapped John. 'You're under—'

He glimpsed the pistol in von Henning's hand and fired, but as he did so he felt a blow on his shoulder that knocked him backwards against the wall. He heard a great bellow of pain as he slumped down on the floor, and wondered if he had uttered it, then realised it must have been made by von Henning. A piercing scream pulsed in his ears. He sensed, rather than saw, the rush of his two soldiers with their bayonets into the room. Then he blacked out.

But it could only have been for a few seconds. He woke to a throbbing pain in his shoulder. Dizzily, he shook himself, until he felt his head was clear again. Von Henning was still lying on his back. One of the soldiers was pulling a bayonet out of the man's forearm. The other was observing the blood on his own bayonet, and John noticed the ragged wound in von Henning's thigh. He wondered where he himself had hit him, because he was certain the Austrian had cried out after he had fired. Then he saw that two toes on the man's left foot were missing. Von Henning was grunting and moaning in agony. The Chinese whore was pressing herself flat against the cupboard, stark naked and wailing. So many naked people, thought John idly. With an effort he sat up. The pain in his shoulder flared, but he believed he could move.

'Well done, men,' he said quietly, stumbling to his feet. 'Can one of you get rid of that woman? She's giving me a headache. Give her her clothes, and one of you find a dressing-gown or something for that bastard on the bed. He's indecent.' As he felt the strong hands of one of the soldiers support him, he knew there was something else he had to say. 'You're under arrest,' he told von Henning, 'for drug-smuggling,' and blacked out again.

He felt better after he had been bandaged and his arm was in a sling. One of the soldiers had had the presence of mind to send for a doctor. A local physician had appeared remarkably quickly, and first John, then von Henning had been given first aid. They had had to order some of the hotel staff to carry the cursing, struggling von Henning to the jeep, but John found that he could walk, although he was still dizzy and his shoulder was agony. With the doctor looking after von Henning, they drove to the military hospital, where John made sure that his prisoner would be kept under guard. He allowed another doctor to clean and examine his shoulder, which was apparently broken, but refused to be taken to the operating-theatre to have the bullet removed. 'I'll come back,' he told them. 'I have to do something first. For the revolution.' They had protested, but he had insisted. 'I'll come back soon,' he said.

By the time they left the hospital and were back in their jeep, it was nearly eight o'clock, and the city was preparing for a new day. John was tired, but he enjoyed listening to the cries of the dumpling-sellers, the excitement and bustle as rickshaws and honey-carts hurried by. He smelt the fragrance from the outdoor breakfast stands, mingled with the wet tang of drains and sewers. Suddenly he was reminded of his boyhood in Canton, going to the fish-market with his mother and sister. Always that mixture of sweetness and stench, he thought, but that's China. We can make a revolution here but we'll never get rid of the smells, and he had laughed, suddenly happy to be smelling the China he loved. He noticed the concerned look on the driver's face. 'Don't worry,' he said. 'I'm not going mad.'

Oh, but it was good to be alive! He looked up at the pale blue sky. From a little square between some tiled houses, somebody was flying a kite. It was fashioned in the shape of a hawk, and whoever was controlling it had great skill because it darted across the sky, rising and diving just like a real bird. He watched it contentedly, turning his head to follow it as the car drove on, until the pain in his shoulder made him wince. He would feel much happier, he decided, if he did not have this pain running down his arm, or this splitting headache.

He was feverish by the time they reached the headquarters building, but he felt a new spurt of energy as he stepped out of the car and trotted up the steps, so fast that the two riflemen had to hurry to keep up. He knew he was going to enjoy what he was about to do. He delighted in the echoes as their boots clicked along the corridor. He pushed open the door to the outer office and noticed the orderly's startled eyes as he rose from his table to protest, but he ignored him, and went straight into Colonel Loong's office.

Loong was sitting at his desk, sipping tea. It would be his favourite oolong tea, thought John, as he observed the pale face and the raised eyebrows. How he loved his oolong! 'You should have stuck to the tea trade, Colonel,' he said conversationally. 'It's more wholesome than opium. Better for your health, anyhow.'

Oh, life is wonderful, he thought – but he was so tired. Dizzy too. Perhaps if he just sat for a moment in Colonel Loong's chair? There was plenty of time to conduct the arrest. He had reached his destination. He had struck a blow for the revolution, for Sun Yat-sen's Three Principles, for the purity of the new China they were struggling to create: the China he wanted for his children – his and Lan-hua's children – in a golden future that was attainable.

Colonel Loong, an experienced officer, knew how to handle two bewildered soldiers, even if they were pointing guns at him. He thanked them for their efforts and told them that Headquarters knew all about the drug-smuggling in which this unconscious officer had been engaged. He was to have been arrested this morning. He apologised that Major Soo had duped them. Knowing that he had been discovered, he had obviously been using them in a last vain attempt to divert the blame, playing the innocent and conscientious investigator of his own crime. It was lucky that he had passed out or otherwise he might have attempted some harm to his superior officer. Whether they believed him or not, the story confused the two soldiers, and when the guard arrived, alerted by the orderly, they were quickly disarmed. Loong had seen to it that by noon they, with John Soo's driver, were on a ferry across the river on the way to a new posting at the front. After that, he had the unconscious John Soo carried to a detention cell, while he went down the corridor to explain to the general, who was also a member of his syndicate, the perfidy and treachery of his subordinate.

The foreigner was treated for his wounds, and a few days later flown back to Shanghai, having been paid in full for the weapons he had delivered according to his contract, even though John Soo had found ways to insert drugs into the delivery for his own nefarious purposes. Probably Major Soo had links to the triads working in the Shanghai dockyards, speculated Colonel Loong.

By the time it was appreciated just how ill John Soo was, some twelve hours after he had been thrown into a damp cell, he was showing all the symptoms of pneumonia. Later it was diagnosed that poisoning from fragments of clothing left in the wound had compounded this weakening of his resistance. Obviously there was no question of him being sent to prison to await trial, so he was kept in hospital under guard. Sadly, the doctors, who had reported his strange behaviour earlier in the day, were doubtful of his recovery. It was decided that, since the prognosis was that he would not survive, there would be no benefit in publicising what he had done because it would cast a bad light on the National Revolutionary Army. For the moment, no charges were made. Colonel Loong volunteered to take the onerous responsibility of selling the impounded drugs on the open market. The proceeds would go towards the expenses of the Northern Expedition, he said.

There were times over the next few days when John's fever abated, but he was very confused, and nobody could make much sense of what he was saying. He seemed to be fixated by a particular revolutionary poster that had been pasted on the wall by his bed when the Nationalists had taken over the hospital. It was a coloured print of a young woman with a rifle strung over her back, holding a book in one hand and with the other pointing a finger in wrath at her imperialist enemies. None of the hospital staff was to know, of course, that this poster bore a marked resemblance to one that John had seen Lan-hua proudly pasting on the wall of a temple in southern Hunan, long ago when his world had been filled with hope, idealism and love. If they had, they might have been touched to think that while his weak body struggled to retain its hold on life, he was sustained by his memory of the long kiss he had shared with her afterwards, while villagers cheered and Kuomintang flags flew, the fresh forces of the National Revolutionary Army had been marching by, and everybody believed in a common cause and the certainty of victory ahead.

At about the same time that John Soo was hovering between life and death in a military hospital, Generalissimo Chiang Kai-shek was returning to the city after a triumphant visit to the front, and Hsuchow in particular, where he had celebrated the great Nationalist victory with his troops. A large crowd had come to Nanking station to welcome him back, and there were bands, anti-imperialist and anti-warlord speeches, cheering children waving Kuomintang flags, and all the pomp that the modest generalissimo found it politic to countenance. Stepping out of his private railway carriage after him came his generals and staff officers, carrying the boxes of official papers that always accompanied the busy generalissimo wherever he went. The crowd cheered them as well.

It was only after the official reception was over that other passengers emerged from his carriage, four bedraggled foreign correspondents: representatives of the *Chicago Tribune* and the *New York Times*, a Dane, who was covering for several European newspapers, and Willie Lampsett of Reuters. They were in high spirits – or three of them were – because they had secured a scoop, news of such stunning importance that it would change the course of the war.

For it had not only been to inspect the troops that Chiang Kai-shek had set out last week from his headquarters. As these correspondents now knew – as *only* they now knew – secret arrangements had been made for a summit with a man who, until recently, had been considered the generalissimo's worst enemy. And they had been there when it had happened. It had been an undreamed-of coup, and entirely unexpected.

Willie, however, was miserable. Although he knew that the scoop would make him famous among his peers and certainly endear him to Reuters, it meant that he had to return to Shanghai, and possibly

Tientsin, and that would take him further away from Catherine even than he was now. She was far away in Wuhan, or on her way there, but every day he had spent covering this war at the front, he had felt close to her, as if they were sharing an experience. A return to civilisation, however, was akin to a prison sentence.

In the year since the Northern Expedition had begun, Willie had thrown himself into his work. Few other correspondents had seen as much action, and to all outward appearances he was still the hard-bitten newsman: he had preserved the cold, watchful exterior and the cynical bravado of his calling, while the depth of his know-ledge and the acuity of his analysis were the envy of his colleagues. But he knew that this was a shell, and that deep inside he had changed. Following his débâcle at the hands of George Airton, the old Willie had been destroyed, and what had slowly emerged from the wreck had been a different man, perhaps wiser, certainly more self-aware and sympathetic to the suffering that he now saw all around him, and above all passionate. In the past, he had played with poetry as a diversion; now he had developed the sensibility of a poet – and he owed it all to Catherine.

It had taken him months to get over the shame and embarrass-ment after George had discovered them in bed together, and the shock when he had discovered that Catherine had left Tientsin. The blow that had shattered his pride, though, had been the knowledge that she despised him. When he replayed that terrible scene in his mind, he understood how pathetic he must have appeared to her. Instead of standing up to George, he had whimpered away like a beaten cur. He had been a coward – and Catherine had seen him for what he was.

At first, he had fooled himself that their love could be salvaged. He had used his sources to track her down at a hospital in Wuhan. He had sat for a day and a night in front of his typewriter with the intention of explaining himself to her, begging forgiveness and pleading with her to return to him, but he had torn up every pitiful word he had written. Some time during that long night he had accepted it was pointless. He knew Catherine: once she had made up her mind about something, she would never change it.

Sometimes now he would force himself to reread his journal

entries during the weeks that had followed: self-recrimination, outbursts of rage against himself, George and Catherine; remorse that he had allowed himself to be used by a designing woman. Usually he wrote of his love for her, abjectly bemoaning his own foolishness in throwing away the pearl of happiness he had held. Gradually these outpourings developed into a bitter, meditative reflection about loss, and the self-knowledge that comes with the dissolution of hope. It had been about then that he had begun to write verse again.

Some of his best poems had been composed by torchlight as he crouched in foxholes under bombardment, or while he snatched a few moments' rest in the chaotic helter-skelter of a retreat. At first the poetry had been erotic and sensual: to obliterate the explosions, the shouts and curses of terrified young men, he had tried to escape into the calm of those afternoons in his bungalow, when the afternoon light crept behind the closed curtains, and shimmered blue shadows on Catherine's white limbs.

When the firing increased, he had lost himself in visions of ivory arms lifting to welcome him, a dreamy smile on lips that opened to meet his own; and he would describe the ocean mysteries of her shining green eyes: sometimes blinding like sunbeam jewels on the water, the flame of a laughing Diana exhilarated by the hunt; at others a flat morning calm, brushed by a soft wind, the serene contemplation of the Mother Goddess acknowledging the devotion of her supplicant, indulgently inviting him to enter the safe grounds of her temple, the soft silk of her fiery red hair tenting over his face during their lovemaking, like the curtains descending behind the initiated in an inner sanctum of a shrine.

Later, during long marches and counter-marches, his writing turned to the Chinese landscape he loved, the mountains and lakes of Kiangsi, the canals and hilltop temples of Kiangsu, but often with something of Catherine that inspired him: the flight of a covey of ducks above a marsh, recalling the day they had spent in Taku; the evening sunlight catching the burned gold of an unharvested cornfield invoking the colour of her hair.

As the war progressed, and he witnessed the brutality of the warlord forces, his poetry became tougher, less Georgian: brittle, full of savage ironies and hard, unsentimental description as he wrote of the columns of refugees fleeing their burned villages; of slave porters collapsing from exhaustion and malnutrition; of the generals feasting and womanising while their troops starved; of opium, which became for him a symbol of the degradation of a civilisation in its death throes. He rarely mentioned Catherine, but his muse revealed herself even more strongly than when he was overtly worshipping her. Sometimes he thought he was writing with her voice: Catherine, with her sardonic humour, her implacable honesty, her courage and defiance, and outrage at unfairness or cruelty. Slowly the vacuum that had entered his soul when he lost her began to be replaced by the consoling belief that she was still with him in spirit if not in fact.

Meanwhile, he did his job, reporting on troop movements and the political cut-and-thrust, filing his stories by messenger or by wire when he could. That was his duty, and he did it well – but he lived for the private moments when he could be alone with his journal and his thoughts, because then he believed he was with Catherine, and found a sort of peace.

After the Dog General's withdrawal from Nanking, Willie had taken one of the last-running trains back to Tientsin to file his stories. Robby, in his sly way, had shown how pleased he was to see his friend return in one piece, and had tried to organise dinner parties, but Willie had declined all invitations, spending his days in the office trying to catch up with the work that had piled up in his absence, and the evenings with his journal. He had not been in Tientsin long when the Shanghai massacre occurred, and he had made his way back south to cover the aftermath.

It was there that somebody had mentioned the Red nurse who had so recently caused such a scandal and who had been the subject of a clever assassination piece in the *Herald*. He heard the name: Mrs George Airton. Ears burning, Willie had gone back to his bureau to look through the back numbers in the newspaper pile his assistant had collected, and found the article. He read it over and over again, furious at its tone and the twisting of Catherine's words, but it was news of her, and that was like a draught of water to an expiring man in the desert. He felt a wave of disappointment and regret when he realised that if Catherine had been caught up in the Nanking Outrage, she must have been there at the same time he was. Then he felt an overpowering surge of hope. She had only recently been in Shanghai. She might still be there. He would find her. He would throw himself on her mercy like the supplicant in his poem, and surely she would see that he was no longer the cold, selfish Willie who had hurt her. He had changed, suffered; she would understand that he had loved her all this time, been faithful to her, and she would forgive him . . .

In his madness, he had searched every hotel, every hostel. He had all his staff out on the streets making enquiries – and, because they knew their job, they had eventually found out that a Mrs C. Airton had embarked on the Chinese tramp steamer, *Kuan Yin*, up the Yangtse to Wuhan. His goddess had again slipped his grasp, and not even his journal could console Willie this time.

Shortly after that he had met Misselwitz of the *Tribune*, who had suggested he accompany him to Hsuchow. And he had agreed, because he could not think of anything better to do.

Willie and his colleagues had gone through laborious negotiations with unhelpful departments in Nanking to get a travel permit. They had experienced excruciating delays when the one engine and rolling stock that the Nationalists had managed to recover in working order after the Dog General's retreat the previous month had failed again and again to appear. When it did, they commandeered a goods van to themselves, but to do so had to fight off hordes of semi-naked coolies who had already overflowed every other compartment of the once proud Blue Line and were clinging to the roof and even hanging on the buffers. They had endured twenty-four hours of hell.

The officers under General T. K. Wang's command had welcomed them warmly. They had been given beer on arrival, shown with courtesy to a room in a Confucian mansion that was to be their billet, and were wined and dined each night in the mess. Their evenings had ended drunkenly and uproariously, watching young officers who had been educated in Europe dancing the charleston and the can-can.

When the generalissimo arrived, they had been given seats three rows behind him on the grandstand outside the city, where a mass rally was being held in his honour. The irony that they were seated under a banner emblazoned with the characters 'Death to the Imperialists and Stinking Foreigners', and the fact that the arrayed ranks of soldiers and political activists were shouting slogans much the same, had not seemed to occur to anybody else. Afterwards the generalissimo had shaken their hands warmly, welcoming them to the National Revolutionary Army.

The day after the rally, however, they had been expelled from the Confucian mansion and taken by armed guard to a solitary building guarded by a picket of fierce-looking soldiers. They had had no idea why they were now *persona non grata*, and it had been with trepidation that they had followed the cold captain, now emphatically uninterested in the charleston, who came at noon with another armed guard and ordered them to accompany him in his jeep.

They had been taken back to the mansion and the banqueting hall, where they found places set for them at a sumptuous feast. There they had seen, in the place of honour beside the sleek generalissimo, a huge, unshaven peasant of a man in grubby private's uniform. Willie had recognised him immediately. It had been the warlord Feng Yu-hsiang, once approved by the world as the Christian general, now vilified as the Red general in Moscow's pay.

He had known then and there, even before both men stood up to speak, that a cataclysmic change had occurred in Chinese politics. The Red general had decided that his interests lay in supporting Chiang Kai-shek and the right wing of the Kuomintang. He was going to abandon his paymaster, Stalin, and his friends in Hankow. Feng Yu-hsiang's army had been Borodin's only hope – but now the Russian and the whole Communist left wing of the party would be isolated. The kingmaker had chosen Chiang Kai-shek. The Communists were doomed.

After the banquet, Willie and his three journalist companions had been among the photographers who had taken pictures of the two new allies standing together, one in crisp-cut uniform with shining leather boots, gleaming belt and strap, smiling shyly, the other a head taller, wearing bulging pantaloons above his puttees and a padded smock of a tunic, glowering from his piggy eyes at the cameras.

It was an unbelievable scoop.

They had applied and been given approval to accompany the generalissimo on his private train back to Nanking. They had sat at the end of the carriage watching the generalissimo doing his paperwork or gazing meditatively out of the window at the passing countryside – the unquestioned new ruler of China.

He had called them over and given them copies of the joint memorandum that he and General Feng proposed to telegraph to the left wing of the Party in Hankow. It called for the immediate dismissal of Borodin and all the other Russian advisers, the combination of their forces under the generalissimo's own command, the dissolution of their so-called government, and the removal at the first opportunity of all political personnel to Nanking.

To have this actual text in their hands had been political, not to mention journalistic, dynamite. The four journalists made a hurried agreement that they would return to Shanghai immediately and co-ordinate their stories so that they could all share the prize.

But in the end it was the Danish journalist, Nielsen, who out-scooped everybody. He slipped away in Nanking and travelled to Hankow, where he delivered his bombshell at Borodin's headquarters before the official telegram had arrived.

When Lan-hua and her colleagues in the secretariat were summoned into Mr Borodin's room they found their leader looking unnaturally white and badly shaken. Lan-hua was stunned when she heard what the paper in his hand contained. It was unthinkable that General Feng Yu-hsiang could have met with Chiang Kai-shek, let alone allied with him. Her immediate response was that this was merely another attempt of the right wing of the Kuomintang to cause mischief. She only calmed down when it became clear that Mr Borodin shared the same view.

Even so, he told them, the rumour was alarming enough that its provenance should be verified. He delegated members of his staff to go to the offices of the various Kuomintang leaders in the city and to the titular head of the government, Wang Ching-wei, to let them know what he had heard and to establish whether any of them had received a communication from either of the two generals.

Meanwhile Lan-hua spent the afternoon taking Mr Borodin's dictation while he composed a telegram to General Feng, repeating the substance of the extraordinary document that the foreign reporter had passed to him, and asking simply whether there was any truth in it.

When she brought him the typed-up draft, he gave her one of his warm smiles, and asked, as he always did, whether she had had any news of her fiancé. Lan-hua had not realised quite how emotional and scared this rumour of General Feng's defection had made her, when her nerves were already strained after weeks without communication from John. To her embarrassment and shame, she burst into tears and poured out all her fears for his safety.

Mr Borodin offered her his own handkerchief. 'Well,' he said kindly, 'we can't allow that state of affairs to continue. Where is Major Soo? Didn't you tell me once that he worked for the logistics department of the Sixth Corps in Nanking, and that he was not very happy with his job? We will think of something. For now, however, Comrade Lei, I need you to dry those tears and take another dictation.'

She reached for her pad and pencil, thinking how lucky she was to be working for so extraordinary a man. She could only imagine what strain he was now under. There was not only the deteriorating situation with Chiang Kai-shek, but a few weeks before he had learned that his wife, Fanya, had been captured by a warlord gunboat on the way to Shanghai; he had had no firm news of her, except a rumour that she had been taken to Peking, where she had been threatened with execution by Chang Tso-lin. Even after the shock of this morning's news, which, if true, would make his position in Hankow untenable, he yet found time to show interest in his colleagues. She knew that in all probability nothing would come of his offer to help her contact John Soo but it was generous of him to show sympathy when he had a hundred more pressing worries.

'Are you ready?' he asked. 'Good, now take this down. "Senior Political Adviser to C-in-C Headquarters Nanking, notification urgent. In view military situation on Central Hepeh front requires experienced engineer, request immediate repeat immediate loan and attachment to Hankow 8th Corps HQ of Major K. S. Soo, currently posted 6th Corps Logistics Nanking. Signed, Mikhail Borodin."'

'There.' He grinned, as she gaped at him. 'Perhaps you would be so kind as to send this telegram with the other. No, don't thank me. I'm sure we could do with an experienced engineer in Wuhan. Anyway, while the United Front formally exists, we might as well do something useful through it.' A stern, glowering look replaced his benevolent smile. 'His excellency the generalissimo may want to be rid of Mikhail Borodin, but while Mikhail Borodin is the official adviser to the Kuomintang, his authority and his wishes will remain unquestioned. Now, hurry. I want an answer from General Feng tonight.'

With the two telegrams in her top tunic pocket, close to her thumping heart, she ran to the telegraph building on the Bund, and personally supervised their dispatch. The weary officer told her to be patient: there would certainly be no reply to either message for at least two hours.

She wiled away her time by pacing up and down the waterfront. The Feng Yu-hsiang crisis had slipped her mind, relegated to insignificance in comparison with the prospect that John would soon be with her. She would move out of her dormitory, she decided, and take a room where they could be on their own. On the day he arrived she would fill it with orchids – no, chrysanthemums, the flower after which she was named. It would be their private love-nest. She would buy stores of the smoked duck and yellow wine he loved, walnuts and fruit, cakes, dried beef, melon seeds and *mantou*. Mr Borodin would give her leave of absence, she was sure. Oh, what a wonderful man he was, she thought. She wished she could do something to relieve him of the heavy pressures he had to bear. That he could think of her happiness when his own wife was a prisoner of the warlords!

After a while, she calmed down: she was behaving like a giddy schoolgirl. A professional cadre, she told herself, would wait patiently for the confirmation before giving way to such undignified elation. Even then she had to use what willpower she had to stop herself looking at her watch every two seconds. The hands were moving so slowly that she wondered if there was a fault with the mechanism, but she knew it was her own impatience.

It had been some time since she had been here. This promenade by the river had been where she had confronted the British soldiers. It was looking very different now. The quays were empty of shipping: she spotted only one freighter and two junks. She was momentarily grateful that the green canopies of the acacia trees blocked out the sinister line of foreign warships that had not moved in months, their threatening guns still pointing towards the shore. But no flimsy barriers of leaves could hide the fact that the city was still under blockade.

The very silence spoke volumes. She could hear, faintly, the murmur of a crowd, chanting slogans, but somehow the isolated sound emphasised the stillness that had fallen over the city. There had been a time when every street of Hankow was a turmoil of protest. Now whole days passed without a demonstration. It appeared to Lan-hua that the revolution had run out of steam.

She frowned as she remembered how John Soo had prophesied the economic collapse. The empty wharves vindicated him. Even if the blockade had not had its effect, the proliferation of unions demanding the right to question any management decision had stifled business. Not long ago Lan-hua had been their most eager supporter, but the excited activist, leading workers on strike, initiating struggle sessions, had become a reflective, more contemplative woman.

She thought that she owed it to the tutelage of Mr Borodin, whose example everybody in his office tried to emulate. He was a master of compromise – 'more Chinese than the Chinese' they sometimes joked, after one of his successful sleights of hand – and, above all, he was a realist. 'Slogans and ideology are useful, Comrade Lei,' he had told her, 'but you must learn to adapt yourself to the reality of the world as it is before you can achieve the world you desire.' When he had sought to curb the power of the unions she had been surprised, but he had explained, 'It is like a child breaking a complicated toy because he does not understand its mechanism. We are fighting for the freedom of the workers, but we should not destroy the existing means of production to do so. Until the workers are educated, we will need the capitalists to run the factories, because only they know how. In that way we recruit our class enemies to assist our cause.'

It had been weeks since she had participated in any demonstration, and she shuddered at the memory of the last one. She had heard one afternoon that there was to be another protest march against the one surviving foreign hospital, and been persuaded by her friends to join. Mr Borodin had given her leave, and she had joined the throng of activists marching under the wide red banners emblazoned with 'Down with Imperialism in the Clothes of Paternalism'. At the hospital gates she had been screaming with the rest of them when the doors had opened and the stinking imperialist who came out to meet them had been . . . Dr Edmund Airton. She had been shocked to see her old friend pelted with vegetables. He had stood quietly, however, repeating patiently in his fluent Chinese, 'We are not political. We have come to help.' When he had been shouted down, he raised his voice to plead, 'If you really want to help the revolution, find a way to bring us medicines. We need them to prevent your brave soldiers dying of their wounds.' All the time he had stared straight at her, and Lan-hua had seen the sad disappointment in his eyes. She had blushed with shame and embarrassment.

Afterwards she had stayed behind and knocked on the gate. The nurse who met her had been hostile, but eventually, when she had shown her pass proving that she worked in Mr Borodin's headquarters, she had allowed her in, and Lan-hua was taken to Edmund's office. 'I thought it was you, Lan-hua,' he had said, his face breaking into a warm smile as he rose to his feet to greet her. 'Sometimes I wondered if you had found your way to Hankow. How jolly good to see you – although I can't say I'm always enamoured of your friends.'

He was interested to hear that she worked with the famous Mr Borodin. 'My, you have gone up in the world,' he congratulated her. 'You're quite the revolutionary now. It may surprise you but I support your revolution, except for some of the stupidities and excesses. What you and your Mr Borodin are doing will, I believe, result in a better China, if you're given time. In all the millennia of this country's civilisation nobody has bothered about the common people until now, and they do need help.' He looked shy. 'Would you like me to show you what we're doing here? It's very little, but there are some good officers who bring their wounded men to us. We could do a lot more if we had supplies and the support of the government.'

He had taken her round the wards. The terrible wounds had shocked her. 'I'm sorry, but that's what war does to people,' Edmund had said gently, when he saw her eyes fill with tears at the foot of a bed where what had once been a human being was now a bandage-wrapped trunk fed by a drip. She had been amazed by the cleanliness of the sunlit room and the efficiency of the white starched nurses as they moved among the patients. 'Of course I have Catherine to thank for that,' said Edmund. 'She's a marvellous matron.'

'Catherine's here?' she had asked in surprise.

'No, but I hope to see her back soon. She's had to take rather a dangerous journey downriver to bring me more medicines through the blockade. When the telegraph started working again I received the good news that she's on her way in a Chinese steamer and should arrive any day. We do need those medicines, Lan-hua, but it's a drop in the ocean. There are literally thousands of soldiers coming back wounded from the central front but we're stretched as it is, looking after just a handful. A lot more needs to be done. Perhaps you could mention that to Mr Borodin. I would welcome him to come and see what we're doing.'

She was proud that Mr Borodin had listened to her. He had mentioned the matter to Madame Sun Yat-sen who had contacted her friends in the United States. Edmund's efforts had been augmented, indeed overshadowed, when a ship flying League of Nations flags had docked in the harbour, and disembarked several American doctors, a mountain of medicines and, it was said, eighty American-trained nurses on an aid mission organised by the Rockefeller Institute. There had been no more demonstrations against foreign hospitals. Some among her colleagues had disapproved of help from imperialists, but, ideological issues like that did not worry Lan-hua any more.

Catherine must have been back some time now, she thought. It would be good if John could meet her. Of course! They had once been friends at Oxford. She felt a little guilty that she had not yet found time to see her, but she had been so busy.

She looked at her watch for the umpteenth time. Only forty minutes had passed. She had a sudden fear. What if he refused to come? John Soo was so honourable that he would hate influence being used on his behalf. She did not care. He had no choice. This was an order from Mr Borodin himself. Nobody would disobey that.

She was back in the telegraph office after only one hour and fifteen minutes. There was a grim expression on the face of the operator as he offered her the flimsy. Her heart sank. The rumours of the alliance between Chiang and Feng must be true, she thought – but the order for John's release might still be given before the 6th Corps realised what had happened. Without looking at the text in her hand, she asked urgently, 'The reply from Nanking HQ? Has that come in yet?'

The man looked surprised. 'This *is* the telegram from Nanking. General Feng hasn't replied yet.'

And it was then that she read the bald words:

'C-IN-C HQ NANKING TO MIKHAIL BORODIN WUHAN REGRET MAJOR SOO DIED OF COMPLICATIONS RESULTING FROM PNEUMONIA APRIL 25TH STOP SEARCHING FOR SUBSTITUTE ENGINEER.'

The telegraph operator had been very kind. He had helped her up from the floor, and steered her towards a chair, muttering that he saw so many tragedies pass by his desk; so many reports of brave men's deaths. 'I take it you knew this Major Soo, then?' he asked, giving her a cup of tea.

She told him woodenly that he had been her fiancé.

'Ah, you'll be inconsolable, then.' He sighed. 'Do you want to go home? I can phone your headquarters to get someone else to pick up the other reply.'

'No,' she said dully. 'I have all the time in the world now, don't I?'

'It won't be long before the other answer comes through,' he said.

She sat in the chair holding the mug of tea, seeing only John Soo's face as he waved goodbye to her from his sampan. The telegraph officer went back to his desk. After about twenty minutes the machine began to clatter loudly. 'I won't be long,' he said. 'It's a short enough message.' He spent some time translating it, chewing his pencil as he consulted the manual of the day. 'Looks like this is bad news too,' he muttered, handing Lan-hua the flimsy.

She read General Feng's reply confirming that the information, which the foreign journalist had passed Mr Borodin, had been correct, and that the official telegram was being prepared. It did not seem to matter any more – although, of course, when she brought it back to Headquarters it had a dramatic effect on all her colleagues, who shouted, cried or slumped, numb, in their chairs. One of her colleagues even banged his head against the wall. Mr Borodin alone seemed to take it calmly, retiring to his private office and closing the door behind him.

She did not tell her friends about John Soo; nor did she tell Mr Borodin. He had enough to think about now, she thought. Since everybody was behaving hysterically, she did not think that her grief would be noticed, and she could not bear the thought of going back to her dormitory. Nobody else seemed to want to go home either, and she took some comfort in their company, sometimes even listening to their angry speculations before the words faded into meaninglessness, and images of John Soo occupied her thoughts exclusively. He had had so many faces, she remembered. One after another, they emerged from her memory: smiling, laughing, serious, tired, sleeping, reflective, angry, excited. She imagined him lying on a hospital bed, alone, far from anybody who loved him – and then she wept.

There was activity of a kind. Some of her friends went back wearily to their desks to continue writing their reports and analyses. Eventually Mr Borodin emerged and told everybody to go home. There was nothing more to be done tonight. He paused by Lan-hua's desk. 'Don't cry for me, Comrade,' he said gently, 'although I appreciate it. Everything will turn out for the best in time. This is not the end of the world. You and your Major Soo will see the revolution triumph. I guarantee it.' Still she said nothing. He went on, 'Can you come to the office early tomorrow, Comrade? I have an appointment with another journalist, a Mr Manners from Manchuria at eight a.m., and somebody must be here to let him in.'

At some point during the long, desolate night that followed, she thought of Mr Borodin's words, and realised that for the first time he had been wrong. 'This is not the end of the world,' he had said. It was for her, she thought. Now she had nothing. Slowly, she began to be afraid, as she imagined the empty future that yawned before her.

Once the two soldiers at the door had frisked him and his pocket-knife had been confiscated, Henry Manners was allowed to enter the dark, marbled vestibule of the insurance building in the French concession that Borodin had taken over as his headquarters. As he waited in the cool shade, he noticed the stained glass in the windows, which seemed to consist entirely of erotic pictures in the *fin-de-siècle* style, of semi-nude damsels being rescued by knights in armour from various kinds of durance vile. He chuckled that such louche *Yellow Book* touches were to be found in the offices of the Red commissar. On the other hand, the famous Borodin probably envisaged himself as the champion of the virtuous workers of China, confronting the dragon of capitalism. Well, he should have known better: Chinese dragons had a habit of consuming everything around them, particularly wishful-thinking knights-errant who thought they had the latest panacea for China's ills.

Despite the aching discomfort in his leg that humid climates such as that of Wuhan invariably intensified, Manners was in a good mood, determined to enjoy this interview.

Actually, as far as he was concerned, there was no need for this meeting now. If General Taro had sent him down here to assess the Communist threat, he could report back that there wasn't any. Even if Borodin and his stooges were stupid enough to hang on and fight, the moderates in the Hankow government, and there were enough of them, would desert. Anyway, as soon as Feng Yu-hsiang brought up his forces, the Communists would be annihilated, as they had been in Shanghai and other cities. The writing was on the wall.

There was certainly no requirement for the second, rather ambiguously worded, part of his assignment, in which Taro had asked him to 'deal with the problem'. Not that he wasn't curious to meet the 'Evil Genius of the Chinese Revolution' whom he had vilified in so many articles. It was rare, these days, that Manners had a chance to gloat.

A rather pretty girl with bobbed hair was coming down the corridor. Miserable face, though, he thought, and shabby little uniform. She had the puffy eyes of somebody who had been crying all night. Probably one of the great man's minions, he decided, devastated by the catastrophe. Well, if the Kuomintang kept to its usual form, they would make short work of the likes of her when they came to Hankow. If he had been in her dainty little shoes, he would be making for the hills – but he gave her a cheery smile when she approached him and asked if he was Mr Manners.

'Certainly am,' he said. 'Is the master ready to see me now?'

'If you'll follow me,' she said woodenly. She led him up the stairs, through a large outer office, and knocked on a door beyond. She turned the handle and stepped aside to let him pass.

Mikhail Borodin was sitting behind a large desk, scattered with papers, a soft light shining on him from the louvred windows. He was wearing a white cotton tunic of the type that Sun Yat-sen had popularised. In one of the top pockets Manners noticed the bowl of a protruding pipe. His thick brown hair was brushed back, and his lips were half hidden by a silky moustache in the English style. There were deep shadows under his eyes, and the skin on his face looked stretched and unnaturally white.

Manners's first thought was that the great Borodin in person appeared rather ordinary and unimposing. He looked like a bus conductor who had had a heavy night out – but there was a grace and elegance to his movements when he stepped round the desk to shake Manners's hand, and he did so with a firm grasp. He was a well-built man, with a trim stomach, late fortyish, fiftyish; probably he'd be a formidable opponent if it ever came to a scrap, and the warm, brown eyes, though melancholy, burned with an intense intelligence.

By the time Borodin had waved him to an armchair, and was

sitting alertly opposite him, Manners had revised his opinion of him. Jew-boy, obviously, he thought: all these Bolshies were, the clever ones – this one had depth. There was a gravity about him too, a natural stillness that indicated iron self-control and determination. There was also, in the ironic, half-humorous glint playing in his eyes, something likeable and human. A man you could do business with, he decided, and discovered to his surprise that he was beginning to respect him.

Borodin smiled. 'Well,' he said, 'you asked for an appointment with Borodin and here he is. How can I help the Imperial Army of Japan? I assume that is whom you represent.'

'Not formally,' replied Manners carefully. 'I'm a newsman. I've come for an interview for my paper.'

'Yes, Mr Manners, we have all read the articles you write for the Japanese propaganda media. Your reputation as a polemicist is well known even as far away as Moscow – but as far as I am aware your métier rarely involves anything as mundane as factual reporting. You are more famous for your colourful invective unrestrained by facts of any kind. So let us skip the pretence that you have come here looking for a scoop. Incidentally,' he added, 'I know as much about you from the Cheka as I do from your recent scribblings. They inherited thick files on you from the Okhrana. I confess I was impressed. In your day, it seems, you were quite the brave chevalier. You were once considered a considerable nuisance to imperial Russia when you were working in Manchuria for British, as opposed to Japanese, intelligence.'

Manners laughed. He liked the man's style. 'It's so very convenient, isn't it, when chaps don't have to go through any complicated introductions? All right, since it hardly matters now, it's true that I was asked to come here by the Japanese authorities.'

'The Kempeitai presumably? That is whom we understand you work for. General Taro or Colonel Doihara, perhaps? Or are you here representing the Kokuryukai? The Black Dragon Society?'

'Let's just say, the Japanese authorities in Dairen,' said Manners. 'They wanted a newsman's assessment of the situation. Fears that you Bolshies were getting a bit powerful. You know the score: Moscow pulling strings, Stalin taking over the Northern Expedition . . . Japs wouldn't have liked that. They have enough trouble with your boys on the Manchurian border.'

'I doubt they would have sent such an experienced secret agent and mercenary just to assess the situation, Mr Manners. I am sure that you were also given other instructions. How were you going to remove the thorny problem of Mikhail Borodin? Were you considering assassination, perhaps?' He smiled.

Manners shrugged. 'That's water under the bridge now, isn't it? After yesterday's interesting news.'

He saw the man opposite stiffen, and for a moment the eyes in the sallow face hardened – but, as quickly, Borodin relaxed, and emitted a short, bitter bark of a laugh. 'Well, it was bound to come out. The Chinese have a reputation for inscrutability and secrecy, but when it comes to privileged information, the place leaks like a sieve. I suppose that, after the supposed news of my imminent dismissal, you're thinking I might welcome assassination as a way out of my problems. Should I consider your visit a philanthropic one, Mr Manners? Are you here to put an old dog out of his misery?'

'Sorry, old boy, but I don't think I can oblige you any more on that score. Doesn't really seem to be the need, does there? You're all washed up.'

Borodin contemplated him expressionlessly. Then he gave another short laugh. When he spoke again it was in the soft conversational tones he had used earlier. 'Let us pretend,' he said, 'that you really are a journalist and I am the leader still of this revolution. Now that Mr Henry Manners has been given his interview with Borodin, what would this famous anti-Bolshevik polemicist wish to ask?'

'All right, then, if that's how you wish to play it. As I said, it's water under the bridge, but I confess I'm intrigued. It's not often one gets a ringside seat at a turning-point of history. How is a man like you going to face up to failure and betrayal?'

'Failure and betrayal?' murmured Borodin. For a moment the soft eyes bored into his own, and Manners had the odd feeling that he had been caught naked, that this man could penetrate his soul. 'I have a suspicion that I know why you asked that question, Mr Manners. This is perhaps a subject in which we both have experience. It could be that there are things we can teach each other. No? Well, let us play our game, anyway. Let me answer your question at face value. It is too early to judge whether I have failed in what I set out to achieve. The struggle is by no means over. I remind you that I have not yet been dismissed.'

'You will be. Madame Sun has spunk. The others don't. Wang Ching-wei's jealous of you, and would be glad of any excuse to be rid of you. Eugene Chen and Sun Fo will blow with the prevailing wind.'

Borodin sighed. 'You may be right. That would still not necessarily mean that everything we strove for will have been a failure. Fires, even after they have been put out, can flare up again from ashes of the original inferno, often in the most unexpected ways. There are young cadres like Li Li-shan and Mao Tse-tung who will have learned something from this débâcle. Comrade Mao has been doing some interesting work among the liberated peasants in Hunan, discovering great wells of support in the countryside. Perhaps the revolution will disappear for a while into the hills and mountains to return stronger when the people are ready.'

'You know as well as I do that every one of them will be hunted down like vermin and exterminated.'

'But not all of them will be caught, Mr Manners,' Borodin said softly.

'All right, if you say so, but the odds are stacked against them. What about betrayal? I also asked you about that.'

'I am merely an adviser, Mr Manners. There will always come a time in any contract when the client wishes to dispense with an intermediary.'

This time it was Manners who laughed. 'Such sanctimony from you? You're Stalin's man in China. You came here to promote the world revolution and Russia's interests. If it hadn't been for you there wouldn't have been a Chinese revolution in the first place. You became the Chinese revolution.'

Borodin raised his eyebrows. 'It is flattering that my enemies consider me so formidable. Thank you, Mr Manners, although I daresay you had no intention of being complimentary – but all the same, you touch a raw nerve. I have been all too successful, at least initially, but perhaps therein does lie a failure – not of the revolution but perhaps my own.'

'You'll have to explain that, old boy. Way I see it, your whole cause is in ruins.'

There was a dreamy, meditative look in Borodin's eyes. 'You were right to say that the motives that brought me here were for a world revolution in which I believed. China was to have been the first stepping-stone in a general struggle to liberate the peoples of the East – but somewhere along the way, I lost sight of that goal, and became absorbed in this beguiling country exclusively for itself. I imagine that I am not the first foreigner to be hypnotised by the colour, the beauty, the allure of five thousand years of civilisation, the charm of these impossible, contradictory people – and I allowed myself to believe, because I so desired it, and because the conditions appeared so right, that instead of steering the great struggle of the suffering people in the way that my masters wanted, I could lead it to a fulfilment of its own. Well . . . as you have said, it does not matter now. What has happened has happened. It is in the nature of this frustrating place that the foreigner with his best intentions is thwarted because ultimately he does not understand, and never will, the deeper currents that flow in the depths of China's lakes and rivers. I brought the revolution to the shores of the Yangtse, I, a foreigner – then China defeated me.'

Manners stared, fascinated, as the man whom he had considered the coldest and most cunning of Bolshevik manipulators spoke of his private hopes and dreams, and he was also appalled. He had come here today to crow over the downfall of an enemy, but he felt an instinctive sympathy and remembered that once, long ago, before he had become an alcoholic and a mercenary, he had had visions of a better world and the part he could play to achieve it. He had once believed in empire – it was as remote from Borodin's ideology as anything could be, but it had been an ideal of sorts. Slowly, over time, he had been thwarted and disillusioned, betrayed and used by the people he had served, and had succumbed to despair. He noticed that Borodin was looking at him closely and imagined a sad compassion in those eyes. Again he felt naked, and at the same time a sense of complicity, as if he were being pulled against his better nature to share this man's predicament. He had consciously to remind himself that Borodin was a Bolshevik, his enemy.

An ironic smile was playing on Borodin's lips. 'I told the journalist, Nielsen, that if you were to send a diver to the bottom of the Yangtse he would rise again with an armful of shattered hopes. Is that not the tragic reality for any of us foreigners who try to make our brief mark on China? Is it not true that history begins with tragedy? The second time it is tragi-comedy. What is your story, Mr Manners? Is it also tragi-comedy? Do you really believe in this Japanese miracle, this modern star of Asia? Or are you like us Russians? We are dreamers but all too often the dreams we have only realise themselves in the delusory comfort of the bottle. I do not drink, as I suspect you do, but perhaps when I return to Mother Russia I wonder if I also will find myself taking refuge in the bottle.'

'If you're lucky enough to be allowed any refuge,' said Manners, suddenly angry, though whether it was with Borodin or himself he could not be sure. 'From what I hear of your Mr Stalin, he is not forgiving of failure.'

Borodin chuckled. 'No, he is not. The revolution cannot fail, so how can a revolutionary fail?'

'You managed to,' said Manners.

'Then obviously I was no revolutionary, was I? Write that down, Mr Manners. Borodin was no true revolutionary. He was an imperialist saboteur.'

'Moscow sent you,' said Manners, bristling under Borodin's savage irony. It seemed that, some time during their conversation, the tables had been turned. 'What was it? An error of judgement?'

'Certainly not,' said Borodin. 'The Party cannot err.' He looked serious. 'I changed after I came here. It is an old, old tale. I am like the Sir Tristram in your English romance who was sent to bring a lady to his king. I loved the lady, and betrayed my king. Oh, this China. What has it done to us?'

'In my experience, old boy, when people moan about their failure, it's usually themselves they have to blame.'

'Well, perhaps you are right, but then China attracts the self-destructive, does it not? It is the great chimaera where all seems possible, and one by one we are sucked into its heartless flame, which burns the hopeful soul even where it most entices. Learn from my example, Mr Manners. Perhaps it is not too late for you.'

'Whether it is or not,' said Manners, 'it will be for you. Where will your dream be when you are sent to a punishment camp in Siberia?'

'Even in Siberia a man may dream,' said Borodin.

'Thank God, then, that I'm not a man who needs to dream,' said Manners.

'Then I pity you,' said Borodin, 'but I do not believe you. I am a Russian and if there is one thing we Russians understand it is suffering. We are born in the cold night of the winter steppes. We arrive out of our mother's womb yearning for the light – but that darkness we were born with is always in us. Every Russian knows how easy it is to succumb to the darkness of the human soul. What I see in your eyes confirms what I suspected when I read your pamphlets. You, too, are a man who has been wounded by life.'

'Is that so?' muttered Manners. 'I thought the rules of the game were that *I* would be interviewing *you*.'

'Ah, yes,' smiled Borodin, sadly. 'But is that not just another example of the futility of the rules we try to set ourselves? Is that not always the way of the world? The interviewer ends up examining his own soul. The manipulator is manipulated. And, yes, the commissar who tries to lead China finds that he has been led by the nose.' He leaned forward in his chair. His haggard face was now close to Manners's, his eyes glinting with a flame. 'So! The man who came to interview Borodin, and maybe assassinate him, what has he learned about himself today? Let us hope that this meeting, which, you told me at the beginning, "hardly matters any more", has had some purpose.'

Confused, Manners could think of nothing to say.

Borodin laughed, not the bark he had uttered earlier but a rich, jovial, affectionate roar. 'Here we two stand at a crossroads, I perhaps to return to Russia, you – to go where? To do what? I wish that the two of us could have met when we were both younger men. When we were both *parfait chevaliers*. Perhaps we could have been friends. I see nobility in you, Mr Manners. You have courage. You would not be here if you did not. What was it that made you succumb to the dark side of your soul? Are you really so different from me? Are we not both wounded kings in the wasteland of our shattered hopes? What Perceval will bring his holy grail to cure us? My holy grail is the revolution. It may yet cure me. Despite all that has happened, I believe. In what do you believe, Mr Manners? What is your grail? Please don't tell me it is the Kwantung army of Japan. That would be too, too tragi-comic.'

He stood up and placed a hand on Manners's shoulder. 'Come, I have enjoyed talking to you, but I have still – for a while – a revolution to run. What have you to do, Mr Manners? I hope one day you will find your grail. If you do, think of Mikhail Borodin.'

It was a more thoughtful Henry Manners who stepped out of Borodin's office. He hardly noticed the pretty girl with the puffy eyes who led him back through the outer room, now full of her colleagues. He walked for a long while through the empty streets, oblivious of his surroundings. The meeting had disturbed him deeply. He had not found a broken enemy at whom he could jeer; instead he had ended up liking the man who had epitomised all he had hated for so many years. He was inclined to dismiss Borodin's words as philosophical balderdash but something had woken feelings inside him that he had not experienced for longer than he could remember. He could hardly credit it, but Borodin had awakened his conscience. The overriding emotion he felt now was shame.

'Damn him,' he muttered. What bloody right had anybody to lecture him? Or pity him?

In the end he dispensed with his intended visit to the golf club. He returned to his hotel and consumed the best part of a bottle of whisky. Then he felt better.

Catherine had spent a busy day with the Rockefeller people, handing over her wards and the administration of the hospital. The humourless Philadelphia matron, who had come to take over the keys, had insisted that she interview all the nurses. Catherine had spent a nervous hour and a half waiting with her charges, as they went, one by one, into what had been her office to learn their fate, and had been relieved when they all had been accepted. In fact, the American woman had congratulated her grudgingly on the quality of their training. Edmund had agreed to stay on for two days so that he could brief the incoming doctors on the treatment he had been giving his patients, but Catherine, who had become attached to the little world she had created and therefore could not bear to see it in the hands of others, had said farewell to her nurses, then gathered her things and left. She had taken a rickshaw to the small hotel on the Bund in which she and Edmund had stayed on their first night in Hankow, so many months ago.

The polished wood-panelling in the lobby, the courteous German manager who greeted her, the homely smell of newly made bread were as she remembered them, but Catherine felt a curious sense of dislocation. The hotel was alien to her. It belonged to a different era of her life. Sadly she accepted that this was just another sign of how she had changed.

She was pondering this now as she strolled along the Bund after dinner. She had been driven out of the restaurant by the noisy conversation of a group of diplomats. They had been celebrating the downfall of Borodin, loudly toasting Chiang Kai-shek with brimming glasses of champagne. 'Borodin won't dare go out by river,' a young American first secretary was saying. 'He's got more enemies between here and Shanghai than a negro in a Ku Klux Klan convention. They'll string him up as soon as look at him.'

'They'll be stringing him up here if he hangs around much longer,' replied his equally youthful British counterpart. 'Not that there'll be many tears for Borodin – but if what happened in Shanghai is anything to go by, there'll be purges all round.'

'Serves the buggers right,' laughed an Australian. 'I'd lop a few heads off some of those Commie bastards myself after what they put us through. But I don't think they'll get Borodin. The intelligence blokes are saying he and Madame Sun have already fixed up an armoured motorcade to take them up through Kalgan and back to Russia via the Gobi.'

'Then let us pray that the wells on his passage turn out to be dry,' murmured a French second secretary. 'It would be ironic, *non*, if such an orator, who has spouted rivers and torrents of propaganda, meets his end in thirst?'

'Something you'll never do, Jean-Jacques, not with all the bloody *vino* you Froggies put away,' said the Australian. 'But I don't mind throwing in a prayer for a desert demise, though my preference would be for the poisonous bastard to get stung by a scorpion.'

'Or by a rattlesnake,' contributed the American.

Walking along the Bund now, the lights from the line of anchored warships twinkling on the water, Catherine wondered why she had not said anything when she passed their table. With what had happened in Shanghai fresh in her mind (how would she ever forget?), she had been disgusted to hear them gloating over the purges that the Kuomintang would bring to Wuhan, and even though she had no respect for Borodin or any politician, she had thought their vindictiveness was vicious and small-minded. There had been a time when she would have assaulted the gathering with all the sarcasm of which she was capable. Or would she? In a vision of self-realisation, she saw herself sitting at just such a table, raising her glass in triumph over Borodin's humiliation. She had hated Borodin and the Bolsheviks with a passion greater than any those young men could have mustered.

But it was not only her passionate hatred that had been purged in the furnace during the long night of hell she had experienced with Fu-kuei: it had been passion of any kind, and Catherine had been a woman who had defined her life by her passions.

It had been a relief to come back to the routine of the hospital: she did her job with her usual efficiency, but the nurses, who had been surprisingly pleased to see the old dragon return, had sometimes looked at her strangely. They had probably been wondering what had happened to her fire.

When Edmund called her into his office one morning, he had been irritable, which she knew was a sign of nervousness. He had taken ages to get to the point, which was that since the arrival of the Rockefeller contingent, their work in Hankow had become redundant. She had accepted this without demur. He had been surprised: he had obviously expected an angry reaction. 'It'll mean giving up everything you've set up here,' he had said, 'leaving all your nurses, starting from scratch . . .' She had only nodded. He had frowned, eyes moist, as if there was something else he wanted to say to her, but she had stood up and told him she would wait for his instructions. 'Will that be all, Doctor?' she had asked quietly.

She had thought long and hard on the boat journey up the river about what to tell Edmund, and in the end decided it would be best if she told him nothing – nothing, anyway, about the horrors in Nanking or Shanghai, or even of the battle on the junk (how long ago that seemed!). She knew that if she told him of the dangers she had faced on his errand, he would never forgive himself for sending her. She could hardly tell him about what had happened to his sister, Jenny, either, because that would hurt him too – so she told him that she and his family had been rescued quickly, all things considered. As for Shanghai, she had been sleeping peacefully in her hotel and had known nothing about it.

But Edmund worried about her. Once he had come across her, late at night, seated in the dying room beside a patient. The boy had been unconscious and there was nothing she could do to alleviate his condition, but she had occasionally passed a wet towel over his sweating chest. Edmund had pulled a chair to the other side of the bed and joined her vigil. Neither spoke. He had hunched forward, his head hanging above his knees. Occasionally he lifted intense eyes and contemplated her. He tried to twist his lips into a reassuring smile. When she began to weep, he put his arm round her shoulders and she had let her head fall against his breast. He had stroked her forehead until the sobbing ceased, and even then he did not let go.

It was not long afterwards that the boy had died. Edmund checked his pulse and felt his heart, then nodded wearily. For a moment she caught a look of despair, but he smiled again and kissed her forehead. 'Time you went to bed, Catherine,' he whispered, 'it'll be morning soon,' and helped her to her feet. Her limbs were numb after sitting for so long, and she stumbled. For a moment, inadvertently, they embraced. She felt his warmth. If it had lasted a second longer, she might not have had the power to let go, but 'Goodnight, Catherine,' he whispered, with another kiss on her forehead. 'Tomorrow will be better.' He had paused at the door. 'We all need you, you know. I need you,' he had added, almost harshly. Briskly he had walked away in the direction of his quarters.

Now, under the shadowy trees, she realised there was a good reason not to tell lies: they were so easily found out. She could not disguise that she had changed. Edmund knew that something had happened to her during her long journey.

She recalled those empty days with Fu-kuei after their rescue. They had hardly spoken to each other during the long hours in front of the fire. They went through the motions of living. They ate together in the dining room. Occasionally they separated to wash or perform other ablutions – but at night they still sat together, neither of them prepared to face the horrors of a solitary bedroom.

Gradually they grasped that Catherine had to go. Yi-liang had made it easy for her: he had handled all the arrangements, bringing the medicines from the Quai de France, telegraphing Niedemeyer and Edmund in her name, personally checking her berth on the *Kuan Yin*. Slowly they focused on the world around them again. Catherine asked Fu-kuei what she was going to do. Fu-kuei considered for a long while, and answered hollowly, 'Rest. Try to regain my strength. Perhaps I'll see if one of the universities here will take me as a teacher of English literature – although, I can't . . . I can't face that now.'

'Will you stay with Yi-liang?' asked Catherine softly. 'He does love you, you know.'

'I suppose so.'

'Even after what he's done?'

'Yes, I think so. I have nowhere else to go.'

'Do you still love him?' Catherine asked.

Tears streaked Fu-kuei's face as she replied, in an almost inaudible whisper, 'Yes.' The deep, brown eyes were almost pleading. 'Oh, Catherine,' she said, 'I feel so ashamed of myself.'

Catherine had gazed at the flames in the grate. 'Don't be. You should be grateful.' She had added bitterly, 'Love's something to hold on to if you can find it.'

She felt Fu-kuei's warm hand squeeze hers. 'And you, Catherine? Do you not have somebody to love?'

And then it had been Catherine's turn to weep. 'I thought so, Fu-kuei. It seemed that all through the river journey, I was waking up to something I'd denied for so long. I'd been so foolish, so blind . . . I thought when I returned to Hankow, Edmund would be there, and he and I . . . But it seems impossible now . . .'

'He will be there, Catherine. Edmund will be waiting for you. You must tell him.'

'I don't think I can, Fu-kuei,' she had croaked. 'Not after that night in front of the furnace. I changed. Something died in me. I can't explain it. I don't believe I would know how to handle the responsibility. It would be unfair on Edmund. I'm so empty. I think I've lost the will to go on.'

Fu-kuei's eyes were blazing. 'You'll find out in time that you're wrong. We mustn't give way to defeat, Catherine. We can't allow those evil men to break us. We're still who we are, beaten maybe, but there will come a day when we'll be strong again and defeat them. You must believe it.'

Catherine had smiled despite herself, and kissed her cheek. 'Oh, my darling Fu-kuei. How glad I am that I found you again. You're such a revolutionary. So determined . . . But I'm tired of everything. I don't think I have the strength any more. Unlike you, I don't believe in anything.'

It had been a bitter parting. Catherine and Fu-kuei clung to each other on the pier like lovers. Eventually Yi-liang had had to part them. Weeping, Catherine had followed him as he carried her bags up the gangplank. Later she had watched their two figures fading on the shore. Fu-kuei, a tiny round bundle in her fur coat, did not wave. She stood where she was, still, solitary and, Catherine believed, strong, her lover hovering by her side.

She had kept to herself on the journey. She hated even to look at the river that had brought her so inexorably to despair. After a while the memories of the furnace dimmed, (she knew those images would never truly erase themselves from her mind) and her thoughts turned to Edmund. The nearer they came to Hankow the more she panicked. By the end of the journey she was dreading him, fearing that the sight of him would crumble whatever minimal resolve she had left. But she need not have worried. She had forgotten how quintessentially English he was. He could not conceal the joy, the relief, the excitement when he bounded up the gangplank, and for a moment squeezed her to him – but it was only a moment. He had instantly collected himself, pecked her on the cheek, picking up her suitcase, blushing as he did so, and safe formality was restored. Within minutes, they were calling each other 'Doctor' and 'Nurse' again, Edmund with wry irony, Catherine with undisguised relief.

She was such a coward, she thought. She leaned against the rails by the waterside, staring into the blackness. She could hear the river out there – that hateful, deceiving river. She was so timid now. Once a resolute Catherine might have considered ending her life by throwing herself into that torrent. This new, empty Catherine did not even have the courage to do that.

'Catherine,' she heard, from the darkness. At first she was so lost in self-pity that she mistook it for the voice of her conscience, but the call was insistent. Wearily she turned from the water to see who the persistent nuisance was. A short figure in a crumpled tunic crept closer. Eventually a pale Chinese face peered into hers. It was streaked with dirt and tears, but the eyes were familiar. 'Catherine, don't you recognise me? It's Lan-hua.'

'Of course I recognise you.' She was startled. 'Edmund told me you were in Hankow. But what are you doing here? It's so late.'

'I tried to find you in the hospital but it was full of American nurses and strange people. Eventually one of the porters told me where your hotel was. You weren't there so I looked here. Oh, Catherine, you must help me. I'm so scared.'

'But – but how can I help you? You work in the government here, don't you?'

The eyes blazed fiercely. 'The government is leaving, Catherine. Mr Borodin is abandoning us. You must help me get out too. Oh, please, Catherine, I have no money and you're my only hope.' Suddenly she slumped to her knees, and to her horror Catherine found that the girl was clutching her skirt. 'Oh, please,' she wailed. 'Please.'

When Lan-hua raised her head, Catherine saw the terror that convulsed her features. 'I don't want to die. I'm too young to die. Please.'

In her bewilderment, Catherine knelt beside her, hugging the wet face to her breast. 'Calm down, Lan-hua. Just tell me what the matter is.'

'They'll cut off my head,' the girl wailed inconsolably. 'I know it – because I worked with Mr Borodin and I have bobbed hair. John told me. There was a girl in Nanchang. They put her head on a pole – and a crow plucked out her eyes! I couldn't face that!'

Catherine felt a shudder of horror, remembering the conversation she had just heard in the restaurant about the likelihood of purges. She remembered what had happened in Shanghai. She remembered the girl in the warehouse with pig-tails who had run away in terror and been shot down. She remembered the young woman who had been dragged away from her lover, screaming, to the furnace. She clutched Lan-hua more tightly. Suddenly the waterfront promenade seemed full of menacing shadows. A shadow moved behind a tree. She felt the cold tingle at the back of her spine that told her she was being watched.

On the other side of the river, beyond Wuchang, she saw a streak of lightning on the horizon, and heard a whisper of thunder. The brief glare had suddenly illuminated the ghostly grey of the warships and the long barrels of their guns. Catherine shivered as a gust wafted up from the water.

She was overtaken by a wave of helplessness. She no longer had the strength to deal with a situation like this. She felt as broken and scared as the weeping girl she held in her arms. The evil in the world was ubiquitous, implacable. Why couldn't life and its problems just leave her alone? She knew that was an unworthy thought, and forced kindness into her tone, although she wanted to shake Lan-hua. Why was she always being expected to cope?

'Is there nobody else who can help you? There must be others in your situation. What about your fiancé? Have you been in touch with John Soo? What does he say?'

Sheet lightning flashed again on the other side of the river. In its white light Lan-hua's face shone with terrible clarity; it seemed to wizen and grow old. 'There is no John Soo. He's dead.' The harsh whisper was followed by a despairing moan and Lan-hua repeated, 'He's dead, Catherine. They sent me a telegram. Catherine, I'm all alone.'

To Catherine, it seemed that all the ghosts of the dead who had populated her life were gathering around her. Again she glimpsed a shadow moving silently round a tree-trunk.

But she had no time to think of that now. 'You're not alone, darling,' she murmured, even though she did not yet believe it. 'You're with me, and I'll look after you. I don't know how but I will. I'm so sorry about John, but I'll think of something. Let's go back to my hotel. We'll be safe there, and in the morning we'll ask Edmund. He'll know what to do. He and I are leaving in a couple of days. We have a berth on a ship. Maybe we can take you with us. If we dress you in a nurse's uniform nobody will see your bobbed hair, will they? That's it, darling. Stop crying. We'll cry together later on.'

With pathetic trust in her eyes, Lan-hua allowed her to take her arm. Catherine hurried the pace in the direction of the hotel, whose welcoming lights she could vaguely make out several hundred yards away through the now gathering rain. Under the trees they were still protected from the downpour, but Catherine had felt the first drops on her cheek and the back of her neck and had shuddered as if she were being caressed by an icy hand. Thunder was cracking overhead, and in the flashes of phosphorescence that preceded them, she peered forward to see if the strange presence she had imagined was really there. She saw no one, only the pale trunks of the trees.

Every step forward into the blackness was an effort of will. She mumbled words of encouragement to Lan-hua but she was convinced that somebody was tracking them. She even believed she could hear the tap-tap of a stick on the pavement above the sound of the rain.

They reached the point where they had to cross the road to the hotel. They were already soaked. Through the sheets of rain the lights in the windows glimmered warmly. They had only to cross the road . . .

Then Catherine saw him, the figure from her nightmares who, in a deep part of herself, she blamed for everything that had happened to her. A man was standing in the middle of the road, cloaked against the rain, the brim of his sodden Homburg curling, leaning on a stick and looking straight at her. She did not need the flash of lightning to reveal the ravaged features, the pouched eyes, the ragged moustache. She saw them often enough in her dreams.

The figure moved forward as if it wanted to speak to her.

The mouth opened, and she saw teeth, which glinted white. He raised a gloved hand.

But she knew this was only an apparition, something she had conjured in this night of fear. She lifted her nurse's cape over her and Lan-hua's heads, gripped the girl, and together they ran past the ghost, up the dripping steps into the haven of the hotel.

That night, after she had bathed Lan-hua and put her into her own bed, kissing her like a child, she checked that the curtains were firmly closed before she lay down on the couch, and she kept the lights burning, as if that would stop Henry Manners, or any other of her many ghosts from haunting her.

16

The Battle in the Dark

From the journal of William Lampsett, Reuters correspondent, Shantung Front, 17 April 1928

Song of a Russian Machine-gunner Far From Home

I saw myself in that boy's wondering eyes –
When I was young I shared his peasant dreams
And just like him I trusted in the lies
That lured our youth from hearth and native streams.
My parents wept like his and shook their heads.
'Who'll give us grandsons who can till the land?'
We left to fight imperialists or Reds
Though what they were we didn't understand.

We startled on his troop upon a plain
Of barley like the home fields we once knew.
He heard a sound and, turning, saw a train,
A child's delight, all shining, metalled, new . . .

I sighted on that wonder sans regret,
Blew out his eyes, and lit a cigarette.

Colonel Ti Jen-hsing waited while General Lin read the orders that had just arrived from the Dog General's headquarters on the other side of the city. Lin was taking his time. His cold eyes contemplated each paragraph with the concentration and meditation that one might devote to a book of philosophy, then turned to his field map.

Ti yawned. As usual he had not been offered a seat. There was not one to be had. They were billeted in what had once been a hotel, but Lin had turned his luxurious suite into the simple quarters he preferred, removing all the furniture and replacing it with his desk, his camp bed, his portable locker and his filing cabinets. They might as well have been meeting in a tent, thought Ti, thinking of his own plush rooms.

Over the last year, as the fighting had moved from the Yangtse into Shantung, back down the railway line to the Yangtse and up to Shantung again, Ti had stood in similar surroundings more times than he could remember. The only difference was that this room in Tsinan, where they had been billeted for the last four months, was illuminated by an electric lightbulb instead of an oil lamp. Even the decorations were the same. The obligatory portrait of Generalissimo Chang Tso-lin hung behind the desk; next to it, on Lin's right, were pinned his maps; the strange picture of the woman with red hair that Lin had purloined from the monastery stared out from the wall to his left, and on top of his locker lay the glass case containing the femur wrapped in tattered imperial silk, that he had seen Lin take from the emperor's tomb. Ti presumed it was some private talisman that would one day find its place among all the other oddities in Lin's mausoleum in Shishan.

He had ceased speculating long ago about his superior's collection mania, his fascination with imperial relics and ancient religions, and his deviant sexual tastes. It was not only works of art that Lin sent back under guard to Shishan; he also collected red-headed Russians for his harem, and priests of all religions for his temple. Ti did not care about his master's imperial fantasies: every warlord was corrupted in his own way; Lin's eccentricities were harmless when compared to the depravities of some of the other madmen who commanded in this army, and he was a brilliant general, which was all that mattered.

Ti's career had prospered since the day he had personally executed Colonel Yen in the monastery courtyard, and learned what it was like to be feared. He had immediately imposed stricter standards of discipline than had existed before, and meted out punishments for the slightest infraction. It had taken trial and error, and attrition during the subsequent fighting, but it had not been long before he had built up a corps of officers, whose ruthlessness and efficiency were almost equal to his own. Above all, he had made sure that they were loyal, not necessarily to him but to Lin, because that was where the ultimate authority emanated, and also the rewards – but Ti made sure that he was the medium for that power and patronage: he passed on the orders and distributed the spoils. And men had flocked to join their division, good men, hard men, because they knew that General Lin was blessed by fortune, followed by victory, and had the surest nose in the warlord army for loot.

After one dangerous action in which Ti, following Lin's carefully conceived plan, had led the Shishan cavalry contingents on a flanking raid round the Nationalists' left wing to one of their major supply depots deep behind the lines – where they had captured wagonloads of matériel, ammunition and bullion – Lin had shown his appreciation by distributing gold coins to his men. For Ti there had been a special reward, but he did not receive it until some time later.

Shortly after they had retaken Hsuchow, the situation had appeared settled enough for Lin to summon one of his Russian concubines from Shishan. When Ti had met her at the station, he recognised the tall, red-headed woman whom a year before he had escorted to the Lungmen caves. She had arrived in a fur coat, despite the heat, and with all the airs of a princess; she had treated Ti like an insignificant underling, making him carry her hatbox, while his men struggled under her trunks and suitcases. Ti had smarted under such disrespect and said nothing. But his opinion of foreign women had been confirmed. This one he particularly disliked, and not only because she stank. After he had delivered her to the general's pavilion, he had wondered what Lin could possibly find attractive in her. That night he had gone to one of the men's stews to get clean.

Two evenings later, he had reported as usual to Lin in his Spartan office. His woman had been installed in more comfortable rooms next door, and through the wall Ti could hear the sound of her singing. Lin had looked up from his papers and observed Ti contemplatively. 'You are a hard-working officer, Colonel, and have done me good service. I am conscious that I have not expressed my appreciation adequately.'

'To do my duty by my general is all I ask,' Ti had replied, surprised. There had been a long pause while the general watched him. The woman next door had been attempting some sort of operatic aria.

'I believe you. One of your merits is that you obey my orders without questioning them, yet you implement them intelligently with a flair of your own.' Then, inconsequentially, he had added, 'Does my concubine's singing please you?'

'It is very agreeable,' Ti had said carefully.

'You lie well.' The general had given him one of his twisted smiles, then his eyes had strayed towards the painting of the red-headed saint. 'Do you find the woman in this picture attractive, Colonel?' he had asked.

'It is a beautiful painting. A rare work of art.'

'Indeed it is,' said Lin, 'but what it represents is important. I once explained to you my interest in ancient religion and history. You have helped me on more than one occasion add religious arte-facts to my collection. It has struck me, as a detached observer, that whatever the religion is – Christian, Buddhist, shaman – its essen-tial aspects are very much the same . . .'

Ti had cursed his luck that he had caught his general in one of his mad moods. Although at first he tried to keep his expression attentive, gradually his thoughts had wandered, but suddenly he became aware that Lin had stood up and was looking at him fixedly, his face only inches away. He had felt a bead of cold sweat on his brow.

'You're humouring me, Colonel. Yes, don't deny it, you believe that I am insane.' The frosty eyes had been mocking, but the general's tone was amiable. 'I am not surprised. You are efficient and talented, but at bottom you are a simple, obedient, unthinking soldier, which is why I employ you. And these are deep mysteries.

'Colonel, a terrible thing occurred when Sun Yat-sen and his Nationalists led a revolution against the decrepit Ch'ing dynasty. Oh, yes, it had to happen. The Ch'ing, like empires before them, was rotten. Sun Yat-sen was right to take the Mandate of Heaven out of their hands – but what he did not realise was that when you destroy an order that has tied together a civilisation for millennia, the inevitable result is a spiritual vacuum that affects everything under heaven and on earth. It is like the wrenching out of a soul, and what is left is a void. Until a new spiritual order is established we become like hungry ghosts wandering in the ruins of our broken mansions. It is not surprising that we find ourselves mired in a state of civil war, or that so many of our young men and women are being enticed by the spurious beliefs of Communism.'

He moved towards the picture of the Magdalene.

'I keep this on my wall, Colonel, because it reminds me of the great task that our generation must undertake to make China whole again, to restore its soul. It is ironic that I must thank Chang Tso-lin for first showing me the way. Several years ago, one of his bureaucrats in Mukden sent me a memorandum. I thought the idea fanciful at first. The document, which had obviously been worked out by a committee, stated that in order to make a placid society, spiritual and political regeneration must go hand in hand. Some clever clerk had the idea that if we combined all existing religions into one then the whole population would be united and satisfied. Obviously none of my colleagues, who were practical men, gave it a moment's consideration, and I, too, nearly filed it away. I would have done, had not something strange occurred. About that time, you see, Colonel, I discovered, in Shishan, relics of our earliest forebears and, to my surprise, I realised the link between our ancestors and the wider primitive world. The origin of all cultures, all religions, is universal . . . And then I saw that absurd memorandum in a different light.

'What do you think, Colonel? Is it so illogical to imagine that a new age deserves a new religion? Oh, not the cobbled-together master plan of a bureaucrat but, rather, one based on the fundamental core of our civilisation, the old, forgotten religion, for that truly combines all belief, and has true, rather than manufactured, spiritual values . . .'

The general droned on. Ti kept on his face what he hoped was an interested smile. Thankfully, these aberrations did not occur often, but he was praying heartily that this one would be over soon so they could discuss the orders of the day. He had been relieved when eventually Lin returned to his desk.

'All right, Colonel, we should get back to business. I was saying I was satisfied with your work, and that you deserved a reward. I have brought that Russian woman here for a purpose. I once had high hopes for her, but she has disappointed me. She lacks spirituality, so I have no more time for her. She is yours, Colonel. I give her to you. My bodyguard will bring her to your quarters later this evening. You may do with her as you will. When you tire of her, as is probable, you may dispose of her as you think best. I suggest to the men's stews. She is no Holy Whore but whore she is in every other way, although she claims to be of aristocratic birth. Anyway, I think her talents will provide an interesting diversion for you at this quiet period of the war. Well done, Colonel. That will be all. Good night.' He had buried his face in his papers.

Now, months afterwards, as he again stood by his general's desk, Ti was still unclear what mad reason had inspired the gift. He suspected, as he had then, that Lin had been testing him. For some moments after the black-bearded bodyguard had carried the woman struggling and screaming into his room and thrown her naked on to the carpet, he had been frozen by indecision. She revolted him, but would he anger the general by not pretending at least to enjoy her? Or was Lin trying his loyalty? He remembered that Yen had been executed after raping a foreign nun. The circumstances were not the same, but he suspected that Yen's undisciplined self-indulgence had lost him Lin's trust. There was another aspect to consider. This woman, even if she was now cast off, had been his master's concubine. Was Lin testing his subordinate's ambition? Was it a trap? He had looked down at the big white body, the wide pelvis, the moon bottom, the red flame of her hair, the blue, bulging eyes that spat hatred and fear – and found her repugnant. He had gagged her, which had stopped her noise, but there was nothing he could do to alleviate the stink of stale perfume and sweat. Then he had remembered the general's suggestion and ordered his corporal to take her to the men's brothel. He had opened all the windows in his room, and taken huge gulps of the fragrant night air.

Next morning, he had been nervous when he reported as usual to the general, but Lin had spoken of nothing but matters relating to the regiment, and had never broached the subject again. A few days later, when Ti had gone to the bordello to seek out his favourite, who reminded him of Lan-hua, the *mama-san* had told him how popular the Russian was with the men. He was confident that he had acted wisely.

He presumed that she was entertaining the Nationalists now. Shortly afterwards, the tides of war had changed, and after much welcome fighting – for Ti there were prospects of loot in either an advance or a retreat – Lin's division had withdrawn to a front closer to the Shantung border, and later to Tsinan, where they had wiled away the long winter stalemate in boredom.

As he watched his general now, reading the papers that described the great push to be launched within the next ten days, Ti felt a flutter of excitement. They had spent too many months in quarters; the men were restless. Nobody dared complain, but he knew from his officers that the week-long manoeuvres he organised for them in the countryside exasperated them. The Dog General had reduced every village in his domain to a state of crippling poverty through his taxes and other extortions; it was rumoured that more than a million peasants from Shantung had fled the province, crossing the straits to seek a better life in the wilder lands of Manchuria. Ti's men had found that what remained was hardly worth scavenging.

He was satisfied that discipline was still good, but the men craved combat, and the opportunities that only war provided. Recent rumours had made the mood of the army more confident, and Ti, too, felt certain, listening to the gossip from Headquarters, that this time they would push the Nationalists beyond the barrier of the Yangtse, and into the fat lands of the south. It was already an open secret that three of Feng Yu-hsiang's divisions had deserted their Bolshevik leader and were even now marching to join the Fengtian forces. This time their numbers would be overwhelming.

General Lin was putting the documents back into their folder. He turned his cold eyes on his subordinate. 'You have read these plans, Colonel. What is your view of the strategy?'

'I approve, General. I think we stand every chance of success.'

'Do you? Alas, I do not share your view. I believe that our revered leader, the Dog General, will be marching our forces into a trap from which it will be difficult to escape annihilation.'

'Sir, I do not understand.'

'Then let me explain to you,' said Lin. He stood up and went over to his wall map. 'The plan is that our Russian friends in their armoured trains will storm down the railway line to Hsuchow, with the infantry in support. Did we not try that last year?'

'Yes, General. Last year we were only partially successful, but this time it will be different. We have enormous reinforcements on the right wing, who will be able to outflank the enemy while they face us.'

'Forces generously provided by our enemy, General Feng Yu-hsiang. Colonel, does that not alarm you?'

'Their generals have been bribed by our generalissimo, Chang Tso-lin. They were disaffected, anyway, by the Bolshevism of their commander.'

'Colonel, since last summer, when Chiang Kai-shek purged his party, there have been no communists in the Kuomintang. We continue to call them Bolsheviks because it is a rallying call, but there is no substantial difference now between our side and theirs. We are all warlords, fighting for power. Did I not tell you once about the spiritual vacuum in this country? We have now reached its nadir. No, Colonel, if you are to understand what is happening now, you should study the ancient histories. We are back again in a period of warring states. Surely, Colonel, even you as a schoolboy read *The War of the Three Kingdoms*? Then, like now, generals were fighting over the carcass of an empire, and which of them eventually succeeded, inheriting the Mandate of Heaven? The one with most guile, Colonel, not the strongest, but the general with most guile.'

Ti was appalled by such defeatism. 'But this is the modern age, General. Surely—'

'This is China, Colonel, and China never changes. Look at the political situation today. Two generalissimos are struggling for the Dragon Throne. One, our venerable leader, Chang Tso-lin, claims to represent the old Confucian values, but what does he do? He sits in the halls of the Forbidden City, afraid to leave it in case he loses it. Meanwhile he wastes his hours in opium dreams of greatness, leaving his fighting to his dog generals. The other, a new man, a young man, a general who cloaks himself in the slogans of the times, waits his opportunity patiently.'

'Chiang Kai-shek can hardly keep his own party together. Last year he was forced out of the country and spent months in Japan.'

'And why do you think he abandoned his position? He had almost consolidated his power. He left because he knew that, without him, all the other contenders for his throne would be impotent to conduct the struggle. He left because he knew that he would be called on to return, and when he did, there would be no one to challenge him. You will find the same story in the annals of the Han, the Tang. Nothing changes, Colonel.'

'But, General, he relies on Feng Yu-hsiang, who everybody knows wants to supplant him. General Feng did not support him last year. He kept his forces back when we made our push.'

'And that was the only reason we got as far as we did, and it was the reason why Generalissimo Chiang "retired" – not because he was overawed by Feng but because he wanted to master him. And do you really believe that Chiang, now he has consolidated his position, would allow three divisions to desert at such a crucial time?'

'They are Feng's men, not Chiang's, General.'

'They are Chiang's men, Colonel. Feng is now his puppet, and is using his vast talents for betrayal on his master's behalf.'

'You mean . . .'

'Yes, Colonel. If I was in command of this army, I would not make a march on the south just yet. I would wait for my so-called new allies, and when they arrived I would exterminate them while they are isolated, and before they have a chance to stab us in the back – but, alas, I am not in command. The Dog General is. Our opium-soaked generalissimo's brightest commander, whose dreams of glory are as fanciful as his master's . . .'

Suddenly Ti realised that his general might be right. 'Then what are we going to do? Do we warn Generalissimo Chang Tso-lin of the trap?'

'And be suspected ourselves of treachery? No, Colonel. We will do our duty and follow our instructions until it is evident that they are untenable, and then we will retreat, as we always do, in good order. I do not have the luxury of being able to go over to the enemy. Shishan is in Chang Tso-lin's domain so I am tied to him. We will all retreat to the north eventually, behind the Wall, and the Nationalists will not be able to follow. The long cycle of wars will go on. Whether Chang Tso-lin survives or not, I will. I have an important task ahead of me, more important than these little wars.'

He moved slowly to stand by Ti, who was startled to find that Lin had put a hand on his shoulder. This was the first time he had ever witnessed the general touch anybody. 'My loyal colonel,' he said softly, his hand sliding over his subordinate's arm almost caressingly, 'you have responded to my training very well. You are no longer the callow youth whose talent I first perceived. You have obeyed all my instructions with dedication and ruthlessness. I now have another task that I would like you to perform for me, not on the battleground but at home. I want you to leave tomorrow for Shishan to prepare the ground for my return.'

'But, General, the division? Who will pass on your orders? This will be an important and complicated battle . . .'

'Your officers will be adequate for the task. You have trained them well, but it is more important now that I have somebody I can trust in Shishan. I am not happy about what I hear of its present administration. We have been too indulgent, and there are many unruly and subversive elements in the city, which Yu Fu-cheng has not, as I have many times requested him, discouraged. I fear, too, that in his anxiety to create what he believes is a socially advanced society, he has himself been affected by liberal ideas, and has wasted revenues on counterproductive experiments. I am appointing you acting governor in my absence. I expect to return to a tidy city. Colonel, do you think you can manage that for me?'

Ti was trying to master conflicting sensations: a sense of disappointment that he would no longer be taking a part in the coming battle, and a surge of elation at this new responsibility. 'General, I cannot thank you for your confidence in me,' he managed. 'But, General, Minister Yu—'

'What about him?'

'How would you like me to deal with him, General?'

Lin's scarred face twisted into its cold smile. At the same time, he affectionately pulled Ti's earlobe. 'I gave you a cast-off once before, Colonel,' he said softly. 'I thought that you dealt with her most aptly. I am sure you will know what to do with Minister Yu.'

Ti stood to full attention, grinning, and saluted. 'Yes, General,' he snapped. He understood his instruction perfectly.

> *Thirty spokes unite in one nave;*
> *the utility of the cart*
> *depends on the hollow centre in which the wheel turns.*
> *Clay is moulded into a vessel;*
> *The utility of the vessel*
> *Depends on its hollow interior . . .*

Catherine was sitting in the pavilion in Bishop Huber's garden attempting to make sense of the tattered translation of the *Tao Te Ching* that she had found in his library. She could see Edmund sprawled on the lawn by the fishpond in serious conversation with the white-bearded old priest, whose saintly, cassocked appearance was compromised somewhat today by the large pair of sunglasses that nestled on his red, avuncular features, and the bottle of Pilsener that he held between stubby, nicotine-stained fingers. Perching cross-legged on the top of an ornamental rock, also enjoying a beer, was the bishop's constant companion, the Taoist monk, Hsiung, who was watching the pair mischievously, his clever eyes twinkling with humour in a face so etched with wrinkles that it reminded Catherine of a cracked egg. The murmur of their voices as they discussed their abstruse philosophy mingled comfortably with the background drone of insects, the tinkle of water from the fountain, and the occasional laughter of pleasure-seekers boating on the glittering surface of the lake that dazzled through the gaps between the trees.

Catherine felt drowsy and contented. She knew that, just over the walls of their sanctuary, the warlords' armies were marshalling, the armoured trains were loading supplies and ammunition, and the generals were drawing up last-minute orders for a renewal of hostilities. In only a few days, the wounded would return up the line, and then their quiet little hospital would be overwhelmed, as it had been the previous summer. For now she did not want to think about that. They were prepared for the worst. The hospital had been cleared of all but the most serious cases. Empty beds waited in the neat, well-aired wards. Professor Niedemeyer's generosity had ensured that the stores were full of bandages, morphine, splints and everything they would require. The scalpels and saws had been sharpened; the buckets were lined up alongside the operating-tables. Only a skeleton staff, consisting of Bishop Huber's nuns, was working today. Catherine had given her own nurses leave to spend time with their lovers and fiancés, who would soon be heading for the front. This afternoon, their chores completed, she and Edmund were taking advantage of the glorious weather. They would be busy enough soon.

She glanced fondly at Edmund, who was laughing at one of Hsiung's gentle gibes at his friend's religion. The bishop and the monk had been arguing with each other for more than twenty years, each convinced of the other's spirituality but pretending to be baffled by the perversity of his beliefs. To Catherine, whose Chinese was not as good as Edmund's, these interminable debates seemed nonsensical: when the bishop talked of heaven and hell, Hsiung would counter with a discourse on butterflies; when Huber patiently argued the existence of God as revealed through the scriptures, Hsiung would express doubts about the existence of Bishop Huber . . . Instead of being exasperated, however, the old Catholic priest would chuckle loudly, as would Edmund, and they would ponder these ridiculous Taoist conundrums as if the laughing sage had uttered some secret of the universe.

Catherine had left them to it, happy only that Edmund, in the friendship and company of these two eccentrics, seemed to find relaxation from the cares of his work. Looking at him now, he appeared younger, more like the humorous, ironical man she had first met. He had lost the tension that had driven him in Hankow. The furrow on his forehead was still there, but the line had softened, the muscles round his mouth become less taut; and it had been a long time since he had revealed to her the pain and despair that had come near to crucifying him the previous year.

> *Doors and windows are cut out in order to make a house;*
> *The utility of the house depends on the empty space.*
> *Thus, while the existence of things may be good,*
> *It is the non-existent in them which makes them serviceable.*

She woke with a jolt. She had been dozing. This really was too perfect an afternoon to be reading obscure philosophy, especially anything as turgid as this. She watched a dragonfly alight on the table, then skim towards the flowers . . .

War, this damned war! She wondered how Bishop Huber and Hsiung always managed to be cheerful. They were as different as chalk and cheese, but she had never known anybody so devoted to the service of their fellow human beings.

Edmund had performed miracles during the fighting of the previous summer to save the lives of the broken, dehydrated bodies that Bishop Huber and Hsiung had been able to bring to the mission from the hell of the railway terminal. Catherine and her nurses had sometimes accompanied the priest and the monk, marvelling at the good humour with which they had slowly won over the suspicious guards, persuading them to open the doors of the ovens that the cattle trucks had become, finally shaming them into allowing them to go into the fly-blown stench. The first time Catherine had seen one of these charnel houses she had thought they had arrived too late, but Bishop Huber and Hsiung had moved among the carpet of bodies, identifying the living from the dead, kneeling down, offering water to parched lips that had not drunk anything for sometimes three days. Afterwards, with infinite patience, the two old men had coaxed those who could still walk to their feet, supporting them down the ramp to the arms of the waiting nurses; by this stage, even the guards had become shocked by the horror, numbly helping them as they brought out the more seriously wounded on stretchers. Sometimes their two mule carts had had to return three times to the station to bring in all the wounded; many, despite their efforts, had died on the way. It had only been the lucky ones who had reached Edmund.

It had been in the railway yard that Catherine and Edmund had first come across them. That had been during the heat wave of July, shortly after last year's big push had begun. Edmund had encountered bitter opposition from the Red Swastika and ferocious greed from the officials of the Shantung warlord. When the armoured trains headed south, he had only just begun to negotiate the lease of a filthy compound on the outskirts of the city, while Catherine and Lan-hua, after weeks of interviewing and training, were engaged in a running battle with the Red Swastika to keep the few nurses who had not already been driven away by threats. They had by no means been ready when they heard that trains full of wounded were coming back up the line.

That morning the languid official in the Dog General's headquarters in charge of medical affairs had told Edmund that it made no sense for money to be spent on the rehabilitation of wounded soldiers in a country where replacements could be impressed into service by a simple raid on a village; it was more economical to leave these peasants to die or recover where they lay – there were plenty more where they came from. Edmund, boiling with anger, had told Catherine to gather her nurses and whatever medical supplies they had at hand. They would set up their hospital in the open air of the marshalling yard! They had not even got near the cattle wagons before they were arrested. Catherine had been terrified that in Edmund's rage he would throw himself on the bayonets of the angry soldiers.

It was then that Bishop Huber and Hsiung had made their unlikely appearance. Catherine, holding Lan-hua, who was weeping with fear, could hardly believe her eyes as first a jovial Catholic clergyman in a white cassock, then a grinning Taoist monk with his hair in a top-knot had good-naturedly pushed aside the rifles of the soldiers and stepped into the circle. The priest, whose white beard reminded Catherine of Father Christmas, had gone up to the angry lieutenant and bowed deeply in front of him. 'Colonel,' he said, in perfect Chinese, 'I can't thank you enough. I have been looking for these people everywhere. I do hope they haven't been bothering you. They shouldn't be here, of course. What a confusion – but don't worry, I will take them off your hands. The Lord Jesus and all the saints bless you, my son,' he had added, making a sign of the cross over the flustered officer's head. 'Come, Hsiung,' he called to the Taoist monk, who was laughing and joking with some of the soldiers. 'Help me to show our guests to our mission. Colonel, many thanks. Doctor, if you and your nurses will follow me, I will show you the hospital we have prepared for you. We will bring the patients later.' And then, to Catherine's amazement, he had turned his head so that he was out of the lieutenant's eyeshot and winked.

Later, in his beautiful mission, he had distributed cold beer, and told them that their arrival in Tsinan had been a blessing from heaven. 'We have everything here for a hospital except a doctor and expert nurses – and here you are. Until now, Hsiung and I have been able to do little to alleviate those poor soldiers' suffering, except for giving them water and suchlike – no, not Pilsener, that would probably kill them – but now, thanks be to God, we can save their lives and give them Pilsener later perhaps. By the way, what is your name, Doctor, and yours, Matron? Mine is Huber. At your service.'

That very evening, in the convent that had already been converted into a hospital, they had operated on their first patients. Bishop Huber had put his Austrian nuns in Catherine's charge.

It had been Wuchang and Hankow all over again: sleepless nights and wearing days coping with crisis, tragedy and unspeakable horrors – but there had been a difference, which Catherine could only attribute to Bishop Huber and Hsiung. The former, through a combination of saintliness and earthy humour, dignity and self-deprecation, had secured the co-operation of the authorities. Hsiung, like some smiling Puck or earth spirit, had always materialised when he was needed. When the nurses were reeling after a twelve-hour stint of surgery and amputation, they would find Hsiung had quietly replaced the buckets of blood, or mopped the floor, or carried away and buried the offal and limbs. Sometimes, when Catherine had been near to swooning with heat but unable to leave Edmund's operating-table, she had found Hsiung by her side, offering a cup of jasmine tea. When Edmund was swaying on his feet with still more wounded to treat Hsiung, happening to pass by, would make one of his nonsensical remarks, and Edmund would throw back his head and laugh; this clearing of his mind would give him the concentration and energy to continue. The nurses told her of the long hours Hsiung spent by the bedsides of the wounded men, asking about their families, listening to the stories of their lives, and of the merriment that seemed to linger in the wards after he had gone.

Once, late at night, Catherine, as was her habit, stopped by the dying room. She had been startled to hear peals of laughter coming from inside, and recognised the voice of a head-wound patient who, earlier that evening, had gone into coma. She had waited uncertainly by the door. A few moments later, Hsiung had emerged and she had been touched by the sadness in his eyes, the age bowing his shoulders. 'The boy's sleeping now,' he had said quietly. 'He will not wake again, but perhaps his last dreams will be happy ones.'

Somehow, over the months, the quiet influence of the bishop and the monk had affected all of those working in the hospital. Slowly she, too, had come under their spell.

When she had arrived in Tsinan from Hankow, she had been suffering from the bleak despair that had overtaken her after her experiences in Shanghai. After they had left Hankow, it had been only the companionship of Lan-hua that had sustained her. During the long journey by steamer down the river to Shanghai, on the ship to Tsingtao, on the train that took them to Tsinan, she and Lan-hua had been inseparable in their misery. She had known that their absorption in each other to the exclusion of any other company had disturbed Edmund, that he might even have been jealous of the protective attention she had devoted to the girl. She had felt sorry for him but in those days, with the emptiness inside her, the fear of responsibility, it had been all she could manage to look after one wounded sparrow.

She had found in their shared mourning for John Soo a focus for the indefinable sense of loss that affected her; his memory was also a link with Fu-kuei. Often, at night, in their cabin, holding Lan-hua in her arms, she had found herself thinking of her as Fu-kuei, and taken a perverse comfort from this surrogate companionship. Catherine had never been one for the fashionable, Bloomsbury-inspired Sapphic friendships of her Oxford college, but she was comforted by the beat of a human heart next to her own in the bunk they shared. Gradually Lan-hua had become calmer. She had started to speak of John not in terms of grief but remembering amusing or tender moments they had shared, but Catherine, listening to Lan-hua's quiet breathing when she slept beside her, found herself thinking of Edmund, which frightened her. She was still not ready. As Lan-hua slowly recovered, Catherine's sense of isolation had grown, and the emptiness returned. She knew she needed something beyond the love of Edmund to heal her, but she did not know what it might be.

The monk, Hsiung, had spent a lot of time with Lan-hua. Catherine, absorbed with her duties, had noticed them walking together in Bishop Huber's garden, and been relieved, because once the wounded from the push had started to come in, she had little time to devote to her. After the first night Lan-hua had shown that she was not capable of being a nurse. She had tried bravely to master her fear of the wounds and the blood, but Catherine had gauged the pallor of her face, and detailed her to work in the laundry. They no longer shared a room, and sometimes days would go by without them seeing each other. She had not been surprised when, one morning, Lan-hua had come to her and told her that she was leaving: she would go to Tientsin to try to find her brother, Lei Tang, from whom she had not heard in months; and after that, to Shishan, to see if her other brother, Ming, would give her a job in his school. Catherine had asked whether she had the money for the train tickets, and Lan-hua had said that Hsiung and Bishop Huber had arranged her passage. There had been little more to say. They had hugged and kissed each other; Lan-hua had wept a little, but Catherine had to hurry to Edmund's side for an operation. Next morning Hsiung had seen her off at the station.

After Lan-hua's departure, Hsiung had turned his attention to Catherine. One rainy morning when she had little to do – a trainload of wounded had been expected in the afternoon – Edmund, the bishop and Hsiung had been arguing philosophy over a cup of coffee in Huber's study. Catherine had been sitting listlessly at the window, gazing at the shifting patterns of the yellowing leaves of an elm tree through the streams of water on the pane. A nurse put her head round the door and called Edmund away. Satisfied that it was no emergency, Catherine returned to her contemplation of the tree. She became aware of Bishop Huber's reflection in the glass, and turned to see him standing behind her, a steaming cup in his hand. 'I did not wish to startle you, my dear,' he said, 'but you looked so pensive and lonely. Excuse me for being a busybody. It is an old man's vice. I was wondering if I could help.'

'I'm sorry, Bishop, but you know I don't believe in any religion.' She regretted her rudeness, but he had surprised her and annoyed her. 'I'm fine. Really I am. You don't have to worry about me,' she added.

Huber gave his rich chuckle. 'No, Catherine. I would not presume to offer pastoral advice. Not in miserable weather like this. That would be too depressing. I thought you might like to talk to my friend Hsiung.'

'Hsiung?' said Catherine, startled. 'Why?'

'Oh, I don't know. It was only an idea, perhaps a foolish one. I find that he cheers me up when I am depressed, and he is very wise, even if he is a pagan. I think we are all travelling in the same direction in this strange journey of life, and there are many winding paths up the mountain. Do you know what the *Tao* means literally? It is the *Road*. He may be able to point out to you a few signposts that you have missed. At the very least he will entertain you.'

Catherine's face had flushed with anger. 'Bishop, I know you're being kind, but I can't study philosophy while we're so busy in the hospital. My time is absolutely filled.'

Huber had looked at her with a gentle smile. 'Ah, fullness and emptiness – such deep, deep concepts. Do you know? There is a verse of the *Tao Te Ching* that goes:

> "Keep the mouth shut, close the gateways of sense,
> And as long as you live you will have no trouble.
> Open your lips and push your affairs,
> And you will not be safe
> To the end of your days."

'My friend, Hsiung, quotes it to me when he thinks I am too busy. He is perverse. He believes himself to be an expert on the fullness and emptiness of the soul. I tell him that, without the Word of our

Lord Jesus, he knows nothing. And he laughs, and thanks me for complimenting him, for nothing is what he hopes to attain. What is one to do with a fellow like that? I am sorry, my dear, I have been presumptuous, and irritated you a little. One day, this horrible war will end, and we will all be less busy. Then, perhaps, there may be time for philosophy – and the well-being of the soul.'

He bowed in his old-fashioned way, and moved back to his armchair. Catherine saw that Hsiung, who had not been paying any attention to their conversation in English, was seated cross-legged, apparently meditating. He opened his eyes and seemed to stare at her with an unfathomable expression. Her heart fluttering, she turned back to the window, but it had misted over.

For the next few days, she had seethed with anger, and shame. It had been as if the bishop and Hsiung had pried into her private affairs, but in moments between emergencies in the ward, she had admitted to herself that the bishop had touched a raw nerve. Over the next weeks, his words gnawed and buzzed in her mind. One late autumn morning – the fighting was long over and the hospital was quiet – she had come across the old monk sitting on his rock in the garden, meditating. She had rounded on him furiously: 'All right, Hsiung, I'm here. What was it you and Bishop Huber wanted to teach me?'

The monk had opened one eye. 'I? Nothing,' he replied, solemnly.

She laughed despite herself. He looked like a comical gnome. 'That's one of your paradoxes, I suppose. By nothing you mean everything?'

He closed his eyes again, and appeared to ponder her question. 'Nothing might be more practical,' he said. 'Bishop Huber says you are very busy, so your mind must be filled with all kinds of ideas, worries and fears. It is difficult to pour wine into a bottle that is already full. The only thing you can add is nothing.'

'On the contrary,' said Catherine, 'I don't think you could find a bottle that was emptier than my life.'

'If that were true,' said Hsiung, 'I would be asking you to teach me.' His face cracked into a mischievous grin and, with surprising agility, he slithered down the rock to stand next to her on the path. 'Come,' he said, 'let us walk together, and see if between us we can find a way of pouring nothing into an empty bottle to make it full.'

That had been the first of many walks in the garden, in the golden autumn and through the snow of winter. Sometimes Catherine thought it ludicrous that she was making a confessional of her life to a Taoist monk, especially to a man who would giggle when she revealed her most terrible experiences. It was not even that he ever gave her any advice that could be considered useful, by any practical terms: he rarely uttered anything that was not paradoxical or obscure, although he listened with full attention, subtly pressing her to reveal more. He had an unerring instinct for the obscured truth, and always knew when she was hiding something or avoiding an issue. Then he would tease her mercilessly until, exploding with anger, she told him what he wanted to know. At other times he would maddeningly steer her off what she considered the point, to focus on details she considered irrelevant, and sometimes distasteful. When, with great emotion, she had described the murder of her friends in the glade, he had shown no interest, but had been fascinated to hear more about the Kirghiz tribesmen; he had dismissed her treatment by the brute in the Cheka, but wanted to hear everything about the friends she had betrayed; when, weeping, she had told him about the horrors she had witnessed in Nanking and Shanghai, she had been appalled afterwards by his eager curiosity about the furnace and the length of time it took for a body in such circumstances to burn. On that occasion she had stamped away through the snow, his laughter pealing behind her.

What seemed to fascinate him most was her childhood – particularly her relationship with Helen Frances, the details of whose tragic life would send him into paroxysms of mirth. Sometimes she wondered if he was mad. When she told him about her search for Henry Manners, he had been more than usually objectionable. 'So much effort, and you couldn't even find him!' He grinned, rocking from side to side.

'You weren't listening. I did find him,' she snapped, her cheeks crimsoning. 'And he rejected me.'

'No father would reject his daughter.' He giggled happily. 'You found the wrong man. What a joke! You'll never become whole if you make mistakes like that. You must start looking for him all over again.'

'You're impossible!' She was seething, half with anger, half with incredulity at the sheer ridiculousness of it. 'The man who was so cruel to me was Henry Manners, my father. There was no doubt of it.'

'No,' he said, 'you have mistaken the shadow for the substance. You must try all over again. This is very important for you, because you need to find a father, Catherine. It's the great lack in your life – but you must choose the right time, when you are both ready. You can't make a dumpling with just pastry or just meat. You must learn to be a daughter, and this Ma Na Si must learn to be a father again. Only when you both know who you are will the emptiness inside each of you be filled. It is the same with your lover, the doctor Airton. You and he are like the swordfighters in the opera *The Battle in the Dark* chasing each other's shadows over the stage. It is very funny for us in the audience to watch your blundering movements as you fail to find each other when you are so close. Oh, you are very funny, Catherine. Very, very funny.'

'I'm so happy I amuse you,' she had snarled. That was another occasion when she had tramped off in the snow.

Yet she had returned for more, because she realised that, uncomfortable as her sessions with Hsiung always were, he made her think, and usually, even when he was at his most outrageous or contradictory, she would discover a lesson later, hidden in his mockery and humour. Slowly she saw that he had been making her confront all her worst memories, her faults, vanities and self-deceptions, and in facing them, to accept them. She hardly knew then whether she was half empty, or half full – but she had found that she was learning to live with herself again, and discovered a sort of peace.

One afternoon, Hsiung had not been in the garden. Instead she had found Edmund standing by the rock. He had been wrapped in his long coat against the cold, and she could see his breath, as he stamped his feet and rubbed his hands. 'Catherine,' he said, surprised. 'I was expecting Hsiung. He told me to meet him here.'

And Catherine had smiled, thinking of *The Battle in the Dark*. She had moved towards him and taken his arm. 'There's only me,

I'm afraid. I guess this is one of Hsiung's pranks. But it has been a long time, Edmund, such a long, long time, since we walked and talked together. Do you remember those happy days in Tientsin? It seems like another life ago.'

He had been nervous and tongue-tied, but she had not let go of his arm. Gradually he had relaxed, allowing her to rest her head on his shoulder. On that occasion they only made three circuits of the garden – the weather really had been very cold. When it began to snow heavily, they had made a dash for the warmth of Bishop Huber's study, and there the two old men had been waiting for them. One of the nuns had made a sponge cake, and Bishop Huber had brought out a bottle of schnapps to pour into the tea. Their faces tingled as they warmed themselves by the fire, and Edmund had made a joke – she could not remember for the life of her what it was, but they had laughed and laughed, while the bishop and Hsiung smiled. She had not felt so invigorated for years.

After that they often met in the garden, and made the circuit arm in arm. Sometimes, in milder weather, they would see Hsiung meditating on his perch. He would grin at them as they passed and Edmund would wave. At first, they did not talk much, content merely to be in each other's company. Christmas that year had been a merry affair. A long table had been set down in one of the wards. Bishop Huber and the nuns had led the carols, then, with Hsiung, had distributed goods to all the patients. Later, Catherine and Edmund had paused outside, following one of their walks. It had been early, only six, but stars were glittering in the sky. There had been the smell of a wood fire, and far away they could hear a dog barking. Bishop Huber's study had reflected an orange square on the snow. In the stillness of the night and the shadow of the porch, Edmund had kissed her.

They had continued their walks as if nothing had happened, but they had crossed an invisible barrier, and they both felt free to reveal to each other something of the pain they had both experienced during the long years of their separation. They had wept silently at the accounts of the other's terrible experiences. By mutual assent, they had drawn a veil over Catherine's life in Tientsin, her empty marriage with George, her despairing affair with Willie and, strangely, it had not seemed to matter any more. It was as if the lost years had blown away.

For a long while they had found comfort in the chastity of their relationship. Neither had been in a hurry to take it to its inevitable conclusion. For a while they rejoiced merely in being friends again. They kissed and embraced, but one or other would break off before things went too far. It had become a gentle game, a protracted courtship. Neither had wished to take the final step that might shatter the precarious peace they had found in each other's company – but they lived for those shy moments when they were alone. Gradually, the intimacy of the garden had filtered into their working lives. They would unconsciously brush against each other in the wards. Their fingers would linger on the touch when one or other passed the salt-cellar at table, or as Catherine handed him the chart at the bedside of a patient. They would catch themselves gazing at each other, some-times losing the thread of Bishop Huber's conversation. Of course, their professional relationship had been entirely correct, especially in the operating-theatre, where there was no question but that they were doctor and nurse. It had been ironic therefore that they should have found themselves in the theatre when the crisis came. Neither had planned it. They had both been exhausted after a particularly harrowing day during which one of their stomach wounds, a young man who had responded well to treatment, suddenly relapsed. Edmund had opened up the stitches and discovered that the anasta-mosis joining two damaged bowel sections had broken down, and leakage of bowel contents had caused peritonitis and septicaemia. He had attempted a perilous operation, cutting the abdominal wound closure sutures and re-entering the abdomen – but despite all his efforts, the patient had died on the operating-table.

Catherine had been returning from the morgue, when she had seen that the lights were still on in the theatre. She had found Edmund leaning against the window-sill, with tears in his eyes. She had put down her tray, taken him by the hand to her room, where she had made love to him, using all the art she knew. He had responded clumsily, after which there had been no need for art. In fact, she had never in her life felt more natural with a man or so certain that she was in love.

When they appeared late for breakfast next morning, in a state of dazed wonder at what they had experienced, neither Bishop Huber nor Hsiung, neither the nuns nor her nurses had said anything – but she had noticed, over the following days, shy smiles in their eyes when they passed her in the corridors.

Afterwards it had been a glorious spring . . .

Catherine, making an effort to keep her eyes open, realised that she had been day-dreaming and forced herself back to the Taoist poem she had been trying to study, if only to make Hsiung happy.

> *A violent wind does not outlast the morning;*
> *A squall of rain does not outlast the day.*
> *Such is the course of Nature*
> *And if Nature herself cannot sustain her efforts long*
> *How much less can Man!*
> *Attain complete vacuity,*
> *And sedulously preserve a state of repose.*

She began to giggle, remembering the previous night, when Edmund, a little tipsy after a session with Bishop Huber's schnapps, had managed to sustain his efforts of cloud and rain long enough to send her into a state of absolute vacuity – but that was probably not what the ancient sage had had in mind.

'What's so funny?' Edmund called, shading his eyes.

'You are.' She laughed. 'And Bishop Huber, and ridiculous Mr Hsiung, sitting on his rock. Come on, I'm bored with watching you three sages counting angels on pins. Who's coming with me to the market? I promised Sister Agnes I'd look for some watermelons, and I need a strong pair of arms to help me carry them.'

'Thank God! An excuse to get away,' said Edmund, scrambling to his feet. 'You'll be saving me from a fate worse than death. Hsiung's already proved the non-existence of Bishop Huber and I fear he's about to start on me.'

Arm in arm they strolled out of the gate, skirting the lake to the vegetable market, where they spent a quarter-hour haggling over the few watermelons left on the stands. The woman was asking three times the normal price for fruit of inferior quality. It was, of course, because of shortages caused by the war, but in their present mood they did not care – they had decided that no shadows would affect them on this sunny day. They allowed the woman to browbeat them and Edmund paid happily what she asked, but Catherine was not satisfied. 'I promised Sister Agnes more melons than this,' she said. 'Come on, Edmund, stop groaning. There's another market on the other side of the main street.'

'That's miles away,' he protested. 'My arms are already numb under this load. I won't be able to operate.'

Catherine kissed him, and tickled him under his shirt. 'That's bribery, Nurse.' He laughed. 'You're treating your superior with enormous disrespect, you know.'

At first they were so preoccupied with each other that they hardly noticed the crowds thickening as they approached the main street. It was only when Edmund had been knocked aside, causing a melon to fall out of the bag – it was snatched up by a darting street urchin – that they found themselves caught in a throng that was pushing forward eagerly to see something that was happening ahead. 'Oh, Lord,' groaned Edmund. 'Now we're stuck. It's probably troops marching off to the front. Yes, there's a line of bayonets moving beyond the heads of the crowd.'

'Edmund, let's turn round. I don't want to have anything to do with the war today.' Catherine felt a chill. 'Please,' she cried. But it was no use: she was pushed from behind.

Edmund had dropped all of the melons now and reached for her hand. 'Don't let us be separated,' he called.

They had been pushed near to the front of the crowd and could see a pale blue column of infantrymen marching down the street. They were in battle kit, their leather belts and the peaks of their caps shining in the sunshine; they had bulging packs from which protruded the usual accoutrements of a warlord army – spades, machetes, pots, pans, umbrellas. Rifles sloped on their shoulders, they were setting a brisk pace, their cloth shoes below white puttees slapping in the dust. The faces appeared confident and cheerful. Some were giving sidelong grins at the crowd. Others waved little flags.

'This is so damned depressing,' Catherine said. 'You know what shape half of these boys will be in when they come back to us.'

'Don't think of it,' Edmund replied. 'Give them their moment of glory. They think they're marching to victory.'

Company after company, they paraded by. Catherine watched, appalled by the youth of the soldiers, until she heard Edmund exclaim. 'What?' she cried.

Edmund had to put his head close to her ear as a great shout rose up from the throng. 'Don't you recognise him?' he said.

She peered through the dust. A new column was approaching, led by a general on a white horse. The men appeared taller than the ones who had gone before, with grimmer, harder faces, and they were marching with more disciplined steps. Now the general was almost opposite them. He was a thin man, slouched in his saddle, wearing a simple private's uniform and a forage cap. As she watched, he turned his head. She saw the scar and froze.

The gleaming eyes were contemplating her as they had done years before in that banquet room at the Yamen in Shishan. Stunned, she saw him flick his reins, and his horse reared as he manoeuvred it backwards and closer to where she and Edmund were standing. He observed her for a long, cold moment. Then his mouth twisted into a grin, revealing his yellow teeth. The disfigured lips shaped words she could not hear. Briskly, he snapped up his arm in a salute, dug his spurs into the horse and was gone. His hard-looking soldiers marched on by, looking neither to left nor right.

She became aware of Edmund's arm round her shoulders. He tried to make light of it: 'There's someone who hasn't forgotten you – you certainly made an impression on General Lin!' but the look in his eyes revealed his concern.

She felt weak. 'Please, please, can we get away?' she begged.

Somehow, using his free elbow, and shielding her with his other arm, Edmund pushed his way to the back of the crowd. Those around them who had noticed the famous general's attention towards the red-haired foreigner gave way instinctively, observing her suspiciously. She struggled to restrain her panic, and it was only when they were free of the throng that she could breathe again. 'Are you all right?' Edmund was solicitous.

'Yes,' she breathed. 'It was a shock – That horrible man.'

'Forget him. Let's go back to the hospital.'

'Can we walk for a bit? I want to unwind.'

They threaded their way through the streets of the Chinese town, eventually reaching the wider roads of the Japanese quarter, with its bank buildings and hotels. When they reached the Yamato, Edmund murmured, 'Shall we take a rickshaw, darling? It'll be a long walk back otherwise.'

She looked up into the tender brown eyes, and wondered how she could have denied her feelings for so long. Impulsively she kissed him, and ran a hand over his brow. 'I do so love you, Edmund,' she murmured. 'Promise me we'll never be apart again.' He pressed his lips to her nose and eyes. 'Edmund – let's go into the Yamato now.'

'Good idea,' he said. 'I could do with a cup of tea. Maybe we can find some melons for Sister Agnes.'

'No, Edmund.' She squeezed his arm closer with hers. 'I don't want tea or melons. I want a room.'

Edmund's eyebrows lifted in surprise, but then he smiled.

The Japanese desk clerk was supercilious when they told him they had no luggage, but they didn't care. They hardly noticed the smirks of the English commercial travellers who shared the lift with them to the fifth floor. When the grinning bellboy had taken his tip, and Edmund had pulled open the heavy curtains to allow the bright pink of the evening to flood the room, they had stared at the huge bed, the carpets, the *en-suite* bathroom, awed by the sudden luxury. The arrangement of the furniture was familiar, of course: Yamato hotels were always the same.

'My God,' Catherine whispered. 'We could be back in that hotel in Shishan.'

'Don't think of it,' he murmured, nuzzling her cheek. 'All that's over now.'

'That's what I mean,' she said. 'It's as if time's telescoped to where we were before, as if none of that terrible stuff ever happened, and we've been given a chance to start all over again. It's as it was always meant to be. Oh, darling,' she whispered, 'you and I have been such fools. Oh, Edmund . . .' He had unbuttoned her blouse, and she felt a tremor through her body as his lips touched her breast. 'I couldn't believe I'd ever be this happy.'

'I want to see you,' said Edmund. 'In the light, where you're meant to be. We've spent too long in dark little rooms.'

She moved into the patch of fire cast by the setting sun. She could see the blazing orb as it hung over the lake, and felt the warmth on her skin as she undressed. In the mirror on the cupboard door she caught a reflection of herself, turning, with shining eyes to her lover, a long, golden body, loosed hair flowing over her curves like burning red lava, the sloping sun's rays catching the motes of dust and enveloping her in a column of flame. Edmund was slowly taking off his clothes, and she waited for him, smiling, stretching out her arms. He stepped into the light and she closed her eyes, letting his hot lips descend on hers, firing her with his breath; she felt his beautiful hands, like those of a sculptor, caressing her breasts, her flanks and thighs, tingling where he touched. She shivered as he entered her, possessing her. Slowly he sank to his knees, and she followed, curling her legs round his back, moulding herself to him, her hair rippling with light and colour as she clung . . .

They were only vaguely aware of the noises of the night, the drunken singing in the early hours, and the unmistakable thrum of a balalaika from a room down the corridor. 'The Dog General's White Russians,' whispered Edmund.

'I'm glad they're Russian,' murmured Catherine, comfortably, content in his arms. 'My first lover was a Russian. No,' she said urgently, 'you're my first lover, my only real one. Kiss me, Edmund, in case I think this is only a dream.' And they made love again, moving unconsciously to the rhythm of the music coming down the landing.

Edmund roused her in the dawn light. He was already dressed. 'We ought to get back to the mission, darling,' he said.

'No.' She pouted. 'Come back to bed.' He sat down beside her and kissed her. 'Now, now, Nurse,' he grinned, 'leave's over.'

'No,' she said, pressing the pillow over her eyes. 'I want this never to end. You and I, tonight, we've abolished war and wounds and revolution . . .'

'I know, my love, but we can't abolish Bishop Huber even if Hsiung can, and he'll be expecting us for breakfast.' She threw the pillow at him, leaped out of bed and, giggling, ran off towards the bathroom.

In the end, however, Catherine was hurrying Edmund, who was struggling with a broken shoelace. 'Come on,' she fumed, opening the door. 'You're like a fussy old man.'

'Ouch, I'm only a decade older than you. Hold on, I won't be a second.'

Laughing, she stepped into the corridor as a door opened opposite her. Stepping out, pipe in his mouth, suitcase in hand, was Willie Lampsett. She was stunned, and he was as taken aback as she was. His face broke into a delighted smile, and his eyes shone. 'Catherine!' he said. 'I've searched all over China for you.'

He dropped his bag and moved across the corridor, his arms opening to embrace her. She stepped back and bumped into Edmund, who was coming out of the door. He put his arm round her shoulders to steady her.

Willie froze in mid-stride, horror in his eyes. Incongruously his smile remained fixed.

'Lampsett!' said Edmund. 'What on earth are you doing here?'

'I might ask you the same thing, Airton,' Willie said. 'I'm covering the war.'

'I have a hospital here for the war wounded,' said Edmund. 'Catherine's my . . .'

'I'm his nurse, Willie, and, as you've gathered, his lover,' said Catherine. 'Sorry, but you might as well know.'

'I see,' said Willie.

As his features crumpled, Catherine felt a pang of sympathy for him. 'How are you?' she asked.

'I'm – I'm fine,' he muttered. 'I'm off to the front.'

Rizhi Angelochek!'

They swung round. Two Russians, with gold-striped trousers tucked into their boots and uniform white smocks, kit-bags over their shoulders, one with a balalaika on his back, were gaping at them.

Catherine thought she was dreaming, but the next minute the crop-headed man with the balalaika had bounded forward and lifted her off her feet, kissing her on both cheeks. 'Oleg!' he shouted at his companion. 'This is Katusha, the *Rizhi Angelochek* of Chertoviche! I tell you of her a hundred times!'

Then Serge Kovalevsky, for it was no other, saw Edmund, and the next minute was kissing and embracing him. 'Edmund! So you are lucky dog who marries my Katusha! I should kill you, because you no deserve her. No man deserve *Rizhi Angelochek*, even poor Serge who will die for her. Oleg! Vodka! We must drink to lucky fellow!' As the other Russian, a short, solemn-faced man with a drooping moustache, fumbled in his knapsack, Serge winked at Catherine. 'Katusha, you tell me true. You love this man? Or he bad to you? If so I kill him with bare hands.' He roared with laughter and kissed Edmund again. 'Joke! You are my brother!'

'Congratulations, Catherine,' murmured Willie Lampsett, bitterly, in the brief silence as Serge opened the bottle. 'It seems you're loved by everybody.'

Serge wrapped a huge arm round Willie's neck. 'What he saying? He rude to my *Rizhi Angelochek*? Never mind. This my friend Willie. Is little mad,' he said, pinching his cheek. 'He brave journalist, but stupid, because he come to die with Russians. Katusha, drink with me. I am full colonel again. Not Preobrazhensky, but work is honourable – well, nearly honourable. Chief Commander Sergei Ilianovich Kovalevsky of armoured train, *Shantung*, at your service! Meet my comrade, Oleg Priapin, chief intelligence officer when not drunk. Today he sober because we go to kill Bolsheviks!'

'Colonel Kovalevsky always drunk,' smiled the other man. 'When drinking he see double. Every time he kill one Bolshevik, he report he kill two. That is why he is colonel and I am only captain.'

'Excuse me, Catherine, I'm going down to check out,' said Willie, snatching a moment while the two Russians were bickering in their own language. 'Edmund, to the victor the laurels and all that. Look after her.'

Catherine leaned forward and kissed his cheek. Willie shrugged her off. She thought she saw hatred in his eyes. 'Willie, be careful. Keep safe,' she said. He gave her a last look and clattered down the stairs.

Edmund was trying politely to refuse a second tot of vodka, and Serge was looking at her curiously. 'Serge, you look after yourself too,' she said in Russian. She linked her arm in his and kissed his leathery cheeks. 'Bring Willie back safe. He was once a friend.'

A solemn expression transformed the big man's face. He glanced at Edmund, then back to her. He nodded seriously. 'I will try, Katusha – but this will be a big battle and we are the spearhead of the attack. Maybe we will need an *Angelochek*'s prayers today, because there will be no mercy for us Russians if the Chinese capture our train – no, it is not suitable for your ears to know what the Chinese will do to us before they shoot us. However, this is what you must know, that every Russian keeps a bullet for himself. I will keep two: one for Willie as he is your friend.' He smiled. 'Who knows? The saints have been good to us so far. I think there will be a day when we will both come back and drink vodka in your hospital. Come, Oleg, it is time. We must go. Think of your Serge sometimes, Katusha, and,' he reverted to English, 'Edmund, you old dog, you keep Katusha safe. You have best woman in world.'

'I know that, Serge,' said Edmund. 'Good fortune.'

'Ah, these hurried meetings!' sighed Serge, lifting his knapsack. 'Brief and tender like a woman's kiss, and then goodbye! But it is war. Katusha, remember Serge, who is still fighting for his honour and a long-dead Tsar! *Dosvidanya*!'

They saw the two Russians into the lift, then returned to their room, and sank into the armchairs.

'"Laurels to the victor",' Edmund muttered. 'I knew Lampsett loved you. Once he as good as told me so. He became one of your lovers, I take it?'

'Not like you,' she said. 'And I'm not who I once was.'

'I know that, darling,' he said. 'It's our generation, I suppose. We're all haunted by ghosts of the past. Sometimes it's difficult not to be affected.'

'I feel nothing for him now. Or not in that way. We're starting again, Edmund, you and I. Didn't last night mean something?' A tear ran down her cheek. 'You mustn't be jealous of ghosts. You mustn't.'

'I'm not.' He smiled sadly. 'It's just . . . Everything seems so fragile. Lin yesterday. Lampsett and Serge today. You've led such a complicated life, Catherine. I'm just terrified of losing you to one of these phantoms from the past.'

Catherine kissed his forehead, his cheeks, his chin. 'We have a future, Edmund. You must believe it. You're only depressed because the past has broken in on us, but we can deal with that. I'll divorce George. Who cares what the world thinks? As soon as this bloody war's over, we'll go back to Tientsin together. Then we'll leave China and all this behind us. Oh, Edmund, I can't tell you how much I love you. This time nothing can come between us.'

They sat together, holding each other. The light of a new day gradually filled the room, restoring the colours.

'It is the war, I suppose,' said Edmund, after a long while. 'We had a bit of a holiday from it, and Serge and Willie have brought it back to us. It's silly to be depressed. Come on, we'd better go. Huber will be worried.'

'Yes, it's the war,' said Catherine. 'But it doesn't matter any more, darling. You and I can face anything if we're together. Can't we, Edmund?'

'Certainly can, Nurse.'

It was a brave attempt at a chuckle, and the weather was shaping for another perfect day, but the shadow that had crept over them in the morning did not leave them when they got into a rickshaw. It accompanied them back to Bishop Huber's mission, and even filled the garden when they met again after lunch for their usual walk.

There were few pleasure-seekers on the lake that day, or the next. The celebrations were over. The soldiers had departed. Everybody in the city was waiting anxiously for good news from the front.

From the journal of William Lampsett, Reuters correspondent, Shantung, 16 April 1928

They have given me a bunk in the 'dining-car'. There is one trestle table, covered with a gingham cloth. The whole compartment is decorated with vodka bottles. They are being used as candleholders, water-containers, vinegar-containers, salt-cellars, ashtrays ... Several bottles stand on either side of a portrait of the martyred

Tsar, Nicholas II. They are stuffed full of burning incense sticks or flowers, like offerings at a Buddhist shrine. Underneath is a plaque with the names inscribed of comrades who have lost their lives in this war. I counted more than thirty, and there is an ominous space underneath for more. The cosiness of this little nest is marred by the shell holes in the sides of the compartment. A small jagged tear just above my head lets in a welcome breeze as we trundle through the hot night, alleviating a little the stuffy smell of incense smoke, stale tobacco, axle oil and borscht. The Shantung was in the thick of the fighting last year. Tomorrow, Colonel Kovalevsky told me, the guns will fire again. He promises me 'an enjoyable picnic'.

This is more like a battleship than a train, and Colonel K is the proud captain, obviously adored by his men, about eighty of them, all grinning, piratical characters, with scarred faces and extravagant mustachios. Every one has been fighting in one war or another since 1914. They are mercenaries, but all of them believe passionately in the 'Holy Cause' and are willing to die to defeat the Bolshevism that has robbed them of their country. They all know what kind of death to expect in the case of defeat. The Chinese loathe and fear them. Yet a cheerier crowd you could never hope to find. They live for the next moment, the next woman, the next drink: of course, they have nothing to lose. Above all, they live for war. These exiled Russians have become like the nomads whom they once fought for empire in the wilds of Siberia. When Genghis Khan sent his armies to pillage the world, adventurers like these accompanied him. The world has come full circle. Now the dregs of the new civilisations are preying on the old, with the most modern weaponry and technology that science can devise.

Before we set off Colonel K allowed me to accompany him as we inspected the train. It is a magnificent beast, like a stegosaurus cased in iron plates. Each compartment is linked to the next by an internal telephone system so that Colonel K, from his command post in the centre, can control the devastating fire of the great naval guns that swing in their turrets at the front and rear of the train. All along the length of it, machine-guns bristle through loopholes. The two steam engines, one at the back, one at the rear, are also encased in heavy armour. At each end of the train are flat cars, loaded with coal, spare rails and sleepers. If these should by misfortune run over a mine, no damage will be done to the fighting machine, but they also provide the wherewithal to mend broken tracks. These warriors are skilled navvies, who are trained to rebuild a railroad under fire. This is a self-sustaining monster, living off the land it destroys — but it is more than coal, steel and weaponry. It is a moving castle manned by brave men. As I walked down the platform with their commander, his little army stood on the roofs of their fortresses or clustered by the doors of the turrets and cheered.

Colonel K thinks we will face our first action when we cross the Kiangsu border at about dawn. The Nationalists are believed to have two armoured trains of their own, which will do their best to prevent our attack, so it will be a duel of monsters. Colonel K and his intelligence officer Priapin are confident. Over dinner we toasted victory in vodka. The men went to their bunks early. Priapin told me that this would be the last decent night's sleep I will get for a fortnight.

I cannot sleep, however, despite the liquor with which I tried to drug myself. All I can think of is Catherine in Airton's arms — another Airton. When I woke this morning, I was ready for war. I dreamed I had seen a vision of my goddess; she had forgiven me and I felt blessed, like a knight endowed with his lady's favours. When I stepped out of my room, I thought I was still dreaming. There she was, as I had pictured her all these years. She was laughing, lighting the dingy corridor with the bright stars of her eyes, her hair loose over her shoulders shining like purging fire. In my ecstasy, I thought those smiles were for me, and that she was as overjoyed to see me as I to see her, and I stepped forward to throw myself at her feet. Then he appeared behind her, her latest lover, fresh from the stink of last night's sheets. And those shining eyes turned cold, glaring at me as if I was detestable in her sight, and she put her arm round Airton's waist, as if to protect herself from me.

I had to endure more. Colonel K appeared, a Russian mercenary, and I watched him plant his kisses on those beloved cheeks, and she responding. No basilisk stare for Colonel K! Am I to believe that he is yet another lover? Airton did not seem to mind him fondling her. Quite clearly hers are favours that can be shared by all. Her lovers are not particular and neither is she. I should have listened to Robby's warnings. He as good as told me that Catherine was making love to Airton at the very time she was fucking me. For all I know she was planning her flight with him all the time. Was I just a humorous diversion? Did she stage my humiliation with George to cover her exit with his brother? And what is Edmund Airton? Her pander? Her pimp? The mind boggles at such cynicism, such perfidy, such depravity. Whore! Whore! Whore!

Oh my goddess! My muse! Why have you left me? Why did you appear in the flesh only to mock me with your worthlessness? After all these years, when I had taught myself to hope again. You are merciless and cruel, for you know that whatever you inflict on me, I will never cease worshipping you. My goddess! My whore! Your ascendancy over me is absolute, yet even you have not the power to prevent me loving you.

It is four in the morning. I haven't slept. I have reread my 'war diary' entry for today. It is undignified, the self-piteous outpouring of a lovestruck teenager, not of a man. Or a poet. There's a joke! Yet I must be a man today, if not a poet. In a few hours this dark capsule in which I lie, steaming towards the front and stinking of men, real men, like Kovalevsky, Priapin and Samsonov, whose snores I hear from the bunkroom next door grinding over the roar of the clacking wheels, and who would laugh me to scorn if they knew I was fretting over a mere woman, and a loose one at that, will propel me into the middle of a battle as fierce as any I have ever seen. War doesn't spare journalists. I have chosen to cast my lot with mercenaries, and share their fate, whatever it is — and it could be a terrible one. The Nationalists will not respect my neutral's armband if they find me in the company of Russians, and even if the Nationalists don't get me, there is the chance that a stray bullet or a shell will. Those are the baron's wages and I accept them.

17 April

10 a.m.

We have steamed into our first trap. Luckily the lookouts were observant and saw the torn-up rails before our train blundered over them, but we were stopped where the enemy wanted us, and shortly before eight, after the rail gang had been sent forward to make the necessary repairs on the line, their shells began to fall. The first exploded in a millet field about five hundred yards away from us while Priapin, Ordozhev, the medical officer, and I were having breakfast. This led to great excitement. We tumbled out of the compartment on to the track, where we found Colonel K and some of his officers peering through binoculars at the horizon. It was flat country dotted with clumps of woodland. In the distance we could see troops moving but they were too far away to identify. They could either have been advance forces from our army or retreating units of theirs. They were not the immediate problem. What Colonel K wanted was to identify the direction from which the shell had come so that we could pinpoint the Nationalist armoured train and return fire. Nobody seemed concerned. The soldiers working on the rails did not even turn their heads.

We did not have long to wait. In quick succession we heard a whistle and a thump, and saw two great fountains of earth and smoke exploding again in the millet field. The second burst only about a hundred yards from where we were standing, but I was the only one who ducked. The Russians had obviously acquired the information they wanted, because there was an exchange of shouts with the gun turrets, and in a moment our big guns swung in the direction of a wood to the south-west. I felt a great slap on my back and saw Colonel K's laughing face. 'Now we exchange visiting cards,' he said. He had hardly spoken before the air cracked with the sound of our guns, and the whoosh of our parting projectiles. Up came the binoculars. Even without them I could make out the neat white mushrooms of smoke appearing behind the wood, two volleys of extraordinary precision. Everybody looked very pleased with themselves.

'Did we score a hit?' I asked Priapin. He shrugged, continuing to peer through his binoculars at the fading wisps of smoke. Colonel K, who had taken off his jacket in the heat and was strolling among his officers in his vest and braces, was casually lighting his pipe. I happened to be looking in his direction when the next two shells struck. I was aware of a bright burst of fire. I heard an enormous explosion and the sound of rattling metal, and the next second I felt clumps of earth landing on my head. I crouched with my head against the buffer. The shell had landed on the track beside the dining-car I had just vacated. Colonel K had not flinched. His tall figure stood erect, as he quietly puffed away at his pipe. I heard a shout and a cry of pain, then saw the doctor running towards the door of the compartment where two men were supporting the steward, Chapin, who was lolling unconscious, the white of his jacket stained crimson. I subsequently found out that his arm had been torn off at the elbow. Priapin was lifting himself off the ground. 'Bad,' he muttered.

'You mean the shell that landed next to the dining-car?' I asked.

'No,' he said. 'That was miss. Not important. See armoured wagon there? They're getting our range.' Then I noticed a severe dent in the metal plates under one of the machine-gun nests on the roof. The gunners were peering down, pointing and laughing, apparently unhurt. Colonel K shouted another order and our big guns fired again, and again, with the same accuracy as before. The little wood seemed to be covered with a white cloud. Through it I saw a column of black smoke. There was a cheer down the line of the train.

'We've hit them?' I asked.

'Probably,' said Priapin. 'Anyway, they leave now. That is engine making smoke. We have first victory.'

As he spoke there was another whoosh, a crack, and a white fountain rose from the other side of the train.

'Parting shot,' said Priapin. He was watching through his binoculars as the black column in the distance became a horizontal ribbon fading to the south.

'What happens now?' I asked.

'Wait till rail is repaired. Maybe one hour. Two hours later,

*expect more trains join us in convoy, Peking and Hepeh. Then we
go down line again with more guns.'*

So that was my first battle. It seemed inconsequential to me,
apart from the loss of poor Chapin's arm, of course, but my Russian
companions were satisfied. They spent the next hour taking pot-
shots at the soldiers in the distance. I saw the antlike figures disappearing into the corn after the first few explosions. Priapin told me
it was good target practice.

'But what if they're our men, not the enemy?' I asked.

'Then we apologise,' he said, giving me one of his rare smiles.

The rail gang, who had worked all through the exchange of fire,
came back, the section repaired. For the last hour we have sat lazing
in the sun. A few minutes ago, the two new armoured trains came
up behind us. Colonel K has put on his jacket and gone to confer
with their commanders. Priapin and Samsonov have brought out
a chessboard and are laying out the pieces. It is unlikely that we
will be going anywhere very soon. It appears that the duel of
monsters is to be a leisurely affair.

5 p.m.

It is one of those bright summer evenings where every leaf of every
tree, every stalk of corn is backlit in stark clarity and colour by the
rays of the declining sun. I am looking at the aftermath of a
massacre, however, and the beauty is obscene . . .

Our three trains made great progress through the afternoon.
Around three o'clock, we hit another obstacle on the track, and
the elusive enemy ahead bombarded us again — with little effect
because when the nine great cannon from our combined force
returned fire they realised immediately they were outmatched:
shortly afterwards we saw the smoke from their funnel disappear
southwards as they beat a hasty retreat. It did not take our soldier-
navvies long to replace the rails, which had only been unscrewed
and thrown down the bank. Then we followed in hot pursuit.

By late afternoon we had so outstripped our own advancing
infantry that it was clear that the troops we suddenly came across
retreating over the cornfields were Nationalists. Through the

*shimmering heat we could even make out their armbands. That is
the only way to distinguish one army from another, these days.
They wear the same motley blue tunics with similar leggings, and
they all carry umbrellas. In fact, this might have been the picnic
that Colonel K described to me last night. The men seemed to be
strolling rather than marching. Most had their parasols open to
ward off the hot sun. It looked like a village harvest procession.
We were rounding smooth hills when we saw them and some trick
of the landscape must have disguised the sound of our approach,
because we caught them by surprise. The more alert ones were
running away, but many seemed hypnotised where they stood,
gaping at us with open mouths and startled white eyes in their
brown peasant faces, still shaded by their brollies.*

*I saw these faces explode into red pulp when the machine-guns
all along the flank of our train fired.*

*Colonel K in his command post spoke briefly into his telephone.
The wheels shifted pace. A few hundred yards further, with a
shudder and whine of metal, our whole convoy groaned to a halt.
The only sound then was the stutter from the machine-guns. I saw
running figures throw their arms into the air and seem to fly as the
heavy-calibre bullets hit them in the back. Some brave souls were
firing their rifles at us. I heard the tinkle on the side of our compartment. They might as well have been throwing pebbles for any effect
this had. Leisurely, our gunners identified the points of resistance,
and knocked them out. Sensibly, most of the enemy soldiers had
lain flat on their faces, hiding in the corn. Our machine-gunners
knew their trade, however, and lowered their sights. A film of dust
and chaff hung over the killing fields as the machine-guns performed
their efficient threshing. Sometimes a knot of the enemy would
make a bolt for it, like flushed hares. They did not go far.*

*There were three gunners in the next compartment. I watched
one of them, a clean-shaven fellow wearing a fur hat, with pink
cheeks and a cigarette hanging from his lips, methodically sweeping
the field. For all the emotion he put into the task, he might have
been a factory hand performing a robotic function he had accomplished a thousand times before. There was indeed something of a
factory workshop about the claustrophobic compartment, the*

rhythmic metal press of the guns, the ringing echoes, the tinkle of empty cartridges like discarded metal filings coiling on the steel floor out of a great lathe. When the ash on his cigarette reached his lips, the gunner stood up and stretched. His companion, a slit-eyed Slav with a long, yellow moustache, adroitly slipped into his place and carried on the process almost without missing a beat. It was a change of shift in the workplace. The relieved hand lit two cigarettes, one for himself. The other he placed between the lips of his colleague, who was concentrating on his task.

Oh, the depravity of our modern age that has turned the killing of men into an automated production process!

Eventually Kovalevsky, through his telephone system, called a halt. The firing in our train stopped; shortly afterwards the shooting from the rear two trains petered out. There was a terrible silence. A pall of mist and smoke hung over the field like an early-morning fog – but soon that cleared too and I heard the chatter of birds as they flew in to peck at the scattered corn. Detachments of our men were moving through the fields. Occasionally we heard a shot. This was no mission of mercy. They had gone in search of loot.

Now I am watching the beginnings of a spectacular central China sunset. The corn stalks are distinct again, but so are the torn bodies scattered among them. Those are not crimson flowers peeping up from the soil. They are parts of men. What have we done? We have brought the poppies of Flanders to take root in an Oriental field. Is this the harvest of modernity we bring? The gift of civilisation and science? We would have been better to leave China to its ancient plough.

11 p.m.

We continue to steam southwards, slowly to avoid mines or ambushes. The men are exuberant. They believe this to be a rout. Colonel K is playing his balalaika and Samsonov, in a deep, reverberating voice, is singing the sad songs that Russians enjoy when they are happy. Only Priapin is worried. He thinks this is all too easy. I am exhausted, and still a little sickened. I have retired to my bunk. I hope I can sleep. Let me dream of my goddess tonight, as she was.

18 April

3 p.m.

I am writing this in a teahouse in the town of Lung-shan. The proprietor was reluctant to serve us but my Russian companions kicked in his shutters. He is happier now that I have shown him real Mexican dollars and, judging by the smells emanating from the kitchen, appears to be cooking up a feast.

We occupied the town this morning without any resistance. The enemy has apparently fled. Our three trains steamed into an empty station yard. While Samsonov supervised the refuelling and rewatering of the engines, Colonel K led a detachment of riflemen to explore the town. He was clearly nervous, and ordered me to remain on the train. Most of the other officers now shared Priapin's worries of last night. The ease of our advance had been too good to be true. We had not seen hide or hair of the Nationalist armoured train since the engagement yesterday afternoon. Interrogation of a railway official, whom Priapin found hiding under a desk in his office, revealed that the train had hurried through the station the previous evening, barely stopping to rewater. Shortly afterwards all the other Nationalist troops stationed in Lung-shan had decamped in an orderly fashion. It was all very mysterious, and there was an eerie quality about the empty streets, where the walls were still plastered with Nationalist propaganda.

Colonel K reappeared about eleven, confirming that there were no enemy troops to be seen. Some of his men were leading pigs and a sheep. Clearly they had found time for looting during their reconnaissance.

The situation became clearer when advance troops from our own side began to arrive about noon. The first stages of the attack had been a brilliant success, or so a colonel in one of Sun Chuan-fang's Kiangsu detachments told us. There had been strong resistance on the right wing at the beginning, but the news of the imminent flanking approach of the Red general's renegades from the west had caused the Nationalists to panic and begin a precipitate retreat. The infantry had advanced without opposition through the night. Their supply lines were now very stretched, but it did not seem to matter because the enemy strength appeared to have collapsed.

I thought back to the meeting in Hsuchow I attended last year between Chiang Kai-shek and Feng Yu-hsiang. At that time General Feng had appeared to be the kingmaker of China – but now, with the main part of his feared Kuominchun deserting him and going over to the warlords, the tide has turned. The Kiangsu colonel had been weary, but quietly elated. He told us that Feng's three divisions should be arriving here very soon, and with their combined weight, we would be on the banks of the Yangtse in a matter of days. I thought. How typical and how Chinese. With all the panoply of modern warfare it is still treachery that carries the day, as it has always done since the time of the Han. What a country! But perhaps it is this pragmatic paradigm, so incomprehensible to the Westerner, that will one day make this country work as a formidable modern state.

After this news, the Russians began to relax. There will clearly be a pause in the fighting until the warlord side has regrouped. Colonel K announced to his men that they had the freedom of the town, whatever that means (presumably to take what they can). We are all to meet back at the train this evening for a roast of the animals they 'liberated' this morning, no doubt with extras they find in the afternoon. I wrote a brief dispatch for the baron that I will find a means somehow to transmit – if I can locate a telegraph – but meanwhile I, too, am enjoying the freedom of the town in the Russian way! Ah, I see that the now very cheerful proprietor has unearthed a jar of samshu as they call their filthy spirit here, and my companions are happy indeed!

6 p.m.

Priapin, who still looks as miserable as ever, told me that Feng Yu-hsiang's deserters have reached the outskirts of the town, and there has been some fraternisation with the Fengtian troops. Our generals are expected to come down in the Dog General's train some time tomorrow (or since this is China, probably the next day, or the day after that), following which there will be a conference on how to conduct the next stage of the campaign. Meanwhile we are in celebratory mood, assisted no doubt by samshu. Poor Chapin's replacement is stripped to the waist and roasting a sheep. I can't make out Colonel K, however. He seems to have sunk into a melancholy despond, strumming his balalaika idly to no distinct tune. Occasionally he and Priapin disappear for long walks. Colonel K, with his arms behind his back, his pipe stuck forward in his mouth, listens to the shorter man moodily. Clearly something is still disturbing them but whatever it is they are not telling anybody. I must go. Samsonov has called me an idle parasite. I have been officially appointed assistant steward, in charge of the garnish. I think that means he wants me to peel potatoes.

7 p.m.

It is very strange. Colonel K has just issued the order that no vodka or other alcohol is to be drunk tonight. We are to eat the feast in two shifts, with half our force at action stations. I can also see that the stokers of one of the engines are lighting the boiler. The men have taken the news philosophically and unquestioningly; such is their sense of discipline and their respect for their commander. I have tried to ask both Colonel K and Priapin what is happening, but both give me the same vague and disturbing answer: 'Security precautions.'

11.45 p.m.

It is near the witching hour. I still have no idea what is going on. Whatever emergency it is, it applies only to the Shantung. I can hear the noise of roistering from the other two trains parked in their sidings. Ours is as silent as a tomb – but every one on board is awake, alert and manning his gun. This in a town we have secured! In our 'dining-car' Samsonov and Priapin are playing chess, but Priapin occasionally goes out between moves to Colonel K who is pacing the sidings. I see the red bowl of his pipe in the darkness.

I am haunted by my usual memories. I always am when I am

alone and nothing is happening, but it is strange how the subconscious works. Unknown to me and inside me I feel that a debate has been raging, and I am dimly gathering some conclusions. For a start, I have come to see what a fool I have been these last two years. I know that I have been chasing a phantom. Catherine is no goddess, nor is she a whore. She is a woman, that's all. Fascinating, flawed, like any of us is flawed. What was that sonnet of Shakespeare's? 'My mistress when she walks, walks on the ground.' Well, so does my goddess. She is the woman I loved. She is the woman I still love — I can't help that — but she doesn't want me. She has never been anything less than forthright about it. She made herself clear when we parted. She was very clear the other day. She has taken another path to mine. It is not one I approve of. I will always be jealous of her other lovers — but I cannot deny her the right to live the life she wants and, frankly, what do I know about her anyway? The Catherine I have allowed myself to become besotted by has probably always been half fantasy. That is the selfishness of love. We create the objects of our devotion in our own self-image. Did we ever get to know each other at all during our furtive meetings in the half-light? I saw her as I wanted her to be. I have continued to see her thus ever since and, in doing so, have cut myself off from life and reality for too long.

The one I feel really sorry for is Robby. No, I have not discovered some new homoerotic urge in me — but I know that he is my truest friend, and he needs me. My God, in this filthy world we should snatch at friendship and love where we find it. There are enough illusions poisoning the fabric of our existence. What is this war, or any war, but illusion? I have ignored Robby for two years, lost in my own selfish absorption, and with what? A dream!

There are lessons to be learned from these simple Russians. They have no illusions — but they have all the great human virtues of courage and strength and, yes, devotion. I have never seen such camaraderie as on this train. Not even in the trenches. They are rough diamonds, every one of them, but they burn with a true fire. They know that their cause is lost. That portrait of the Tsar is a symbol of their exile, not of any serious belief that their old empire can be restored. They live for each other, battling on even though they know what, ultimately, the end will be, and they enjoy what little life gives them today because there may be no tomorrow. If truth were to be told, I feel rather humble in front of a man like Kovalevsky. He is as good a commander as any I have seen on any front. And to think that I was jealous of him because he kissed Catherine! I should be ashamed.

No, Mr Lampsett, you have been a fool. You have betrayed your friends and you have betrayed yourself. I don't know if I will survive this war, but if I do ...

Something is happening. Kovalevsky has just bounded into the compartment and shouted orders in Russian. Priapin and Samsonov have followed him to his control post. I think I understood a few of the words he said — 'It's a trap' — and something about Feng Yu-hsiang.

12.10 a.m.

All hell has broken loose. Our machine-guns are firing along either side of our train, and it sounds as if a hailstorm is clattering against our armour. The yard is full of soldiers shooting at us. I recognise the uniform. It is the khaki of Feng Yu-hsiang's Kuominchun. So, we have been tricked. They never deserted at all.

I am snatching glances out of the slit. It looks like the Peking has been overrun. I see hand-to-hand fighting in the yards. I can see the bodies all around our perimeter where our machine-guns have mown down the first attacks.

Slowly we are beginning to move. The whole train is juddering. It must be pushing at some obstacle along the line.

Yes, the Peking has been overrun. My God, it is exploding in flames, and I hear the sound of our own guns.

Kovalevsky has fired at one of our own trains at almost point-blank range, destroying the gun turrets. I can't see the Hepeh but our guns are still firing so he must be meting out the same treatment to it ...

I am in the control tower now with the colonel. He has given me a pistol and mimed that I should use it against myself in the event of capture. For the moment it seems to be stalemate because the enemy cannot get near our machine-guns. We are still trying to push the obstacles, whatever they are, out of the way. Samsonov is gathering a company of riflemen with bayonets. They have set off towards the front of the train.

Colonel K is walking round the control tower smoking his pipe, occasionally slapping me on the back before growling something into the internal telephone. He is laughing with Priapin, who is stationed by the observation hole with his customary pair of binoculars.

An enormous crash and the whole train rocks. Another. I think they have brought up cannon. Our own guns are firing back. We cannot hear ourselves above the screaming, banging noise. It seems that only one of our big guns is still firing. We are being pounded at very close range. The train is rocking.

Flames are coming from the door of the next machine-gun compartment. It is an inferno. A gravy of human fat is dripping out on to the steps.

A shell has hit the side of our control post. Priapin is dead. Colonel K is, I think, wounded. One arm is bleeding, but he is still shouting into the telephone. I hear a . . .

Catherine, Catherine, Catherine . . .

It was last summer all over again, but worse. Edmund had decided that, with the sheer numbers of wounded, it made more sense to leave the hospital in the hands of Dr Chen and the nuns, who would treat the less serious cases, whom Bishop Huber could more easily bring there by mule cart, while he and Catherine set up a makeshift surgery in a tent in the marshalling yard. Such was the panic in Tsinan that neither the authorities nor the Red Swastika protested. They were more concerned with finding a way to escape the doomed city, following the example of their leader, the Dog General, who had already decamped in a motorcade with his mistresses and his bullion.

Hsiung had worked tirelessly to bring the patients from the carriages, helped by two soldiers who, over the months, had become his friends. Edmund and Catherine, after nearly twenty-four hours on their feet, were performing their tasks mechanically. She had lost count of the arms and legs they had amputated, the skulls they had trepanned and the guts they had somehow sewn together. They exercised a ruthless triage. Sometimes a torn and bleeding body would lie on the dripping operating-table for only a few seconds before Edmund would silently shake his head, and Hsiung would shrug, then carry away the dying man, replacing him a few moments later with another bleeding carcass, whom, this time, Edmund might examine and try to save.

Life and hope had become a matter of ruthless mathematics. Finally it was Hsiung who appointed himself timekeeper. Inevitably, in his tiredness, Edmund's hand slipped. They cauterised the spurting artery. The man might even have lived, but when that operation was completed, Hsiung called a halt and ordered Edmund and Catherine to rest. They lay on the ground in their red-drenched clothes. Many soldiers would die because of that hour and a half's sleep, but their renewed energy when they woke would save others. Such was the remorseless equation of life and death.

Some time during the second day they noticed European features on the bodies passing over their table. Catherine's dull mind remembered another war. These were Russians. It did not seem strange. By that stage she felt that her whole life had been spent standing by an operating-table. Circles turned. Bleeding bodies were all the same whatever the length of their noses, and one hacked-off arm was like another. One patient looked familiar. He had golden hair. There had once been another stomach wound with golden hair. She could not remember his name. Feodor? By the time she remembered, Edmund had shaken his head. Hsiung carried the body away.

The light suddenly darkened. A big man was silhouetted in the open flaps of the tent. He was holding something in a blanket, which he laid gently on the table. Carefully, Edmund unfolded the cloth, and Catherine saw the burned flesh, the unrecognisable skeleton of a face from which all the skin had fallen away.

'This man's dead,' said Edmund, wearily.

She recognised the voice that replied: 'I promise to Katusha I bring him back,' said Serge. His voice broke. 'I'm sorry, Katusha. I could not save him. I'm sorry.'

Edmund was looking at him closely. 'You're burned and wounded yourself, man,' he muttered. 'Lie down on the table and let me examine you.'

'No,' said Serge. 'No matter me. I finished. All trains destroyed. Only mine return, but it is also finished. No guns. Few men. I only come for Katusha. My promise. Here,' he added. With some difficulty he reached into his pocket, and painfully extracted a charred, leatherbound notebook. He proffered it to Catherine, and mumbled in Russian, 'This is yours. He probably wanted you to have it. It is poems. Writings. Your name is everywhere.' He shrugged. 'He must have loved you, poor fellow. He died bravely. Like all of my comrades, he died bravely. That is something to remember him by.'

Catherine knew she should feel something, say something, but she was too numbed, too tired. Thankfully, Hsiung had folded the blankets over the burned corpse on the table. She could not for the moment equate that skull with Willie's face, or even take in that he was dead. She took the book, and slipped it into the pocket of her blood-sodden apron without looking at it. She wanted to get back to the routine. She wanted Serge to go.

'Hsiung, you look after him. Ask Huber to take him to Dr Chen,' she heard Edmund saying. 'We'll all talk later.'

'No,' said Serge. 'I leave Tsinan. Not good for Russians when Nationalists come, and I am too well known. Katusha,' he said, kissing her cheeks, 'I find you again one day, and then we grieve together for lost friends.'

'Goodbye, Serge,' she managed. She gripped his two large hands. 'Thank you.'

The big man's features twisted, as if there was something he was struggling to say. Then his shoulders slumped. He turned and left. Catherine became aware that both Edmund and Hsiung were watching her with concern.

'What?' she said irritably.

'Are you all right, Catherine?' Edmund asked. 'Shall I get another nurse to stand in for you for a while?'

'No, I'm fine.' She sighed. 'Let's get on with it, shall we?'

A few minutes later, she was holding down a shredded leg while Edmund sawed carefully at the hip.

* * *

Martha looked back to those early days of the civil war as a period of undreamed-of happiness.

With General Lin and his army away from Shishan, Minister Yu Fu-cheng was left in control of the city and protected them. The school thrived, and whole months went by when they were not in the red. Martha even managed, through careful housekeeping, to save some money.

What really pleased her was that Ming, who had become morose and aged with the strain of running and teaching in a school in such a hostile political environment, had regained the boyish optimism with which she had fallen in love. It was as if the Northern Expedition had lit a fire in him. He would rush out eagerly before classes to buy the early-morning papers and, over coffee in the common room, study carefully the reports of the various armies' progress. He would bang the table with his fists when he read of a Nationalist victory, and stride whistling down the hall to the classroom to reposition the flags on the wall map that showed the triumphant southern advance. The Kuomintang banner that she had eventually persuaded him to take down was now back in its proud position above his teacher's dais.

It sometimes worried her – especially when Yu Fu-cheng, during their Sunday meetings at Old Man Yu's, censured her husband mildly for his provocative actions – but she said nothing, so overjoyed was she to have Ming happy and affectionate again. They had not made love for more than a year, but one night, after falling into bed as usual after a tiring day, her head had hardly hit the pillow before she was woken by the sensation of his hands on her breasts. Then she saw Ming's grinning face above her, his soft eyes tender with love, and he told her that he wanted a baby who would be born into the new China. She pulled him down to her, weeping with gratitude that her husband had returned to her.

The holiday lasted only as long as it took General Chiang Kai-shek to reach Shanghai. The subsequent slaughter of the Communists, and the even more terrible massacres in Wuhan after the expulsion of Borodin, had strained Ming's faith in the Party and, of course, he feared for his sister, whom they knew had worked in Hankow. After much soul-searching, he persuaded himself that the Kuomintang had been right to do what it had, however horrific, because ultimately the Communists owed allegiance to Russia rather than China – but it cost him an effort to make this mental adjustment and it did nothing to calm his fears for Lan-hua.

They had had to wait weeks to find out if she was all right. In the meanwhile, Ming fell back into his former depression. His spirits revived temporarily when the telegram arrived from a Catholic mission station in Tsinan, and he laughed at the thought that his Communist sister had found refuge with the Church. That night they made love again, and for a few days harmony was restored.

Shortly afterwards they received a letter from Lei Tang, containing two items of news. First, he announced that after many hardships he had found a job: the merchant from Kaifeng who had bought the Lei mansion had taken pity on the plight of his family and had offered him a position as a porter in their old home; he, his wife, his children and his grandmother had been given a servant's room, and his patron had even been generous enough to allow Tang to rear his pigeons. The second item of news concerned Lan-hua, who had arrived with no money, wrote Tang; she had, however, scorned the housemaid's job that Mr Ti had kindly offered her in his family apartments, and insisted that she wanted to go to Shishan to burden her second brother. Tang apologised for this skittishness on Younger Sister's part, saying that he feared she had annoyed Mr Ti, but since he did not have alternative means to look after her, could Second Brother please help to find her a job? He added the date and time of the train on which she would arrive.

Martha and Ming did not know whether to laugh or cry at Tang's stupidity; they were mortified that he had allowed their family to be humiliated yet again by the father of Ti Jen-hsing, and had not the wit to understand that the generosity for which he was so pathetically grateful hid only a desire for further revenge by this upstart provincial merchant on his former benefactor. They were appalled that he had thought of involving Lan-hua. Martha and Ming went to the station in the Japanese town to meet her – the first time Martha had been there since her humiliation the previous spring – and there was a joyful reunion with many tears.

They celebrated her safe return extravagantly, blowing a month's savings in an expensive restaurant, but Martha did not begrudge it for she saw how much it meant to Ming to be reunited with his sister. Together they mourned Lan-hua's lost fiancé, and eagerly exchanged news of Catherine, Fu-kuei and other mutual friends; they sighed over Elder Brother's sad decline into imbecility ('You know he's become a peasant, Ming,' said Lan-hua. 'You remember how we joked about "Slippers to slippers in three"? Well, it's happened. He was working as a watchman outside a brothel when I found them. He'd even tried being a rickshaw-puller, till his lungs gave out. His awful wife runs a small laundry for a little money, and is a tyrant to Grandmother who just lies on her bed looking at the wall. The children are starved. That's why I went to see Mr Ti. I know it's humiliating, but it's a roof over their head at least. They only got the job because of me. I think the old man wanted to add me to his collection of concubines. I played along giving him sweet smiles until Elder Brother and the others were settled, then made an excuse and said I had to come to Shishan. I don't think even the Tis would have the face to throw out Tang now: the old man has already boasted over town how kind he has been to his former patrons. And, believe it or not, Tang's happy. He has his pigeons.')

For those first three days, the only topic they did not touch upon was politics. Martha changed the subject every time it threatened to come up because she knew that after the split between the Kuomintang and the Communists, brother and sister would be divided. In fact, the day before Lan-hua had arrived Martha had taken down the portrait of Chiang Kai-shek that Ming had placed in the common room on the excuse that it was torn, but really it was because she guessed the effect it would have on her sister-in-law.

Inevitably the row happened, despite Martha's efforts, a day after Lan-hua had taken her place as assistant teacher in Ming's history class. She stamped out, face red with fury, complaining that Ming's lesson had been a panegyric about the murdering generalissimo. After the lesson, brother and sister shouted at each other, while Martha and *Hsiao* Hung sipped their coffee and waited for the storm to blow over. It never really did, although Ming and Lan-hua finally agreed to disagree, and to avoid direct confrontations.

Martha did her best to be a peacemaker, trying to persuade both that the only real enemies were the warlords and, surely, whatever side of the socialist spectrum one stood at, it was encouraging at least that Chang Tso-lin's side appeared to be losing the war. She pleased neither brother nor sister: Lan-hua told her that she was no longer interested in a war that consisted merely of one warlord fighting another, and Ming repeated his hurtful complaint, now sadly all too frequent, that Martha was a foreigner, so how could she hope to understand? For a long while, Ming and Lan-hua did not speak to each other. Lan-hua helped *Xiao* Hung in the kindergarten class, and Martha became an unwilling go-between between the factions. The strain was intolerable, and Ming was wretched and irritable. There was no talk now about making babies for a new China, which was ironic, thought Martha, because he had his wish, although she had not yet found an occasion to tell him. For two months now she had been certain she was pregnant.

One day Yu Fu-cheng called at the school. He arrived unannounced just after they had closed for the day. For several months they had not been to Old Man Yu's lunches, and Martha, who answered the door, was staggered by the change in the minister's appearance. The little man was almost unrecognisable in an ill-fitting Western suit, and there was no trace of his usual bonhomie. There was certainly no sign of the customary twinkle in the eyes that flitted from side to side of his round spectacles; the hand holding a battered leather suitcase was shaking. It was as if at any moment he expected to see a ghost, thought Martha, who was amused until she realised, with a shock, that he was in a state of terror.

He only seemed to relax when he was inside the door, but he would not leave the corridor or put down his suitcase. 'Ma Ta,' he whispered, 'I cannot stay. I have to hurry to the Japanese town and catch a train this very evening to Dairen. I have only come to warn you before I go.'

'Warn us?'

'Yes. You should leave too. You must persuade your fanatical husband and his deluded sister that it is no longer safe here. You probably have only a few days. I cannot risk staying because I will

627

be their first target. Listen,' he said, reaching into his pockets for a wad of notes, 'this is not very much, but it will buy the three of you train tickets. If you come to Dairen, look for me in the Yamato hotel. I will leave a message there where you can find me.'

She felt a little faint. She was scared by what he had said, even though she did not understand. 'Minister Yu, can you not tell us what this is about?'

'I'm sorry,' he said, looking at his watch. 'There is little time. I am to be replaced by Colonel Ti, who will be arriving tomorrow to assume the governorship of Shishan. Never mind how I heard. I have friends. Listen, Ma Ta, you are sensible, unlike your husband. The war is going badly. Chang Tso-lin has only a month, two months at most, before he will be forced to retire from Peking. He and all his forces will retreat beyond the Wall. Then there will be purges throughout Manchuria of disloyal elements. You know he sacked his prime minister, Mr Wang, a few weeks ago. He is in hiding now under Japanese protection in Dairen. I fear I must do the same.' He grabbed her hand. 'I'm sorry, Ma Ta. I had hoped to hold on to my position. I still retained faith in General Lin, but it seems I was too trusting. The fact that he is sending Ti Jen-hsing, one of his most ruthless executioners, shows me that I am to be proscribed. Organisations, like this school, that I have been involved with will also be subject to persecution, especially since your husband so stupidly insists on flying his Kuomintang colours. It will soon be dangerous for all of you. I have told my father that he, too, should leave but as you know he is stubborn.' A sad smile crossed his tense features. 'I don't think they will hurt a harmless old man but, please, Ma Ta, persuade your husband. Let my flight be a token of my sincerity. I'm sorry. I cannot do more.'

Martha was dizzy with alarm. She had to support herself against the wall. 'Minister Yu, won't you tell my husband what you told me?'

'No,' he said. 'He will argue and strike poses. I haven't time. You persuade him, Ma Ta. Only you know how. If he won't listen, then at least save Lan-hua and yourself. Her Bolshevik past puts her life in danger, and your foreignness, since you took Chinese nationality, will not protect you. I beg you all, be prudent. Now I

must go. I do not dare to wait any longer.' He had already opened
the door and was peering from side to side, as if he expected the
house to be watched. Outside, a driver was waiting in his official
car. He scuttled across the pavement and into the back. He rolled
down the window and she saw his round spectacles reflecting the
evening light. 'I'm sorry' was the last thing she heard, before the
car rolled off towards the city gates, picking up speed.

It was useless. Neither Lan-hua nor Ming would listen to her.
Martha was sure from Lan-hua's reaction that she was scared, but
since her brother was sitting on a moral high horse, it would be
too much loss of face for her to do anything but the same. Only
Hsiao Hung, who said nothing when Martha broke the news, took
her seriously: next day she did not turn up for work, or the next,
and when they made enquiries at her lodgings, they found that she
had taken a train back to her parents' home in Harbin, not even
waiting for her wages.

For a week nothing happened, but the atmosphere in the city
had subtly changed. In the marketplace Martha heard the rumours.
Colonel Ti had established himself in the Yamen. He had held a
great banquet there for the authorities in the Japanese town. On
the Chinese side only soldiers had been present. All the senior civil
officials in the administration had been sent home, pending investigation of their activities. It seemed Minister Yu had not been the
only official who had fled. Charges of corruption would be laid
against those who had remained. Meanwhile taxes would be
reassessed. The shopkeepers were scared; they expected triple the
impositions that had been put on them in the past. When Martha
went to her bank to withdraw her housekeeping money, she had to
join a queue that stretched round the block; when she neared the
front she saw soldiers stationed at the door pasting up a notice that
all banks and money-lending establishments would be temporarily
closed 'by order of the state'. Essential monies could be withdrawn
only with stamped approval from the Yamen officer in charge of
investigating 'corruption, smuggling and other anti-social activities'. Martha slipped quietly away.

Later that day they heard of the confiscation of Yu Fu-cheng's
father's estates. The old man had protested and been beaten up,

then arrested 'for his association with the criminal activities of the outlaw Yu Fu-cheng'. Colonel Ti did not waste time. The first trial of 'the collaborators of the traitor Yu Fu-cheng' was held two days later in a closed court in the Yamen. Afterwards, two members of Minister Yu's government were executed in the public square, their heads placed on the city gates. Old Man Yu was sentenced to penal servitude in the tin mines in the Black Hills. The official bulletin pasted on the wall of the temple later praised his young wife, whose patriotism had impelled her to report her husband's Nationalist sympathies and whose evidence at the trial had revealed the extent of the sabotage of the economy that he and his son had effected for their financial gain. The bulletin ended with a warning that interrogation and confessions of these malefactors had revealed the existence of other conspiracies and anti-social activities that would be immediately investigated. Good citizens were encouraged to report any suspicious behaviour of their neighbours.

Martha pleaded again with Ming to leave before it was too late. She pointed to the fact that hardly any students were turning up for classes, kept away by their scared parents. The only ones left were the two Chow girls, daughters of the superintendent of the hospital that Yu Fu-cheng had set up, who was as fanatical a Nationalist as Ming. She asked her husband what he was trying to prove by flying his dumb flag and preaching what could only be interpreted now as open sedition. Ming did not reply. He blinked at her behind his dusty spectacles. She saw madness in his eyes. He fumbled with his books of Sun Yat-sen's speeches, and muttered that he had to prepare for the afternoon lesson. Lan-hua, sitting at the other end of the table, observed them sardonically. 'Don't bother, Martha,' she said. 'Don't you realise my brother's a patriot? He's going to win the revolution here all on his own.' And she laughed. To Martha she seemed as mad as her brother.

That night Martha told him about the baby, begging him, for the child's sake, to give up his stupid crusade. 'We can go somewhere else and start again,' she told him. 'For God's sake, Ming, things are moving in our direction now. The Nationalists are winning. Chang Tso-lin's about to leave Peking. What are we achieving by staying on here?' He lay rigid on the bed beside her.

'I love you, Ming. Can't you see that?' she pleaded, stroking his cheek. He flinched away. She wondered if he had even heard her. Then she saw that he was weeping silently. Eventually, exhausted, she slept.

Catherine and Edmund returned to the hospital when the first fires lit the skyline, and menacing crowds of looters roamed the streets. Hsiung and Bishop Huber still made forays to the railyard, but fewer trains were making their way back now, and the hospital was full in any case with the patients whom they had already treated.

The Nationalists were expected any day, and as usual terrifying rumours circulated of the terrible vengeance they would exact. Catherine had to spend as much time with her nurses as she did with the patients, attempting to calm their fears. Hsiung, as usual, was a pillar of strength. Laughter found its place among the tears.

She hardly saw Edmund outside the surgery. This was not the time for lovemaking. The shadow that had hung over them since that morning in the Yamato was still brooding, intensified by the sudden onset of the war, darkened in some indefinable way by Willie's death.

One evening, while Catherine was checking the morphine supply in the dispensary, she became aware that Edmund was watching her from the door. His hair was untidy. He was unshaven. He was exhausted after a twelve-hour stint at the operating-table. She wanted to rush over to him, smooth the curl on his forehead, stroke those tired cheeks – but something prevented her.

'What was in that journal?' he asked.

'I don't know. I haven't read it. It's in a drawer.'

'You should read it if you loved him.'

'If you're so interested, why don't you read the damn thing?' She could not believe she had snapped at him like that.

'I wasn't his lover,' said Edmund.

'God, Edmund!' She hunched on a stool. 'Why are we quarrelling? I love you. I haven't seen Willie for two years. All right, he and I had an affair. I had many affairs. You know that. I slept with him to get back at George, or because I was snatching at any straw to get away from a life I hated. That wasn't love. I know what love is only now. It was you who taught me, darling, and I'm yours. Haven't you grasped that yet?' Her anger erupted again. This was so ridiculous. 'Anyway, Willie's dead, isn't he? What on earth do you have to be jealous about?'

Edmund sighed, and put his hands in the pockets of his surgical coat. 'Perhaps because he is dead,' he muttered. 'I don't know, Catherine. I'm tired, and everything looks so difficult. There are so many ghosts that sometimes I'm not sure I have the strength to fight them all. And you're my brother's wife,' he added softly.

'Well, whose fault was that?' rounded Catherine. 'Oh, I'm sorry, I'm sorry.' She slipped off the stool and hugged him. He did not respond, just hung his head, stiff in her arms, and gazed at the row of medicines. After a moment, Catherine moved back to the stool. Both were silent.

'It's so complicated,' he said.

'It's the war, that's all,' said Catherine. 'You're exhausted. So am I.'

'Yes,' he said.

'When it's over we'll go away together,' said Catherine. 'To somewhere far away from here, where none of this will matter any more.'

'Yes,' he said.

'I love you,' she said.

'I love you too.'

He went back to his operating-table. She went back to her ward.

Hsiung was sitting next to a young man who had been blinded by shell fragments, some of which were lodged so deeply in his brain that Edmund had been unable to remove them. The explosion had also shattered his eardrums so he could not hear. Hsiung was carefully lifting flowers and herbs to the nostrils that protruded from under the bandages; one at a time, a rose, a bunch of lilac, posies of honeysuckle and thyme . . . He saw Catherine and smiled at her. 'We are all of us fighting in the dark, little one,' he told her. 'Sometimes it is when the lights begin to turn on that one is most blinded and confused.'

'But isn't that the dawning of certainty?' she asked. Surreptitiously she looked at her watch, pleased to humour him because she was so grateful for what he was doing to help, and his kindness to the wounded soldier had touched her, but she was anxious to get on.

'It is a milestone, perhaps, on the long, long road that stretches behind you.'

'Behind me? I'd rather hoped I was moving forward.'

'Is there a difference? My friend the bishop always tells me I am terrible about directions, but on reflection I think it is more interesting to go backwards. Anybody can decide what lies in the future for them, but the past is always full of mystery. Especially for you, Catherine, but I am glad you have decided to make that journey, although I will be sorry to see you go.'

'Am I going anywhere?'

'Oh, yes,' he said. 'And very soon. There's nothing more for you to do here.'

'Really?' she replied. 'Well, I'm sorry to disappoint you, Hsiung, but actually there's rather a lot. There's a man there for a start who needs an injection of morphine.'

'Goodbye, Nurse,' he whispered suddenly, in English. It was extraordinary. He had mimicked the exact timbre of Edmund's voice. She thought it a joke in bad taste, and hurried down the ward, angry that she had wasted time with him. She also felt a prickle down her back, aware that the strange eyes of the Taoist monk were still watching her.

The soldiers arrived for them exactly an hour later. Catherine and Edmund had been called by anxious nurses to Bishop Huber's study, Edmund protesting that he was about to perform an operation. They found the bishop at his desk, looking at a sheet of paper with an official chop, while behind him stood a burly, black-bearded soldier without any insignia of rank that Catherine could perceive. Nevertheless there was something familiar about him. She was more alarmed by the two soldiers with bayonets who were guarding the door, and the look of despair on Bishop Huber's face.

'I'm sorry, Edmund, but these are orders from what remains of the Dog General's government for you and Catherine to leave Tsinan. No, please, don't protest. I have spent the last few minutes protesting on your behalf. This paper says that the Nationalists are expected here within twenty-four hours. It is an order for all foreigners to be evacuated because they do not want to run the risk of another Nanking Outrage. There is a special Blue Train leaving the station in two hours, and you must be on it. It does not mention me or my nuns. Apparently we have been here so long that we are considered Chinese. I'm sorry, Edmund, I see no alternative. These men have threatened that they will close the hospital and arrest all of our staff if you do not comply. And I think they mean it.'

Of course they did argue. Edmund refused point-blank to go. The black-bearded man's response was to say nothing but point out of the window. Once again Edmund saw his old friend, Dr Chen, who had arrived only two weeks before, pinioned in the arms of soldiers and being slapped by a corporal.

An hour later, they were under armed guard on the way to the station, their holdalls and Edmund's medical bag on their knees. Catherine recognised the familiar signs of a hurried retreat: blackened, looted buildings; soldiers loading mule carts with their booty; the scared faces of the few civilians who saw this military convoy hurrying by. Edmund was seething with rage, muttering, 'I'm coming back. I'll find a way to come back.'

It was madness at the station but, with bayonets, their escort shoved the desperate people aside. The Blue Train was parked at a special siding, ringed by troops. The once-polished carriages of a service that had been a nationwide marvel of luxury in time of peace were filthy and rusted, but even so Catherine was shocked to see something that reminded her of a normal past. Most of the carriages were being used to carry troops. With unusual discipline in a warlord army, these battle-hardened men were waiting in patient squares to be embarked. The black-bearded man took them to one of the first-class carriages at the front, watched them aboard, then shuffled off towards the rear of the train. They found themselves alone in the upholstered splendour, except for two armed guards and, of all incongruities, a cabin attendant in the uniform of the Blue Line, who offered them a gin and tonic.

'There's something fishy about this,' muttered Edmund. He had calmed a little, but was still fidgety, frowning out of the window. 'Where are all the other evacuees?'

'Perhaps we're the only foreigners left,' said Catherine. 'You know the British consulate in Tientsin sent a message advising all nationals to leave when the fighting started.'

'There's a whole colony of Japanese here, Catherine. I see none of them.'

'Perhaps they feel they're adequately protected by all the Japanese troops stationed in Tsinan.'

'Maybe,' he said. He attempted a smile. 'I suppose there's a bright side. At least you're being taken to safety. That's a relief for me. There may be something in what they're saying about the Nanking Outrage.'

'Oh, surely not,' said Catherine. 'Even Chiang Kai-shek wouldn't let that kind of thing happen again. It's just the warlords putting on a last desperate gesture of defiance to ingratiate themselves with the Powers or something.'

He pulled up the window and stuck out his head. 'The last troops are on board,' he said. 'We'll be setting off soon. Hold on. The men guarding the cordon are packing up too. Looks like they're coming with us.'

His face was grim when he turned, but again he tried to smile. He took Catherine's hands and peered intently into her eyes. 'I do so love you,' he said softly. He leaned forward and kissed her. Relieved and delighted, she responded warmly. He was looking happier when he rested back in his seat. 'Well,' he said, 'if we're to be Shanghaied we might as well enjoy it. You said you wanted us to go away together, didn't you? Here, boy,' he clapped, 'where are those gins and tonic you promised us?'

'Coming, Master!' she heard.

Edmund stood up. 'Get a move on!' he shouted angrily.

This staggered Catherine: she had never heard him raise his voice to a servant.

Edmund reeled slightly, jolted by the train as it started to move along the siding. At the same time the flustered cabin attendant rushed down the aisle with a tray. 'Come on, you lazy bugger, where are our drinks?' he yelled. She saw the two guards at either end of the train, smiling at this predictable foreigner. She was blushing with embarrassment. Edmund turned to her, with a soft, yearning expression in his eyes. 'Goodbye, Nurse,' he whispered.

The cabin attendant appeared. Edmund kicked his tray so that bottles, glasses, ice and lemon clattered against the ceiling. He reached for the brass coat hook that hung above the window, pulled himself up and swung his bent legs outside. As he disappeared Catherine screamed. Terrified, she saw the two guards running forward, fumbling with their guns, and rushed to the window, blocking it, so they could not fire. Out of the corner of her eye she saw a tall figure darting across the tracks towards the crowded platforms. A soldier tried to pull her away. She bit and struggled. She clung to the rifle, but was knocked back into her seat. By then it did not matter. The train was picking up speed. The soldier pulled his head in. '*Meile!*' he muttered. 'Nothing!'

Both soldiers glared at her. While one covered her with his rifle, the other went to the next carriage. The black-bearded man returned, following another man. Catherine knew then why she had recognised him earlier: she had recalled a bar in Tientsin and a banquet in Shishan where he had also walked behind his master. She also knew the small man in the white suit who came up behind.

General Lin settled comfortably in the seat vacated by Edmund, and smiled his sinister smile. 'I am sorry that your friend has so rashly declined my invitation to travel with us,' he said. 'The city will be extremely dangerous when the Bolsheviks arrive. I hope he will be all right. However, I am relieved that you are still on the train, because it was you I intended to save. I have been worrying about you ever since I saw you by the roadside in Tsinan. War is uncertain, but one tries to do favours for one's friends where one can. Translate,' he ordered the man in the white suit.

'There's no need,' said Catherine. 'Where are you taking me?'

'Excellent, you have learned Chinese,' he said. 'Of course, it has been many years since I last had the pleasure of your company, and you are intelligent, like your father, as well as beautiful, like your mother. Your talents should not surprise me. It is no mystery, by the way, where we are going. To Tientsin, of course. Do you not have a husband there?'

'You seem to know a lot about me, General,' she said, trying to control her turbulent emotions, 'and I may sound ungrateful but I resent your high-handed intrusion into our lives. We did not need to be saved, and I do not wish to go to Tientsin. What you have done is abominable, whatever your intentions.'

The general chuckled. 'You are so like your mother,' he said. 'I was almost sure when I last saw you, but subsequently I confirmed who you were. There was an element of the child in her as well. It is characteristic of children not to know what is good for them and perversely to set about their self-willed course, resulting all too often in their own harm. It is the father's role to steer them on the right path.'

'I am not a child, General,' she bristled, 'and you are certainly not my father.'

The snake-like eyes observed her. 'No, Catherine, you are not physically my child, but I am an old family friend. I could say that I knew your mother intimately. I think of you as my child. In a spiritual sense, of course. I even cherish a hope that one day you might think of me as more than a father. Sadly,' he sighed, 'that must wait until after this war.'

Abruptly he stood up. 'Alas, duty calls me away. You cannot imagine the amount of work a general has to do, and I am a man, as you will discover, with many serious responsibilities, both on the battlefield and, even more importantly, in Shishan. One day you may visit me there, perhaps. I believe you still owe me a dance.' He gave his low, breathy laugh. 'I trust you will be comfortable. If you require anything, you have only to ask.'

She was left to herself for the rest of the journey. For a long while she gazed out of the window, thinking about Edmund.

She was proud of the courageous thing he had done. She wished that she, too, had found a way to leave the train. Somehow, she told herself, she would get back to Tsinan, because that was where her duty lay – and her lover.

She missed him, but she did not feel as empty and isolated as she had before. With that whispered 'Goodbye, Nurse' and 'I love you' he had left part of himself inside her.

As the train rolled on she began to think that it might not be a bad idea to return to Tientsin. She would have to divorce George one day – he would do the decent thing, she was sure. There were ways of arranging divorces in a manner that society seemed to accept, and in which the woman's good name was preserved. Not that she cared about her reputation any more, but Edmund would not want a scandal to upset his parents – and there would certainly be a scandal if a divorce went through citing one brother against another. Robby had once told her of a Russian lady who provided a professional co-respondent's service for honourable husbands; he had told her that half the divorces that came up to court had private eyes' photographs, taken in this woman's boudoir. George would be game for that, wouldn't he? She didn't want any of his money.

The thought of Robby, however, brought her back to reality. Robby would be devastated by Willie's death. How was she to tell him?

His diary – she hadn't thought of it since Serge had given it to her: she had not wanted to be reminded of that nightmare skull face and the burned skin wrapped in a blanket, but now, she thought, perhaps she should read it. She would have to one day. She owed Willie that at least. Perhaps there might be something in it to comfort Robby. She stood up and took her holdall from the rack, fumbled under her clothes until she found the leather journal and unclasped the strap. She had hours to kill. She might even enjoy some of the poems.

She was already weeping before the long golden evening outside the window had become night, and the cabin attendant had switched on the lights. Occasionally she glanced at her pale-faced reflection in the pane, framed by its fiery red hair, and turned away, hating to look at it because it had been that vision that had driven Willie to such self-delusion.

She forced herself to read on to the conclusion. At first, she had been crying partly for herself, partly out of sympathy for a high mind brought low. By the end she was grieving for a friend who had got over his madness and come to terms with himself. She felt a tragic sense of loss because, had he lived, his poetry and his visions for China and the world might have spoken for a generation, the lost generation of which she was a part. And she cried for all the others like him, whom she had known and who had died in useless, futile wars, never living up to their promise.

She determined that she would return to Edmund in Tsinan, however difficult it would be. She thought of Hsiung and Bishop Huber, their kindness in the wards and their selfless dedication to the patients. Reading Willie's diaries had humbled her. She did not love him, but she felt that she owed him something. For all Hsiung's tedious philosophising, she realised, his lessons were in his actions, not his words. It was service to others that counted. She felt a sudden sense of joy. Edmund had known that from the beginning. It was why he had returned.

She laughed. Perhaps the old monk's paradoxes made sense after all. She had never fully understood this until now: she had had to leave to arrive.

As she dozed, she thought of the old monk, with his wizened face. He was such a strange bird. Journey backwards, for heaven's sake – and that extraordinary coincidence that the words he had spoken in Edmund's voice were the last words Edmund had said to her . . .

She woke with a start when, next morning, the train jolted into Tientsin. Lin's black-bearded bodyguard escorted her off the train to the rank of rickshaws waiting outside the station. She was relieved that the general did not appear.

With a light heart, she gave the rickshaw boy instructions for Meadows Road. Her heart was bursting with excitement at the prospect of the life that lay ahead of her.

17

The Wolf Time

From the Journal of William Lampsett, Reuters correspondent, Tsinan, 15 April 1928

There is a lot more at stake tonight than the happiness of William Lampsett breaking his heart over a woman. A battle is about to begin that will define the future of a nation, and perhaps the world. Great forces have been stirred in this continent. The old Chinese empire is waking after centuries of sleep.

The ancient dragon has shuffled off its scales, and finds that the new skin itches. It tosses and turns. Every frustrated snort from its nostrils fires the hearts and minds of men to revolution and civil war; every irritable scratch of its talons tears further the feudal fabric that has resisted change for thousands of years. I have witnessed the cruelty and degradation that have resulted: burned homesteads, famine, the rapaciousness of warlords, the collapse of any order – but this is only the dragon adjusting to new circumstances. The suit will fit one day and shine more resplendently. I believe this passionately. This terrible war will end, and out of it will be forged a new China, a better China. Whoever wins – the Confucian Chinese warlord in Peking or the reformist Chinese warlord in Nanking – it will be China for the Chinese. The dragon will be comfortable again.

All that is to be determined now is the pace of change, which is what this battle will decide. Whatever happens, a powerful new force will take its place in the councils of the world, something not Western, not socialist, certainly not a liberal democracy, something unique and Chinese. And the awakened China will be strong.

Nations and Powers, who over the last centuries have used and abused her in her somnolence, beware the dragon's revenge!

When the orderly ushered him into the office, Henry Manners was surprised to see the general and his subordinate, Colonel Doihara, bent over what appeared to be a metal cage on a piece of newspaper on Taro's desk. It looked out of place in the otherwise elegant room, and stank.

'Ah, my friend, Henry-san. It is good of you to accept my invitation.' Taro welcomed him in with his usual good humour. 'You are in time to witness a little experiment. You did not know, perhaps, that Colonel Doihara is a naturalist in his spare time. He is sharing his hobby with us today.'

Doihara bowed curtly, the cold eyes expressionless. Manners nodded back. There was no love lost between them. He knew that Doihara was Taro's main link with the all-powerful Kokuryukai, the Black Dragon Society. In Taro's outer office he had seen two of the young firebrands associated with its more violent conspiracies, Colonels Seishiro and Komoto. Something more than a zoological experiment was clearly being planned today.

'Come over, Henry-san. Take a look,' said Taro.

In the cage were three rats. One was a large, glossy monster with fierce red eyes. The other two were separated from the bigger one by a mesh fence in which there was a latch that could be lifted with a loop of string. The two smaller rats were skeletal creatures with torn fur, scratches and bites; one was in a worse state than the other, cowering at the edge of the cage while the other prowled in circles over the straw.

'What of it?' said Manners, carefully. 'Doihara breeds rats. So what?'

'He breeds cannibal rats,' said Taro. 'He has trained them to eat only the embryos of their own kind. Once a day, he places baby rats through this aperture in the compartment containing the two small rats. They fight over the food because there is never enough. No food is given to the larger rat, but while the other two are fighting, Colonel Doihara opens the little door leading to the other cage. The big rat enters and takes what he needs. Neither of the others dares to challenge him. Anyway, they are too absorbed with denying the other a share. The result is that the large rat strengthens but the other two weaken. He is apparently content with this arrangement. Recently, however, one of the two small rats has sickened. It cannot defend itself. The balance of power is affected. It will be interesting to see, do you not think, what the big rat will do? Colonel Doihara and I have a bet on the outcome. Would you like to wager too, Henry-san?'

'I'll leave these games to the two of you,' he said.

'Oh, you disappoint me. I had taken you to be a gambling man,' grinned Taro. 'And as a journalist you must be interested in our current affairs.'

'What have rats to do with current affairs?'

'Do you not see similarities with the China of today? Warlords and nationalists struggle. The Powers, including imperial Japan – perhaps particularly imperial Japan – profit from the chaos. But what happens if only one Chinese contestant is left in the game? What happens if China unifies? The Nationalists seem poised now to take Peking, and I cannot see Chang Tso-lin offering effective resistance for long. He seems to be in the same piteous state as that poor animal whimpering against its cage there. What will the larger rat do now? Or the other smaller one, for that matter? Will it defend its turf against a larger predator? Fight him too?'

'Is that how you and Doihara see yourselves? As rats?' asked Manners.

'Big ones, Henry-san. Big ones.' Taro gave him an expansive smile. 'Now, let me explain our wager. Colonel Doihara is a pessimist. He believes that the two small rats will finally understand that they must take on the big rat if they are to be left any of the food, and that there will be a bloodbath in the cage with uncertain results, because two rats against one, even if one is weakened, will neutralise the power of the stronger one. I have more faith in the wisdom of Nature, and the cunning of species. I believe that the large rat will come to an accommodation with one of the two small rats. He will perhaps assist one to eliminate the other – then wait, like any sensible statesman, knowing that time and strength are on his side.'

'You put a lot of faith in the intelligence of rats,' said Manners.

'Rats are very intelligent,' said Taro. 'The successful ones. Let us begin our experiment.'

From a small container Doihara took two pink embryos and dropped them through the aperture on to the straw floor of the cage. Immediately all three rats stiffened, their whiskers and fur bristling. The stronger of the two small ones bent over an embryo and gulped it. With half still hanging from its mouth, the rat shrieked at its companion, which seemed to collapse, shrinking into itself at the side of the cage.

Doihara lifted the flap that controlled the door between the compartments. The big rat ran through, a sinuous movement of black fur, and stopped in front of the rat with the embryo in its mouth. There was a long, tense pause – then the larger rat struck, not against its squealing challenger but against the weak rat on the side of the cage. Its teeth sank into the back of its neck. There was a flurry of little limbs, and it was over. Manners watched in disgust as it began to eat its victim. The survivor of the two smaller rats appeared transfixed, staring at the big black shadow worrying the remains of its former cellmate. The embryo hung unmasticated from its teeth. It began to shiver, perhaps with fear, as it watched the dismemberment with its beady eyes.

'I win my wager,' said Taro quietly. 'There is a new status quo, Henry-san. Do not tell me you did not find that instructive.'

'The large rat will go for the other eventually,' said Manners. 'Doihara will get his bloodbath.'

'In time, but Nature is unhurried,' murmured Taro. 'There is a beautiful order to its process, do you not think?'

Manners laughed. 'What are you two planning now? I know your little parables and metaphors, Hideyoshi. There's always a sting in the tail. What are you trying to tell me? That Japan is going to eliminate Chang Tso-lin now he looks as if he's going to be defeated? Take over Manchuria? You must be mad if you think you can get away with that. More to the point, why are you telling me? What have I to do with it?'

General Taro rang a bell on his desk, and waved to the orderly to take away the cage. 'Let us sit down comfortably,' he said. 'You will find your whisky in its usual place. Doihara-san, do not go. What I have to say to Henry-san concerns what we were speaking about earlier.'

Taro sighed. 'Henry-san, of course you are right. Real life, as opposed to a pure experiment conducted under laboratory conditions, is complex. It is true that a weakened Chang Tso-lin is of little use to us and, yes, many of us dream of furthering our imperial ambitions, but we must not forget that we are speaking of someone who in the past has been a loyal ally. In any case, Japan is a civilised country, a founder member of the League of Nations. That any of us, even the most patriotic firebrands in the Kwantung army who believe that Manchuria is ours by right of blood, should be connected with assassination or unlawful annexation, is unacceptable, unthinkable. It would be terrible indeed if Chang Tso-lin should be killed. On the other hand if, in hypothetical circumstances, the train, say, in which he was travelling home were to be blown up by a bomb, planted by a Nationalist, it would lead to chaos, Henry-san, social unrest. We would be concerned for our citizens. If the situation got out of hand, if Manchuria descended into anarchy, well, in those circumstances the Kwantung army might have to reimpose order, but it would do so reluctantly, forced by events . . .'

'The Kwantung army would exert a peace-keeping role,' said Doihara.

'A peace-keeping role. Exactly,' said Taro, smiling.

'None of the other Powers could blame us,' said Doihara. 'We would be making the territory safe for our citizens.'

'Absolutely correct, as you British did when you took over Egypt to reimpose order in the last century. I believe you have been reimposing order there ever since. Anyway, it is forty years later and your troops have not left. Of course, the Suez Canal is one of your imperial interests as the SMR in Manchuria is one of ours.' Taro grinned broadly, but Manners did not take the bait.

'And just how hypothetical is it that Chang Tso-lin will be blown up in his train?' Manners asked softly.

'It is such an unpredictable, dangerous world,' said Taro, 'who knows what the Nationalists might be plotting? It is an interesting speculation, however. Generalissimo Chang is a well-protected man.

Doihara-san, hypothetically, how would you set about an assassination like this if you were a Nationalist? One could hardly plant a bomb on his train, could one? He would be bound to have the train searched thoroughly before it left the station.'

'A bomb could be planted on the line, General, to explode under Chang Tso-lin's carriage,' said Doihara. There was nothing speculative in his voice.

'I suppose they could do it that way,' said Taro. 'It would have to be well concealed. Yes, the Nationalists could put a bomb on the line, under a railway bridge, perhaps – but trains travel fast, Colonel. How would they guarantee that the plunger is pressed exactly at the moment that the generalissimo's carriage is above it?'

'The engine driver at the front of the train would decrease speed to make sure,' said Doihara.

'Yes, that would work,' said Taro. 'But, Colonel, Chang Tso-lin has his own loyal drivers. The Nationalist assassins would somehow have to switch them with men of their own.'

'An English official in the China Railways, if given inducements, might arrange that,' said Doihara.

'No,' said Manners. 'I won't do it.'

'Do what, Henry-san?' Taro enquired mildly.

'I see exactly where you're leading. You want me to persuade my railway-official contact to assist with this assassination. I've done enough dirty work for you. I won't be involved in the murder of Chang Tso-lin. I told you that I wanted to retire.'

Taro rose slowly from the armchair and yawned. He went back to his desk and sifted idly through the papers in his tray. As if inconsequentially he picked out a sheet covered with Chinese characters. 'I am so busy these days, Henry-san,' he murmured. 'You would not believe the sort of things that demand my attention, the favours people ask of me. Take this one. It is from one of Chang Tso-lin's subsidiary warlords with whom we are involved in the opium trade.' He slapped the side of his head. 'Of course, how stupid of me! You know him, Henry-san, from long ago. It is your old friend, Lin Fu-po. Or, rather, your enemy. I remember now, there is some sort of vendetta between you, isn't there? And you once asked me to remind him that you are under my protection.'

Manners's blood chilled. 'If you think you can scare me by threatening me with Lin . . .' he began.

'I wouldn't dream of it. No, as I said, I had forgotten about your connection. This letter is not about you anyway. It is about a woman. Lin is a strange man. Well, every warlord is eccentric. They are all corrupted by power to a greater or lesser extent. Lin is something of a collector. He collects statues, paintings and monuments for his mausoleum. I believe he has plundered half of China in his antiquarian zeal. Some of the things he collects are very odd. I am told he has in his possession the thighbone of one of the emperors. And a whole Neolithic skeleton to which he attributes extraordinary powers. He has some weird ideas, too, about ancient religions. His mania for collection goes beyond mere artefacts, however. He likes to collect people, Henry-san. Priests and *rinpoches*, whom he corrupts. And women, Henry-san, for his harem. Red-headed women particularly. I cannot think why. There is no accounting for sexual taste, is there? Well, we have helped him from time to time. Colonel Doihara has contacts in all the vice-rings, and in the past we have steered the odd Russian woman of the right colouring in his direction. These are only friendly favours for a partner in our commercial enterprise. As you know, the opium supply from the Shishan area is important to us – but recently, Henry-san, Lin has become importunate, not to say troublesome. In this letter he threatens to cut off our opium supplies unless we do him a specific favour. Not satisfied with the other women we have sent him, he has apparently seen one who fits his extraordinary requirements and, would you believe it?, wants us to kidnap her for him. Apparently, twenty years ago he had sexual relations with her mother and now thinks the daughter is just the thing. As I said, there is no accounting for sexual taste. I suppose we will have to do it for him – after all, business is business – but it will be tricky. She is an Englishwoman, living in the international concession in Tientsin. I assume that is why he is asking us to arrange it instead of snatching her himself.'

'Who is she?' Manners croaked, although he knew.

'Well, that's the most extraordinary coincidence,' said Taro. 'Do you remember some time ago I had the foolish idea that a young woman called Catherine Airton was your daughter, and you always denied it? Believe it or not, it's the same woman. Lucky for you she isn't your daughter, or we would have an embarrassing conflict of interest on our hands . . . What's the matter, old friend?'

'You bastard,' Manners muttered, his knuckles whitening on his chair arm.

'Of course,' Taro continued, as if he had not spoken, 'there may be other ways to deal with this matter, equally complicated and troublesome, but the truth is that General Lin has begun lately to show signs of unreliability. His sanity is questionable, as this request makes clear. He has also become rather remote from daily affairs. Recently we have been dealing with his deputy, a young officer called Ti, for whom our Captain Fuzumi in the SMR garrison in Shishan has the highest praise. He has sometimes said in his reports how much more efficient it would be if Ti were running Shishan instead of his boss. I imagine that if we can organise a kidnapping we can presumably organise a coup. It might even be easier. Of course, the most important issue for us is how to ensure a continued supply of opium. What would you advise me to do, Henry-san? As an old friend?'

'What guarantee will you give me?' whispered Manners.

'Guarantee?' Taro laughed. 'Have you not heard the old Chinese expression: "An agreement between gentlemen is as a glass of clear water handed between friends."'

'Tell me what you want me to do,' said Manners, defeated.

'I would have another whisky if I were you,' said Doihara, smiling for the first time.

Lao Tang danced with delight when he saw Catherine on the front porch. Half laughing, half crying, he pulled her upstairs to show her how he had kept all her things exactly as she had left them because he always knew that one day Missy would return.

She looked at her dresses hanging in the cupboard, the scatter of makeup and jewellery on her dressing-table, and felt as if they belonged to somebody else. After she had bathed, she stood for a long moment in front of the chest of drawers before she picked out a pair of panties and a chemise. But even as the soft silk rippled over her skin, she felt that she was putting on a stranger's clothes.

And she was thrilled by the sense of liberation she experienced. An intruder in her own bedroom, she realised how long had been the journey she had travelled since last she had stood in front of this mirror.

She was no longer the glittering, tinselled Catherine, whose image still grinned out of a photograph on the window-sill in party costume with George. She was not yet certain who the new Catherine might be, but she had gone a long way towards finding out, and she looked forward to getting back to Tsinan to learn more. What she was sure of now, with a certainty that stiffened her spine and spread a glow through her limbs, was that she no longer wanted *this*.

In the rickshaw coming here she had thought how wonderful it would be to be clean again, to consign her shabby nurse's kit to *Lao* Tang's laundry while she put on a comfortable frock. Now, running her eyes over the extravagant dresses, she felt a surge of revulsion. She was about to confront George. She was going to make the break from her former, idle existence. She would not wear borrowed clothes to do so.

Laughing, she unclipped the suspenders and stripped the shimmering silk off her legs. Down came the frilly panties. Over her head rustled the delightful Canton chemise. Naked, she bounded back to the frayed leather holdall in the corner of the room, and tipped its contents on to the bed. Out cascaded the folded woollen skirts, the simple blouses, the sensible drawers and brassières, the capes and headscarves, the single cheap frock, the rubber wash bag, her sandals and everything else that had marked her life for the last two years, and she smiled with affection for these worn items that had accompanied her. They seemed to define her happiness.

But following them, fluttering out from the bottom of the bag, flapping to rest on Willie's charred diary, was a note. She recognised the paper immediately. It had come from the pad on which Edmund had scribbled his prescriptions.

Standing naked by the bed, staring at it, she felt chilled, although the room was warm, and goosebumps prickled on her legs and arms. It had not been there when she had packed the holdall. Edmund must have hidden it when she was not paying attention, thrusting it deeply under her clothes so that she would not find it immediately. She gazed at it, not wanting to open it. If Edmund had used the few moments while he was packing his things to write a letter to her, then taken such precautions to conceal it, it was unlikely to contain good news. Her blood rushing, feeling a little dizzy, she picked it up.

Dearest Catherine,

You will understand why I have made my escape from these soldiers. I cannot abandon my patients. What may break your heart a little is that I have also decided that it would be better if we do not see each other for a while.

Not until I am sure that you are sure – absolutely sure – that you want me.

Oh, I know that you gave yourself generously, and that you believe you love me – but your love for me has grown in the unnatural circumstances of a war, and partly, I fear, as a refuge for your damaged spirit after the terrible experiences you have suffered. You are such a creature of life, but our love has flourished in an atmosphere of death and destruction. What haunts me is the fear that it will not survive the reality that peace will bring, when our difference in age and social conventions may bite again. You need time on your own to determine what you feel.

Your first reaction will be to rebel against these words. Your stubbornness, courage and resourcefulness, your sense of duty will prompt you to find a means to return to Tsinan. I will not welcome you. Nor will Huber. I have spoken to him, and he agrees.

Believe me, the thought of losing you withers my soul – but I ask for a separation of six months. That should be long enough for you to decide if you really want me. If you do, then I am yours, and we will find a way. If not, I will always remember the two happiest years of my life with my angel by my side. I love you, darling, I love you more than life,

Your Edmund

Eventually, after she had cried, after she had laughed, after she had absorbed this new disappointment, and deposited it in that pocket of her soul where she kept all the other disappointments; after she had locked the folded note, along with Willie's journal, in the drawer where she had consigned to oblivion all the memories of a life she wished to forget – photographs and keepsakes of her mother, her father, Marya, Olga, Mamasha, and Edmund (because his photograph had ended up there, too, when she had married George) – she spent an hour in front of the dressing-table and made up her face to look like that of the stranger in whose room she had found herself. She put the discarded underwear back on, then picked from the wardrobe a colourful looking dress – a slip of white silk, patterned with green leaves and strawberries that matched the colour of this stranger's hair – and put on a pair of the stranger's red shoes. Then she went downstairs to George.

He was waiting in the living room, unchanged, wearing an immaculate pearl-grey suit and waistcoat that she remembered, with a tie and matching handkerchief in the pattern of his racing colours that she had once given him for Christmas. He was leaning in his habitual place by the mantelpiece, smoking his usual cigar, running a hand over his sleek, centrally parted hair, and grinning at her with his white teeth.

'Well, well,' he said. 'Ravishing as ever. I'd expected you to be grim and starched like Florence Nightingale after a bad day in Scutari. Trust you to break the mould, Catherine. Most heroines tend to be rather plain. Coarse features bring out the inner Christian light or some such. Appropriate for prayer meetings, and salutary portraits in the corridors of girls' schools and reformatory establishments . . .'

'Hello, George,' she said coldly. 'I see you've not lost your penchant for sarcasm.'

'I'm not being sarcastic at all, old girl. News is all over town that you're back. Some story was picked up from the Chinese papers about how you were rescued in the nick of time by a Chinese general from the sack of a burning city. You're a heroine. No question. Two years of devoted work with my bro saving lives. You're up there with saintly Willie, whose martyrdom is bringing tears to every matron's eyes.'

'Really?' she said. 'I thought I was the scarlet woman who'd gone off to live in sin and support the Bolshevik cause.'

'No, no, that's old hat. Nobody gives a toss for Bolsheviks nowadays, and you've been out of the news for so long that your peccadilloes are *passé*. Anyway, all your subsequent good works have laundered any dirty linen you left behind. You've got to understand, old thing, how public opinion works. You see, now that it looks as if the war's about to end, and good old General Cash My Cheque is apparently no longer the rabid Red monster but the great white hope of civilisation and commerce, we're all quite keen to have a few war heroes of our own up our sleeves so we can join the celebrations and suck up to the winner. White man keeping his end up, that sort of thing. Poor Willie fits the bill perfectly, of course. Newspapers love dead correspondents, but you're up there by a nose, no doubt of it. Play it properly, we could have you as the loyal keeper of the deceased martyr's shrine, the high priestess of Willie's memory, with me, Robby and his other friends as mournful pallbearers. We might even make Robby a vestal virgin. It could run for weeks.' He puffed happily at his cigar.

'Tasteless as ever. How's Robby coping?' she asked.

'Oh, everybody's bearing round. Sending him flowers, that sort of thing. Not that that will help him. Now that his protector has joined the ranks of the dear departed, what he probably needs most is cash. He spends half the day unconscious. Odds are being laid in the club whether he'll be sober enough when the will's read. Presumably that's what he's waiting for – but Robby's an irrepressible cove. He emerges in the evening for parties, and sits there like Grief on a Monument while the old ladies cluster round and ask him to tell them what a great fellow Willie was. Sort of like a plump Patroclus mourning Achilles – or was it the other way round? Anyway, you'll see him tonight and you can decide for yourself. The Aglerns are putting on a bash for him.'

'What on earth makes you think I'll go with you to a party, George?' she asked.

'You're my wife,' he said. 'I'm going. Invitation's open to you too, old sport. What an extraordinary question.'

'After two years you expect me just to pick up where I left off?'

'Well, why else have you come back?'

'To ask you to give me a divorce, George,' she said.

He laughed. 'That old tune,' he said. 'Out of the question now, old girl. Can't have heroines going round divorcing their husbands. Wouldn't look good at all.'

'I'm in love with Edmund,' she said hollowly, thinking of the letter.

'Like you were once before?' He smiled, looking at her steadily. 'And where is dear Edmund? On the next train up from Tsinan? No, he can't be, can he? There won't be any trains for a while. Truth is, he's not coming, is he?'

'He has his hospital to look after,' she said.

'Yes, my dear, certainly he does. Is that what he told you? "Catherine, old chum, pop up to Tientsin, would you? I'm a bit busy now, but you go off with this obliging general and get a divorce from Georgy. When you're ready, come back and I'll welcome you with open arms." With a few "You're mine forevers" mingled in, of course. Did he throw you a bit of pocket money while he was about it? Or is trusting old Georgy expected to provide room and board while these proceedings take place?'

'I thought you might be gentlemanly about it.' Her voice was so small as to be almost inaudible.

George observed her, taking a long pull on his cigar. 'Truth is, noble Edmund's done it again, hasn't he?' he said. 'There are horses like that, you know. Hyperions in the paddock. Great, gleaming, shining things, full of stamina. Look like real winners in the flesh. Punters put all their money on the nose, but when it comes to the starting-gate, they shy away – and there are always good excuses afterwards. Oh, yes, mucus on the lungs, state of the ground, too wet, too dry – but the truth is, they ain't runners. Don't have it in them to commit, and always for the best of reasons. In Edmund's case, selfless ones. What did he tell you? That he wants you to be sure? Or has he established some sensible period of time in which the two of you should be apart while you both think about things rationally?'

Catherine lowered her head, tears in her eyes.

'Have you never thought why Edmund spends his life hiding up mountains or rushing off to wars?' continued George. 'It's very honourable and all that, saving lives, serving humanity, risking his life for others. It's also rather easy, believe it or not. Oh, there are tough decisions, sure. Save this man, leave that man to die, but that's all process. A bit dispassionate when you come to think of it. When it comes to the big decisions of life, ordinary things like commitment to another human being, marriage, society – well, he's not so good at finding his way round that, is he? Life's a bit too scary when actual responsibility's involved. Tell me, Catherine . . . No, don't. I'll tell you. This affair of yours is quite a recent thing, isn't it? And you made the first move, didn't you? You took the initiative, and he followed you meekly to your bed. Am I wrong?'

Keeping his eyes on her, he moved to an armchair and sat down.

'You've been down there together for – what? Two years? And, no doubt, all that time he gazed at you with big mooning eyes and repressed emotion, but he didn't say a thing, did he? I know my brother Edmund, you see.' Savagely he stubbed out his cigar in the ashtray. 'I knew all along you weren't fucking him, Catherine, whatever gossip there was around, because I knew as soon as you did he'd find some noble excuse and send you back to me, as you've come now, with your head tucked inside your damned tail.'

'It wasn't like that,' she said slowly. 'You're a bastard, George. A bastard.'

'And you're an adulteress, my love. As I've always told you, we're a matched pair.'

'I've changed, George. I'm not that Catherine any more.'

'Yes, darling,' he said. 'And I'm Old King Cole. I'm sure I'm being very remiss. I should be asking after your holiday. Just take it that I'm overwhelmed with pleasure that you're home again. As we all are. Oh, by the way, Jenny phoned. They're back here too. Longing to see you. Lionel was even singing your praises at the club this morning. You see what weathercocks we all are. I promise you, it'll all be very easy. You can just slip into the old groove. I wouldn't be surprised if they clap you when you make your appearance this evening. Maybe for best effect you should wear your nurse's uniform, but I'd just as soon you didn't. Dowdiness doesn't suit you.'

'I hate you!'

'That's the passion I like to see. I'll offer you a deal, Catherine, because fair's fair, and I always was a betting man. It suits me to have you back on my arm again for a while. I'm rather tired of playing the poor, put-upon husband deserted by his dearest. And you're smelling of roses now, so I'll enjoy basking in the fragrance for a bit. Haven't had much success with old China Coast for a while. If you play along, I'll give you a divorce when I'm ready. Two years? Three? How about that? I'll do the decent thing, all *mea culpas* on me, and give you a fat settlement. Alternatively, if my dear brother does come back to claim you, I'll do the same, with double the settlement, whenever he appears. I'd be very surprised if he does, but you're welcome to live in hope.'

He opened his cigar box, and picked out a Corona. 'In the meanwhile, we'll go back to the same arrangement as before, shall we? Oh, and, Catherine, if you do pick up any of your old habits again, please be discreet. Nobody in the world could be more complaisant than long-suffering George but, remember, we do have a name to uphold here. If you shame me, I'll take you through the courts and throw you out on the world with nothing. If you try to run off again, I'll do the same, for desertion.' He gave her his most amiable grin. 'Does all that sound fair, darling? It's so nice to have you back. Old Tang thinks he's in cook's heaven. He's missed you dreadfully, as of course have I. Shall we say seven thirty in the hall? I think your grey and white taffeta may not go amiss tonight. Something a little sober. After all, we're still in mourning for poor Willie, aren't we?'

She went to the party, as George had known she would. That first evening, she told herself she was only doing so because she owed it to Robby. It was a face-saver of sorts. Before she left, wearing the white and grey taffeta as George had requested, with her white gloves on her arms and her South Sea pearls round her neck, she unlocked the drawer and brought out Willie's diary. He had written about his friendship with Robby shortly before he died. Perhaps that would comfort him, she thought.

She was not, of course, the sparkling Catherine she had been before, but nobody expected her to be. They did not clap her, but everyone came up at some point to congratulate her on her bravery. Old Mr Aglern had tears in his eyes when he greeted her, and Lionel, who was basking in his recent promotion as number two at the Maritime Customs Service in Tientsin, proposed a toast to her, retelling the story of her selfless nursing 'while bullets flew and cannons roared' during the Nanking Outrage, at the same time paying due deference to the heroism of his 'darling Jenny', who was blushing at the other end of the table. George preened, although he hid his smugness well under the mask of stern solicitousness that he had developed for the occasion, while he escorted her round the room, keeping a firm hand on her arm, as if he was concerned that memories of the terrible things that had happened to her might overwhelm her; once or twice, when nobody was looking, he gave her a wink.

Of course, Willie Lampsett was the hero of the hour, and tributes to him flowed. Everyone recalled an act of friendship or generosity that Willie had shown them, and there was much speculation about how far he would have gone, had he not met such an untimely end; his brilliant perception and analysis would certainly have brought him into politics once he returned home, Aglern pontificated.

Catherine kept quiet, watching Robby, who was sitting on Mrs Aglern's right, with equally splendid matrons on his other side and opposite him. Pale and puffy-faced, he also maintained a dignified silence, except for the occasional snuffle, after which he would dab his eyes with a mauve handkerchief that he took from his sleeve.

It was only when coffee had been served, and the gentlemen had returned to the sitting room, that Catherine had a chance to talk to him alone. In fact, it was one of those tragic moments that the assembled throng had been anticipating: the occasion for the heroine to comfort the hero's friend. Rather obviously, they were left alone together in an alcove.

Robby embraced her, bursting into tears. 'We both loved him, Catherine,' he sobbed. 'I don't know what I'm going to do now. Only you understand how I feel.'

'He was thinking of you just before he died,' she said, taking his flabby hand.

Robby pulled it away. His features twisted into a snarl. 'How do you know that? He never thought of me, not after he met you. He left me for those bloody wars for two whole years and the few occasions he came back he could only talk of you. I hated you, Catherine. He called you his muse, even after the diabolical way you treated him.'

'I know,' she said. 'I'm sorry.'

'Sorry won't bring him back. You as good as sent him to his death. I think sometimes he wanted to die and that was why he took on all those dangerous assignments. Because of what you did to him. Oh, I'm sorry, Catherine. I didn't mean to say that.'

'You had a right to,' she said. 'I can see that's how you might look at it. Listen, Robby, I've not told anyone, but I saw Willie just before he went off on that last campaign. In Tsinan the day he left.'

Robby stared at her.

'It wasn't a happy meeting,' she said. 'He was very bitter – but I promise you, Robby, he was getting over me by the end, and he was remembering how only you had been his true friend. Here,' she said, reaching into her bag. 'This is his diary. I'm giving it to you. There's a lot about me in it, and it's very painful, and private, but he would want you to have it. He knew how much you loved him.'

'How – how did you get it?'

'One of the Russian survivors from the train brought it to our surgery. He knew I'd been a friend of Willie. I kept it for you.'

'But if it's about you, don't you want it?'

'No,' she said. 'It's not really about me. In the end all I am is a sort of muse, as you say. It's about Willie. It contains his poems. It's him, Robby, speaking from the page. I'm sure he'd want you to have it, to cherish his memory. It'll be his private voice that you can keep with you in the long years ahead.'

Robby was staring at her, the book between them. 'Thank you,' he whispered. 'I'll look after this with my life. Catherine, you're my only friend. Those things I said about you . . .'

She lifted her arms, and allowed him to cry on her shoulder. When he was calmer, he kissed her on both cheeks, and put on a brave smile when George, a cigar between his lips, came to collect her because the Aglerns wanted to be photographed with her.

* * *

Over the next few weeks there were more social engagements. She went along with them, playing a part.

The night after the first party she had lain in her bed, sleepless, considering her options, and decided that she had none but to accept George's distasteful terms. George had been a bastard, but at least he had promised her a divorce. He had been fair in his way. He had behaved in character. She could handle George.

But Edmund's letter had unsettled and hurt her. Oh, yes, she acknowledged angrily, he had behaved in character, too: he was such a damned gentleman. She had chosen to fall in love with a saint – what was she to expect other than scrupulous unselfishness? If it was unselfishness . . . She realised, to her shame, that George's snide and all too perceptive comments had rattled her; part of her had ignominiously believed them. And he was right: this wasn't the first time Edmund had let her down. He had once played the coward before when he had run away to his sanctuary up a mountainside.

But that was so long ago, she told herself. The circumstances had been different. She had been a giddy girl, and Edmund had been weak, recovering from the effects of the Great War. During the last two years they had both changed. What they had endured, they had endured together. Life had hardened them, made them stronger. Their shared experience at the front had forged an unbreakable bond.

She forced herself to reconsider his letter. He said he loved her. He had certainly behaved as if he did right up to when he had left her. She remembered his kiss and the tenderness of that whispered goodbye. Was it not sensible for him to concern himself about the practicalities of their affair? And wasn't there something generous and self-sacrificing, courageous, even, in his giving her the freedom to decide? She resented that he still felt he had to put their love to the test – she wished he could have trusted her more – but she thought she understood his reasons. Willie's re-emergence must have upset him. Was he not doing, as he always did, the honourable thing? His letter had been harsh, but it offered hope. He did say it would be only a six-month separation, and then, if she still wanted him, they would 'find a way' . . .

Eventually her spirit and her sense of honour rebelled. She

determined, despite her fears, to give Edmund the benefit of the doubt. She owed him that. She owed it to herself. Without Edmund . . . She could not bear to think of it . . .

And, after all, a wait in Tientsin would not be onerous. She could shine at parties sleep-walking. There was even something comical about the way she was being lionised; it revealed, like nothing else, the hypocrisy of this lotus world. If George wanted her to perform she would: she would dazzle them – and then she would walk away on Edmund's arm, without looking back, without even bothering to show her scorn.

Towards dawn, she had stretched in the soft sheets and smiled. She might even enjoy it. It was a small price to pay for divorce, honour and freedom.

Meanwhile peace was coming. The warlord forces were retreating in disarray towards Peking. The word was that Chiang Kai-shek would be in the capital within a month. Now there was no praise high enough for the man of the hour. Catherine listened sardonically at dinner parties to businessmen praising his ruthless treatment of the unions, diplomats approving his moderate approach to the treaties question, society women forgiving him everything because he had recently married a Christian woman: Soong Mei-ling, sister of the wife of Sun Yat-sen. Not a few church groups wrote to him asking him if he might consider becoming their patron. Catherine thought it ironic that Jenny, who had been raped by his soldiers, had thought fit to buy a portrait of him at a charity do. Jenny had tried to explain to her: 'It'll please Lionel,' she said. 'People are now saying that whatever happened in Nanking was committed by renegade warlords or Communists, not Nationalists. Don't you see, darling?' she pleaded. 'Lionel says we must draw a line under the past because we have to work with these people. It's in everybody's interests.'

Catherine had laughed. 'Well,' she said, 'if you can draw a line under what happened to you, I'm delighted for you. I'm not sure that I can forget so quickly.'

Jenny's eyes were as large as soup plates with anxiety. 'Catherine, you won't tell? You promised.'

Catherine was happy to go along with any nonsense. She didn't care. She was just waiting for the six months to be over, and for Edmund to return.

Of course, she had no means of anticipating that Robby, once he had read his friend's diary, had recognised that the last testament of a war hero and poet would be journalistic dynamite, and the publication rights would guarantee him a fortune. The diary's publication in serial form in the *Peking and Tientsin Times*, three weeks after Catherine's return to society, and its later syndication to other newspapers around the Far East, was a sensation, both literary and controversial. Robby soon had the income to turn Willie's former bungalow into a chic nightclub, famed for the cocktails designed by the now wealthy proprietor. 'Willie's Bar' became a popular haunt of journalists and socialites alike: they enjoyed Robby's racy conversation as much as their speculation on his relationship with his handsome young Chinese partner, who poured the drinks. Due acknowledgement had been given, of course, by his grieving friend and torchbearer to Willie himself, whose poems were printed and framed on the walls, alongside photographs of the great war correspondent on his various campaigns. In keeping with the legend, there were a number of photographs also of the love of his life, the scarlet woman who had driven him to his tragic death. Those in the know would tell each other that the room on the side, furnished in rather louche Oriental style with a Chinese bed and opium couches, where Robby sometimes allowed gentlemen to entertain their Russian escorts, had been Willie's bedroom, where the great liaison had taken place.

To give him his due, George had taken the serialisation and subsequent scandal philosophically. It offered him a chance to give Catherine another witty little lecture on the vagaries of public opinion. He even congratulated her – it was good going even for her to transform herself from Florence Nightingale into Mata Hari in less than a month. Of course, he added, any deal that they had had was now off. 'You've committed the one unforgivable, my dear. You were found out. Doesn't leave me an option, I'm afraid. Caesar's wife and all that. You do understand, darling?' Since Catherine was now ostracised by society, he continued, she was hardly likely to be receiving any invitations so there did not seem much point in continuing the masquerade. He told her to look on the bright side. She would get her divorce, but without the settlement. He might take his time over it, he added, as he packed up his clothes to move into the club. There would be at least a few months' mileage for him in the role of the noble betrayed husband. 'Chaps are saying I'm Generosity in the Pageant allowing a fallen wife to stay on in Meadows Road. I've been demonstrating so much stiff upper lip lately that it hurts,' he joked.

Catherine knew, of course, that he was waiting for her to beg, and inevitably she did. 'All right, Catherine,' he said. 'I won't do anything about a divorce until those six months Edmund promised you are up, and if he does come back for you within that time I'll make myself look like the guilty party, and give you a trousseau to be proud of. Not that I think he will, but hope's eternal! It'd be the comedy of the season if he did. After all this, for you to appear in court as the innocent and me as the adulterer? My reputation for *noblesse oblige* would be guaranteed for ever!' And, laughing, he had left the house with his bags.

Catherine found herself alone again, secluded in the house, with nobody to turn to, no money, and not the slightest idea of what she would do. Between them the brothers had trapped her in limbo.

Colonel Ti himself arrived with a platoon of soldiers. They had already kicked in the door before Martha and Lan-hua tumbled into the corridor. They saw the bayonets and Lan-hua screamed. They ran down the hall to the classroom where Ming was teaching the Chow sisters. He ignored the eruption, and continued to write his Nationalist slogans on the blackboard. Martha and Lan-hua backed away when Ti entered the room. Martha noticed that Captain Fuzumi was with them: he leaned against the doorway, smiling at her and bobbing his head in a polite bow.

The two girls were hunched together on the bench. One was weeping. Ming turned, carefully placing his chalk on the tray. He glanced coldly at Ti, and said, 'If you have official b-business with me p-p-perhaps you can wait in the common room. This lesson will shortly be over.'

'This lesson is already over,' said Ti. 'By official proclamation of the Yamen this school is closed. And you, my friend, are to be investigated for treason.'

'I d-do not recognise your authority to close this school,' said Ming, 'and there is no t-treason in teaching the principles of our republic. Please leave. You are disturbing my class.'

Ti laughed. 'This is quite a reunion, isn't it? Lan-hua.' He acknowledged her with a nod. 'I heard you'd come here. Revolution disappointed you, did it?' He shrugged. 'It's rather sad. The Lei family was so respected in Tientsin, but look what's become of you. My father tells me he had to rescue your doltish brother from penury. He's pathetic, but at least he isn't a traitor, while you, Lei Ming, are hypocritical even in your sedition. You preach the virtue of being Chinese yet you live with a foreign whore. And, Lan-hua – well, you're pretty as ever, but where's your bobbed hair? Are you trying to hide the fact that you're a Bolshevik? You, too, are under investigation, by the way.'

He turned towards the weeping students. 'And who do we have here? Whose little minds have we been poisoning today? Well, well, it's Dr Chow's daughters. What a small world. One of these days we will have to visit the hospital. I have been receiving the most unfavourable reports about your parents' activities . . .'

'Don't you dare touch those children!' shouted Ming, stepping down from the rostrum.

'They look grown-up to me,' said Ti. 'What are they? Seventeen and sixteen? They're already attractive women, don't you think, Sergeant?' He nodded to one of his men, who grinned, showing broken teeth. 'Anyway, quite old enough to know right from wrong, and to understand what treason is. Perhaps there is hope for them. You can be sure I will be lenient with them, if they give evidence voluntarily against their parents. I don't need evidence against you, old friend. I see our enemy's rag hanging on the wall. Sergeant, pull it down.'

'You will not touch it!' shouted Ming, pressing his back against the flag. 'I will not let your bloodstained hands defile it!'

'Ming, please,' said Martha. Ti laughed. He glanced at Fuzumi, who grinned back as if they were sharing a private joke

Suddenly Ming stood to full attention. His eyes shone. He raised his head and began to sing the Kuomintang anthem. '*San min chu-yi, wu tang suo chong . . .*'

'Silence that noise, Sergeant,' said Ti. Martha shrieked, and so, a moment later, did Lan-hua and the girls as two of Ti's men ran forward and began methodically to hit Ming in the stomach with the butts of their rifles. Somehow he managed to keep upright. The men stepped back to allow the sergeant to swing a heavy, iron-tipped cudgel. Blood poured down the side of Ming's face, staining his moustache, his gown and his scarf, but his mouth continued to croak out: '*Yi chian min-kuo, tuo chin ta lu . . .*' The sergeant swung the cudgel again. Ming staggered. His hand clutched the flag. It draped over him as he fell, his dazed eyes blinked above the white sun that half covered his face. He still tried to sing. The sergeant, using all his strength, swung the cudgel down again, and Ming was silent.

Martha, yelling incoherently, ran forward. One of the soldiers brought his rifle butt down on the back of her head. She collapsed on her knees, but tried to crawl through the desks towards her husband. The soldiers began to kick her in the head and the stomach. She felt something break inside her and an agonising pain in her womb. She could no longer move.

'People's stupidity always amazes me,' she heard Ti say. 'It wasn't as if we had come to arrest them – yet. Mind you, the violence demonstrated by this teacher and his wife was certainly treasonable. Don't you think so, Sergeant?'

'Yes, sir, very treasonable.' She heard the sound of boots clicking over the floor. She tried to force open her eyes. She saw Ti approaching Lan-hua and the girls, who were cowering behind one of the desks.

'Just look at them,' Ti said. 'You can see the guilt on their faces. What are we do with them? I suppose we had better get on with the interrogation of this one, the Communist sympathiser. I'll handle it, Sergeant. Upstairs, I think. Meanwhile you had better get rid of these poor, corrupted children.'

'Yes, sir,' said the sergeant. 'Excuse me, sir.' The muttering voice became confidential. 'You did say they were both adults, sir. There's a table in the next room. Me and my men could . . .'

Ti laughed. Martha saw him brush the hair and cheeks of the girls with his gloved hands. Lan-hua clutched them closer to her.

'N-no-o,' Martha tried to cry, but all that came out was a croak.

'Come, come, Sergeant, where do you think we are?' Ti turned. 'We're not on campaign, you know. Anyway, there'll be time for that later, once we have investigated their parents and find them guilty of sedition.' He smiled. 'They're sweet little things. But we are dealing with their teachers today.' He clapped his hands. 'Let go of them, Lan-hua, my pretty. Off you go, you two. Do give my best wishes to your father and tell him I'm looking forward to calling on him soon.'

The Chow sisters, whimpering, sidled past the soldiers. Fuzumi stepped aside to let them pass, giving another of his polite bows.

'Captain Fuzumi,' Ti said, 'have you seen enough? I think you can report that we have been attentive to the complaints of the SMR.'

'Oh, yes, Colonel. My superiors will be more than satisfied. Do let me know the results of your — interrogation of this Communist suspect.' He squealed with mirth.

Martha must have blacked out. When she looked up again the Japanese was gone. She was not sure how much time had passed. Through the mist that was covering her eyes, she saw that Ti had grabbed Lan-hua's hair and twisted her body so her spine arced backwards. 'It has been a long, long time since I had a conversation with her,' he was telling his sergeant. 'I knew her before. Did you know that? Oh, yes. It is about time that we were reacquainted. My dear one,' he added in a whisper, viciously pulling back her head, 'do you know there has been hardly a day that I have not thought about you? My pretty fiancée, do you still believe I'm not good enough for you? Sergeant, watch these two. I am going to take her upstairs now to conduct her interrogation in private.'

Blearily Martha watched as he dragged her friend out of the door by the hair. She heard the thump of his boots, Lan-hua's squeals of pain and the brush of her body up the wooden stairs. She swooned again.

She came back to her senses, and the pain; her dress was wet with blood from her miscarriage. She concentrated, however, on moving her body, inch by inch at a time, towards where Ming was lying under his flag. After a long while, she managed to touch his ankle.

The soldiers watched her progress, laughing and egging her on, while they waited for their commander to finish his rape of the girl upstairs. He was obviously taking his time about it, they joked. Who wouldn't with such a pretty thing? After a while they got bored of watching Martha, and lit cigarettes, chatting about the basketball match that was scheduled against the SMR garrison that weekend.

Eventually they all left, after smashing the furniture in the classroom and confiscating all the books. Martha felt no pain any more. She lay there, watching them. When they were gone, she used all her strength to pull herself closer to Ming, who was unconscious and breathing heavily through his broken face. She rested his bleeding head on her bosom and sang an old Yiddish nursery song that she remembered from childhood. Then she lay for a long time listening to the quiet around her. The far-off street noises seemed only to intensify the silence. After a while, she became aware of Lan-hua, slumped beside them. Her clothes were torn, she was bleeding at the mouth and her face was covered with bruises. There was a vacant expression in the slit of the one eye that could be seen. There were criss-cross wounds on her cheeks and forehead, which Colonel Ti had cut with a razor to destroy her beauty.

'Lan-hua,' Martha whispered. Her own voice, almost inaudible, startled her, and temporarily confused her. 'You have to get help for us.' She struggled to make the right words. 'A – a doctor.'

Lan-hua stared at her. She began to cry, and the eye became invisible among her welling tears.

'I know, sister,' Martha muttered. 'I know.' She felt Lan-hua's cold hands clutching her own and saw the battered face move closer. The cracked lips were quivering and the childlike face behind the destroyed features seemed to plead.

'They won't win,' Lan-hua sobbed. 'They won't – they won't win.'

'No, sister,' Martha said. She felt very tired. With the arm that was not holding Ming she reached for Lan-hua, and gently pulled her head to rest on the other side of her breast.

'There are revolutionaries in the hills.' Lan-hua was crying. '*Hong huzi*. Guerrilla fighters. Resisting. They'll win one day. We can join them. We can . . .' Her cries ended in a flood of sobbing.

'Yeah, sister, sure we can,' Martha murmured, stroking Lan-hua's hair. 'Sure we'll win. We'll all go together, you and Ming and me, and find the freedom-fighters. When we're better.'

She was so tired. She would sleep for a while, she decided, and then she would work out what to do . . .

When, later, Dr Chow, alerted by his daughters, arrived at the school, Lan-hua had been the only conscious person in the room, and there was little sense he could make out of her. She was murmuring some revolutionary song, a vacant smile on her damaged face. He thought he had arrived too late, but the others were alive – if barely. He had no time to treat them there, and Lan-hua was no help to him, so he had to get his wife and daughters, whom he had left with their hurriedly snatched possessions in the mule cart, to come in and carry them. With Ming, Martha and Lan-hua concealed in the back, it was nerve-racking for the family when their cart passed the guards at the city gates. Dr Chow's wife had to put her hand over Lan-hua's mouth to prevent the mad girl from singing.

The newspapers still came to Meadows Road. At least George's malice had not extended to cancelling the subscriptions, or perhaps it amused him to think that she was keeping track of what was going on in the outside world. Once, during one of his infrequent visits to the house to collect his golf clubs and check his bills, he came into the sitting room and saw her studying the latest war analyses in the *Peking and Tientsin Times*. 'My, darling, you're becoming quite the military expert – a regular Clausewitz,' he had told her. 'We'll have you lecturing soon at the Retired Servicemen's League! "Musings of an English Nurse on the Campaigns of General Cash My Cheque!" Alas, old thing, I don't think a study of warlord troop movements will be any horoscope to determine the day dear old bro flies back here on Cupid's wing. War's long left Tsinan and there's nothing to have stopped him hopping on a ferry from Tsingtao already, if he'd really wanted to. Surely he must know that the Tientsin service is running again. But you keep at it. As I've said before, hope's eternal. Would you like me to send you the steamships' passenger manifests along with the newspapers?' And he had left, chuckling and whistling. On another day, when he was checking the mail waiting for him on the hall table, he had sighed and said, 'Don't see any love letters from Edmund here. What a shame!'

Catherine would ignore him, refusing to speak to him unless she had to. It was an irony, she thought, that having been ostracised by society she had imposed Coventry on the one person she could talk to – but there it was. She did not care. Society no longer interested her. She knew that if she had wanted it there was a set in the city who would have been happy to see her. Shortly after the publication of Willie's diaries she had received a number of visits from young men she had known, sometimes intimately, in the past, bringing flowers and consolation. She had slammed the door in the faces of the eager Johnnies, Ruperts and Freddies, and later told *Lao* Tang that she would not be at home to any caller.

Her only female visitor had been Jenny who, red-faced and embarrassed, had come one dusk heavily veiled, terrified and thrilled at the same time by her courage in breaking social convention. 'Lionel doesn't know I'm here,' she told Catherine, 'but I just wanted to tell you how brave I think you are. You're a liberated woman and we're all being beastly to you. Just to let you know that there's one person in Tientsin who supports you utterly. Utterly,' she emphasised. 'And if there's anything I can do to help you as you once helped me, I will.' Catherine had thanked her and asked what she proposed to do. Jenny had looked uncomfortable, and said she could not think of anything at the moment – things were a little difficult – but if anything changed she would be the first to put out a helping hand. Catherine had hidden a smile, and offered her more tea. Only as Jenny was leaving did she suddenly remember why she had come. She glanced nervously at the shadows in the corner of the room, then pulled out an envelope from her bag. 'This is from Mother,' she whispered. 'It was inside a letter she sent me.

The one I got was dictated to Father because she finds it difficult to write since her stroke, but your name on the envelope seems to be in her own handwriting.' She sniffed as if she resented this mark of favour. 'I haven't looked at what's inside. I only opened the envelope by accident. Gosh, is that the time? I really must go.'

Nellie had only managed to write a few words, obviously with great effort. The spidery letters were difficult to decipher, but with tears filling her eyes – for the first time since she had received Edmund's letter – Catherine made out: 'Darling Goddaughter, keep courage, hope, follow your heart and you will win through. You always have our love, Nellie.' There was a scratched postscript. 'What the world thinks, never mind!!'

Her first wish was that Edmund had been there to read it. It seemed like a blessing and an absolution – but as the weeks went on, and she heard nothing from him, George's taunts returned to haunt her. She found herself becoming irritable with *Lao* Tang. She would pick up a novel she had read twice before and throw it against the wall after a chapter. She would play her old records and turn them off mid-flow. Once she wrote a long letter to Fu-kuei, but she did not receive a reply, which added to her anxiety.

The news of the war did nothing to cheer her. Again, she felt the effects of George's poison. Three armies were poised to take Peking. Generalissimo Chang Tso-lin had spent a month negotiating with Chiang Kai-shek and the Japanese, and had finally moved his headquarters out of the capital taking his special pale blue train (once the Empress Dowager's) to Tientsin. The newspapers described the grand reception at the station. He was not expected to stay. His son, Chang Hsueh-liang, was organising the retreat of Fengtian forces to Manchuria. Elaborate efforts had been made to save face, but the truth was that Chang Tso-lin had given the field to Chiang Kai-shek. There had hardly been any fighting during the last two weeks: only advances by one side and retreats by the other. It depressed her to acknowledge that George had been right again. There would be little work in a war hospital for Edmund to do now. What was keeping him in Tsinan? If that was where he was. She had written to him about her impossible situation after the publication of Willie's diary, adding that there was no reason to wait six months; but either her letter had not arrived or Edmund did not want to reply.

She felt deserted, and bored.

She tried to suppress the howling fear inside her. What if George had been right? What if Edmund really was running away? And she savaged herself for her cowardice, because she knew that the one thing stopping her getting on a train or a boat was the fear that Edmund would reject her. On those occasions she would cling to the six months like a mantra because it staved off a decision and allowed her to hope at least a little longer.

So the dreary days passed.

One afternoon – she had picked up her old habits again and was lying late in bed – *Lao* Tang knocked on her door and told her she had a visitor.

'Who is it? Tell them I'm not at home.'

The name *Lao* Tang gave her made her sit up. 'Tell him to wait in the sitting room,' she called.

The dark pouches under the cold blue eyes, the mockery in the appraising, arrogant stare, the bedraggled moustache and sallow cheeks, the flushed nose of a soak, and the untidy grey hair were exactly as she remembered. He had settled himself comfortably in George's armchair, his stick on the carpet beside him. His hands were linked on his chest. He did not attempt to get up when she came in.

'What a pleasure,' he drawled. 'I came to see your husband, but your servant told me only Missy was at home. You're certainly the more attractive option, especially since you've dropped the nurse's drab.'

'George hasn't lived here for a while,' she said coldly, keeping her position by the door. 'You can find him at the club.'

'So I gather – but I don't want to go to the club. It's a bit too conspicuous for the business he and I need to conduct. I prefer to keep a low profile, these days. You know how it is. Perhaps you could get your man to send a discreet message to him that I'm here. Meanwhile you and I can have a little chat. I seem to remember you were once anxious to have a chat with me. About a paternity issue, wasn't it?'

'I don't know what business you have with my husband, Mr Manners, but you have none with me. You made yourself unpleasantly clear on where you stood the last time we met, and frankly I'd just as soon drop it.'

'Hoity-toity!' He laughed. 'You know, you really are like your mother. Not just in your looks. Don't worry,' he added. 'I understand. If you don't mind my saying so, you also made perfectly clear how you feel about me when you ostentatiously ignored me in Hankow. If I really had been your father, as you once tried to claim, I might have felt a mite upset to be cut.'

'So that *was* you stalking us in the rain.'

'I wouldn't have put it like that. Bit difficult to stalk with a game leg but, yes, young George told me about your good deeds down south, so since I was in town and at a loose end, I thought I might renew old acquaintance. You haven't got any whisky, by any chance? It's been a tiring ride down from Dairen. Dash of soda. No ice.'

She went over to the drinks stand, and poured a tumbler for him, then went to the hall, telephoned the club and left a message for George. She returned and sat down in a chair opposite Henry Manners. 'What business can a man like you possibly have with George?' she asked.

He smiled. 'So he never told you? That doesn't surprise me. George and I go back a long way, my dear. Knew him as a little boy, before even you were born. After that meeting of ours in Mukden, I realised I'd been a little abrupt, and next time I was in Tientsin I looked him up. Discovered a mutual interest in railways, as it happened. I have good relations with the SMR up north. Was able to help him out from time to time. In fact, we've been doing business off and on for years.'

'He never told me,' she said.

'Well, freight matters and such things are infinitely boring. And you and I didn't exactly hit it off, did we? He probably didn't want to hurt your feelings. Anyway, staying in the background is more my style. Not that I didn't continue to maintain a close interest in what you were doing all these years. I hesitate to say "in a paternal way" as that may send the wrong signals – perhaps "godfatherly" would be more appropriate. You've impressed me, my dear. If I was your father, as you once believed, I would have been damned proud of what you did during the recent war. And I wouldn't have been overly upset either by this great scandal you seem to have stirred up. I've read that pathetic journalist's diary. Only fools can't see you come out well from it. I wouldn't worry too much. These things blow over. That's been my experience, anyway. Your mother lived her life with passion. You have inherited something of that from her – but you've a strength she didn't have, an ability to look facts in the face, and a cool calculation that will stand you in good stead in adversity. A ruthlessness, perhaps. Maybe you inherit those qualities from your father. If I were he I'm sure I'd like to think so.'

It was extraordinary. Part of Catherine wanted to throw him out of the house – it was outrageous that he should be talking about her so intimately. On the other hand she was fascinated: there was something in the intensity of his gaze, although he was speaking in the light, ironical tone with which he had started, that made her think he was trying to give her a serious message. And underneath her hatred for this man, she felt again that old longing for a father . . . Was he finally, in this circuitous manner, coming round to admitting the truth?

'But Tom Cabot didn't have those qualities, did he, Mr Manners?' she said carefully. Somehow she kept her voice steady. 'All my mother ever told me about him was that he was a brave English fool and a cricketer. The only lover my mother had with the qualities you described was yourself, Mr Manners.'

'Don't go down that route, Catherine,' muttered Manners. 'I'll only give you the answer I gave you before.'

'What are you trying to hide from, Mr Manners? Why do I frighten you so much?' she asked. 'You can't deny that you and Helen Frances were lovers. I have photographs of you together in Japan. I've been to your son's grave. I even remember you telling me the most wonderful stories, and playing with me when I was a little girl. I adored you. Why won't you admit it? Is it because you're ashamed that you're no longer a paragon, a heroic spy or whatever you once were?'

'Where did you hear that?' he snapped.

'A British diplomat came to see me, wanted me to persuade you to stop working for the Japanese.'

'Pritchett,' he muttered.

'I think that was his name. Listen, I don't care any more. If you wanted to make me hate you, you were successful. I despise what you did to me in Mukden, and I despise everything I hear about you now. If you have business with George, I don't want to know about it. It's probably as murky as everything else you seem to be involved in. If you don't want to be my father, that's fine by me. I'm not sure that I want to be your daughter any more – but, for God's sake, if we have to sit here facing each other, let's at least speak the truth. I know you're my natural father. I have your own letters as evidence. It doesn't make me proud. Whatever you once were, you've degenerated into something else. Thank God Mama isn't here to see you – but your continued denial of paternity makes you even more pathetic in my eyes. It's . . . cowardly!' She clutched for words. 'And downright dishonourable.'

'After that I could do with another whisky.' Catherine was disconcerted to see that Manners's blue eyes were twinkling, and he was grinning at her indulgently. 'Bravo!' he said. 'What a peroration!'

'So you're going to continue to deny it?' she said. Exasperated, she got up and poured him the whisky.

'If you think you have evidence, what does it matter if I deny it or not?' he said. 'You can believe what you like, my dear. Listen,' he said, 'do you want me to talk to George? It seems he's treating you shabbily. Your marriage may be on the rocks, but he should do the decent thing by you. Free you to marry his brother, or whomever it is you're in love with.'

She stared at him. 'How dare you? What on earth gives you the right to pry into my personal affairs?'

'I was your father a moment ago,' he said, languidly sipping his whisky. 'Can't have it both ways, you know. If I am your father I have a damned good right to worry about my daughter's welfare.'

'Well, you can't have it both ways, either,' she snapped. 'And why the devil would George listen to you?'

'*Touché.*' He grinned. 'George might heed the words of an old family friend, and a business partner of long duration.'

Catherine looked at him scornfully. 'I wouldn't accept any help from you if you were the only thing standing between me and penury,' she said.

He laughed. 'My dear girl,' he said, 'what makes you think that you aren't in that situation already?'

'You're despicable,' she said.

'Please yourself,' he said. 'My goodness, but aren't you like Helen Frances? The years could have rolled away!' He laughed again, a strangely rich, exuberant outburst from such a wreck of a man. 'Mind you,' he chuckled, 'you're better behaved than she was. She'd have been scratching my eyes out by now.'

'Manners, what are you doing here?' said a voice from the doorway. George, his hair streaked on a sweating forehead, looked uncharacteristically flustered, although his white ducks and Aertex shirt were, as usual, immaculate; but that he hadn't changed into something more formal indicated he must have hurried straight from the tennis court. He was frowning, and he had spoken without a trace of his usual irony. 'This is rather unorthodox, isn't it?' he said. 'I wasn't expecting to see you for another month.'

Henry Manners settled in his chair. 'Bit of an emergency's cropped up, old boy,' he drawled. 'Powers that be want your help.'

'We've dealt with all the freight for this month,' said George. 'There was no hitch as far as I know.'

'It's something rather more important than that, I'm afraid. More a passenger than a freight problem. You know who's leaving the station tomorrow? At two p.m.? A special train north? Ring any bells?'

George was still frowning. 'Chang Tso-lin? That's a purely Chinese affair. What's it got to do with me?'

Catherine saw Manners smile, lifting his eyebrows significantly and nodding at her.

George appeared to notice her for the first time. 'Yes, I see,' he said, making an effort to settle his features into a bland smile. 'Catherine, dear, would you mind? Mr Manners and I have something to discuss. Could I ask you to wait in your room? Sorry. I'll call you when we're finished.'

Puzzled, she stood up. 'Take as long as you like. My father's come to see you, not me.' George glanced at Manners, confusion on his face. Manners shrugged. With a bitter smile she flounced out of the room.

A short while afterwards, stepping on to the landing, she heard angry voices from behind the sitting-room door.

An hour later George knocked. He was still grim. 'Listen, Catherine,' he said, 'I'm leaving now, but I've invited Mr Manners to stay for a couple of nights. He shouldn't disturb you. It'd be decent if you had dinner with him, but you don't have to. Sorry, old thing,' he added lamely. 'He shouldn't be in your way.'

'No need to be sorry,' she said. 'It's your house, isn't it? I'm just one of your chattels waiting to be discarded.'

'Thank you, Catherine,' he said, not rising to the bait. 'I appreciate it. I'll – I'll make it up somehow.' With sloped shoulders, head bent in preoccupation, he retreated down the stairs.

By the time *Lao* Tang called them to supper Henry Manners was drunk. He had not dressed for dinner: he was wearing the same old suit that he had had on in the afternoon, dishevelled after his sojourn with the whisky bottle in the sitting room. They passed the soup course in silence. Manners swayed in his seat. He appeared to be making an effort to control his shaking, but that did not prevent him drinking George's claret. Catherine watched him with mounting disgust.

'So,' she said, after *Lao* Tang had served the steak and vegetables, 'how was your business meeting with George?'

'Very satisfactory.' He glanced at her slyly.

'A passenger problem?' she asked.

'You could say that.' He wore a smug smile.

'It sounds mysterious to me,' she said. 'Why did George mention Chang Tso-lin? I assume it was his special train you were referring to. Is he leaving for Manchuria tomorrow?'

Again, that sly, knowing smile. 'He'll certainly leave for Manchuria,' he said. 'Hasn't any choice. The Jappos have given him an ultimatum. Come home and everything will be forgiven. Great peacemakers, the Jappos, you know. They've given an ultimatum to Chiang Kai-shek as well. No more squabbling, children, or we big boys will have to step in. The kiddies are being separated. Chiang can have China, and the Old Tiger of the North can go back to his lair in Mukden. Or that's what Chang Tso-lin thinks.'

'Well, isn't that the case?' asked Catherine, coldly. 'All the newspapers say he'll run Fengtian as a separate state with Japanese blessing.'

'That's what he'd like – but not everybody's happy about it,' he said, picking his words with a drunkard's precision. 'Kwantung army's not too pleased. Those soldier boys see things rather differently from Tokyo. They're the ones who have to deal with these backbiting warlords. Men on the spot. Old Chang Tso-lin may not get the welcome he expects.' He started to laugh and coughed over his wine.

'What's that supposed to mean?' continued Catherine, watching the wine dribble down his chin.

'Nothing,' he said – but there was still something knowing in his grin.

'Anyway, what's this got to do with you and George? What are you two scheming?'

'George is a railway official.' Manners smiled. 'In charge of the points,' he sneered. 'If you want to check that a certain train will arrive at a certain place at a certain time, you consult a railway official. Nothing odd in that, is there, my dear?' He grinned at her archly, as if he had made a clever point.

'That still doesn't tell me what you and he have to do with Chang Tso-lin. I can see why the Japanese want Chang to get back to Fengtian, but I don't see what sort of role you have to play, or George. It doesn't need a senior railway official like him to ensure the train leaves on time.'

'Leaves on time, or arrives on time?' he said archly, tapping his nose. 'Maybe that's what you should be asking.'

Catherine felt that he was playing with her. She was bored with this. 'Whatever you're up to, I don't like the sound of it. It smacks more of politics than business to me.'

'Business, politics – there's little difference nowadays. Anyway, nothing to worry your pretty head over. A woman and politics . . . A woman and politics . . .' It sounded as if he was trying to remember an epigram, but he gave up and pushed his beef with his fork.

'I know your politics,' she said. 'I've read your disgusting articles.'

'They are pretty dreadful,' he acknowledged, after giving it a moment's ponderous thought, 'but give me my due. They're heart-felt.' He reached for the wine decanter. 'By that I mean, of course, they tell me what to write and I put my heart into it.' He laughed bitterly. 'Thus do we professionals earn our dirty wages, and keep the wolf from the door.'

He appeared to meditate on this for some time. Catherine was fascinated by the play of expressions on his face – bitterness, self-hatred, disgust, anger. She thought she should feel sorry for him, but as she looked at him, she realised with surprise that this man, whom she had once followed across the world, meant nothing to her now.

'Wolves, did I say? That's what they are, you know. Taro, Doihara. The Kempeitai. They'll eat all of us one day. You mark my words. Give them time. They won't let a tinsel general like Chang Tso-lin keep Manchuria. They want it for themselves. They want the whole of China too. They'll bide their time, creeping through the woods with their cold, calculating eyes, waiting till the sheepdogs are asleep and the fold is unsuspecting. They'll stage an incident, step in to restore order. Oh, they're wily and calculating and patient. I know them, you see. The joke is, who set them up in the first place? Trained their armies and navies? Gave them industry? Supported them against Russia? Made them what they are today? It was us, Catherine. Christ, Catherine, it was me. All my life, soldiering on for king and country, doing what? Helping the Japanese. And now they have my soul. You said I was dishon-ourable this afternoon, and a coward. You don't know the half of it . . .'

'I don't want to,' she said, putting her napkin on the table. 'You're drunk.'

But he was ruminating on what he had been saying. 'Wolves,' he said. His eyes softened. 'Well, I can't keep them from my door. It's too late for that. But I can try to keep them from others' doors. You've grown into a beautiful woman, Catherine. I wish Helen Frances could see you now. Yes, I can still do my best to keep them away from my innocent little piggy, before they huff and they puff and they blo-o-ow your house down!' The blue eyes blinked, and for a fraction of a second, she glimpsed a different man. 'Remember that? Your mother and I used to read you that story long ago. In those days you were such a bright, inquisitive little creature, sitting wide-eyed in your little *yukata*. You loved stories. Loved me to sing to you too.' He began to hum a tune. It was a sad, haunting melody, familiar too, a Japanese nursery song. She had forgotten it, but as he murmured the words, she froze, as memories dredged themselves from deep inside her unconscious.

She was standing on the shoreline of the Inland Sea. The moon was shimmering silver ribbons on the waters. Lights from the fishing-boats were bobbing in the dark patches between the islands; a fragrant smell of pine was wafting from the hill, and her uncle was singing her favourite song: *Aka i Kutsu* . . . Tears were rolling down his cheeks as he sang, and she thought this strange, because adults don't cry, so she pulled his sleeve to ask him why he was sad. He turned to her with a smile and told her that it was because it was a song about her. It's a story about a little girl with red shoes, he said, who has to go away with a foreigner 'from the port of Yokohama, over the waves'. She laughed with relief and told him not to be silly: she wouldn't ever go away from him and, anyway, she didn't have any red shoes – and, of course, he laughed too and kissed her, and his soft moustache tickled her cheek . . .

She wrenched her mind back to the present and her dinner-table, where a ravaged old man whom she detested, a parody of the uncle she had loved, was singing softly the same words: '*Aka i Kutsu* . . .' All she could feel was anger, and resentment. He seemed to sense her mood. Abruptly he stopped. With a shaking hand, he poured the wine into his glass, spilling several drops on the tablecloth. He sipped it, and put the glass back on the table as if he did not like the taste. 'Sorry,' he muttered. 'Tactless of me.' He lowered his head. When he looked up, he observed her with the same watchful scorn that he had shown her when she had come into the sitting room that afternoon. 'Catherine, you don't want me as your father, you know,' he said. 'Best leave things buried as they are. Don't you think, old thing? Trust Uncle Henry on this one. It's better that way for both of us.'

She stared at him. 'There's another bottle on the sideboard,' she said. '*Lao* Tang will give you coffee if you want it. Excuse me. I'm not feeling well.' He gave her a nod. She left the room quickly, maintaining what dignity she could, then ran up the stairs. Collapsing on her bed she began to weep.

When she rose next day he was not in the house. *Lao* Tang said that he had left shortly after eight, having consumed three cups of coffee and a brandy. She felt restless and put on her dressing-gown, then went downstairs to have her morning cup of tea in the sitting room while she read the papers. Idly she glanced at the headlines. Generalissimo Chang had made a speech saying that, in the interests of peace and the Chinese people, he was retiring to Manchuria because he had failed to defeat the Communists. He was taking his seal, the banner of the Grand Marshal of the National Pacification Army, as well as all important state files to Mukden, which would be the true China's capital in exile. There would be a military parade to see him off at the station in his private train.

She sipped her tea and turned to the editorial page. It contained the usual pompous pronouncements and speculations, but one paragraph caught her eye:

So the Tiger of the North is returning to Manchuria with his tail between his legs. As his special train rumbles through the night what will he be thinking? The bandit who dreamed he could become an emperor and failed. He still has his armies and his borders, protected by the patronage of the Japanese, who have been his friends in the past. But in the cruel world of politics a failure has no friends. Until now the Japanese have supported him, saved him on more than one occasion, used him as their puppet – but will they consider him useful in the future? It is well known that the more radical officers in the Kwantung army resent the fact that they have to share power in an area of China that they believe is theirs by right of conquest. Is their old warlord client now supernumerary to their needs? His return will be ignominious. Perhaps there are elements within the Japanese imperium who would prefer that he did not return at all . . .

She froze, remembering her father's drunken words of the night before. 'Wolves . . . that's what they are . . . Taro. Doihara. The

Kempeitai . . . They won't let a tinsel general like Chang Tso-lin keep Manchuria . . . They'll stage an incident, step in to restore order . . . Old Chang Tso-lin may not get the welcome he expects.'

She tried to remember what else he had said during dinner, that strange, debauched dinner in which he seemed to have acknowledged her as his daughter, and she had run away – but it was not the childhood memories that she was thinking about now: it was what he had said about the train. Something about George being in charge of the points, and making sure the train arrived on time.

The words shouted from the editorial: '*Perhaps there are elements within the Japanese imperium who would prefer that he did not return . . .*' What had her father been implying? She remembered his arch tone, the mocking look in his eye – and, beneath it, something else. Self-disgust. Anger. Shame.

Her father had said that the Japanese would stage an incident. Her father was a Japanese agent. He would know their plans.

And, slowly, it dawned on her. He had not been referring to the train arriving in a station. All along he had had in mind another sort of rendezvous. Why would a Japanese agent want the assistance of a senior railways official?

Unless he was plotting to sabotage a train . . .

The cup began to rattle in its saucer. She had to put it on the table. From the hallway she could hear *Lao* Tang whistling as he went about his dusting. The normality of her surroundings, the familiar sofa, George's phonogram, the grate in front of the fireplace, the racing prints on the walls, made her pause. Was she going mad? How could George be involved in an assassination? George was a playboy. Hearty George. Life and soul of every party, caring only for pleasure and the finest clothes . . .

There was another side to George, she knew, which he had shown to her: the cruelty, the calculation, the amorality . . . With a chill she acknowledged that George might indeed be capable of murder; he might be capable of anything, if it suited his selfish purpose. She tried to rebel, asking herself, What could he possibly gain by it? And remembered a conversation that she had had with Robby many years ago. He had pressed her, in his irritating fashion, about George's luxurious lifestyle, asking how he could afford it on a railway official's salary. She had not been interested, attributing the question to Robby's gossipy envy: as far as she was concerned, George's money flowed as naturally as champagne. But now she asked herself, and it was as if another piece of a child's puzzle had fitted into place. Where did he get his money for the round-the-world cruises, the stables, the diamonds, the parties, the motor-car? Simple. From her father. After all, what possible business could her husband have with a man like Henry Manners, the Japanese agent, unless it was something criminal and profitable? Freight-handling, her father had said. She imagined that was a euphemism for smuggling. Of guns? Of opium? Yes, her husband was certainly in a position to 'help with the points'. She had read once that the Japanese were China's biggest smugglers of opium. Was that their dark cargo? Their dark secret? Only now there was a darker secret. She was sure of it. They were plotting political murder.

She remembered the time she had seen the generalissimo. He had been with his three grandchildren and they were all wearing pompous military uniforms. He had seemed such an insignificant little man, so ordinary – yet it had been he who had brought the whole country into a state of civil war. His death might embroil China in another war, this time with Japan.

She had no idea how they planned to do it. Smuggle an assassin on board? Or a bomb? Yes, George could pull strings at the station. And all the world would believe the Nationalists were responsible – that would be the point of the conspiracy, after all, to give the Japanese a chance to deploy their armies to restore law and order. 'They'll stage an incident,' her father had said.

No doubt her father and George were only small cogs in the mechanism of a much bigger conspiracy, minor players, but they had a part to play none the less. That made her both the daughter and the wife of international assassins.

It took her some minutes to absorb this. She saw George's smug features, her father's haggard sneer. Between them they had already made a mockery of her life and her dreams. Both had let her down. They were each despicable in their way and she had come to terms with that – but to think that they were murderers as well! She felt filthy, defiled. And, however irrational it seemed, she could not avoid a feeling of complicity. They were both men she had once loved: she had lived with them, shared her bread with them. One of them had fathered her! She felt tainted, as if she herself was to blame because of her association with them.

As she was recoiling with shock, a verse that Hsiung had taught her from the *Tao* nagged at her mind like an irrelevant insect:

> *Those who know do not speak;*
> *Those who speak do not know …*
> *Success is the hiding-place of failure;*
> *But who can tell when the turning-point will come?*

Yes, it was a hideous irony. It would be a joke that would make Hsiung rock on his perch. She had spent weeks locked in this house, frustrated by the lack of activity, cut off from life, indulging her self-pity, while all along she had been at the heart of a conspiracy of world-shaking proportions. She had had the means, had she known it, to prevent a catastrophe, but she had been too preoccupied with her own little concerns.

Was it too late? Could she do anything to stop it? At the end of the day this was only another crisis of Chinese politics. The man who would die was not guiltless: the blood of a nation was on the thin, elegant hands she had seen folded in his gloves as he inspected his troops. She and Edmund had been mopping up the blood he had spilled these two years. One set of monsters would kill another monster. Was there anything even to grieve over?

But his death might cause another war – a greater war. Was she to stand by, knowing what she did, knowing who would perpetrate the crime, and do nothing about it?

This is your father, your husband! She was chilled by the implication. George is the brother of the man you love! The son of Nellie and Edward Airton who had been kind to her and accepted her into their family! The social scandals that had been preoccupying her were nothing compared to the disgrace of murder – or conspiracy to commit murder, because it was the same.

She had seen the ravages of a civil war. Suddenly she thought of the family on the junk that had taken her down the river: the lithe younger brother climbing to the top of the mast and laughing for the joy of youth and life, the old woman with her shrine below, and the babies playing on the deck; the tranquil calm of an evening when the fishermen cast their nets . . . She could not stand by and do nothing, whatever her relationship with the Airtons.

With a sudden surge of energy, she threw aside the newspapers and ran up the stairs to her room. All the malaise and depression of the last weeks evaporated; she felt a firm sense of purpose, certainty, calm. Perhaps she might not be successful – but she could try to make amends for what her father and George had done. Yes, it might be painful for Edmund and Nellie, but if they were the people she thought they were, they would understand.

Suddenly it appeared simple. She had rarely known such clarity. She felt as if a shining light had illuminated her soul. Perhaps this was the awakening that Hsiung had talked about. Something beyond herself was calling her to help, to serve, and nothing else mattered.

Hurriedly, she scrambled into her clothes. Unconsciously she had grabbed the nearest dress to hand, her nurse's uniform. It was only when she was tying her shoes that she came down to earth with a thump: she had no idea of what she intended to do. She saw a mountain of obstacles. Who on earth would believe her? What proof did she have? Anybody in Tientsin who heard that the disgraced Catherine Airton was trying to regain notoriety by spitefully accusing jolly George of political murder would laugh.

That didn't matter, she told herself. Think! You can work it out. Who would believe you? She knew how important this was. Who would believe that renegade Japanese officers were launching a murder plot for which the Nationalists would be blamed? The Nationalists would believe her, but how was she to get in touch with them? Their armies had not yet reached Tientsin. Only international intervention would be powerful enough to put pressure on Japan. She could go to the British consulate. No, they would laugh at her too. The British consul had been at that dinner at the Aglerns and had showered her with effusiveness but would be the last person to help her now.

The answer came in a flash. Suddenly she thought of the diplomat who had once come to the house to talk about her father. Pritchett, he was called. She had told her father about him only last night, and he had known immediately whom she meant. Pritchett the spymaster – that obnoxious and rather sinister man who had upset her and whom she had thrown out of the house. But he had given her a card, telling her to contact him if she ever needed help. Yes, Pritchett was the one man in the world who would believe her. He knew Manners. He would know, too, how to use this information, working through his influential channels.

She ran to the hall and yelled to *Lao* Tang to order a car. She went to her writing desk, and scribbled out everything she knew. This would be the basis of a telegram. When she read it, she had a moment of doubt. Everything seemed so circumstantial, so insubstantial. No, she was sure Pritchett would understand. The envelope to her lips, she had a vision of Nellie's face, then Edmund's, and saw the pain she was about to inflict – but it was only momentary indecision: deep inside her she knew they would understand, and want her to do what was right. And if they didn't? Well, it couldn't be helped. She felt strong, invulnerable, and more certain than she had felt at any other time in her life.

Licking the envelope, thrusting it into her handbag, she ran down the stairs – and saw Henry Manners in the hall.

He was standing as she had seen him once before, in a flash of lightning on a wet night in Wuhan. Again, he was cloaked against the weather. The brim of his Homburg had curled in the rain that was beating on the pathway outside the open door. Again, he was leaning on his stick, looking straight at her with those cruel, pouched eyes, but this time his expression was one of infinite sadness.

'Hello, Catherine,' he said quietly, blocking her way. 'This is the second time I've seen you in a nurse's uniform. You looked purposeful the last time as well. Might I enquire where you're planning to go?'

'It's – it's none of your business. I have to go out,' she said. 'Will you let me pass please?'

His answer was a sigh, and a gentle shake of his head. He had fixed his cold blue eyes on hers. His expression was not exactly threatening, but behind the tragic resignation there was something implacable. She sensed desperation, as if he was on the borderline of self-control.

He spoke, however, in an easy conversational tone. There was no trace of his usual sarcasm. 'I've been back some time. Call it sixth sense, if you like. I was worried about you. It seems I had cause to be.'

Her eyes flared under his searching gaze, but she could not think what to say. She seemed paralysed. He nodded slowly. 'Well, it was my fault. I was indiscreet last night in my cups. There is a pathetic desire in all of us to confess, to seek absolution. I'm sorry. It was unfair of me – weak of me – to burden you with secrets. It's ironic, isn't it? The best intentions are liable to cause the greatest harm.'

'You must let me pass,' she said, finding her voice, but she could see already that it was no use. With a half-smile on his lips, he seemed to be reciting something. She recognised the verse:

*'For each man kills the thing he loves, by all let this be heard
The weak man with a bitter look, the brave man with a sword.'*

It was then she noticed that a revolver hung from his right hand.

Yu Fu-kuei and Yang Yi-liang had also been reading the newspapers in their house in Shanghai. They had arrived back that morning after a long sea voyage that had taken them to Japan, the Philippines and Australia, returning by way of the South Sea Islands and Hawaii. They were having a light lunch before they unpacked. Fu-kuei had seen the letter from Catherine in the pile of correspondence waiting for them in the hall and was looking forward to reading it when she had some time alone. She had thought often of her friend during the last year. Of course, the headlines announcing Chang Tso-lin's decision to return to Manchuria had put everything else out of their minds, and they were poring over the papers as they ate their dumplings.

'What do you think, Yi-liang?' asked Fu-kuei. 'Is the war really over? Will Chiang Kai-shek pursue Chang over the border?'

'Anything's possible,' he said. 'I don't see what he would expect to gain from it, though. He's about to enter Peking in triumph as the unchallenged leader of China. He'd have to face Japan if he wanted to take on Chang Tso-lin now. Why would he risk war with an imperial power now he has almost everything he's ever wanted?'

'So you think China's really at peace? No more plots and conspiracies?' she asked. She smiled. 'That's the secret policeman's view?'

He laughed. 'I'm no longer a secret policeman. Thank goodness I don't have to have any views on matters like this any more.'

She reached over and put her hand on his, squeezing it affectionately. They smiled at each other. 'Do you regret that?' she asked.

'No,' he said. 'Not a bit. It was the best decision I ever made.'

His sudden resignation a year before had surprised everybody. After the part that he had played in the suppression of the Communists, the government in Nanking had publicly thanked him for his patriotism. He had been promoted to the rank of full colonel, and been made second-in-command of the whole security apparatus in Shanghai. He had been seen as one of the coming men in the Kuomintang. Invitations had poured into their house from the most distinguished generals, politicians and businessmen. Since he was unmarried, there was speculation that he would make an alliance with a daughter of one of the highest-placed families.

He had refused all invitations, which if anything had added to his reputation and mystique. An article in one of the gossip magazines had described 'The Man with the Secrets' and drawn a portrait of a devoted public servant working tirelessly and selflessly in the background, conducting secret wars against enemies of the republic, keeping his own life a mystery. It was rumoured, the article said, that his counsel was heeded at the highest levels of the Party, hinting that he was a confidant of the generalissimo himself.

One morning, however, after he and Fu-kuei had spent a long weekend by the lake in Hangchow, he had called at his superior's office, told him that for 'personal reasons' he could no longer fulfil his tasks and requested immediate release from the service. The general had been difficult, telling him that at this critical period of the country's history, he could not be spared; Yi-liang had then felt compelled to draw the general's attention to various photographs taken in a male brothel, as well as carbons of certain monetary transactions with arms-dealers and opium-traders, and it had been surprising how co-operative he had become.

A week later Yi-liang and Fu-kuei had returned to Hangchow

where they were married in a quiet civil ceremony. Two weeks after that they were sailing across the Yellow Sea for Japan.

They kept to themselves on the ship. They were content to ignore the curious glances of the other passengers in first class, who were no doubt speculating on the identity of this elegant and obviously wealthy Chinese couple who stood for hours on the after deck gazing silently at the sea.

They had spent two months walking in the mountains of Hokkaido, staying in small hotels or in temples. In the Philippines they rented a cottage by an extinct volcano. In Australia, Yi-liang hired a car and they drove the length of the continent. They wanted no other company than their own. There were too many ghosts they had quietly to exorcise. There was little of their former passion in their relationship – but neither wanted passion: too much had happened for either to believe any more in absolutes of love or devotion. They took comfort in that they had learned to forgive each other. For the moment they were content that they were friends. That they could not help each other directly to confront their own demons – each had to face and conquer their own guilt and pain – was in itself a bond. Suffering together was a form of companionship.

In the beauty of a dawn over the red sands of the Western Australian outback, or in the mountains that rose to cloudy heights above blue lagoons in Tahiti, or in the cracked volcano landscape of the Big Island in Hawaii, they found that they could sublimate for a while their private anguish in something bigger than themselves and, slowly, they began to appreciate life again. In their awesomeness these landscapes taught humility at first, and later offered hope that, however they had failed in their own little lives, there was a bigger universe that could absorb and accept them – and that was the first step in accepting themselves. Healing followed gradually. They became lovers again, taking comfort from each other's body.

On the voyage back from Hawaii across the blue ocean, they were laughing again. In Yokohama, where they stopped for a week before the last passage to Shanghai, they had gone to an expensive restaurant and enjoyed a feast; later they went to a performance of

Noh drama, and giggled afterwards when they discovered how incomprehensible the other had found it. By the time the ship was sailing between the familiar banks of the Whangpoo, they were eagerly discussing what they would do. Fu-kuei would teach. Yi-liang believed that one of his childhood classmates might offer him a job in his company. By now they had spent most of the money he had saved. Neither cared. They looked forward to a long, uncomplicated life in obscurity, and found joy in the thought.

They finished their dumplings, and unpacked their trunks. It was a bright, sunny day, and Fu-kuei suggested they celebrate their first afternoon back with a walk on the Bund. There might be a grand sunset over Soochow Creek, she said. It would be wonderful to see the bustling sampans again. Yi-liang went into the garage to check the Rolls-Royce, which had lain idle for more than a year. Laughingly Fu-kuei wiped off the oil that had smeared his cheek when he had crawled under it to inspect the suspension. 'Let's dress up,' she said. 'One last time before we become humble teacher and lowly clerk.'

She chose a red cheongsam, and Yi-liang his white suit and boater. They got into the car and sailed out of the gates. They passed the local park, and Yi-liang threaded through Chapei until they reached the road adjoining Soochow Creek. They drove past the granite mass of the post office. On their right they could see the tall buildings of the Bund. Just before they reached the bridge across the creek, they stopped at a set of traffic lights. Fu-kuei enjoyed the bustling sights of the city around her: a Sikh policeman ticking off two coolies loaded with bags of cement, a group of young students strolling by the river, a prosperous *tai-tai* in her rickshaw, a musician on the corner playing his *er-hu* to a crowd of idlers. They exchanged smiles.

Yi-liang was tapping his fingers on the ridge of the open window, waiting for the lights to change. 'You know, there's never really an end to anything,' he said.

'What are you talking about?' She smiled.

'Secret conspiracies. Chang Tso-lin. Chiang Kai-shek. The Japanese.'

'I thought you'd given up working out secret conspiracies,' she murmured.

'Oh, I have.' He laughed. 'That's just the uninformed speculation of an ordinary man in the street.'

She reached out her hand and took his. 'Do you think we can
be ordinary?' she said.

'I can.' He grinned. 'Nothing ordinary about you, though.'

They saw a burly crew-cut man making his way towards their
car through the parked traffic. He had a brush and a bucket and
no doubt wanted to make some cash cleaning their windscreen. He
leaned in at the window and smiled, showing a wide gap in his
teeth. Yi-liang shrugged, lifted the hand that was not holding Fu-
kuei's and waved at the windscreen. The man grinned in acknowledgement. Fu-kuei saw his head disappear as he reached into his
bucket . . .

It was a moment before she recognised that what he had pulled
out was a sawn-off shotgun, and the words he was shouting,
'Traitors! Murderers! Betrayers of the revolution!' at first made no
sense to her. She saw Yi-liang turn towards her, opening his mouth
as if to say something. She realised they were still holding hands,
and that the pressure of his flesh was a small comfort. Then she
heard a deafening explosion, the sound of breaking glass, and found
herself, as if caught in the slipstream of one of those big waves she
had seen on the beach at Kahlua, swirling through a black whirlpool
towards a shining, white light.

'You were so pretty as a child,' Henry Manners said. They faced
each other like duellists from opposite ends of the sitting-room
carpet. Vaguely he kept his gun trained on *Lao* Tang and his
daughter, *Hsiao* Meng, who were tied up on the sofa, their eyes
bulging over their gags, but he was nervous, and from time to time
would get up from his armchair and limp back and forth across
the rug. Catherine watched him carefully, trying to judge how far
she could provoke him. If she could only grab his gun. She was not
afraid for herself but he had threatened to hurt *Lao* Tang.

'How can you think you will get away with this?' she asked. 'I
know now. So will other people.'

'In a few hours it'll no longer be important,' said Manners.
'Afterwards you can make what accusations you like. Nobody will

believe you. Anyway, it won't matter if they do or they don't. China will have entered a new stage of politics and Japanese annexation of Manchuria will be a *fait accompli*.'

'And you're proud of that, are you?' she taunted. 'You don't care that it might lead to new wars, new bloodshed and more misery for millions of people?'

He hung his head. He sighed. 'Listen, Catherine.' His voice trembled with urgency. 'What I'm doing here, with George, is – necessary. Mine is a complicated life, and things aren't always as simple as they might appear. Sometimes one is forced by circumstances . . . The world we live in . . .'

'Nothing is complicated enough to justify murder,' she said. 'Father.'

'Please don't call me that.'

'But you are my father and you know it,' she said. 'That's why you sang me a sentimental song last night and why you keep telling me how proud you are of me. Do you think I'm proud of you? Do you think by pointing a gun at me and tying up my servants I'll admire you? Respect you? Love you?'

'Look,' he said, in an attempt at a reasonable tone, 'I was in two minds about coming to your house in the first place. If I could have I'd have made contact with George some other way. The last person I wanted to involve in this is you. God!' he shouted suddenly, and she realised how tense he must be. 'Don't you understand that the only reason I'm doing this – that I've done any of this – is to protect—' He stopped himself. He had risen to his feet. He was breathing deeply, although his cheeks were bright red.

'Go on,' she said. 'Protect what? Your good name? Is that what you want? Your daughter's respect? Bit late for that, isn't it?'

He glared at her, his lip quivering. He was shaking. His face was twisted with anger, but his eyes were . . . pleading.

'My God,' she said slowly. 'My God, how wrong could I have been? That's not what you meant at all, is it? Good Lord, you thought you could protect *me*, didn't you? Me! That's what you were going to say, wasn't it?' She gave a harsh laugh. 'You poor, poor man.'

'And what if that is the case?' snarled Manners. 'Do you have any idea how dangerous are the people I have to deal with? What they will do to innocent bystanders who get in their way? Silly, idealistic young girls who don't know what's good for them.'

'That's it, isn't it?' Everything suddenly made sense to her. 'Those Japanese you work for . . . they know you have a daughter . . . and they're – yes, they're blackmailing you, aren't they? That's why you've always kept a distance. Why you pretended to reject me. Because they've threatened to hurt me if you don't do what they say.'

'That's nonsense,' he muttered, glaring at her.

'That night in Wuhan. You really wanted to talk to me, didn't you? You meant what you said last night, that you've been keeping tabs on me. You've been watching over me all along.'

'Catherine, leave it,' he barked.

'My God, if I had only known.' She felt tears bubbling in her eyes.

'How dare you?' he shouted. 'How dare you pity me? I've told you a hundred times. I – am – not – your bloody father.' He had moved closer to her. She could feel his spittle on her face.

'Oh, you're pathetic,' she screamed. 'Who are you trying to delude? It's too damned late anyway. I don't want anything to do with you, you despicable . . . failure!'

He roared with rage, and raised the hand in which he held his pistol to strike her. She waited for the blow. He grunted and turned away, shaking. He made his way to George's drinks cabinet where, hands quivering, he poured a heavy shot of whisky into a tumbler.

Catherine saw he had placed the revolver on the side of the cabinet by the cocktail shakers. She ran towards it, but he was too quick for her and grabbed her wrist. With her other hand she scratched at his face. He ducked back. Her right wrist slipped his grasp. In her fury all she wanted to do was scratch and bite. She tore at the lapel of his jacket because it was the closest part of him she could reach. She pulled harder and heard the lining rip. Something heavy – his wallet – thumped on to the floor. 'Damn you,' she heard him cry and felt herself thrust on to her armchair, but as she was falling she saw the pictures and newspaper cuttings on the carpet, all portraits of her . . .

Catherine stared, amazed. She saw a small girl in a pinafore with a young Helen Frances on a Japanese shore. She saw herself in nurse's uniform on the eastern front, in velvet academic hat and gown at Oxford. There were photos of her at parties, with George, at society balls, with naval officers, smiling, glittering, laughing, teasing . . .

Manners stood frozen above her. Her eyes met his. As she watched, his taut features crumpled. With a groan he hurled himself into an armchair and covered his face with his hands. She saw the old man's shoulders shake as he broke into uncontrollable sobs.

She stood up slowly. She noticed that the revolver had fallen off the cabinet. She paused irresolutely for a moment, then kicked it under the coffee-table. She quickly untied *Hsiao Meng*'s and *Lao* Tang's gags, but lifted a finger to her lips indicating that they should be quiet. 'Please forgive us, *Lao* Tang,' she murmured. 'It's terrible what we have done to you, but my father is very upset.'

'This – this bad man your daddy, Missy?'

'Yes,' she answered. 'Please forgive him. He's not a bad man, really. He – he didn't mean to hurt you.'

'Oh . . . Family trouble, then, Missy? Like when I go crazy at *Hsiao Meng*?'

'Something like that.' She smiled. 'It's all over now.' *Lao* Tang nodded solemnly, but still looked bewildered.

'Go and make us some tea, will you?' she said, untying their bonds. 'And please, this is a secret. Between us. Okay?'

'Okay, Missy,' *Lao* Tang and *Hsiao Meng* promised. Chattering together, they left the room.

Catherine walked over to where her father was sobbing on his chair. She lowered herself on to its arm and embraced him, pressing her cheek to his. 'It's all right,' she said. 'It's all right, Father. It's not too late. It's never too late.'

'I – I feel so ashamed,' he muttered through his sobs.

'I know,' she said. 'I know.' She kissed his forehead. 'I've been wanting to do that since I was a little girl.' His face contorted as tears ran down his haggard cheeks. Lightly she stroked his hair. 'Listen,' she whispered, 'we both have to make amends now. For all these wasted years. We have to do something together now.

Something good. There's still an hour or so before the general's train leaves. We must warn him. Will you help me, Father? Please. I need you. Your daughter needs you now.'

Slowly, he nodded.

The car had to drop them outside the station concourse. No vehicles were being allowed through and a cordon of soldiers was pressing back the large crowd that had gathered to see the marshall make his departure. Troops in full battle gear were lined up in squares in the courtyard and a military band was playing mournful music that jangled in cacophony with the booming drums of a troupe of lion dancers and acrobats. As they pushed their way to the front of the onlookers they could see the white plumes of the official party disappearing through the large entrance into the station. Catherine noticed that her father was looking worried. 'We haven't much time,' he muttered. 'The troop inspection and the ceremonies are over. He'll be boarding within minutes. George will have switched the drivers by now. Damn. Come on. Do you have the pass I gave you? Let's hope these soldiers aren't too punctilious.'

He went up to one of the guards, who told them to step aside. 'My orders are that no one goes through,' the youth shouted.

'But these are official passes,' her father was explaining, in his most authoritative Chinese.

'My orders are that no one goes through,' the soldier repeated, crimsoning and rattling his rifle.

Catherine pulled at Manners's sleeve. 'I see a colleague of George's over there. That Englishman walking across the yard. Geoff!' she screamed. 'Geoffrey!'

Somehow her shrill voice carried over the hubbub. Geoffrey Earnshaw, who was in charge of the signalling department, came up to them, and hailed her over the soldier's shoulder. 'I say, Catherine, what are you doing here? And why are you wearing nurse's togs?' he asked cheerfully. 'You've missed the show, you know. It was quite splendid, really.'

'Never mind that!' she cried. 'Look, can you help us? I must see George. It's really urgent. Can you get this man to let us through?'

'Mmm, don't know about that,' he said doubtfully. 'George is rather busy at the moment. And these security fellows are being a bit tiresome today.'

'Come on, Geoff. Please.' She put on her most flirtatious voice. 'Promise I'll dance with you at the harvest ball.'

'Ooh, bribery!' laughed Geoffrey – but he spoke to the guard in curt Chinese, flashing an impressive China Railways identification badge. Beleaguered on both sides, the young soldier relented. 'Now, what's the name of this old fellow,' asked Geoffrey, 'so I can sign him in? Who is he? Your father?'

'Yes, he is,' cried Catherine, over her shoulder, as she pulled Manners through the barrier.

'You are a card.' Geoffrey grinned. 'Here, hold on. You can't just rush off like that. I'll get into trouble.' But Catherine and her father were already running as fast as they could through the lines of soldiers. Their own passes worked to get them into the station and they ran through the hall, their feet and Manners's stick echoing on the marble. 'It's platform eleven,' he panted. They had to go through three more armed barriers before they reached it, each inspection of their passes taking valuable time. Catherine looked wildly at the station clock. They had only ten minutes: the train was due to leave at two o'clock.

The platform was crowded with troops. They saw over the heads of the soldiers the official party. Catherine recognised Generalissimo Chang, who was talking to a group of men in top hats, clearly a civic delegation. He was already standing on the steps of his private carriage. Further down the platform another band was playing. Catherine was shivering with frustration. She wanted to scream a warning, but she knew that in this hubbub she would not be heard. 'We must get closer,' her father shouted in her ear. 'I see someone I know. Colonel Machino, Chang's military adviser.'

'He's Japanese,' Catherine shouted back.

'But he's not connected to the Kempeitai. He's loyal to Chang. Follow me.'

It took an interminable time to get through the press. They still had fifty feet to go when they saw Generalissimo Chang wave at the crowd and disappear into his carriage, followed by his staff officers in their plumes. 'It's all right,' Manners called. 'Machino's still on the platform. Oh, damnit. I see Doihara. By the engine. Keep your head down.'

But it was too late. Over the heads of the crowd, Catherine saw two figures standing by the locomotive at the front of the train. One was a Japanese officer, whom she vaguely remembered having seen before. The other was George – who was staring directly at her. She saw him frown, pull at the Japanese officer's sleeve and point. Horrified, she saw the Japanese shout something at the engine crew, then the two men began to push through the crowd in the direction of the official party. 'Hurry!' She saw rather than heard her father mouth the word, his eyes glittering in his agonised face.

Over the noise of the band she heard a whistle, followed by a shriek from the engine. The porters were moving down the train, slamming doors. The band was playing the Fengtian anthem. The men in top hats had taken them off and were holding them to their chests. The platform clock read two minutes to two. They had ten feet to go. She could see the broad back of the Japanese officer in whose direction her father was heading. She could hear him shouting, 'Colonel Machino!' But it was not Colonel Machino who turned. It was another officer, somebody whom she had also seen before. She recognised the cropped white hair and the handsome features. General Taro. He was smiling at them.

With a hiss and the grinding of gears the locomotive began to pull the train slowly away from the platform. The band reached the climax of the anthem. The carriages gathered speed. In the relative quiet after the music had stopped she heard General Taro address her father: 'Henry-san, what a pleasant surprise. This beautiful lady must be your daughter. At last you see fit to introduce me. And, moreover, it is a complete family reunion – because here also, if I am not mistaken, is your son-in-law.'

George and Colonel Doihara had come up behind him. She had never seen George look so grim. Doihara made a signal with his gloved hand. She felt something hard pressed discreetly into the small of her back. She turned her head and saw that a Japanese soldier was standing right behind her.

Smiling and chatting to each other, the dignitaries dispersed, including the Japanese colonel, Machino, who nodded at Manners as he passed him.

'What are you going to do with them?' she heard George ask General Taro. 'They know.'

'Know what, Mr Airton?' asked Taro, equably. 'That the generalissimo's train has left the station? That our loyal ally is on his way to Mukden, not stopping until he gets there?'

'The crew,' George muttered. He was sweating with fear. 'They know we switched the crew. We bribed the new ones with opium to slow the train for the bomb. What if Manners and Catherine tell?'

'You have a vivid imagination, Mr Airton,' said Taro. 'Colonel Doihara, do you know of any switch of crew? Or,' he chuckled, 'of a bomb?'

'No, General,' said Doihara. 'One would assume that any Nationalist perpetrator of a hypothetical attack, if that is what Mr Airton is imagining, would make sure that the engine was destroyed as well as the generalissimo's carriage. I would guess that the bodies of the warlord's original crew would be found in the wreck of the engine. In such an unlikely circumstance.'

'Of course they bloody will be,' hissed George. 'We made sure their bodies were loaded in with the coal. But what of my three men?'

'Your three men, Mr Airton? Have some of your railwaymen disappeared? How frustrating for your company. But I see that as no concern of ours. What a lurid imagination your son-in-law has, Henry-san. I would have thought he was touched in the head.'

'It's no use, Catherine.' Her father turned to her. 'Taro's right. We can't prove anything now. Or halt the train. We were just too damned late. Hideyoshi, unless you're planning to murder us in Tientsin railway station, I'd be grateful if you'd tell your men to stop prodding their pistols in our backs.'

'Oh, I'm sorry. Everybody is so security-conscious nowadays. Colonel, please.' Doihara waved again and the two Japanese soldiers who had been standing behind them stepped back.

'You're – you're letting them go?' gurgled George.

'If they have anywhere to go to,' said Taro quietly. 'I think they both know that they will have to go very far very quickly if we are not to meet again in less pleasant circumstances, and very soon. I am sure that Henry-san, my old friend, understands that. You too, Mr Airton, would be advised to think exactly what is in your best interests. In your case, I do not see that our business relationship need end, although Colonel Doihara will in future be your controller, now that Henry-san has apparently resigned. Now you must excuse me. I have work to do. An appointment with Colonel Machino, who is wondering why he was ordered so suddenly to remain in Tientsin. Goodbye, Mrs Airton, it is most pleasant to have met you. I am sorry that our acquaintanceship has been so brief. I will not wish you a long and happy life because that would be pointless. Doihara-san, let us go.'

'You're going to fry in hell, Hideyoshi,' said Henry Manners.

'Oh, I doubt that hell will be any worse than our present existence, Henry-san. I will join you there one day perhaps. You will arrive long before I do.'

He gave them each a formal bow and, accompanied by Doihara and his soldiers, followed the crowd that was dwindling towards the exit in his usual unhurried and dignified gait.

Catherine felt faint. She clutched her father's arm. She saw George staring at her, hatred in his eyes. It was the first time in her life that she had ever seen him . . . rumpled. His mouth opened and closed. He blinked as he wiped the salt sweat pouring into his eyes. His cheeks, usually so pink, were a sallow yellow. He hovered for a moment, then ran after the Japanese.

'I was a slave like that,' she heard her father say. 'I'm free now – thanks to you.' He was looking at her strangely. Lightly, he brushed her lips with his finger. 'Oh, Catherine. I've always loved you, you know. And your mother. I never ceased loving her. She'd be so proud if she could see you now. I meant that when I said it the other day. Was it just yesterday? It seems the universe has turned since then. Don't worry about Taro's threats by the way. I can deal with those. I'll drop you at home. You must stay there. Don't go out. Ten days should be enough. Maybe more. Maybe less. I'll let you know. You will be safe. I'll have made sure of that.'

'I – I don't understand,' she said. 'And – and what you said earlier, about the assassination attempt, is there really nothing we can do?'

'Not in time to save Generalissimo Chang,' said Manners, looking at her with the saddest expression. 'Sometimes . . . evil wins, and there's nothing you can do to prevent it, however hard you try. I know about that,' he added. 'It's a hell of a world, really.'

'I can't believe we're going to do nothing,' she said. 'What about Mr Pritchett? Or – or Chang Tso-lin's forces left behind here? Surely they can wire ahead and stop the train?'

He smiled fondly. 'If anybody would believe us they could, but that's not the way bureaucracy works in this country. We have no proof, Catherine. Taro knows that. It would take a brave official to stop his generalissimo's train on an unfounded story. From two unlikely foreigners? Machino might have done something but Taro will have squared him by now. And Pritchett?' He laughed. 'He would probably believe us, but he would do nothing about it. Intelligence agents like Pritchett play a long, long game. Taro knows we're powerless. That's why he could let us go. At least for now.'

'So we do nothing? After all that?'

'I didn't say I would do nothing, Catherine. We can't save Chang, but we can thwart their main plan – maybe. We will make sure Pritchett knows the real story, that it was not the Nationalists who were behind this. That might give ammunition to the Powers to pressure Japan behind the scenes. Given time, we can probably get the true facts to Chang Tso-lin's son. If he can find a way to get to Manchuria from wherever he is and take the reins of power quickly, then maybe we can stop the breakdown of order that will be the Japanese excuse to mobilise. The game's not over. You'll have to trust me, I'm afraid. But now my priority is to take you home.'

'The Young Marshal. I met him once,' she said inconsequentially. 'He was a nice young man.'

'Oh, my darling Catherine,' he murmured, 'how I love you.'

The next afternoon, when she rose, the newspapers were waiting by her breakfast tray. They all bore similar headlines, and one or two had photographs of a crumpled railway bridge on the outskirts of Mukden, and the crushed remains of a train. Generalissimo

Chang Tso-lin had apparently been taken alive out of the carriage that had been passing directly over the bridge when the bomb had exploded, but he had been unconscious, bleeding from terrible injuries, and was not expected to recover. The assumption was that the Nationalists had been responsible for setting off the bomb, although Chiang Kai-shek's headquarters emphatically denied this. An editorial in one of the newspapers expressed fears that this assassination attempt would play into the hands of the right-wing elements within the Kwantung army and the SMR garrisons, which had now been put on full alert throughout Manchuria. Senior members of the Japanese community were demanding that their army should annex the Manchurian provinces to restore stability under Japanese rule. Generalissimo Chang's office had reported that he was hanging in a state between life and death. If he should succumb to his injuries before the rest of the Fengtian army had managed to retreat north, the editorial threatened, the world should expect to see the banner of the Rising Sun flying over Manchuria within a few days.

She wept, for herself, for her father, for China.

She had heard no news from Henry Manners for ten days, although he had promised to call. She was back to her life of limbo. She passed the time reading the papers.

At the beginning there was indeed a lot of speculation that the Japanese might react precipitately, but the wounded generalissimo did not die – every day bulletins came from his mansion that he was taking food, that he had regained consciousness, that he was recovering. The Japanese armies waited. There was much speculation about the whereabouts of Chang Tso-lin's heir, Chang Hsueh-liang, the Young Marshal, who had been with his troops south of Tientsin when the bombing had occurred. Somehow he made his appearance in Mukden (there were rumours that he had crossed the border in the guise of a woman). A few days afterwards, when he had secured the reins of government and control of his father's armies, the announcement came that his father, Generalissimo Chang, had passed away. Whether he had been alive or not in the intervening period since the assassination attempt, everybody agreed that the daily health bulletins had been a skilful trick, buying time. After Chang Hsueh-liang's return, he had been assiduous in cultivating the Japanese. The fiction that the Nationalists had committed the crime was formally acknowledged, but with no breakdown in order and a smooth transition of leadership, the Japanese had no excuse to intervene. The crisis passed.

And still she heard no news from Henry Manners, although what she read in the papers had made her hopeful. She remembered that he had told her he would contact the Young Marshal. It was strange. Despite General Taro's threats she did not feel in any particular danger. Her father had told her she would be safe. She trusted him.

After a while the papers no longer spoke of the Manchurian crisis. Such political news as there was concerned the arrival in Peking of the Nationalists and the establishment of a new unified government. The editorials were triumphant. China was at peace. The prospects for trade had never been better, and, best news of all, the question of the status of the Treaty Ports had been indefinitely staved. After a few days, China's political stories returned to the obscurity of the central pages and the headlines reverted to matters of more moment to the foreign community. There had been new developments in the ongoing bloodstock debate at the Jockey Club.

But there was still no word from her father. She was becoming alarmed.

Lao Tang came into her bedroom one morning, beaming with delight, bearing two letters. 'Missy!' he shouted in Mandarin. 'It's come! A letter! It's from Tsinan! Master Edmund!'

'What?'

'Yes, Missy!' He was almost yelling. 'It's from Master Edmund. He's answered you at last.'

Catherine saw the yellow envelope on the tray. She recognised the writing. She felt as if all her newly found strength had drained from her body. Part of her wanted to rip the paper apart and devour the words – hoping, hoping that this was the answer for which she had waited so long. But what if he was writing to say he had changed his mind?

Lao Tang saw the pain on her face and smiled. He switched to his most comical pidgin. 'Open, Missy. Must belong good news. Otherwise why Master Edmun' takee trouble, hiyah? No Chinee write bad news. If bad news best say nothin' 'tall.'

'Oh, *Lao* Tang,' she whispered. 'He's not Chinese.' She gazed at the old servant with wide, scared eyes.

'Maybe you read other letter first. Must also belong good news. From you daddy. It same-same han'-writing from before-time when he write Master and Master tell me hide letter from you.'

She froze. Her father? Why had he written to her? Somehow she had always expected that he would turn up at her door. It was a big, bulky envelope, more a packet than a letter. With trembling fingers she opened it. A thick wad of what looked like transport manifests fell over her sheets. She ignored them, scrabbling to get out the two thin sheets of writing paper that remained in the envelope. Trembling, she read:

My dearest Catherine, my beloved daughter (you cannot imagine the joy I feel in writing that word), I must be brief. I am about to go on a journey, and the ship will soon depart.

First, you will have read the newspapers and know already that the situation in Manchuria is stable. I cannot tell you what I have done but, as I promised you, I have been busy. We did not save the generalissimo but those who need to know are aware of what really happened, and that might have been contributory to the positive result. You should know that had it not been for your bravery and example things might have been worse than they are. I am so proud of you. The Japanese military and thugs like Taro and Doihara will continue to plot. One day they may be successful, but fore-warned is forearmed.

Second, more importantly, you are safe. All along that is what has mattered to me most. Again, I cannot give you all the details, but there was not a moment that your house was not watched. Today I have given instructions for that watch to be lifted. I can tell you categorically that you are no longer in any danger. The slate is wiped clean or, rather, the books are now balanced. A trade has been made and I have not the slightest doubt that the terms of the contract will be met. General Taro is a brute but he likes to think of himself as a samurai and honourable. He will honour the bargain.

That's the sum of it really. I'm afraid that the journey I have to go on will be a long one. It is necessary. It relates to the bargain I have made. A woman as clever as you will read between the lines, however artfully I try to conceal the unpalatable. I do not want you to be sad, or upset, or grieve in any way. Know that I travel joyously. I am the beneficiary of my deal. In fact, no father could ever be more privileged than I am to make what for me is an insignificant sacrifice.

Anyway, I owe an expiation for the harm that I have done in my rather worthless life. In this way I make more than amends.

Think well of me if you can. I did always love you.

There, I am getting sentimental and I did not want to be.

You are so like your mother. *Et vera incessu patuit dea.*

Be happy, my dearest. Be yourself because that is perfection. Find that doctor and get married. It sounds as if he is a bit of a ditherer, that lover of yours. I wouldn't have been had I been in his shoes!

I hear the ship's horn calling the passengers to board. It's only a few hours across the bay, and they'll be choppy seas on the way – but I'm immune to seasickness. You've made me so, my darling. I can face anything now. I've never been happier, or more sure.

I love you,

Your father

PS Money matters, I forgot. A lawyer will contact you in a few days. My fortune, such as it is, is yours. It is an ill-gotten one, but perhaps you can put it to good use. PPS And, yes, the attached. It relates to certain railway-related transactions that I conducted over the years with that no-good husband of yours. If you send it to the railway authorities, you will have enough material here to put him away for life, if Doihara doesn't get to him first, that is. At the very least, you can use the threat of it to divorce him on any terms you desire. What an old rogue your father is: his last advice to his daughter is on how to blackmail!

It was several minutes before she could control herself. She remembered his sad smile as he had dropped her at her door and how, after he had kissed her, he had walked quickly down the path, with the erect shoulders of a soldier striding purposefully to battle, not even turning his head. She understood now that he had determined on what he had to do to protect her, and that he had known even then that he would never see her again.

She remembered the kind, gentle uncle of her childhood, and the nobility of his letters to her mother. She thought of the song he had sung to her, about the little girl travelling over the seas. She thought of the father she had searched for all her life, had found, and now lost again, but this time because of his love for her.

Standing by her bedside, *Lao* Tang flapped his hands in alarm. Eventually, he could contain himself no longer. Picking up the other letter, he thrust it towards her. 'Please, Missy, no cry. Read this. *Lao* Tang savvy sure-ting belong good news, same-same Missy wanshee hear. Please, Missy, no makee sad.'

'Oh, *Lao* Tang, I can't . . . I can't think of anything else now.' She thought her heart was breaking.

'Belong bad news you daddy, Missy? He go 'way 'gain?'

'Yes,' she sobbed. 'He's gone away for ever, *Lao* Tang. For ever.' Tears were falling down her cheeks. 'He's . . . he's . . .'

But how could she put into words the tragedy? Or even comprehend the courage, the nobility, the pride of this final act of his life? For she had read between the lines, and understood the only bargain that General Taro would accept.

Lao Tang sighed. Then he clicked his tongue, and said firmly, 'If you daddy leave you, sure-ting must have velly good reason. *Hsiao Meng* and me plenty savvy he love you. He good man even though he tie up *Lao* Tang and hit on head. You daddy, he never likee see daughter sad. Opposite. You daddy, if he here present time, he same-same wanshee you read other letter also, makee he muchee happy.'

'But how do you know?' she wailed through her tears. 'I couldn't bear it if . . . if . . .'

'I know, Missy,' he said in Chinese. 'Trust *Lao* Tang. Here. Here, let me open it for you . . .'

He tore the envelope apart and passed the single piece of paper gingerly towards her. It was a page torn from Edmund's prescription pad. Her heart sank, remembering the last letter he had sent. After what she had just read, she could not face rejection. Not after this.

'Read it. Please, Missy. Please,' begged her old servant, gazing at her woefully.

There was only one paragraph, written in Edmund's untidy scrawl,

Catherine, I've just read your letter. It's taken weeks to get to me, and now I know what a blithering idiot I've been. Selfish, fastidious, conventional, jealous when there was no need to have been. I've imposed a cruel trial on you, for which I do not deserve to be forgiven, but if you do forgive me I promise by all that's sacred that I'll never be so foolish again. Or leave you. Ever. So I'm taking the next Tientsin train (I have Bishop Huber's blessing, as well as a kick up my mental backside from Hsiung. I've also, for what it's worth, had an absolute broadside from Mother). I'm only sending this note to prove that love has faster wings than a mailman. I fully intend to be at your door before this arrives – and then you can rage at me or spurn me or do whatever you like, but it'll be water off a duck's back to me, my darling, because I know now what you've always known and I've been too dim to realise. That we're made for each other, and nothing on earth can come between us. You'll see there'll be no getting rid of me now. Oh how I love you, Catherine, how I kick myself for not coming to my senses sooner, Your Edmund.

She was stunned. She stared at the astonishing words, hardly daring to believe her eyes.

Then she heard *Lao* Tang chuckle. Furious, she grabbed him by his collar. '*Lao* Tang,' she said fiercely, 'how did you know this was good news?'

'Because I bloody well told him it was,' she heard the familiar voice. 'Hello, Nurse.'

'Edmund!' she screamed, and found that she was crying all over again.

A moment later, *Lao* Tang, straightening his collar but wearing a very smug smile, went out, treading softly as was his habit, even though he knew that at this moment not even an earthquake could disturb the couple on the bed. Then he quietly closed the door.

EPILOGUE
The Rising Sun
1929–1930

On Sept 18th 1931, in the middle of the night, soldiers of the Kwantung army laid a bomb on a railway track in far-away Mukden. Of course, I was blissfully unaware that such a momentous event was going on. To be truthful, I have very little memory of anything at all that happened during the following three days, because we had had a party to end parties to celebrate the opening of my new restaurant. But when I recovered, I found Tony, the dear boy, in tears. He told me that the 'Mukden Incident', as it was called, had been blamed as usual on the Nationalists: the Japanese had mobilised their army, attacked the Young Marshal's troops, and driven him out of Manchuria, mopping up his subsidiary warlords one by one along the way. I had never realised that Tony had such patriotic sentiments, but it gave me the excuse to dole out more than the usual dose of TLC . . . No more of that.

I suppose it was a highly significant moment in history. Everything followed from there. The annexation of the north-east was tantamount to a declaration of war against China. Fighting broke out near Shanghai in 1932 and again in 1937 after the Marco Polo Bridge Incident, and that led to full-scale Japanese invasion over the Wall. Some say that was the true beginning of the Second World War.

Why I mention it, however, and the reason why the event remains so vividly in my mind, is that, though I did not know it then, my life was about to change for the better . . .

From *A Chinese Cocktail – Life and Times in Good Old Tientsin*, Robert Berry, 1955

General Lin was spending more of his time now in the mausoleum he was building for himself outside the city.

He had not, as he had threatened the overbearing Japanese general, stopped the profitable opium trade. Old Man Yu's and other confiscated estates were yielding a richer crop than ever before. He had made his point, though, and was satisfied that General Taro would accede to his demands. It had been a mark of good faith that Taro, as a down payment, had handed over to him the Englishman, Ma Na Si. Lin had made sure that his old enemy's end was a terrible one: his bodyguard was subtle in the ways of torture and Ma Na Si had lasted ten days before he died. The man's bones now had a subsidiary place in his collection.

But satisfactory as his revenge had been, the father was not the daughter: Lin had made clear to General Taro through his inter-mediaries, Colonel Ti and Captain Fuzumi, that his patience was not inexhaustible.

His forbearance and his firm bargaining had paid off. It had been inconvenient that the Japanese had allowed the woman and her new husband to escape to Tsinan, where, unsuspecting, they had been allowed to return to the hospital from which he had extracted them. But now General Taro had fulfilled his long overdue promise, and Lin expected delivery of the fox-fairy's daughter within a few days.

Today he had had himself driven, with his faithful bodyguard, to the mausoleum. He had spent the day examining his collection of treasures and was now inspecting the two thrones – imperial ones that he had looted from a museum in Loyang. They had pride of place in the Great Hall, around which he had assembled the sacred relics he had picked up on his campaigns. There, against the wall, was the great statue of Kuan-yin that had come from the Lung-men caves. There above the altar was the portrait of the Magdalene. There were Madonnas and crucifixes, Shivas and Buddhas, strange shamanistic totems and straw effigies, even a pottery cast of a woman, though it was a distortion of the female form, with pendulous breasts, a round belly and a crude vulva protruding above the crouched legs. He had had great trouble securing this stone-age representation of the Earth Mother, but he was certain it was authentic; he had placed it reverently between the two huge stone phalluses that the American archaeologist had discovered in his excavations. That was not all. On a table in front of the altar was a huge, grinning skull, with sloped forehead and large jaws. General Lin had the American, Niedemeyer, to thank for it too. It rested next to his most sacred relic, wrapped in faded yellow silk: the thighbone of the Emperor Ch'ien-lung. Lin was proud of his collection. He believed that there could be nothing quite like it in the rest of the world.

His black-bearded bodyguard interrupted his reverie. 'It's Colonel Ti with the Japanese, Fuzumi,' he grunted. 'Do I let them in?'

'He brought the Japanese here?'

'I'll tell them to wait outside,' said the bodyguard.

'No, bring them in,' he ordered. He was impatient to know of the arrival of this last living item that would complete his collection. If they had come all this way from the city they must have news. He would greet them from the throne, he thought.

He waited, feeling in his fiery blood the emanations from the relics.

The two officers entered through the great stone doorway, and saluted.

'Speak,' he said. 'What news do you bring me of the woman?'

'There's been a change of plan, General,' said Ti.

'What did you say?' He could not believe the insolent tone. In astonishment he saw that they were reaching for the pistols in their holsters.

'Stop them,' he shrieked to his bodyguard, but too late. Ti and Fuzumi had levelled their Mausers at the bodyguard, who was gazing at them, dumb with astonishment. Together they fired, and the big, bearded man staggered backwards clutching his chest. They fired again and he fell onto the paved floor, moaning. Ti walked leisurely to the body and fired into the man's head.

'General,' Ti turned to face him, 'we do not need to disturb you any longer. We will leave you to enjoy your collection.'

'Wait,' he called. 'The fox-fairy? You were bringing me my fox-fairy. Where is she?'

The two men glanced over their shoulders. He could see the mockery in their eyes.

In his rage and fear he ran forward, suddenly realising what they intended to do, but the sole of his boot slipped in his henchman's blood on the marble paving. When he scrambled to his feet again, it was too late. Ti and Fuzumi were closing the great stone doors. 'I forbid you,' he screamed, but before he could reach them, the doors were sealed.

He turned, bewildered. In the flickering candlelight the faces of the statues seemed to mock him. Only the calm features of the Magdalene above the altar gazed at him with her usual benevolence.

She continued to do so until the last candle went out.

The sun was setting as Colonel Ti and Captain Fuzumi set off along the macadam road that linked the temple complex through a mile of poppy fields to the city wall and the small postern gate that led to the Yamen.

The half-constructed mausoleum and temple were bathed in pink light. Fuzumi stared at the extraordinary buildings. The complex was modelled on an imperial tomb, with a turreted wall round a high earth mound and temple courtyards before it, only these were of half-Chinese, half-Corinthian design. Their semi-finished carvings were the same eclectic jumble of mythologies that he had seen in the extraordinary hall, where they had disposed of Lin. Something about the shape of the main hall reminded him of Chang Tso-lin's palace, which he had once passed in Mukden. It reflected the same *folie de grandeur*, he thought. It was artificial, unoriginal and ultimately banal. As the convoy drove down the Spirit Way, he noticed stone elephants, horses, lions and mythical beasts that had obviously been pillaged from real imperial tombs round the country, mismatched because they came from different epochs: Sung lions, Ming camels, Ch'ing warriors. Even the memorial *beis*, dragon-surmounted tablets raised on the backs of turtles, were still inscribed with the glorious deeds of Aisin-Goro princes and other scions of past dynasties.

'This is an extraordinary tribute to hubris,' he said. 'Don't you think it's symbolic somehow of everything the warlords have attempted to achieve this last decade in China?'

'What do you mean?' asked Ti.

'Look at it. It's a monument to failure, to the thwarted pretensions of two-bit bandit kings who thought they could become emperors by wearing stolen clothes. Those bones Lin kept as talismans . . .'

Ti laughed. 'Lin's mad. He has been for years.'

'Yes,' said Fuzumi, contentedly, 'but he's not unrepresentative. I sometimes think all the warlords were like jackals, gnawing on the bones of an old empire.'

'Then what are you, my friend?' Ti enquired. 'If the warlords have stripped the country bare, who profits? Are you not the real scavengers, the wolves waiting to take the spoils? We Chinese have a long perspective, you know. You're just the new barbarians at the gates.'

'We're not barbarians, my friend.' Fuzumi looked hurt. 'Is that what you really think?'

'I don't care what you are,' said Ti. 'I do my job, and serve any master who profits me.'

'You will profit now,' said Fuzumi. 'You are in control.'

'Am I?' asked Ti. 'Don't I know what the Kwantung army and the Black Dragon Society are planning? You failed once when the Young Marshal outsmarted you. But you won't let it happen again – next time.'

'No, I don't suppose we will,' said Fuzumi, yawning. He gave an order to his driver to go faster. 'It's chilly,' he said. 'We should not perhaps have taken an open jeep. Mind you,' he added, 'it's a beautiful sunset. By the way, how are you planning to celebrate tonight?' he asked. 'Now our new partnership is secured. In General Lin's harem, perhaps?'

'I am not interested in those filthy foreign women,' said Ti. 'They disgust me.'

Fuzumi looked at him curiously, a twinkle in his eye.

'No, there was only one woman for you, wasn't there? You were careless to let her go after you punished her. You should have anticipated that those two schoolgirls would run to their father and that he would come to the school and rescue the Leis before he fled with his own family. We Japanese would've finished the job properly. Do you know where she is now, your Lan-hua?'

'I neither know nor care,' muttered Ti.

Fuzumi chuckled. 'Many Communists have joined the *hong huzi* in Mongolia. An intelligence report I read the other day described an American woman who had been seen with one of these bandit bands – quite a fierce fighter, I gather. Perhaps you should send your army, now you are in command, on an expedition out there.'

'I'll be busy enough here,' said Ti. 'I'm sure the Kwantung army, when it eventually moves against the Young Marshal, will be more than competent to deal with any side operations against *hong huzi*.'

'We will deal with a lot more than bandits,' said Fuzumi. 'When the day comes.'

He watched for a while the sun setting over the hills. How appropriate, he thought, as he glanced at the flag that was flapping on the bonnet of the car. The pattern exactly resembled the sinking globe. There was the big red ball in the middle of it, and stripes, like a sun's rays, spreading to all sides of its white surface. He had always appreciated the symbolism, but he had never seen it reproduced so perfectly in the natural environment.

One could see symbolism in anything if one thought about it, he supposed. And destiny.

The rickshaw man, sweating after his exertions, dropped them outside a row of stuccoed cottages at the top of the hill. While Edmund helped to untie the heavy pram from the rickshaw frame Catherine, her baby in her arms, looked round her at the wonderful panorama of mountains that rose jaggedly to a clear blue sky. Below her, spread out like a map, were the grid-like streets of Dairen, the Russian-designed city with its wharfs and shipping traffic beyond. In the distance shimmered the yellow hills behind which lay Port Arthur and the naval dockyards, where Japan's Northern Fleet rode at anchor.

She was surprised by the cosiness of the little garden, and how neat were the flowerbeds on either side of the path leading to the front door. In one corner there was a patch of carefully raked white gravel, surrounding ornamental rocks, *bonzais*, and a miniature Japanese *pailou*. She had not known what to expect, but such signs of domesticity did not fit her image of a home that had once been the residence of a spy.

Outside the door hung a string of bronze Japanese bells. They made an attractive tinkling peal as Edmund shook them. A diminutive woman with flat features and a kindly, inquisitive face opened the door. She was wearing a traditional kimono and bowed as she greeted them. She saw the baby, and immediately her mouth curved in a wide, warm smile.

'This is grandson, *neh*?' Her voice was also warm and attractive. Her brown eyes peered at Catherine and Edmund. 'Looks like father, maybe,' she said.

'We think he looks like his grandfather,' said Catherine. 'The nose, the black hair, the blue eyes. Would you like to hold him, Haruko-sama? We – we consider you to be his grandmother.'

The woman's eyes widened, and filmed with tears, but she leaned forward and took Harry in her arms, folding him under her kimono sleeves, and cooing over his staring blue eyes. 'Please,' she said, 'come inside. I have some tea . . . and . . . and cakes prepared.'

She took them through a wood-panelled hall to a small sitting room, in which there were neat sofas and chairs. Sunlight streamed through the window and Catherine could see flowers and trees rising to hills beyond. On the windowsill, next to a portrait of her father, was one of herself.

'Henry loved that picture of you,' said Haruko, stroking Harry's lips with her finger. 'He carried it with him wherever he went. I always packed it in his suitcase for him. Only the last time, before he went to Tientsin, he left it behind. I think he knew he might not come back.'

'I'm so sorry,' said Catherine.

'No, don't be sorry,' said Haruko. 'I believe he was happy at the end.'

Later, when Harry was sleeping in his pram, and they were seated round the small fireplace, Edmund returned to the subject.

'It was through the bank that we heard about you,' he said. 'When their representative came to Tsinan and read the will. He gave us your address, and that was when Catherine wrote to you. We thought it only fair that you as his widow should have the larger portion of the estate.'

'I apologise,' she said. 'I did not reply to your letter for a long, long time. I understood, and appreciated your generosity. But . . . You must see that it was only then that I was certain of Henry's death, and after that I was . . .' She bowed her head. A tear glistened in her eye. 'Not well . . .' she continued. She leaned forward impulsively and took Catherine's hand. 'I'm sorry,' she said. 'I was angry with you. I blamed you for taking my husband from me.'

Catherine had tears in her eyes too. 'I understand,' she whispered. 'I do understand.'

Haruko sat back on the sofa. She dabbed her tears with her sleeve. When she was finished her posture was erect, her chin was lifted proudly, and there was a gleam in her eye. 'Catherine,' she said, 'one day I will tell you the story of Henry and me. Of our love, which was a deep love. There was always another in his heart,' her eyes levelled with Catherine's, 'but I – I understood that. Your mother was never a problem. I honoured her memory. You should know that I am daughter of samurai,' she said, 'and Henry always . . . respected me. When I knew him first, he too was like samurai. He was proud, brave, noble. But later . . .' A look of pain flitted across her cheeks. 'I could not reach him any more. I do not believe he changed. Not inside. He was still the samurai I married, but too long we were without honour.' Her voice rose. 'These Taros. These Doiharas.' She almost spat the names. 'Too long has my country been shamed. And Henry was forced to do many things. Shameful things, because he was trapped. And later it was to protect you.'

'Oh, Haruko,' murmured Catherine. 'You must have hated me.'

'Yes, I did,' said Haruko, 'sometimes. But I loved you too, because he loved you. Do you know, Catherine? He wrote to me before he returned to Taro and the Kempeitai. He told me of his bargain. It was a loving letter, like the ones when we were young and parted by circumstance. It was as if my old Henry had come back to me, full of courage, and decision, and joy. He also wrote of you, and I knew that it was you who had brought him back to duty, and responsibility. Made him samurai again!' Her voice rang out.

'It took me months,' she continued softly, 'but then this spring – perhaps it was the blue skies – I realised I must not be angry with you for what you did, but I should honour you and thank you for saving my husband from his shame.'

Before Catherine or Edmund could stop her, she sank off the sofa on to her knees, and bowed, her head pressed to the floor between her outstretched arms.

'Oh, Haruko,' Catherine cried, lifting her to her feet and hugging her. They were both weeping. 'Don't. Please. Please forgive me. We – we must be a family now that we have found you. You and Edmund and Harry and me. We – we have a wonderful home in Tsinan. There's the hospital and our good friends. You must come, and be with Harry and see him grow. Oh, please, Haruko.'

'The . . . the baby,' Haruko was muttering between her tears. Harry, awakened by the weeping, was wailing in his pram. She stumbled towards him and picked him up. Catherine and Edmund watched, hand in hand, as she rocked him, eyes shining as she muttered and cooed, like any grandmother playing with her grandchild for the first time. Harry stared up at her with his clear blue eyes, reached up a tiny hand and touched her wet cheek.

Later still, when clouds had descended over the hills outside the window, and dusk was darkening the sky, Catherine asked Haruko to tell her about her father, what he was like. She had known him so briefly, she said.

Haruko laughed. 'Tell you about Henry Manners?' she said. 'I don't know where to begin.'

Afterword

As a child growing up in Hong Kong in the 1950s, my mother used to scare me when I was naughty with the words: 'You'd better watch out or Chang Tso-lin will come and get you.' I knew nothing then of the historical warlord whose armies had terrorised north China in the 1920s. I imagined I was being threatened by some sharp-fanged, rolling-eyed devil or ghost – but for my mother, a little girl growing up in the International Concession in Tientsin, Chang Tso-lin and warlords like him were more than bogeymen to frighten an impressionable child. No wonder that the words used by her Manchu *amah* to persuade her into good behaviour should reverberate a quarter of a century later and have an intimidating effect on her son.

Fifty years on, living and working in China, I have visited Chang Tso-lin's palace in Shenyang and his fantastic mausoleum in Fushan. I have seen photographs of him and know his full story, from his bandit origins to his violent death. I have even dined with one of his great grandsons, David Lie, a respectable Hong Kong businessman, who proudly told me about his ancestor over claret and cigars. I know now that Chang Tso-lin, tyrant as he was, was not the worst of the warlords. In fact, in some quarters he is seen as a patriot of a conservative Confucian kind and a worthy, even honourable, opponent of Chiang Kai-shek . . . Yet even now I wake sometimes from a dream in which the terrifying monster of my childhood imagination returns to haunt me.

When one day my editor at Hodder, Carolyn Mays, invited me to write a sequel to *The Palace of Heavenly Pleasure*, I remembered this nightmare figure, and I determined that my next romance would be set in a period of history in which I might exorcise Chang Tso-lin's ghost. I also remembered other stories my mother and grandmother used to tell me about their lives in north China in the 1920s, and decided to weave them into my tale.

So members of the Airton family of *Palace* return as thinly disguised versions of my own forebears: Dr Edward Airton's career continues to follow that of my great-grandfather, David Muir, who became chief medical officer at the Kailan Mining Administration in Tientsin after the First World War. I have made George Airton an official of the China Railways and he goes duck-shooting in his private railway carriage before breakfast, just as my grandfather, Guy Newmarch, did in his. Catherine and George sip cocktails at the Reuters bungalow when the black flag is lifted in the evening. That is how my grandparents used to start their evening rampages, when it was the real-life Reuters correspondent, Edward Ward, and his friend, Rupert Bibby, who entertained them. (I hasten to add that their fictitious equivalents, Willie Lampsett and the waspish Robby Berry, bear no resemblance to their real-life counterparts beyond the black flag and the cocktails.)

Nor has my heroine, Catherine Cabot, any resemblance, beyond her name and the colour of her hair, to my grandmother, Katie Newmarch, although I have allowed her to share some of the latter's real-life adventures. From her first-class railway compartment, my grandmother really did watch the Battle of the Parasols that starts this novel. She, too, was evacuated to the naval vessels at Peitaiho during the warlord scare of 1924, and she, like Catherine, once bearded the warlord, Wu Pei-fu, when he had the temerity to camp his soldiers on her lawn. I have also given my Catherine some of Katie Newmarch's prejudices: my mother once told me that she was born in the seaside resort of Chinwangtao, rather than the more popular British-frequented resort of Peitaiho, because British naval officers wore beards and my grandmother preferred dancing with clean-shaven US sailors from the American ships that summered in Chingwangtao . . . Perhaps the less said on that subject the better: they were colourful times . . . But, wild as Red-haired Katie might have been in her Gatsby-style Tientsin youth, she never behaved as badly as my Catherine. In the afterword to my first novel I wrote of how my ancestors would be rolling in their graves if they knew what I had done to them in my fiction. They will continue rolling through this book.

The twenties are nowadays a forgotten period in Chinese history, one of anarchy that preceded the better-known thirties when China was invaded by Japan – but they were the crucible years during which all the movements that were later to affect China's history – Nationalist and Communist – were established.

No novel could do justice to the complicated events that took place, and this is not intended to be a history. For all that, I have attempted in my simplifications not to be too cavalier with the facts. Warlords as terrible as the Dog General, Chang Tsung-chang, he of the Three Don't Knows (how many soldiers he had in his army, how much money he had in his bank and how many women he had in his harem) did exist, and the 'Christian General', later 'Red General', Feng Yu-hsiang, was quite as perfidious as I have portrayed him, although he is something of a hero in Communist histories of today because he ultimately ended up on the Nationalists' side. Similarly, all the setpiece historical events – the Fengtian-Chihli Wars of 1922 and 1924, the May 30th Movement of 1925, the Northern Expedition of 1926–8, the Nanking Outrage and Shanghai massacre of 1927, as well as the assassination of Chang Tso-lin in 1928 occurred more or less as I have described.

I was particularly keen to write about the Soviet adviser to the Kuomintang, Mikhail Borodin, whose contribution to the rise of the Communist party in China tends to be passed over in chauvinist Communist (and Nationalist) histories – but it is an extraordinary fact that for a while it was a foreigner who led the Chinese revolution. I have based my description of Borodin's last days in Hankow on eyewitness accounts, and in his conversation with Henry Manners I have used expressions he himself used to describe his 'tragi-comedy'. Borodin's experience was that of most foreigners who attempt to change China. He told the Danish journalist A. Krarup Nielsen, 'The revolution reached as far as the banks of the Yangtse river. Let a diver go down into the yellow stream, and he will come up again with his arms full of vanished dreams and thwarted aspirations.' I recommend Nielsen's war memoirs, *The Dragon Wakes*, to any reader who wishes to find a colourful (and factual) account of the Northern Expedition. I hope Nielsen's shade will excuse me for transposing some of his experiences – the scoop of the Chiang-Feng summit in Hsuchow, his account of being with the Russians on an armoured train – to my fictional journalist, Willie Lampsett (as I have transposed some of the experiences of the real-life English nurse, Florence Farmborough, to Catherine). Writers of fiction rapidly realise that it is difficult to invent stranger things than actually happened, and my pillage of memoirs and diaries is my homage to those who have gone before.

I am sure that, for all my care to be accurate, inevitably I have got the history wrong in parts, and for this I apologise. The one wilful historical error was to have the ransacking of Chien-Lung's tomb take place in 1924 rather than 1928, because I needed to give my fictional General Lin the bones of the title. I hope this *lèse-majesté* will be forgiven by the emperor's spirit. Another historical liberty I have taken is to ascribe the murky Japanese plots being hatched in the 1920s to unsettle China to be the work of the Kempeitai, although its official role was mainly internal security rather than subversion. In fact several intelligence organisations and loose gatherings of young officers in the Japanese military were involved in imperialist conspiracies, for example the ultra-patriotic Sakura Society; the Ketsumeidan, the Blood Brotherhood League; and the Kokuryukai, the Black Dragon Society, which I have mentioned in passing. The assassination of Chang Tso-lin is often written about in terms of 'free enterprise' by young firebrands in the Kwantung military such as Colonels Komoto Daisaku and Itagaki Seishiro – but we can assume a higher-level sanction was sought before they embarked on their enterprise. I hope experts on the period will forgive me for simplifying things for the sake of my story and attributing the layers of scheming to a convenient hold-all, the later notorious Kempeitai, in which I have placed my villain, General Taro, and the historical *éminence grise* of Japanese sabotage in Manchuria, Colonel Doihara Kenji, infamous even then as 'the Japanese T. E. Lawrence'.

I have no doubt that I will offend somebody by my spelling of Chinese names, for Chinese orthography is always a minefield. What I have done, as far as possible, is to use the spelling that was current at the time (except where I have my characters speaking Chinese, when I have used the easier Pinyin). The eagle-eyed reader may notice some discrepancies in spelling of names with those in my first novel: the former Major Lin Fubo, for example, is now General Lin Fu-po. As I said, Chinese orthography is a minefield ...

But the Chinese have a saying: 'Painting legs on a snake.' This is a novel, a fiction, an adventure, a romance, and any concern about historical accuracy is secondary to the main purpose of telling a story. If my reader enjoys this tale only half as much as I did writing it I will be more than half satisfied.

I would like to thank my family for suffering my absence from their life on the long weekends I spent writing, and my employer for allowing me days off China business, even throwing in a sabbatical so I could complete the novel in time for my publisher's deadline. I would like to thank all my friends whose scholarship and knowledge of the period is greater than my own and who brainstormed and gave me ideas. In this context I would include, of course, the aforementioned David Lie, who is not only a descendant of Chang Tso-lin but is married to the descendant of Chang's enemy, Kuo Sung-lien; and Richard Rigby, who wrote the seminal work on the May 30th Movement before entering a successful career as a diplomat. I have benefited enormously from the encouragement, inspiration and criticism of David Mahon, Liu Lu, T. C. Tang, Hua Shan, Peter Batey, Maxim Moskalov, Alan Babington-Smith, Simon Helan, Philip Snow, Piers Litherland, Viktor Ma, Brian Outlaw, Deborah Swain, Tessa Keswick and Humphrey Hawksley. I owe a debt I cannot put into words to my agents and editors, Araminta Whitley and Peta Nightingale, and later Hazel Orme, who between them helped me turn an unwieldy manuscript into what it is today. Araminta and Peta have lived this story for two long years; they certainly know my characters as well as I do. Without them there would be no *Emperor's Bones*. Finally I would like to thank Carolyn Mays and all her colleagues at Hodder and Stoughton who believed in this novel even when for me it was a barely formed idea.

Adam Charles Newmarch Williams,
Hotel Paradiso, Amandola (A.P.), Italy
May Day 2005

ADAM WILLIAMS

The Palace of Heavenly Pleasure

'A rattling good read . . . this is as good as an
adventure story gets' *The Times*

China 1899. A weakened Dynasty watched helplessly
as western powers encroach on its land. But driven by
drought and hunger, a secret society is preaching
rebellion.

Unaware of the forces broiling around her, a young
English girl arrives in the city of Shishan. Life is picnics
and tiger hunts for the foreigners. But for Helen
Frances there are other, more dangerous delights. For
the Boxers are massing secretly in the forests and hills.
Soon Helen Frances and the other westerners will find
themselves in enormous peril.

And at the end of the road, the Palace of Heavenly
Pleasure beckons: a brothel overlooking an execution
ground, its scented rooms offer safety – at a price few
would be prepared to pay.

'An epic historical and romantic story as well as an
impressive first novel' *Sunday Mirror*

HODDER